HEARTSTONE

THE WEEPING GROVE

by

NICHOLAS RINTH

www.nrinth.wordpress.com

Cover Art, Design, and Illustrations by Fabian Rensch
www.fabianrensch.com

ISBN 978-0-9988216-4-1 (Print)
ISBN 978-0-9988216-5-8 (Ebook)

PRINTED IN THE UNITED STATES OF AMERICA

FIRST EDITION

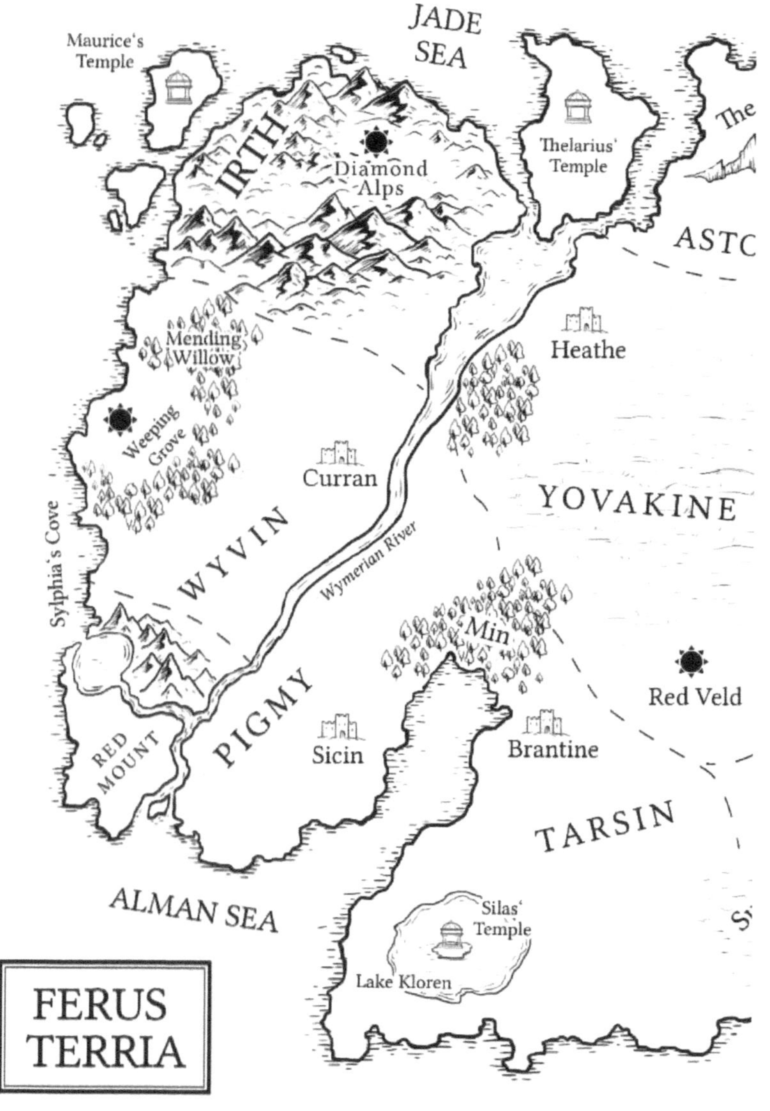

Maurice's
Temple
JADE
SEA
IRTH
Diamond
Alps
Thelarius'
Temple
ASTC
The
Heathe
Mending
Willow
Weeping
Grove
Curran
YOVAKINE
Sylphia's Cove
WYVIN
Wymerian River
Min
Red Veld
PIGMY
RED
MOUNT
Sicin
Brantine
TARSIN
ALMAN SEA
Silas'
Temple
S
Lake Kloren
FERUS
TERRIA

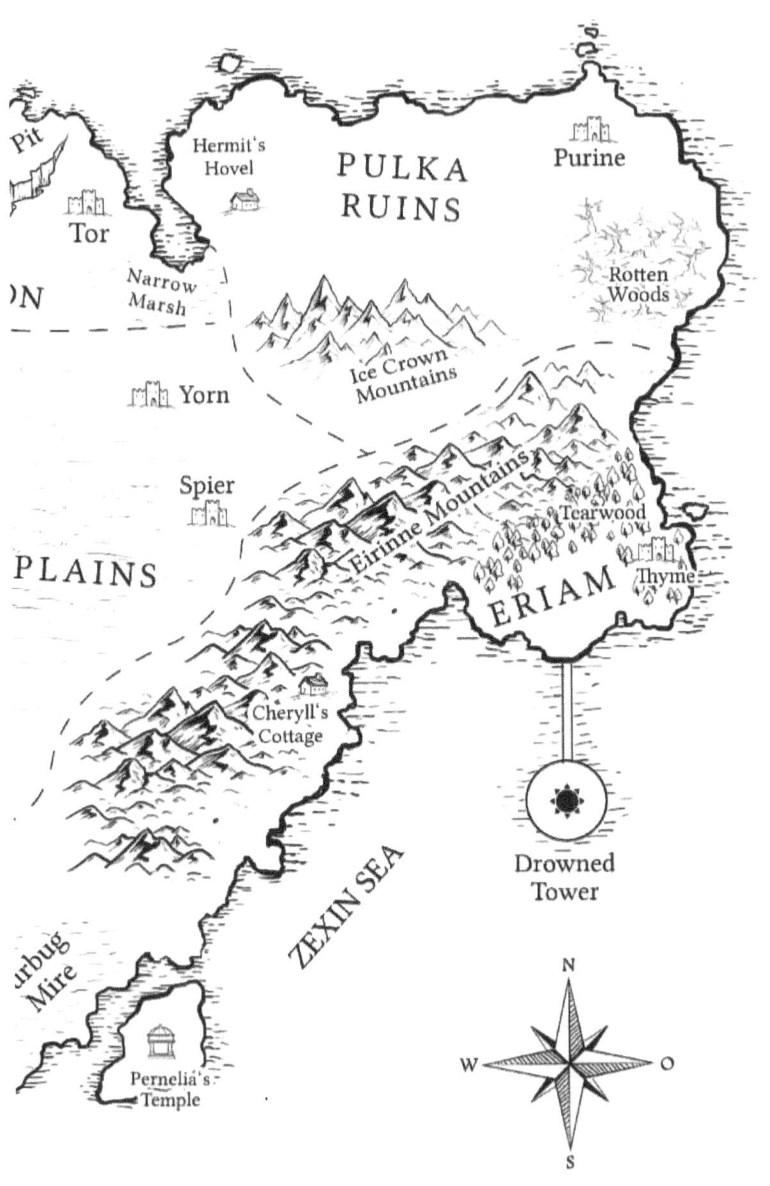

Pit
Tor
Narrow Marsh
N
Hermit's Hovel
PULKA RUINS
Purine
Rotten Woods
Yorn
Ice Crown Mountains
Spier
Eirinne Mountains
Tearwood
PLAINS
ERIAM
Thyme
Cheryll's Cottage
ZEXIN SEA
Drowned Tower
urbug Mire
Pernelia's Temple
N
W
O
S

Excerpt from, "Creator, Practitioner, and Nebbin: An Inclusive Introspection" originally written by Silas Drayr.
First published in 340.26. Oak Age as part of the series, *Secular Divinity: The Great Conjurer's Message.* Legacy Collection of Select Historical Texts. Edition 03. (Volume number 11: Clarity.)

Translated by: Scholar Madeleine Wynt and Brother Endall Vale

"There are those that believe themselves destined for greatness. It's a self-call that rattles their bones. As intangible and true as the wild air at their backs, urging them forward; one hand on their shoulder, a breathless whisper in their ear, teaching them how to best use their wings.

Those are the ones that fall prey to the beguiling beauty of their own feathers. Even as they grow more weary with each new leap. More gray with the passing of the seasons. Most of these acclaimed chosen go deaf. Others blind. Their senses become clouded by sheets of unfurling white, until they're veiled entirely by shadow. Ignorant now to the world's suffering. Few are left with their humanity intact or their values spared, though that's assuming they had any to begin with.

Then there are those whose feet stumble, and through a hapless twist of fate, they fall into the arms of timing and need. A human mistake in a world built from human horrors. The worst of which, arguably being that their paths are thrust upon them. Because more often than not, the roads they walk are shaped by blood and steel and foul magic.

It's the kind of path no man ever wishes to find himself upon. It's barely walkable, lined with corpses as it is, but leaving it is a feat only gods and dead men can speak of — and even then, they only tell tales of envy and regret. But I walked with one such man, and I know the secret of those that didn't give up this path, this only just life...

... There is none.

Navigating the road back to dawn is an impossible endeavor. Corners vanish along the way, edges are shrouded entirely by shadow, and bridges burn like beacons for one, blinding instant, before they're nothing more than ash, so all that's left to do is sprint toward the infant sun of tomorrow.

But these awkward, ill-prepared champions are the ones that fight for their place under the heavens. That go against the mundane accounts of the gifted and the blessed and struggle to exist, despite their flaws, despite that one crucial cord that they so obviously lack. Because they bear within them a deep love for the sky above their heads and the ground beneath their feet. Perhaps more, if anything else truly mattered. But when all of the words that need to be said have been spoken and action is no longer a must, very few effects garner enough merit to be considered vital. Others might contend this view, and they wouldn't be wrong—that is their truth.

The one I express here is simply my own.

It is the truth of a man who bore witness to the world trembling before glittering orbs and unwavering conviction. Seduced by sheer difference, even the most powerful of Mentalists fell to their knees, grasping for the slipping remnants of their empire of terror and despair. Because when hope, despite cruelty and hardship, is coupled with an unwavering sense of determination, society itself can twist, shatter, and be repaired into something new. I, more than anyone else, have seen those stark lines of division bend and blur, until all that remained was splattered paint.

At the end of it all, I realized one thing: the truly great don't have magic or power or even wings. They are simply those that have the will to carve out a future that they can call theirs—and theirs alone. They are the creators that press fresh steps into the sand, so that the lost might follow them to a new home.

I was led by a great man.

Once."

1

The world spun on gossip.

It was a millennia-long pastime that Cheryll could never escape. No matter which corner of Ferus Terria she found herself in and no matter what company she kept, people were still people. The Nebbin spoke of their farms and of the noblemen that married beneath their station, of those frugal and of those that spent enough money on new silks in an hour to feed six families for a month. They talked animatedly about the latest scandals and observed keenly the problems of the Institute. The Nebbin ruminated over Institute affairs far more than the practitioners themselves. Who, contrary to popular opinion, spoke very little of politics and even less of their own magic.

Most practitioners blathered about mundane events. From their awful supper to apprentices burnt by errant fireballs. They liked to whisper about the latest love affairs and made it a point to know more about the families of those that led them rather than the leaders themselves. Recently, Cheryll found her own family a topic of conversation. It started after a small horde of eastern practitioners were escorted back to Eriam by Conjurers from the Veld. Jack and Sylvie's names were thrown around more times than she was comfortable with. Frankly, Cheryll was just glad to know that they managed to do what she'd asked. She knew from experience that Monet was impossible to deal with.

Cheryll only realized that they were talking about her son when she caught a mousy little girl asking one of the bumbling old men from the Drowned Tower about Jacques. The man simply looked at her with his dead eyes and even deader hair, before putting a finger to his lips. He taught her about curiosity and what it did to little girls instead.

Good man, she thought. *Why can't people understand that secrets shouldn't be picked at and dragged out of the dark before they're ready?*

She wondered if he was once part of the Tower's Assembly, but didn't care enough to ask. He didn't look keen on talking anyway. If he wanted to make himself scarce, then she had no qualms about letting him.

As the weeks pressed on, Cheryll heard more people asking the same questions and throwing around the same stories—and that was exactly how she caught the two practitioners standing a distance away from her now. They were huddled together before Tearwood's line of trees, behind a particularly large rock that no one ever bothered to look behind because of the forest's terrifying atmosphere. But Cheryll had come to know Eriam's shores well, and she knew all of the nooks that people hid in to avoid their work. It was also where she went when she wanted to be alone.

Hidden past them were the more dutiful practitioners that remolded stones and enchanted pillars, before heaving them off to the Amorphs in charge of building the base of the Institute. Gavinists bent iron to their will, creating pipes and webbed stands that would be used as the Tower's foundation. It was a demanding job. One that the pair before her undoubtedly sought respite from.

They spoke with their heads bowed and their fingers cupped around their mouths, ignorant to the fact that she'd been standing there for a good five minutes before they arrived. The woman had a grimoire hanging from a long chain that disappeared somewhere inside her robes, while the man had a distinctly protruding jawline. Cheryll didn't recognize them, but that was true for most of the practitioners here. She only kept in mind the few that were intent on going out of their way to help her—an ill-tempered Healer named, Olivia, who returned to Eriam with a gaggle of tiny children and no less than eight exhausted preteens, and a man with a mole under his eye called, Levin.

If they wanted her to take them away once she was finished here, then they did a good job of making themselves stand out. As far as she was concerned, hard workers were always welcome.

"Move!" the Grimoire Holder suddenly yelled. She shoved her companion to the side as a practitioner half their age sauntered near the trees to set up a trap for the local Snuff. Cheryll would've laughed had she not wanted to remain hidden. She leaned further against the tree instead, watching on as the two began whispering heatedly to each other.

"Don't get mad at me because you weren't hiding right," Protruding Jaw bit out, but took three steps back all the same. "What do you want? If it involves touching, then sorry to say that I'm not interested."

She glanced scathingly at him and breathed in through her nose, grasping for composure. Eventually, she decided against responding to the crude remark because the words that left her mouth weren't at all what Cheryll had been expecting.

"You're the one that told me to call you if I had news about any of the Tower's practitioners!" she yelled.

"I don't see why we have to hide."

"Of course we have to hide. This is big."

"Spit it out then."

"Jack and Sylvie survived!"

"*Obviously.* Half of Thyme saw them wash up on shore."

"Will you let me finish? They were on the lower floors of the Assembly Tower when it blew, and—"

"You're insane," he cut in. "There's no way they could've crawled their way up under all of that rubble. They were passed out and injured on the top floor. The waves brought them to the shore. End of story."

"No, I swear!" she insisted. "Those that saw them say they were enveloped in something when they first washed up and that Master Dace placed a homing spell on Jack which led them back."

He looked skeptical. "And where did you hear that?"

"From Sphen," she said matter-of-factly, "who heard it from Daniel, who heard it from Therin, who heard it from the Bels twins, the younger of which, heard it from one of the children that likes to hang around Olive."

Protruding Jaw pinched the bridge of his nose in sudden grievance. Cheryll was compelled to do the same. But before she could stalk away, a juvenile boy made his way towards them. The two unsuspecting practitioners stiffened at his intrusion, but he didn't stop to reassure them. His weary eyes swept over the pair, seeming to place them in the same category as the rest of the foliage. Cheryll wanted to laugh at that. But she restrained herself when she caught him scanning the lines of trees, searching for something… or someone. Did the boy know she was hiding?

She stepped forward. A strip of light illuminated her face just enough for the boy to catch the shadow of her figure under the heavy shade. His eyes brightened immediately, and he let out a relieved breath as he rummaged around his pack.

A courier?

The two gossipers that she hadn't caught the names of took that moment to flee, both berating each other for not noticing her sooner. Cheryll did laugh then, soft and fleeting. Their red faces were the most amusing things she'd seen in weeks.

Cheryll waited patiently until the boy produced an outrageous pile of missives from his pack. His eyes gleamed in accomplishment as he presented them to her. He seemed to deflate when she simply blinked at the offending amount, while mentally debating even acknowledging their existence. Cheryll didn't want to reply to *all* of them. Most were likely repetitive words of gratitude anyway.

Contrary to what her peers seemed to think, rebuilding the Drowned Tower was an easy task. Or rather, being in charge of the effort was. Cheryll didn't understand how so many failed to see that. She'd received dozens of letters from esteemed scholars to ordinary practitioners. Barring slight differences in wording, they all read the same. They thanked her for actually doing her job. If they thought that too mundane a topic, then they wrote about how much they empathized with her and all of the trouble she was going through; how *hard* it must be to be away from her family.

Cheryll didn't know what to make of it. What she was doing wasn't trouble; it was barely even a worry. What was signing a few documents, barking orders at her men, and searching for quarries compared to the hardship that the eastern practitioners faced while watching their home crumble in a matter of minutes? How could having food to eat and a spacious tent to sleep inside of compare to the fates of those that were apprehended by slavers during the chaos? So many were carted away, while she deemed it more important to salvage what she could from the wasted knowledge leagues beneath the Zexin Sea.

The world acted as if leading them was some grand feat when Cheryll hardly lifted a finger. Her Hunters were adept enough to work autonomously. Those originally from the Tower were the same, if not quicker, considering it was their home that they were piecing back together. Still, they continued to shower her in gratitude. So much so that the thought of opening another letter was enough to sour her mood. Truthfully, Cheryll had half-expected to receive posts filled with mockery at the fact that someone as destructive as her was actually helping construct something. But if her work didn't progress smoothly, then she supposed that would've been more unsettling. Cheryll claimed very few blunders throughout her long career, and she wanted to keep it that way. Their gratitude was certainly better for her image than their venom.

The boy cleared his throat, still holding the envelopes.

Cheryll snatched them away. She glanced at the names and dropped the ones she didn't deem urgent back in his open hands. She ignored the way the corners of his lips wavered with each one she let fall.

"Destroy these." She made a move to drop the rest of the pile into his unsuspecting arms when her hands suddenly stilled over a thick envelope that bore the familiar wax seal of the Vanguard Circle's crest along its opening. Her name was written just above it. Handing back everything else, she clawed the wax off with her blunt nails, uncaring for the red stain that it left on her fingertips.

She read:

Cheryll,

By now, I'm sure you've heard all about the Alps' isolation and the terrible things happening within the Council. I'm afraid it's all true. I barely got this dispatch out to you. If I didn't have so many friends on the Council, then I'm sure I wouldn't have. I don't know how much I should tell you or how much you've been able to find out on your own, but just know that I'm safe.

Although... I have been suspected of murder.

Don't worry! It's not as bad as it sounds. I've been confined to my study is all. I'm just thankful that they didn't throw me in the dungeons. Honestly, I'm more concerned about you and Jack. I hope they don't apprehend him when he arrives. He'll unleash the infamous Hallan-Dace temper on them, and then I'll have an entirely different mess on my hands. What if he decides to never return to the Alps after that?

I won't stand for it. Absolutely not.

However, I was hoping that you might... risk returning here, that is. I'd appreciate your aid and your company. I never noticed how awful this office was until now. I have all of these young practitioners guarding my door, acting as if they stand a chance should I actually decide to leave! They're a headache.

Speaking of annoyances, the wind has carried news about the practitioners there and their complaints about your unwillingness to erect a new statue of Pernelia. I hope they aren't giving you a hard time. I know that you don't have the time to find someone skilled enough to make something so large (and so expensive), but do try to be... less austere about it. At least smile when you deny their wishes. Refusals hurt, love. Explaining the reason behind your decision can go a long way.

I'm sure they'll understand... and if they don't, I will make them. Work calls. I must be going now. I pray for your safe and timely return. Don't keep me waiting too long.

Yours,

Leonas Dace

Cheryll read the closing line three times. Her eyes drifted to the bottom of the page where her husband's name was etched unnaturally deep. She knew him well enough to know that the heaviness of his hand served as an indicator of his focus. Strangely enough, the harsher his grip, the less interested he was in whatever he wrote—and it showed. His writing lacked its usual plump curves. The loops she so often suffered through were stiff, curled almost as an afterthought. His *a*'s were thin and his *i*'s weren't dotted in all of the right places.

Her gut churned in unease. There was just something *wrong* about the entire letter. Cheryll scrutinized the way the ink blotched intensely around the first few letters of his name, before it fizzled out into smooth nothing. It looked almost as if he couldn't move his pen away fast enough; as if he didn't want to suffer the extra second it would take to sign their shared name. But the fact that it was there in the first place made her question the letter's contents. Leonas never signed his correspondences to her with Dace. If it was a new good habit that he wanted to adopt, then he would've mentioned it. Leonas always felt the need to talk about the nonsense that went on inside of his mind. It didn't matter how pressed for time he was, Leonas never skimped on details in his letters to her, especially not his own self-gushing.

Cheryll read the closing again. But this time, she sneered. The words were bold, the rest of the message loquacious. But it was nowhere near enough to be her husband. That final line was demanding... very much like him. But it was also voracious in a way that sounded nothing like him. It was blunt. It was impatient and gauche. It was a little too everything.

Leonas didn't write it. He couldn't have.

Then who did?

Cheryll promptly ripped the page in half and let the wind carry its pieces to the sea. The courier stepped back at the sight of her bitter expression. Smart boy. But definitely not one of her husband's men. Leonas trained them until even their souls developed callouses. Cheryll didn't recognize his face, so he wasn't one of Roderek's either. All Hunter candidates had to first be evaluated by her and the other captains, but since she was gone, they couldn't rightfully appoint any new greenhorns. If nothing else, her peers were sticklers for tradition.

Someone from the Research Division then? Her eyes thinned. *What in the world is he doing dispatching messages?*

"Who sent you?" Cheryll watched the boy stiffen. She didn't wait for him to gather his courage. "Do you work for Javis? Has he finally gotten over his indolence and left that lonely lab?"

"I—no, wait, I," he stammered, his eyes shifting.

"What? Straighten your back. Speak clearly."

"Yes!" he corrected. When Cheryll lifted an eyebrow at him, he blushed to the tips of his ears. This time, she waited for him to stutter out a proper answer. "I work for Master Javis, but Elder Avarrin was the one that sent me. I think he thought I was from Elder Dace's division because he had this terse look on his face when he handed me that letter that you just..." he paused to tilt his head woefully at the scattered pieces. "He said that it was from my leader and that it needed to be brought to you... but Master Javis is my leader. Still, I didn't think it would be smart to disobey an order from the Head of Corre—Elder Dace!"

Cheryll smirked, despite herself. He'd obviously heard the stories. If not that, then the screams. He was part of the Vanguard Circle after all, so she wouldn't be surprised if it was the latter.

"And you just left?" she asked, a little impressed.

"Never!" he denied fervently, then lifted his robes to expose his ankle. A familiar spell was curled around it. "I asked Master Javis for permission first. He cast this, then helped me escape."

"Escape?"

He scratched his cheek, sheepish. "The north is closed off right now. I don't know the details, since I'm always locked away in the lab, but it must've been important for Master Javis to let me go, instead of handing the task off to someone from Elder Dace's division. This is the first time I've been outside Irth in seven years! I wasn't expecting so much… dirt."

Cheryll disregarded his excitement. Ignored, too, the way he shifted on the balls of his feet and scuffed the grass beneath him in wonder. Did Javis know that the letter wasn't written by Leonas? Or was he just as ignorant as the boy he sent? No, that was impossible. Javis preferred keeping to the shadows for the simple fact that they held truths those involved were blind to. The true question was, did he permit it to be sent because he wanted her to return or because he was trying to warn her away?

Did something happen to Leonas? She frowned at the thought. *Of course something did.*

Even if the rest of the letter was full of lies, she was at least sure of that. She'd never been fond of Javis. It wasn't a stretch to say that she disliked him the most out of all of the Vanguard Circle's heads. He was obscenely messy, grew burgundy colored molds in the armory, and had an ungodly habit of writing over anything within reach whenever he had an idea. Even ancient documents that would turn yellow if breathed on the wrong way.

… But he was also the most trustworthy of the three—even more so than Leonas, who wasn't beyond lying through his teeth or using outright coercion to get what he wanted.

"You didn't see Leonas yourself?" Cheryll asked, startling the boy back to attention. "Did you hear anything about him before you left?"

He didn't speak. But the apologetic look in his eyes was answer enough.

"Stay for a while," she went on. It wasn't a suggestion. "I must… *thank* Javis for sending you. There's a gifted Healer here— Olivia. She usually checks on the children at this time. Have her tend to you. I won't have a tired Amorph flying back to the Alps.

I have enough worries and I certainly don't want to be blamed should something happen to you because of your poor condition."

With that, she left him to care for himself. She disappeared inside her tent to scribble out a brief message to Javis—and no one else. But before she knew it, she found herself jotting down Leonas' name on the far side of the page, and then there was an entire corner littered with scrawls meant for him. As if Javis needed to know that she was too busy daydreaming to write him properly. Cheryll sighed in agitation. Balling up the paper, she started again. She was hyperaware of the death grip she had on the quill, alternately shocked and annoyed that it hadn't snapped yet. But it lasted all the way until she signed the bottom with her name. It was a quality item. She'd have to talk to that Thyme merchant about sending a few to the Alps. She was certain Leonas would love it.

And because she couldn't resist, she wrote him a missive as well. To the true Leonas. Cheryll spilled her disappointment at the imposter's ineptitude and at Leonas' incompetence with the entire situation. She didn't approve of his allowing someone to run around and make a mockery of him. Just what kind of trouble did he get himself into? It must've been extreme if someone would go so far as to impersonate him—easily one of the most terrifying men in the Alps.

But even if he was in such an obvious predicament, she couldn't bring herself to return. Not when she'd be walking into such an apparent trap. She'd be damned if she played into someone else's hands so willingly. Because once she did, what then? The last thing Cheryll wanted was to be used against Leonas in whatever new scheme the bastards in the Alps concocted.

For the moment, all she could do was sit, wait, and grit her teeth. She'd send a few Hunters back with the boy to figure out where Javis stood. The rest would gather what was left of her legion. Hopefully Leonas didn't scar them too badly. Although she doubted it. He was notorious for that.

As soon as she finished penning the eight-page long rant, she read it over and grinned at the amount of threats riddled within. A small, buried part of her hurt because she'd never been soft enough to write words of warmth. She didn't have fluffy edges made of cotton and visible affection. Cheryll knew Leonas would've liked to receive something more than her candid reprimands, but ultimately, she didn't care. And when it came down to it, neither did he. He'd assured her on numerous occasions that he valued her lectures more than the spineless nothings others could offer—he needed them. He wanted someone he could stand beside, not another nobody that he had to push forward.

Cheryll swiftly threw the letter into a tiny fire pit just outside her tent. It was meant more for light rather than warmth. But it made a good paper disposal, too. It wouldn't do if someone found her writings to him. Worse, if it fell into another's hands. So, she stood there and watched it burn into ash, feeling almost lazy in the glow of the flames. It was such a waste—of ink and of effort. But Cheryll consoled herself with the thought that she'd much rather say the words to his face than have him read it and smirk each time she veered off topic to scold him about something else. She wanted to make him suffer her voice. A part of her also wanted to hear his never-failing responses, but that thought was quickly submerged in the deepest, darkest pit of her mind along with her worry for Jack and her current annoyance with her position. There would be time to properly ponder and question and feel—later. Now was not.

Cheryll returned to her tent. By the time she reemerged, the sun was long past its peak, burning pink and orange over the Zexin Sea. The practitioners had settled around various campfires for a late luncheon. Cheryll searched the crowd for Javis' messenger. She found him huddled between Olivia and two small children. The biggest, dorkiest smile she could ever imagine a boy having graced his lips, and he looked extremely well-rested. Olivia had obviously replenished his stamina. If nothing else, the boy responded to orders well. Better than her husband; two times better than her son. Cheryll appreciated that.

Just then, a sliver of white caught her eye and she turned to find the letters she'd told him to get rid of piled high beneath a flat stone.

Cheryll smirked.

Well enough.

2

There was a flower inside of his cell.

Leonas stared at it, bewildered by its presence. It had five snow-white petals and an aquamarine stem that slanted pathetically to the side from the lack of nutrients. It was a local snowdew, he knew. Not because he was intimately familiar with the flower's appearance, but because it was the only flower hardy enough to grow in the north. Cheryll liked them, though not enough to pick, and he wasn't one to gift something so breakable.

How it grew between the enchanted stone floors of his dungeon, he would never know. Perhaps the previous occupant had nicked it before his capture and planted it there? That would explain its lackluster appearance, as well as the coppery tang of fresh blood in the air. It was a stubborn thing though. He'd give it that. Almost as stubborn as the rising sun every morning.

Leonas felt sorry for it. He felt sorry, too, for the big black rat that scurried up to the plant, snout first, sniffing the foreign object. It plucked a good portion of its leaves off with its claws. The rat rolled it between them, before chowing. Leonas watched impassively as it ate. He stared at the rat's dark eyes; they were too small to belong to an Amorph. Although he really didn't need to look at its eyes to know that it wasn't one. Few Amorphs went so far as to mimic disturbing characteristics like boils, and this rodent's head was covered in them.

For one senseless moment, Leonas envied the creature that was able to roam where it pleased and eat at its leisure. Unlike him, who had to sit idle and learn how to tell the time by his meals. He'd always had bizarre sleeping patterns, but they turned even stranger here. It was then that Leonas realized just how drab his dungeons were. To others, it might've been terrifying because of the constant screams that echoed in the background or the distant sound of trickling water droning on and on. It was enough to drive any person insane. But to him, it was simply dull. There was no sunlight here. The only illumination came from the door. Whenever it opened, shafts of torchlight would dribble in to stain the cold floor with waning bursts of orange and gold.

There were moments when he admired the warm colors, but more often than not, the one thought that occupied his mind were his peers, and where each of them fell on a scale from one to senile. Because what kind of backwards thinking did it take to believe that locking him in his own territory was a good idea? It would've been smarter to keep him in one of the common cells in the Council's prison. Better, too. The cells there were smaller, crammed wall to wall with a low table and a cot he'd undoubtedly be too large for, but it was still better than... *this*.

His cage had iron bars on the side closest to the door and metal welded in gridded patterns along the outer portions. They had holes that were smaller than his fisted hand. Inside, he had a wooden bucket and enough empty space to drive him mad.

Not even a mound of hay, he thought, while thinking of the Council's prison. *I'd take thin cotton over solid stone any day.*

He wasn't about to voice his complaints, however. It was his own fault for keeping his cells this way. And, in the end, this worked for him. Leonas knew every crevice of his dungeon. He knew each corridor like the scars on his body… perhaps even better. There were faulty bricks and blind spots in key areas that only he'd be able to fully utilize. He'd discovered ancient paths that not even the other heads of the Vanguard Circle knew about. Leonas had even carved out a few of his own. So, if they believed this an adequate punishment, then they were wrong.

His division was strictly meant for breaking minds and

shattering wills. It was arrogant to think themselves capable of doing such a thing. Especially to him. He was the best, and that's why he was named Head of Corrections in the first place. Or did they just keep him here for the sheer irony of it all? Perhaps it was a slap on the wrist. A sign to reflect over his actions.

Adult time-out? Leonas thought with a grimace. It certainly seemed like it. He had no chains around his ankles and the ones clasped around his wrists were so long, he could stretch his arms out in full. That was a luxury he didn't afford to anyone in his cells, regardless of their station.

Then again, Leonas hadn't fought them, so perhaps they didn't think it necessary to restrain him. That, or he had too many friends speaking up for him on the Council. But somehow, he doubted it. Most were too green with envy, while others were angry at him for previous transgressions that he'd probably fail to recall. The few that weren't sore with him were the quiet sort that would defend him with actions rather than words.

"Demented bastards," Leonas said, more for the sound of it than the sentiment.

Well, if they allowed him the freedom of pacing the confines of his cell as he pleased, then he wouldn't complain. Never mind the fact that he'd never do such a thing in the first place. He wasn't some caged tiger that needed to prowl back and forth to relieve tension. Leonas wouldn't give them the satisfaction of seeing his displeasure. So, he sat quietly, seething in his unease and mulling over all that had happened. As much as he hated to admit it, all he could do now was wait for news from his lackeys.

On cue, a door in the distance creaked. Leonas heard the thunderous pace of hurried footsteps approaching his cell. Not a moment later, and his iron door flew open to reveal an older man with tired eyes and a crooked smile.

"Elder Dace," he greeted.

His voice didn't have the same grit as Leonas' men, but the lines on his face spoke of past grievances that could've made him one. He stuck his head outside of the door to confirm that they were well and truly alone before flashing him a golden coin with a finely chiseled 'T' on its center.

A Tipping? Leonas examined his plain features, from the black eyes to the large belly hidden behind a stained apron. The seams of his trousers were giving away at the knees. *How... ordinary. But if that was true, then how did he get in?*

The fact that he was able to sneak inside was as disconcerting as it was wonderful. While Leonas appreciated being passed along information, he didn't need the added stress of knowing someone could so easily break through his defenses.

"And here I thought I wasn't allowed visitors," Leonas said, flashing him his usual smile.

A momentary expression of wariness crossed the man's face, before he schooled it enough to grin back. "One of your men led me inside," he explained, much to Leonas' relief.

His pride would've been shattered if the guard rotation he'd spent weeks working on had been seen through so easily — assuming those codgers on the Council were still using it. They'd be hard-pressed to create a system that worked better than his. But Roderek wasn't known for his inefficiency. He must've assigned a few new patrols by now.

That would explain this... breach.

"And why would they do that?" Leonas asked cryptically.

The man reached into his trousers and pulled out four sealed letters. They were creased at the edges, but otherwise unopened.

"I was ordered to pass these on."

Leonas didn't say a word as the man left them by his feet. The staring contest that ensued wasn't one that he found particularly uncomfortable, but the man clearly did because not a minute into it and he was already bringing out his pocket watch. He looked at it in such a fake manner that Leonas wondered why he didn't just leave. There was no need to give an excuse or to say goodbye. It was the proper thing to do, but Leonas never much cared for propriety. Besides, he was locked in a cell. No need for good manners in a place like this.

With nothing more than a point at the time and a half-hearted salute, he left, nearly slamming against the door in his mad dash to get away. Leonas was more taken by the door's harsh closing than his departure. There was a sort of finality to it. The door shutting meant that he was once again trapped with that vile rat.

Oh, how he longed to see Cheryll.

If she was here, then she would've demanded an audience with the Council. Her intimidating stare might've even gotten him out. Thelarius only knew how many of the Elders cringed back at the mere sight of her. But Cheryll wasn't here, and Leonas had no intention of letting her return. Lest the more jittery Elders do something he'd make them regret. For now, they were still unsure of their boundaries regarding his strange situation, and they were hesitant to overstep them. That was enough.

Leonas stared at the letters for a long time, eyeing their seals from across the room. One had that 'T' that he just had the pleasure of seeing, another had the Council's mark embossed boldly on its front, while those remaining held the seals of the Vanguard Circle. One was from his subordinate, no doubt.

And the other? he wondered, inching towards them.

He opened the Tippings' missive first, knowing it would be the easiest to stomach out of the four.

I've recently made contact with your scout. My peers find your terms acceptable. As promised, your men in the Gelid Mountains have been led to the Mending Willow. They were granted entrance under the Dace name. The Grove seems to be in disarray, however. The colleges are fighting about something.

My men informed me that the Zenith Council has approved the Grove's request to abolish their Union. Do you confirm this?

Euphemia

Leonas' eyebrows raised, bewildered by the inquiry. The Council wasn't against dissolving the Union, but they didn't exactly approve it either. They wanted to focus on the Summit, then have the new leader make the big decisions to display the strength of the position. Any announcements that brought attention away from the importance of a new Grand Elder would surely be frowned upon. So, why now? Who was influential enough to call for a vote? And who took his place in it?

Shaking his head, Leonas tore through the rest of the pages, needing to find out more. If worst came to worst, he'd break out and work from the sidelines. He had friends on the Council and the trust of his subordinates in the Circle. If he really wanted to, then he could disappear from the north altogether. But even in his muddled state, he knew that was reckless.

Not yet, he told himself, as if trying to grip the words. *Not yet.* He quickly broke the wax seals of the rest.

Leonas,

I can't believe those fools apprehended you! Then they had the audacity to start a meeting... and even a vote! Roderek has taken full control of the Council. Very few are willing to go against a Drakone, and even less now that you've been accused of killing Dels. Vaklas in ah vashen. Your support is dwindling, and I have no idea what's going through Roderek's head.

The Grove has been given permission to dissolve their Union following the Summit. It was formally announced six days ago, and the colleges have already begun preparing for the shift. They've requested our aid on numerous occasions since your lockup, but the Elders are in total gridlock. They can't agree long enough to send men to the Grove to help deal with the angry Potens.

Borris has left to see to the problem himself. It's a disaster, I tell you! He said he was going there to escort Arch Poten Cole here for the Summit, but even a child could tell that was a lie. He's worried about his home, and I'm not sure if his presence will do anything to mollify the situation.

I don't know what you think you can do while locked up in those dungeons, but if you're going to do something, let me in on it, too.

Personally, if you can. I don't think I can stomach talking to your men anymore. They're stoic and relentless. I hate how intimidation never works on them. I can only hope that they believed my intentions were pure and that this dispatch has reached you safely.

I've reached out to Victor. He said he'll help you in any way he can. He told me to tell you that he has proof. Something about someone being able to contend with Drakone blood? I assume it's a secret that you want kept between you two until the time comes, so forgive me for this, but I'll be wringing the answer out of him.

Rocous

Leonas,

*I retire to my lab for a few weeks to skip out on preparations for the Summit with nothing—**nothing**—on my mind but the simple expectation that everything will be finalized upon my return, so imagine my surprise when I'm suddenly called upon to take your place in a senior council meeting over the fate of the Weeping Grove's Potentate Union. I almost dropped acid on the messenger from the sheer absurdity of the news.*

Although what I find most surprising is that you're locked away. I never thought you'd allow yourself to be taken prisoner. Before today, I never even considered you being one a possibility. But as I looked back on all of the years that I've known you, I realized that you've always had an impressive track record of enemies, Leonas. Frankly, your ability to aggravate others has astounded me for the last three decades... so perhaps it was a naïve thought. You were bound to get into serious trouble sooner or later.

As a scholar, I can't wait to see how this pans out. As a fellow Head of the Vanguard Circle, I want to resolve this swiftly and quietly. My research is already under heavy scrutiny. I don't want every other aspect of my work to be subjected to the same treatment. So, let's get to the bottom of this, shall we? You can expect a visit from me soon.

In other news, you should hear the thinly-veiled insults that some of the other Elders are saying now that you're gone... and far away from them. (Though not far enough for the spite in their tones if you ask me.) I'm not crass enough to mention names. Although I have a feeling you'll find out who they are anyway.

[Blots of ink mar the page.]

... I've been summoned by the Council again.

It looks like I don't have any more time to write to you, so I'll cut the pleasantries here. Someone is impersonating you and has sent a dispatch to Cheryll pleading with her to return. Fret not, for I've warned her away. Not directly of course. She'll understand once she sees one of my men delivering it instead of yours.

For now, just know that I'll be taking your place on the Council until further notice. I've also sent one of my men to inform me about what's going on in the Grove... just in case.

Burn this.

Javis

Leonas didn't need to be told twice. As soon as he read the signature at the bottom, both letters were already half-gone. He knew the Alps closed their gates, but he didn't realize they'd go so far as to publicly announce the dissolution of the Grove's Potentate Union. Especially since they couldn't send out any practitioners to aid the colleges should those still loyal to the Potens decide to fight to keep their power. The colleges might think them apathetic to their struggle, which could be a cause for future resentment.

He could already imagine the complaints—'how could you lot decide something so crucial when you knew you were in a state of imbalance?' The Weeping Grove was their only source of *Orivellea*. They couldn't allow such dissatisfaction.

Knowing this, why would they still decide to do it?

Leonas wearily rubbed his eyes at the suddenness of it all. Despite what he liked to claim, the Elders weren't all bumbling old men. They were certainly past the age of recklessness, but they still had their wits about them. Most preferred to leave things as they were than risk change, especially at such a crucial time. If they did this, then someone must've forced the issue. Leonas mentally went through the missives again in his mind.

Was it Roderek? He's the only one with enough sway in the Council to force such a thing. But what would he gain from it? Dels is dead, but that isn't enough cause to turn Roderek into a fool. His sister then… no, she has no ties to the Council. No motive either. Her skills aren't worth noting. It can only be him. Why would he do this though?

Leonas stared at the ceiling above him, willing it to answer. But of course it didn't. He was left to ponder on his own.

How and when did Javis get a message out to Cheryll? Is she on her way? Leonas shook his head in answer to himself. *Of course she isn't. Cheryll wouldn't risk it. Looks like I'll have to place my trust in Javis for now. But will he really contend against the Drakone family?*

Only time would tell. He'd have to wait for more answers for now. This wasn't the moment to break out and hide. In fact, being cooped up in his dungeons was a blessing. It was the best place to be for information. He couldn't be accused of committing any more crimes here. They weren't interrogating him; the Elders weren't that stupid. Leonas could stomach sitting alone for a few more weeks if need be.

He stared at the ashes on the ground. The haze around his mind ebbed away. Resolution gradually took its place. He had more than enough time to think about this, much more than he knew what to do with. He'd devise a plan and get all of his ducks in a row—later.

For now, Leonas opened the final letter, wondering if there could be worse news. It would be hard to top this. Hopefully his subordinate had something good to report.

Elder,

    News has reached the Alps: Arch Poten Verne and her husband are on their way for the Summit. They rejected the Counci's offer to provide escorts.

Leonas choked.

Vidal is coming?

His smile alone was taxing enough to keep others far, far away. Vidal had mastered the art of political speech at the tender age of eleven—and had chosen the route of most impertinence ever since. Not that Leonas was any different, but he doubted the Council would be happy about it.

Well, having my partner around is still a relief.

They wrote each other when time permitted, and Leonas knew that Vidal had only become more prone to erraticism as the years hummed on. He'd always been unpredictable and a little too daring, but now his decisions bordered on thoughtless. Plans, no matter how meticulously crafted, always had a hole or two. Vidal's plans, however, had twenty, and they were all glaringly obvious. Even the greenest of tacticians could spot the missteps. It was as if he made them in-the-moment from knowledge based on pure intuition rather than actual fact. But even though they were wild leaps of faith, somehow they always ended just the way he wanted them to. Vidal's luck was inconceivable, and he'd clearly gotten used to winning by the skin of his teeth because he'd grown bolder over the years.

The Elders wouldn't appreciate that unflinching confidence of his—they hadn't before—and their long-standing disapproval of his wife wouldn't help smooth things over. But Monet was a Thareen, so they'd be forced to respect her ways.

Although, Leonas amended, *the Council's tendency to steer clear of Vidal might work in my favor. If anyone can talk me into getting out of here, then it's him.* His greatest friend had a tongue sharper than a whip, and ten times more cutting. *It would be better if I could leave without breaking out, lest the others turn sides and believe me guilty. I don't want to look like a criminal.*

He chuckled at the thought.

For everything he'd done during his time as the Head of Corrections, he was so much worse. Felons didn't hold a candle to the crosses that marked his record. A day of his memories could easily give someone night terrors for years. Half a month could shove a weaker-willed man over the border of insanity in an instant.

Is that why the others on the Council were so quick to believe those that suspected me? Well, not that it matters. It wouldn't be much of a revelation anyway.

Leonas made a career out of destroying lives—innocent and guilty alike—and he'd do it again in a heartbeat. He settled back against the sad corner of his cell that he'd dubbed his napping place. It could hardly be considered comfortable, but nothing around him could. Leonas drizzled the ashes of his subordinate's dispatch over the floor. They fell hypnotically over the stone blocks, blending in with the darkness of the granite.

The destruction of the east marked the end to many things. The ripples were still being felt across the lands, instigating a plethora of new beginnings that affected the other Institutes in ways that were only now becoming apparent. If this had occurred when he was thirty years younger, then he would've loved to explore Ferus Terria with Vidal to see those minute changes happen for himself. But he supposed that getting a birds-eye view wasn't so bad either.

Vidal will have far better luck getting me out of here than anyone else in this godforsaken land, Leonas thought, no, he knew. So, he shut his eyes and exhaled a tired sigh.

He could wait until then.

3

Sleep came in fitful bursts for Tiv.

Sprinkled behind the darkness of his lids were brutal, horrifying dreams of torture and unrest; of a dark, dank cell, and magic just beneath his skin, singing in his veins, searching for a way out—and finding none. In the background, the piteous screams of someone familiar rang. It was never clear enough for him to attach a face to the voice. He didn't know anyone that cried like a wounded animal. But whenever he came to the realization that the screams belonged to a child, a young boy he only knew lucid, he'd wake, panicked and half-shouting.

Sometimes he'd wake on his own. Others, by a shake from the practitioners that he travelled with, and once by an accidental blow to the head by a boggled Philip and a laughing Dalis. Neither breathed a word about how that particular incident came about, and Tiv didn't ask. But he didn't make the mistake of sleeping anywhere near them again.

Today, however, he was awoken by the scent of burning.

Tiv's eyes flew open, and for one, disoriented moment, all he saw was red. But then the moment passed, his vision steadied, and he found himself face to face with that tongue-less Elementalist, who still, after a solid two weeks of travel, refused to give her name. So, in a magnificent display of his creativity, Tiv had taken to calling her, Ruddy. It wasn't exactly feminine, but she never complained. Glared, sure. They couldn't keep calling her *'you'* and *'hey'* though, so it stuck.

But her name wasn't the problem now. The problem was the burning grass under her glowing hands and how dangerously close they were to her face. To *his* face.

Without a second thought, Tiv used his pack to slap the growing flames. The effect was immediate. Ruddy jerked away, blinking her eyes wildly in incomprehension. She didn't seem to understand what was happening until she saw the urgency in his eyes. Ruddy looked down to see that her arms were lit up to the elbow. She took a deep, calming breath, mastering her magic and forcing it down. There was nothing artful about the way her brow creased or how she struggled for breath. But her actions were open and intent, telling him that it really was an accident and that she wasn't trying to kill him in his sleep like those slavers in the dungeons.

By the time she got her magic under control, Tiv knew that there'd be no more sleep to be had tonight. Both for him and for the unfortunate people around them that groaned when they realized what had happened.

"Are you alright?" Tiv asked.

Ruddy nodded mutely, before falling back down with her legs pressed up against her body and her arms tucked safely to her chest. She turned away from him. Her actions were jerky and terse. Still so proud, despite being so small. He didn't know how that was possible, didn't even think it could be, and he wondered if she loathed seeming so reduced before so many people. If it were him, and he'd lost control of his powers like a newborn babe, then he'd be humiliated.

Tiv didn't bother speaking again, knowing she wanted to be left alone. Instead, he got up and looked north, toward the outer line of the Weeping Grove. The trees were old and thick. They reminded him of Tearwood, except there was no unrelenting fog here. No army of giant toads lingered inside, prepared to kill any trespassers… at least he hoped not.

Deeper in, just on the edge of his vision, he saw strange trees. They had few leaves and many branches that curled inward and held yellow balls of light that shooed away the darkness. He was eager to see them for himself, but even he wasn't reckless enough to go in alone and risk getting on Dalis' bad side. Not again.

How does someone go from terrifying to utterly agreeable that quickly anyway?

Just as the thought crossed his mind, Tiv found the Healer in question standing a distance away with his arms crossed and his mouth set into a thin line. Tiv had never seen Dalis sleep, and yet he looked as well-rested as the rest of his little band. Perhaps even more so. Some days, he had the look of a nobleman with a full belly and fuller pockets.

Does he sleep with his eyes open? Or is it just his magic at work?

Either way, it couldn't be healthy. It didn't matter how sturdy or skilled he was. There were some things that people, no matter how much they tried, just couldn't do. Especially not for extended periods of time.

Wallowing in pain was, perhaps, first on that list.

Dalis was loyal, courageous, and unapologetically himself. He looked forward—to the future or to whatever it was he believed in—but there were times when Tiv caught him isolating himself and staring down at his hands as if questioning his place amongst them, questioning what in the world he was doing with his life. On an especially memorable occasion, he found Dalis with his fingers gripped so tightly around his dagger's hilt that the blunt ridges framing it drew blood.

Today wasn't one of those days. Dalis' expression was more than pleasant. His mood, amicable. Yet, the air around him kept Tiv away. And when Dalis cursed in a language that sounded like vultures feasting, Tiv knew better than to casually approach. What followed the curse was a dozen dark mutterings in an entirely different dialect than the one before. The words of the second were gentle on the tongue and pleasant to the ears. It was too soothing for the naked hate in his tone.

As if sensing that he was being watched, Dalis turned, catching Tiv's gaze. Tiv almost looked away. Almost. He'd already been caught. There was no use feigning innocence now. But that didn't make stepping up any easier.

In the end, it was Dalis who called him over. With nothing more than a tight grin, Tiv found himself jogging until he was standing right beside him.

They both stared at the forest beyond.

"The Mending Willow," Dalis said. "Beautiful, isn't it?"

"It's dark," Tiv said, for lack of a better word. "Looks like a normal forest to me."

"That's just the outer line. The trees change deeper in."

"Change?"

"You'll see soon enough." Dalis grinned secretively. "Honestly, I'm shocked you decided to stay with us. You could've gone to the Veld like some of the others or even back to the Tower. It's being rebuilt, you know? If you want to leave, then you should. While you still can. Once you're back inside another Institute, leaving becomes ten times more complicated… but you know that."

"I do."

"Then what are you waiting for? I won't tell anyone."

Tiv shook his head. "I'm not worried about that."

"You don't owe me anything," Dalis said easily. He understood Tiv's inner turmoil without him having to say a word. Dalis fixed him with a kind stare that was reminiscent to the look he had when he'd found him in that rotten cell. "I didn't go there expecting to rescue you."

"You did anyway," Tiv said… or he thought he did because the voice that broke the air between them was harsh even for him and thick with emotion. It was hard to believe it belonged to him. To his overwhelming relief, Dalis took one look at him and let the topic drift to a pain less jagged, blunted over enough that it no longer hurt him to errantly think about.

"Are you really okay with this?" Dalis asked. "Coming to an Institute you don't know anything about isn't easy. The Grove is different from the Tower. Far different."

"I've already made up my mind," Tiv said, resolute.

"You shouldn't leave what you can't replace," Dalis said, avoiding his gaze. "Take it from the guy that may or may not have lost his sister."

"As the guy that may or may not have lost almost everyone he ever cared for, I'll tell you now that the thought of starting new doesn't sound like such a bad idea. And for the record, I didn't leave anyone. Rather, I was kidnapped because of my own carelessness."

"That's all the more reason to return. You should let them know that you're alright."

"No need." Tiv shrugged. "If I know my friends, then they're already out looking for me. They aren't the type to sit still. Master Celaris, if he's still around, is more than likely helping reconstruct the Drowned Tower. And Jack… Jack is… there's nothing left for me to return to. Not now anyway."

"Don't take this the wrong way." Dalis sighed dramatically, before flashing him a light-hearted grin. "But I have to say that I'm a little relieved."

"Relieved that I have no one to go back to?"

"I just said not to—" he cut himself off when Tiv mimicked his smile. Clearing his throat, he said, "I'm relieved because I can leave that Elementalist in your care. She's touchy. I have a feeling she'll bite me if I so much as look at her the wrong way."

Tiv's eyes widened. "So, I've been demoted to babysitter?"

"Hey, you owe me remember?"

"You *just* said I didn't!"

"Stop living in the past."

"You—"

"Anyway," Dalis smoothly interrupted, "it's not a bad idea to watch her. She's incredibly talented for an Elementalist. More an asset than a hindrance… when awake at least."

Tiv paused. He knew that Dalis had never seen her properly use her powers. Even he hadn't, and he'd spent the better part of the week by her side, afraid she might accidentally hurt herself.

He prompted Dalis to continue with a low hum of controlled interest. But when Dalis only smiled in response, his eyes just begging him to ask, Tiv looked away. He knew Dalis just wanted to tell everyone that he liked to gossip. Tiv had been around him all of a week, and he already knew how he operated. Dalis wasn't a complicated man. When he saw the opportunity for a few split seconds of harmless fun, he took it. He always took it. But it was one thing for Dalis to spread false rumors, despite his knowledge of the contrary. It was an entirely different, more aggravating matter when everyone agreed with him, despite *their* knowledge of the contrary. Curiosity battled with frustration in Tiv's mind. Eventually, the former emerged the winner.

"How do you know?" Tiv asked through clenched teeth.

"She breathed fire in her sleep," Dalis said simply.

"Is that even possible?" Tiv looked back at Ruddy, still cocooned in her own limbs.

"That's the first time I've ever seen someone do it actually. Do you think she did it subconsciously? She was asleep after all. Bu—oh!" Dalis exclaimed, catching the attention of a few of the more alert Conjurers, as he whirled around in excitement. "Do you think she accidentally…"

"What?"

"You know…"

"Know *what*?"

"Do you think she burned her tongue off?"

Tiv blinked, caught between amused, bewildered, and utterly unsure how to react to such an insensitive remark. He didn't know which was worse: that Dalis was joking about it or that he might actually be serious. Before he could decide, his face must've morphed into something like aversion because Dalis took two steps back and held both of his hands up, already prepared to placate him.

"Bad joke," Dalis said. "Right. I get it. *Bad* Dalis."

"I don't suppose you can heal her?" Tiv asked, remembering his previous kindness and mercifully changing the subject.

"I'm not a miracle worker."

"But you *are* skilled."

"Well, I won't deny that." Dalis grinned. "But I know of only one Healer that had the power to regrow limbs, and if the stories are to be believed, that was Maurice. It's a shame he didn't pass on his secrets."

"There's no one else? Really?"

"Don't believe me?"

"No, I do. I'm just surprised. There are over two hundred Healers in the Grove alone, and you're telling me that not a single one of them can help her speak again?"

Dalis paused to deliberate his answer. It didn't take long.

"There is one."

"Who?"

"Arch Poten Cole."

Tiv stopped himself from questioning his skill as soon as the title registered. He'd almost forgotten the weight it held in other Institutes. Growing up in the Tower, on top of rarely interacting with what little was left of the Cephas line, there was never any reason for him to pay attention to the rank—or the power behind it—but now that he was here, Tiv wasn't opposed to learning more. Not just about Arch Potens in general, but about Lucian in particular. Was he at all like Columbus Cephas? Or any of the others he'd studied under in the Tower?

He knew little about those that ran the Grove, and though he tried to remedy that during their journey, no one volunteered to tell him more. From the way Dalis' eyes shifted to the camp behind them in avoidance, Tiv knew he wouldn't either.

Just what are they hiding? Tiv wondered.

"You should go back to sleep," Dalis advised, interrupting his thoughts. "We have a rough morning ahead of us."

The sheer certainty in his voice kept Tiv from disagreeing.

***

The Mending Willow was, in a word, mesmerizing.

It was so filled with old enchantments and even older magic that once their troop stepped past the first line of trees and into the encompassing darkness, Tiv felt his magic surge, then hum contentedly in his veins.

Refreshed, he thought, fanning out his fingers, *but from what?*

Tiv brought his magic closer to the surface, until his hands were alight with a luster so blue, it appeared white. He jumped back in disbelief when, for reasons beyond his own admittedly limited knowledge, his blood warmed to an almost suffocating degree. While not unpleasant, he certainly wouldn't call it the opposite either. Tiv felt almost… crowded. In his own body. But when he glanced at the others, particularly those native to the Grove, they all seemed to be at peace with the feeling of outside forces blatantly needling under their skin.

It's natural, Tiv reassured himself. *It's only the difference in environment. They'd be just as amazed if they went to another Institute.*

But even he wasn't fully convinced.

The trees sang to him here; to the deepest parts within his core. They quested in an endeavor to bring the unknown pieces of him to the surface. Because even he wasn't sure what version of him dwelt beneath all those layers of flesh and bone. When everything else was stripped bare and all that remained was the magic he utilized and the soft, rotten base that made the rest of him—*him,* what kind of person was he? He certainly wasn't noble, though he wouldn't call himself wicked either. Would whatever was hidden here notice that?

Tiv rubbed his temples to expel the thoughts. There was no use dwelling over his own nature. He wasn't interested in finding something like that out in a place like this. But it seemed as if the trees were trying to coax the answer from him, discontent with his decision to battle against them.

He lurched to a halt, suddenly knowing why he felt so uncomfortable. The forest felt akin to being in the old sectors of the Drowned Tower, where ancient spells ran deep, and magic deeper. Except this was more widespread. Far more.

With every inhale, he could smell the rawness of the spells. He never knew magic had a scent. Never even considered it might. Until now.

"Enthralling, isn't it?" Dalis asked.

Tiv turned to find Dalis looking up at the trees and exhaling deeply. Utterly satisfied by it all. He nodded, uncertain how to voice his thoughts, all the while deciding that enthralling just seemed… right. No more words passed between them, and neither tried to fill the silence. That was done by the excited gasps of those around them when they ventured deeper in.

The leaves that had been numerous enough to block out any vestiges of light slowly disappeared, falling to the ground in heaps of brown and black, yet it was still dark regardless. Tiv had no doubt that this was some sort of enchantment to keep men away. He could only hope that they weren't lost like so many others. The lack of life in their surroundings was hypnotizing enough to halt the others in their tracks, but the western practitioners made sure to keep them moving at all times. It was obvious that they were used to escorting others through the forest, and Tiv wondered if this was a part of their regular duties or if they treated navigation of the forest as an initiation of some sort. The same way newly chosen practitioners in the Tower were required to patrol the distant corners of the Eirinne Mountains.

Tiv watched, fascinated, when the looming trees shifted with each step they took. First into thick, thorny branches that curled both out and in, creating whorls that seemed to him like the errant strings of a half-finished web. Meant more to ensnare than to bear fruit. It was as if they'd entered a dream world where even the trees took on different roles. Then, when it seemed as if all traces of life was lost, hundreds of tiny lights guided them farther. They grew bigger and brighter, growing in number, until they filled the entire scope of his vision.

He screwed his eyes shut for a spell longer than usual, hoping it would help them adjust. Tiv swallowed a shout when Dalis abruptly gripped his shoulder hard enough to bruise.

"Keep your eyes open," Dalis ordered. His voice brooked no barter. Tiv obeyed, only to gasp when he found himself in complete darkness. If it wasn't for Dalis' hand on his shoulder, he might've believed himself alone.

"I," Tiv looked frantically around him, "I can't see!"

"Relax, I've got you." Dalis tightened his grip. "You're safe. Just find the lights and don't close your eyes. You'll get lost if you shut them for too long."

Where would I end up? Tiv was tempted to ask, but bit his tongue. Resisting the urge to rub his eyes to make sure they were actually working, he comforted himself with the thought that he wasn't lost, and then did his best to find the lights again.

They appeared slower this time like stubborn children that needed to be cajoled away from their parents. One by one, they emerged all around him, until they surrounded him completely. He breathed a sigh of relief when he saw his companions again. Their faces were a mix between nervous and amused, as they grinned reassuringly back at him. Tiv tried his best to return it. But his heart pounded loud and heavy in his chest, keeping him on edge, despite how aware he was of his own safety.

Tiv was caught once again by the soft glow of the lights. He looked up at the trees he thought dry and bare, only to find globes of yellow, both large and small, sitting in the spaces where the branches coiled. They sat still, engulfed by nature. Each orb was just bright enough to illuminate half a foot around them. But with their numbers, it wasn't hard to see the entire forest.

Magic? Tiv thought. But he'd never seen magic quite like this before. Vines were draped like curtains around them, blessing the forest with all of the vivacity and charm he'd expected when he first stepped inside.

"What's with this place?" Tiv wondered aloud.

"Every twig, every blade of grass, even the air is enchanted," Dalis explained. "Magic runs all the way to the land's core and past the trees in the sky."

"I don't see any raw veins though. Are they underground? I

didn't know the Mentalists buried those."

"They didn't."

Tiv stopped, his eyes widening. "Then how does the Grove supply all this?"

"It's the job of the Grove's Arch Poten to supply the Mending Willow with magic," Dalis revealed, grinning when Tiv's jaw slackened. He nudged him forward, forcing him to move with the rest. This was no time to be stopping. "Arch Poten Cole took it to the next level though. On his first day as primary apprentice, when he was asked to supply the inner lights as a test, it was so potent that just blinking made half a dozen seniors lose their way. He's learned to control it better since then, but even closing your eyes for an extra second is enough to blind you."

"So, they're some kind of amplification device?" Tiv asked.

"In a sense." Dalis shrugged. "If you're really interested, you can ask the Primordians. They're a scholarly college that know everything worth knowing. They've studied the orbs extensively. You'll find a lot of them inside. We use them for light."

"It was hard getting used to at first," Philip chimed from in front of them. "We've all become better escorts ever since Lucian received his title."

From the corner of his eye, Tiv saw a particularly intense light, and he reached out before conscious thought could tell him otherwise. He was so close. And it had appeared out of thin air, as if begging to be noticed. How could he not try to grasp it? But Philip caught his wrist before his fingers could even brush against the strange orb's surface.

"Don't," Philip warned, his eyes sharp and dangerous in the sparse light. "They're extremely sensitive to magic. Touch it the wrong way and you could lose a hand."

"Or what's left of it anyway," Dalis remarked, earning him a glare from his partner.

"Tasteless as always, aren't you?"

"I try."

Tiv ignored them, unable to muster an ounce of thanks for

Philip's defense. He swallowed his fear and his shame, making a conscious effort to keep his hands to himself. Through some glorious twist of fate, the attention was taken off of him when a strangled yelp cut through the silence. The sound could only be described as guttural.

Whirling around, they all smiled as soon as they saw Ruddy futilely try to steady herself after tripping on a root partially above ground. She quickly noticed their attention, and Tiv suppressed a laugh when she glared heatedly at them until they gathered themselves enough to turn away.

An Elementalist's gaze was always chilling. That was something everyone, no matter their walk of life, could agree on.

As they walked, Tiv's eyes wandered to a patch of wildflowers by the base of a tree. He noted how the shadows swayed there. They shifted whenever a practitioner passed by and covered the light. But that wasn't what interested him, no, what really caught his eye was the tiny bug that sat on one of the flower's petals. It was lightly colored and blended well with its surroundings, but he'd taken the shape of an insect enough times to know how they acted.

And that was no insect.

Someone from the Grove? he speculated, watching the Amorph borough deep into the flower's center. The fact that they were being monitored couldn't be good.

In an effort to ease his nerves, Tiv breathed in his surroundings, appreciating how his magic hummed in response. Despite his initial doubts, the rush of heat in his veins was starting to feel good. Now that he knew where the magic stemmed from, he felt better about its presence around him.

It was often said that an Institute was only as great as its head. But to supply the entire forest with magic at such a young age, and on his own at that, the Grove's Arch Poten was simply extraordinary. If it was possible, then Tiv wanted to meet him. To see the second coming of Maurice for himself. To see the one responsible for keeping the Mending Willow so well preserved.

It was unlike any place he'd ever seen. Granted, he hadn't seen much of Ferus Terria, but he knew in his gut that no other place could compare. They lived in such tandem with nature that it was a wonder the Drowned Tower was actually the best Institute for Amorphs. He could easily imagine himself soaring through the trees here or, better yet, perching on top of the thick roots and idly scratching at the moss. It would be a challenge to glide under all of the branches, but it would be one he'd happily accept.

This was a good place for an Amorph—a good place for *him*. Assuming the Grove was less strict when it came to their individual freedom, then the Grove was his wildest fantasies brought to life. Tiv didn't know enough about how the west ran to know how long their practitioner's leashes were, but Dalis and everyone else he'd met seemed happy enough. No one complained when they were ordered to return, so it couldn't be that bad. Still, the Grove was undergoing a shift in power. And as with all great change, great discord must've preceded it. If they were actually demanding that the Zenith Council transfer power to the colleges, then their restrictions must've been bothersome enough to annoy the majority of their population.

Tiv wanted to ask about the current situation, but he knew they wouldn't give him any answers. Not now. He'd been asking about the Grove for a week, and no one seemed keen on speaking to him. He doubted a step into the Mending Willow would change that.

Is it because I'm an outsider? he speculated, unable to think of any other reason for their silence. But before he could ponder over it any further, he stopped in his tracks. Tiv didn't put much stock in signs. But the armed guards waiting for them at the Grove's entrance was one he couldn't deny.

They all went very still, as the guards hastily formed a half-circle in front of them, effectively cutting off their path to the Grove's winding entrance—a raised dirt road framed by long rails on each side. The rails were crafted out of branches and vines, but even from where Tiv stood, he could tell that the wood was too thin and too light to be of any real use. They seemed more for aesthetics rather than safety. Judging by how old the timber looked, Tiv didn't have to ask to know that very few had suffered accidental falls here. Orbs of light interrupted the rails. Each one sat a meter away from the next. They sat upon blunted wooden pikes with intricate carvings where magic coursed, blue and strong, keeping the orbs alight. It was a long road, however, and the spheres were dim in the darkness. They provided just enough light to see the next.

Unlike the path, the Grove itself was clearer. Lit by dozens of larger orbs, held steady by coiled, finger-like extensions made of timber. They were attached to the branches. Though by what, he couldn't say for certain. Each extension was covered by a wave of leaves that kept him from getting a proper look, but he knew enough about nature to know that they were definitely artificial.

It's carved, Tiv realized. *Who in their right mind decided to build an Institute into an oversized log?*

The large, hollow trunk that acted as the Institute's base was lined with moss and splashes of white wildflowers. Holes in the bark served as windows, while additional structures had been crafted along the ends of the thicker branches for more room. From what he could see, the main branches had been pitted as well. No doubt used as central walkways to get to the more important parts of the Institute. More rooms stuck out from above, hanging like fruits all around the tree's crown. Some were in plain sight, while others were hidden entirely by the foliage. The leaves were thicker here. More bunched together. But even that couldn't fully mask the light of some of the bigger orbs.

The sight was so majestic that Tiv stepped back, cowed by the sheer magnitude of it all. Even the double doors were something to behold, surrounded by sentries as they were. Every inch was polished, stately perfection. The wood was so dark it appeared black under the light. Each door was six times Tiv's size and twice as thick. He couldn't fathom how many men it took to open it. Moss covered a good portion of the door's surface, though he could still make out several deer heads engraved upon it. Two were even fashioned into expensive knockers as homage to Maurice.

"Dalis," Philip called, already stepping forward.

"Right behind you," Dalis said. He squeezed Tiv's shoulder, flashing him and everyone else a reassuring smile, before following his partner.

Though this was their home, and there were easy-going grins on their faces, Tiv had the distinct impression that they were throwing themselves to the wolves. So, as they walked up to the line of scowling men, Tiv moved forward with them, shoulders taut and prepared to defend, but a woman he didn't recognize caught his elbow and dug her nails into his skin to hold him in place. She was two whole heads shorter than him, but just as wide and every bit as threatening.

"Don't," she warned.

But she didn't have to speak. Her expression alone was enough to hold him in place. Dark and unfriendly. Her eyes had the same shape as the Mistress', and they shone with the same silent promise. She wasn't that vile woman though, and he relaxed when he realized that. It was impossible to fear someone that willingly travelled with men like Dalis; the honest sort that braided their sister's hair; that swallowed no less than seven raw eggs because of a lost bet. Dalis was good, but he wasn't stupid or naïve. He'd never accept someone that didn't share his values.

So, Tiv watched, rooted to the spot, as Dalis and Philip walked up to the man in the middle. He wasn't particularly impressive, and despite how generous he was with his assessment, Tiv failed to find any noteworthy qualities that separated him from the rest. The man beside him, on the other hand, gruff and portly, with hair the color of dried leaves. He had a long sword at his hip and an oversized maul on his back. Now, he was dangerous.

"Tobias," Philip greeted, smiling amicably.

"That's Sir Alcove to you," the guardsman said, shutting him down completely. "Show some respect, deserter."

"Name-calling already?" Dalis interjected, shrugging like none of this concerned him. "Didn't your mother teach you manners? And, well… *not* to lie? We both know that if the Union considered us deserters, then we wouldn't have made it this far. Since we did, I'm assuming they're still deciding what to do with us. So, let us through. I'm tired and hungry and in need of a long, hot bath. Have you ever crossed a swamp before? The smell sticks like you wouldn't believe."

"Winded as always." Tobias heaved a long-suffering sigh. "You don't need to tell me things I never asked about. I don't care about your problems, Sirx."

Dalis' eyebrows scrunched, all traces of humor disappearing from his face. "You want me to be serious then? Fine. Let us through, Tobias."

Tobias crossed his arms. "And if I refuse?"

"You really want to play with me, *sih tovash?*"

"Watch your mouth, Sirx!" another guard yelled, stepping forward to point the tip of his spear at him. "Or I'll shut it for you."

"I'd like to see you try." Dalis laughed. Shrill and mocking. "But shouldn't you two be taking your own advice? You're in the presence of Gavin Rhone's primary apprentice. He outranks every one of you."

"Not for long," Tobias remarked.

"What was that?"

Before Dalis could draw his dagger, Philip pressed the palm of his hand over the hilt, locking it in place.

"We aren't here to pick a fight!" Philip roared, raising his voice to a startlingly forceful degree. Dalis tilted his chin up in response. Defiant and unyielding. But Philip didn't back down either. He glanced sternly at him until his fingers eased, and he averted his gaze—pride shattered, but composure regained.

They were both red in the face by the end of it.

Everyone looked tensely between them. Silent spectators,

waiting with bated breath for either of them to speak. Their attention was swiftly directed at Tobias, who sneered in disdain.

"What are you all standing around for?" Tobias barked at his men. "Take these two to the Slates. The Union will decide their fate." He gestured vaguely to the rest. "And escort the rest of this… garbage heap to the Red Scripts' common room. Let Master Rhone sort through them."

No one moved. Their minds were too stunted by the sudden turn of events to properly register the command. But the others beside Tiv seemed to have no such misgivings. From their faces, Tiv could tell they'd already resigned themselves to this. That they were fully prepared to go and suffer the consequences of their actions. And yet… they grouped themselves in such a way that they fully surrounded those they released from captivity, just as prepared to protect them should the guardsmen decide that coarse treatment was the best way to display their power.

"Don't make me repeat myself!" Tobias shouted, snapping the guardsmen from their stupor. His voice was halfway between furious and exasperated. "Hurry, before the Elder sees."

That got their attention, or rather, everyone's attention. Mouths hardened into thin lines and shoulders went rigid. The guardsmen moved with an urgency akin to desperation. They were wound so tight that it was a wonder they were able to walk at all. The guards pointed the sharp edges of their weapons at them, but it was their eyes that urged them to move more than anything else. Demanding and pleading all at once. A strange look for those supposedly in charge.

Philip made a show of waving his hand. It was an order for them to come along quietly and save their questions for later. The others tensed in apprehension at that, but all Tiv could think about as he was led away from the Mending Willow and closer to the Weeping Grove was that he really didn't want to see another Elder. Not now, and never again. But his desires were worth nothing in the face of what awaited them.

***

The Weeping Grove was livelier than he thought.

From the little he'd heard on the way, Tiv had expected solemnity and an aura too grave for joy. As soon as he stepped inside, however, he was greeted by three dozen smiling faces and the excited babble of curious onlookers, all staring at their little ragtag band. Beside him, practitioners waved, excited to be home. But all Tiv could do was flinch away from the sudden burst of light that assaulted his senses, as he tried and failed to shake off the white spots behind his vision.

Someone placed their hand on his arm, guiding him forward with the rest. He heard the guards shooing away the crowd, and by the time he reopened his eyes, very little of them remained. Tiv looked to the side, his eyes widening in surprise at Ruddy's jittery appearance. He hadn't expected her of all people to help guide him. It was usually the other way around. When she caught him staring, however, she dropped her hand, as if burned, before distancing herself from him.

It was all done in one, jerky motion. Decidedly clumsy. Like an inebriated watchman that caught on just a second too late.

Tiv rolled his eyes when she pursed her lips and tried her best to ignore him. It was worth a shot, but he wasn't one to be snubbed for long. Especially when he so easily stepped in her way. He nodded his head in thanks, startling her for the briefest of moments, before she turned her head away with a huff. The skip in her step betrayed her inner glee.

Funny thing, acknowledgement. Sprinkle it with a dash of gratitude and it went a long way.

As Tiv examined his surroundings, he noticed that even the guards had dwindled. There were only four of them now. Two in front and two at the rear. They were either extremely skilled or just confident that no one would attempt to run away now that they were inside the clutches of the Institute. The latter seemed most likely. But then one of the guards at the front tilted his head just enough to shower them all with an infuriating smirk, even going so far as to couple it with a meaningful twirl of his axe, and Tiv couldn't help but scoff at the man's arrogance.

Thankfully, the axe-wielder's companion was less prone to showing off and directed them to a door at the end of the hall. It had a golden plate tacked upon it that read, *Red Scripts.*

"We're here," the guard said.

"We know," one of the practitioners stepped up. He was whipcord thin with a style that could only be described as daring. "Half of us are from this college. Do you really think we—"

"Watch your mouth, whorespawn!" the arrogant axe-wielder interrupted, aggressively waving his weapon at him.

The practitioner seemed to undergo an emotional deepfreeze at the remark because harmless cheek turned into passion, passion into fury, and fury into nothing at all. When he spoke again, his voice was a barely controlled whisper, "What did you just call me?"

"Are you deaf?" the axe-wielder sneered viciously. "I sa—"

"Cool it." Lyss stepped up. His hands glowed blue, and the temperature dropped in reaction. "Both of you."

"Lyss!" the practitioner yelled. "You can't just expect me to sit and take that!"

"He's from the Lafertti Clan," Lyss told him, as if that explained everything. "That makes him an ass by default. But *you* don't get to drag the Scripts' name down by picking a fight with trash like him. Not while I'm here."

The guard stalked forward, face red and lips curled up into an awful sneer. Obviously done trading insults. He raised his axe high into the air, prepared to split Lyss' head into two gory pieces, when the door suddenly opened. It hit the adjacent wall, echoing loud enough to split the tense air that had settled as swift and silent as the dust around them. Light trickled over their faces, as a man with wrinkled cheeks and a prominent frown stepped out, stunning everyone just long enough to distract them from their anger.

"Master Rhone!" a woman called from the crowd.

Rhone paid her no mind. He simply turned his head, slowly taking the time to glance at each and every one of them. His gaze was the piercing sort that reminded Tiv of some of the stricter Masters in the Tower. It was as if he was evaluating them all in that brief instant, combing through those he recognized and those he didn't, searching for any injured, and trying to assess the extent of their wounds with just his eyes. When his narrow gaze finally settled on Lyss, Tiv's breath caught in his throat. There was something profoundly ominous about the way he cocked his head to the side at the sight of the man's axe. Like the first flash of lightning before the coming cackle.

The guard still held the axe high over his head, but now it was gripped so tightly that the steel hilt looked ready to bend under the pressure. Whether that was from fear or his pent up rage, Tiv couldn't say. But the nervous sweat that ran down his brow was unmistakable.

Rhone took another step forward, and the guard immediately straightened into an upright position. His axe shook along with his hands. Tiv had to consciously keep his own from doing the same.

"You've all just returned," Rhone said with such vehemence that when the light from the door faltered and waned, Tiv pegged it on his voice, "and already you're picking fights with the Lafertti Clan?"

A chill fixed the room. Every practitioner in the immediate vicinity took a collective step back at his tone, seared by a sea of fire conjured by their own imagine. If Rhone was bothered by their fear, he didn't show it. His face was a chaotic mix between disappointed and livid. The latter was winning.

"Where's Philip?" Rhone asked, his eyes sweeping the crowd once more. "Don't tell me he's still out there."

"Both Philip and Dalis were taken to the Slates," Lyss said, sidestepping the guard and bowing to the waist in respect.

"They did lead them," another voice spoke up, and everyone

swiveled around to see a beefy older man leaning on the door. The sheer wideness of his shoulders was impressive. He had a well-trimmed beard that covered everything from his cheeks to his chin. It was a striking shade of black that contrasted sharply with the dull gray of his hair. His eyes were rounder than Rhone's, but no less intimidating. "It's no surprise they were locked up. The Union is afraid they'll try something again. We can't blame them for being cautious. Those two were able to gather this many practitioners. I assume they'll be calling us soon to preside over their trial."

"But Master Flax," came Lyss' immediate protest, "what about us? They weren't the only ones that left. I won't leave them to be chained and put down like disobedient dogs, while the rest of us get away scot-free."

"Who said the rest of you are free?" Flax asked, rolling his head around a thick neck. "Your fate will be decided with them."

"The rest of you were brought here upon Poten Pramm's request," one of the guards said.

"Pramm?" Rhone repeated, incredulous. "Why would she do us any favors?"

"As the representatives of the Closions and the Scripts', you should be familiar with all your members. She'd like you to separate them, make a list of all their names, and identify whoever else they brought along. Afterwards, you'll be granted permission into the Slates to speak with your primary apprentice."

"Oh? And why are members of the Lafertti Clan being so obedient to a Poten of all people? Have you forgotten that it was your college that started all this mayhem in the first place?"

"If you'd like to speak on their behalf," the guard went on, pointedly ignoring him, "then they'll be waiting for you in the Clave. You're free to bring whomever you wish."

"No crowds," axe-wielder added.

"So, she wants us to comb through all these new faces for her." Rhone pinched the bridge of his nose. He stared at them, silently taking note of the large number of Amorphs. His eyes lingered on Ruddy, who took a step behind Tiv to shield herself from his gaze. But she was too late. He'd already gotten a glimpse at her eyes. "Silas help you all."

"They'll need more than just Silas on their side to get them out of this mess," Flax remarked, waving a hand to shoo away the members of the Lafertti Clan. He waited until they disappeared down the hall before speaking again. "You leave to find your family and return without a single one of them. Who are all these people?"

"They're," Lyss paused, choosing his next words carefully, "captives. We found them in Hermit's Hovel. Just past the marshes. They were taken by the She's Disciples."

"I heard about that," Rhone said. "So, it was you that took them down. This'll work in our favor. But I doubt it'll be enough to excuse your leaving. Please tell me you captured their leader."

Lyss shook his head. "She's dead."

"Of course." Rhone sighed. "Where are they from?"

"A mix of places. The ones here are mostly from the Alps." Lyss tilted his head towards Tiv. "Except him. He's from the Tower. We parted ways with those from the Veld on our way back."

"None from the Grove?"

"A few. No one we recognized though. Their bodies were filled with maggots by the time we arrived. But we brought back their robes and any belongings they had on them just in case."

Rhone grimaced, before turning to look directly at Tiv. He straightened, prepared to answer any of Rhone's questions, but when he merely flicked his wrist in a gesture for him to step aside it was apparent that he didn't care about him, only the Elementalist he stood before. Tiv hesitated, looking behind him to meet Ruddy's wide and unblinking eyes. Though her face was set into a determined scowl, it was easy to tell just how nervous she really was. Tiv nodded at her. A brief warning that he was moving, before actually doing so.

Ruddy stood there, shifting on the balls of her feet, ready to flee at the first sign of danger. She was the only Elementalist among them, so it was obvious that she'd be singled out. And though she had her peers from the Alps beside her, they were all too young and too afraid to step up. So, Tiv did so in their place.

He didn't reel back like so many others when Rhone's eyes zeroed in on him. Not even when the Master raised his eyebrows in question. The look in his eyes reminded Tiv of his own Master. Celaris had a way of scrunching his brows that made others skid back and curse. But this wasn't Celaris, and Tiv knew that if he didn't explain himself soon, Rhone would be a lot less forgiving. He had that kind of face.

"She can't speak." Tiv pointed at his mouth for emphasis. "They cut out her tongue."

Profound silence washed over the hall.

Rhone and Flax stared at them, their expressions caught somewhere between disbelief and impolite interest. They briefly turned to meet each other's gazes, staring just long enough to wage a silent argument, before turning back, decision on both their faces. They had an air of mutual agreement that told the others everything they needed to know. Their fates, as far as their representatives were concerned, had already been decided.

"You two," Rhone pointed at Tiv and Ruddy, "are going to accompany me to the Slates and the Clave. An account of your… experiences might prove useful. As for the rest of you, line up. I want Closions on the left and Scripts on the right. Those without a college, go to Flax. I'll need a list of all your names and any immediate family you might have in the Alps."

As they parted into clusters, Tiv became acutely aware of Rhone approaching, of Lyss' scalding stare burning a blister on the back of his neck, of Ruddy's furrowed brow—the one thing that betrayed the mask she wore. It gave him a glimpse into the inner turmoil she felt.

Tiv schooled his expression into one of careful neutrality. The thin line of his lips was as formidable as the magic he wielded. He didn't waver, hardly even twitched, despite the fear that settled in his stomach like a pit of endless quicksand. From the corner of his eye, he saw someone across the room jolt away, eyes wary and knees shaking, as if trying to escape the suffocating pressure Rhone's mere presence exuded.

"Nervous, scared, or angry?" Rhone suddenly asked once he was close enough to speak comfortably without raising his voice.

It was then that Tiv noticed his clenched fists. They weren't tight enough to draw blood, but his nails dug crescent moons into the palms of his hands.

Forcing himself to relax, he met Rhone's gaze. "Angry."

The Red Scripts' representative regarded him carefully. His head cocked to the side in amusement.

"At?" he inquired.

"Right now?" Tiv asked, though he didn't wait for an answer. "The Grove's Potentate Union."

"Good," came Rhone's reply. The corners of his lips turned up in satisfaction. "We all are."

4

The Slates was a quaint place.

Tiv would even go so far as to call it charming. Although the lights here were noticeably dimmer, the orbs casting a morose glow upon the prisoner's faces, it wasn't a terrible place to be. Certainly nothing like the cells he'd been holed up in. But then again, nothing was. He'd been surrounded by rat droppings and puddles of his own blood then. There was always fungus along the outer corners of the room, sprouting through the moss ridden cracks like weeds. Persistent and undying. That, coupled with the personal bucket they so graciously gave him, cautioned anyone from breathing too deeply.

Beaten and trapped behind bars, while left to die with the metallic scent of iron and gore wasn't a fate he wished upon anyone. But Tiv didn't think the Slates appealing because of his own past experiences locked inside of a slaver's den—though that was definitely a good reason—he thought it simply because he'd been in nicer, well-kept places that actually seemed more menacing. Places like the common rooms in the Drowned Tower.

The east had numerous grand halls that were subdivided into smaller ones over the years. They weren't meant to lock practitioners up anymore, and were instead kept for the sake of history. Remnants of the Mentalists hung from the corners in the form of portraits of old powers with strict faces and strange names that he could hardly pronounce; sets of long, iron chains half-hidden behind shelves; unsteady chandeliers with pointed edges that could pierce through bone, and if that didn't kill you, the rust surely would. But it was as if the Grove had been wholly purged of that era. Stripped bare until all that remained were aging scriptures tucked away in archives that no one bothered entering. It was just so... different from the east.

The aesthetically carved holes and the long curtains of vines were mysterious and inviting. It urged him to keep moving. His eyes roved over cells sliced inside the giant tree that made up the Institute. How they did that was anybody's guess. He would've thought that the outer edges of the wood would snap or coil in strange ways, but that wasn't the case. Tiv's gaze lingered on the engraved words just above each cell. It was written in a tongue that he didn't know how to read. Each separate mark gave off just enough light to glow in the relative darkness.

Enchantments? he wondered.

Tiv's eyes met the striking red orbs of a rugged man with a tattoo on his face. He tapped mindlessly against the metal bars with his long nails. It was weak at first, unsure, still trying to find a tempo. But once he had, it grew steadily louder, and the man exhaled, visibly pleased with himself. His breath turned into something between a snort and a groan halfway out, and Tiv rubbed his ears, not knowing what to make of it. For a second, he'd sounded more bovine than human.

Focusing instead on the rhythm of his fingers, Tiv realized quickly just how strong it was. It droned on and on, sticking to his brain. And while it was stable now, it was also a hundred times more irritating. Thankfully, the sound didn't carry the deeper they went.

In the cell beside him were two practitioners. Boys with eyes too sharp for their youthful faces. They whispered words that were lost in the air over their heads, seemingly unconcerned with their fellow inmate's antics. That they were all alleged criminals seemed to be the only thing the prisoners had in common because as Tiv discretely inspected every chamber, he found each person distinctly different from the rest.

Most criminals could be stereotyped. They looked a certain way, and in the end, you just knew. Here, however, he saw a tall man with glasses balanced on the tip of his nose. He flashed Tiv the most innocent smile he'd ever seen on an adult. Across from him was a little girl that looked barely eight. She had dead eyes and an even deader countenance.

One of them was even asleep. It was an older man in what was once Master's garb. The robe was nothing more than torn cotton and gaping holes now, but that color was unmistakable. Even from five meters away, Tiv could smell the alcohol on him. It followed like a plague. How he got his hands on anything other than the usual prisoner's slop was a mystery, but he was more curious about whoever had the courage to risk slipping it to him.

Sleep fled in the presence of fear, and with everyone else jittery in their own ways, Tiv could only guess that he'd been here a long time. He doubted he'd be leaving anytime soon either. His comfort was almost offensive. But Tiv snubbed the urge to wake him. He knew from experience that an unwelcome visitor wasn't the most pleasant thing to wake up to.

"So," Rhone began, pulling Tiv from his thoughts, "Lyss said you were from the Drowned Tower?"

"What of it?" Tiv asked, rising to his full height. There was something more than the passing twinges of curiosity in Rhone's voice. Something he hadn't heard in a long time—assessment. Since Tiv had every intention of staying here for the foreseeable future, making an impression ranked high on his priorities. He wasn't some sheep that would quietly join their herd. The sooner they knew that, the better.

"You have my condolences." Rhone gave him a solemn nod, and nothing else. There wasn't an ounce of pity in his eyes. Tiv would've hugged him had his dignity allowed it. "I didn't catch your name."

"Tiv," he said. "Tiv Grovegg."

Rhone's eyes widened a fraction. The action was fleeting, yet so unbelievably controlled that Tiv wondered if he'd let him see it on purpose. But of course that couldn't be true.

"Celaris' primary apprentice?" Rhone asked.

It was Tiv's turn to look surprised. "You knew my Master?"

"Not personally. Rather, I knew Orpha." Rhone gave him a rueful smile, before he drew an imaginary line across his eyes. "I blinded him."

Tiv stilled, his stomach filled with rocks from shock. Rhone blinded Orpha? One of the largest and most terrifying Amorphs in the Tower. Orpha could transform into a griffin for Pernelia's sake! The only reason he died was because some otherworldly force was brought into the mix. Tiv's mouth opened and closed. He tried to find the right words, anything to convey just how bewildered he was by the revelation. But for the first time in over a decade, he found his vocabulary lacking.

"It was a training accident." Rhone stopped when he realized that he wasn't following. "He never forgave me."

There was a pregnant pause, and in it, Tiv found his voice. "I wouldn't have either."

"Neither would I." Rhone shrugged. He watched the corner of Tiv's mouth twitch up into an uncertain smile, before turning to the Elementalist that trailed a good distance behind them. "I'd like to know your name as well. But perhaps we should've gotten you a quill first."

Rhone halted, his fingers rubbing the stubble on his chin.

Against the grain, Tiv thought listlessly. His eye twitched involuntarily at the sound. Like boxes being torn. He rubbed his ear in appeasement, while silently cursing his animal-like senses.

Rhone didn't seem to notice, as he busied himself with looking down the hall, then back from where they came. He did that a total of four times. Each longer than the last. It didn't take a genius to figure out what he was thinking. When Rhone faced them again, decision in his eyes and in the way he squared his shoulders, Tiv already knew what he was going to say.

"I'll go with this young lady to grab what she needs," Rhone declared in no uncertain terms. This matter wasn't up for debate.

"While you tell Philip and Dalis to prepare to stand trial before the Union. We'll return once I find her something to write with."

Rhone pointed in the direction of the eerie darkness, and Tiv peered inside of it. It was as if something loomed within. A being of metaphysical dread that would start whispering in his ear as soon as he drew near. Tiv saw a few prisoners amble closer to the bars of their cells. They pressed their bodies up against the metal rods and stared curiously at their little group. The creases on their hands grew like webs as they squeezed their cage. Their eyes slinked over him. Psychological rakes that made his skin crawl. Intuition told him that they were gauging his skill, but that didn't stop him from shivering. Tiv gritted his teeth, trying to will away the sting of his own apprehension.

The walk was more terrifying now that he knew he'd have to brave it alone. It was starting to look more and more like the long row of cells he'd passed before he was forced into the manor's basement. Visited by unwelcome guests every evening, starved for days on end, and left to rot alone with his thoughts. It reminded him of the days when the only thing he had to look forward to was the rain.

Tiv *hated* the rain. It didn't wash away anything.

"They're farther down the hall," Rhone told him. "Keep going. You'll find them."

Rhone waited for him to nod, before motioning for Ruddy to follow. The Elementalist spared him a glance. Worry creased her brow, and she looked like she wanted to take him with her, but then Rhone stopped as well, and her wants no longer mattered in the face of his stern glare.

Tiv didn't bother watching them disappear. He turned, wanting to find Dalis as soon as possible. Despite his impatience, however, his pace was slow. Cautious. He walked like he had a glass full of wine and he was ordered not to stain the carpet. Attentive eyes scalded the back of his neck, making his skin itch, while simultaneously threatening to burn holes into him.

Silas' holy pyre, Tiv thought, his brows knitting together.

Don't these people have anything better to do than leer?

It was a blessing that life dwindled the farther he went. After a few more minutes, he found himself in a section of the Slates that held few prisoners and even fewer guards. The captives there were indifferent to his presence. All cold and unfeeling. Even their skin had taken on a mild greenish pallor. No doubt a product of their time spent rotting in their cells. One thing was clear though: they'd given up on life a long time ago.

Maximum security? Tiv speculated. But he already knew the answer. The way the guards held themselves spoke of more than just mediocre skill. For a second, Tiv considered the possibility of him accidentally passing the duo. He'd been lost in thought since Rhone and Ruddy left. As he looked at his desolate surroundings, the more that feeling grew.

Am I even allowed here?

On cue, one of the guards stopped to shoot him a berating glance. It was a tacit order to finish whatever business he had quickly... or else.

So, Tiv continued walking, his doubts quelled by the man's silent threat. There was no way he passed them. Even if he did, he wasn't about to turn around and give the man a reason to call him stupid. His pride wouldn't allow it. And when two familiar voices bounced on the walls around him, he knew he'd made the right decision.

"Can I ask a favor from a Creator I'm not sure I believe in?"

"Dalis," Philip said, beyond frustrated with him. "Stop being dramatic."

"Don't get annoyed," came the immediate rebuke. "The guards will just find this funny if you do."

"What did you just... you're actually *trying* to anger them?" Philip asked, then immediately regretted doing so.

Dalis drew in a deep breath, before exhaling through his nose. He was clearly spent by... well, Philip didn't know exactly. But his friend shot him a look that openly questioned his intelligence. Philip didn't mind that so much as the fact that Dalis was actually losing his patience—with him no less. As if he had the right! Philip contemplated just knocking him out altogether. At least then he'd have some peace.

"Isn't that obvious?" Dalis asked.

"No!"

"It isn't?"

"Thelarius, free me," Philip grumbled. "What exactly do you hope to accomplish?"

"Okay, you're upset. I get it. I used the wrong word. Look, I'm not trying to *anger* them," Dalis emphasized. "I was just hoping to annoy them a little. I thought that maybe they'd let us go if I did it well enough."

"What kind of ridiculous way of thinking is that?"

"Oh, back off. You're ruining my perfect plan!"

"Your perfect plan is flawed."

"Your personality's flawed."

"Real mature."

"Can you blame me?" Dalis sighed. "We've been trapped here for days, Philip. Days!"

"Barely an hour."

"In your time."

"And what alien clock do you run on exactly?"

Tuning them out, Tiv exhaled a breath he hadn't even known he'd been holding. He was glad to hear that they were doing well, despite the exasperated glances the guards threw their way whenever one of them spoke. Frankly, he was surprised none of them actually tried throwing them out. This was a hallway meant for silence. Voices boomed unnaturally here. And from the way the guards rubbed their ears, it had been a long time since they received anyone willing to break it.

Dalis and Philip kept talking as he approached. Tiv slowed his pace to a ginger skulk when their voices grew. Judging by how his friends carried on, Tiv didn't think they noticed just how much their prattling really affected their wards. Or maybe they did, and this was all just a part of Dalis' elaborate scheme.

Tiv shook his head of the thought.

Best not to read too much into it, he decided.

They either weren't all that concerned about what was going to happen to them or they were just hiding it behind their usual jousting. Tiv couldn't read the subtle lilts in their voices well enough to say for certain, but if they could keep their fates from their minds, then he supposed he could, too.

"Don't worry, Dalis," Philip said gravelly. Tiv stopped to give them a minute. "I'm sure Master Rhone is coming to get us."

"I know," Dalis replied in the same tone. He coughed once, and then in a louder, higher voice, said, "But for now you can enjoy skipping your duties and spending your day here with me, your funny, *funny* partner."

"What's gotten into you?" Philip asked. "You possessed?"

Tiv heard the scuffle of shoes and the unmistakable boom of a merciless slap to the back.

"Right, right. Enough bad jokes," Dalis hissed the final letter like a snake. "I get it. Just... don't coat your hands in gravel again. Are you trying to kill me?"

"Of course not," Philip denied. "What would I do with your body?"

"*That's* your concern? You—"

Tiv took that moment to reveal himself. "Nice place," he coolly interrupted, failing to hide his satisfaction when they both jumped at his sudden appearance.

"Nice?" Dalis repeated after a moment, shock making way for incredulity. "These markings suck the magic right from your bones. I can use a little, but... ugh. I can already feel the headache coming. And did you see these walls? They've been reinforced with so many complex enchantments that I doubt even one of the leaders of the Vanguard Circle could break free."

Tiv paused, taken aback by the unexpected rant. He'd expected a few questions regarding his presence, maybe even an ill joke about how their positions had reversed, anything, but the exasperated outburst he got.

"You're not planning on breaking out anyway," Tiv blurted out when he realized that Dalis was waiting for him to respond. "I know prison cells, and it isn't half bad in there. So, what's the big deal?"

"I just don't like my current options." Dalis threw his hands in the air, as if imploring the Creator to knock some logic into his current company. "Did you know that there are only two ways to leave this place? Up those stairs you just came through or... digging down. You don't want to go there."

"Why not?" Tiv asked, before he could stop himself.

"The Mentalists didn't choose the name Slates because it sounded pretty," Philip said. His words were little more than weak whispers, as if he was afraid someone would jump out and reprimand him. "They chose it because that's exactly what it is. A cover for the pit underneath."

"Pit sounds too nice," Dalis butted in, earning himself a disgruntled scowl from his partner. "It's more like a... tomb. Crypt. Mass grave. It's the Institutes base. Literally built on the backs of slaves, and where we are, where we're standing, is right on top of it." Dalis leaned in, his voice was so low that Tiv had to strain his ears just to hear it. "You should see it, Tiv. All the dust. All the bones and maggots piled on top of each other. That's where all the dead slaves went. Where all the practitioners that aren't given a trial go, and where those that overwork themselves in the *Anv—ow*!"

"That's enough," Philip said harshly, further digging his elbow into Dalis' ribs. The Healer winced, but shut his mouth. Tiv's stomach flipped at the uneasy look they shared. But before he could question their behavior, Philip spoke again, purposely easing his tone into something lighter. "I've only ever heard stories, but is it true that the practitioners in the east don't bury their dead?"

Tiv blinked, his mind reeling at the sudden shift in subject. It was a blatant and incredibly graceless attempt at recovery, but it worked well enough. The stifling tension around them eased into nothing, and he was held by how easy Philip made it seem.

"They light them on fire, then let their bodies drift off in small boats across the Zexin Sea," Dalis answered when Tiv didn't. "The boats are made of cedar wood and covered in rodent blood to attract Pernelia's ravens." He leaned down and shoved his face close to the bars, drawing the Amorph from his thoughts. "Speaking of the Tower, didn't you say your partner was with my sister? Tell me about him."

"Jack? He's an Elementalist. Arrogant, foul-mouthed, and hot-temp—" Tiv coughed loudly, cutting himself off when he saw the frown on Dalis' face. "I mean... great. Jack's great."

"Well, that makes me feel *so* much better."

"Jack's," Tiv struggled to find the words, "aggressive, but considerate... when he wants to be. He knows how to handle himself and is strong enough to protect those that can't."

"Strong enough to escape a crumbling Institute?"

"Yes." Tiv met Dalis' gaze, daring him to say otherwise. They stared at each other for a long moment, and Tiv couldn't stop the swell of pride he felt when Dalis looked away first.

The Healer sighed, then rolled his shoulders like he was preparing for a fight. "I'll hold you to those words."

"And I'll stand by them."

"Brilliant. Now, do you mind telling us why you're here?" Dalis finally asked the question Tiv had expected at the beginning of all this. "I have a newfound respect for you if you're here because you actually think this place is nice. I can't stand it."

"We know," Philip muttered, earning himself a glare.

"I'm here," Tiv said pointedly, "because Master Rhone told me to tell you two that you'll be standing trial before the Union when he gets here."

Silence.

They blinked at him, dazed by the news, before...

"Open with that!" Dalis yelled, reaching between the bars to grab him. He growled in frustration when Tiv stepped back. A mere inch out of reach.

"You're the ones that kept bringing up strange topics." Tiv shrugged. "Which reminds me, I saw a Master in a cell on the way here."

"Leinus Pavlov," Philip answered, peeling Dalis away from the bars, so Tiv could step closer. He wasn't surprised when the Amorph chose to stay where he was. Tiv was smart, he'd give him that.

"What did he do?" Tiv asked.

"What didn't he do?" Dalis countered. "He's a former representative of the Lafertti Clan and once great head of the Vanguard Circle's Corrections Division. Leonas Dace bested him in a duel. He stayed in the Alps for a while afterwards, but got addicted to some local poultice made of Ireldium. It blackened his lungs and ate away at his liver. Even shut down a kidney from what I heard. Long story short, once he stopped getting his fix, he became violent and attacked a few apprentice Hunters. That was five years ago. The Zenith Council voted to bring him here, and he's been rotting in that cell ever since. Though members of the Lafertti Clan still come around to cater to his... cravings."

There was a moment of silence, where all Tiv did was blink at them, before, "... Okay."

Dalis faltered. "Is that all you have to say?"

"There isn't much else *to* say," Tiv defended.

"Leave him alone, Dalis," Philip interjected. "We need to think about what *we're* going to say at the trial."

"You know better than I do that there's no swaying the Potens." Dalis scoffed, straightening his robes and donning the air of someone old and exhausted with life. "I knew what would happen if I left. I made my choice, and I'll live with it. If that means I'll be forced to work in the Anvil, then I'll live with that, too."

"It won't be a very long life then," a voice interrupted.

They turned to see Rhone blended into the dimness of their surroundings. He stood tall and imposing against the shadows, hands by his side, observing them in a way that made their blood run cold. Ruddy was behind him, cradling a writing set and a bundle of paper to her chest like a personal gift from the Creator. To her, maybe it was. She was smiling, oblivious to the way the hall seemed to darken as soon as Rhone spoke. The look in his eyes was enough to make their backs stiffen in unease.

Tiv tried to speak, to dispel the tension, but his throat was dryer than the barren wastelands of the Pulka ruins right now, and when Rhone's eyes glossed over him, he suddenly found it very important that he kept his mouth shut as tight as possible.

"I see you two are well enough to talk about the Grove's internal affairs," Rhone said, making them all flinch. "Let your tongues wag like that before the Union, and she won't be the only one in need of a writing set."

They shivered at the implication, but neither were stupid enough to make excuses. Rhone eyed them for a minute longer than necessary, and Tiv had the distinct feeling that he did it just because he liked watching them squirm. He'd bet what was left of his fingers that he was right, too. But before he could be properly awed by how intimidating he was, Rhone was already turning away.

Rhone gestured to one of the guards.

"I'm taking them to the Clave," he said. The sheer authority in his voice made him unquestionable. But it was the gruffness brought about by experience and age that gave it that final demanding touch. "Give me the keys."

The guard gulped audibly, his arm stuck out so quick that Tiv feared he might snap his joints with the motion. The keys in his hand trembled. Subtle and intermittent, but real. They stilled only when Rhone snatched them away from his clammy fingers. Tiv barely managed to control his laugh at the sickly pallor of the guard's skin. He'd been here for less than an hour, and already, he knew who he never wanted to be on the wrong side of.

✳✳✳

Tiv ignored the clatter of people as Dalis and Philip were led to the Clave.

Ignored, too, the derisive look of the other practitioners that whispered behind their hands and sneered in open disdain as they passed. The main section of the Grove had many floors, but very few walls. Rails were carved from where there was once whole sheets of bark, providing a pleasant view in exchange for privacy. Tiv could only question the safety of such low banisters. How many children must've fallen over the ledges? Dozens, surely. And out of those, how many had survived the fall? Half? A third? The Grove's history was a long and enduring one—and children, no matter their generation, never changed. Always jumping first, and only looking back when their lives were in danger.

Tiv's gaze lingered on the upper walkways. They were different from the ones below. Secluded by leaves and odd plants he'd never seen before. Their rails were higher. The support beams along each corner was thick and carved with herds of running deer. Older practitioners lingered there. Adults well into their years. The long trail of aged faces was broken only by the occasional, fresh faced adolescent. They were quiet and paid scant attention to the floors below them. There was obviously some kind of internal hierarchy associated with each section of the Grove.

They're segregated. By age? Tiv speculated. He eyed the younger men and women among them. Their faces were rounder than their peers, but they didn't have the same jittery disposition that usually hovered over those that felt out of place. *By rank,* he amended. *Do they all belong to the same college?*

He didn't know, and he didn't ask. Instead, Tiv continued to watch them interact from below. They sat in circles with low tables between them. A half-open pouch sat on one of them, plump with gaudy silver coins that were too bright and too tempting not to garner a second look. The men there were noticeably more relaxed than the rest. They leaned back and spoke civilly with one another, as if they were all old friends. Two tables over, however, sat two women that were both red in the face. One mouthed off, while the other sat with her fists clenched in what looked to be restraint.

Somehow, Tiv expected more privacy between each table. But due to the limited amount of branches large enough to carve into, the Grove's overall structure left little room for the construction of extra, more sequestered lodgings.

But even that was something to gape about.

The Grove truly was a sight. With its high ceilings and strangely shaped rooms. It had an openness that bordered on inconceivable. The sort of spectacle he'd only ever seen in Thyme's markets during harvest season. People strutted about on spiraling walkways, talking about Institute politics and some Master's awful headdress, while others leaned on the rails, fearless, despite the wood's age. There were dozens of floors, some more congested than the rest. On a particularly bright one, he saw half a dozen practitioners huddled over themselves, discussing the significance of an ancient scholar he only vaguely recalled reading about as a child.

Primordians? Tiv guessed, then wondered what section of the Grove they were assigned. There were two Elementalists among them, speaking with no less fervor. Intellectuals, despite their power. He was sure that if they displayed their skill, they'd be taken to the Alps for special training. As an Elementalist, it took a special kind of screw up to not be invited to the Alps. Maybe it was the competition of others like them that they feared? Or... did they just love their college *that* much?

Tiv turned when a Healer with chestnut hair yelled for her friend six floors above her. An Amorph, he noted, freckled and gangly. Before he could blink, the Amorph transformed into a white bird he'd never seen before, beating heavy wings and swooping down to perch on his friend's shoulder.

It was enough to make him want to shift and follow.

He restrained himself when they turned a tight corner, right inside one of the Grove's many branches. The sound from the main hall bounced along the walls in the new space. Tiv looked up to find that the high-ceiling had been replaced with something much lower. The same spheres of light hung closer here, strung together like lanterns. They cast a cheerful glow over the path, as it thinned and steepened, before eventually shifting into stairs.

Unlike the Grove's trunk, walls framed this area, turning it into a large tunnel. Every surface was carved with stills of life inside the Institute and old symbols that's meanings were lost to time. There was a bear, roaring, forever locked in battle with a pack of wolves. A hawk, perched on a broad man's shoulder. Beside him, a woman was caught gaping at an open tome. There was even an entire area dedicated to three men, drunk around a tankard. They had manacles on their feet and collars clasped around their necks. The key to their chains nowhere to be found.

"Enjoying the view?" Dalis asked from behind him.

Tiv forced his eyes forward, ashamed by the question. Dalis and Philip were about to be judged by the Grove's Potentate Union, and here he was, gawking at everything else. As if any of it mattered.

"You don't have to pretend you aren't interested," Dalis went on, clasping his shoulder and grinning knowingly. "It's new. It won't be tomorrow. Enjoy it."

Tiv paused, considering the offer. It was a generous one. Still, it wasn't right for him to… he couldn't just… he was a guest here, and would be for a long time. There would be more opportunities to look around without the weight of a trial lingering over his shoulder.

"I'd rather hear about the Grove's Union," Tiv decided after a moment. Dalis looked as if he was about to reprimand him for his solemnity, but Philip cut in before he could.

"There are many purists among the Potens," Philip began. "Especially here. The Weeping Grove is the only Institute with an unbroken line of blue-bloods. The families that rule now were the same one's appointed by Maurice, himself, and no one dares contend with them because of it. They were supposedly chosen based on wealth, intellect, and blood. Maybe even charisma. No one really knows for certain. But that doesn't matter now, does it? The only thing that matters is that they're there, and they don't take kindly to practitioners with Nebbin blood in their line."

Tiv recoiled at his words.

"Don't worry," Dalis assured. "What Philip's trying to say is that they hate everyone. I mean, who doesn't have a little Nebbin blood in their veins? You can count the families on two hands. It just so happens that a good number of those families happen to be a part of the Grove's Potentate Union. Besides, it's not a crime to marry a Nebbin."

"They don't see it that way," Philip said. "Nebbin are blemishes on the family tree to them. Nothing more."

"Thank the Creator we wiped out an entire mansion full of them, right?"

"Enough," Rhone interrupted. All it took was a glance. Backs straightened, mouths clamped shut, and all that remained was silence.

When Rhone turned back around, it was only to step purposefully onto the platform that sat at the very top of the stairs. They followed, much more hesitant. Their tentative gazes swept over the menacing double doors that stood before them like the gates to the underworld. Except instead of skeletons, it was decorated with an impossibly large elk head. It was mounted at the very top in honor of Maurice.

"I hate this place," Dalis muttered under his breath.

"I would, too, if I were you," a dewy voice crooned, drawing everyone's attention away from the top of the door to the bottom of it, where an old crone stood, hunched over with a vile grin. She had wild, unkempt hair that covered her eyes and a large robe that brushed against the wood beneath her. "We've been here for some time. I was beginning to think you weren't coming."

"Poten Pramm," Rhone acknowledged. "I apologize for the delay. Fetching them took longer than I anticipated."

"Of course, dear. I understand completely." Pramm smiled

again, before brushing away the hair from her face.

Dalis and Philip jolted back, immediately craning their necks up toward the ceiling as if to pray to Maurice for mercy. Tiv and Ruddy blinked at them in confusion. They were so confident on their way here, it made no sense to call to the First Zenith now. But when neither of them looked like they'd be straightening anytime soon, they looked forward again...

... then shrunk around the shoulders in fright.

Tiv would've screamed had his voice not bent in his throat at the gruesome sight.

Pramm's eyes were sewn shut.

The edges of her lids were an angry red, but there was no blood or lingering inflammation to suggest recent torture. Even if there was, this was an Institute that specialized in healing. It wasn't a stretch to believe that at least one person would be skilled enough to free her from those awful pieces of string and properly bandage her eyes.

Punishment, Tiv realized, as he struggled to close his gaping mouth. That was the only reason no one bothered to heal her. *It's some kind of punishment... but for what?*

"Come now," Pramm urged, amused by their discomfort. Was it their fear she smelt or could she hear how loudly their hearts were pounding? Not that it made much of a difference. "You've kept us waiting long enough."

5

When Ethil was first led away from the snowy deathtrap that was the Gelid Mountains and to the balmier, more natural woods surrounding the Weeping Grove by a group of Tippings—*Tippings!*—she'd pinched herself awake so many times that Myrrh had to swat her hand away from her upper arm like a child that ventured too close to the stove. And exactly like a child, she was both demeaned and frustrated by her meddling. Because of all the people in the world, Myrrh was the one person she expected to share her doubts. The Tippings tried to kill them. *Kill.* They almost succeeded to.

Ethil was tempted to shake some sense into her. But as soon as their leader flashed Dwyn and Myrrh a scroll that slowly began burning when they broke the wax seal over it, the two Hunters were more than willing to follow after the group. Like they weren't a bunch of dangerous assassins. Like they wouldn't just turn on them when they remembered that there was more coin to be found in slavery than escorting.

Their jobs had clearly gotten to their heads because as far as Ethil was concerned, she was the only sane one in their entire entourage. Though that didn't come as much of a surprise, seeing as how their party consisted of a deranged Hunter that liked to speak to his crab, a fat man with a horrific scar across his forehead, and two other men that grunted more than they spoke. The two were covered head to toe in multiple layers of dark cloth. But few things were easy to hide from cautious company, and

Ethil had gotten a glimpse of their skin when they passed a creek along the outskirts of the Mending Willow. One look at the blisters and angry red lines that marred every surface was enough to make her forget her resentment. Ethil rushed forward with her hands up, magic flowing from her fingertips, bright and blue and needing to ease their suffering.

Their refusal had been crushing... yet, not as well.

She'd tried. Ethil offered her help, despite her better judgment. Her conscience was clear. If they didn't want it, then she wouldn't force it onto them. And if it just so happened that those injuries gave her an advantage when they finally came to their senses and turned on them, then all the better.

Her worries, as it turned out, were for naught. They made it to the Mending Willow without mishap. The Tippings even went as far as to escort them to the entrance of the Weeping Grove before silently taking their leave. Dwyn flashed the men at the gate a golden button with the symbol of an insect emblazoned boldly onto it. Somehow, she doubted it belonged to him. It was a family emblem. A very influential one by the looks of it. Ethil doubted Leonas kept easily recognizable faces in his party.

Did it belong to the Dace family then?

It must have because the guards opened the Grove's doors with a mouthful of apologies and repeated assurances that they were free to roam until their company was able to see them. Who exactly they came here to see, however, eluded her.

Though she didn't think Myrrh or Dwyn knew either. Because the way they looked around the Grove reminded her of the few freshly appointed Masters she'd met as a child. When someone was caught stealing flasks from the labs, and they, with all of their newness and lack of experience, were forced to peer into every nook and cranny of the Tower's extensive dorms for evidence. Anything out of place. Any tiny hint that would guide them to where they needed to go or who they needed to speak to because they weren't capable of commanding the same respect their older peers held. They didn't yet have the kind of importance that others would just crack in the presence of; the kind that would never be told to wait.

Briefly, Ethil played with the thought of Roderek Drakone being told to amuse himself until someone could make time to see him… then shook her head until her hair was frazzled and the world spun. That wouldn't end well. Not at all.

Ethil didn't bother fixing her hair. The Grove's practitioners didn't much care who they were or why they looked so rundown anyway. They simply passed by without even a nod in their direction. Dwyn and Myrrh weren't speaking either, and on the rare occasions they did, it was always in snipped sentences and annoyed grunts. More boar than human.

Tired of whatever feud they had going on, Ethil took to watching her surroundings. It wasn't much different from the other Institutes she'd lived in. Embrocologists fiddled with their brews and excited adolescents screamed at each other from across the halls. There was the occasional madman that ran down the corridors though. He always went on and on about his latest discovery, while his peers brushed him off as if he'd discovered *'the cure to stopping hiccups'* every other day.

Nestled in the more secluded areas were the younger, more talented practitioners that were given special training. There was an almost innumerable number of Healers with the occasional Elementalist and Amorph sprinkled in between. Strangely enough, Conjurers made up the bulk of the practitioners here. They hurled weak tunnels of flame toward their Masters in front of shelves laden with books. None of them seemed to pay heed to the fact that parchment burned just as well as wood.

Ethil spent a long time watching them. Caught by how weak their magic was compared to those she'd met in the Alps or to the few memories she had of Jack and Sylvie, and how their powers seemed to burst from their bodies. Volatile and deadly. She'd seen Jack fight during border patrols along the Eirinne Mountains. His magic was a hurricane that spiraled with the promise of destruction. In contrast, Sylvie's flames were always under her control. But they were no less devastating. Targets were burned with a disturbing cruelty only precision and the fullness of someone's attention could bring; and if given enough fuel, Sylvie could be provoked past discipline. They were similar in that neither of them were ever reluctant in their actions. Once they made up their minds, the game was already over.

Ethil wondered if these bright eyed children would grow up to be like that. It was a frightening thought. But one that must've made their Masters proud. Measuring progress was so easy when what you were evaluating was visible—the size of a flame, the strength of the wind, the density of a spire of ice risen from the ground—even someone like her, who had no experience with teaching, could see the difference between those that excelled and those that struggled to improve. Still, prowess in a classroom was no replacement for true experience. In the end, all that truly mattered was if they could strike when it counted. Once they were tasked to go on patrols, then the true stars would shine.

She found herself staring at a particularly mad cluster of practitioners. They watched their surroundings with wary eyes, as if expecting the Grove to fall on their heads in a moment's notice. The group crept from room to room with their necks cocked in strange angles. Each one had bags under their eyes that made it seem as though they spent every waking moment alert, waiting for something they knew would come—and furious that it was taking so long.

As she watched them, Ethil listened in on the conversations of those around her. It was mostly gossip and internal affairs. Some discussions, she was happy to hear. Others, she wished she could erase from memory. Like that one about maggots found in the kitchen sinks or the other about a pair of apprentices found fornicating in one of the libraries. It wasn't all awful though. As the days pressed on, Ethil heard talk of a group of runaway practitioners that willingly returned to the Grove. They had a group of freed slaves with them.

While she hadn't been able to see them for herself, Dwyn

had, and he looked absolutely miserable about their arrival.

"Don't mind him," Myrrh told her, as they made their way to the crowded areas of the main trunk where those that instigated the mutiny—if it could even be called that—would pass through to reach the Clave. "He's just sore because his sister was one of those that left. She cast a long shadow. The kind that stretches back into childhood. If she gets ousted before he can surpass her, you'll see the full force of his inferiority complex."

"Shut up!" Dwyn said venomously. "I'm *right* here, you thrice-damned squeak."

"Is that the best you can come up with?"

"It's the only thing your feeble brain can comprehend."

Myrrh's smile fell. "What did you just say? You demented, crab-loving pe—"

"They're here," Ethil interrupted, silencing them.

The rest of the practitioners didn't cease their clatter, rather they only seemed to grow louder once the group finally rounded the corner that led away from the Grove's underground prison. They weren't physically flanked. Not really. Eyes from all over, from every floor and every branch, turned on them. There was nothing subtle about their glances and some even had the audacity to spew whatever they were thinking right in their faces.

"Why are these walks always so noisy?" Dwyn commented, rubbing the shells of his abused ears. "What exactly do these people hope to accomplish? Look, they're just ignoring them."

It was true.

While their eyes did occasionally shift when one practitioner ventured a step too close, for the most part, they disregarded them completely. An impressive feat considering their ragged appearances. Though not one she couldn't understand. Because to Ethil, those malicious strangers were nothing more than colored hazes, muttering broken strings of nonsense that her ears didn't care to register. But that wasn't anything new. From the moment they left the Alps, their entire journey had been nothing more than a massive blur that seemed more like fantasy than reality. More the effects of her own disillusioned mind... because it was disillusioned. Surely, it was. She was in the Weeping Grove, where all Healers dreamed of going, and yet, all she felt was weary, numb, and a touch of something else she couldn't put her finger on.

Being dragged around by Myrrh left little time for private grief. Time passed quicker than she thought possible. The world spun and the sun continued to rise over the horizon. Some days moved faster than most, stewed into a pot of mundane hours. Then one day, without her realizing, the jagged edges of her memory wore down. Just blunt enough for her not to get cut by errant recollections whenever she found a tome that seemed a little too familiar or a goose that would lead into a private joke only Duward would understand. She never had the chance to properly shield her heart from the potency of sorrow. It merely swept past and moved right along. Superfluous emotions like that were unnecessary, no, outright ignorable in the face of what she'd seen since the Drowned Tower's fall.

It was only when she saw Tiv, walking with a wondrous look in his eye and lines she didn't remember him having that the memories came rushing back. Astonishing, how one look at someone could bring back a flood of feelings that had been absent for months.

Tiv! Ethil wanted to shout, but refrained in fear of catching the livid gazes of the practitioners around them. Their little group had clearly gotten on the wrong side of someone they shouldn't have. Though they had some supporters in the crowd that kept the others in line, calling his name still wasn't worth the risk.

Ethil gaped once she finally got a good look at him. Was her memory of him just skewed or had he always been so thin? No, there was no way. Tiv was all broad shoulders and cut steel. Jack was the lean one.

But now she wasn't so sure.

The robes he wore swallowed him, and even with them on, she could tell that only withered remnants of muscle were all that was left of his arms. His cheeks were sunken in, his hair was greasy, and his face was more angular than she'd ever seen. Tiv's bones jutted out in all of the wrong places. The excess weight loss even seemed to affect his posture. He unconsciously hunched over himself, as if it hurt to stand.

This sinewy person before her wasn't Tiv. It couldn't be. Tiv Grovegg was the textbook definition of an Amorph—animalistic gait, broad at the chest, and quick, despite his size. The hollow man before her looked like he could keel over and die at any minute. He was so spare, she actually feared he might break his leg if he so much as stumbled.

His hands, Ethil lamented. *Creator, what happened to his hands?*

As a Healer, she was accustomed to spotting injuries most tried their best to hide. Usually it was a burn or a sprained ankle from something silly that they didn't want to explain, but nothing like this. Sure, Ethil had encountered worse. She'd healed knife wounds oozing with infection, legs torn apart by shards of ice, and at one point, she'd even seen a man with his blackened arms raised to big, empty space. But that was different. *This* was different. Those were casualties on the field.

Tiv was… he was…

They rescued potential slaves, didn't they?

Ethil swallowed.

She looked again. This time, she searched his face, his eyes, how his mouth curved this way and that, as if struggling with which emotion to express. That was all unmistakable. The ferocity was still there. Tiv was still there. Just shrouded in a layer of thick, blackened stress that had yet to be scrubbed away. Eventually, they filed through a smaller corner. When Ethil turned to her companions to suggest that they follow them, the words immediately vanished. Eaten by the monster in her throat.

How could she say anything when Myrrh looked like *that*?

With her large eyes opened wide in disbelief and her jaw slackened in the most exaggerated manner she'd ever seen. It was reminiscent to the expressions she remembered her having in the east, where she was just another apprentice ceaselessly striving for approval.

Not all an act then, Ethil decided, finally putting to rest the question about her long undercover performance. But deep down, she knew that already. If Ethil didn't know what Myrrh was looking at, then she might've teased her for her openness. But she did know, and Tiv's condition wasn't anything to laugh about.

Dwyn, however, wasn't so considerate.

"So, the tall one's missing a few fingers," Dwyn said, making them both flinch. "As if you've never sliced off one or two during your time under Master Dace. I know her methods. Elder Dace talks a lot about them. So, stop your ridiculous gaping and follow them!" With that, he went ahead. His Peose pinched its pincers energetically at them from its position on his shoulder as if urging them to abide by his keeper's wishes.

Myrrh exhaled a shaky breath. Her small frame bobbed with the motion. But before Ethil could offer a sympathetic ear, Myrrh was already hurrying after her temporary partner.

It wasn't a long walk.

They trailed just far enough behind to escape notice. Dwyn and Myrrh had even taken the extra precaution of shifting into tiny lizards. They crawled along Ethil's robes, hiding between the folds of loose fabric. They were so light that she could hardly feel them. As Ethil ascended the tall flight of stairs that led to the Clave, she seriously considered the idea that they'd just leave her to fend for herself and attach themselves onto Tiv or one of the others in his group. But the notion was trashed as soon as she set foot on the large platform.

The Clave, as it turned out, was guarded by a woman with a stooped spine and a nest for a head. Her entire body seemed to shift toward Ethil, somehow hearing her incredibly light steps, before she wrinkled her nose in distaste. Ethil was tempted to do the same. The crone smelt like incense and arrogance. The sneer on her face was enough to deter even the kindest of visitors.

"Slink back to whatever hole you three crawled out of," she hissed. "I won't have Hunters listening in on Grove business."

How she knew Dwyn and Myrrh were even there was a question for the ages. But all Ethil cared about now was the bewildered group that had turned to see who the crone was yelling at. For an unbearable instant, her gaze locked with each of theirs. Four were unfamiliar, and of those, all were unfriendly. She caught Tiv's eye last. He looked at her in disbelief; both eyebrows raised, mouth slightly parted. He wanted to speak. That much was obvious. But they hardly knew each other. So, there was very little to say. Even less that needed to be said with any urgency.

Before either of them could decide how to react, the door slammed shut, separating them once more.

***

"The look on your faces when you saw that guy," Dwyn howled. "What is he? An old flame? Did he play you both? Because let me tell you now that I doubt he's gonna be much fun with such few digits."

"It wasn't like that!" Ethil yelled, horrified.

"Sure it wasn't." Dwyn grinned. He leaned back into his seat, handing his Peose a small rock that it gladly rolled in circles on the walnut table between them.

They were in one of the private rooms in the Closions' quarter. It was a cozy place filled with warm colors and even warmer lights. Flowers grew above them. Judging by the vibrancy of their petals, they were well cared for. The room itself was littered with furniture that sat low enough to brush against the bottom of their knees while standing. Each tabletop was filled end to end with silver dishes piled high with an assortment of fruits and sweetened bread. Every now and then, practitioners would come in to exchange the empty plates with new ones or add even more to the table. Needless to say, they'd eaten their fill as they waited for Dwyn's sister to arrive. It was at least nice to know that the inner sectors of the colleges were more comfortable than the common grounds.

"Seriously though," Dwyn went on, "who is he? Someone from the Tower, right? If he even has Myrrh in a tizzy, then he's definitely high up on the ladder."

"High on the…" Ethil trailed off, unsure of what he was implying. "If you're asking if he held some sort of position in the Tower, then he was a primary apprentice."

"Called it!" Dwyn winked. "This girl doesn't bend for just anyone."

Myrrh promptly threw the closest thing she could find at him, which, coincidentally, was his crab. The crustacean landed on his face with startling accuracy. Ethil had a feeling that Dwyn didn't dodge on purpose though, not wanting to hurt his crab, despite the fact that it was now unintentionally clawing his eyes out and leaving enough scratches to make even water sting.

"*Vaklas,*" Dwyn cursed. He fought against the sudden urge to transform and just have at her. "Alright, I get it. Neither of you want to talk about your ex. And here I thought women liked talking about love."

"Then between the three of us, doesn't that make you the feminine one?" Myrrh quipped.

"Fine with me, man hands."

"Dwyn," a woman interrupted.

They turned to find an older woman with frown lines framing her lips and nose, aging her past her years. She had long arms that unbalanced her smaller legs, and the fat prayer beads that were wrapped around the entire span of her forearm only brought more attention to the fact. More circled her waist, serving as a makeshift belt for her robes. Though she didn't wear the garbs of a priestess, the sheer amount of beads suggested a certain amount of piety. As did the golden emblem of Maurice that gleamed around her neck.

She has the same eyes as Dwyn, Ethil noted.

By the door, stood another woman with impressive scars littered all over her hands and forearms. There were a few half-hidden by the collar of her robes, suggesting more across her chest. Nothing about the way she watched Dwyn's sister suggested friendship. It was too soft. Too careful. It was clear to all that she was a concerned lover.

When she caught Ethil looking, she flashed her a sheepish smile that didn't at all fit the profile Ethil had built in her head of a cool and distant Conjurer. But before Ethil could apologize for staring, she'd already turned around to watch the hall, making sure no one interrupted them.

As soon as Dwyn saw them, the smile on his face curved downward into an upset grimace. "Sister," he greeted, while crossing his arms. As if his displeasure wasn't obvious enough.

"Don't make that face, Dwyn," she chastised, though her expression mirrored his completely. "It makes you look like a hound. The terminally ill kind."

"You're one to talk." His gaze purposely lowered to her rumpled clothes and the bandages wrapped around her neck. He'd gotten paper cuts and non-lethal nicks from errant arrows dozens of times, but he'd never been injured there. That wasn't a place for a simple injury.

Dwyn wrinkled his nose when he caught the robust scent of *Sicivine*. It was often used when infection had set in and all of the usual means to get rid of it weren't enough. Most practitioners knew it by smell alone—rotten eggs and the heavy musk of charred timber. Few wounds were grievous enough to warrant such a potent salve. Fewer, still, the excessive use of it. Dwyn saw the green spread under her chin. It curved all the way up to her ears, making them glisten. There weren't many capable of getting so close to his sister. Her opponent was undeniably skilled.

"Shouldn't you get yourself checked by a Healer?" he asked, not even trying to hide his commanding tone. Dwyn pointed at his own neck for emphasis. "I'm sure they could fix that for you."

"Did you pick up that forceful urging from Elder Dace?" his

sister replied. There was nothing scathing or playful about the way she said it. It was all cold intensity. "It's a good tone. Strong. Assertive. It suits you."

"Thank you?"

"But don't use it on me."

Dwyn rolled his eyes.

"I just returned," his sister went on when his jaw clenched shut. "But I'm sure you already know that. I'll get my wounds checked once things have calmed down, or better yet, I'll tend to them myself once I get a proper night's rest."

"Can you afford to wait that long?" His eyes shifted briefly to the woman by the door. "They must be bad if you've got Daisy following you."

"It's not fully out of concern. Master Flax is testy right now. He doesn't want us roaming around on our own."

"I still can't believe you actually left." Dwyn sighed. "What were you thinking?

"That our cousin is missing."

"Did you even find him?"

Her eyes sparked at the question. "Cut to the chase," she said, putting a hand on her hip in impatience. "Why are you here, Dwyn? I know this isn't a family visit. You hate the Grove, and I doubt Elder Dace is so laidback that he'd allow you to run wherever you please."

"I'm here to investigate."

"Investigate what?"

"What do you think?" he asked meaningfully.

She clicked her tongue at him, before turning to Ethil and Myrrh. She sized them up, and they instinctively straightened their shoulders in response. There was pride in the way she lifted her chin, but nothing to suggest arrogance or contempt.

"My name is Vivian. I'm a member of the Closions."

"Myrrh," she introduced, standing. "Hunter Division."

"Good to know the Alps hasn't abandoned us entirely," Vivian muttered. "How many Hunters are in the Grove now?"

"Seven," Dwyn answered.

"So few?"

"Having more than five in any Institute is unheard of."

"Now, that *is* news." Vivian turned to Ethil. "And you are?"

"Ethil," she paused, "from the Drowned Tower."

"The Tower?" Vivian echoed, tilting her head in thought. "That must be hard on life expectancy."

Ethil leaned back in surprise. "W—What?"

"We recently found an Amorph from the Tower in a slaver's den past the Narrow Marsh. He's a tough one. The rest of the prisoners on his floor were all dead."

"Sister!" Dwyn yelled.

"Don't be so sensitive," Vivian muttered. "She can take it."

"Not everyone is like you."

"Don't coddle people, Dwyn. It's unlike you." Her fingers glazed over the wrapping around her neck, as if she wanted to scratch the skin beneath. "Now that introductions are over, what do you want? I'm sure there's a reason you were waiting for me here instead of slinking around the Institute doing your jobs."

"We were hoping you could tell us more about what's going on between the colleges," Dwyn revealed.

"I've been out for weeks. Do you really think I know anything about what's currently happening?"

"No, but I didn't ask for fresh information, did I? Outdated news is still news."

Vivian gave him a bitter look. "As far as I can tell, the overall dilemma is still the same. Livid underlings and conceited leaders. Both sides have only beeng getting worse over the years."

"Are the Potens still mistreating practitioners?"

"What do you think?"

"Has it gotten worse?"

"The Alps has finally allowed the colleges to take full responsibility over the Grove's affairs after the Summit, so *of course* they're abusing their power. They don't have much time left. While I don't condone what they're doing, I do understand it. I'd be venting all of my anger, too, if I was suddenly ousted from the only job I've ever had."

"Turnover," Dwyn suddenly said in an effort to steer the conversation away from her usual rants. "Let's talk about that. How much do you know about the change in leadership?"

"Stop asking stupid questions, Dwyn."

"The answers might be obvious to you, but confessions are part of my job. I need to hear you say it, not rely on guesswork."

"Creator," Vivian cried, exasperated, "you need to get away from the north. Spend a holiday in Yorn or something."

"Just answer the question."

"I don't know much, okay?" she said. "I've heard the basics: the Potentate Union will be dissolved, and the representatives will take their place."

"I don't understand," Ethil cut in. "Aren't they just creating a new Potentate Union?"

"That isn't the point," Vivian said sharply. "The Grove needs new leaders. The ones on top were blinded by their power long ago."

"We've heard, no," Myrrh amended, "we've *seen* a few fights break out since we've come here. If the colleges are finally being allowed to govern, why are they fighting?"

"There has always been in-fighting amongst the colleges. It's become rougher over the years, but never so openly violent. Out of all of us, the Lafertti Clan has pushed for dissolution the hardest and so expect more power now that their pleas have been answered. Some are still playing good. Doing the work of the Potens and feigning ignorance, but the majority are acting alongside their representative, using more... active means to get what they want. It seems like a trick to me. Like they want people to believe them divided. Not that it would do them any good. Their protests have already reached the Alps because we've received a number of letters regarding their behavior over the past few months. They've always been a hot-blooded bunch, but they knew where to draw the line. Reckless abandon doesn't further colleges. Every child knows the consequences of disgracing their house. This is no different. But recently, they've been acting as if they're above dissolution themselves."

"Are you suggesting that someone is using them?" Dwyn questioned, bewildered by her words. "An entire college?"

"They could be backing them," Myrrh cut in. "Have any of their Masters changed within the past year?"

"None that I know of," Vivian answered. "My colleagues in the Red Scripts', however, suspect that they have a backer in the north. An Elder no doubt. From one of the older families. Very few can make a college as old and powerful as the Lafertti Clan move, and those that can are frightening."

"But why would an Elder meddle in the Grove's affairs?"

"The bigger your castle, the more restraining it becomes. Maybe they wanted to branch out? There are many warmongers in the north. Those looking to show off their skills mostly. Then there are those that would incite chaos simply to prove a point or to achieve their own personal goal. Whatever the case, it doesn't matter. Not now. But whoever suggested a public announcement is clearly not a friend of the Grove... or any of the colleges."

"What do you mean?" Ethil asked. "Didn't the Zenith Council announce their decision, so that the colleges could properly prepare to take the Potentate Union's place?"

"It would seem that way." Vivian shrugged. "But people aren't always so patient."

"You're saying they don't want to wait? Why not? If they'd just sit back for a few more weeks until the Summit is over, then they'll be able to—"

"Not a single Arch Poten has even arrived," Vivian interrupted. "They're afraid the Zenith Council will renege on their promise or that the current Potentate Union will somehow convince them otherwise. All valid assumptions. But rising up without the support of the Alps' will only divide us. The Potentate Union does still have backers. The other colleges have tried to reason with the Lafertti Clan, but most have only resulted in unnecessary conflict. It doesn't help that many secretly agree with their methods. The Elders aren't fools. I'm sure they took the spirit of the Lafertti Clan into account. They knew those fools would start something. Like I said... someone unpleasant is pulling the strings."

"I can't think of anyone that would benefit from sparking conflict in the Grove," Myrrh muttered. "In the Alps, sure... but the Grove?"

"Then you aren't thinking hard enough," Vivian said. Blunt and merciless. "Incite violence here and the next target would obviously be the Alps. Aren't they under isolation now? The Vanguard Circle's forces won't be able to help us should something happen, and the practitioners here aren't forgiving enough to pardon being abandoned. They're creating animosity. The struggle that will surely arise here is just another step. The masses are powerful, and if left to their own devices, they can be very aggressive. Revolts are one of the worst things that can happen to those on top. Can you truly think of no one that wants to show what a lack of control can do to an Institute? No one that can take advantage of that fear to enforce their own rule?"

Myrrh was silent as over a dozen faces came to mind. Though one did stand out among all the rest. One she was too afraid to state.

"But to go so far..." Ethil trailed off.

"Necessary casualties," Dwyn said insensitively. He shooed away the topic, earning him glares from all three women in the room. He stood, picking up his crab and adjusting his robes, clearly preparing to run off somewhere. "I've heard enough speculation to last me a lifetime. It's time I did my job. I wasn't chosen to have opinions on the Institute's politics."

"This is why I rejected the Vanguard Circle's offer," Vivian said. "Can't you at least pretend to care?"

"I heard the previous head of the Corrections Division is in the Grove's underground prison," Dwyn said, ignoring her remark. Along with the way her eye twitched in annoyance.

"What of it?"

"I'd like to meet him."

"And I suppose you want me to set up the meeting?" Vivian said, incredulous. "You're joking."

"I'm not."

"You're insane then. He's the Lafertti Clan's previous head. He isn't someone you can just whimsically decide to meet. You might work under Elder Dace, but you're nowhere near as important. Keep acting like it and you'll wake up one day with a dagger pressed to your throat."

"If you can't help, then just say so."

Vivian snarled. "If you want to meet with him so badly, then you need permission from one of the representatives, their primary apprentices, or one of the four direct apprentices of the current Lafertti Clan's head, Master Zacarias."

"What about your college? Can't you just speak to your representative on my behalf?"

"The Closions are under careful scrutiny at the moment. I can try, but I can't promise you anything. I doubt Master Flax wants to give the Potentate Union another reason to incarcerate our practitioners."

"What about his primary apprentice?"

"Gregor has a stick for a spine. You can't count on him to pass the salt, let alone grant you entrance into the Slates. Though he's Master Flax's son, he's shown no ability to lead. Candidates are already being sought out to take his place. His sway in the Grove is shaky at best."

"Then who *can* I count on to help me?" Dwyn asked, frustration leaking into his tone.

"Master Ivy of the Sanct Union," Vivian said after a moment's contemplation. "But she's not one to do favors without asking for something in return, and debts to her are paid in sweat and blood. Still, she's there should you have need of her. You can also try seeking out Master Rhone's primary apprentice, Philip. Of all the next heads, he's the most mild-tempered. Watch out for his companions though. He tends to walk with two or three people at any given time, and none of them should be taken lightly."

"They've assigned him guards?"

"Not at all. Most are friends. Others are tag-alongs looking to learn something. Philip is... well-liked by the Scripts."

"Just the Scripts?" Dwyn questioned. "Do the other colleges have a problem with him?"

"Only a scant few are personal," Vivian assured. "You'll find that most of our grudges are inherited. The practitioners in the Sanct Union have an especially long memory."

"But aren't the inherited ones the most difficult to resolve?"

"It depends on the grudge."

"Of course." He sighed. "So, where's Philip now?"

"In the Clave."

Dwyn paused.

He exchanged a glance with Myrrh, who merely shrugged her shoulders and grabbed an entire loaf of sweet bread from the table. A silent argument seemed to run in the air between them, before Dwyn caved in with a sigh.

"After all this, I have to wait again?" Dwyn groaned. This was going nowhere.

A flicker of affection finally flashed in Vivian's eyes. The corner of her lips tilted upward, and she reached out to ruffle his hair. Dwyn's response was an annoyed click of his tongue, as he tried to unsuccessfully back away from her touch.

"It won't be long now," Vivian promised.

He hoped not.

His hope was realized sooner than he expected because not even a second later, the door was flying open and someone came barreling into the room. An Amorph, they quickly realized, as he stopped to breathe before them. He was smaller than most, with a pair of thin, round spectacles on his nose. His hair was shaved along the sides, the top hanging pathetically in front of his face, clearly mussed in his mad dash to get to them.

"Are you from the Vanguard Circle?" he asked between pants.

Dwyn straightened. "Who wants to know?"

"I'm terribly sorry for not getting in touch with you sooner," the Amorph said, reaching into his pockets to pull out a letter with a broken wax seal. He opened it to show them a page full of elegant handwriting and the Dace family seal stamped in navy blue along the bottom. "Elder Dace sent word some time ago, telling us that he'd be sending someone to check on things. I would have come to you sooner, but I've been stuck tending to... other problems. There was a small cave-in in our tunnels, you see, and—"

"Can you get us into the Slates?" Dwyn asked, disregarding his excuses.

The Amorph looked taken aback for a moment. "The Slates? Why would you," he stopped to swallow when he caught sight of Dwyn's raised brow, "y—yes, I can."

"What are you waiting for then? Lead the way."

"I'm sorry, but I can't right now."

"Why not?"

"As I said, there was a small cave-in inside our tunnels. I've been digging it out for the past week, but then I heard that the two of you had arrived, so I rushed here. It'll take a few hours to clear." He breathed deeply. "I... I promise this isn't a common occurrence. *Please* don't report it to our Captain."

Dwyn rolled his eyes, before falling gracelessly back into his seat. His wiry frame molded to the chair like wet leaves to the ground. His legs bounced up and down in a classic sign of impatience.

"Thelarius, help me," Dwyn said after a moment, "I *hate* waiting."

6

Still caught in a daze from seeing such a familiar face, Tiv stalked forward, tracing after Dalis without really seeing him. He didn't realize how their footsteps echoed ominously or how the atmosphere shifted as soon as they stepped through the door. All he noticed was the world softening at the edges, blurred by the warm lights that glowed somewhere high above them. There were no more intricate carvings here. Just wood. Dark and spicy.

Tiv stopped when Philip grabbed his shoulder, preventing him from moving forward. Out of instinct, he looked up, his eyes instantly locking on a man that was impossible to overlook. He was tall and broad at the shoulders, donning a feathered cloak that only made him seem more vigorous. His eyes swept over them with all the subtlety of a blazing bonfire in the dead of night. The very pressure of his presence seemed to spill into them, before settling around the room. As if the air itself surged forward to do his bidding, reshaping to fit those around him in a private bubble that only he commanded. Though from the distinct cobalt blue that glazed over his missing fingers, Tiv knew that couldn't be the case. He was a Healer. A very intimidating one at that. A trait most Healers in the Grove seemed to share.

A Poten? Tiv wondered, but from the way Rhone merely locked eyes with him in brief acknowledgement, Tiv doubted it. *A Master then.*

"That's the Primordian's representative, Caius Varron," Philip whispered. "Smart *and* deadly. Don't make eye contact."

Listening, Tiv looked behind the man instead, where the stern-faced Potens sat. They rested in high chairs that were arranged in a semi-circle. Each was built slightly uncomfortable to caution anyone from staying too long. High above them hung a chandelier made out of gridded iron and bone. Tiv hoped they weren't human. But somehow, he doubted it.

As his eyes swept over them, he couldn't help but notice how most of the Potens looked mediocre compared to the intimidating Healer he'd first seen. They were all dressed in the same flowing robes. Though the embroidered patterns on their chests differed in the way they coiled, it wasn't enough to truly stand out. Not in the same way Poten Pramm did with her terrifying eyes and greasy smile. The scare he'd gotten from her was enough to traumatize him for life.

Shoulders sagging in disappointment, it was only when he caught sight of a young boy seated at the very heart of the room did he remember just where he was—and how disrespectful he was being by not standing his straightest.

There was no doubt this time... *he* was the Arch Poten.

And here he was, standing before him with a room full of his advisers. Men and women hardened by years and spoiled by wealth. They could declare him a deserter, and every single practitioner across Ferus Terria would be obligated to capture him. Tiv shivered at the thought.

Not wanting to think about it, he examined the Grove's leader instead. The boy's chair was taller and more elaborate than the rest. Framed by animal skins and precious stones embedded into the wood. A snow owl was perched on the back of it. Streaks of wild blue sprouted from its feet and extended upward over its head and body, twining like branches across its wings.

A Peose, he noted absently. It had been so long since he'd seen one. He'd almost forgotten how brilliantly their veins pulsed. Bright and hazy. Like storm lanterns lit during a downpour. The owl stared at them just as intensely as its unsmiling master… and they stared right back. Not in scrutiny or defiance, but in awe.

Many things could be said about the revered Arch Poten of the Weeping Grove, and Tiv had heard them all. A common one was that he was a child, too quiet and too inexperienced in the ways of the world to lead an Institute; his Master had died before ever having groomed him for the position. Another was that he was submissive. Prone to daydreaming. He always wandered a step behind his domineering Potens, content to hand over the reigns. But the one that trumped any ill complaint against him was that he was a sensational Healer. The sort of prodigy that only came about once every age.

He was such an asset that the majority of practitioners both in the Grove and out of it didn't think it a stretch to call him the Crown Age's second coming of Maurice. To underestimate his abilities was a display of ignorance. The unforgiveable sort that would either get someone a boggled look or endless bouts of pity-filled laughter.

What many failed to mention, however, though perhaps acknowledged in the furthest recesses of their minds, was that Lucian Cole was… indisputably beautiful. An ethereal being made to walk the mortal realm. With a sharp jaw and aristocratic cheeks, further enunciated by startlingly blonde hair, he looked almost too perfect to be real. Tiv swore that, for a split second, a shaft of light had shined down upon him because before he could even register, he was squinting.

The boy was dazzling. And he was what—twelve? Thirteen? Some things just weren't fair.

"Welcome," Lucian greeted, his blue eyes glittering.

Tiv muffled the urge to groan in envy. Though he was young, he spoke with a quiet forcefulness that he was sure would one day turn into a rich smolder. The slight frown etched into his features wouldn't be considered sour or severe, but a form of striking displeasure. A constant shroud of seriousness that would no doubt get him compliments from his peers.

Tilting his head in an effort to find a flaw, Tiv noted that he seemed almost feeble from a certain angle. He was nowhere near becoming a man. Though Tiv faulted his apparent delicacy on the large overcoat he wore. It dwarfed him. The deep scarlet didn't suit his features just yet. But it would. Soon.

Growing up, Tiv had overheard many things from the adolescent girls in the Drowned Tower. They believed things that he could poke holes straight through the logic of. Such as how only unfortunate looking men appreciated assertiveness in a woman or that everyone sought gentleness from their partner. Young, innocent notions. Too general to be true. But Tiv did find one of them to be somewhat accurate. For the moment.

Only those blessed in the face had the capacity to brood.

With a sigh, Tiv turned just in time to catch the bespectacled expressions of everyone else in the room, save for Rhone and the other Potens, who were evidently used to being in the boy's presence. There was a long minute of uncomfortable silence where everyone just stared at each other, until finally, Rhone cleared his throat. A harsh and guttural sound. It was followed by an undignified yelp, courtesy of Dalis, as he and Philip were pushed forward.

"Pardon these two," Rhone said, though his tone suggested that even he couldn't find it in himself to forgive them. His voice was like lava erupting over a tree revered for its hardiness. Harsh and merciless. "They're tired from their journey."

"Ah, yes," one of the Potens spoke. He had a fledgling smile on his face that exposed his missing teeth. "Care to explain why you decided to leave with an entire group of well-trained practitioners behind you? Without our permission or the permission of your representative at that."

"Isn't it obvious?" Dalis tilted his chin up high in defiance. "I was looking for my s—"

Philip elbowed him in the gut before he could finish.

"We heard about a slaver ring operating along the outskirts of the Narrow Marsh," Philip explained, only half-lying. "We decided to investigate in the hopes of finding some of our missing peers from the Drowned Tower."

"That isn't enough reason to leave," another Poten argued. "Why didn't you bring this information to us? We would've sent out a search party, or better yet, sent word to the Circle. There are others more adept at handling these types of investigations."

"I know there are. But you'd need to verify the information before contacting them. How long would that take?"

"How incompetent do you think we are?" he roared. "You'd rather desert than wait—"

"We were ready then. There was no reason to wait."

"So, you don't deny deserting?"

"If we deserted, then why would we return?" Philip sighed in resignation. "Are any of you even listening to me?"

"Why would we? It's practitioners like you that blight our Institute... or perhaps it's that impure blood running through your veins that challenges us?

"If you got rid of every practitioner with Nebbin blood, then you wouldn't preside over anyone," Philip said.

"Watch your mouth, boy," Poten Pramm suddenly said. Her tone was a thousand times ruder. "You're not a representative yet. Just what have you been teaching him, Rhone?"

Before Rhone could speak, Dalis interjected, raising his hand like his opinion mattered to them. "I actually *like* living," he said as stoically as possible, "and I'm no glutton for punishment, so I'm not agreeing with Philip because he's my partner, but because he's right. If we deserted, then why would we return? The reason we left was simple. Ever since the Tower fell, no one has listened to our appeals for search parties. Not even when we reported that we'd lost contact with a number of our family and friends."

"If you're trying to convince us that your *desertion* wasn't purely due to your own selfish reasons, then you're failing miserably," one of the Potens said obstinately.

"I'm not," Dalis bit back. "What I'm trying to say is that in the Red Scripts' alone, twenty-three of our members have yet to hear from their families from the Tower. Even after reporting this, none of you would give us the permission we needed to leave."

"Do you count yourself amongst them, Dalis Sirx? Because we received a message from your father. He attempted to explain the brashness of your actions to us."

"Why would my father—"

"Your sister hasn't been found yet, has she?" The Poten gave him a slimy smile. "Sylvie Sirx, primary apprentice to the Tower's Arch Poten. A lofty title. A *family* title. Assuming she doesn't have any children, that title would go to the next of kin. Is the title of Arch Poten something you'd like to claim as your own one day?"

Dalis' eyes widened. His jaw clenched in anger at what the man was insinuating. "I wanted to bring her back to the Grove with me! Not..." he wrinkled his nose, disgusted by the mere thought. Breathing deeply, he tried to steer the subject away from their clearly senile ramblings. "Why would I ever want to be Arch Poten? Everyone knows that's just a glorified puppet's sea—"

"We didn't find her," Philip interrupted, clasping Dalis' shoulder hard enough to bruise.

"Then why return at all?"

"Because we heard about the Alps' decision to abolish the Potentate Union." Dalis reveled in their infuriated expressions. "And even if I didn't find her, that doesn't change the fact that our quick action saved lives. Which is more than—"

Philip squeezed his shoulder even harder.

It was out of respect for Master Rhone that Dalis resisted the urge to curse Philip to the Creator's side and back in every language he knew. He settled for a displeased grimace instead. One that conveyed every single one of his grievances. Along with the promise of a long and bothersome retaliation.

Unfortunately for him, Philip had grown used to those looks over the years—and even better at ignoring them. So, it was with perfect composure that Philip faced forward, mouth straight and shoulders squared, still holding him in place and fully prepared to keep on doing so. All of this, despite the fact that the Potens had already begun speaking amongst themselves, turning their sorry excuse of a trial into a debate about a fitting punishment.

Like they couldn't hear every single word of scorn that left their mouths.

As the mild grumbles and hand-covered protests turned into shouted disputes, Dalis knew their fates would be decided soon. It was just as he suspected—and surely what everyone else did as well—this was no trial. They'd already deemed them guilty from the start. This was an interrogation, tacked with a more pleasing title for the public's sake. Nothing more.

At least that's what he believed until Lucian intervened.

"Enough."

His voice was quiet, but it carried like a howl in the night. A demand for obedience. Even Poten L'nara, the loudest of them all, stopped shouting. The impassioned speech of sending them to suffer for a decade patrolling the forest died in her throat as surely as a candle blown by a gust of wind.

They stared in silence, tense and unbreathing, until Lucian sighed. Just dumpy enough to convey his boredom. There was an air about him that suggested exhaustion, but from what, no one could say. The world, maybe? It was a familiar look to anyone, and it was one he wore well, so it only seemed right. Though certainly not for someone his age.

Lucian leaned back in his seat, cradling his cheek in his palm. Behind him, his Peose unfurled its massive wings. As if it could sense that its keeper desired their attention. It was a moving sight, albeit a useless one. Lucian had their attention ever since they stepped inside the room. All he had to do was speak.

"More than half of you are prepared to decide their fate based on your own reckless anger," he began, tone drawn and jaded. "This isn't a trial. It's a tit-for-tat of backhanded insults and useless questioning. I'm tired of it."

Dalis would've cheered had he not been so stunned by the declaration. It was selfish. Positively childish. But only because it came from a child's mouth. He was sure that if someone older and harsher like Master Flax had said the same, he'd be scared witless.

Before Dalis could recover, Lucian was already directing his gaze at him. "You say you returned because of the... luckless decision that the Zenith Council has made regarding our Union. But I'm interested to know if you accomplished what you first set out to do."

"No," Dalis said, as steady as his suddenly parched throat allowed. "I didn't find my sister."

"No news either?"

"Nothing," a pause, "nothing concrete."

Lucian didn't even blink.

"So, that means you did hear something," Lucian concluded. "From who? A survivor from the Drowned Tower?" His eyes shifted to look over Dalis' shoulder. They glazed downward for the briefest of moments, and Dalis knew he was looking at what little was left of Tiv's hands. There was no question in his tone when he said, "You heard it from the Amorph."

"Tiv Grovegg," Philip answered. "Primary apprentice to the late Master Pyrne Celaris. We found him beaten and tortured in a basement in the Hovel."

"I've heard stories of the Amorphs in the east," Lucian said. "And I'm sure they did as well, so I doubt they were short on buyers. Was he just a special case? Answered back one too many times? Or did they stick you in a ring, forcing you to fight until your knees gave out? One finger every time you fell?"

While the majority of people flinched at his words, Dalis actually laughed. It certainly didn't seem like a joke, nor did his tone imply it. But the humor was right up his alley.

"You've been listening to too many stories." Dalis grinned, finally finding his composure. There was something about discovering common ground in ridiculous things that reminded him that Lucian was, indeed, human. "Nothing so elaborate though. He was tortured. That's all."

"But why?"

"For answers," Dalis revealed. He and Philip had agreed to keep their findings a secret from the Union, but having never spoken to Lucian directly, he was pleasantly surprised to find that he wasn't at all like he expected. The boy was nothing like the Potens he sat beside. "When I found the woman responsible for keeping Tiv and the others locked up, she claimed that she was seeking the secret to our magic circuits. The idea came to her when she saw an *Orivellea* in an Elementalist's head. She was trying to recreate them."

"Did she succeed?" Poten Pramm asked.

"Of course not," Philip cut in. He shot Dalis a brief, withering look. "But she did know that they were made in the Grove. If she knew we made them, then no ordinary practitioner leaked that information. All those she supposedly questioned didn't know anything about how they were made."

"Are you accusing us of something, boy?"

"It always circles back to accusations with you lot," Dalis interjected. "What we're saying is that someone that knows about the Anvil has switched sides. If the Nebbin find out the—"

"We don't need *you* to remind us of the consequences!" Poten Pramm stood. "Have you forgotten that you're in the presence of outsiders, Dalis Sirx? Learn to hold your tongue."

"They've suffered more for the Institute's secrets than any one of you!"

"Who are you to make such baseless claims? Don't speak of things you know nothing about. And as for those unfortunates you found in the Hovel, they're practitioners. They'll live and they'll die for the Institute, regardless of whether they know what they're dying for. It's not our fault they suffered so. They can only blame themselves for getting captured."

"You can't be ser—"

"Is this the Elementalist you were speaking of?" Lucian abruptly asked. His question was enough to silence everyone around him a second time. He waited a moment. Then two. Before, "Well?"

The girl bobbed her head once. She stepped out from where she was half-hidden behind Tiv.

"How long were you in that woman's captivity?" Lucian went on, unperturbed by their shifting eyes at the sudden topic. They were clearly trying to be as delicate as possible with her. Admirable, but ultimately, a waste of his time.

She got on her knees, dipped a quill in a bottle of ink, and wrote on an empty page. No one asked why she did. Once she was done, she held it up for him to see. The others, curious as they were, couldn't help but take a peek as well.

'*204 days,*' they read.

The temperature seemed to drop around them.

"Can you confirm their story about your captors?"

She nodded.

"Good." Lucian said. "I've decided."

All of the Potens turned to him, staggered by the declaration.

"Wait, Lucian!" Poten L'nara shouted. "Just what do you mean by that?"

"I want everyone they saved from the Hovel to give me a complete written account of their experiences. We'll send a copy to the Council, which they can use however they please. To scare the younger apprentices, I suspect. I, at least, want to read about what they were saved from before making a decision. In light of this, the punishment of those that left will be decided upon my return from the Summit. For now, they'll be tasked with patrol duty inside the Mending Willow until further notice." He turned to Rhone. "Double Demar Spells will be placed on each of them to keep them from wandering too far — one by Master Varron and another by Master Ivy. You're free to place your own if you wish. If they so much as step outside of the forest, they'll officially be declared deserters, regardless of their reasons."

"Consider it done," Rhone agreed, before the Potens could protest the decision.

"Lucian," Poten L'nara tried to reason. "Think about what you're saying. Such a light sentence, even if it is temporary, will make us seem —"

"We can't drag this trial out any longer," Lucian interrupted, meeting the gazes of his angered council. "I guarantee you that the Closions and the Scripts will break that door right down if we do. And have you forgotten that Elder Borris is also here? We've kept him waiting long enough. He's already asked to inspect the Anvil four times since he arrived and he'll undoubtedly be curious about the practitioners they found in the Hovel. If everyone's accounts line up about a woman seeking *Orivellea*…" he trailed off, looking at each of them meaningfully, "we'll have a rat to deal with."

Before the gravity of his words fully settled, he was already turning back to the tongue-less cause of their grief.

"Your name?" he asked.

She bent to write again. *'Cera Verathin.'*

"Verathin?" Lucian repeated, not missing the way everyone in the room turned to the girl with renewed interest. "Daughter of Elder Gillot Verathin?"

A nod, and suddenly, Lucian was on his feet, heading toward her with purpose fueling his gait. He was a few inches taller, kneeling as she was. Using that to his advantage, he placed his hands over her cheeks to hold her in place.

His Peose circled the air above him, cawing at nothing in particular. They watched as Cera opened her mouth, reflexively trying to give her protests voice. It came out as a string of garbled nonsense until she forced her jaw shut. Lucian ignored her wails in favor of allowing his magic to course through his veins. His hands glowed bright. Before him, Cera closed her eyes in terror. Shoulders tensed, teeth locked, and fists clenched—one by one, as if her mind was going through a checklist of how to prepare for the pain she was so sure would come.

Lucian knew from the way she balked that memories chased each other inside of her mind. Those were wounds he couldn't heal. Mental scars that made a person soften in some places and harden in more. They always had the tendency to reopen. One press and that was it. But… physical ones. Those he could fix. Those he could *erase*.

His magic didn't pour into her. Not yet. First, it prodded along the surface, finding superficial scratches. Ones that those they'd placed in charge of tending to her weren't skilled enough to heal. A straight groove that spanned the roof of her mouth, scar tissue on her back, a tiny fracture along the base of her head, and joints that would've creaked had she been at a healthy weight, and the most obvious problem of all—

Lucian forced her mouth open.

She screeched, tears prickling her eyes, as Lucian inspected the clean line of her teeth and the saliva welling between the crevices with a cold detachment that made her shiver.

The rest stared on in morbid fascination. It lasted all of a minute, and no one was shocked when Tiv was the first to gather his wits. The Amorph reached out to grab Lucian by the collar, but before he could even take a step, he was held back by Philip and Dalis.

"Consider this a gift," Lucian said to her then. "One I hope your father will remember once the Grove's Potentate Union has been dissolved."

And then his magic rushed out of him.

The light that burst forth from his hands was so bright, she closed her eyes. She couldn't see the path it travelled across her skin, but she could feel it, could imagine it as it lit up every vessel on her face, focusing on what was in her mouth for one insane instant, before speeding down her neck, her torso, and even her lower extremities, where any wounds she'd suffered had long since healed. Most, through natural means.

Cera opened her eyes, despite the glare, unable to breathe at the sight of him. He was larger than life. Surrounded by light and goodness. Behind him, a translucent shadow that mimicked his pose, was Mauri—

His magic dug deeper.

It went further than anyone else's magic had ever gone before. Healer or otherwise. Maybe even further than her own. It was so potent that stray tendrils went straight between her ribs to adjust the frantic beat of her heart. They settled inside her head in what felt like a soft stroke, calming her frazzled nerves, and subtly apologizing for the earlier scare he'd given her.

She never knew magic could feel so alive.

Cera closed her eyes again, except this time, in reverence. She waited to feel that overwhelming sensation once more, to drown in the feeling of purity given form, but then… *nothing*.

It was gone. Lucian was already walking away.

Cera fell forward, gasping, tongue slithering inside of her—

She gasped and stacked her hands over her mouth for fear that it might escape. Everyone looked at her then, questions in their eyes and in their throats. Even more were hidden in their poses, frozen as they were. But none could find it in themselves to give those questions voice. Cera didn't humor them, her eyes were too busy following Lucian, who was already opening the stately double doors.

He was obviously using her as a distraction; as a means to slip out while they wondered if he was actually able to do the impossible—to heal a missing appendage. Besides, he had no more to say. He'd already made his decision, and whether the Potens agreed or not, his word was indisputably law. Still, Cera couldn't help but feel abandoned. He couldn't just leave. Not here. Not now. Not after all of that.

"Wait!" she yelled, then gasped again. This time, it was accompanied by several sharp inhales around the room. Even a shriek of surprise and a complaint from Poten Pramm, who didn't understand what was going on.

Cera's hands flew back up to cover her mouth, but by the time she recovered, Lucian had already gone.

✳✳✳

Philip sighed, as they walked down the long flight of stairs that led back to the Grove's main hall. Their surroundings weren't nearly as interesting as they were going up. But then again, they didn't fear what awaited them at the bottom.

The Potens had left first, cursing them on their way out. One even scrunched his face in distaste. Like he wasn't a living embodiment of animosity. Varron and Rhone followed after a few minutes, making sure to put a good amount of distance between themselves and their uppers. They were much more civil, even though they had a lot more reason to be angry with them. The two masters talked amongst themselves. Mostly about Demar Spells. They were trying to work out an agreement about who went to who. Rhone wanted as many of his men as possible under Varron rather than Ivy. A sentiment Philip backed. That woman was cracked somewhere in the head. He wouldn't be shocked if she used the spell for her own personal amusement.

Philip stopped. Speaking of vile humor…

"Creator, you're easy," Philip said. He slapped Dalis' arm with the back of his hand, making sure he knew who exactly it was he was talking about. "One bad joke and Lucian has you eating out of the palm of his hand."

"How dare you!" Dalis exclaimed, offended. "It wasn't a bad joke. It was brilliant! Brilliant! Did you hear how easily he let his imagination run away with him?"

"I did, and you're an awful person for laughing."

"Oh, shut it. Don't tell me you weren't surprised. He got us good. Having us think he was some stick-in-the-mud. I didn't know he scared the other Potens so much. He's so quiet that... now that I think about it, have you ever even heard him speak before? Two sentences tops, right? Seeing him talk was intense. Creator, look, my hands are *still* shaking. I need flatcakes and a deep dish of Roco sauce."

"Of course you do," Philip muttered under his breath. "That entire conversation essentially got us nowhere. We're still going to be punished when he returns from the Summit."

"Not too badly, and it wasn't a complete waste. Ru*d—err*." Dalis flashed her an apologetic smile. "Cera's alright now."

"So I am." She rolled her tongue. Even her vocal cords felt astounding. Like she'd never screamed a day in her life.

"That's the best thing I've heard all year," Dalis said. "Now, let's go before Lyss loses his mind and convinces everyone to free us from the Poten's clutches."

"I wish he'd taken the time to heal my hands," Tiv said.

"And who are you the son of?"

"Dalis!" Philip admonished.

"I know, I know. Sorry." Dalis patted Tiv twice on the shoulder. "Don't worry about your hands! You're a fledgling of the Red Scripts' now. We hold our brothers close. We'll bring you to see him again tomorrow. I'd like to do it now, but we can't. You heard what he said—there's some hotshot Elder wandering these halls. It isn't good to keep someone like that waiting."

"You're actually looking forward to seeing him again, aren't you?" Tiv asked, suspicious.

"Am I that transparent?"

"Like glass."

"Well, since I'm so honest, I was hoping you'd be the same." Dalis stopped to point at a group of practitioners waiting at the end of the stairway. Two men and three women. He recognized only two of them. "You froze when we saw them at the entrance. Friends of yours?"

"Acquaintances," Tiv answered, not missing a beat. Nothing short of Jack's appearance could phase him after what he'd just witnessed. "And not all of them."

Before introductions could be made, a practitioner dressed in buttery leather ran up to them. He carried two swords and a battle axe in his hands. Daggers of all sizes were fastened across his chest, and there were no less than four quivers on his back. They heard the snikt of clasps opening, as he wordlessly handed Dalis a dagger. The Healer stared at it, stunted by the suddenness of his arrival, before realization sank in.

"What happened?" Dalis asked, nicking it from his hands.

"Is the Lafertti Clan stirring up trouble?" Philip pressed.

"Nothin' like that," he assured, before looking around to see if there was anyone else from the Scripts among them. He found none. "Patrollers found two practitioners an' a Nebbin wanderin' the Willow. They did some routine questioning, y'know how it is. The ones they found were real touchy though. I heard the pair let loose their magic after a few words, but that could jus' be 'cause it was Tobias talkin'. He's, well, I don't gotta explain. Anyway, they're strong for hotheads. Real heavy-duty types."

"Properly trained then?"

"Probably primary apprentices once upon a time," the boy said. "As soon as their magic came out, all of the lights along the outer forest just blew! They've got the whole Grove in a tizzy. Tobias wants backup, an' Master Rhone said that as of today, we're in charge o' that."

"We're helping Tobias?" Dalis grimaced.

"We're *dealing* with intruders," Philip corrected.

"Right, of course." A pause. "So, we're *not* helping Tobias?"

"Thelarius, save me."

Not wanting to deal with his partner's antics, Philip turned to Tiv and Cera, who were already nodding their heads at his unspoken request.

Off to the side, Vivian and her entourage were led away by a similar errand boy, except much younger; a new addition to the Closions no doubt. He could only harbor a guess as to where they were headed, but it must've had something to do with assessing the state of the orbs. There were more than forty enchanters in their college, and he knew for a fact that Vivian was one of the more skilled ones. But were her companion's enchanters as well?

Philip was about to ask, but there was a flash of light, and then only two of them remained. *Amorphs,* was his first thought, before he recalled Poten Pramm's threat in front of the Clave. *Not just any Amorphs either. They're from the Vanguard Circle. What do Hunters want with us?*

He stared at their absent places for a second longer, before shaking his head. It didn't matter now. They were gone, and he had his own work to do. He'd have Vivian introduce them later.

"Let's go," Philip ordered, leading them out.

7

Vidal's mood wasn't at its best today.

The morning was cold, the hour early, and already, two dozen messages had arrived for him from all across the Yovakine Plains. Half were sent by his runners. They either reported about slavers growing too bold or mercenary groups on the move. Vidal knew very little about the men suddenly scurrying out of whatever holes they'd been living in while the Fetters ruled. He knew that they had a few scuffles here and there over land or, more often, a woman, but nothing bloody enough to attract his attention... until now.

Recently, they were being contracted under a common employer. A nigh traceless stranger that went by the name, Lynol. Despite their best efforts, none of Vidal's men were able to secure an accurate description. Let alone a witness. For all he knew, even the name was fake. But the stories surrounding him certainly weren't. He knew that only because they all ended the same—with blood filling lakes as wide as oceans.

Lynol used the power of messengers, ink, and gold; he knew better than to trust people to deliver messages. Vidal learned that early on when one of his runners came home missing an eye and cursing all owls in more tongues than even he could speak. From the way his runner spoke of them, it was as if Lynol's owls stayed true to their nature, despite their apparent training. They were relentless predators taught to serve, kill, and nothing else.

If Lynol was the Fetters' enigmatic third leader, then Vidal wouldn't be surprised. The man was extremely cautious. Nevertheless, Vidal had no doubt that he'd have more information soon. Once the Tower's practitioners were sent back to their rightful home, he'd have dozens of Amorphs and Conjurers under his command. He was almost looking forward to working them to the bone. Most had grown lazy running errands for Monet's aging Potens.

For now, all he needed to do was wait. Vidal could be patient when the time called for it. He flipped through the letters, separating those meant for him and those for his wife into neat piles. Monet's was considerably larger. It was as if every one of her practitioners sent her a dispatch. While skimming, he noticed that they could all be boiled down into one sentence: *we're doing our best, but problems are mounting.* Complete garbage. But, he conceded, they were short-handed, so maybe they really were trying their best.

They could only send out so many men, and the list of casualties were always endless. Slavers and mercenaries were skilled; their instincts honed by experience. Which was only heightened by desperation whenever they faced off against someone with magic. The overconfidence of some practitioners didn't help either. But they were wrong if they thought reinforcements would help them deal with their Nebbin foes. A group's strength didn't lie in the sheer number of combatants, no, Vidal saw what so many didn't want to admit. The Veld needed more Healers. Plain and simple. They needed those capable of caring for the weary and mending the wounds of the injured. Not muscle heads that would eventually end up in the same state.

But with the Grove sorting out its own affairs, more Healers was nothing short of a miracle. He'd seen too many of those recently to know that he wouldn't be getting another anytime soon. Vidal supposed they could ask Cheryll for a few volunteers from the east. Monet, however, was adamant against asking for help. Her pride faltered to no one. Especially during times of adversity. It was her greatest strength and her greatest weakness.

Luckily, Vidal had no such reservations. He quickly penned a request for aid and handed it to one of the half-awake guards outside his door for immediate delivery. Monet would be furious. But this was no time for stubbornness.

To his astonishment, the guards assigned to protect him looked twice his age and three times more stern. None of them seemed very lithe... or alert for that matter.

Did they scare people off by glowering at them? Vidal didn't discount the possibility. Or perhaps they were just scowling because they didn't like what he was wearing? Now, that *was* something to properly antagonize over. The robes he wore were so plain, it physically pained him. Whenever he caught a glimpse of his reflection, he grumbled until someone came to see if he'd unintentionally hurt himself. Did he seem like the clumsy type? Oh, he hoped not.

Vidal missed the comforts of his office in Yorn. Filled with portraits of Monet and the silence only a city full of careless Nebbin could bring. He'd been away too long. Surely, the House of Silver Strings needed him. Never mind that none of his runners had yet to send a dispatch stating otherwise. He was *sure* that they needed him to run his auctions, entertain those pesky nobles, and waste money on any reputable painter that happened to pass through the city.

Because if they didn't, then he'd lose his mind.

He envied Jack and Sylvie; able to run off to the Grove just because it suited them. Vidal had no doubt that they were enjoying themselves now that he wasn't around to poke fun at them. Riling them had become a pastime, so when he went up to check on them one morning to do so again, he wasn't startled to find them gone.

And without a word of farewell, Vidal thought dejectedly.

He comforted himself with the fact that he'd soon be off on his own little journey. Once Monet finished her preparations and their daughter was properly hidden away, he'd be able to leave this place. It was such a hassle how, despite the Veld's Potentate

Union holding strong, they still fumbled at the thought of their Arch Poten leaving. Being one of the top leaders of the Institute was so much work. Even as a child, he was against it. In fact, he distinctly recalled making an elaborate vow before a sleek statue of Thelarius that he'd never put himself through such pain.

I have to remember to congratulate Leonas for all of his years as Head of Corrections… maybe I can do that now? Writing a personal letter in-between all of this work wouldn't be frowned upon, would it? Vidal didn't care what they thought about him, but he didn't want them to speak ill of Monet. *There's no one here, so I should be fine. It'll only take a minute.*

As soon as he wrote his old friend's name, however, he heard the door creak open. "Just a moment," Vidal said, hurriedly stuffing the page under a pile of unopened scrolls.

The person on the other side didn't heed his warning and simply strolled in like they belonged there. Before Vidal could get upset over it, he found Monet standing there, fully armored and holding a crisp letter that looked too fine to be from anyone but a member of the Zenith Council.

Vidal couldn't help the smile that tilted his lips at the sight of her. "Monet!" he exclaimed, jumping from his seat. "What brings you here?"

"This is my office," she replied, acidic. Monet looked up just long enough to give him a steely glare, before burning the letter with a spark so bright, Vidal was forced to look away. By the time the dots in his vision subsided, she was already reclaiming her seat and opening the scrolls he'd been trying to will out of existence for the last hour. "Did you go through these already?"

"Some, well, no, more like a few. I'm surprised you noticed."

She pointed at a neatly stacked pile beside her desk. "You organized them. You've always been a neat freak."

"Only by comparison. Your table's a mess. I don't know how you find anything."

"I don't need to find anything. I have to read and answer everything here eventually."

Vidal laughed, foregoing answering in favor of basking in the spike of contentment he felt now that she was by his side. He settled himself across from her. Vidal watched her lips purse and her quill sweep ink across the pages for a long while, until eventually, his gaze was drawn to the ashes left by the Zenith Council's missive.

"So," he began, slow to test her mood, "did the Council have anything interesting to say?"

Her hand stopped. Ink blotted the page. Monet looked at him, either unaware or simply uncaring for her ruined letter. "They're glad I'm going, and they hope to see me soon. They also mentioned you. I didn't bother reading that part."

"And?"

"That's it."

"You're lying." Vidal's eyes narrowed. He ran his fingers over his brow to show her that her own was wrinkled. "I can tell."

Monet sighed, finally dropping the quill and offering him her full attention. "They touched upon a rather delicate subject concerning Cheryll and those two children that you're so fond of. The letter was purposely vague. Though they did order us to bring them along if we happened to meet them."

"A little late for that, isn't it?"

"Exactly." Monet shrugged. "But they're nothing, if not prepared. They also had a bit about what we should do if they'd already passed through and we don't know their whereabouts— and it's *ridiculous*. They want me to send someone to warn them not to pass through the Grove. As if I have a man to spare for such an inane task! They're trained practitioners, aren't they? Surely, they can handle a little danger."

"Yes, I'm sure those two will be just fine," Vidal agreed. "The Council only sent that order because they want them to head straight to the north for the Summit. I find it hard to believe that they're that concerned for their safety though. Besides, that argument makes absolutely no sense. The Grove and the Alps have always worked together, and despite the Grove's current situation, there's no safer place for them to be. Their family names mean a lot in the north, so they'll mean a lot there, too."

"But the Alps is under isolation now."

If Vidal had a drink, he was certain he would've choked in astonishment. Instead, he stood abruptly. His chair scraped against the floors, making Monet wince, but he couldn't be bothered to apologize. Not now.

"What?" Vidal asked. "Why would the Diamond Alps ever isolate themselves? The other Institutes look to the north for direction. Always have and always will. Especially now that the order to dissolve the Grove's Potentate Union has been made public. Isolating themselves is a fool's move."

"It was necessary, or so they assured. An Elder has been murdered. They didn't mention who, but it's someone important enough to stir the rest of those half-dead fossils into action. A Drakone maybe. Or one of the Vanguard Circle's leaders."

"Impossible," Vidal muttered, his mind racing. "The heads of the Vanguard Circle all rank in the top ten most powerful practitioners alive today. They're nigh untouchable. Even I'd be worried about facing off against one of them. Ambushed or not, the light from their magic is so strong, it's blinding. People would notice, and then they would talk. But then again… who would be stupid enough to kill a Drakone?"

"This is all just speculation," Monet said, trying to assuage him with her tone. "It could've been someone else."

"Your instincts are rarely wrong, but," he fell into his chair and flashed her an ambiguous smile, "jumping to conclusions is."

"I'm glad you can still see reason," she said, before returning to her work. "Now, get out of my office. I can't work with your incessant staring. I've already spoken to the Union. If I finish all of this by noon, then we can leave tonight."

"And Elise?"

"Looking for you."

"I should be going then." Vidal straightened his robe.

"Oh, wait," Monet suddenly called.

The word was quick and clumsy as it left her lips. Vidal turned just in time to see her take a ragged breath, as if steeling herself for a challenge. Monet dropped her pen once more, and his vision funneled, arrested by her every move and still, even after all of these years, unable to fathom the extent of his own emotions. She was a drop of dark blue ink in a field of perpetual gray. His heart throbbed with unmanageable heat, but it wasn't unwelcome. It spread. Hot. Like blood and poison and stars too close for him to see. Vidal treasured every second of it.

"Yes?" Vidal asked when she didn't continue. He prompted her with his eyes and two steps forward.

"It's nothing," she said hurriedly, seeming to come to her senses. Monet picked up her quill and pressed it back onto the page, pointedly avoiding his gaze. "Don't take too long."

"Is there a reason for me to rush?"

"... I'll be waiting for you here."

Vidal's cheeks flushed, and he did nothing to hide them. They'd always been traitorous things. Especially when it came to her. But they stood no chance really.

Because oh, how he loved her voice.

***

Their voices were like acid to his ears.

The courtyard was packed with people, all talking at once. Some shouted nonsense across the yard, while others leaned in close and whispered, better only because of their discretion. Though that didn't change the fact that they still added to the jumbled mess that assaulted his senses the moment he stepped out of Monet's office. Vidal cursed his own observance when he caught tidbits of conversation—*'Oh, Lydia's pregnant!'*, *'I met the most delightful old man yesterday.'*, *'Did you see that Amorph circling around outside? What a flaming showoff!'*—every word that left their mouths made his ears bleed. How could they even understand each other over the noise?

Moments like this made him deem his stellar hearing a flaw.

Because even though he wasn't interested in what they had to say, his mind registered, processed, and filed all of it away for a time when the information might be useful. Truthfully, he was more interested in the beetles. They were out in droves today, and he knew his daughter had a particular dislike for them after one attempted to ram itself in her open eye. Twice. Elise had come crying to him, screaming murder well after he'd batted it away with a particularly vicious flick of his wrist. It wasn't something he wanted a repeat of.

Is that why she's looking for me? Vidal speculated, the strings of amusement crooked his lips. *To summon a gale? Or maybe I could burn them all into ash. I doubt Monet would be happy about that. She'll have my head if I ruin any aspect of the Veld's precious environment.*

Vidal's fingers twitched. The thought just made him want to do it more. But it wouldn't do for him to act on the urge, so he busied himself with turning to the nearest guard instead. A man. Shorter than most, but lean with a well-defined jaw and long hair.

A Conjurer, Vidal deduced, though he had yet to see his eyes. He could tell from the way he held himself. Not as proud as an Elementalist, but jerky enough to be one. His fingers kept twitching, ready to raise them should the need arise. Healers and Amorphs never focused on the distance between their enemies and their hands.

As if realizing he was being watched, the man turned, then immediately straightened when he saw just who was eyeing him. Vidal almost didn't want to look away, too caught by the way the man squirmed. But remembering that Elise was looking for him, Vidal flashed him a merciful smile to which the man exhaled a breath of relief, before he did another sweep of the crowd.

Vidal noticed a young boy point up, and he followed his finger toward the impressive circular motions of four birds above. Amorphs. They were too far for him to discern what kind of birds they mimicked, but they were dark enough against the bright sky for him to make out the long, ominous circles they cut across the air.

The Veld had a visitor. Four, to be exact.

Two of the birds swerved left, as the rest flew down.

Practitioners and… Nebbin? Vidal fought the urge to smirk in delight. *This should be interesting.*

Making his way to the wall their guests were reportedly situated behind, Vidal caught the attention of some of the guards and fanned his fingers in an upward motion. They looked skeptical, glancing at each other with the sort of nervous apprehension men only had when commanded by someone that wasn't their leader, but they got over it soon enough. All it took was a wide, impatient smile, and half of the people in the courtyard were already running to draw their weapons, while the rest formed a defensive half-circle around the wall.

A portly Amorph was the one to place his hands upon it, feeding the wall with his magic. It lit brilliantly. The blue of his magic was so intense it looked white as it bled into the walls, forcing not one, but three panels up into the sky. The chatter in the yard ceased immediately, drowned by the sound of stone brushing against stone and grime falling. The smell was worse than the screeching abuse his ears were forced to suffer. The walls needed a thorough cleaning. Frankly, Vidal was astounded that Silas' mark was still able to appear, despite the centuries of grime.

Vidal looked to the side just long enough to find two of the Veld's Potens step outside, prepared to reprimand him and all those that actually listened to the unvoiced command he'd given. Their lips were so pursed, Vidal wondered if their expressions were forced.

Did they swallow lemons before coming out?

Vidal disregarded them in favor of looking at the Amorph talented enough to move so many of the Veld's walls. He had an incredible amount of magic for one person. But he was also twice Vidal's size, so sheer body mass could've been a factor. Vidal was only further impressed when he was still able to sprint out of the way of all the falling dirt without wobbling.

I wonder how big his magic circuit is? Vidal mused. He knew more than a few people that would be tempted to crack his head open just to find out. Thankfully, none of them resided within the Veld. All thoughts of dissection left him when the dust finally cleared and four people made their way inside. The guards closest to the opening raised weapons and hands alike, fully prepared to deal with them should they prove a threat.

A man with red hair and black eyes stepped forward. He whistled, impressed. "Creator's piss, that was a fancy door," he said in a clear Astonian accent. The thick layer of bewilderment only made it worse.

"And some welcome," another Amorph chimed in. He was smaller than the first, but no less wide-eyed.

"Look at all these men." One of the Nebbin that Vidal was infinitely more interested in finally came into view. He had shaggy hair and stubble that looked as unkempt as the rest of him. His eyes were more cautious that a wild animal's, and the calluses on his hands proved that he'd seen his fair share of hardship. "How is *this* a welcome? I told you we wouldn't be wanted here."

"If they didn't want you," the red-head rebutted, "then they wouldn't 'ave opened the door, yea?"

"Sound logic," Vidal finally interrupted.

The newcomers turned to him with a start. They each weighed him in their own ways, while Vidal signaled for the others to stand down. They were obedient enough, and to his utter delight, the Potens that lingered on the sidelines remained there, clearly deciding to wait and see what he planned to do. He'd definitely be called up to their meeting room after this. Vidal just hoped that the privilege of questioning them first would be worth it.

"Welcome to my temporary world, extras," Vidal greeted.

"What?" the smaller Amorph questioned, before shaking his head in abrupt dismissal. He was clearly used to dealing with all sorts of people. "Are you the Arch Poten here? No, wait, isn't the Veld's Arch Poten a woman?"

Before Vidal could answer, the sole woman among them spoke, "All I know is that the Arch Poten here is a Conjurer. None of us have actually seen her… or him?"

"So, you don't even know that much."

"Shouldn't *you* have learned this in the Tower?"

"Don't tell me you're that four-armed Elementalist?" the red-head abruptly asked, his eyes were wide and disappointed. "I thought you were supposed ta be fifteen feet tall with muscles the size of melons!"

"I don't know," the shaggy-haired Nebbin chimed in. "He does seem pretty beefy under those robes."

The red-head wrinkled his nose in distaste. "Imagine him naked all you want, but don't go sayin' that stuff out loud, yea? Perv solo, boss. I just had lunch."

"I didn't mean it like that, you li—" he cut himself off with a sharp exhale, then rubbed his temples in slow, circular motions. Vidal had a sneaking suspicion that he did that often. "Weren't you two looking for someone?"

"Tiv!" the red-head shouted. It was loud enough to startle everyone around him. "You lot wouldn't've happened ta come across a stray Amorph 'round here, yea? Tall guy. Goes by the name Tiv Grovegg. Has a violent scowl and a good right swing."

"Can't say that I have," Vidal said, looking at one of the older practitioners off to the side for confirmation. "I'm sure he'd be welcome here though, and if you point us in the right direction, I'll be able to send a few men out."

"That's real nice of you." He grinned. "The name's Khale."

"Vidal Verne."

"Catchy."

"And your partner?"

"Pom," Khale introduced, pointing. "An' these two Nebbin are Drage an' Celina."

"Is he even interested in who we are?" Drage asked, but his words were drowned by Khale's louder voice.

"We heard about those slavers you offed and thought maybe

our friend might be with you," Khale went on, happy that Tiv wasn't kidnapped by some slaver ring, yet crestfallen by their lack of information.

"The Fetters in the Pit employed Nebbin," Vidal revealed. "It's too dangerous to own someone with magic unless you have the proper binds, and even then, the risk of Hunters interfering isn't worth it."

"What about the Disciples?"

"The Disciples? You haven't heard?" Vidal asked, stunned. He looked at each of them, searching their eyes for any sign that they might've been lying. That this was all just a farce, so the Veld could open their doors. He found nothing. "A large group of practitioners from the Grove broke them. They killed everyone, then burned the place down. No one knows why. Last I heard, they were on their way back to the Grove."

"You hear that, Pom?" Khale exclaimed, his eyes lighting up. "The Grove might have Tiv!"

"Don't get so excited," Pom rebuked. "If they have Tiv that means the slavers really did get him."

Seeming to realize the gravity of the situation, Khale folded in on himself once more. "Right."

"But why would he be with slavers?" Vidal asked.

"They got a big haul of practitioners from the Tower when it fell," Pom said.

"So, he's from the Tower," Vidal said, nodding to himself. "That explains it. The Tower's practitioners are easy pickings for the more skilled groups. I've come across quite a few that were chained up and sold off to old, eccentric rich men. The Veld has opened its gates to them, despite our circumstances. And with the disappearance of the Fetters, we've finally found ourselves with enough men to guard some of the more… faint-hearted practitioners back to Eriam."

"Real nice of you ta open up for 'em," Khale said. "There were a lotta greenhorns in the Tower. I don't think they'd be much use ta you."

"Are you from there, too?"

"Me an' Pom here were born an' raised in the east, yea?" Khale leaned on his partner for emphasis.

"Tell me, did you curse or did you pray when it fell?"

"What?" Khale asked, caught off guard.

"I just want to know what kind of person you are."

"I... cursed. A litany of curses." Khale knew he said the right thing when the corner of Vidal's lips quirked up. "Forget that though. If you want, we can help guard those gomers back if some of yer men ain't up for the trip."

"Oh?" Vidal lifted a brow. "I thought you were looking for someone. Don't tell me you're giving up already."

"The Veld was our only real lead, an' we can't just leave the others ta mooch off a' you, yea? We'll do our part."

"Unless..." Pom spoke up, taking a moment to shove Khale away from him. "Did any of your men happen to come across an Elementalist named Jack? Jacques Dace? He has dark hair and some really itchy fire fingers?"

Vidal's eyes thinned. "Is he a friend of yours, too?"

"He is," Khale said. "That maroon was Tiv's partner. But last we saw him, he was headin' three floors too deep in the Institute's Assembly Tower. Jack's a survivor though. We're sure he's out here somewhere, an' if anyone can find Tiv, it's him. He's got a real talent for snaggin' turkeys."

"Jacques Dace is currently on his way to the Weeping Grove," Vidal said with an ambiguous smile. "Why, he left with your Arch Poten not six days ago."

"He's alive?" Pom asked, astounded.

"Of course he's alive!" Khale smacked his head. "Didn't I just say that? An' did you say Arch Poten? Master Cephas is there?"

"Sylvie Sirx," Vidal corrected, reveling in their astonishment. "With Columbus Cephas' body missing, his primary apprentice has been forced to don the mantle."

"They still haven't found him then," Pom muttered.

"Just be glad that Sylvie's still around, yea?" Khale said. "She was deep down in the boonies with Jack when the Tower fell."

"Well, sorry if I don't share your disgusting optimism."

"Care ta repeat that?"

"I said—"

"That's what I thought," Khale interrupted with an overly jubilant nod. "Wonder how they escaped though. I mean, a lotta the crowds in the higher floors didn't even make it. Especially the Healers. You reckon they're just good swimmers?"

"I doubt it."

"An' now they're runnin' 'round on their own. Think they're just killin' time together? Sight-seein' an' all that?"

"As if." Pom scoffed. "This is *Jack*."

"Your point?"

"He's got the words, 'Return to the Alps,' stamped across his forehead and glowing bright pink! They're probably heading there now. And if Sylvie's our new Arch Poten, then she needs to attend the Summit."

"Oh!" Khale exclaimed, dropping a fist into an open palm. "I forgot about that!"

"How do you just forget about something that huge?"

"I gotta pay attention ta the little things, yea? Else I'd never see you."

Pom palmed his dagger's hilt.

Vidal left them to their squabbling. His gaze drifted toward the two Nebbin silently eyeing their surroundings. The way they scrutinized the area made it seem as though they were trying to find an escape route. Who would be the easiest to overpower? Who was important enough to take hostage? Which direction would they be safe from magic? Vidal found his eyes drawn to the man. He looked familiar, but not enough for him to attach a name to his face.

A slaver? Vidal thought, but swiftly dismissed the idea. Khale and Pom wouldn't be with him if he was. *A nobleman? No, too shabby. A merchant? Too unfriendly. A mercenary then?*

Vidal paused to smile at him, not missing the way Drage's

hand inched closer to whatever it was he kept concealed inside of his leathers before smiling back. His expression looked genuine enough. Perhaps it was. Whatever the case, Vidal was certain that he'd been reaching for a weapon.

Definitely a mercenary, he decided. Vidal wasn't familiar with no name lackeys, so he must've been a leader of some sort. That, or on his way to becoming one. *If he's the leader, then he might be of some use after all. But why would these two be travelling with mercenaries? Are they deserters? No, since they're from the Tower, then they either left willingly or they were separated. But couldn't they search for their friend on their own? Unless these Nebbin can offer them something. What though? A warm place to return to? Information?*

There was only one way to find out.

"I'm afraid," Vidal began, "that I can't let you accompany Monet's men back to the Tower."

Vidal ignored their questioning glances in favor of signaling to the gathered practitioners around them. With a wave of his hand and a stony glare that spoke of severe consequences should they decide to question him, they dispersed. Most were quick to leave. The ones farther back took a few moments to realize what was going on, before following the others in their quest to get as far away from Vidal's sight as possible.

From the corner of his eye, Vidal saw a few practitioners head toward Monet's office to inform her of what was going on. Farther away, the Potens told anyone close enough to prepare their meeting room.

Now, how much time will she be able to buy me until that Union of hers drags me away? Vidal wondered. Not that it mattered. No matter how much time she bought, it still wouldn't be enough. Of that, he was certain.

"Come with me," Vidal said, already turning on his heel. He couldn't squander the little time he did have. "We have a lot to discuss."

8

The room Vidal led them to had seen better days.

Various weapons were propped along the walls, built more for appearance than practical use. It was a testament to the Veld's former wealth, as well as the once glories of the now storage room they stood in. Old linens and broken crates surrounded them. Most would undoubtedly be used as tinder for the winter.

Khale watched with a fake smile plastered on his face as Vidal looked twice down the hall, before closing the door behind him with all the finality of a cat cornering its prey. There was something about the way his eyes slinked over them that put every muscle in his body on edge. It was the sort of feeling he got deep in his gut whenever he morphed to join a swarm of ants. Those he passed would always turn his way, their brains only large enough to know that he was strange and not the reason behind his apparent disregard for their incessant hunt for colony supplies. To them, he was a vagrant member that needed to be reported to the queen.

Over time, Khale made a game of it. How long could he trick them into believing he was just another mindless drone like the rest of them? His record was four days. It had gotten him into a new level of trouble with the Tower's Assembly, but Khale basked in the thrill of not getting caught too much to care about the consequences. What was one or two weeks of scrubbing the baths compared to the experience of a thousand and one eyes trained on him? He felt almost like a newly appointed Hunter sent to blend into one of the Institutes.

But it was different with Vidal. The Elementalist didn't want to report him. He wanted something else entirely. Something Khale couldn't even begin to fathom. But he did know one thing, whatever Vidal sought wasn't something he could simply escape by transforming back into his original self, and that terrified him. Suddenly, finding Tiv seemed like such an insignificant thing. He wanted to be back in the easy company of his friends in the Chattering Crow, with their coarse humor and honest smiles.

As if reading his thoughts, Vidal flashed him a wide, mocking grin, instantly giving him indigestion. Idly rubbing his stomach in a sorry attempt to calm it, Khale turned just in time to see a dagger catch Pom's eye. His partner stalked towards it like it was the flame of Silas calling him to the next world. Pom whistled, tilting his head back to stare up at it in appraisal. His expression was caught in a strangled mix of impressed, respectful, and reverent. Frankly, Khale was amazed that he hadn't started bowing yet. With how wide his eyes were, Pom could kiss the damn thing and he wouldn't have questioned it— maybe a freaked shout, sure, but not one question—but all Pom did was stare. He didn't even try swiping it even though no one else was paying attention to him.

Khale glanced at the dagger, not seeing what he found so interesting. It looked pretty enough, and though it was a bit too gaudy for his taste, it was certainly better than most daggers he'd seen. But that was it. It was nothing more than a forgotten trinket now. Settled like the dust around them. He felt almost bad for it. Weapons were meant to be swung. Exerted. Exercised in the heat of battle. Not put on display for people to watch dull.

"Do you like it?" Vidal asked, his voice startling everyone but Pom, who had eyes only for the blade before him.

"I *love* it." Pom gawked. With an edge sharp enough to pierce armor and a hilt adorned in expensive black steel, the weapon shimmered against the wall. It was a streak of richness in an otherwise dull world, shining with a light too bright for the senses. This dagger was beauty incarnate, and Pom was more than willing to flank his hip with beauty.

"Can I keep it?" Celina asked, suddenly by his side.

"Of course," Vidal agreed, not missing a beat.

Pom stood there, gaping, as she took the dagger down from its place. His eyes lingered on each of her movements. From the way she reached up to grab it, to how she adjusted it on her belt with a ghost of a smile on her lips. By the time she stepped away, patting his shoulder twice just to mock him for his slowness, the protest in his throat was as dead as his faith in humanity. He cursed instead, loud and angry, finding satisfaction in the way Celina rubbed her ears at the resounding echo.

"That's a nice look on you," Vidal said, smirking and looking every bit like the monster he was. The look Pom threw Khale then was so fierce and so pitiful that Vidal stifled a laugh. Pom wasn't even trying to hide his desperation anymore.

"What did you want to talk about?" Pom barked when he realized that Khale wasn't going to step in to help him, too busy laughing himself. Damn red-headed chicken.

"I was curious..." Vidal trailed off, ignoring the tart look Pom threw him. It could curdle milk. His good mood had obviously taken a dive out of the nearest window, and Vidal reveled in it.

"About?" Drage prompted, impatient.

"You," Vidal gave him a winning grin that curved his bloody orbs into little crescents, "or rather what you do."

"I take silver and turn it into dead bodies," Drage said, stone-faced. "What's it to you?"

"Yea, why're you interested in him of all people?" Khale intervened, making all eyes fall on him. "He'll bleed you drier than a two-penny whore. I've seen the astonishin' amount a' coin he charges. I get that he runs a murky business an' all, an' some folks are real into that type a' thing, so I won't give you any lip for swingin' his way, but Drage ain't exactly fresh cream, yea? I can guarantee that you'll get a lump on yer jewels if you try."

Drage choked. "I'm not diseased!"

Khale raised his eyebrows. "You really gonna take the word

of a pigeon over me?"

Vidal blinked painfully slow. He didn't even have the heart to feel offended by what the redhead was insinuating. "Did you just call him a pige—"

"Forget the little details," Khale interrupted, waving a hand as if to brush the topic aside. Drage bristled and was expertly ignored in the same second, as Khale's expression took a turn for the serious. He looked as if he'd just eaten a lemon and was trying very hard not to wrinkle his nose. "I thought we were here ta discuss Jack. This ain't a game ta us, yea?"

"Nonsense," Vidal said, unable to help himself. "Of course this is a game."

"Then I forfeit."

"You can't do that. You don't even know the rules. And there's really no reason to rush now, is there? Your important friend can take care of himself. So, humor me a bit. You look like someone that likes to have a little fun. In fact, you remind me of someone I once knew. A man. Just as tall, except thicker around the waist. He always struggled for discipline, but deep down, he craved to abandon it. In the end, he lost control of himself."

"You talkin' 'bout you?" Khale asked, unimpressed.

"Oh." Vidal beamed. "Do I look like the repressed type?"

"His point is," Pom cut in, annoyed on Vidal's behalf, "don't bother going against yourself."

"Exactly." Vidal nodded approvingly.

"Why didn't you just say that then?" Khale asked, pursing his lips in exasperation. "I don't like mind games."

"I see why you're friends with Jack."

"Why do I feel like yer insultin' me right now?"

"Are all practitioners so carefree?" Celina interjected.

"Creator, no!" Vidal exclaimed, offended. "I assure you that I'm a special case."

"Why do you sound so proud of that?"

Vidal only smiled vaguely. None of them were fooled by his pleasant expression. Despite the ease in which he held himself, they could all see him for what he was—a man carved from steel and hardened by blood. Like a snake in the grass, watching first and striking when presented the opportunity. Doing just enough damage to cripple a little more each time, then letting the pent-up fear take care of the rest. Getting swept up in his pace seemed inevitable, but they'd be foolish to let their guard down.

"Are you a Poten?" Pom asked, cutting through the silent tension that Vidal's smile brought. He'd never met someone whose grin had the ability to drain more than refresh.

"Thelarius forbid," Vidal answered. "I'm a Master. The title was bestowed upon me years ago in a different institute. But I work here now, and as far as I'm concerned, that title holds very little value to anyone of real importance."

"Little value…" Pom trailed off. "I didn't know the Institute allowed swapping."

"If you're wealthy enough."

"You?" Khale stared dubiously at him. "Wealthy? You need ta hire some new tailors then, yea? All those colors must be gettin' ta yer head. Ain't no way yer loaded."

"Shut up," Pom whispered harshly, before stepping on his partner's foot. "The Verne family owns half of the Yovakine Plains, you flaming idiot."

Khale choked.

"Enough about that," Vidal said, ending the topic before it could even begin. Though his voice was light, it demanded obedience. "My rank and family don't matter. All you need to know about me is that I have considerable sway within the Institute and that I'm married to Monet Thareen, Arch Poten of the Red Veld. I'll be accompanying her to the Alps to attend the Summit soon."

"You? Married?" Khale went on, flabbergasted. "The Veld's Arch Poten must be incredible, considerin—"

"You're dreadfully confused," Vidal interrupted. "Part of the reason she's so incredible is because she's married to me."

"… Conceited, aren't you?"

"Just honest."

"Hey," Drage called, nudging Khale with his boot. "Weren't you concerned about some guy named Jack?"

Khale paused, his jaw slackening at how easily the subjects shifted out of his control.

"Jack… right," he said, dazed. Khale rubbed his knuckles under his chin in an odd gesture of concentration that caught the attention of those around him. "You said he was with Syl, yea? That they're on their way ta the Grove. But what're they doin' takin' the long way 'round? If yer goin' ta the north, then couldn't they 'ave hitched a ride with you?"

"I don't know what those two are up to," Vidal lied. "But if you're so curious, then why not follow them? They could stand to see a few familiar faces. Especially after all that's happened recently."

"Across the Plains?" Pom asked. "Or in the Alps?"

Vidal turned, genuinely stunned by the question. Being in the Veld had obviously left him ignorant to the information that ran so quickly across the rest of the Plains because he hadn't even heard about the Alps' isolation until Monet mentioned it. Just how much did they know? And how did they get their information? Did they have a mole in the Alps? He doubted the existence of an agent skilled enough to elude all three heads of the Vanguard Circle, doubted that Leonas would allow any agent to live for long even more. Unless… the agent had some sort of worth Vidal couldn't see. That, or the information was purposely leaked by someone in the Zenith Council looking to stir up trouble by telling the rest of the world that the Institute's most feared practitioners were officially under house arrest.

Those unfortunates that were left outside to twiddle their thumbs would no doubt be making themselves scarce until the self-imposed isolation was lifted. The curious ones would go to the Grove to watch how the practitioners dealt with the news of their Potentate Union's abolition. But with word of the Alps closing themselves off, Vidal doubted they'd play nicely.

Then there was also the threat of deserters coming out of hiding. The talented ones, usually old Hunters that knew best how to evade their kin, raked in piles of enemies throughout the years. Mostly Nebbin they'd betrayed or were deceived by. Vidal doubted they'd let this chance go. He certainly wouldn't. It was an opportunity to get rid of overly stubborn enemies without the risk of Hunters stabbing them in the throat as soon as they tired.

Leonas should've reached out to me by now, Vidal thought. The fact that he didn't meant something was going on. *I need to return. Soon.*

"Has word about the Alps already spread to the cities in the Plains?" Vidal asked, realizing that he'd been silent too long.

"To the larger ones," Celina answered. "It's not exactly public news. Not entirely reliable either. No one knows who started the rumor. Some say it was a merchant, others a drunk practitioner. From what I've gathered, word is still spreading across several underground channels. The larger mercenary bands should know about it by now. Which means the smaller ones are next. But those fools are never quiet, so it's only a matter of time until it spreads to the common folk." She paused to glance at him. "… Is that a problem?"

"No, of course not," Vidal replied instantly. Any trace of shock that was once on his face was quickly replaced by his usual smile. "I take it you're well-acquainted with these… channels?"

"You've got the main head of the Hellion right here." Khale elbowed Drage, who shot him a glare acidic enough to scald. "An' me an' Pom here are bonafide underlings, yea? They take care of us, we take care of them. It's a relationship!"

"How reassuring," Vidal said, ignoring Drage's glower. He could tell at a glance that the man was important in some way. Someone useful he could whisper his darker suggestions to. But to know that he was already accepting of practitioners, well, Vidal didn't think he'd be so lucky. "I advise bringing some of those mercenary friends of yours to the Grove then. The practitioners there have grown wary over the years. It's rare for them to let outsiders inside their domain. Especially practitioners from no-name families. You could use the extra muscle."

"You're telling him to bring *my* men into an Institute full of jittery practitioners?" Drage's eyes thinned in a mixture of suspicion and disbelief. "Are you insane?"

"So people say."

"Don't drag me into your Institute's games, you cocky bastard!"

"Me?" Vidal laughed. "Drag you into Institute politics? Never. I wouldn't dream of doing something so crass. Our struggles don't concern you. I just thought you'd like to help one of your *underlings* find their lost friends. It's a mess there… or rather, it's going to be."

"What do you mean by that?" Pom asked, worry creased his brow.

"I mean that everyone is so neurotic these days. Always quick to draw upon their magic, flailing their hands like they aren't as deadly as any blade. Especially the pair you're after. Jack and Sylvie are eruptions waiting to happen. It doesn't help that they stumble into the worst of trouble, always arriving just as the situation escalates. You'll want more than one person watching your back if you decide to chase them. I had an entire horde behind me and none were left unscathed."

"Seems I'll have to decline then," Drage said, patting Khale harshly on the shoulder before he could protest his decision. "Sorry kids, but that sounds like more trouble than it's worth."

"Really?" Vidal drawled. "I don't think you're seeing the big picture. Reckless as they may be, their potential isn't anything to scoff at. Dace and Sirx are famous names among practitioners. Sylvie is currently the head of the eastern Institute. With more experience, the Zenith Council would welcome her as an Elder. And Jack is the son of one of the most influential practitioners alive today. Give him a few years, and he'll become the same. If you help them, I guarantee that the reward will be worth it."

"You're really endorsing those kids," Drage said, seemingly

disinterested. His hum of contemplation betrayed him. "But this is all assuming they live that long, and from what you've said about them, I doubt they're the sort to die old and wrinkly. I'd rather sit and drink somewhere than risk bleeding for two brats I don't know."

"Then why not drink here?" Vidal offered, gauging Drage's reaction. To his credit, the mercenary captain didn't even bat an eye at the suggestion.

"Drinking isn't the same without all the boisterous drunks in the background. And I've got the palette of a pig farmer. Cheap alcohol reminds me of home."

Vidal looked offended. "Our alcohol's cheap. Who said our alcohol isn't cheap? I'll put them straight."

"You don't really think I'll just agr—" Drage cut himself off once he processed Vidal's words. "Wait, *what*? Is that something to brag about?"

"Stay," Vidal ordered. "You'll come around."

"I highly doubt that."

"You will," he insisted. "Just think of this as a favor to me."

"And why would I ever want to do you any favors?"

"Because as soon as I reach the Alps, I'm going to officially declare Jack my primary apprentice," he revealed, internally rejoicing when Khale and Pom's jaws dropped in disbelief. "You might not be interested in them or in our traditions, but I'm sure *I* can help you in some way. Isn't the Hellion based in the Plains? The Verne family has never been against associating themselves with Nebbin."

Before any of them could recover, the door creaked open. They all turned to find a little girl with puffy cheeks and brown eyes staring up at them. She was dressed in practitioner's garb, though the color of her irises suggested anything but.

Before any of them could question her, she threw the door open and stepped inside with all of the confidence of someone that had every right to be there. The first thing they noticed was that her robe was covered in a myriad of things. Dirt, mud, flour, a few others they couldn't name. The scents blended, wafting into the storage room's stale air and turning it sour. Their confusion about her lack of magic was momentarily forgotten in the face of the sudden, horrid odor.

She eyed them in the exact same manner Vidal had been doing since they stepped inside the Veld. With keen interest at first, and then nothing at all. Like their worth as people had already been decided in her mind. Except to her, they were nothing more than particles of dust floating about.

When she was done with her minute assessment, she turned to Vidal. Her lips tilted downward into a pout that deepened as her eyes met red.

"I've been looking for you!" She crossed her arms like she needed to physically emphasize just how livid she was.

"And I was looking for you," came the unperturbed reply.

"Really?"

"Really."

"Why would I *ever* come here?"

"And yet, here you are."

Vidal stepped forward then. He smothered her against his robes to block her from their view, then proceeded to urge her back outside. Judging by the indignant flailing and the muffled whines, she wasn't happy with his treatment. But Vidal didn't care. In fact, he looked to be enjoying her reaction.

By the time they reached the door, it was clear to all of them that Vidal was done talking because he grabbed the iron handle with the same solemnity he had when he first entered. He stopped just long enough to address them a final time.

"Feel free to stay the night," Vidal told them, "but don't linger. I won't be here come morning, and Monet's Potens aren't nearly as welcoming."

***

"Who does he think he is?" Drage complained, taking a deep swig from the bottle Vidal had one of his lackeys bring to their room. It was a modest dwelling with just enough space for two double decker beds and a small, round table. While it looked to be cleaned and aired out often, age had taken its toll, leaving streaks of brown and orange in the ceiling's corners. "And did he call this wine cheap? If he considers this cheap, then I don't even want to know what he thinks expensive is."

"Well," Khale began, "he didn't exactly grow up skint."

"He grew up flaming absurd." Drage clicked his tongue. "Like I need some twisted rich heir in my life. I've got enough going on as it is."

"I thought a rich boy with a keen interest in you was every woman's fantasy. He looks like he'll buy you things. Personally, I think the Chatterin' Crow could use some fixin'. If you ask *real* nice, you reckon he'll pay ta have it renovated for you?"

"Are you really making more prostitute jokes right now?"

"I didn't say one thing 'bout sellin' yerself. Not one. But if you wanna do it, I suggest not announcin' it ta the rest a' the world, yea? I actually like bein' able ta sleep at night."

"I'm going to knock your teeth out one of these days, you Astonian cu—"

"Stop right there!" Khale admonished. "Or I might just feel insulted, yea? No one wants that."

"Yet you insult me at every turn."

"Hey, I have *some* class. You don't see me insultin' you with foul words like that. It ain't creative. Bad for the brain, the soul, an' the mouth."

"So, you admit to insulting me?"

"Well, I never exactly tried ta hide it."

Drage pinched the bridge of his nose, wholly and utterly done with him. He needed sanity. He needed anything, anyone else... just not Khale. "Where's Celina?"

"With Pom," Khale said, crushing his hopes with two measly words. "They're watchin' the inborns train in the yard. Scopin' out the competition an' all. Maybe even showin' off a tip. Pom likes ta keep his knives sharp, an' he ain't exactly humble."

"You didn't want to join them?"

"I don't know no fancy swordplay." Khale shrugged and sat down across from him. "Besides, someone has ta ask what yer plannin' on doin'."

"Blunt as always." Drage groaned in frustration. "But isn't it already obvious? I don't exactly have a choice in the matter."

"There's always a choice."

"Of course you'd think that. Didn't you see the look in that Verne bastard's eyes? Does he seem like the type that'll take no for an answer?"

"Try an' see for yerself," Khale suggested, making him groan again. "At least y'know the Veld ain't out ta get anyone. No warped eradication scheme like you thought, yea? They got bigger problems on their hands."

"Your Elementalist friend seems to be right in the middle of those problems."

"Not surprisin'. Jack's got his fingers in lotsa things. He's always been curious 'bout all the thorns the Institute snags their silken robes on. Probably corrupted Syl, too. He's good at that."

"You speaking from experience?"

"Observation. Jack's got a stubborn streak a mile wide, but yer off yer eggs if you think I'll let anyone rope me inta somethin' I ain't interested in."

"Let me ask you this then, do you think Verne is telling the truth? That your friend actually passed through here? He could just be using you… using *us*."

"I can live with that," Khale dismissed. "Look, I've seen Jack spew fire an' rock enough times ta tell you just how hot-blooded he is when he's left ta his own devices. Jack's rash, yea, but he's our best lead ta Tiv. So, we'll follow it. I'm not goin' ta force you ta tag along, especially knowin' the Grove's gonna get messy. The Hellions full a' loyals. They'll bleed for whoever you tell 'em ta bleed for."

"Your point?"

"That's dangerous, but useful."

"Way to state the bleeding obvious." Drage rolled his eyes. "That's what I'm there for. It's my duty to make sure they don't risk their lives for some idiot."

"Exactly," Khale stressed. "An' as much as it pains me ta admit this, me an' Pom, we're not worth no dozen lives. Creator's ashes, we're hardly worth one."

"At this point, they wouldn't be risking their lives for you or Pom. They'll be doing it for the Hellion. Like I said, do you really think a man like Vidal will accept no for an answer?"

"He didn't seem ta be pressin' you," Khale argued mulishly. "Sure it ain't just in your head? He did have a weird smile. The pressure-exuding kind. But that don't mean nothin'."

"Khale," Drage stressed, "he offered the Hellion his name. Even if I said no, the others would question my decision."

"Let the bitches bark. Better yet, tell 'em ta stuff it, yea? Last I checked, you were the leader."

"And create animosity?"

"They don't even know about his offer!"

"You think he won't leak the information?"

Khale sighed, infuriated. "For someone that acts so carefree, you sure like ta fret."

"Because this isn't just another slimy bastard with too much money to spend!" Drage yelled, slamming his hand down on the table. The bottle he'd been drinking from tipped over, shattering against the ground and sprinkling shards of glass around them. "No matter how you look at it, it's a good opportunity for the Hellion..." Drage trailed off, coughing twice, before saying in a quieter voice, "and do you really think I'd leave two of our own to fend for themselves?"

Khale opened his mouth to retort, then closed it as soon as he processed the words. His response lodged itself somewhere in his throat, as the scent of the malt around them seeped into the air just as quickly as it did through the threadbare parts of his boots. For a long, unnerving moment, they just stared at each other. The awkward tension between them was palpable. Then,

Drage turned away, and Khale knew with absolute certainty that the light dusting on his cheeks wasn't from the alcohol. He barely drank a quarter. Drage was no lightweight.

"Look what you made me do!" Drage suddenly yelled, pointing at the wasted alcohol now decorating their shoes. "Call someone to send another one of these damn bottles over, and get Celina while you're at it! She needs to send a message out to those drunks in Brantine, before I change my mind."

Khale just stood there, blinking at him.

"Didn't you hear me?" Drage glared.

"Me an' Pom," Khale muttered. His tone was slow and full of realization. "We're real lucky, y'know? Always have been."

"What are you going on about now?"

"Nothin'." Khale grinned, already walking out the door. His toes were wet and the crunching glass definitely wasn't good for his boots, but that didn't seem so important anymore. "Anythin' you need, boss."

9

When the sun set and their abused feet demanded rest, Jack and Sylvie settled in a dilapidated village just past Min. It was close enough to the Wymeran River that they could hear the familiar rush of water, but unimportant enough that it held no mark on Ferus Terria's atlas. Even Vidal hadn't deemed it necessary to leave a dot when he updated Jack's graffitied map a few days before they left the Veld.

As they walked through the town, Sylvie couldn't help but think that perhaps they'd be better off camping outside. From the looks of things, it wouldn't make much difference. Atrophied men leaned against their hovels, their cheeks sunken in, and their eyes swollen. They were barely able to life their heads without swaying to the side. In contrast, gaunt children chased each other on top of houses. Insultingly energetic for children so underfed. They climbed like monkeys and shouted loudly, despite the hour. Their parents were nowhere to be found. The rest, drunkards and whores, were split between brazenly calling out to them and staring on in wonder. As if they couldn't believe their derelict village actually had visitors—Sylvie couldn't either.

The village reeked of deprivation.

What were they thinking? She wanted to say they hadn't been, but that wasn't entirely true. Jack, wordless and grumpy from their trek, had decided to walk through the village. If it was in an attempt to find a better place to sleep, then it was a futile one. But Sylvie had continued following him. Too tired to object, and painfully aware of the angry gray clouds spreading above them. Despite the coming rainfall, the village was filled with heat. Perhaps it was a lingering effect of the season. The scorching sun was particularly ruthless in the Plains.

She regretted not taking a detour. There were dozens of other hamlets. Farther and more expensive, but so much better off. Here, she wouldn't be shocked if they stumbled across overturned wagons and alleyways full of rotting bodies. It didn't get much lower than this.

Sylvie found a row of gambling rings in the far corner of the village. Just past their sorry excuse of a market. A lone bar, turned brothel, sat beside it. It was the liveliest building of all. Gaudy lamps hung from its roof, illuminating the dirty ground in a light so green she winced. Her nostrils flared, assaulted by the scent of fish and something she couldn't place, but insulted her nevertheless. She wrinkled her nose when she caught a whiff of manure emerging from an alley they passed. At the end of it, were two boys shoveling the mess and piling it all in filthy bags. Sylvie couldn't help but feel sorry for them. Shoveling shit was a thankless task.

Being so close to a body of water and having no neighboring cities to contest with for land, Sylvie would've thought them better off. They certainly had all the advantages they needed to flourish. But it seemed that most would rather spend their lives on women and drink than suffer the hardships of farm work.

Well, it was their life to waste. She had her own to live.

Sylvie stopped when Jack stilled. Confusion chased nervousness across her features when he didn't speak. She didn't dare break the silence, however. Had he somehow read her thoughts? Oh, he'd mock her endlessly for thinking like him.

Jack turned to her, back slouched and lips drawn into a rigid line. His eyes were distinctly alert under his hood. That was when she registered the deep voice calling out to them.

Sylvie whirled around just as a pair of unsteady footsteps drew too close for comfort. She stepped back immediately. The red-faced man tilted his head in bewilderment, his hazy eyes unable to comprehend how she'd suddenly gotten so far. But for all of his slowness, he seemed to realize that he wasn't going to figure it out because he snorted instead. If it was at his own expense or because he found something funny about her, Sylvie neither knew, nor cared to.

"Hello," he greeted with a wide, deviant leer.

Sylvie's fingers twitched in apprehension.

Before the familiar light of her magic could seep out, she grabbed her hood and readjusted it over her eyes in an effort to ease her nerves. It didn't help. But distantly, she thanked the Institute for their preference for large hoods and unisex clothing. She didn't want to cause a scene. Neither did she want to deal with an angry drunk. So, in light of ignoring him, she simply lowered her voice to an unnatural degree.

"Hello," she replied in a pitch that was unbelievably forced.

Jack had the audacity to snicker.

The man, inebriated as he was, scrutinized her in surprise. Clearly not expecting the deep tone. He tried to peer at her face from under the hood. To no avail. Sylvie gripped her cowl tighter when his breath fanned over her skin. Tart and rotten. The man didn't seem to notice her dismay, as he exhaled deeply through his mouth. It was followed by a hiccup that had her back tensing in frustration.

He stared for a minute longer. His gaze drifted to Jack, who was laughing behind his hands. Bleary eyes flickered back and forth. His face morphed into one of thoughtfulness, before traces of understanding washed over him and he clicked his tongue in disgust. His face blanched a specific shade of green that suggested illness. Jack sobered in an instant, already knowing what the man was thinking. But before he could give him a piece of his mind, the man stuffed his hands in his pockets and stalked away. He stumbled to a shady corner where three scantily clad whores batted their lashes at him in expectance.

Jack damned him twice under his breath, before walking away. The smooth lines of *Iarre* slipped from his mouth before he even knew he was cursing. He purposely snubbed the smug grin on Sylvie's face when she caught up to him. Her stride was shorter than his own, but she moved fast enough to keep his pace. She didn't tease him outright. Though she might as well have because the incessant skip in her step annoyed him to no end, and the way her entire face lit up as she mocked him in her mind made his brow furrow in exasperation. He held himself back from sighing, not wanting to give her the satisfaction of a reaction. She was definitely doing it on purpose.

They walked until they found themselves in front of a downtrodden shack, long abandoned by its owners, if the broken lock and thick blanket of dust were any indication. It was big enough for two cots and a bucket, but it held none of those. Only a leaky roof, a barred window, and an empty, rotten smelling barrel. It was likely used for collecting rainwater once upon a time. Shocking, that no one had thought to steal it.

Jack was quick to step inside. He eyed the broken roof with caution, and took extra care to seat himself under what was possibly the only patch of ground safe from holes and webs, but still close enough to the door for him to bolt should the need arise.

Sylvie was less careful. She settled beside the shack's only window and rubbed the dust away with her sleeve. If she squinted, she could see the shadow of Curran's gates just past the Wymeran River. There was movement on the other side. But it was too dark for her to make out what they were doing.

"Syl," Jack called, holding his hand out. He said nothing more. Only wiggled his fingers expectantly. But it didn't matter. She knew what he wanted.

Rummaging in her pack, she threw Silas' journal at him.

He caught it with ease and immediately opened it to where he left off. They'd taken to pouring over the great Conjurer's memoir ever since they left the Veld. Never mind that they'd already finished it four times. Each. It was an interesting read, and there were some entries written entirely in code that they weren't able to decipher. Jack had obsessed over it for the better part of the week. He'd tried to blend *Íarre, Yövín, Wysûvium,* and a dozen other dialects that he knew bits and pieces of, but it was all for naught. Thelarius and Silas' code was either based off of a language long dead or personally crafted from scratch. Both were equally likely. Neither option changed the fact that it would take him years to crack, and that was with the proper books at his disposal. They didn't have that kind of time.

"What do you make of it?" Jack asked vaguely. He didn't bother elaborating. She knew what he meant.

Sylvie breathed audibly, and for a moment, he thought she was sighing at him. It wouldn't be the first time. But then the moment passed, and he shivered when he realized that she was trying to drill holes into him with her eyes. She sought his attention—his full attention. Jack didn't give it. He forced nonchalance over his features out of reflex, while he flipped carelessly through the journal's yellow pages. The sides felt fuzzier than usual from the weather.

"Does it really matter?" Sylvie asked eventually.

Jack tried not to look offended. "Of course it does."

"Then ask *her.*"

Jack heard more than saw Sylvie shift. She pressed her face back against the window, openly disinterested in the subject. She'd made her thoughts on the matter clear when she first found him hunched over the pages like a madman.

Sylvie wanted to leave the specifics to someone more knowledgeable. They weren't scholars. It was the logical course of action. But Jack didn't want to leave it to someone else when they had a chance to figure it out for themselves. It may have been a waste of energy and time, both of which they only had so much of, but it was worth it. Sylvie, however, was stubborn when she wanted to be, and he knew from previous experience that she wouldn't be moved by his speeches. Or at least... not easily.

Jack supposed he could follow Sylvie's advice. He could grit his teeth, grab the Heartstone from under her collar, and demand answers that *she* may or may not give.

But unbeknownst to her, he'd already tried.

He did it two days ago, while she slept. *She* didn't even grace him with a response. Talking wasn't hard. Neither was being ignored. Jack sat and took it. Yet, he counted the ordeal amongst the most difficult things he'd ever experienced in his life. It was right up there with that time he got overpowered by a deserter when he was seventeen. He almost died then, and he had the scars to prove it. It was definitely harder than when he fell out of a window when he was four. His terrible landing skills weren't what made the affair unpleasant, rather it was the walk back up the winding halls of the Alps' public archives. His mother waited at the top to scold him. Cheryll Dace was the single most terrifying woman he'd ever known—and she was his mother for pity's sake! He deserved an award.

But if he received one for getting close to Sylvie without getting half of his face burnt, then he thought it well-deserved. She stirred at the slightest sound. Sylvie slept like an animal left to fend for itself in the wild. Her magic bled from her whenever she slept. The pads of her fingers would glow blue and fill with heat, before pulsing in time with her heart. It was something Jack thought only happened to children during their uncontrollable years. Clearly, he was wrong.

Jack wasn't flame retardant. He almost had his hair singed. Twice. It didn't help that whenever he spoke, she'd move again. Frankly, he was amazed that she hadn't woken herself up with her constant tossing. The grass under her had been crushed in a matter of minutes. It couldn't be comfortable.

"Jack," Sylvie called, snapping him from his stupor.

He turned to find her offering the Heartstone he'd tried so hard to grab all those nights ago. She was closer than he expected, holding the stone right up to his face. The weight of her gaze stripped him of strength and breath alike. Jack leaned back against the weathered gray wood behind him to escape from it, on the pretense of getting a better look at the terrible rock. It was still translucent. Still bright and strange and beautiful.

But he didn't expect anything less. It was a symbol after all. A symbol of beings that shouldn't exist and of everything in this world that lacked light.

"What?" he asked, defensive.

"Are you going to ask?"

Jack stared at it for a tick longer, eyeing the darkness that swirled within. If he looked close enough, he could make out each individual tendril. Seamless and languid. The presence within was quiet. Tame once again... for now.

The wisps meshed into a tiny, condensed ball that reflected his face back at him. In the blackness, he couldn't find the shadows in his eyes. All he saw was red. Untainted red. He missed it. He missed what the color of his eyes once represented.

"No," Jack said eventually. He grabbed her hand with both of his to close her fingers tightly over the Heartstone. As much to get it away from him as an answer to her question. Jack's fingers lingered. His insides twisted, tingling and treacherous, before he moved away. His arms fell limply back to his side, as he told her, "You should rest."

It wasn't an order, but it clearly wasn't an option either.

"And you?" she asked.

"I'm leaning back, aren't I?"

Sylvie didn't answer, choosing instead to inspect him. She searched his face for something only she knew. Jack met her gaze head on, his chin tilted upwards and his eyes filled with a kind of boldness that was distinctly his own. Sylvie wasn't deterred by the thin line of his lips or the displeased tightness of his jaw. If anything, they spurred her on. She knew him well enough by now to know that if he disliked her attention, he'd say so.

She reached out, her finger ghosting over a bulging vein on his temple. Jack felt her press against it, before tracing its length. The blunted tip of her nail dug gently into the tender skin, and the elastic vessel squished back in obedience.

Her eyes were so bright and so focused.

His chest heated, despite himself.

Jack swallowed thickly. He kept his eyes on her face. This close, he could smell her. Crushed mint leaves and smoke. With... soil? Jack pinched himself, willing the thought away.

He watched her inspect what little she could see of the Orive Crystal embedded on the side of his head. She looked like she wanted to say something, to mutter a reassurance he'd undoubtedly scoff at, but she clenched her jaw in preference. Her eyes gave him a glimpse of the mental war she waged within herself, before she shut them away, hiding from his scrutiny.

No words passed between them.

Slinking back to her previous position, Sylvie prepared herself for what would undoubtedly be a restless slumber. But it was better than nothing. In the meantime, Jack busied himself with flipping through the well-worn pages with an absent hand and an even more absent mind.

He stopped at his most favored passage and read:

_07.02.OA_

I met three children today. Naïve, little things. They said they wanted to be just like me, to serve the Institute, and to fight for what's right. While it's flattering, I do think that whoever's embellishing them with such polished tales needs to stop. I fought for what I believed in. Nothing more. The fact that the rest of the world deemed it justice was because of Thelarius. If anyone should be given praise, it's him. And if anyone should be idolized, it's those with better temperaments.

The new generation should focus on peace and goodness and light. Though I suppose there is a certain... allure to wiping out the enemy. Still, there's no need—absolutely none—for them to seek out the whispered promises offered amidst all the gore. They're young. The paths before them are endless. There are better, more diplomatic ways to solve problems. Maurice and Pernelia taught me that.

If I had been alone with them, I would've told them not to bother searching for glory. For it's found on the backs of rotting, twisted corpses of men and women with eyes exactly like theirs. It's in the blood *caked beneath your fingernails that never disappears no matter how much you scrub. I've lived long enough to know that when you look back on all of the war and the strife, on all of the violence you wrought, the hardest part isn't dealing with the cries of those left to grieve or putting up with the phantom aches your body suffers every morning from wounds long since healed...*

So, I offer these words to my children and to their children's children that hopefully come across this journal, if nothing else, remember this: the hardest thing to look at isn't the mangled carcasses after a battle or the faces of those left behind, it's the little mirror above your dresser, showing you the ghost of that child soldier you killed in the heat of the moment.

I'm sorry.

Jack traced the old, blotted scrawl.

Silas was a wise man. Experienced in more ways than one. If they were forced to hand over this journal once they reached the Alps, then he'd be sure to tear this page out as a memento.

***

The Great Conjurer, Silas Drayr, was born to make war. Not settle in the verbose discomforts of politics.

Thelarius knew that well. Though his friend had been groomed for a position of leadership within the Institute, the only thing he'd ever wanted and the only thing he'd ever pushed for was its change—and he did so in the only way he knew how. By unleashing fire. Displays of power were considered normal, even necessary, before the four of them rose to the top. They were common still, although growing fewer now that Maurice and Pernelia took to settling disputes by presiding over them rather than allowing practitioners to square off against each other. Thelarius didn't have that kind of patience, so he let them be. He wanted to continue learning about the world. To see the gap between Nebbin and practitioner shorten with his own two eyes. There wasn't much left for him to do in the Alps now that the larger battles had been won.

Silas was similar. He rarely bothered with the minute details, although he did remain aware of them. So long as things changed for the better, then he was perfectly content to let his friends squabble as they pleased. Silas learned the ins and outs of his new job at his own pace.

During the rare times when they all fell into disagreement, arguing over something that could be dealt with quickly if one of them just yielded, Thelarius could see how much they differed from Maurice and Pernelia, who were made for this world.

He wasn't claimed by some sense of inferiority, but neither was he awed by their skill. Thelarius was just tired of being at the center of everything. He realized this one day when Silas came to him with bags under his eyes and cheeks as hollow as logs. He kept mumbling word salads. But before Thelarius could question him, Silas had produced a list from his robes. It was longer than most of the scrolls in the archives and labelled, "ENOUGH," in big, bold letters at the very top. Thelarius read the first few lines, then stopped to take the long list in. He couldn't believe that Silas had actually taken the time to list all of the things that bothered him, and then left it for him to peruse.

Thelarius had never seen such a blatant order.

Absently, he recalled that the latest on that list had a lot to do with the Pulka scholars. Silas was wary of them, and it wasn't just because he disagreed with their comments about his black-feathered spaulders. Thelarius knew better than to ignore his friend's keen instincts. But Maurice was just as committed as the rest of them to their cause—perhaps even more so—which was why Thelarius paused whenever the scholars overstepped their boundaries with their questions or when they crafted strange gems that the voice in his head warned him to watch out for.

Thankfully, Silas' guard didn't affect his cordiality, and the few times it did, Alaina always managed to temper him. The Conjurer laughed when appropriate and spoke when necessary, but there was only so much he could take. So, when Thelarius stumbled upon Silas standing by himself on top of the tallest building in the north, he didn't question it. And when he spread his arms out, head tilted to the sky, before lighting up into an unrestrained pillar of fire, Thelarius simply watched on.

Silas looked at the sky the same way a vagrant looked at a warm hearth through frosted windowpanes. His cloak burned, un-enchanted as it was. But the rest of his clothes remained unaffected. The air blurred, and Thelarius felt licks of heat caress his cheeks. Silas' flames weren't filled with warmth or the crackling sense of protection that only fire could bring. They were angry. Each spark was chockfull of threats that promised a slow death to any that stepped too close.

Thelarius couldn't help but do just that.

Careful, she warned. But there was no need. Silas wouldn't hurt him. His oldest friend was the tortured sort that had a knack for helping others find themselves, but could never do the same.

Nevertheless, Thelarius nodded. Because he knew that *she* wouldn't let him move if he didn't. The tendrils that always wrapped around him when *she* was upset made every hair on his body stand on end. The experience wasn't exactly unpleasant. Just… abrupt. Surprising. The darkness *she* ruled warmed him in ways that Silas' fire didn't; in ways nothing else truly could. It was vast and encompassing, always bursting with heat.

"Thelarius," Silas called, reeling him from his thoughts. His flames receded back into his body, lingering on his shoulder as if to burn the last vestiges of his already ruined cowl before they disappeared completely. "What are you doing here?"

"I found something good."

He searched several pockets, before finding what he was looking for. Thelarius held up his prize—a sweet bun. Lightly browned and filled with jam. It was freshly baked. Sort of. Silas wasn't sure how long he'd been standing there, but it looked fairly new. It was then his eyes zeroed in on the bite mark that Thelarius futilely tried to hide with a napkin.

"Of course you bit it."

"Be grateful that I saved you one at all." Thelarius broke off another piece just to spite him, before handing it over to the now grumbling Conjurer. "Alaina is looking for you. Something about replenishing her stocks."

"She has you running around now, too?" Silas shook his head. "What am I saying? Of course she does."

"What are you doing up here?" Thelarius asked. "You've got a stack of paperwork on your desk, and if you don't do it soon, I'm afraid Pernelia might have me finish it. So, please come back down. Oh, but if you're trying to become a human beacon to guide the Amorphs back before the blizzard hits, then carry on."

"I have a stack of paperwork?" Silas gave him a sour look. "You don't happen to mean *your* stack that you carted to my study two nights ago so you could have someone to moan about work to, do you?"

"I didn't bring it to moan! I brought it to show you the unholy amount of things they need my signature for."

"It's still your work."

"It's in your study."

"Thelarius," Silas said evenly, "it needs *your* signature."

"Like you've never forged my signature before. It isn't exactly complicated and no matter how hard I try, I can never get my *t*'s to loop the way I want them to. How do you do it? You always get them so thin and perfect."

"We all write differently. I thought I told you that before. It makes no sense to compare—"

"—When we each have our own natural strengths and weaknesses," Thelarius finished the *'focus-on-improving-yourself'* speech he'd heard so many times before. "Yes, I know."

"I'm glad to know my lessons stuck."

"Of course they did. But Silas, in this case, I've settled on a goal that I want to reach."

"Just don't lose your own personal touch in your attempt to reach that standard," Silas advised. "But you're not here to talk about handwriting, are you? What do you want, Thelarius?"

"What do you mean I'm not? Maybe I am."

"Fine then. But you still can't leave your work for me to finish just because you don't want to do it."

"Nonsense! Of course I *ca*—*w*ait." Thelarius paused and looked at him with wide eyes as if seeing him in an entirely new light. His eyebrows drew together in thought. "You didn't even deny it when I said..."

"When you said what?"

"When I..."

"Spit it out."

"Have you really forged my signature before?"

There was an age of silence, where they both blinked blankly back at each other. Distantly, the echo of laughing children could be heard somewhere below them. It was followed by the loud bang of a dozen fallen crates and four stunted curses. Thelarius swore the birds chirped louder on purpose.

Silas was the first to break.

Pinching the bridge of his nose, he muttered a defeated, "Creator, give me strength."

"Which contract?" Thelarius went on. He was bouncing back and forth on the balls of his feet now. His eyes were alight with wonder. "Was it the request to send more Amorphs to explore Redmount? I know you're curious about that place. Or maybe it was *th*—*o*h!" His jaw slackened and he took a step back in sudden, knowing shock. The betrayal on his face was clear. "Don't tell me it was the Revin Salve requisition? Because I saw a new supply in the Healer's Quarters a few nights ago, and I know that I didn't approve of them. I locked the paper up. I know they're for pain relief and we need them, but I can't stand their scent! They reek of old socks and closet. The smell sticks to your hands and—" Thelarius cut himself off, blanching at the thought.

"I did no such thing," Silas said, taking a satisfying bite of his sweet bun. The slight smile on his face fooled no one.

"You traitor," Thelarius accused. "And to think I gave you my last sweet bun."

Behind you, *she* suddenly said. Dour enough to kill his mood.

Thelarius straightened. His shoulders were taut with tension, as he turned his head just enough to catch a glimpse of dark robes and an ornate tome. Vaguely, he noticed Silas' eyes narrow for the briefest of instants. If it was because of the sudden change in his temper or because of the intruder before them, he didn't know. But it didn't matter. It was gone a split second later. Hidden behind a careless shrug and a sleepy smile.

That was all Thelarius needed to know who was there. Really, his friend was overprotective to the point of insult. Just because he didn't always see eye to eye with the man, didn't mean that Silas needed to watch out for him as well.

"Maurice," Silas greeted, noting the tension in the air. The animosity was palpable. But he couldn't blame Maurice for his anger. He and Thelarius had gotten into another petty argument not even two hours ago. Before Thelarius could even think about addressing the Healer with him present, Silas patted him twice on the back in farewell.

"You're leaving?" Thelarius asked, though what he meant to say was, *'Please don't leave me alone with him.'*

'Don't drag me into your fights,' was Silas' unvoiced response. Or maybe it was, *'Work it out yourself.'* Thelarius wasn't quite sure. His bothered face looked a lot like his 'you-deserve-this' face, but what Silas did say was far clearer.

"I'm going to see Alaina. Be sure to pick up your work from my study later."

Forget dignity. Forget pride. Thelarius didn't value either that much anyway. His eyes begged for him to stay. When that didn't work, his tongue did.

"Wait, Silas!"

***

Jack was reading her letters.

That was the first thing Sylvie noticed when she woke, sore and dazed from sleeping in a strange position. She heaved upon waking, so she concluded that she must've been gasping in her sleep. The second thing she noticed was something dripping on her. She looked up to see slow, but steady droplets of rainwater trickling down her face and soaking her collar. From how damp her robes and the rest of the shack were, she could tell that it had been pouring for some time. Her eyes reflexively fell to the world outside. It was foggy and gray, masked by the heat-filled rain.

Cracking her neck, she rubbed at the aching spot between her shoulders. Why did she ever think it was a good idea to sleep while sitting? Her muscles were tenser than before she'd rested. They protested with each movement. Sylvie couldn't even stretch without pain filling her senses.

"Bad dream?" Jack asked her, though his eyes never left the page in front of him.

"No."

"You were tossing and turning. Assuming you're not lying, then you must've seen—no, I hope you saw another memory. I don't think we can continue being friends if you tell me that you fantasize about your great ancestor."

Her eyes widened. Two bright spots appeared on her cheeks and with a voice too loud for her newly roused state, she yelled, "What?"

"You were mumbling '*Silas*' in your sleep," Jack explained. The corner of his lips quirked up in an uncertain smile. "Please tell me it was a memory."

Sylvie grimaced, but instead of answering him, she asked, "Why are you awake?"

"What? Wait, no! Don't answer with another question! I'm serious here, Syl. It was a memory, right?"

"Of course it was!"

"Sweet Pernelia." Jack sighed in relief. He slumped back against the muggy plank behind him. "You can't just leave something like that hanging. What's wrong with you? My sanity is on the line here."

"You didn't answer my question."

"I'm awake because I wanted to avoid that." He waved vaguely at her. "Don't you remember what happened last time I had one of those dreams?"

"You had tension headaches."

"Exactly. My body suffers enough. I don't need my own mind going against me."

"How'd you even know I'd have a dream? Have you finally developed some sixth sense?"

"If only. But there's no way I'm putting myself through that again. So, I'll be counting on you to tell me what you see."

"You can't stay awake forever, Jack."

"Watch me," he dismissed, then buried his nose back in her journal. He kept rubbing the buttery leather cover, and she found herself staring as he did. Sylvie wasn't sure what he found so interesting about the letters she'd written, but she left him be. Jack had an enraptured look in his eyes that told her that she wouldn't be able to hold his attention no matter how much she tried. She turned back to the window in preference.

Their current situation reminded her of the hostel back in Thyme, where she and Jack holed up after getting soaked to the bone in the Forest of Tears. That building had been decrepit, too. But it was still more comfortable than the shack they were in now. She regretted not appreciating how good she had it then. They'd even offered them two rooms. Two! At this point, even one sounded heavenly. Preferably one without holes in the ceiling.

Her thoughts grinded to a halt when she saw two figures in the rain. They were close enough for her to hear the sound of their yells over the downpour, but not enough for her to make out their words. They might as well have yelled in another language... then again, perhaps they were. She couldn't tell.

Sylvie shimmied closer to the windowsill and lowered her head as they approached.

Are they searching for shelter? she wondered. *Or did they follow us from the village? No, it doesn't matter.*

They were coming closer.

If she squinted, she could just make out their faces. They were harsh, stern-faced men. All wrinkles and hard lines with flat planes for faces. One of them was shivering so badly his skin had taken a pallor similar to her own. They were bigger than she thought they'd be. Even as hunched in on themselves as they were, she could tell that they easily towered a good foot over her.

"Jack," she whispered without turning.

The urgency in her tone was enough to spring him into standing, and before she knew it, he was by the door. He froze it shut without a second thought. The frost spread along the walls and over the glass windowpane, cracking as it went. By the time they were encased in a square of ice, both men were outside.

Jack motioned for her to move, so he could sit by the door. His ice seemed to pulse whenever he came in contact with it. With a wave of his hand, the glitters of hoarfrost spread farther up the window, thickening the already dense coat there.

They pressed their backs against the wall and waited.

One of the men practically rammed the door in his haste for shelter. It didn't even budge.

"Huh?" he mumbled, confused. "It won't open."

"Let me try," his companion said. There was another thump, but the door didn't give. They tried again and again, growing more aggravated with every hit. With a battle cry, they both slammed their shoulders into the door. It shook, but otherwise stayed in place.

Jack smiled, pleased with himself.

"Maybe we should let them in?" Sylvie whispered.

"They'll rob us in our sleep."

"You weren't sleeping anyway."

"I'd like the option."

"We can't just leave them out there."

"I beg to differ." To emphasize his point, Jack coated the bottom of the door with another layer of ice. "If they just walk a bit more, then they'll reach the village. It's less than eighty steps away. They'd have to be blind not to see it. The fact that they haven't left this decrepit shed yet means they know we're here."

On cue, one of them spoke, "Are you sure they're in here?"

"That's what Yeva said," his partner answered in a deeper voice. "There's a window over there. Try that."

Sylvie frowned at the smug look Jack sent her then. She purposely twisted away and listened instead to the man's boots as he scuttled closer. She pressed her back against the wall, but quickly realized that there was no need.

"Damn this rain!" the man cursed. "The window's all foggy. I can't see a damn thing."

"Idiot." Jack snickered under his breath. The cool mist his ice expelled wrapped around them. It dropped the temperature just enough for discomfort.

"Well, don't just stand there," his partner said. "They definitely heard us by now. Just break it."

"I ain't gonna risk gettin' shards a' glass all over me. 'Sides, I won't be able to fit through those panels even if I tried!"

"Then break the door, idiot."

Jack had an excited gleam in his eye when he saw the man's shadow rise, as he pulled back his fist. Magic against brawn. The victor was clear. If nothing else, Jack was immensely confident in his abilities. But before he could even see the Nebbin try, a spray of frozen specks fell over his head and eyes. Jack wiped them away with an aggravated curse.

Within the span of a breath, he jumped away from the door. Sylvie was right behind him. She muttered something too low for his ears to catch. Just as he was about to tell her to speak louder, he stilled at the sight before him. The man's partner, in all of his agitation to get inside, had punched a hole right through the door. Both wood and ice caved under the force of the blow. Jack's magic made quick work of blocking the gap, inadvertently locking the man's arm in place.

"Brawn wins, huh?" Jack said, amazed. It reminded him of Tiv. His face fell at that. Before he was even aware of it, his hands were up and splayed, prepared to freeze the offending limb.

"We should leave," Sylvie said, knowing they wouldn't find any reprieve here.

Jack tore his eyes away from the door. "That's the plan," he said snippily. To her credit, she didn't even narrow her eyes at him. "It's been the plan for weeks, Syl."

"I meant now."

"In this storm?"

"It'll pass."

The Elementalist eyed her warily. Jack really didn't want to run around in the rain. It was better to wait it out, then travel at their own pace. That was the smart thing to do. Hell, it was the obvious thing. Especially since they had Silas' journal. Whether the rest of the world knew it existed or not, it was still considered a treasure of the Institute. Any practitioner he knew—and would ever know—would kill him for risking it in such spotty weather.

And that, ultimately, was what shaped his decision.

Jack couldn't stop himself from chortling. He looked between her, the door, and the panicked shadow outside of the window. Both of the men outside were screaming now. One, because of his trapped arm. The other, for another reason altogether. Concern for his friend? Fear? Both were a waste of energy. Jack's eyes fell to the sack that hung from Sylvie's shoulder, where Silas' priceless memoir was tucked away.

Oh, they'd be so angry at him.

And he was going to enjoy every second of it.

Feigning reluctance, Jack sighed. Loud and rich like molten lava. He'd meant to tease her a bit. But from the way Sylvie's eyes lit up, he knew that his mouth was probably twisted in an entirely different emotion. One that betrayed his inner desire to prance outside in this dreadful downpour. Traitorous thing.

"And what about them?" Jack tilted his head toward the door. "They'll continue screaming if we just leave them here. I don't know about you, but I really don't want a cross, pitchfork brandishing mob chasing us all the way to the Alps. Plus, I really don't think we should be letting these guys go. They're trying to kill us, Syl... or mug us *at least*. That's just tonight. Who knows what they'll be doing tomorrow."

Her eyebrows scrunched together. She regarded him in a curious way that made him think of Elise and her big, brown eyes. Jack resisted the urge to rub his neck in discomfort. His gaze ventured off to the side, before he decided that he was chicken shit for doing so and he met her eyes again with something like defiance. They stared at each other for an uncomfortable amount of time. But just as he was about to break and ask her to blow a tunnel of flame through the back wall so they could leave, Sylvie's voice stopped him in his tracks.

"I never told you to stop."

He opened his mouth to argue, but stilled mid-way once her words registered. Jack gaped like a fish out of water. Sylvie, on the other hand, simply nodded her head obligingly at him. She took two steps back, rolled her shoulders like none of this concerned her, and then dug into her pack to double check her belongings. She wrapped her things in an extra cloak, while simultaneously shoving smaller trinkets to the bottom of her pack where they'd be safer.

All the while, Jack continued to stare. He wasn't ready for the spur of excitement that coursed through his veins then. His insides were giddy from the unexpectedness of it all. Jack hadn't felt this eager to use his magic since his days in the east; remnants of it already seeped from his skin. They froze part of his robes. The cloth would undoubtedly become crisp and wrinkled once it finally dried, but none of that mattered now.

He turned back to the door. A wild smirk split his lips. Although he felt slight confliction at what he was about to do—and what she so easily condoned—it was squashed as soon as he held his hands up. Absently, Jack noted that they were shaking with thrilled vehemence, before ice leapt from his fingers.

The men stopped screaming long before the final vestiges of warmth left their bones.

10

The Wymeran River was a waking nightmare.

Its waters sprinted toward the Alman Sea, stopped only momentarily by jagged rocks that forced it to swirl in dozens of whirlpools like chunks of stew in a deep pot. The roaring storm above them only added to the fierceness. Rain blanched the color out of everything. Wind blew wildly, provoking the waves to rise and fall and rise again, moving higher with each passing second. They buffeted the masses of stone and spilled onto the high shore, but neither yielded under the river's ill-tempered caress.

The pair stared at it, entranced by the chaos. Jack was the first to look away. Wrestling with the mop of his hair, he took in their surroundings with a thoughtful, dragging absorption.

The river wasn't small by any means. They couldn't just wade across with ropes and hope for the best. It was wrathful, strong, and deep. They'd need a small boat and proper conditions to even think about crossing. But as he walked with Sylvie toward the shore, standing just outside of the water's reach, he realized that even a boat wouldn't cut it. Remnants of split oars and broken timber were littered along the coast; the rest of their pieces carried off into the night. Jack could venture a guess as to where the men and women that manned them were.

There were broken fishnets on the other side of the river, but not one dock. Perhaps the locals thought it a waste to build something that would undoubtedly give during times like this. Jack both cursed and commended them for their judgment. The former only because it didn't help them now.

Sylvie pointed at something in the distance. Jack squinted until he found the brooding shadow of Curran's outermost building. The city was so close to the water.

Where are the guards? he wondered, then frowned when the answer came to him a second later. *Snug inside their homes.*

Either their captain didn't want to lose any men to the storm or they were confident that no one would venture out into this madness—likely both. Suddenly, Jack felt sorry for all of the Hunters that were always forced out into awful conditions. But he quickly shook his head of the thought when a shiver wracked his body. Now that they'd stopped running, he realized that he was freezing. It felt like his muscles stopped producing heat hours ago rather than the mere minutes they stood there.

Noticing his discomfort, Sylvie lit a fire immediately. She kindled it between her fingers. They crouched to better huddle over the warmth, while making futile attempts to better cover their already soaked heads.

Jack crowded dangerously close to the flame, not caring if he burned. "I'm going to freeze a strip of water," he yelled over the rain, then pointed at the river for emphasis.

He waited for her to nod, before dashing closer to the waves. Jack moved quicker than an arrow. He focused solely on bridging the gap between him and the rolling water, building mental calluses against the wind that tried with all of its might to sweep him off of his feet. It almost succeeded, too. Twice.

Jack raised his arms higher with each step to shield himself. He carried on until he felt the cold wash of water soak his shoes. Close and harrowing. Upset by his tenacity. The river was akin to an angry cat that had yet to feel the warmth of a human's touch. Overflowing with mistrust and impossible demands—and right now, it demanded that he prove himself.

He wasn't one to disappoint.

Invoking his power, he crouched down and plunged his hands into the muddy ground. It felt like the fleshy veneer of an open wound. Viscous. Damp. Slick with foul substances he didn't want to know the names of. Jack almost gagged at the thought. He would've been pulled right into the river's depths had he not buried his heels deep into the dirt, but his clever thinking did nothing to improve his mood. There was nothing enjoyable about being caked in mud after all.

With a strangled exhale, he unleashed his magic. It spilled all too happily from his veins and over the water's surface, cracking as it went. There were a thousand sharp snaps, followed by the hum of white mist, as it blew out and added a layer of chill to the already dense fog around them. The protesting flood of warm water was quick to follow. It hissed under the path of ice he conjured, slowly melting it from the bottom and forcing Jack to add another layer.

Jack saw more than heard Sylvie approach. He caught the orange flicker of her flame as it cast a warm light all around them. Her long shadow stretched over the trail he made. The corner of her shoulder was lost in the water's black depths. Jack shot her a sideways glance and gestured for her to hurry. He didn't want a repeat of what happened at the Drowned Tower's bridge. There was no way he was going to be almost killed by nature's temper a second time. His pride wouldn't allow it.

Thankfully, Sylvie didn't need to be told twice—or even once for that matter—she was already moving ahead of him. Her mouth drew into a thin line as she put one foot on the ice, testing its strength.

Finding it adequate, she grabbed his hand to help him up, before rushing along. Swift enough for urgency, but careful enough not to slip and bruise her chin. She obviously wanted to get this over with as soon as possible. The rain, however, kept them from just mindlessly sprinting across.

Jack trailed behind her with his eyes on his feet. He tugged her back when she moved too fast and nudged her forward when it was safe. Four times, he saw large air bubbles form beneath him and forced her to stop, so he could add another inch to the ice. Absently, he noticed that he was coating her hand with mud, but promptly let the thought go once they were more than halfway across. If he was going to get dirty, then it was only fair that she did, too.

"I thought the Wymeran River was sweet and soothing," Sylvie said through chattering teeth. "That's what all the books said."

"They lied," Jack said, his tone scalding. He only vaguely recalled the stories about how pleasant this place was. The tellers were obviously out of their minds. The Wymeran River was as bad, if not worse, than the Zexin Sea which was famed, *famed* for being the most terrible waterbody in all of Ferus Terria. Those damn bards and scholars could say all they wanted about it, but at least that had a stable bridge. At this point, he'd even settle for a flimsy one. Reinforcing an existing walkway was a thousand times better than literally walking on ice.

"Even Master Cephas told me that he adored his time here," Sylvie went on, her brow creased in focus.

"What was that old bag doing all the way out here?" Jack asked before he could stop himself. Sylvie wrenched his hand forward in disapproval, almost making him bloody his nose against his own magic.

Jack bit back a retort. He deserved that.

"He was fishing," she told him, satisfied that he hadn't grumbled.

Jack couldn't imagine someone like Columbus Cephas fishing, so he didn't try. To him, he was the nagging head of the Assembly whose lectures he most liked to avoid on account of their length and the manner in which he said them. Not wanting to recall the particulars, he went back to staring at his feet. Jack absently counted each step. He got to eleven, before crashing into Sylvie's back and sending them both sliding forward. He grabbed her arms out of instinct, as he tried in vain to steady them both.

Sylvie's knees wobbled in uncertainty. He would've laughed at her terror-stricken face had they been on stable ground. They weren't though, and he feared his ice might crack from the echo—

oh, but they were so close. So, so close. One laugh couldn't hurt.

"Don't just suddenly stop," he rebuked instead.

Sylvie didn't speak, only pointed.

His eyes followed the clear line of her hand, before slinking up to see a woman standing on the shore. She had skin as black as tar and a dagger on each hip. Her eyes were the color of oak. But they weren't rough like wood, they were captivating in a way that reminded him of dribbling honey. The woman held a lamp in front of her face. Its soft light was dampened by the rain, though it didn't shade it completely. The remnants made the shadows behind her dance.

She inched toward the ice he crafted in wonder. Angling a hand over her brow, she bent forward and peered at their faces. Jack's stomach churned in worry. His fingers twitched, prepared to lash out should she deem them a threat. He was a muddled mess of grumpy and cold right now, and he didn't think he'd be able to keep a level-head should she decide to show him just how skilled she was with her blades.

But then the woman straightened. Her arm lowered in what looked a lot like relief, and she flashed a wide, exhausted smile at them. Waving her free hand, she called out, "You Vidal's men?"

Her accent was so thick that he had to take a minute to decipher her words. But once he did, Jack exhaled a shaky breath of relief that he hadn't even known he'd been holding. It escaped in a rush of hot air that made Sylvie's hand tighten around his own. Her own relief was more obvious—a content squeeze of his fingertips, the low bending of her core—he could feel her body droop from how close he was.

Eventually, Jack collected himself enough to respond.

"We are."

Her smile broadened. "I've been waiting for you."

***

The woman, whose name Jack still didn't know, waited three nights for them. And of course they arrived at the worst possible time. Jack was grateful that she didn't complain. In fact, she didn't say much at all. She spoke in clipped sentences that brooked no barter. Each word that left her lips was a command—*'Let us in. Open the gate. Get out of my sight!'*—one that the people obeyed. It left them with little else to do but trail after her.

She guided them through the sleeping town of Curran. A haven full of mossy squares packed with gray-stone buildings and iron gates. Above each walkway, were pointed spikes fixed onto metal rods that could be dropped in an instant. A remnant of a bloodier time. They led to open plazas lined with stalls that were abandoned by their owners because of the storm. A few of the frailer ones fell over, scattering splinters over the gravel path.

They passed rowdy pubs and closed houses. The windows showed laundry hanging from wires across the rooms. They were tied around the strangest things; a chair sitting precariously over a table, the antlers of an animal's head mounted on the wall, one was even wedged between a stack of books piled high enough to reach the ceiling. At one point during their walk, they reached an entire street filled end-to-end with brothels. Every now and then, they'd find someone peeking outside for any stranded—or frightfully desperate—customers. Jack kept his hood on just in case. But with a scowl as unapproachable as his, he doubted anyone would even think to come near.

Like a focused hurricane, the woman took sharp turns and climbed stairs by threes and twos. She would occasionally turn to make sure they were still there, but she didn't slow her pace. Eventually, they reached a modest building with a lamp hanging over the wooden entrance. There was a faded sign above it that neither of them could read. But it was definitely written in the trade tongue because they could just make out the beginning of the word, "Nest."

The woman threw open the door, startling the young boy inside. He had shaggy blond hair, brown eyes, and a mousy face that would've been handsome had his ears been a little less bulging. They were large enough to catch and hold anyone's attention. The boy seemed to realize this because as soon as he saw them, he reached for a cap haphazardly discarded on a nearby table. It was old and big. Clearly not his.

"Conor," the woman called. "Get towels."

The boy was quick to comply.

In under a minute, they found themselves seated with towels around their necks and plates of bread lathered with dripping honey before them. It settled in a warm pool at the bottom. The woman was even kind enough to provide a pitcher full of something hot and thick that neither knew the name of. But that didn't stop them from drinking it greedily.

Across from them, Conor sat with his fingers clutching the edge of the table. He peered at them with wide, curious eyes, while his caretaker disappeared into another room, presumably to change, now that her guests were taken care of.

Conor had such a look of utter concentration on his face that Jack couldn't help but raise his eyebrows in wonder. Toweling his hair one final time, he deliberately moved slower to give Conor a chance to avert his gaze. But when he looked up and the boy still hadn't stopped, Jack did what he did best—he glared at him. In all of his juvenile innocence, however, Conor only leaned forward, trying to peer deeper into his eyes. Not at all realizing how uncomfortable he was making him.

"Is there something on my face?" Jack asked Sylvie.

"No," she said, not even sparing him a glance. Her eyes were fixed on her food, though she made no move to eat any of it. As if she was afraid they'd make her pay for it once she did. She already drank her fill though, so Jack saw no reason to hesitate.

"You should eat, Syl."

She only frowned in response.

Knowing he wasn't going to get through to her any time soon, Jack reached out so that half of his arm lay on the table between them. Conor watched, fascinated, as Jack directed two of his fingers at him. With a twitch, ice sprang from them and froze the flame of a nearby candle. The boy yelped, falling from his seat and toppling the chair so harshly that one of the planks on its back snapped in half.

Sylvie bumped her elbow against his in silent reprimand. But she couldn't fool him. He saw the amused curve of her lips that she futilely tried to hide, and he grinned knowingly at her. By the time he tore his gaze away, Conor was already standing. The boy stared at the floor, drawing circles on his thighs and looking every bit like the child he was. Terrified, excited, and ready to bolt at the first sign of scolding.

Jack's lips twitched in amusement. He hid his expression behind a hand. "Did you need something?" he asked.

"You should've asked that first," Sylvie chided.

"I wanted to scare him a bit."

Conor peered tentatively up at them, before dropping his gaze again. The third time he did it, Jack started eating and gestured for Sylvie to do the same. There was no need for them to starve while waiting for him to dislodge whatever plug he had clogging his throat. But the portion was small and they were famished, so it wasn't long before they were once again left to wait... and wait they did. It took him a long time to gather his courage. Neither of them liked to be kept waiting and Jack's scant patience was already near its end.

The boy looked up at them, then down at the floor a grand total of eleven times, before Jack stopped counting. When a full five minutes passed in silence, Jack finally made a move to stand.

"I'm going to look around," he told Sylvie, who hummed in acknowledgement. Her eyes were distant and half-open. Jack was about to tell her to come with him to rest when—

"Wait," Conor spoke, making them both fall still.

His voice was lower than either of them expected. It would be deep and guttural by the time he grew into a man. But for now, it still had that youthful innocence all children shared. They watched, as Conor looked up and down one final time. His ears burned red from whatever was on his mind.

"You... you have..."

"Spit it out, kid."

"You have pretty eyes," he said in a hurry. As soon as the words left his lips, he clamped both hands over his mouth. Sweat fell down his brow and his eyes were so wide they looked as if they might pop out of their sockets.

"I have…" Jack trailed off, caught completely flat-footed by the compliment. "What?"

Conor's blush deepened and before they could stop him, he ran deeper into the house. His steps were followed by the loud bang of a door slamming shut, telling them that the conversation was over.

"You have an admirer," Sylvie said, laughing. "That's cute."

"It's *disturbing* is what it is."

"Elise liked you, too."

"Shut it!" Jack yelled, looking around desperately. "Vidal has ears everywhere. I'll be hanged if someone hears that."

His tone only made her double over herself.

"You never told me how popular you were with children, Jack," she went on, clearly opting to ignore him. "If only they knew how you really are."

"Oh, and how's that?"

"Vicious. Grumpy. Bad-tempered," she listed off. "With a tendency towards… well, I don't want to say violence, but…"

"I wouldn't hurt a fly."

"I've seen you ice dozens of people, Jack."

"They weren't flies."

"And very fussy," she added.

Jack's shoulders sagged, alternately resentful and resigned, as she laughed louder at his expense. He settled for violently glaring at his fingernails until the nameless woman reappeared again. She looked more relaxed now, with her fresh clothes and damp hair. The first thing she did was inspect them, visibly pleased when she saw their overclothes dripping from a wire over a basin and their plates licked clean.

"I hope the food wasn't too pedestrian," she said.

"I've had to put up with her cooking for weeks," Jack said, sour from Sylvie's teasing. "This is fine dining in comparison."

"Oh, like your cooking's any better," Sylvie argued.

"You charred the rabbit I caught, Syl."

"And you threw a poisonous mushroom in the stew!"

"I was distracted because you burned the damn meat!"

Already sensing that they weren't going to stop anytime soon, the woman intervened.

"I haven't introduced myself yet, have I?" she said just as Sylvie opened her mouth to retort. And like a flash of peace between heaves of storm, her words brought them back to the matter at hand. Without looking at them, she righted Conor's fallen chair before settling into it with all the grace of a seductive Madam. "Excuse me for that. I wanted to get out of the storm."

"I hadn't noticed," Jack muttered, only to choke when Sylvie elbowed him in the ribs.

"My name is Jovie," she went on, ignoring his remark. "Vidal's ears here in Curran. Though truthfully, there isn't much to hear nowadays with the Grove so quiet."

"I'm Sylvie," she introduced, as Jack breathlessly chimed in his own name. He rubbed his abused side, not even trying to hide his disdain.

"I believe I was originally supposed to expect you late next week. Imagine my shock when I received word from Vidal that the two of you had decided to depart early. Few deliberately opt to change his plans. I waited outside every night because I thought you'd get here sooner."

"Jack," Sylvie scowled at him, "insisted we leave earlier than usual, so as to avoid Vidal's compa—any unwanted attention. Unfortunately, that meant leaving behind our ride."

"I didn't see you disagreeing at the time," Jack cut in. "And *you* were the one that said not to disturb the rider."

"He was in bed with his wife."

"Your point?"

"He would've cursed you out and woken up the entire

Institute. Then Vidal would've come, and we still wouldn't have a rider."

"We could've at least taken the horses."

"I don't know how to ride one," Sylvie mumbled. But Jack heard it as clearly as if she'd shouted it in his ears.

"You…" he blinked. Very slowly. "Please tell me you're joking."

"We lived in the Tower!" Sylvie defended. "I never needed to learn."

"You're both such pale things," Jovie intervened then.

Jack snapped his mouth shut to hold in the retort dancing along the tip of his tongue. Jovie smiled when Sylvie glanced gratefully in her direction. Leaning her chin in the palm of her hand, she compared their sickly pallor with her own much darker hue.

"I thought it had something to do with the cold," she went on. "Seems I was wrong."

"Oh, I'm sure part of it was definitely from the weather," Sylvie said. "We're both much warmer now though. Thank you for having us."

"Vidal asked, and I agreed. There's nothing to thank me for. I couldn't very well say no. Not to that man. But if anyone deserves platitudes here, it's you two. I heard you helped deal with the Fetters holed up in the Pit."

"Something like that," Jack said evasively.

"You can't fool me." Josie smiled. She slouched against her seat, only to grimace when the broken back almost snapped under her weight. "News travels fast around these parts. Especially Vidal's network. He's been after that particular group for a long time. Of course the Veld and their blasted Union never let him make the moves he wanted. They're too risky, or so they claim."

"You know a lot about the Veld's inner workings," Jack paused, then added, "for a Nebbin."

"I was a former runner for Vidal," she revealed, the corners of her lips curled in nostalgia. "It was a physically demanding job, but I do miss the thrill that came with it."

"That explains the daggers then."

"I'm surprised you noticed! It was pouring death out there. But those are more for intimidation than anything else. I've lived quietly here since I had Conor, and I'm sure my skills have rusted more than my blades. Though I do house the occasional stray every now and again. But as I said, there isn't much for me to do now. You two are the first visitors I've had in months. The last was a real spender. He slept in every brothel on Bale Street and boasted about it, too."

"You mentioned that the Grove has been quiet recently," Sylvie interrupted, before they ventured into a topic she really didn't want to know the details of. "Do you know why?"

Jovie stared at the ceiling for a moment, chewing her bottom lip in thought. The only sound in the room came from the pitter-patter of rain outside and the constant thumping of her foot against the ground. After what seemed like an age, she finally turned back to them with an uncertain look in her eye. Neither could tell if it was concern or suspicion that clouded her gaze — probably both. But what she had to be worried about, they couldn't say. Curran seemed peaceful enough, and it was doubtful that the practitioners would do anything to harm the Nebbin here. From what they knew, the Grove relied heavily on them for basic resources. That wasn't something to just throw away.

"I don't know," Jovie finally said. "But I do know that it started when Arch Poten Cole took control. The boy's only a year or two older than Conor. I'm amazed they even considered him for the seat, never mind actually allowing him to sit in it. But I haven't heard any complaints about him, so things must be going well. Although, now that I think about it, I haven't seen many practitioners around these parts since his initiation either. The few that do come are all tight-lipped and always quick to leave. They look healthy enough, but... oh, never mind all that."

Jovie abruptly stood.

She almost toppled the chair all over again, but managed to catch it before it hit the floor with a relieved sigh. She didn't look like the type that had enough money lying around to afford new furniture. Thankfully, they still had leftovers from those phony silk dealers that they dealt with before arriving at the Veld. It was more than enough to finance their stay. Vidal had also given them a considerable sum for their travels... just in case. If this didn't count as a 'just in case' situation, then Jack didn't know what did.

Jovie gestured for them to follow her. But Jack promptly received another elbow to the ribs before he could take one step. He glared viciously at the culprit, just knowing that he'd have an ugly, yellow bruise in the morning. Sylvie didn't seem to care. She only pointed meaningfully at the plates until Jack cleaned them with a huff. While she made quick work of melting his ice around the table's only candle.

"Oh, don't worry about the mess. You two must be tired," Jovie said, though she seemed the weariest of them all. Now that they were fed and out of the rain, they noticed the dark bags under her eyes. Even darker than her skin. She really had been waiting a long time for them to arrive. "Vidal told me that you two were on your way to the Grove. If you're important enough for him to send here, then I'm sure they'll let you in."

"Are they letting practitioners through?" Sylvie asked.

"All the ones that have come through Curran looking for a guide to the Alps never returned, so I assume they are. Really, it's the north you should be worried about. They've isolated themselves up there."

"We heard. Even the Nebbin are talking about it. Though no one seems to know why exactly. Something about a problem in the Council?"

"I don't know the details. But I'm sure the practitioners in the Grove will have more answers for you. Though you should really wait for the storm to pass first. A day or two at the most. It's dangerous to venture off into the Mending Willow in this weather. They say the trees are enchanted. They'll trap you if you don't keep your destination in mind. I've gathered a few books for the two of you to sift through until then. Vidal requested them. They're upstairs."

"Books?"

"History mostly," she said, missing the way Jack's face scrunched up in dread. "He said you were interested in Heartstones? I had a few sitting in my closet. Old, dusty things. They don't sell for much around these parts. I was actually planning on shipping them off to Spier for a few silvers, but I left them in your room in case either of you wanted them."

"We can pay," Jack offered, but Jovie waved him off.

"Just buy something in the market for Conor, will you? That boy has the biggest, most effective puppy eyes I've ever seen, and that's not just a mother's bias. I'd get him something myself, but times have been hard recently. What with the skies being so temperamental. And Conor has such… fine taste. I don't know where he got that from."

"Consider it done."

Jack and Sylvie shared a glance, simultaneously excited and distressed by the thought of seeing another stone. How did they look? How were things put inside? Maybe they could even find out those magic words the people used to open it.

But would theirs even open for them? It was an old thing—no doubt older than the rest—so perhaps it needed a different incantation. But more importantly, did they even dare try?

No more words passed between them, as Josie led them deeper into the house, and hopefully, closer to secrets behind the stone.

11

"Find anything?" Sylvie asked.

Jack grunted in response.

They'd been reading all night. Somewhere between arguing points and sharing pointless anecdotes, Jack took to sprawling across his bed with a book in his hand and a pillow under his feet. Those he lost interest in were left in growing piles around him.

Sylvie sat on the floor against her own bed, with her own stacks of books scattered haphazardly around her. Where Jovie got them from and how she was able to scrounge up enough silver to afford them all, she couldn't say for certain, but she could hazard a guess.

Did Vidal send money along with his message? she wondered. It was likely. *We owe him far too many favors.*

Regardless of how correct she thought she was, Sylvie still made a mental note to ask Jovie about it in the morning. It wouldn't be long now. From the cracked window, she could already hear a few early birds opening their doors and cursing loudly at the leftover drizzle from the storm. They stomped heavily into puddles. The little splashes sounded loud and angry in the tranquil silence of the infant dawn. Somehow, she doubted Jovie was an early riser. But even if she was, her exhaustion would surely keep her in bed well into noon.

There was no rush.

So, Sylvie leaned back and made herself comfortable. She caught herself staring at the dried plants hanging on top of their door. *Vanibrime,* she recognized, noting its thick, wood colored stem and bell shaped head. It looked harmless up on the wall, but she could tell at a glance that its thorny shoots had been carefully removed, along with its poisonous roots. Sylvie couldn't help but stare at it, impressed that Jovie hadn't been deterred by its usual appearance.

It may have seemed like an old, rotting decoration to some, but any good embrocologist knew that Vanibrime was prized not for its beauty, but for its medicinal value. When all of its toxic portions were removed, its scent was fresh enough to clear even the most clogged of sinuses, making it perfect for those that suffered from allergies in the spring. If boiled with Wanewood and Vellian Nettle, it could be turned into a potent salve to ease muscle pains.

But why does she have it? Sylvie wondered, then answered her own question a second later when her gaze wandered around the room. It was clean... yet filthy. Before they commandeered the area, the bed had been made and all the furniture sat in its rightful place, but now that they'd shaken things up a bit, she could also see that the sheets had holes along the edges, likely from rats, and that a thin blanket of dust coated the nightstands and dresser. With the help of a little candlelight, more of it was illuminated floating about the room.

Jovie wasn't lying when she said that she hadn't entertained anyone in months.

Sylvie hummed, willing away the thoughts and focusing back on her research. She thumbed through a particularly thick tome that's text was so small, she had to hold it up to her nose just to read it. Even Jack, with his clearer vision, had given up on it after twenty minutes of craning his neck low enough to give him a lasting ache that he was still grumbling about.

Flattening the page, she read:

Docks were built along the coast, but none could conquer the Wymeran River's volatile waters. The waves rose higher and stronger each time they rebuilt, until the Weeping Grove grew tired of losing resources. Slaves were pricy, and with flash floods constantly laying waste to their crops for the last decade, they had little coin to spend. They used it to hire Conjurers from the Red Veld instead.

But their fortunes changed during the thirtieth year of the Iron Age when esteemed Mentalist and Healer, Thomas Tenby Orvalis, founded Curran's first apothecary. It caused quite an uproar during the time, attracting all sorts of visitors. From scholars in Pulka to the heads of the Vanguard Circle. Everyone wanted to see the modest shop—the only establishment in all of Ferus Terria to offer enchanted goods and tonics outside of the designated Institutes. The matter was so controversial that practitioner's protested outside of its doors for years after its opening. Eventually, Orvalis was forced to shut down. Some say he'd grown tired of the hateful screams, while others claim his storage houses were burnt to the ground by a slighted neighbor.

Regardless of how it ended, it encouraged others to start their own trade, and Curran eventually became a hub for—

Sylvie leaned back and groaned.

She was beyond exasperated.

"Giving up?" Jack asked, smiling crookedly at her. His eyes sparkled. Smug *and* triumphant. She hated it. "You see why I hate history now? It's too condensed. There's too much information that you'll never remember once you've read all of it, and the paragraphs are so tight that you end up skimming *at least* half."

She wasn't about to admit that she'd done just that. Her eyes were sore and no amount of rubbing made the tiredness go away—it only made it worse. But it wasn't the sheer amount of information that bothered her, it was the size of the text. She could only imagine how red her eyes would be if she decided to go through the entire book.

Redder than Jack's, she mused.

He lifted an eyebrow at her tickled expression, but let it go shortly after. Seemed even he wasn't in the mood for mindless teasing. Instead, Jack spread himself farther on the bed. He drew in a deep breath, then exhaled it in one slow, satisfied motion.

"This isn't the best room," Jack began, "but its still heaven compared to that shack."

Sylvie only nodded in agreement, as Jack listlessly ran his finger over a finely printed moth decorating one of the better looking tomes. Excluding the one he was currently reading, it was the only book that wasn't piled and put away. Instead, it sat directly under his hand. He even dog-eared the page, obviously deeming it important. But from the way he was able to trace over the jagged lines of the moth's wings, then follow the curve that formed a half-circle around its top, all without looking, hinted at more than just familiarity. He'd memorized the symbol. Had actually taken the time to sit down and intimately study it. But Jack couldn't have learnt something so detailed in the short time they'd been here. He was engrossed in so many other books that he wouldn't have had the time.

Something he already knows, Sylvie guessed. *But why would he bother marking the page?*

"What is that?" she asked, knowing she wouldn't get an answer just by staring. Jack shot her a quizzical look. So, Sylvie nodded toward the book under his hand for emphasis.

"Oh," Jack said, dazed. He glared at his hand in disapproval, before removing it from the page. "This is a biographical account of all the members of the Zenith Council from the middle of the Silver Age to just before the start of the Crown Age." He tossed it to her. "It's pretty interesting."

"Interesting?"

"There were some real loons back then." Jack chortled.

"Like who?"

"I don't recall their names, but there was a woman that used to hunt Snuff, then tear off their ears, so she could use them as money pouches. There was another that was arrested on multiple occasions for boisterous intoxication and six, *six* public displays of nudity. He got kicked out for that."

"Was he ill?"

"I don't doubt it."

Sylvie half-heartedly acknowledged him with a grin. She easily found the page he'd dog-eared. Sylvie ran her fingers over it, delighted by the powdery texture of the parchment.

"Oh, you meant that." Jack glanced at it, before wrinkling his nose in distaste.

"Remon Decius Dace," she read. "Your grandfather?"

"The only one worth mentioning. He was an intolerable man, or so the stories say. He passed long before I was born. It was apparently due to some fatal tumble down three flights of stairs. Tragic *and* dishonorable. It's there. You can read all about how he smashed his teeth, before falling on his own dagger."

"You shouldn't speak ill of the dead."

"Tell that to the rest of the world. Remon Dace was known for his dexterity. There was no way he would've died tripping of all things. The Vanguard Circle only wanted to save face."

"What do you mean?"

"Well, my father told me that one of the prisoner's in the Circle's underground ward escaped and killed him. Stabbed him three times. Twice in the stomach and another just above the heart. Of course they couldn't just admit that one of their captives broke out. Thankfully, security's been better ever since my father was appointed head."

"Should you really be telling me something so scandalous?"

"It's old news," Jack dismissed. "My father's made his peace with it and those responsible have already been punished. It's a dead rumor now. Though in your case, it's more like a fun fact."

She laughed at that, then mentally chastised herself for doing so. Not wanting to look at the smirk adorning his lips, Sylvie occupied herself by tracing the wings of the moth in wonder. His family name had been written under it in elegant script. Beside it was a rough sketch of Remon. He had a full beard and the same sharp eyes she'd grown so accustomed to. His lips were thinner than Jack's own and flanked by frown lines.

"I didn't know you had a family symbol," Sylvie said, impressed and stunned all at once. It only escalated when Jack matched her surprise with his own.

"You don't?" he questioned.

"Why would I? The Sirx name isn't wealthy or influential. Not outside of the Alps anyway."

"But your father's an adviser to the Zenith Council. What about your mother? Your grandparents? Or… did he rise that high on his own?"

"My mother was from the east, and so were her parents, and their parents before them. On my father's side, my grandmother worked as an archivist in the restricted libraries in the north, while my grandfather worked as an adviser for the Council."

"A family of advisers is still impressive." He gave her a rueful smile. "But somehow, it doesn't suit you."

"How about Arch Poten?"

"That's better."

"I should hope so."

"If you want to be something more, you could always go by Drayr now," Jack suggested, smiling. The glare Sylvie shot him then only made the corner of his lips tilt higher. "I was joking. Well, half-joking. Can you imagine the perks, Syl? If they let you into some kind of secret room, promise you'll bring me."

Sylvie ignored him in favor of pointing at the moth. "Why this?"

"At least say you'll try," Jack grumbled, before saying in his usual tone, "it's a moth."

"Clearly."

"I've heard people call it a cursed butterfly before, so you can't blame me for elaborating."

There was old, bottled frustration in his voice that she couldn't help but smile at. "Why a moth?"

"Resistance when bound. Determination when cornered," he recited. "Remain vigilant, despite the flame."

"You have a creed, too?"

"And our own cheese," Jack retorted. "All three were made a long time ago by Maverick Dace. I don't know much about him, save that he preferred to go by Sirius. No one really knows why. My father suspected it was because he liked what it meant—*burning*. Maverick was apparently quick to raise his flames against anyone that so much as breathed in his direction."

"His genes carried well."

"... Say that again?"

Sylvie grinned. "What about your father?"

"My father?" Jack raised an eyebrow. "Why do you ask?"

"All of the books only mention his successes. They say little about him as a person." She paused, then added, "And if he's anything like your mother, I think I'll hold off on meeting him."

"My father's an entirely different kind of aggravating." Jack grinned when she sighed in despair. "As much as I hate to admit it, he's a lot like me... or is it the other way around? You get the point. Father has about as much patience as a goose and none of the fancy feathers."

"You think of yourself as a goose?"

He gave her a look that she grinned at. "His personality is... livelier. It slips into every room. He's also prone to picking up strange habits, then dropping them the following week. Once, he took to forcing food into my hands every chance he got. As if I might starve if he didn't."

"That sounds nice actually."

"It *was* one of the nicer ones now that I look back on it." Jack shrugged. "He has this way of frowning that makes it feel like he's chastising you though. It isn't pleasant. But enough about that! That isn't interesting. If you really want to know something amazing, then I read something that would fit the bill."

"And what's that?"

Jack gestured vaguely in the direction of a particularly tall pile of books. "Thelarius' Peose."

"I didn't know he had one." A pause. "Were there even any Peose back then?"

"It was one of the first successful ones. He had it for a day, then had to give it up for research."

"What was it?"

"A chicken." He breathed deeply, as if trying to contain a laugh. "An angry, dirt-conjuring chicken."

Sylvie choked on her own saliva at the mental image. She coughed harshly, slapping her chest until she could breathe again... a good two minutes later. When she looked back up at Jack, he was grinning in amusement.

"That can't be true," Sylvie disputed.

"Maybe. Maybe not." Jack shrugged. "The book was referencing an older text. For all we know, it could've been written by a hallucinating old man."

"Let's just assume that until proven otherwise. It's..."

"Lame?" Jack supplied. "Stupid?"

"Very."

With that, he leaned back and reached out to play with one of the empty Heartstones Jovie had left for them. The stone was clear and pearlescent. It shined differently from the one Sylvie carried, but it was no less beautiful. It was easy to see why people wore it for fashion.

He rolled the stone between his fingers. He'd clearly given up on finding the words to open it. Sylvie didn't bother rebuking him for his easy surrender. They could always ask one of the townspeople in the morning. But now that the conversation had fizzled out and there was nothing left for them to do, Sylvie was caught by the thought that they really should've asked Jovie. Asking, however, had completely slipped her mind. All she could think about then was figuring out how the stone worked. But that was easier said than done.

Jack seemed to think the same because his book already lay forgotten on his chest. He hummed a soft tune under his breath. It wasn't gloomy, but neither was it jolly. Though it sounded as if it could've been. If Jack's voice was clearer. Louder. If he put more effort into the song. But he didn't, and she didn't ask him to. Sylvie didn't want to risk the very high possibility that he'd clamp his mouth shut and turn away instead.

This is leagues better than his grumbling. When he repeated the same tune for the third time, it suddenly became familiar. *A children's song?* she wondered, smiling at the thought.

She'd definitely heard it before, though not enough to distinctly recall what came next. Knowing she'd never be able to focus with him humming away like that, Sylvie promptly dropped her book and reached over the piles around her to grab Silas' journal. She flipped gently through the pages. They sported new dog ears along the corners and had more creases than any journal should be allowed to have, but at least it hadn't been ruined by the storm. She'd buried it under layers of her clothes, much to Jack's displeasure, but he should've known better than to think that she'd actually let anything happen to it.

Sylvie fiddled with the corner of the page, as she reread Silas' final entry. The ink had yellowed, but the words were written harshly enough for them to not have faded completely. Her fingers traced them. They were bunched together and slanted awkwardly to the left. For someone that wrote thousands of documents throughout his life, Silas had horrid penmanship.

Did he hold his quill like a spoon? she pondered seriously.

She found drawings along the outer edges of some of the pages, but disregarded them in favor of inspecting the journal's cover. It was a tattered thing. There were patches here and there to help keep it together. But even those were coming undone. After a quick observation, she deemed it uninteresting, and soon enough, she found herself playing with the journal's spine instead. It had an almost tube-like quality to it.

Flattened by age, she guessed, while occupying herself with the loose strings at its base. There was a brown square along its middle, noticeably newer than everything else, but stained enough to look rattier. The cloth was unfastened on the higher corners, and Sylvie resisted the urge to find a sewing kit.

She knew that Jovie had one. That sort of thing was a must for mothers with young, curious children. But Sylvie doubted that she'd appreciate her rummaging around her home.

Appreciate it less, if she bothered her in the middle of the night for something that could wait until morning.

Sylvie ran her fingers against the spine and debated just going to bed. She hadn't gotten a night of proper rest since leaving the Veld. It was beginning to take a toll on not only her mood, but also her appearance. The bags under her eyes rivalled her satchel in weight.

Without much thought, Sylvie flattened the side of the cover's spine, then pushed the ugly, loose cloth back into place. She did that twice, before...

... She stopped.

Sylvie stared at the spine in confusion. She'd expected to feel the hard resistance of the stack of pages within. Instead, she was met with something softer. She pressed again. This time, she measured the gap between where the spine began and where the pages were bound. Not even half an inch. The space was meant to go unnoticed. Had she not been paying such close attention, then she wouldn't have given it a second thought—but she was. Oh, she was.

Sylvie squeezed a vertical line upwards until there was a noticeable crease along the journal's side. *How did this break? Age?* she speculated. *Or maybe they purposely left it like this, so the journal could bend properly?*

Sylvie knew little of the making and binding of journals, but... she dragged the nail of her thumb harshly over its width. The smoothness of the cloth was interrupted by a small groove near the side.

Not for bending, she realized.

Sylvie pried the cloth off immediately. The sound of it ripping was enough to have Jack up in an instant.

"What are you doing?" he asked, staring at her like she'd sprouted a second head.

"There's something inside."

She undid the stitched thread. It wasn't hard, so much as tedious. By the time she was finished, Jack was already crouched before her. His gaze was fixated on her fingers.

There was a rust-colored paper inside. No doubt stained by the leather after so many years. It must've been rolled at one point, but now it was only flat. Sylvie did her best to remove it without damaging the edges. It slid out with ease, though it looked as if it might crumble if they breathed on it the wrong way. They watched with bated breath as she opened it bit by bit.

"A map?" Jack crowded closer. He squinted in interest.

There were notes scribbled along the sides. They had a distinct quality of frenzy and frustration. As expected, most of it was illegible. But Sylvie's eyes sped through the words all the same, trying to make sense of anything she could. She quickly found that it wasn't Silas' penmanship that was the problem, but that everything was written in the same code that made up most of his journal.

"This map is definitely outdated, but look." Sylvie pointed at a few place markers and the four branches of the Institute. They were all clear. As was the original text that stated their names beneath them.

"*Yövín*, huh?" Jack caught on, easily recognizing the letters. "Is this a map from the Yovakine Plains or did other cities speak *Yövín* back then?"

"I don't know," she answered honestly, before pointing at a few blank points. "Sicin and Brantine haven't been marked."

"Neither has the Ice Crown Mountains. How old is this thing?" Jack grabbed the other side to better flatten it between them. His eyebrows creased at how fragile it felt under his fingertips. He double-checked the words, but still failed to spot anything familiar. "Do you see a date anywhere?"

Her own eyes roamed all four corners of the map once more, before she shook her head. "If it was in here, then it's probably from the Oak Age."

"Did Silas write anything in *Yövín*?"

"Not from what I can see. Wait, look at this." Sylvie pointed at a blank spot where Thelarius' Temple should've been. In its place was a circle and more unintelligible words. She looked at where the other temples should've been, too, but found no marks for them either. Only Thelarius' had a circle. "Think he wanted to go here?"

"It's possible. But if it isn't marked, then that was just uninhabited land at the time. Unless... do you know if Silas was in charge of the temple's construction?"

"He might've been. When were the temples built?"

"I read that somewhere." Jack reached backwards to grab one of his discarded books. He flipped hurriedly through the pages, stopping only to skim a few paragraphs, before going again. Finally, he paused and squinted at a sentence lost between a particularly large chunk of text with a black and gray picture of a plant on the other side. "Thousands of workers were hired to build the temples during the first year of the Oak Age, but their construction was officially started six days before the welcoming celebration when—" he cut himself off when he realized the book was about to go off on a tangent, "—it's from the Iron Age then."

"What was Silas doing at the time? If he was working on construction, then we can rule this place out for now. But if he circled the area after he found out about Maurice..."

Jack groaned. "There's too much information from the Iron Age. We've got the time of the Mentalists, Thelarius' revolution, his upbringing, how he met Pernelia, and about ninety more major events! We'll never find the right books we need here. We can check, but we're better off looking in the Grove's archives."

"Well, we were going to look through there anyway." Sylvie shrugged. "How do we even get to Thelarius' Temple? I heard it was surrounded by enchanted stone giants."

"Golems," he corrected. His face seemed to light up at the mention of them. "And yes, it is. There's no less than twenty, and that's just on the outside. My father used to tell me stories about them when I was young."

"Bedtime stories?"

"He was good at voices. Problem was, all of his stories were true. Even the darker ones. So, I could never get any sleep after. Looking back on it, that's probably why he told them."

"Sounds tough."

"It was. Sometimes. But I learned a lot from them. Like this." Jack brought out his own map. Newer, but no less packed. He pointed at the area across Heathe, direct enough to tell her that he meant the empty space and not the words he'd written. "To get to the temple, you need to be ferried from here by one of the temple's brothers. If you knock on their door unaccompanied, they'll set off their golems."

"Like Pernelia's then. Well, without the oversized guards."

"Exactly. But the brothers don't come out unless an Elder requests it. There's bound to be one or two Elders in the Grove. That's where they make Orive crystals after all. It's only right that someone remains there to keep an eye on the delivery."

"I don't know. They might all be in the Alps for the Summit."

"It's been delayed for ages, Syl. I'm sure they don't expect it to happen anytime soon. Arch Poten Verne only just agreed to go to the north, and they have no idea where you are right now. But I'm sure Vidal will keep the fact that he saw us a secret... or maybe he'll tell them, then just make up some excuse. I can never tell with him. But he is curious about the stone, so he'll definitely buy us as much time as he can."

"I think he'll tell them. Tell them, then smile vaguely to avoid any personal questions."

"That sounds like him." Jack sighed. "In any case, even if there aren't any Elders in the Grove that doesn't mean we can't pay a boatman to take us there."

"It's going to be a hefty sum."

"We aren't skint, but," Jack flashed her his most mischievous grin, "if you really want to save, you could always use your fancy title to convince them. Say you're seeking Thelarius' blessing and all that garbage. They'll listen. They like noise like that."

"I didn't know we already decided to go," she said, amused.

Jack shrugged, before comparing the maps again. His fingers

brushed against the odd writing. "It would be easier if we could read this code. I'm sure Silas said something about it in here."

"We could always ask *her*."

"If *she* knew, then *she* would've said something by now."

"Yes, but I think *she's* still sore about what happened in the Pit. *She* hasn't spoken at all lately, and those dreams are becoming much more frequent. Do you think *she's* ruminating?"

"Do we really have to take *her* feelings into account?" Jack countered, avoiding the question. If *her* musings caused them to dream so vividly, then he didn't even want to know what that meant in regards to their connection with *her*.

"That's what Vidal said."

"Oh?" His eyebrows pinched. "Are we following him now?"

"He's your future master, Jack. You could at least try to respect his words."

"I do."

In fact, Jack was simultaneously awed and terrified of the man. Vidal was someone he aspired to be. Not completely. Never completely. But Vidal was the closest embodiment to Jack's ideal practitioner. Powerful enough to be recognized, smart enough to be trusted, and influential enough to do whatever he pleased. In Jack's mind, that went beyond the vague simplicity of respect. What he felt was more encompassing. Too grave for esteem and too real for reverence.

"But," Jack went on, "that doesn't mean I'm never going to question him."

"Even when he looks like he knows exactly what he's talking about?"

"Especially then. Looking like you know isn't the same as actually knowing. His suggestions could just be gibberish. It wouldn't surprise me."

"It can't hurt to try them though." She held her hand up and gave him the wisest expression she could muster. "Let's wait for *her* to speak to us of her own free will. Everyone needs their space. I'm sure *she's* aggravated about being trapped in here."

Jack grumbled something unpleasant under his breath, but let it go. He looked toward the unshielded window and peered at the still gray skies above them. The winds had finally calmed. Even the drizzle had died. If he listened carefully, then he could hear the townspeople making the most out of the brief respite.

It looked like it would pour again though. Soon.

Sylvie followed his gaze. The nagging thought that they still needed to ask about the words to open the Heartstone lingered in the back of her mind. Though she had yet to decide if it was even worth trying. They might just end up causing unnecessary problems.

"Looks like it finally stopped raining," Jack suddenly said, looking out the window starred with fog, then, as if reading her thoughts, "should we try to get *her* out of there then? We can check a few bookstores while we're at it."

"You promised to get something for Conor," Sylvie added.

"I'll leave that to you."

Her protest fell on deaf ears as Jack made his way to the door. He took one of the spare stones on his way out.

***

Bathed in the bleary glow of the sun, Curran was a different world. The stone buildings that shone like silver were now dull and swathed in moss, and the rust along the spiked iron-gates was clear for all to see. Most were closed, sealing away the parts of the city that were damaged in the storm. The few that were kept open for carts to pass had half-awake guards stationed beside them. An errant chicken had even begun pecking at a particularly tired guard's boot, with the man none the wiser.

Jack recognized many of the tight alleys they came across. Most were passages into darker parts of town. To streets filled with pubs and brothels that would lead them deeper into the city. Women donning heavy scarves around their necks came to and fro with their heads bowed and their shoulders tense.

The people were incredibly cheerful as they ambled about.

Jack didn't know if it was to make up for the apparent lack of luster in their surroundings or if they were really just that happy, but he quickly grew tired of their demeanor. It was enough to make anyone never want to leave their house again. He'd willingly return to the Drowned Tower as a permanent homebody if everywhere he visited was like this. Their voices were loud, and their responses were louder. They smiled so widely at everything that when a sturdy-looking fisherman shot one his way, Jack reeled back in distrust.

They zeroed in on them like bored housewives, prying for the latest gossip. Jack couldn't control the scowl that marred his lips when a teenage girl purposefully bumped into him in an endeavor to catch a glimpse under his hood. When she stepped back in fright, he knew she saw his glower. Perhaps even his eyes. Sylvie didn't elbow him for his cruel expression this time, and that alone was enough to lighten his mood. But not by much.

They carried on, dodging dozens of wooden barrels left out to gather lingering droplets of rain. Come night, those barrels would be filled to the brim. If the sharp scent of dirt and wet tree bark was any indication. It was suffocating.

He looked up. The clouds above them were gray and still heavy with rain. Jack stared when an especially thoughtless boy set out a blue pale with no bottom. He had the biggest, most triumphant grin on his face.

Shaking his head, Jack took a quick step back when Sylvie pulled him by the elbow before a wagon full of vegetables could trample him. After that, they both silently agreed to avoid the more crowded areas.

Their steps led them to a dingy, broken cart on the side of the road. Its back was deluged with books. Jack would've been happy had he not caught sight of someone hiding in an adjacent alleyway. Picking one of the lighter books up, he pretended to skim its pages, while he stared at the moving shadow from the corner of his eye.

"Someone's watching us," Jack murmured just low enough

for Sylvie to hear.

She shrugged, unconcerned, choosing instead to immerse herself in a particularly thick tome the length of her forearm. "It's just Conor."

"Wonderful." Jack sighed, focusing on the volume in his hands. It was separated from the rest of its series, he realized, slighted on its behalf. Jack didn't bother turning when he called out to the boy. "Well, don't just hide there, kid!"

There was a girlish yelp, followed by a crash loud enough to turn more than a few distant heads. Even Sylvie swiveled, hard cover forgotten, as she tried to peer into the darkness of the alley. She took a few cautious steps forward with her hand raised half-mast in concern.

Jack tilted with her movements. His legs pivoted to keep her in view before he could stop himself. But then she stilled, and Jack peered around her only to find Conor emerging from the alley with his hands clasped in front of him and his eyes fixated on the ground. His expression could only be described as guilty. For a while, no one moved. It was only when Jack realized that Conor wouldn't be lifting his head anytime soon that he turned back to the cart and picked up his book again.

Sylvie followed him, albeit hesitantly. Her eyes were drawn to the boy every few seconds as if compelled to stare by some unknown force. When Jack handed her an unbound manuscript of rare gems, however, she was finally distracted enough to stop.

"Do you have anything on Heartstones?" Jack asked the wobbly old coot managing the shop. "An enchantment book would be good, too. Even if it's just history and not actual formulas."

"Fans of magic, are you?" He startled when they both looked up at him just long enough to show their eyes. "Oh, practitioners! Ain't seen a lotta you around recently."

Suddenly feeling self-conscious, Jack adjusted his hood.

Sylvie buried her nose back in the book, not wanting to deal with his yellow grin. It was the smart choice. But Jack had already asked, and there was no one here to talk in his place.

"Now, don't go fixing your clothes," the man chided. "You should be proud of those eyes! Creator knows I wish I had magic coursing through my veins."

Oh, if he only knew how easy it would be for him to have such powers. That particular secret would surely incite chaos all around Ferus Terria.

"I don't want to draw attention," Jack said.

"I see, I see." The man nodded enthusiastically. "But to answer your question, lad, no. I don't have anything about those enchanted stones, but I do have this finely trimmed little pocket book of Zenith chants, and this one here," he held up a smaller volume with a weathered red cover, "came straight from the Diamond Alps! A compilation from the greatest scholars the world has ever seen. They're all about the First Zenith's disappearance."

"Two-hundred pages of speculation then. Hardly worth my time." Jack had always preferred cold, hard facts over theories. "Dozens of those are published every year, and all about the same topic, too."

"Ah, you would think. But see here, this gem was authored by Diana Sicii, praised scholar and devout follower of Thelarius. She was granted permanent admission into his temple to study the engravings there at the tender age of twenty and three. Such a bright woman."

Sales talk. Jack tried not to grimace. It was hard when he wanted nothing more than to boot himself because it was actually working.

"I'm sure," he went on, "that a practitioner like yourself could find something usef—"

"Enough already," Jack interrupted. "I get it, old man. I'll take the damn book."

He smiled. Wide and victorious. "Shall I add his, too?"

Jack turned to find Conor gaping at a picture book riddled with folklore and ancient wives' tales older than everyone in his family combined. Sylvie shot him a pointed look from the corner of her eye that told him to agree… or else. He was tempted to say no just to spite her, but not enough to risk the repercussions. While her threats were often just empty barks, he wasn't keen on getting on her wrong side. Especially not with her being his only companion on this long journey. Sylvie could be unpleasant when she wanted to be.

He didn't know why she was being so demanding though. He'd get it even without her silent threats. Jack had promised after all, and he was no liar.

Jack sighed, waving a hand in defeat. "Sure, sure."

"Thanks, boy. Not many around these parts stop to take a look at my wares, so I appreciate you taking the time to. It was a pleasure."

"I know it was."

"You've got spunk, and about a thousand more lines than I had at your age. Word of advice, boy. Stop for a while, look out, and breathe to take it all in. I was young, too… once. Eyes bright and ready to travel the world. But look at me now! Managing a stall and selling off my only friends. Curran has a way of keeping you here."

"I'm never going to end up a book merchant, old man."

"You say that now, but blink and before you know it, forty years have passed."

Jack did so. Slow and deliberate.

The old man laughed. He turned to Sylvie and pointed one wrinkly, spotted finger at Jack's face. "This boy's full of it!"

Sylvie raised an eyebrow, arresting them both with a judging glance, before, "Oh, I know."

"Don't just agree," Jack muttered, and then pointed hotly at the old man. "Look here codger, I'm telling you now that that won't happen."

His response was a patient smile.

"So," Sylvie interjected, stepping closer and lowering her voice, "you wouldn't happen to know how to open those

Heartstones, would you?"

The man reeled back, staggered by the sudden question, and then shook his head almost reflexively. Before they could feel disappointed, however, Conor raised his hand high into the air, almost smacking Jack in the nose. The boy didn't seem to notice. His entire face was alight with excitement as he shifted on the balls of his feet, happy to be of help.

"Really, kid?" Jack crouched, partly so he could look Conor in the eye, and partly so he could avoid any more unexpected hand raising. "You know how to open them?"

Jack held the book he'd just bought for him between them like a prize. Conor's eyes were glued to the faded green cover, and with a little more prompting, he nodded in answer. Everything now an afterthought in the face of his gift. Jack had to battle with himself to keep a straight face. He didn't want to tease the kid too badly, lest he run off again.

Sylvie placed her hands over Conor's shoulders, grabbing his attention for a split second. "Can you show us?"

"I can!" Conor yelled proudly. His face split into a wide grin as he rummaged inside of his pockets. He pulled out a folded paper and shoved it in her face.

Sylvie blinked twice in shock, before taking it.

Jack was quick to hand Conor his prize. The boy bounced in glee, before running a finger reverently over the first page. Jack rolled his eyes at that, then busied himself with looking over Sylvie's shoulder. When she didn't unfold it immediately, he prodded her back in encouragement.

They swiftly realized that it was torn from a journal. The words were handwritten, but the penmanship was too fine to belong to a child.

Sylvie squinted at it. While the language wasn't ancient enough to be unrecognizable—many older enchanters still used it regularly—it still wasn't one she knew how to read. Thankfully, there was a translation written in the trade tongue on the bottom:

'The god of dusk is stirred to wakefulness in empty space.'

Much good it did her though. She could hardly pronounce the tongue in which they needed to be said.

"Can you read this?" she asked.

"This is… *Ognum.*" Jack nicked it from her hands. He took a moment to mouth the words, before saying more confidently, *"Vina da fhrûs grïëvan dere ven lahs ri*—number?"

"That doesn't sound right."

"*Rillas,*" he clarified. "I've seen it in a lot of older enchanting manuals. I'm sure it means number."

"*Grïëván,*" Conor suddenly corrected. "And it does."

They turned to him, naked bewilderment on both of their faces. Conor reached into his shirt to show them his stone as way of explanation. It didn't shine as starkly as theirs did, but they could see miniature reflections of the personal items he kept inside. A few sacks, a spare change of clothes, a chest filled with toys, bottles of water, and a… cupboard? Jack resisted the urge to ask about it and focused instead on the way Conor turned it over to show them the number seventy-two engraved beneath.

"They all have numbers, see?" Conor said excitedly. He flaunted the number again, making sure they got a good, long look at it. "You have to say it after the words to open the stones. I don't know much *Ognum,* but I do know all of the numbers, so I can open yours if you want me to!"

Jack reached into his pocket to check the stone he took before leaving. Rolling it over in his hands, he saw the number ninety-eight cleanly carved on the bottom.

"Syl," he called urgently.

"I know," she muttered, already unveiling the stone around her neck. It flashed brilliantly. But no matter how many times she turned it, she couldn't find a number. It was wishful to think she even would. If it had a number, then they would've noticed it long ago. They fiddled with it enough times to memorize every curve, the way it bent light at certain angles, even how it felt against their fingertips.

Trying not to let his disappointment show, Jack turned back

to Conor, who was fixated on the stone in Sylvie's hand. She hurriedly put it away once she noticed his attention. But by then it was already too late. His curiosity had been piqued, and like any child that had yet to learn the importance of restraint, he wasn't at all subtle about it. Conor stood on the tips of his toes, tilting dangerously forward in an attempt to peer down her cloak.

"Easy, kid," Jack said, forcing him down with a hand. "Just where do you think you're looking?"

"What's wrong with that stone?" he asked in an impressive display of his own naiveté. "It had no number. I saw it."

The first thing that came to mind when he said those words was that they should've waited until they were alone to bring it out; should've checked it behind the safety of locked doors and closed windows; at the very least, should've stepped away from all of the prying eyes now on them. They were surrounded by snooping townspeople that weren't quick enough to turn their heads when Jack pinned them with his gaze. Few were discrete enough to not break out into excited runs when they saw that he was a practitioner. Really, they should've...

As if it mattered. Conor had amazing eyesight.

Their impatience had gotten the better of them. It was as simple as that. Now, they had a curious child on their hands that knew *exactly* what he saw, and from the way he puckered his lips in determination, he wasn't about to let it go. Children could be so ridiculously single-minded at times.

Unfortunately, Jack wasn't one to lie. Not even to a boy that would be better off not knowing. But that didn't mean he wasn't going to skirt around the truth for as long as possible.

"What *isn't* wrong with it?" Jack said evasively. "Possessed. Ancient. Cursed by the gods. The refuge of a more heinous being. Damn thing is a tall tale come to life, and honestly, when it comes down to it, it's whatever you want it to be."

"Whatever I want?" Conor shifted, puzzled by his words. "I don't get it."

"Good." Jack waved his hand between them as if to brush

the topic aside. "So, why were you following us, kid?"

"Your deflection skills are awful." Sylvie laughed.

"Don't call me out on it," he whispered back harshly. She was right of course. But even if they were less than stellar, their banter was distracting enough for Conor to drop the subject.

"The streets are beginning to fill," Sylvie observed. "There really aren't any practitioners around here, are there? Do you think the Grove's isolation has anything to do with what's happening in the Alps?"

"I doubt it," Jack muttered. "The Grove has closed its borders more times than any of the other Institutes combined. For all we know, the Alps closed their gates because of *them*."

"Why would they ever do that?"

"Maybe they wanted to spice things up by mimicking them? Creator knows they need better role models up there."

"Can't you answer seriously?"

"There's no point. We'll see for ourselves soon enough."

Sylvie sighed, but hummed her agreement nevertheless. She looked up at the darkening sky in apprehension. Her stomach dropped to her feet, and like a bogged-down donkey, she felt the weight of something unknown settle over her shoulders.

"We should go soon," she told him.

"Yea, I'm sure Jovie's waiting for us."

"I meant to the Grove."

"... You've been in a rush for a while, Syl. What's wrong?"

"I have a bad feeling."

Jack lifted an eyebrow. Sylvie was antsy. That much was obvious. She wanted them to keep moving, and while he was never one to disagree with rushing, this was different. She'd been this way ever since they left the Veld. If they found a village, they never stayed for more than a few hours. If they camped, it was never for the night. And that was starting to take its toll. He knew he couldn't have been the only one affected by the lack of sleep.

Did she want to go somewhere? Or was this all really because of some bad feeling welling up in her gut? Instincts were good. But a night of proper rest was better.

"We should stay the night," Jack maintained.

"What if we're caught in another storm?"

"Then we'll stay for longer."

"Please, Jack?" she pleaded.

He looked at her, terrified—*terrified*—by the resignation in her voice. It surged through him. Lofty and encompassing. Like a physical burden made more real by the solemnity in her eyes. He stared even when she turned away, deterred by his sharp gaze. Jack watched how her mouth curved in displeasure, how her eyes searched the houses, half-ashamed by her own plea and half-desperate with the desire to leave this place. The two emotions battled across her face.

"Why are you looking at me like that?" she asked.

"What's wrong, Syl?" was his response, unwilling to relent.

But even as he asked it, Jack knew that she didn't have an answer. He saw it in the way she opened her mouth to speak, then closed it a second later. Sylvie wasn't selfish with her thoughts—not with him—especially not if they might be in any kind of danger. But seeing her pause, searching for an explanation that she didn't know how to give, struck him in places he didn't think possible. It was a piercing effect. One that he wanted to be rid of immediately.

"If you really want to, then we can leave tonight," Jack assured after a second's deliberation. He had to consciously remind himself to school his expression when she turned to him with a grateful twinkle in her eyes.

"Really?" she asked.

"We got what we came for. Anything about Silas and Maurice, we'd be better off trying to find in the Grove's archives. I heard they have a college full of scholars there. I'm sure they'll have more information than this place."

"What?" Conor intervened, shoving his way between them to peer imploringly up at Jack. "Are you leaving already?"

Jack stared, bewildered by his bereft tone. "We are."

"We want to go back to your house before it rains," Sylvie elaborated, knowing Jack wouldn't lie to the boy. Not even a small, white one.

"I can show you the way!" Conor volunteered.

They stepped aside in the face of his jubilant skipping.

***

They were greeted with a warm meal and a well-rested Jovie upon their return. When they caught her hopping around the kitchen, humming an old tune about the Zexin Sea that they'd heard shouted by retired dockhands back in Thyme, any former thoughts of her being a night owl were promptly expelled. Jovie was naturally active, and her lithe figure made her look graceful as she flitted about, stooping low to grab pans or stretching high for something else entirely. Scars littered her skin. Remnants of a former life. They were birthed from cruelty, no doubt, but she made them beautiful by how proudly she wore them.

Jovie had suffered a migraine during the early hours of dawn and apologized for her health even as she served them their meals. Glazed beef with roasted stalks of something local and green that neither of them could pronounce the name of. On the side, were buttered slices of bread.

She was a good host, and though Jack didn't care for being doted on, it was easy to see that she went above and beyond the call of duty for those under her roof. Not an easy feat, he was sure, considering that *they* counted among her guests.

They were... pricklier than most.

Jack told her so, not understanding why she felt the need to apologize for something so trivial. They'd stayed under shoddier conditions, and her home was a haven in comparison. Besides, migraines were more than enough reason to hate the world. He remembered the last time he suffered one, and gladly shoved the memory away a second too late. It was like an army of ants had crawled over his head, biting here and there just to assure themselves that he was still in pain. It didn't help that Tiv had laughed mockingly at him, and then had the audacity to leave an oil lamp on his desk. He still hadn't gotten back at him for that.

"You don't need to apologize for that," Jack said. Not in an attempt to ease her misplaced guilt, but to mollify his own discomfort from it. As soon as the words left his mouth, however, he instantly regretted them. Jovie flashed him an amused smile, while Sylvie stared like he'd grown a second head. Her eyes were wider than he'd ever seen. Beside them, Conor continued eating his fill, ignoring them in favor of his newest book that he not so sneakily peeked at under the table.

"Here I thought you were a jerk in every situation," Sylvie said, bringing another spoonful of vegetables to her lips. Her eyes never left his, and though they weren't quite set into her usual challenging glare, he took it as one all the same.

"Hardly," Jack muttered under his breath.

Sylvie rolled her eyes, and Jack rolled his right back, making sure she saw it. The neutral line of her lips turned up then, lifting her entire face with the motion. Her eyes crinkled with delight and another thing entirely that he couldn't name. It was hidden just beyond the layers of joy that she displayed like fine armor.

Jack's thoughts were lost to the heat pooling in his stomach at the sight of her. His gut churned just enough to make him uncomfortable.

Her grin felt like a blow to his chest. Though it was certainly softer than what he was accustomed to. In that moment, he knew that she'd be the death of him one day. Yet, he found himself undisturbed all the same. Perhaps that was the most disturbing thing of all. He wasn't the chivalrous type. Had never been. Noble, gallant—those were all words he gladly used to describe everything he wasn't, and had no intention of ever becoming— fuzzy descriptions like that were meant for those selfless enough to sacrifice themselves for someone else's world. Those that cared little for their own well-being in the face of the greater good. He didn't fall into that particular category of demented.

But the protective fury that bubbled in his chest whenever he saw that smile wasn't one so easily denied. He was so far gone, he felt almost like his father. Which was a ground-breaking feat, considering he believed his own demise preferable to being so smitten. He was glad that part of him hadn't changed. Jack still felt that death—by anything, even slipping over his own ice along the Wymeran River—was better than surrendering himself to her... or to anyone.

"Jack," Sylvie called, snapping him from his reverie.

His head cleared just enough to register them all staring at him. Even Conor had abandoned his book, finding whatever expression he wore at the moment more interesting than pictures of dragons and regal heroes. He doubted it was, but the kid sure had a knack for making him feel uncomfortable.

"What?" Jack asked, glaring at the last slice of bread on his plate. His hand flew up to cover his lips, shielding his traitorous mouth from their view.

Sylvie stared at him for a second longer. Her eyes narrowed in assessment, before she turned away. "Jovie was asking if you were finished."

Reflexively, Jack's eyes flitted to the woman. She was still staring at him. Although her gaze was more knowing than the rest, observing him with a keen perception that came only from experience. Jack looked away, before she found something even he was still too afraid to confront. Something too warm and too tender for him to touch. He wasn't ready. Not yet.

He stood in an effort to relieve the tension winding through his shoulders. Jovie watched his every move, trying and failing to catch his eye. She waited for him to speak, to say—anything. But he didn't. Jack only gave her a brisk nod, answering the question he hadn't heard, and then made his way upstairs. He needed to be alone. To salvage the tattered remains of his dignity and shove his growing emotions somewhere deep and dark, where he wouldn't have to deal with them. Not now anyway.

"Where are you going?" Sylvie asked, before he was out of earshot.

"To pack," he answered. "Didn't you want to leave tonight?"

Jack smirked when her face shifted, first in agreement, then in horror, as Conor looked at her with a betrayed gape that completely swallowed his round face.

He left her to deal with the boy, feeling better with each step he took away from her voice. It was defensive and remorseful all at once. He even heard a hint of poorly hidden annoyance in it that would surely be hurled his way in the not too distant future.

Knowing that, he took his time bundling up their belongings. Though there really wasn't much to pack in the first place. Everything was still neatly tucked away.

After stuffing a few books into his already overflowing pack, he was done in a matter of minutes. Still, he lingered. Jack dragged his feet across the room, inspecting things that hadn't even garnered a second glance from him before. Like the hanging plants left to dry or the unlit candle in the far corner. He moved entire piles of books that ought not to be moved and smoothed out the sheets three times, despite their perfectly unrumpled states. Jack even fumbled with the dusty closet. The lower cabinets were stuffed with winter cloaks and a carton of forgotten hair ties, while the higher ones were chockfull of children's drawings and old buttons. Worthless. By the time he reached the final drawer, he didn't even care enough to look anymore. He simply closed it and circled the room again.

In his mind, all he saw were hooded eyes, a warm hearth, and an old archive crammed wall to wall with shelves. Entering that archive was undoubtedly one of the best decisions of his life, and if he ever found those two sneaking lovebirds that made him feel unwelcome on his own floor within the Drowned Tower, then he'd thank them profusely.

Sighing, Jack fell against his bed, more the buckling of his knees than his own will. But it gave him an excuse to fix the sheets again, so he didn't care. Coming up here was obviously a stupid idea. Instead of organizing his thoughts, all he did was trap himself with them. He almost wished *she*'d come out and speak.

What am I doing? Jack wondered at last. The sanest thought to grace him since their meal. He swallowed the groan of despair that threatened to escape his lips. Before he could properly curse himself, however, the door swung open.

Sylvie stepped inside. Half-furious and half-amused. Both vanished once she saw his distress. Jack wanted to say something smart about Conor, but the room turned sharp at the edges from her entry. He didn't know how she did that—didn't want to know—so he closed his eyes in preference. She was making him dizzy. That couldn't be a good sign.

"You smell like ginger," Sylvie said, then wrinkled her nose.

Jack's eyes snapped open, caught off-guard by the comment. Truthfully, he'd expected sweat or dirt, but... "Ginger?"

"And cold."

He stared at her.

Very slowly, he lifted his sleeve to his nose. He was met with nothing. Though in retrospect, he should've known that already. Still, the fact that he smelt like ginger of all things bothered him in ways that he wasn't prepared for. Did she really think he, no, there was no use dwelling over it.

Sylvie had obviously lost her mind.

"Are you ill?" he asked, only half-joking.

"Hardly," she repeated his words back at him.

Her tone was teasing. Maybe even a little provoking if he squinted. But Jack contented himself with that answer and massaged the space between his brows, glad that his other, infinitely more infuriating thoughts had left him in the face of her strangeness.

He was about to sigh in relief when they suddenly returned, full-force and stronger than ever as soon as she sat beside him.

"What." It wasn't a question.

"Did *she* say something to you?" she asked.

Jack lifted an eyebrow in confusion.

Sylvie gestured down, before pressing her fingers to his hand. Heat erupted from where they touched. A furnace of white, hot fire. It mellowed out a second too late, sizzling down notch by notch until only softness was left. Less intrusive. Less steady. It reminded him of candlelight. Like the heat at the leading edge of a storm. Jack pulled back and ran his hand down his thigh to numb the sensation. It was only when he did so that he realized that it was clenched tight enough to turn his knuckles white.

"*She* didn't," Jack assured, opening his fists.

Sylvie knew better than to doubt him.

"Have you finished packing?" she asked instead.

It was a safer topic. More urgent as well. Something he could answer without feeling like there was sand shifting beneath his feet. Still, it irked him because she knew that there was nothing to pack. Knew even as he first made his way up to their room. It was a kind gesture though, and he wasn't bothered enough to not appreciate it.

"Yes," he said, making a show of looking around.

"Are you ready to go?"

Jack couldn't hold back his smirk. When he answered, even his expression was certain.

"Always."

12

Sylvie was anxious.

That much, she'd made clear to Jack whenever she'd disturb him in the middle of the night after a long, useless dream of the First Zenith, and despite her own exhaustion, she'd demand that they keep going. They weren't in any rush to get to the Alps. Sylvie didn't doubt Vidal's ability to mollify the Council. Neither were they fully equipped to answer all of the questions the Elders would undoubtedly shoot their way regarding the Tower—or even the Veld. They weren't in any rush to reach the Grove either. Archives could wait. Her brother could wait. *She* could wait.

But as soon as Sylvie saw the whorled, steel-gray clouds roll across the sky, clotting the air like dread during ages of plague, the fear of being caught in the rain intensified. It urged her on, despite the blisters that dotted her heels.

Ever since they'd left the Veld, the world brought rain, rain, and more rain. It flooded entire walkways, destroyed gardens, and threatened to make even the sewers brim. It didn't help that they were always caught in it. Her constant hunching forward for warmth was starting to take its toll on her back. So, it was only a matter of time before Jack got suspicious of her desire to brave it. She'd actually expected him to ask about her sudden rush to get to the Grove sooner. Sylvie had even fabricated a series of half-lies about wanting to see her brother, but it felt wrong to say something like that to Jack.

Jack, who was so honest, it hurt.

So, when he first asked in Curran, she didn't answer; when

they stepped through the dense line of trees that marked the beginning of the Mending Willow, and he asked again, she only shrugged and told him the only answer she could give—she was scared of getting trapped by the rain.

Her fear was hardly worth nights of disturbed rest, but it was the truth, and in the end, that was the only thing he'd accept. Better to be honest from the start, than lie and risk losing his respect, or worse, his trust. Jack, perceptive as he was, understood what she didn't say. She could tell from the way his eyes abruptly softened in sympathy; from the way he hummed in acknowledgement. His fingers reached out to squeeze her shoulder in brief comfort, before falling away.

Neither of them wanted to be stranded, helpless to the plight of friends near enough to save. Never again.

And for a long while, it was quiet between them.

They walked. Pale wraiths amongst obscure trees. Their steps echoed in the forest, despite their attempts at silence. It reached a point where Sylvie debated removing her shoes altogether. If it wasn't for the sharp rocks hidden in the heavier patches of grass, she might have.

Sylvie directed her attention to everything the Mending Willow had to offer instead. It brimmed with life. The sudden shift from field to forest was so stark, it was as if an imaginary fence had been built to signal where the more regal plants were allowed to grow. Even her magic flowed more serenely in her veins, calmed by the remnants of even older magic in the atmosphere. It was enough to make her dizzy. But she'd gotten used to ancient, overbearing presences that lingered in the wind, and this was no different. On the contrary, it was better. Less malevolent. Less overwhelming.

There were lights in the distance. Small orbs that grew as they approached. Closer, were shrubs even she didn't know the names of. They sat in clumps below trees with thick branches and thicker trunks. The trees didn't bow, despite their obvious age. Each bore purple flowers that blossomed in the shade. Plants with leaves broader than the average man were scattered around them. Below those, she found tiny buds she'd only seen in books in the Drowned Tower's archives. Their stems had medicinal properties and their roots could be used for tea, but more than that, she couldn't say. It was amazing how they could survive with such sparse light. Even more amazing was the fact that they weren't submerged by the unending—

Sylvie stopped.

It had been raining enough to depress her, and yet, there wasn't even a drop of dew on any of the plants. No puddles. No muddy ground. No musky air. As she looked up, Sylvie realized that even the sky was gone. A roof of leaves sat in its place.

Jack carried on another ten feet, before he realized that she wasn't following. "What's wrong?" he asked, half-turning. Jack did a quick, subtle sweep of the area. Only when he was sure that they were alone, did he flash her a smirk. "Don't tell me you saw a frog?"

"No!" Sylvie denied vehemently.

"Then what?"

"There's no water."

"Isn't that a good thing?" he asked, miffed by her response. "Or do you want to get soaked again?"

"Hardly."

"Do you," a pause, "miss the rain? I could freeze your clothes if you want."

"Jack," she stressed, then spread her arms out in indication. Sylvie looked him dead in the eye. "There's no water."

There was a moment of muddled silence, before his eyes widened in realization. Jack looked down. He dug his shoes into the soft, dry dirt. It was dark, but naturally so. Pliant, too, he noted. Very fertile. Farmers could make a fortune here. The Grove wouldn't be losing much. From the overgrowth, he could already tell that no one cared for this place—or this section at least. Perhaps they had gardeners deeper in. It would be foolish not to. Even someone like him, with his limited knowledge of plants and their properties, couldn't deny their usefulness. If not for medicine, then for food.

But, Jack amended, that was beside the point.

It wasn't long before he mimicked Sylvie by looking up in a futile attempt to see the sky. All he saw were leaves that were conjoined enough to give him pause. It was the sheer amount that staggered him rather than the fact that they blocked the world above. Because from where he stood, perfectly between two large trunks, each with only one fledgling branch extending outward above his head, he should've been soaking in the rain.

"The trees are enchanted," he guessed.

"Shouldn't we have sensed something earlier then?"

"There's enough magic cramped in here to suffocate someone. Maybe it affected the flora in some way. Or—"

"They were purposely enchanted?"

"Exactly." Jack nodded. "It surrounds an Institute, so there must be *something* wrong with this place. We're probably being watched right now. I doubt the Grove just leaves the forest unattended. It's the perfect place for Amorphs."

"We haven't been stopped yet, so I don't think they patrol this far out."

"Guard the inner forest and let nature take care of the rest, huh?" Jack muttered to himself. "Smart."

"But these enchantments are all active," Sylvie said, as she peered over his shoulder to check if there were any gaps for rain. There were none. "Assuming it encompasses the entire forest, it must require a huge amount of magic to sustain. Where's it all coming from?"

Her question made Jack search the nearby foliage with more vigor. Anything for a sign that their senses weren't off. "No enchantment symbols. No magic veins. But... I can feel it in the air. Maybe they run underground? For all we know, there could be a vast network of tunnels down there."

"And then what? The magic is exuded by the trees?" she finished, irrationally disappointed when he shrugged. "How many practitioners do you think it takes to run this place?"

"It's hard to say. But without exhausting my magic circuit, I could probably activate a small segment for a few hours. Skilled enchanters might fare better."

"Do you think an Elder could do it?"

"Maybe," Jack said, frowning in distaste when one of the smaller plants caught his eye. It was so audaciously yellow that his senses felt offended just by the sight of it. The top sported tiny flowers crowned by even tinier leaves. When he went to touch it, the leaves closed in like the guards of a noblewoman, flanking their charge and effectively shutting it away from his wandering digits. He wasn't petty enough to reach out and crumple it.

"That one's too mature," Sylvie said from behind him. "Garrispore is picked and dried while the flowers are still buds and the surrounding leaves have yet to grow. They're used as a numbing agent. By the time they've blossomed, they're already too strong. A few touches can cause temporary paralysis."

"So, the leaves were actually trying to protect me?"

"Something like that."

"... What's wrong with this place?"

Sylvie grinned, before jutting her chin forward. "Only one way to find out."

"Right," he murmured. "Stay close."

As soon as the words left his mouth, the air grew thicker. Backs dipped forward, hands flew to throats, and for a single, terrifying instant, the oxygen around them was so dense, their lungs struggled to expand.

Sylvie looked around in panic, only for her eyes to widen at the sight that lay before her. The path was bare. The trees above them were dry and long dead. Their rotten branches were coiled in on themselves as if they'd been that way from the start, but that couldn't be. Sylvie blinked repeatedly, trying to make the illusion go away. When that didn't work, she closed her eyes and scrubbed them with her hands in an endeavor to get rid of the insanity that invaded her senses.

When she opened them again, all she saw was black.

Stifling a scream, Sylvie placed a hand over her face, making sure that her eyes were still open—even going so far as to check that they hadn't disappeared from her sockets. She breathed a sigh of relief when they were still there. Her eyes were fine. It was irrational to think otherwise. The only viable explanation then was that it was too dark… that could be remedied.

Sylvie's used her magic. She felt it course through her veins, warming her blood and igniting everything from her fingers to her wrist. Her magic had manifested. She felt the heat of her flames even if she couldn't see it. Her free hand grasped the Heartstone around her neck in reassurance.

"Syl!" Urgency laced Jack's tone. "You there? Light a fire."

"I'm trying," she said, pouring more magic into her hand. She heard it roar to life, smelt the smoke it let out. It was there. She was sure of it. Yet— "I can't see it."

"Wait! Stop!" he shouted. Jack grabbed her forearm. It was sudden enough to startle out the scream that she'd been keeping at bay into the resounding darkness. "Silas' flames! I could feel that from a meter away. Are you trying to torch me?"

"Of course not! I just… I ca—" She stopped when she heard something shift ominously above them. Jack's grip on her forearm tightened. Not a second later, and they were assaulted by the smell of burning wood. "What is that?"

"I think you might've burned the branches above us," he said, already holding up his hand and blindly unleashing his own magic. The sound of ice cracking over wood made Sylvie reel back, but Jack didn't let her move too far from him. Once he was done icing their surroundings, the hand on her arm slid to her wrist. "Alright. Light that fire one more time, Syl, and be *careful*."

Sylvie obliged.

She concentrated on making it smaller this time. Sylvie felt Jack's fingers and the heat of his body beside her, but she didn't know how close his face was to her palm. She doubted he'd take it very well if she really did burn him.

They both felt heat erupt from her fingertips. But…

"So, we're blind now," Jack said, exasperated. "*Fantastic.*"

He made a move to step forward, but Sylvie jerked him back. She didn't need to see his face to know that he was glaring at her, or, more accurately, in her general direction.

"We're not moving," she said obstinately. "You're going to run into something."

"Well, we can't just stay here."

"Someone will find us eventually."

"Do you really think this place gets a lot of visitors?"

"*Jack.*"

That berating tone of hers was something he needed to develop a good defense against, but for now, "Ten minutes," he acquiesced. "Then we're going."

"Ten minutes is hardly—"

"Find the lights!" a voice shouted. "Open your eyes and find the lights!"

"Creator's teeth!" Jack hissed. He made wild turns, inadvertently pulling her along with him in his attempt to locate that voice. "Isn't that…"

"Conor?" Sylvie finished.

"Did that brat follow us?" Jack resisted the urge to break into a run. "How does he even know how to—"

"Find the lights!" Conor repeated, drowning out the rest of Jack's question. "You can't stay in the darkness for too long."

Sylvie stepped on Jack's foot when his grip tightened again. She'd have an angry purple bruise come morning, but that didn't matter now. All she cared about was getting her sight back. So, she did as instructed. Sylvie focused until she found the small orbs of light she'd seen in the distance, before the world turned barren and the wind had been knocked out of her. They were closer now. Bigger. They glowed in the darkness. But not so much that she flinched away. Instead, the spheres were soft, reminding her of the waning flame of candlelight.

And then the darkness was gone.

Sylvie blinked, gasped at her returned sight—everything around her seemed starker somehow—then did it all over again. The first thing she noticed was Jack. His eyes were open, his mouth drawn into a thin line, but from the way he didn't react when she waved a hand in front of his face, she knew that he was still stuck. Then, half-hidden behind a tree with his eyes peering curiously up at her, was Conor.

She opened her mouth to call out to him, to ask him what in the world he was doing, but as soon as her eyes met his, her jaw locked in shock. Like water cradled in cupped hands for too long, all of the color drained from her face. She went rigid at the sight of him. Her shoulders stiffened in inexpressible terror.

Without warning, Sylvie grabbed Jack's arm with her free one and pulled him towards her. "Jack," she called urgently.

He could almost smell her fear. "What's happening, Syl?"

"Do as he said."

"But—"

"Do it!"

Taking a deep breath, Jack's face shifted into neutral. His free hand went up to rub his temple, as if willing himself to concentrate. Then, before she knew it, his eyes were open. He blinked a few times in rapid succession. Once his eyes adjusted, they flickered briefly over to her, searching for any injuries, before they flew to the child that had the audacity to follow them. Jack's mouth opened in a quick reprimand...

... before he snapped it shut.

"*Vaklas!*" Jack cursed, reeling back and almost tripping on his own two feet in an uncharacteristic display of fear. He pointed a shaky finger at the boy, who had familiar black tendrils in his eyes. "*She* can possess people now? Flames! Get him away from me, Syl."

And just what did he expect her to do about it?

"*She* could always possess people," Sylvie reminded.

"Only those with Orive crystals!"

"Is this why *she* hasn't been speaking to us?"

"You mean *she* was out searching for victims?" Jack's knees bent into a defensive stance. "Don't tell me he's going to end up like Rior?"

Her fingers traced the Heartstone, immersed by how it reflected light like the watery streaks of fresh tears. The tendrils were still inside, coiled and shifting towards her, as if it acknowledged her stare. *She* couldn't have actually left, right? How could *she* when Sylvie could so clearly see and feel *her*. *She* was right there. A heavy presence cloaked around her body at all times. If *she* left, truly left, then there was no way Sylvie wouldn't have noticed. But if this really was like Rior, then did that mean *she* could split pieces of herself? But then why didn't *she* do that from the start? Sylvie supposed someone could've planted an Orive crystal inside the boy… but when?

There were too many questions.

Before Sylvie could even ask one, Conor fell to his knees. The veins around his eyes seemed to expand, growing to be as noticeable as Jack's. His face spoke of pain. Though nothing came from his lips. Not even a cry for help. But it was clearly too much for him to handle because not a moment later and he was on all fours, coughing, holding his stomach and applying force in a poor attempt to keep what burned inside of him still.

An impossible task.

She'd seen Rior succumb to sheer pain. She'd seen Serach wail in agony. While those black tendrils escaped them both, coming from the deepest bowels of hell to wrap around their bodies and —*consume*. There was no way Conor would succeed in controlling that mass of energy. Jack barely could, and it actually liked him. Her point was proven when he vomited, smearing blood and stomach acid on the brown, dusty soil, before collapsing right into it.

And then... nothing.

Only spent silence and the putrid stench of mothballs.

It was promptly broken by Jack, who shifted from his stance. Sylvie took that as a good sign and stepped forward, only to be pulled back by a domineering hand.

"You shouldn't get too close," Jack warned.

"We need to see if he has an Orive crystal," she argued.

"We will. Just... not yet."

"Jovie must be worried."

"If she wasn't the one that planted a crystal inside of him in the first place." His grip tightened around her elbow. "Give it a minute, Syl. Don't forget that nasty choking habit of *hers*."

Before she could even mutter her assent, she heard another voice. It was faint. A mere whisper carried by the wind. But she heard it. Sylvie knew better than to doubt her senses. She looked around. Her eyes darted to nearby bushes and up into the trees. There wasn't anything dense enough for a person to hide in. An Amorph though... they could hide in plain sight.

As soon as Jack noticed her cautious gaze, he wordlessly shifted his attention to their surroundings. Having had an Amorph for a partner, he proved far more skilled than her at finding them. Within seconds, his eyes had already settled over a black beetle the size of a button. She hadn't even noticed it, hidden in the shade as it was. It crawled upwards at a sluggish pace, seemingly indifferent to their attention.

Sylvie knew better.

"What do you want?" Jack questioned venomously.

The wings on the beetle's back flapped. Almost vibrating. For a long moment, all they did was stare at it. Their shoulders were stiff in apprehension.

"Forget it then." Jack sneered, then raised a glowing hand. "If you want to keep hiding behind that form, then be my guest. But don't use it to spy on us. I'm going to give you five seconds to shift and get out of my sight because right now all you're doing is wasting the planet's air supply."

Sylvie counted to one.

Ice leapt from Jack's hands, faster than any normal Elementalist. Sylvie stared, not even startled by his impatience at this point. The beetle, on the other hand, hastily flew upwards, fueled by a savage desire to live. Its reaction time alone was enough to reveal the bug's true nature. The beetle ended up on a leaf attached to an unsteady stem. It shifted on the plant, steadying itself with the sort of impeccable balance she doubted any regular insect had.

There was a flash of light, then a man stood before them.

He was of average build with brown hair that was slightly longer at the front. The fringe covered his eyebrows and gave his head a comical walnut shape. His nose and cheekbones, however, had an aristocratic tilt that added to his favor. He had no visible weapons on his person, and the robe he wore fitted him in such a way that seemed as if he'd had it personally tailored.

"That's more like it," Jack said, smirking at the scowling Amorph. "Not much of a looker though, are you? Ever thought about sweeping your hair back?"

"Oh, like you're one to talk." Sylvie shot back. Despite her casual tone, her eyes never left the man before them. He looked harmless. But the same could be said for many practitioners. "Were you planning on killing him?"

"I just wanted to rattle him a bit."

"Well, he's rattled."

"And quiet," Jack said loudly, snapping his fingers to ascertain his deafness. When the Amorph glowered in response, he put his hand down. "I'm assuming you're from the Grove? We don't mean any harm, we're—"

"Not supposed to be here," the Amorph interrupted, before crossing his arms authoritatively.

"We're practitioners," Jack continued. "And we have just as much right to be here as you."

"That remains to be seen."

"Who's going to judge us? You?" Jack scoffed, then turned to Sylvie. From the way he kept his back to the Amorph, she knew he was done speaking with him. "Why is it that whenever we enter a forest, some meddlesome Amorph always shows up? If the Grove explodes, I'm taking a detour to throw that bleeding stone straight into the largest volcano in Red Mount."

"I don't think I'll survive another cave-in," Sylvie agreed, while Jack stepped off to the side. He inspected the nearby shrubbery, leaving her to speak to the Amorph in his stead. "I'm sorry about him. He's not one for idle chatter."

"Your partner?" the Amorph asked, struggling to keep his voice even. But judging by how he kept grinding his teeth together, Sylvie knew that he was failing.

"Something like that," she waved the subject aside. "What did you need from us?"

"Your names and branches," he paused, then tacked on, "as well as the one that sent you and your reason for bringing a Nebbin here."

"I'm Sylvie. That grump over there is Jack," she pointed a thumb in his direction. "We're originally from the east. We were sent here by Hunter Captain Cheryll Dace from the Vanguard Circle. As for the boy, he's the son of an innkeeper that we met in Curran. He followed us here without our knowledge."

The Amorph raised an eyebrow. "You expect me to believe a child followed two Hunters without either of them noticing?"

"We aren't Hunters."

"Then why would a Hunter Captain—"

"Nessler," someone suddenly barked.

They all turned to find a snarling man emerge from the trees. He was smaller and leaner than the Amorph, with a better haircut and a plainer face. There were thick lines on his forehead and around his lips that spoke of constant anger. The newcomer had the same black eyes, though they could already tell from his entrance that he was nowhere near as patient. Sylvie and Jack looked at each other for a brief instant, before they both zeroed in on the sword at the newcomer's hip.

"Tobias!" Nessler called.

"What are you doing all the way—" Tobias lurched to a halt at the sight of them, "—who are they?"

"They said they were from the Tower."

"And you believed them?" Tobias questioned. "That's on the other side of Ferus Terria, and those are clearly Veld robes. I know it's bad in the Plains, but you two will just need to squat somewhere else. The Grove isn't accepting refugees."

"They say they were sent by a Hunter Captain."

"Convenient excuse." He pointed at their ankles. "Come on then. Show me your Demar Spells before you go. We need to make sure you aren't deserters."

Sylvie's eyebrows rose in disbelief at the man's quick refusal of them, their orders, and of refugees in general. There was no way they were going to turn back now just because some patroller told them no—and she definitely wasn't about to show off her unmarked ankles. That was just asking for trouble. Besides, Jack wasn't one to quietly comply with such blatant demands. Especially if they involved him presenting the brands he so detested.

"Isn't there a Master we can speak to?" Sylvie asked.

"Like I'd fall for that," Tobias said. "I'm not letting you anywhere near the Grove. Now, hurry and show us your Demar Spells. We don't have all day."

"No," Jack said with a glare acidic enough to scald. His chin tilted high in defiance, as the tendrils in his eyes swirled. "We introduced ourselves and gave you our reasons for being here. What more do you need? Let us through. Our business doesn't concern lackeys like you."

"It's our job to make sure deserters and lying scum like *you* don't get anywhere near the Grove."

"I *don't* lie," Jack said, more out of habit than an actual attempt at a retort.

"That in itself is a lie!" Tobias yelled. "*Everyone* lies. Hunter, deserter, Nebbin. There's no exception. And until you show me proof that you're telling us the truth, then as far as I'm concerned your business is our business."

"Yea?" Jack lifted a smoking hand, coated up to his wrist in frost. "You want to bet your life on that?"

"Jack," Sylvie called in warning, though she already had her own hand up. Fire blotted the air. Her gaze lingered on Nessler, whose eyes thinned in attention. "Stop provoking them."

He only smirked.

"Back me up, Syl," came the expected response. Followed by the cold press of fingers on her shoulder. That was all the warning she got, before he rushed forward.

When she felt the familiar chill of ice spraying at her back, she immediately turned to release a tunnel of flames aimed at Nessler. The Heartstone responded. It warmed her chest. That lullaby they'd grown so familiar with caressed their ears, thousands of voices bellowed into the open air. It made their magic flow faster and stronger in their veins. They almost lost control of the sheer volume that was expelled from their hands. Both Amorphs yelped in surprise at the strength and speed of the oncoming elements, just barely escaping the torrent of ice and fire by shifting into something tiny tht neither could see.

Wood cracked, courtesy of Jack's ice. Behind him, trees caught fire, spreading and burning everything in its path. The lights in the area flickered from the discharged magic. The surrounding orbs brightened intensely for one insane instant, then waned as soon as their magic dissipated. Jack and Sylvie only had time to spare each other a glance, before the orbs went out and shrouded them all in would-be darkness. If it wasn't for the currently burning forest, Sylvie had no doubt that they'd be lost again. But that didn't mean it was a better alternative.

"Now the forest is on fire," Sylvie said. "Happy now, Jack?"

"That was your fault!" Jack replied harshly.

He ducked just in time to avoid a particularly lethal swipe by an angry bird. It was tall and menacing, but more than that he didn't know. Smoke clouded his vision, and the sweltering heat wasn't helping.

Its species didn't matter now. Only that it was out for blood.

There was a sudden roar to their right. Jack turned, realizing before he even caught sight of the creature that one of them had turned into a bear of all things. He both loved and hated fighting Amorphs.

"This way," Jack yelled, hoisting Conor's unconscious body over his shoulder like a sack of potatoes before taking off.

Sylvie huffed, as she chased after him.

They made it a few meters, before the bear caught up. It barreled forward, jaws open and paws outstretched. They rolled out of the way just in time to avoid being tackled. They collided roughly with a large web of exposed tree roots. Conor's body flopped a few feet away, lifeless, while the bear crashed straight into a tree that snapped like a twig from the impact. The Amorph didn't seem too distraught. It shook its massive head, willing away the pain as if it was nothing more than an annoying pinch.

Jack and Sylvie gaped, despite their aching bodies. Above them, the other Amorph circled the air. It cawed loudly. No doubt signaling other patrollers in the area.

"We're splitting up," Sylvie said in a voice that brooked no barter. "*You're* taking the bear."

"Me?" Jack scrunched his nose in disbelief. He argued with her even as he busied himself with checking Conor's pulse. "*You're* the one that hit that brown-haired one. You take him!"

"How do you even know that's him?"

"Look at how big he is! There's no way that thin pipsqueak morphed into *this*."

"You don't know that! And *you're* the one that provoked them in the first place. Take responsibility!"

"If you had just introduced us properly, then we could've avoided this nonsense."

"I did introduce us!"

"Well, they didn't believe you!"

"How is that my fault?"

"You're the diplomatic one, Syl!"

She pushed him forward angrily, whirling around only to spew a tunnel of fire at the oncoming bear. Her magic made more lights around them flicker. Sylvie gasped when one exploded, immolating the tree it had been attached to.

"The lights are bombs?" she shrieked, covering her ears.

"Who cares?" Jack scolded. "Just keep running!"

Jack headed to a denser part of the forest out of reflex. Areas with tightly packed trees often had thick roots that were mostly above ground, which would make it difficult for larger animals to travel. It was clever, to be sure. They would've died a long time ago if they didn't know how to use the terrain to their advantage, but the same could also be said about their chasers. Because as soon as they stepped foot in the area, there was a flash of light and then the bear disappeared.

Those after them were residents of the Grove. Neither doubted their knowledge of this forest, which meant only two things: they'd either need to capture one of them and force the man to guide them to the Institute or pray that they stumbled upon it themselves. Sylvie doubted fortune favored them so. Though there was always the hidden third option of asking *her* to lead the way. But with Conor currently slumped over Jack's shoulder, they weren't inclined to ask *her* for anything right now.

They hid behind a thick tree with their backs pressed against the wood. Sylvie stood, vigilant, as Jack crouched to seat Conor on top of his feet.

"This place rules out most large animals," Jack muttered, busily checking the boy for any injuries. "I just hope he can't turn into something agile… like a leopard."

Sylvie tensed. "What about a snake?"

"One problem at a time, woman."

"No, Jack, an actual snake!"

Sylvie shoved them roughly forward, while releasing her magic. Jack only had his battle-honed reflexes to thank when he twisted to narrowly avoid smashing into Conor. He tumbled straight into a patch of pink wildflowers instead.

The world spun around him, but with a rough shake of his head, it came back into focus. In the span of a breath, he lifted himself off of the ground in order to see the snake she'd been talking about. It was olive green with dark spots and familiar black eyes. Its body was coiled on the branch above her, partially burned. She'd missed its head... or rather, the snake had curled away at the last second to sacrifice a part of its body instead.

Smart, Jack praised, despite himself. Few survived a direct hit from a Conjurer, and the Amorph clearly knew that. Still, a torched torso was just as bad. The shifter was injured now, and with no Healer nearby, no matter what he turned into, he'd still bear those burns. Jack wouldn't let him transform again.

"Syl, move!"

That was all the warning he gave her, before his hands gushed ice, freezing both snake and tree alike. Sylvie heeded him just in time. She covered the top of her head with both hands and screwed her eyes shut, as she leapt out out of the way of his oncoming frost. There was a blinding flash of light that made them both reel back. Though that didn't keep Jack from discharging his magic. It was only when the light died down that he finally forced himself to stop.

When they chanced a peek up at their handiwork, they both stilled at the gruesome sight before them.

The Amorph was frozen mid-transformation. His snake-like jaw was opened wide, exposing fangs that dripped with venom. At the bottom was a row of half-formed canines and molars. The Amorph's black eyes were engorged, with only a thin slime-like substance covering them. It oozed down onto the tree. His head the only thing spared by Jack's ice. A patch of what looked to be fur sat on top. The Amorph's body was still long and burned, though strange appendages protruded from its once limbless form. A human arm was twisted up into a sick angle with half-formed claws situated near the end.

What was he trying to transform into? Sylvie wondered, noting the patches of tiny hairs littered all along his form. The Amorph's head writhed, bobbing up and down so frantically she feared he'd unintentionally break his neck. The guttural moan that suddenly left his monstrous mouth was enough to anchor her back to reality.

"He's... alive?" Sylvie sputtered in disbelief. "How long can an Amorph survive like that?"

"Not long," Jack said, pulling her hands away from her head and helping her to her feet. "Free him quickly, Syl. We could use a guide."

"You check on Conor."

They nodded at each other, before hurrying to their tasks.

Sylvie made quick work of Jack's ice, careful not to cause any more damage. She warmed the Amorph just enough so that he could shift back into his normal form. It was a slow process, slower than she'd ever seen. Even when she compared it to the beginner transformation classes of the children in the Tower. The light around the Amorph was soft, as if he knew that something terrible would happen if he decided to pump more magic through the pores of his skin.

She watched, fascinated, as his long body shortened, before thickening. His limbs appeared, followed by ten, wriggling fingers and leather covered toes. His clothes were a mess. No doubt irritating his new burns. Sylvie saw the patches of hair lengthen to form a full head of brown. Proof that Jack had been right; this really was the patient Amorph she attacked. Her lips thinned at the thought.

Well, there was no point feeling sorry now.

Nessler coughed violently, before falling from the branch that was now too thin to hold his much larger frame. Sylvie reached out to help him, though she only really took care to make sure he didn't fall on his face and further damage his already charred torso. An injured Amorph was better than a dead one, especially if they were told to explain the reason for their aggression once they reached the Grove.

"*Filan vahs*," Jack cursed, appearing beside her after settling Conor against the large tree they'd been hiding behind just moments ago. "Is he alive?"

"Yes, just unconscious," she answered. "Though he'll need a

Healer. Sooner rather than later."

"Do you have anything on you?"

"A few tonics and balms. I have an ointment for burns, but not for anything this serious. Even if I did, it would take time to apply. We'd be better off searching for a Healer." Sylvie paused to look at Conor. "What about him?"

"The same. Though it might have been shock in his case. He got a little bruised when we fell into those roots. It's nothing a little salve won't fix. If he suddenly wakes up though, I'm pointing him in the direction of Curran and leaving him to fend for himself."

"Jovie's going to kill you if you do."

"I'll take my chances. Better Jovie than *her*."

"You say that now."

"And I'll say it a thousand times," he declared. "My magic doesn't work on *her*, remember?"

"Right." She exhaled, thinking, before, "We should go. Nessler won't be of much help now."

Jack didn't argue, but he did give her a startled look that she tilted her head at. "You..."

"What?"

"You actually remembered his name?"

Before she could respond, there was a rustle from the bushes behind them. They turned just in time to see two men emerge. They were a good foot taller than either of them, and had wary orange eyes. They wore buttery leathers instead of robes, but the deer patches stitched proudly over their hearts served as proof of their affiliation.

There was another sound to their right that had them subtly moving their eyes. Three men stood there. Two Healers armed to the teeth and an Amorph with sharp eyes crouched on the branch of a tree. There was an Elementalist to their left and a litter of more Amorphs both behind and above them.

They were surrounded. When did that happen?

"*Vaklas,*" Jack swore. His eyes drifted briefly to Conor, then to the burnt Amorph everyone around them seemed to be eyeing. "Care to try another introduction, Syl?"

"Your friend needs a Healer," Sylvie began, gesturing with her chin to the cataleptic Amorph at their feet.

"He does," one of the Conjurers in front of them said. He crossed his arms in an authoritative manner. "So I suggest you step away, before you get hurt, little girl."

"Don't be soft, Avin," someone said from behind them. "That ain't no little girl. You saw how she hurt Nessler. Get rid of them."

"He's still alive, isn't he?" Sylvie intervened, whipping her head around to find who had spoken. "And he was the one after us. We tried to explain why we were he—"

The next moments came in an intense roar.

Before she could even finish her sentence, the Elementalist to their left held up a hand and summoned a gust of wind so powerful it blew them both several feet back. Jack let out a string of colorful invective, as he reacted by freezing the ground a good distance in front of them. Everything from the flowers to the Conjurers were covered in hoarfrost. His magic moved far quicker than any of them anticipated, courtesy of the erratic tendrils whirling in his eyes. Jack's ice snaked up to their waists, locking them in place. Silently, he prayed to anyone that would listen that they didn't have an affinity for fire.

Sylvie, in the meantime, set her sights on the Amorphs behind them. She lit the ground on fire, creating a wall that cautioned anyone from jumping in recklessly. Trees were torched and more lights exploded, no doubt exposing their position. They both knew that they needed to deal with the Elementalist first. It was the proper thing to do; it was what their opponents were doing. Sylvie could see them subtly trying to surround Jack. But she didn't have time to help him at the moment.

She pivoted and dropped gracelessly to her side, effectively dodging an arrow that came far too close to hitting her knee. She rolled as another was aimed at her head. Off to the side, Jack throat punched an Amorph that was too close for comfort. The man keeled over and Jack mercilessly stomped on the heavy guards decorating his shoulders. There was a crush of steel and blood, before he ran to shield Conor from a particularly sharp blade aimed at his nose. Jack was quick enough to release a spike of ice from the ground to trap the weapon at the hilt, though what he wasn't prepared for was the arrow that came from directly above him.

A Healer was perched atop a large bird that was so steady, it could only be an Amorph. The Healer held a bow poised in his direction. Jack didn't have time to discharge more ice, only turn just enough so that the arrow tore through the deepest muscle of his shoulder instead of his neck. He bit his tongue in an effort to stop the scream that bubbled violently in the back of his throat.

His eyes filled with baleful fury, even as Sylvie ran towards him, conjuring a tornado of flames that licked uncomfortably at his skin. Those around them reeled back at the sudden ring of fire. Three practitioners he couldn't see were already icing a path. But he didn't have time to focus on them because within the span of a breath, his robes were torn and peeled away. Jack winced, as panicked eyes carefully assessed the exposed wound. It was nothing more than a stinging, starred ember on his skin. Red and barely swollen. It wasn't deep enough to truly maim, and—for the moment—he considered it shallow enough to ignore.

He was fine. There was nothing for her to be concerned about. He could still feel his fingers. He could still bend his elbow and lift his hand half-mast. His wound was merely a shadow of a thought in the face of the trouble before them; a shadow blown away by terrible euphoria. So long as she didn't pull the bolt out, then he wouldn't be spurting blood like a fountain anytime soon.

Jack would've squeezed her hands in reassurance if he didn't think words would be worth more.

"I'm fine, Syl," he told her, his watchful eyes never leaving the Conjurers futilely trying to ice the fire in front of them. If nothing else, that being in the Heartstone made for a good power boost. Though it was the armed practitioners from above that he was really concerned about.

Where did they go? Jack wondered, failing to stifle the disquiet in his mind. How Sylvie could so easily ignore their presence, he would never know. But he made a mental note to ask.

"You're *not* fine," Sylvie bit back, rifling through her pack for a rusty orange tonic that she pressed to his lips. "Drink."

"Stop it." He pushed the vial away. "Have all the explosions made you deaf or do you actually think I'm lying? If I say I'm fine, then I am."

"You aren't, so stop insisting that you are, you mule."

"It's *my* body, Syl. I think I have final—"

"That arrow was poisoned."

Jack stiffened at her words. His heart faltered momentarily. He didn't doubt that she knew what she was talking about. Sylvie had told him stories about the poisons she'd seen and the ways they slayed their victims. From the wild, incomprehensible ravings of Nebbin that crossed the wrong man to the frothing black spittle of animals slowly eaten from the inside. Even Jack had witnessed the swift and deadly work of some of his peers that coated their knives with translucent sheens of purple and green. Each drop guaranteed a cruel death. But seeing as how he wasn't writhing in pain and coughing out his weight in blood, he very much doubted the killing effect of the poison circulating inside of him.

A sleeping agent? Jack speculated. He squinted in a poor attempt to focus his suddenly blurred vision. It didn't take long for him to down the bitter brew she forced into his mouth. *I can't feel my fingertips though, so it could be used for numbing... maybe both.*

He hoped that the mystical tendrils residing inside of him would be kind enough to take care of it. Jack wanted to brush Sylvie off, to tell her to grab Conor and make a run for it while he distracted them, but a strong gust of wind blew his words away. They bent in his throat like the tips of the fire burning around them. He opened his eyes just in time to see a dark-haired man yank Sylvie backwards by the arm. Sylvie was quick though. Her other hand raised in an instant. She was prepared to burn the man's face from his bones.

Jack, however, was quicker.

His fingers wrapped around the stranger's forearm, freezing it up to the elbow. He ignored how his shoulder ached in protest at the sudden movement.

Jack paused, realizing a moment too late that there was a dagger pointed at his jugular. Sharp and lethal. It drew a drop of blood that ran like boiling water down his throat. It was an intense contrast to the coolness of the weapon's steel edge, and Jack snarled at the sensation. His fingers twitched with the realization that this practitioner was a lot better trained, though that was obvious just by looking at him. It was evident even in the way he swung his blade; some never attained that level of finesse. But Jack didn't have time to gush over this man's skill because his instincts were getting the better of him. His brain kicked into overdrive, trying to figure out the best way to get out of this mess. He mentally debated whether or not his magic would be faster than this man's dagger. It was uncomfortably close, so Jack doubted it… but he had to try.

Coming to a decision, Jack tightened his hold. He was about to give his magic free reign when—

"Dalis?" Sylvie whispered.

The cold-eyed Healer slanted his head ever so slightly to look at her. As soon as he did, his jaw slackened and the grip on his blade relaxed unexpectedly.

Jack tightened his hold over the Healer's arm even more, his mind failing to register the name or its significance. Around them, the other practitioners were stopped by another, likely higher-ranking group. A new Conjurer was among them. He had an air that was infinitely more confident than the rest, and when he brought his hands to the ground, Jack saw why.

The earth was torn asunder.

Sylvie's flames were smothered with an efficiency that made

Jack's throat go dry. The trenches that emerged even swallowed the explosions of nearby orbs that were offset by the intense burst of magic.

Beside him, Sylvie abruptly reached forward, grasping the Healer's robes with clumsy, sausage-like fingers. Her face was filled with the kind of astonishment Jack only saw in the eyes of temple-goers and the depraved.

"Dalis!" she repeated, shouting now.

"S—" the Healer swallowed, "—Sylvie!"

Dalis shook Jack off, barely even noticing his half-frozen arm or how his dagger clattered to the ground and almost stabbed him in the foot. Dalis was too busy crushing her in his arms.

Jack grabbed his head in agony at the sudden rocking motion. He was forced to back away from Sylvie, who clutched desperately at the Healer's back. Jack cursed viciously when his scapula accidentally hit Conor's hard head. He moved to the side, all the while apologizing to the boy under his breath.

As soon as he settled against the tree trunk, Jack noticed how the other practitioners stiffened at Dalis' proclamation. He tried to connect the Healer's name with the familiar one from his memory—

Her brother, he recalled, too late for surprise. *Thank Silas.*

Jack knew little about him, save for what was written in that history book—turned partial-memoir—and the few stories that Sylvie had regaled him with during their travels. But it was enough for him to know that Dalis would separate land from ocean to keep her safe. It also helped that Dalis belonged to an influential group. The Conjurer he came with was definite proof of their authority. Jack just hoped their word would be enough to get them out of this mess and safely into the Institute.

Western practitioners were more cautious than he thought. And contrary to the rumors regarding their tranquil natures, they were *incredibly* easy to provoke. It was fun. But he wasn't expecting this much damage.

In retrospect, he really should have.

Jack raised his good arm and rubbed his throbbing temple in a sorry attempt to soothe the dull ache there. Distantly, he heard that lullaby urging him into slumber... or perhaps that was just his imagination. The poison was definitely spreading. And now that he was focused on the wound, it *hurt*. Every heartbeat throbbed from shoulder to wrist with unwelcome, unmanageable heat. His hands shook and clenched with every wasted endeavor to master himself. It wasn't long before Sylvie pulled away from her brother to kneel in front of him. Her face filled his vision.

"Jack," she called, tapping his cheek. "Jack, stay with me."

Then, without warning, a different face was in front of him. Similar, but altered enough to be plain, despite his failing senses. The person in front of him now was tanner and more squared than he was used to. Jack saw laugh lines framing pale pink lips. They contrasted against the deeply creased forehead.

Dalis, Jack realized. He must've said it out loud because Dalis answered with a vague hum. Then, faster than he could track, Dalis' hands were coming closer.

"Sylvie," Jack murmured, as much to remind himself of her presence as to feel the name in his mouth.

"I'm right here," she answered, appearing in the corner of his vision. "Relax, okay? Put your arms down and calm your magic. Dalis is going to heal you."

"That was a member of my college that hit you," Dalis confessed. He inspected the wound. His magic prodded like a curious child around the area, waiting for permission to spread.

"How do you know?" Sylvie asked.

"We coat our weapons in a special oil-based blend made from Garrispore, Dourpot, Bisweed, and Hyxtrot. They're all extremely effective on their own, but when mixed together and allowed to circulate, they work even better. After four hours, it starts eating through your insides. Thankfully, I'm here to help. Though you'll probably be vomiting for a day or two." Dalis touched the arrow, making Jack clench his teeth. "I need to pull the bolt out, before I can get to work on the poison. Don't worry.

You'll be unconscious for it."

"Good," was all Jack managed to hiss out. He appreciated the explanation, but his tongue felt thick in his mouth. Just what did that poison do exactly?

Dalis grinned reassuringly.

"Jack!" another voice called this time.

It was loud and worried enough to make Jack's stomach drop to his feet. Twisting toward the voice was a chore, but with his own mounting curiosity and the fear of someone brashly tilting his head in their direction, he mustered enough strength to catch a glimpse of black eyes and a mop of frazzled hair.

Jack stared.

He knew that face.

"Tiv?" Jack asked, doubtful, at the same instant Dalis whispered, "Sleep."

Before he could even entertain the thought of hallucinations being a side effect of the poison, his entire body was compelled to relax. Jack slouched forward, nestling against Sylvie's shoulder like a drowsy infant. His nose felt hot against her skin. She said something his ears failed to catch, but it was warm and soft and a thousand times more reassuring than Dalis' easy grin.

Jack's sight blackened at the edges, darkening more as the seconds ticked on. This time, he allowed himself to yield to it. Because for now, for the moment, he was safe—and he fully trusted Sylvie to keep him so.

The rest of the world fell away, as he succumbed to the world of dreams.

13

Jack opened his eyes to find himself in a lavish room.

The Drowned Tower, he knew instinctively. He'd been in the restricted areas enough times to recognize it at a glance, though it was certainly brighter than he remembered it ever being. Jack could tell that he was in one of the older archives because he recognized the stack of royal red blankets folded in the far corner of the room. Though it was much, *much* cleaner than his memory served. Dark wood tables littered one side, supporting what must've been three dozen scrolls. Bookshelves lined the far walls, their spaces were filled end to end with knick-knacks and leather-bound tomes that sported faded words on their spines. Their covers were old, but flamboyant. A riot of color amidst the dreary wood. There were seats sprinkled around the area, but only one of them actually looked good for sitting, cushioned as it was. The rest no doubt functioned as stepping stools.

Jack raised his head, marveling at the glory around him. The stones around him sang. The ancient torches mounted on the walls and the thin candlesticks made him feel at ease. Raw veins of magic pulsed across the room. Protecting. Fortifying. They chased away all of the bad things in the outside world.

He didn't find it strange that he was in the Drowned Tower. Rather, he found it strange that he was standing. Opening crusty eyes after what felt like an age-long slumber only to wake up and find himself on his feet just didn't make any sense… though none of this did really.

I'm dreaming, he thought, wanting to laugh at the fact.

It had been a long time since he dreamt—like *this*. He'd adamantly avoided sleeping for longer than a few hours every day for the past week, not wanting to get caught in *her* games. Sylvie had no such qualms, and was all too happy to reiterate whatever she saw. Not that it was anything important. The things she dreamt about were mere passages. Fond memories in the midst of all the chaos that they truly wanted to know more about. Perhaps that was *her* kindness. Gifting Sylvie with warm recollections of her ancestor was thoughtful, but having him witness all of the bloody, hateful times in her stead had him stilling his tongue from singing *her* any sort of praise.

When Sylvie woke, she sighed.

When Jack woke, he screamed.

He just hoped this time would be different.

Jack caught his reflection on a fat oval flask. It was stretched, but not enough to fully distort the sharp eyes and dark hair that were distinctly his. He ran his fingers over his face, making sure he wasn't just seeing things.

"I'm actually me this time?" Jack said aloud. He didn't know if he should be glad or frightened. But when dark tendrils shot out to wrap around his torso, he settled for the latter. Jack reached up. His hands glowed out of instinct, afraid he'd be choked. But as soon as the wisps framed his shoulder blades, they stilled.

Welcome, came that dreadful voice.

Jack shivered.

He hadn't heard *her* in so long that suddenly having *her* invade his ears again made his gut churn in old terror. Jack's fingers twitched in apprehension. His hand was already half-raised, fully prepared to ice himself should *she* try something.

Why was it that *she* had no problem speaking with them in their dreams, but as soon as they were back in the real world, *she*'d lapse into silence as if *she*'d never visited them in the first place. *She* spoke when *she* wanted them to do things, usually unreasonable; *she* spoke even more when *she* subtly urged them toward certain places. Jack had to wonder why *she* didn't just direct them from the start. It seemed to him that *she* already had their course mapped out for them.

Is she trying to teach us something? Jack thought, but immediately shook his head. *That's absurd. But then… why bother? Is it some unspoken favor to Silas? Allow his ancestor to learn and grow, so that there's not another repeat of history? The Drayr name holds a lot of weight. No doubt enough to change many things. But with the information she spills and all this evidence we've come across to back it, anyone would do.*

Jack gripped his head, trying to make sense of it all.

Even in slumber, his mind ran.

He distinctly recalled Vidal insinuating that *she* had feelings. Human ones. A product of *her* time inhabiting practitioners no doubt. But even though *she* seemed to be on amicable terms with Silas, Jack doubted *she'*d go so far. *She'*d made it clear from the start who *she* wanted to return to. That ancient being was loyal to only one man—why that was, didn't matter.

It's for Thelarius, his mind supplied. *Does that mean she chose Sylvie because Silas was his closest friend? It's sentimental, but… maybe. She could also just feel safe with someone of his line. Well, none of this changes the fact that she wants us to learn the truth for Thelarius' sake, so what he built can be corrected. The Demar Spell for one. I'd be glad if they used that vile thing for what it was originally created for.*

Jack paused.

But we're already on her side. Why not just lead us to where she wants us to go? Or maybe… she doesn't know where to go? he mused, while staring at the shadows shawled around him.

Ferus Terria had changed drastically from the time she first roamed it with the First Zenith. Cities were built, farmhouses renovated, and entire acres of forest burned and ploughed into flatland. He couldn't fathom how that black trail of *hers* worked, but he recalled it only ever zeroing in on something specific when the destination was an old, prehistoric landmark or they were somehow trapped inside the area itself.

His eyes widened in realization.

So, *she* wasn't an all-seeing being after all. That bolstered his self-confidence somewhat. *She* directed them only to what *she* already knew and to what *she* felt nearby. *She* was like a living embodiment of magic itself, so it would make sense that *she* was more sensitive to the subtleties of their surroundings whenever they were caught in a confined area like the Pit or the Tower. But that still didn't explain the long periods of silence.

Then again, he could reason an explanation for that as well. *She* could've seen something they didn't in every place that they visited. They didn't bother searching every nook and cranny of the Pit or even the Veld—and Jack didn't doubt her ability to read Silas and Thelarius' code. Perhaps *she* subtly translated it, gathering information from the areas they passed, then directing them when new information presented itself.

It was a good theory. Although riddled with holes primarily due to his lack of knowledge regarding the entity in question. But it was all he had right now.

'*Then ask her,*' he remembered Sylvie say to him in that shack. He cursed her in his head, but followed her advice all the same.

"What are you up to?" Jack gave in, finally asking, finally talking to *her* again of his own volition.

You seek an answer for a question that you've just realized the answer to, *she* said, confirming his thoughts with a mere sentence. But he wanted to hear *her* say it.

"Humor me."

Every action, every word, is all for the one I seek.

"We know that, and I'm sure you know very well that we'll take you to see Thelarius. We'll go where ever you want us to. We want answers just as much as you."

Silence.

Jack should've expected that, but he waited for *her* to respond anyway. After a minute passed and all he heard was his own erratic heartbeat, he took a deep breath and continued, "Okay, answer this instead, why not just possess someone else and be on your way? Why bother staying with us at all?"

Silas' kin is the closest I have been to Thelarius. Silas understands. He always has... only Silas will return me to him.

"If you're so confident in Sylvie, or rather, *Silas*, then why even bother possessing Conor? What's the point?"

There are threats in this world that I cannot shield you from. Confined as I am—within you, within Aethilium greviya—I have no reign, nor do I wish to derive you of your own. With the boy, it is different. He wanted to follow. He carries inside him dustings of Orivellea, courtesy of another failure that sought to copy Thelarius.

Jack ignored the unintended jab. He was one of those failures. But who had given Conor an Orive crystal? Vidal? It was likely. And Jack could guess the reason why, too. That awful master of his probably used the boy to see how much Orive one could consume or embed into another without powers emerging. Did Jovie know? He doubted it, but it wasn't impossible.

"Flames!" Jack yelled, running his hands through his hair.

Borrowing the boy was far less unsettling.

"Less unse—do you hear yourself?" Blood and fucking ashes, it felt like he was reprimanding a child. "You can't do that!"

Fury blinds. Had I forced control over you, Silas' kin would have been livid.

Jack pinched the bridge of his nose and—

—stopped.

What? he thought. Before he could gather his wits to say something cutting, a man burst through the door. He opened it with such force that the hinges whined from the stress. The thick planks slammed against the adjacent wall with a resounding boom that made Jack wince.

Jack didn't think, only moved. He dove to the floor and clumsily rolled out of sight. Jack crouched behind a chest half his size. Only when he was sure that the man hadn't noticed him, did he chance a peek to see just who he was.

He was met with orange eyes, broad shoulders, and wild hair. The neutral expression on the man's face was one he was intimately familiar with. Though instead of the regular robes expected of a practitioner, the man donned blood-stiffened leathers that were threaded at the knees. Jack could smell its fetid stench a good fifteen feet away, sepulchral and desolate. It was the perfume of long-dead soldiers, chilled winds, and blackened steel. And it only grew stronger as the newcomer drew past where Jack was hidden to examine the overburdened tables in the corner of the room. From the ease of his gait, Jack doubted the blood was his.

"Silas," Jack said, before he could stop himself. He slapped a hand over his mouth as soon as the word escaped. But against all odds, the Great Conjurer didn't seem to hear.

He cannot sense what he does not know, she revealed, *or what has yet to exist. This is an old memory. Your presence is no more important than the dust gathered in the air. No matter what you do, you cannot interfere.*

Jack hesitated, not quite believing that. "Weren't you inside Thelarius?" he whispered. His voice grew louder with each passing second, testing the truth in her words. "How could you possibly show me things that Silas did alone?"

Perhaps you should look again.

Jack surveyed the room a second time. He paid special attention to the nooks unilluminated by the candlelight. In the far corner of the room, hidden behind a tiny chest much like the one he'd crouched behind, was Thelarius. He was taller than Jack, and thus, further bent at the knees. His spine curved downward into a low bow. But from how easily his joints caved in and to the side, Jack knew that wasn't a position he was unused to.

Thelarius had his hands clamped over his mouth, stifling his breaths. Jack walked over, purposely stepping louder than usual as he did. He took a moment to examine Silas' beguiling lips and proud nose. The stress lines drawn over his face grew deeper as he read the scrolls in front of him. The symbol of a clover adorned the top—no doubt the insignia of a long dead house. Jack looked at Thelarius next. He had longer hair and a beard. Thelarius was far scruffier than his friend. He also looked healthier than Jack remembered. The whipcord thin practitioner that Jack had found himself inhabiting on more than one occasion was finally as big as the statues masons carved ages down the line. It was as if Thelarius was finally eating right.

How many scholars and artists would kill to be in my position? he wondered. The thought alone made pride swell in his chest. The tendrils cloaking him reacted to his spirit, spreading outward across his skin like wings.

"If someone isn't on the verge of death," Silas said suddenly, his voice was low and intimidating, "then they're very well about to be."

When Thelarius emerged from his position, Jack stepped aside out of instinct. The Elementalist swept past him with sure, confident steps. His back was straight, his chin high, as if he hadn't just been hiding behind a chest not even half his size.

"A missive arrived from your wife." Thelarius picked up a sealed letter at the far end of the desk and threw it on the stretch of table between them. "See?"

"Tell her I was thinking of her," Silas said, then picked up a different scroll in preference.

"Why don't you read it?"

Though it was posed as a question, Jack wasn't naïve enough to think that Thelarius was giving him an option—and neither did Silas. Immediately dropping the scroll in his hands, Silas grabbed the note and broke the wax seal in one smooth movement. His eyes roved over the letter twice, before he burnt it in his hands.

"Anything interesting?" Thelarius prompted.

"She has... concerns."

"Concerns?"

"About my working here."

"Now, why would she be concerned about that?"

"You tell me, Thelarius." Silas eyed him warily. "You left the Diamond Alps so suddenly, and then made your way all the way here to the Tower. When I go to follow, what do I find? You wandering the halls in the middle of the night, chasing shadows like a madman. If you're feeling nostalgic, I hardly think this is the place for you to return. You were chained here."

Thelarius paused to rub his chest. "I met *her* here."

"No one, but you and I are privy to that. The Pulka scholars are angry at you for leaving. The north needs you now."

"You didn't need to follow me."

"Yes," he said with finality, "I did."

They stared at each other. Both unblinking. Both unwilling to yield. The light from the torches bent and waned, casting a sad glow on their faces and the rest of the room. They looked tired — of fighting, of meetings, of politics, of *everything*. It wasn't a look Jack was unfamiliar with, but to see it so clearly gave him pause. To witness the downward slope of broad shoulders, the deep etches across their foreheads, the graying hair... they were regarded as gods during his time. This made them human. Their effort seemed real. Solid and tangible. Like something he'd be able to grasp instead of just read about and absently realize whenever he saw a family of Nebbin wandering the lands, unchained and wholly free from any burden but the one naturally brought about by life and their own liberty.

"Why have you come here Thelarius?" Silas went on. "Did *she* tell you to come?"

"*She*'s gotten noisier." Thelarius struggled to find the words. "More vocal about leaving the Alps. It's not safe, *she* says."

"Is there a threat that we don't know about?"

"*She* believes there is."

"I didn't realize *she* had instincts now." Silas paused. "Is *she*... human?"

"No," came the immediate response. It was said with such conviction that any doubts Silas might've had were immediately expelled from his mind. "But *she*'s learning to be."

"How is that possible?"

"I don't know." Thelarius slouched, tired of it all. His

shoulders fell, heavy and overburdened. He balanced the weight of the world there; the weight of every hope and dream that both practitioner and Nebbin had across Ferus Terria. "I heard Pernelia's cousin died in the Grove. The short one… Kervan."

"I thought you didn't like him. In fact, I distinctly recall you calling him a pretentious weasel."

"He was, but I'm still concerned. It had something to do with riots in Curran?"

"The people were opposed to the concept of Peose. Kervan's death gave the north a reason to put an end to them. He was a necessary casualty."

"They're all necessary, aren't they?"

Silas wrinkled his nose. "I don't like it either, and I'm not here to argue with you."

"Then why are you here?" Thelarius pressed. "You should return. I'm sure Alaina misses you. How far along is she?"

"Four months tomorrow."

"I hope your child doesn't have your eyes. I don't think I can handle two pairs of the same look."

Silas said something that was lost to Jack, as he busied himself with looking between the two once more. He compared their statures to his own—they were similar where it counted. In the shoulders and face. Though he lacked the distinct lines that marred their foreheads, and they, the pulsing blue veins along his temples. Down here, in the older sections of the Tower he used to practice his magic in as a child, they looked likes regular practitioners. Together, they were simply partners that paid no heed to each other's lofty titles or their individual abilities to spin the world on its head.

Jack continued to stare listlessly at them, lost in his thoughts. Frankly, their conversation bored him. There wasn't anything truly important about it, and while it was pleasant enough, their voices held a peevish undertone that irritated him. In part because the voices of men long dead were inherently grating, and in part because whenever Sylvie was annoyed, she spoke in that same displeased tone that Silas did. Her lips would purse the same way, too. And when her eyes narrowed, the space between her brows knitted together, forcing one higher than the other. Silas had incredibly virile genes if generations down the line his mannerisms still remained.

"Why are you showing me this?" Jack suddenly asked. "I already know you suspected Maurice. It was written in the letters from Thelarius that Silas kept."

You wanted this, did you not? These bloodless recollections.

"Why even bother showing me anything at all?" Jack walked to the two chattering practitioners. His hand hovered over Thelarius' robes. He could touch him. Touch a god. But even if this was a dream, even if he'd actually inhabited his body before, it still felt like he'd be profaning the past. "These aren't my ancestors. I could do without their memories."

This is lost history. Where the questions you now have were first asked and where Thelarius was once again enslaved. Here, in this dark dungeon, he became a captive of his interest — an interest brought about by the traitor, Maurice.

"Let Sylvie tell the world about the intricacies of the First Zenith's relationships. I want to know exactly what happened to Thelarius. Where did he run off to? How were you taken away from him? Did he come here to get away from Maurice or is he just looking for the reason why you suspected him?"

Everything ended and began here. Where Thelarius was found, where questions were answered, where failures were first wrought.

"Are you saying Maurice came after Thelarius here?"

In the future, in your past, Pernelia's sanctuary was once considered haven for all. The secrets kept by these walls are old and valuable.

"Then why are you showing me this nonsense? Why not show me those *valuable* secrets instead?"

Twice, your impatience has stunted you.

"What—"

Jack stopped mid-sentence when Silas suddenly conjured a burst of fire, propelling it toward a bookshelf in one of the unilluminated corners of the room. The force of the blast was so strong that Jack had to cover his face with his arms in a sorry hope to shield himself. Silas' magic burned furniture and trinket alike. The papers served as fuel, while the old, flammable ink and ancient metal knobs on the ornaments ignited, making sparks fly from the wreckage. Clouds of smoke blew upward all at once, only to meet the ceiling, and descend around them instead.

He saw two flashes of white light seep through the heavy exhaust around him, but couldn't find their source. Opening his eyes by a slit just made them water in protest, so Jack was forced to wait until the smoke dissipated.

What he saw after didn't disappoint.

The once burning bookshelf was now encased in a solid block of translucent ice. It looked sweaty in the soft glow of the nearby torches. Menacing, too, if one were to look at it on its own and not know the cause. How Thelarius was able to move through all of that gas might've been a mystery to some, but Jack could see the dark tendrils that sprouted from the man's shoulders, marking a trail from where he'd once been standing to the half-charred bookshelf he was now kneeling before. The darkness swirled around him in much the same way it did to Jack now. Their eyes were both the same tainted red.

A Ferrsink was on the ground before Thelarius. Sections of its fur were covered in hoarfrost, while the rest had been burned to expose the now black skin beneath.

Jack ambled closer, having never seen one for himself. It was a small rodent with tall, thin ears and a monkey-like body that existed before the Crown Age. They were hunted to extinction when embrocologists realized that their bones could be grinded down and used as fertilizer for the more stubborn plants that didn't appreciate being taken out of their local environment. It didn't help that the people in Tor had a taste for them either. Their meat was either boiled in stews or baked for more elaborate dishes. Ferrsink meat was found frequently on the dinner tables of many homes, especially during the colder months when yield was little and butchering a larger animal would be too wasteful.

Thelarius leaned over and slid one of the Ferrsink's eyelids up to expose pure black orbs.

"A spy?" Jack and Silas said simultaneously.

"It's likely." Thelarius tore the sleeve of his robes off to cover the Amorph.

"Who sent him?" Silas asked.

Jack watched from his position, as Thelarius' jaw locked at the question. He knew the name that settled on the tip of his tongue, but Thelarius stubbornly kept his mouth shut in silence.

This is the beginning, *she* said in his ear. ***Now allow me to show you the end.***

Her whisper was all the warning Jack received, before the ground shifted beneath his feet. Jack lurched forward. His vision distorted around the edges. Black tendrils encircled him. They wrapped around his neck and waist, and for one senseless moment, he swore he saw Thelarius glance his way, as if he could see what the darkness he commanded was doing. But even that sliver of sight was quickly obscured. *She* encompassed him until nothing remained. That unholy lullaby pealed like bells in his ears. The wisps moved in time with it, creating a distant, edgeless expanse that blended all into one until only he was left.

The tendrils felt cold and wet against his skin. Like soggy bandages wrapped too tightly around bruised flesh. Jack missed the snug, gentle blaze of fire; of worried eyes framed by dark hair that never failed to provide it.

Just as the thought passed, something tepid pooled in the pit of his stomach. It was a welcome change. One that distracted him from his lack of sight. He felt himself floating, the ground long gone beneath him. Nothing anchored him here. Only his thoughts and the knowledge that none of this was real. The pervading warmth was soft at first, bleeding into his veins. A steady trickle of comfort.

Then, all at once, it became unbearable. The forgiving stream turned into an all-out gush of heat. It erupted from his core. Every heartbeat throbbed from head to toe. But Jack wasn't ignorant enough to not realize its source.

He'd been broken down and stitched back together again enough times to know how Healers operated. How their magic dripped into someone's skin with the same meticulous precision an expert tailor displayed with his needle. Their magic was versatile. An almost sentient being that prodded first to find the weakest spots before entering.

Jack felt that happening now.

Except this was different from the soothing exploration he was used to. This was a flood of magic that forced its way inside of him. Intense. Demanding. Magic with only one purpose—to hurt. It dug around his insides, threaded in his limbs, and pierced its way between the soft, pink tissue of his organs. It flanked every layer of muscle, trying to tear him apart at the seams.

And then he was screaming.

Jack didn't know when the bindings around his eyes vanished, but there was no time to worry about such banal concerns. Above him, stood a man with graying hair, half-concealed by his robe's triangular hood. His hands glowed the same color as his eyes. As far as looks went, the man had a decidedly plain face. His eyes and lips were framed by premature wrinkles that concealed his age. There was no demented smile. No wicked glare. Only concentration.

The man's sanity scared him more than he'd ever admit.

Jack tried to move away from the explosive pain the Healer's hands caused, but something hard was behind him, and he unintentionally slammed the back of his head into it in a move so harsh that he swore the base of his skull cracked from the impact. He smelt the rusty scent of iron. Felt it around his shoulders, too. Again, he tried to get away. His movements were jerky and graceless, fueled by the same kind of life-threatening desperation he'd felt so many times before. Only this time, there was no escape. His wrists and ankles were bound by magic-draining fetters that clanked with each involuntary rise of his chest.

Jack wailed when more magic poured into him, high enough to split his own ears with the sound. Between the hazy blurs of hurt, he realized that he was laying atop a stone slab. It reminded him of the heinous tributes in the rural parts of the Plains, where they worshipped violent gods.

His entire body was sore and laden with exhaustion. The parts he could see were either bruised or sported cuts from a beating he didn't remember receiving; and this man, this *Healer* did nothing to ease the burden.

Jack's frantic eyes met his calm ones. In them, he saw his reflection. Peach-toned skin and wide, round orbs. He didn't recognize his features. Even though he knew in the back of his mind that he wasn't in his own body, that still didn't make the evidence any less surprising. But it comforted him, somehow, knowing that this pain wasn't his. That everything happening now had already passed and he only had to endure it for as long as that sadistic thing inhabiting him saw fit.

The man stopped to stare deep into his eyes. Listless, as if *he* was the uninvited spectator in all of this. Jack saw an echo of the strong man he'd observed mere minutes ago in his stare. He, or rather, Thelarius, was fraught with despair and confusion—all layered on top of something else, something entirely more terrifying that he didn't want to give name.

Jack felt the ugly emotions course throughout his body, rushing like the tide across sand. A mass of animosity that made his head pound with a vengeance. He knew this feeling well. It was fury. Pent-up rage. The blackened intent to do nothing but hurt and kill and cause harm in ways he fully knew himself capable of.

Before he could even think about mastering himself, the Healer's hands were glowing again. That evil blue that Jack promised to never again associate with light.

Jack watched as the Healer reached toward a table beside

him, where dozens of oddly shaped flasks sat. Beside them, in a ceramic bowl littered with tiny symbols that he couldn't make out, were Heartstones. Unmarked and utterly transparent. They were soaked in a black, viscous liquid that reminded him of the pool of flesh-sizzling acid in the Pit.

The Healer dipped his glowing hands in a separate bowlful of it. Jack flinched when the concoction bubbled. He heard the protesting hiss as the dark fumes it exuded escaped into the open air above. Jack knew for a fact that his hands were boiling right now, yet... he didn't even blink. The Healer merely removed his blistered hands, shook them twice for good measure, before moving to stand over him again. Jack could already see his wounds healing.

His eyes widened.

"Maurice!" Jack suddenly yelled in a voice that didn't belong to him. It was creaky. Half-choked out from the sheer dryness of his throat. "Wai—no. Stop!"

He didn't seem to hear.

"Come out," Maurice whispered, before his hands settled upon him again.

Distantly, Jack heard *her* screaming as well.

✳✳✳

Sleep came in broken bursts after that, interspersed with violent dreams of Thelarius and waking moments as foggy and blurred as his rippled reflection.

When Jack awoke, truly awoke, he found himself in another room. It was less luxurious than the one from his dreams. He was surrounded by wood and the smell of pine. The walnut furniture and warm, earthy decorations of the room made the stress of waking less awful. Jack's head throbbed. Not from pain, but from the distant memory of it. It was as if his mind was still trying to reconcile what he'd experienced with the ordinariness of now.

Jack laid there for a long while, blinded by heat as if he held a star. He stared at the ceiling and went over everything he'd just witnessed. It was a lot to take in, even more to speculate about. But one thing was for certain: he was *never* sleeping again. He didn't care what other people said, didn't care if he needed it or not. If it was stay awake forever or go through that hellish affair a second time, then the answer was obvious. Surely, Sylvie knew of a tonic that could keep him up for eternity. And if it made him a little grumpier than usual, then so be it.

He shifted so that he laid on his uninjured side. His forehead and back were slippery with sweat. The sheets beneath him were drenched. Even his throat felt raw. Had he been screaming in his sleep? It was likely. Suddenly, he was glad that he was alone... yet annoyed by it at the same time. Irrationally so.

Where's Sylvie?

He wanted to shout her name, to spring out of bed and find her, but thought better of it when his gut churned. Jack heard it make a strange noise that had nothing to do with hunger. Was that his body's disturbing way of reassuring him that it was doing all it could to rid itself of the poison trapped inside of him? He hoped so. Jack didn't need stomach problems on top of everything else.

Didn't Dalis say something about vomiting? Jack thought. He took a deep breath, as if a wave of nausea might hit him at any moment. When nothing did, he sighed in content, and then in displeasure as soon as he remembered that he was lying useless in bed. *I just woke up, and I'm already sick of this place.*

Deciding that it was safe to get up, Jack inched his way to the edge of the unbearably flat mattress. He groaned in despair when the nausea he was dreading came full-force. He didn't relent, however. No matter how much of a struggle sitting up was. Though he did take one too many breaks to catch his breath.

During his final effort to sit, he winced when he accidentally raised his arm in an angle that his injured shoulder didn't agree with. Jack inspected it once he finally managed to straighten. Absently, he noted that someone had changed him into a pair of cotton trousers. Bandages were wrapped around the wound. Jack reached up to take a proper look, but his hands shook so bad, he could barely unwrap the bindings.

It doesn't feel worse, Jack thought, *but it doesn't feel better either.* He cupped the area. *Mostly dry.* He pressed his nose to it and reeled back in the same instant. *And lathered with antiseptic.*

So, it was healed. For the most part.

Lingering soreness then? They could've at least left me a tonic.

Knowing it would be better to leave his shoulder alone, he made a valiant effort to stand instead. But just as he was about to, a voice from outside of his door made him still.

"Hey, wait!" he heard. Male. Early teens, judging by the pitch. "Can I come with you?"

"You know you can't, Niv." Another boy. Older, but still young. His voice was mousier than his companion's.

"Oh, c'mon! Please! I've got a ton of questions for the guy."

"They can wait."

"You say that because you didn't see them! How they just, y'know, boom! Hands out and spewing magic like they didn't care if they burnt their circuits."

"So, they're reckless?"

"No," Niv stressed. "They have a secret technique, I tell you. I've never seen magic travel that fast in my life!"

"Too bad, Niv. You know the rules. Even if I am just doing a check-up, if Master were to find out, then—"

"What about me?" another voice intervened. A woman this time. Their master, if her words and their sudden silence were anything to go by.

Jack watched with narrowed eyes as the shadows under the door shuffled, before it swung open, oiled and mute. When he lifted his gaze, he was met with three pairs of astounded blue eyes. Eyes that he'd just developed a rather potent aversion towards. His hands balled into fists at the mere sight of them coming closer.

Jack bit his tongue, not wanting to say anything cutting. He needed to focus on getting answers—where Sylvie was currently dominated that list. Next, was how to request an audience with their Arch Poten, while the creation of the *Orivellea* and the details of the Grove's current situation were lost somewhere in the middle.

Before he could even open his mouth, however, the youngest of the three Healers, with his chestnut-colored hair and doe-like eyes, leaned dangerously forward. Jack was surprised he didn't fall flat on his face.

"I didn't think you'd be awake," he said excitedly.

"Leave him alone, Niv," his companion warned. "He was poisoned. We need to do a chec—"

"What's wrong with your eyes?"

Jack stared in silence up until the question registered. When it did, he didn't even try to contain the string of wrathful *Íarre* that left his lips.

14

Jack was astonishing.

There was no other word for it. No other way to accurately describe exactly how Sylvie felt when she caught him standing in his room, chewing out the juvenile Healer in charge of recording his progress with all the vigor of a child lost in the throes of unreasonable rage that characterized only the worst of tantrums.

Jack despised being attended to. Despised, what he deemed, unnecessary check-ins even more. If that wasn't clear before, then it certainly was now. The poor boy just so happened to come in at the wrong time... and obviously regretted that decision with every fiber of his being. Sylvie could practically see him praying to the Creator. She didn't blame him. Especially since his fate was apparently bad enough to get him scarred for life by one of the most explosive Elementalists in Ferus Terria.

The boy's tome was shaking in his hands and his breathing took a turn for the ragged before Jack even finished speaking. When Sylvie peeked at his face, she was unsurprised to find it as pasty as her own. But that wasn't what she was so amazed about. She'd been on the receiving end of Jack's flaring mood swings enough times by now to know when he was irritable, and how utterly insistent he was about making everyone within forty meters of him aware of the fact.

It was his constitution that she found so unbelievable.

The Healer in charge of him, a freshly appointed master with olive skin and ebony hair, had explicitly told her before she left his room that Jack's body was still suffering from the after effects of the poison and that getting up would only result in nausea and vomiting. In fact, just one look at his pale skin and thin frame was enough for the woman to conclude that he was in desperate need of bed rest. So, she ordered her apprentices to watch over him and make sure he stayed where he ought. Unfortunately for them, Jack wasn't the most cooperative of patients.

Maybe I should've warned them? Sylvie thought. *Well, it's too late for that now.*

"Leave the boy alone, Jack," Sylvie told him once she finally gathered her wits. "And for Pernelia's sake, let him do his job."

Jack whirled around at the sound of her voice.

"Look who finally decided to grace us with her presence," Jack said caustically. His nose wrinkled in jealousy at the sight of her fresh robes. "It's about time, Syl. I've been asking about you for the past two hours."

"I heard," she said, waving his anger aside. "And while you were spending your time here sleeping—"

"Suffering in my dreams, you mean."

"*—sleeping,*" she looked pointedly at him, "I was with Dalis."

Jack paused to roll his tongue against the inside of his cheek. She could almost hear his thoughts race. Jack debated continuing this little argument, but thankfully, he conceded.

"Where's Conor?" he asked instead.

"With Dalis."

"Did you ask him about *her*?"

"I did." Sylvie looked briefly at the Healer still behind him, making sure to choose her next words carefully. "He didn't say anything important. One minute he was at the edge of the Mending Willow, the next he was waking up in the Grove. Dalis is finding someone to escort him back to Curran tonight."

"Did they heal him properly?"

"Yes," she assured. "He's fine, Jack. I promise."

"Good."

"But—"

"There's always a but."

"—he did mention wanting to see you before he left."

Jack pursed his lips. "Anything else I need to know?"

"Nothing that can't wait until you're discharged. Master Gaddis, the head of this ward, said that you needed to stay here and recuperate for another day or two. *Stress-free*." Sylvie paused to smile at him. "Your deathly pallor worried her."

"You and I both know that I don't need to be here," Jack said, heated once again. He pointed an emphatic finger at his face. His skin looked gray under the light. "I *always* look like this."

"Well, they don't know that."

"But you do."

"And what am I supposed to do about it? I can't rescind a Master's order."

"Of all the infernal excu—*filan vahs! Avina rolin a shiden!*" he shouted in an impressive display of his creativity. The boy beside her recoiled. If it was from Jack's tone or if he actually understood his words, Sylvie couldn't say, but she prayed it was the former.

"Not in front of the children, Jack."

"He's older than you," Jack told her, stifling the brief spark of amusement he felt when Sylvie turned to the Healer with wide, disbelieving eyes. "But that isn't the point. You're an Arch Poten, Syl. The *least* you could do is rescind an order, especially from some fledgling Master that looks even younger than Pom!"

The Healer straightened at his words. "*A*—Arch Poten?" he stuttered, while backing away.

Sylvie turned just in time to find every nervous tick she'd ever seen suddenly manifest itself. The Healer's eyes shifted to the side, his lower lip trembled, his knees quaked, and he even began wiping his hands over his thighs in an effort to rid himself of the sweat. She would've dismissed him had she not been so taken aback by how anxiety seemed to radiate from his pores. His panic spilled into the air around the room, giving it the distinct scent of old fear that had become so familiar to her. It was as if he made the surroundings themselves terrified of her presence.

Unfortunately for him, Jack swiveled at the sound of his

breathing. In under a second, his mislaid fury was once again directed at their unwelcome guest.

"Why are you still here?" Jack sneered. "Go tell your Master that I'm more than capable of walking, despite my, oh, so fragile constitution."

"Yes! Of course! Right away!" the boy shouted. His gaze dropped to the floor, before he tacked on a hesitant, "... sir."

Jack smirked.

"Satisfied?" Sylvie asked once he left.

"Somewhat."

Sylvie sat on the chair by the foot of his bed. There was a desk before her filled with what looked to be medicinal notes and... journal entries? No, they weren't detailed enough for that. The only thing of any import were the tonics administered.

Patient logs then, she decided. This was no ordinary room. Certainly not one kept for guests. Though she should've known that from the start. It had all of the signs of occupancy. From the half-withered flowers by the windowsill to the pink mug on Jack's bedside table.

As she surveyed the room, Jack took it upon himself to frown at his pants. She knew he wanted to change, but Sylvie brought their packs to the room Dalis had given them in the Red Scripts' private sector, and she hadn't thought to bring him a new set of robes. Mostly because she believed he'd still be asleep by the time she returned. He'd been in bed for the better part of the day, and from Master Gaddis' report, he wouldn't be getting out of it soon. She'd clearly underestimated Jack's ability to prove people wrong because here he was, awake and wound with energy.

"You can leave, you know?" Sylvie said. "No one's forcing you to stay, least of all me."

"There are guards in the hall," came the half-hearted reply.

"Kick up another fuss. I doubt they'd stop you."

"One is enough."

With that, Jack fell back into bed. He curled on his side and turned his back on her to effectively end the conversation. Sylvie stared at him for a second longer, watching him breathe in a slow, almost controlled manner. He wasn't one to give in so easily—had never been. But when she saw the way he caved forward, his shoulders curved in on themselves as if trying to will something unpleasant away, she knew why he did.

He is feeling bad, she thought.

Jack really was astonishing. To be able to chew someone out while claiming health was an impressive feat. Though she didn't know if that just made him prideful or an idiot. Perhaps both.

Sylvie swept a hand over her face in exasperation. She leaned back and accidentally elbowed a nearby flask in the process. Too slow to catch it, the bottle fell to the ground. Sylvie winced a moment too late, then felt foolish for doing so. She should've known better than to think it would shatter. That was an Embrocologist's flask. The kind abused by practitioners in the field; the very one she'd used hundreds of times before. It wouldn't break so easily. Instead, it bounced twice, made a grand spin on its narrow throat, and then rolled away, still whole.

"What are you doing?" Jack asked, flipping so he could look at her. "Don't you want to explore the Grove? You'll get chunky if you continue to sit around. Only livestock are worth more big."

"Weren't you asking about me just a moment ago?"

"I was wondering where you were, not ordering them to drag you here. Feel free to leave if you're going to drop things."

She scowled. That was sour. Even for him. "What's got you in such an awful mood?"

"Other than the poison?" His eyes fell to the Heartstone that dangled over her chest. The light was still visible, despite its place underneath her robes. "What do you think?"

Sylvie followed his gaze with a frown. She grabbed the stone to take a proper look at it, but was distracted when Jack suddenly averted his gaze with a loud, exhausted sigh.

"Why is it that I get all of the bad dreams?" he said.

"What happened?"

"I saw him."

"Who?"

"Maurice," Jack spat. "I was there when he extracted *her* from Thelarius. He did it deep in the bowels of the Tower on that disgusting hunk of grit in the restricted sections. Maurice sealed her into that stone, coating his hands in a brew of black liquid that burned every," he cut himself off to breathe, "I remember screaming, Syl. So much screaming."

"Tell me everything, Jack."

It wasn't a request, and they both knew it.

***

Sylvie leaned forward as Jack recounted his dreams. Now that he was actually telling the story, he realized that there wasn't much to say—an argument, sprinkles of pain, a dead Ferrsink— but what he could tell, he relayed vividly. No detail was spared. From the scant torches that illuminated the lavish room he'd first woken up in to the stress lines on Silas' face and how his expressions reminded him of her. Jack didn't particularly care for those little details, but he remembered them nevertheless. He also knew enough about dreams to know that they faded quicker when shared. Jack didn't want to recall this for a second longer than he had to. He'd let Sylvie remember in his place.

She soaked all of it in. By the time he finished, her entire body matched the stiffness of his own. Sylvie stared at him, trying to find something in his eyes. If she was searching for a hint that he was lying, then she wouldn't find one. She'd never find one.

When the minutes ticked on, and she still didn't speak, Jack met her gaze head-on. "Well?" he asked.

Sylvie suddenly stood.

"I'm going to find Dalis," she declared, the words flying from her lips. "We need to meet the Grove's Arch Poten. This is Maurice's Institute, so they probably have something in their archives regarding the creation of *Orivellea* or old journals of some sort. We need to get permission to enter. We also need to ask if someone can ferry us to Thelarius' temple."

She strode past him towards the door.

His eyes lit up in alarm. Jack leapt from his position on the bed. He did his best to ignore the wave of nausea that assaulted him, as he seized her wrist. She turned sharply at the contact. His grip was tight enough to bruise. Realizing this, he tore his hand away, burned by the thought of accidentally hurting her.

Jack wobbled with the loss of purchase. Sylvie reached out, gripping him by the elbows to steady him.

"What's wrong?" she asked.

Jack didn't answer.

Instead, he glared at his hand, trying to will it to obey. But his self-control had long ago splintered into nothing. He found his fingers clenched around the hem of her robes, wanting her to stay, despite the prideful denial resting on the tip of his tongue, just waiting to be given voice.

They stood there for a long time, staring each other down. Both lost to the tension between them. Until finally, when the questioning look in her eyes became unbearable, when Jack had mastered himself enough to unlock his jaw and look away from her captivating gaze—the words spilled forth. Toxic and biting and entirely like him. In the hazy blaze of his own mind, however, he could only recall his lips forming the word, 'leave,' followed by a string of derisive *Íarre* expletives that left of their own volition.

He hated it.

Hated the way she shuddered, and how he felt it all throughout his body. Hated the way he could scarcely remember what even left his mouth. He especially hated the way she reeled back like a puppet yanked by its strings. For an instant, Sylvie's face fell. Her eyes closed just enough for her to crush away the immense, inexplicable disappointment, but then the instant was gone, disappearing like a flock of startled birds.

Sylvie lifted her chin, visibly upset with him, inadvertently showing him that she was no puppet. She was here. She was real. Defiant and unyielding.

Creator, he wanted to kiss her.

A part of him *really* hated that.

Jack stepped back, repeating his personal mantra of *'are you insane?'* in his mind in a sorry endeavor to bolster his self-control. This wasn't good. This couldn't happen because... because...

Why not? he suddenly wondered. *Why can't this happen?*

Jack grimaced, absolutely furious with his thoughts.

"Do you want to come with me," she paused, "or do you want me to stay here?"

His jaw clenched at his own transparency. He didn't want to answer that, but neither could he lie. Jack looked her straight in the eye and let his deadpan expression tell her instead.

"What do you think?"

"I think that we have a lot to do," Sylvie said with all of the patience that he didn't have. "And that I can get a lot more done on my own. You can barely stand, Jack."

"But I *can* stand."

Just as he said it, the door swung open, effectively knocking Sylvie straight into Jack's chest and sending them both to the ground in an ungainly mess of limbs. Jack's head hit the floor with a loud thud, but he didn't even have time to think about the pain welling there as Sylvie's weight dug into his ribs. Her joints pressed against all of the tender places that were still sore from the concoction of death currently rotting his insides.

"*Vak—*" the curse died once he covered his mouth with his free hand. He tried to keep the bile rising in his throat down with nothing but will and a prayer.

"What are you two doing?" a voice asked from above them. It was vaguely familiar.

Dalis, Jack's mind supplied. Sure enough, when he opened his eyes, Dalis and Conor were standing above them. They were accompanied by two practitioners that he didn't know.

"I didn't think you'd be awake," Dalis went on, unrepentant. He didn't even bother offering them a hand. "Let alone trying to get frisky with my sister."

"Dalis," the practitioner beside him called with the air of a long-suffering companion. "Leave them alone."

"Learn to knock," Sylvie said, cross. She dusted herself off, before pulling Jack up to stand beside her. He didn't want her help, and he would've told her so had his insides not felt like they were being wrung like a wet cloth. He was afraid that if he opened his mouth, something sour, disgusting, and *wet* would come tumbling out instead.

"I wouldn't count on it, Syl," the practitioner said, before turning to Jack. "The name's Philip, and this here's Lyss. He'll be escorting Conor back to Curran."

Lyss gave a curt nod in acknowledgement, before his eyes focused on Sylvie. He looked her up and down with his brows furrowed in thought. "This is Sylvie?" Lyss craned his neck to get a better look. "You've grown a lot. How long's it been? Sev—*no*, eight years? It's hard to believe you're related to Dalis."

"Back off, Lyss," Dalis warned.

He gave her a lopsided smile, before turning to inspect Jack instead. "Dace, right? I thought you'd be taller."

Jack bristled at his words. "I'm taller than you."

"But I'm bigger overall," Lyss countered. "You're whipcord thin, but a little *too* wispy if you ask me. Fighting Amorphs must be rough for you."

"At least I'm not a disproportioned *via ler*—"

"Anyway," Philip interrupted, already knowing where this was headed, "Dace... Jacques Dace. I've heard a lot about you."

"His parents, you mean." Dalis chortled.

"No," Philip stressed, "I heard about him from—"

He was cut off when Conor suddenly sprang forward and grabbed the cloth of one of Jack's pant legs. Unaware that his little fingers were, in fact, digging painfully into his thigh, Conor stared up at him with tears in his eyes. If it was from worry, Jack didn't know, but it made him uncomfortable. The silence in the room certainly didn't help.

He looks good, Jack noted distantly. *Healthy.*

Whoever had healed him had done a splendid job. He had no scratches or blossoming bruises, just flawless skin and big, round eyes that stared unwaveringly at him. It was strange to think that he'd been writhing in pain mere hours ago.

"What?" Jack asked as evenly as possible. He didn't know how to deal with kids. They were so fragile in comparison, and were awed by everything. Even someone as explosive as him.

Conor motioned him down with his free hand. He flapped his fingers in a cute way that Jack would've sneered at anyone bigger for doing. Jack dropped to his haunches, allowing Conor to put his lips by his ear.

"She said she was sorry."

Jack's blood ran cold.

"Cute kid," Dalis said, blissfully unaware. "I thought he only spoke to Syl though. Did you two place some kind of silencing enchantment on his tongue or is he just shy?"

"You just have an untrustworthy face," Philip said.

Jack ignored them, as he stood up on shaky legs. Absently, he noted Sylvie eyeing him. Her face was set to neutral. That lasted for all of a second, before she bent down so that she was level with Conor.

"Is everything okay?" Sylvie asked, then frowned when all she got was a silent nod in response. Without warning, a warm hand gripped her shoulder, and she shifted her gaze. "Jack?"

"Will you be alright?" Jack asked, ignoring her.

Conor gave them a reassuring smile, clutching his little hands in front of his chest, before moving to stand beside Lyss. He grabbed the practitioner's hand with a determined look on his face. "I—I'm ready to go home now."

Lyss looked between them for a moment, before shrugging his shoulders in a decidedly dispassionate manner. "Alright, kid. But remember we aren't coming back if you have something else you need to say."

"I don't," Conor croaked, averting his gaze. His hair was so long, it completely shrouded everything up to his chin.

"We'll be going then."

"Take care of him," Sylvie said.

"I got it," Lyss assured. "It was nice seeing you, Sylvie."

Lyss fanned his fingers out in a half-hearted wave. Beside him, Conor looked back one final time. His childish features morphed into something worn as the door shut behind them.

They stared on in silence, before...

"I despise being kept out of the loop," Dalis commented, watching the exchange with interest. "But I also hate sticking my fingers into pies that don't belong to me, so I'm going to imagine the kid said something grisly. Maybe something about those horrifying paintings he saw in the halls on the way here."

Philip groaned. "Creator, spare me."

"Before I forget," Dalis went on, reaching into his pockets to pull out three vials with a white, cloudy liquid inside. He held them out to Jack, who grimaced at the sight. It looked like soap. Jack bet it tasted like it too. "Don't give me that look. This is for your own good. Drink one every morning on an empty stomach and you'll be as right as rain in no time."

Jack took them with a bereaved sigh.

"Thanks," he muttered, despite himself.

"While you two are here," Sylvie began, saving them from lulling into another tense spell of silence. There were secrets between each of them that neither wanted to share. Questions, too, and answers. Ones that no one wanted to give for fear of exposing something they believed only they knew. "I was hoping you could lead me to your Arch Poten. A Poten would do, too, if he isn't available. I have a little request."

"The Potens aren't people you'd like to meet," Dalis said. "They're an aggravating bunch. While I don't think they'll eat you alive, they'll definitely make you want to do it yourself just to escape them. Besides, power is shifting soon. Can't whatever request you have wait until the representatives take charge? At least you'll get an audience without a dozen side-eyes."

"More leeway, too," Philip added.

"I only need permission to enter the archives," she insisted.

"You don't need permission for that," Dalis said. "They're right down the hall."

"Not the public shelves. I need to see the restricted sections."

"I didn't think the day would come when you, of all people, would ask to go see something like that. Did you turn into some weird enthusiast while I had my back turned?"

"I'm being serious, Dalis. This is important."

"I get that. I'm just surprised is all. What else do you want to do? Apply for Peose contracts? Travel the corners of Ferus Terria? Have you considered joining the Vanguard Circle?"

Sylvie shot him a scathing glance that he only grinned at.

"I really am surprised though," Dalis defended. "Stunned. Flabbergasted. Maybe even a little suspicious. You've never been interested in much outside of your own bubble. I bet whatever you're involved in is big too. Your last letter didn't say much, so I'm assuming you found yourself a good influence since then?"

Jack raised his hand. "I'll take full credit for this one."

"I should've known. Hopefully that fire you managed to light under her doesn't get her into too much trouble. I'd have to play the big brother card then, and I really hate doing that. You two seem close. I don't want to be the one to separate you."

"It's a little too late for that."

Dalis raised an eyebrow. "You've got balls to say that to my face, I'll give you that. But I'll play along. Just what do you mean by *too late* exactly? If you try anyth—"

"Could you two focus?" Sylvie intervened. "I said I needed to go to the restricted sections. Don't just ignore what I have to say because you want to run your mouth."

"You're as square as ever," Dalis said. "Why do you need to go there anyway?"

"We're trying to learn more about the *Orivellea.* They're produced here, aren't they?"

Philip and Dalis shared a glance.

"They are," Philip said, wary. "What do you want to know?"

"Who oversees their production," Jack interjected, "and where they're being produced."

"I think you best keep those inquiries to yourselves for now," Philip advised. "It may not look it, but the Grove is in a state of unrest, made even worse with your flashy arrival. It also doesn't help that almost immediately after sending word to the Grove that the Potens would be replaced, the Alps officially closed their gates until a new Grand Elder has been appointed. The Potens have been lashing out, and the people here feel abandoned. Most want to speed things along with force, while others—the wide circle of elites within the colleges that have benefited from the Potens reign—are doing all they can to prevent that."

Dalis nodded grimly. "It's not just the elites though. There are still a lot of ingratiating practitioners out there looking to curry favor with the Potens because they don't actually believe they'll be overthrown. Things are a mess right now. One wrong move and things could go south, Syl. Having an Arch Poten hounding our annals isn't what we need."

"Shouldn't you be focused on getting to the north as soon as possible?" Philip asked. "I know Arch Poten Cole is preparing to make his trip soon. An Elder even arrived to escort him, and I heard from my Master that Arch Poten Verne has already sent word of her arrival. You're the only one left."

"The Summit isn't my number one priority," Sylvie said, undeterred by their reasons. They were good ones, to be sure, and all valid in their own right, but they had other things to do, different places to go. Rushing past those points wasn't an option. "I need to learn more about the *Orivellea* first, then find someone to ferry us to Thelarius' temple. You mentioned an Elder? Could you introduce me? I need them to make a request to the temple to have one of their priests carry us across the Jade Sea. The sooner, the better."

"Why all the detours, Syl?" Dalis asked. "What's going on?"

"Things I can't explain right now."

"Well, you better start because that flimsy excuse isn't good enough for me—for any of us. The Grove needs the Summit to officially begin. That can't happen when you're off sightseeing."

"I can tell you about the crystals," Philip interrupted, glaring at Dalis in a not so subtle manner. "The Potens supervise their production, but the college representatives and a collection of their highest-ranking practitioners know about it as well. As for where they're being produced, there's an open space directly underneath the Grove, past the quarry of dead slaves called the Anvil. It's a restricted area, where few are allowed. Those that are don't visit often."

"Syl," Jack said, urgency lacing his tone. The Anvil sounded suspiciously like the Pit. Jack didn't even want to think about who was forced to work down there or where they got their... ingredients.

"I know," she whispered, then in a louder voice asked, "do the few that have access know how they're made?"

There was an age of silence, where Dalis and Philip looked at them like they'd each sprouted two extra heads, and then screamed murder at the change.

"How..." Dalis trailed off. His tongue darted out to wet his lips. "How much do you know?"

"How much do *you* know?" Jack shot back.

"That answers that. Let me rephrase, *how* do you know?"

"How do *you* know?"

"Stop repeating everything I'm—"

"We found out in the Pit," Sylvie revealed, ignoring Jack's heated glare. "They had an entire lake there. We destroyed it."

"That was you?" Dalis sputtered. He looked between them. "And wait, wait, wait... they were making Orive crystals there? Really? Who was leading them? A deserter?"

"A Nebbin."

"But how did a Nebbin find out about—"

"Does it matter?" Jack asked. "If they're being made here, then you guys are just as bad. You do know that they use live— *filahn vahs!*" Jack cursed when Sylvie's elbow slammed into his ribs. He rubbed the aching spot, as she retracted without a word. "What's *wrong* with you, woman? You *know* I'm still recovering!" he hissed. "*Vina sara lerna ceravesan!*"

"What did you ju—" Sylvie cut herself off with a quick shake of her head, not wanting to get into a petty argument with him. Not now. Not when they had more important things to discuss.

She gave him a look that he knew all too well. He was in trouble. *Him.* That just made his temper flare.

"You *elbowed* me in the ribs!" He snarled, though the way her face shifted into a mix of irritation and repentance made him feel slightly better.

"Because you're too *loud*, Jack," Sylvie chided. "What do you think you were about to yell? For all we know, someone could be out there listening."

Jack clicked his tongue.

"Flaming insufferable," he muttered under his breath, then in a louder, more controlled voice, said, "I'm assuming you two know how the crystals are made?"

"We aren't happy about it either," Philip defended. "Ending their production has been brought up countless times over the last age. But it's hard to garner support for something most people don't even know about. What do you think would happen if the Grove's leaders made this issue public? Chaos... of biblical proportions. Personally, I never even understood the purpose of their creation in the first place. For Peose, okay, that may be good enough. Animal companions were necessary during Thelarius' time when most practitioners were still split between his beliefs and the lingering traditions of the Mentalists, but making crystals for Elementalists? Why do they even need such an intense power boost? They're considered the most powerful type of practitioner even without the implant. On top of that, many die from the procedure as infants. If you look through older records from the second half of the Oak Age, you'll find that some scholars have actually suspected that it causes impotence. Chances of death *and* infertility. What's the point?"

"I thought it was used to channel their magic," Dalis said. "That much power in one body? There's no way only one magic circuit could handle all of that for longer than a minute."

"So, you don't know?" Sylvie asked, keeping her voice as flat as possible.

"Know what?" they asked simultaneously.

Jack and Sylvie shared a glance.

"You want our support, don't you?" Dalis asked. "If you keep us in the dark, then—"

"We want your help," Jack interrupted. "Whether or not you support us doesn't matter."

"Well, if you want our *help*, then you're going to need to tell us exactly what's going on because right now, I see no reason to bring either of you anywhere near the Elder, let alone the Anvil. In fact, I have half a mind to drag you two to the Alps myself to get this damned Summit over with."

Jack saw the reluctance in Sylvie's eyes, but not a moment later and she was already closing them with a sigh, hiding them from his attentive view. She nodded once to him in a way that told him her decision, before sliding the bolt in place on the door. Her eyes roamed every corner of the room with so much caution that Jack could practically feel the heightening tension between Philip and Dalis. Jack grabbed the sleeve of her robe and tugged her back to his side, in part to get her to stand still and in part to anchor himself to something as steady and stubborn as her.

He didn't need to ask about the stone. Not when he could see it glowing beneath her robes.

"Do you have his journal?" Jack whispered.

Sylvie reached into her robes to hold up another Heartstone attached to a thick chain around her neck. Less bright, this one. Not translucent either. There was a number engraved on the side that was mostly covered by her fingers, but he could see the dual curves of an eight on it. Jack squinted and saw Silas' journal inside—it was a tiny thing. There was a pack, too, though it wasn't one he recognized. Had she gotten a few emergency supplies while he was sleeping? She should've put their everyday bags in too, but he supposed she only wanted to open that particular stone when it was absolutely necessary.

"Are you sure?" he asked, before blatantly tilting his head at their curious audience.

"Yes," she answered.

There wasn't a speck of hesitation in her voice. Jack exhaled noisily at her coolness. He wasn't feeling so nauseous now. Only the unexplainably vivacious rush of spilling secrets he knew he shouldn't be was left.

"So," he began, turning to face the pair, "how do you want me to start this, Syl?"

Dalis was the one to answer. "From the beginning."

The Healer's words went ignored, however. Jack continued to stare at him as if he didn't exist.

"Just the facts," Sylvie said eventually. Her grip on the Heartstone tightened. "They don't need to know everything."

"Facts… okay. So, number one, I don't lie." Jack raised his finger as he said it. "And two, we aren't insane."

***

"Wait, let me get this straight," Dalis said for possibly the hundredth time in the past hour.

Jack groaned. "Oh, for the love of Sil—"

"Don't you dare bring my ancestor into this," he said sharply. "I'm just trying to make sure I have everything right."

"Can't you do that later? We're wasting time."

"You shouldn't even be up, so as far as I'm concerned you're opinion regarding anyone's time is moot."

"You can heal me, can't you? Use that sweet magic of yours to balance me out. Just for a little while."

"So you can do what exactly? Run around and put everyone else on edge too?"

"Of course not," Sylvie intervened, making everyone turn to her. She had settled on Jack's unoccupied bed as they delved deeper into their story. "Like I said, we just want to poke around the archives and see the Anvil for ourselves. Interfering with your problems isn't on our agenda. We don't want to get caught in the middle of whatever internal conflict the Grove is having."

"Especially not one that looks like it could turn into a full-on bloodbath," Jack added. "If those that don't know about what lies beneath the Institute were to find out, then we'd never be able to leave. We just want our information and that's it."

"Exactly," Sylvie agreed. "Now, you said you'd help us if we told you, and we did. I'd like to meet that Elder now." Sylvie paused to look pointedly at them. There was no bargaining in her eyes. She was an Arch Poten now. Nothing less. "And," she added, before they could speak, "if either of you have access to the Anvil, then I think it would be best if you took Jack with you, so he can take a look at what's happening."

"You're settling into that Arch Poten position just fine, aren't you?" Dalis grimaced. "Alright, Syl. You win. I'll take you to the Elder."

"I'll escort Jack to the Anvil," Philip volunteered.

Dalis looked at them suspiciously. "Promise me you two won't do anything stupid."

"I don't know about your partner, but it's not like I go out of my way to find storms of shit to jump into." Jack ran a hand through his hair in aggravation. "Trouble has a tendency of following me, but *sure*, if it'll make you feel better. I'll try."

"Tiv talks back a lot, but nowhere near as much as you," Dalis remarked. "Not even three hours in your company and I can already see that you have a habit of using that tongue of yours to spit venom. One day, I might just cut it out."

"Dalis!" Philip yelled.

Whatever comeback Jack had died an early death as soon as his words registered. "Did you just say Tiv?" He swallowed. "Do you mean, Tiv Grovegg?"

"He's your partner, isn't he?" Dalis asked, though he already knew the answer.

"He's here? *Actually* here? I wasn't hallucinating?"

"Do you want to see him?"

"Of course I do!" Jack shouted. "I haven't seen him since the Tower fell. He's—"

"Missing a few pieces," Dalis interrupted with an ambiguous shrug. "Don't do anything stupid in the Anvil, and we'll take you to him after."

Jack's jaw locked, not wanting to reveal his true intentions. Because he knew for a fact that he was going to *destroy* the place. The Anvil would be little more than ashes and rubble once he was through with it.

"Oh, you have an excellent glower!" Dalis went on. "Very forceful. It's a lot darker than most. Absolutely delicious, if I do say so myself. No wonder Sylvie likes you."

"Dalis!" Sylvie shrieked.

"I'm joking, Syl." Dalis raised his hand, palm up, beckoning Jack towards him. "Come on, I need to fix you up a bit."

Jack stepped forward, briefly glancing at Dalis' hands as they settled over his shoulders. Dalis squeezed his shoulders once, his fingers glowing blue, before his magic washed over him like a soothing stream of fresh water after a long day. The effect was immediate. Jack's stomach settled and his muscles loosened, but before he could thank him, shouts erupted from outside the door. The four of them turned toward the sound. It was just loud enough to penetrate the walls, but distant enough that they couldn't make out any of the words. They heard the jeers though, and the echoes of magic released into the air. Judging from the rapid burst of sound, it was... fire? Wind? Maybe wind.

"What's going on?" Sylvie asked.

"Members of the Lafertti Clan are probably picking another fight," Philip answered.

"With who?"

"Poten supporters? Scholars? Some poor practitioner that looked at them the wrong way? Does it really matter? We should go, before they *really* get into it. They're a rowdy bunch. Noise follows them like a shadow."

"I'm all for leaving," Jack said

"I'm sure you are."

Jack ignored him and focused instead on rolling his neck and shoulders as soon as Dalis stepped away. He flexed his fingers, then shook his legs out to work out the kinks. He felt amazing. No protesting joints or heavy limbs. He felt sprightlier than he had in a long time. Dalis was a sensational Healer. There was no doubt about it.

"Good god, I feel *alive*," Jack said. "Thanks."

"He can show gratitude!" Dalis teased. He smiled widely at him, before rummaging inside his pack to throw him a faded blue shirt with loose threads all along the hem. It had obviously seen better days, but Jack wasn't about to complain. "You're welcome, and don't worry, you'll be in good hands down there. I trust Philip with my life."

"I would hope so," Philip remarked.

Jack slipped the shirt over his head. It was larger than he would've liked, the neckline hanging loose and exposing too much of his collar, but the overall fit down his torso was well enough that it didn't dwarf his frame. The cloth could definitely use a dip in boiling water for a few minutes. He'd have to remember to do so before he returned it to Dalis.

When he noticed Sylvie step closer, her arms suddenly rising up and over his head, Jack bent lower out of instinct, allowing her better access. Before she could even take a step back, he felt the cool weight of the Heartstone against his chest. He saw its blinding glow, and he knew, without a sliver of doubt, that the soft whisper of protest in his ear wasn't just his imagination. He was more than happy to give it a louder voice.

"Why are you giving this to me?" Jack asked straightaway.

"You're going to the Anvil."

"And you'll be out there with those loons," he argued. "You need this more than I do, Syl."

"*She*'ll keep you safe."

"*She*'ll kill me without you there."

"Don't assume things, Jack. It's not a good habit."

"I'm not assuming anything."

"Then where's your proof? *She* hasn't tried anything even remotely harmful since we left the Tower."

"That's because *she* actually likes you." He rolled his eyes. "I can't even begin to imagine why."

"Blood and ashes, Jack. Must you always be so difficult?"

"I'll be fine down there."

"Just take it."

"Look, if I get choked, then it'll be on you. Do you want that kind of stain on your conscience?" He paused. "And if something happens to you, then—"

"That's on me too." Sylvie sighed. "I get it, okay?"

"No, that's not it," he said sharply. "I was going to say that if something happens to you, then you better start screaming for me, pride be damned, but if you want to take the blame..."

"Who's the one with the inflated sense of pride between us?"

"Inflated?" Jack repeated, affronted. "If my pride's inflated, then it's for good reason. You do realize that I've saved you just as many times, no, probably even more than you have me, right?"

She sighed, exasperated. "Just go already."

"Gladly," he said, grasping the stone. "As soon as you take this. I said it once, and I'll say it a thousand more times if I have to, you need this more than I do."

"I don't—"

"If something happens, I," Jack bit his tongue. *Speak,* he urged himself. "I can't do this without you, Syl. Don't make me."

Her eyes widened.

"Cute," Dalis said dryly. He had no qualms about physically butting into their conversation by stepping between them. Dalis nudged Sylvie toward the door with an annoyed grunt.

"Stop pushing me," Sylvie complained.

"We're going, Syl. The way he's looking at you is making me queasy."

"*Filan vahs,* we aren't done yet!" Jack protested, but his voice was drowned by the clatter of practitioners in the distance as Dalis swung open the door and pushed Sylvie outside all in one smooth motion. "Sirx, wait! She really needs to take this back!"

"We'll see you in a bit!" Dalis waved jovially in farewell. "Take care of him, Philip."

Jack made a move to chase after them as soon as the door slammed shut, but Philip yanked him back by the elbow.

"Not so fast," Philip said. "We have our own schedule to keep, so let's stick to it."

"Syl's—"

"Have a little faith, Dace. There's no safer place for her to be than with Dalis. He broke the laws of the Institute to find her. She's family."

That got to him. Jack stilled, and even though he didn't miss Philip's triumphant grin, he wasn't *too* bothered by it.

"It's just," Jack paused, struggling to find the words, "it's been a while since we've been separated. I end up getting a little insane when she's not in my sights."

"A little?"

Jack glared.

"The two of you are in good hands," Philip assured. "Now, let's head down to the Anvil, before the fighting outside eases and our perfect distraction disappears."

There was no objection this time.

15

In the end, Tiv was once again dragged into another mess because of this fatal flaw: he hated waiting.

Tiv counted himself among the unlucky few that always happened to be at the wrong place at the wrong time. When Dwyn questioned him before all of this began, he regretted not just leaving him and his little ragtag group to their own devices.

"Why are you following us?" Dwyn had asked. "Shouldn't you be, oh, I don't know, waiting for your partner to wake up?"

"They said he'd be out for another day." Tiv shrugged, grateful when neither Myrrh, nor Ethil commented on Jack's condition... or his own for that matter. Missing so many fingers wasn't so common that it could just be brushed aside after all. "I hate sitting around doing nothing."

He didn't bother saying that he was also scared to be left alone. Dalis was with Sylvie, Cera was with Rhone, Philip was off getting the rest of his fellow Red Scripts' in line, and Jack... that idiot was passed out in bed. His partner was as pale as he'd always been. The sort of gray pallor that was uncommon in the Grove. But to Tiv, he looked unbelievably healthy. In fact, if it wasn't for the way he sweated enough to soak the sheets, then Tiv wouldn't have believed there was anything wrong with him in the first place. He didn't know when it happened, but Jack had evidently begun having night terrors. He spoke incoherently in his sleep, threw his head left and right in a frantic manner, even his legs would twist and jerk, as if he was trying to escape something in his dreams. Tiv knew the feeling.

He'd never had a problem with solitude before. Recently, however, Tiv would remember things. Wicked smiles that made shivers run down his spine; shameful moments where he wept; cold, metal-plated fingers that grasped at his hair and clawed at his skin, bruising it, leaving trails of red that stung long into the night. There were days when he'd purposely scrape his back against the raw stone or struggle against his bindings until his wrists chaffed in an effort to stay awake because he feared that if he slept, then he might miss his rescuer's cries.

That was a hope that died quickly in those dungeons. Yet it was still one he found himself fantasizing about often late at night when the rain would come to wash over him.

Tiv never wanted to feel that way again.

So, for the second time that day, Tiv found himself in the Slates. Though this time, he wasn't walking alone, and he knew from the sketchy entrance Dwyn had led him through, that they weren't allowed anywhere near the area.

The opening was a tiny thing, smaller than even his fist. A literal rat hole with an enchanted doorway that guaranteed secrecy. It was hidden inside one of the many common rooms within the Grove, behind a dark wooden dresser that looked as if it hadn't been polished in a century. Metal plates were attached to the legs, while thick, rusted nails kept the fixture bolted to the floor. Above it, sat a colorful cornucopia overflowing with fresh fruits and dried flowers.

Tiv had his doubts, but both Dwyn and Myrrh had assured him that it was safe and that Hunters used it often to meet with each other in secret. Their profession made them liars by nature, so he didn't really put much worth into their words. But since the only other option was waiting outside and keeping an eye out for any curious onlookers with Myrrh and Ethil, he was more than happy to follow Dwyn. There was no way he was going to stand there and suffer through their unvoiced questions.

So, here they were.

Two mice, scurrying inside the vast network of tunnels that

ran in-between each of the prisoner's cells. Veins of raw magic ran along the top of the passageways, providing a faint glow that illuminated the way forward. They were meticulously carved to fit the tunnels, so Tiv knew that these couldn't be the same veins that supplied the orbs of light all across the Grove. Which meant someone else's magic ran through them, and should that flow suddenly cease, then they'd be left to wander in the dark.

Who's supplying it? Tiv wondered. *And from where?*

Tiv took note of each dead-end they passed. Every one of them should've opened up into a cell within the Slates, but instead, they were blocked by several inches of solid wood with exploding enchantments set around them, in case someone found it and tried to force their way through.

They were all the same. All, save for one.

Tiv saw a faint light at the end of a slim tunnel. It was half-blocked by another rat, whose tiny head snapped sharply in their direction.

"Mox," Dwyn said in that deep voice of his.

"Dwyn!" Mox moseyed forward, meeting them halfway. His voice was squeaky and strangely fit for his form. "I heard from the others, but I didn't think you actually came."

"Elder Dace sent me." Dwyn swiped his paw in Tiv's direction. "This is Tiv Grovegg."

"Does he work for Elder Dace, too? Or is he a Hunter?"

"Neither."

Mox's tiny head tilted to the side. His snout twitched at the revelation. "Then why is he down here? This place is only for—"

"He's a friend," Dwyn interrupted, effectively silencing him.

Tiv didn't know anything about the inner hierarchy within the Vanguard Circle, but Dwyn definitely outranked him. He found evidence in the way Mox submitted so easily to his words, his head slightly bowed in his presence. Mox's tiny claws clicked against each other, exposing a nervous tick. Tiv didn't know that there were Hunters like this, too. Or was this just an act to get him to lower his guard? It was likely.

"How is he?" Dwyn asked, peeking at the hole behind him.

"He doesn't look worse," Mox said carefully. "That said, he doesn't look better either. He's been drinking more. If it's because he's on edge or just bored, I can't say for certain. He won't talk to me. Says he'll only talk to someone under Elder Dace."

"That's what I'm here for," Dwyn declared, before dashing forward on all fours.

The pair watched him go, struck by his quick departure, before gathering their wits and following after him. Once they reached the end of the tunnel, Dwyn motioned for them to stay put, as he walked outside on his tiny hind legs. How he was able to maintain his balance was a mystery that Tiv wanted to unravel, but his thoughts left him as soon as Dwyn spoke.

"Master Pavlov," Dwyn greeted.

Tiv gaped at the name, sneaking his tiny head outside of the hole to get a better look at the man. He was actually awake this time. His eyes were small and the color of wheat. Their orange hue had dulled with the years. His beard, on the other hand, was full and coarse, covering thick lips. Though he still donned the same ratty robes, now that Tiv got a closer look, he realized that the man was strangely clean. No, not just clean. Leinus Pavlov was practically sterile. Unheard of for a prisoner. Even more so for one located down here. Tiv had gotten a glimpse of most of them, and he doubted that they were given enough water to bathe. But seeing as how there was an open Hunter's hole connected to Leinus' cell, Tiv could only think of one explanation.

Special privileges, Tiv concluded. *So, it's not the Lafertti Clan helping him, but the Vanguard Circle? Why would they do that?*

"You one of Leonas' men?" he asked.

Even from his position, Tiv could smell the tart scent of alcohol. It seeped into Leinus' pores, and he embodied it happily.

"I apologize for the delay," Dwyn said after a moment.

"Delay?" Leinus laughed. Cold and unfeeling. "Don't apologize for something as unreasonable as time. It's not as if I count the hours. What matters is that you came. Leonas has left me here for so long that I was beginning to think that he'd forgotten about me."

"Unlike some, Elder Dace would never forget about one of his own," Dwyn said sharply.

"Is that a jab at me?" Leinus bared his teeth in a wicked smile. "I have my faults, but don't forget that Leonas strived for years under my leadership, before he eventually contended for my position. He's the product of my methods and far more rotten than you could ever imagine." He spread his arms, showing off the depravity around him. "Even here, you can see what a slave driver that man is. I'm old. Too old. Surely, there are younger, sprightlier sleeper agents he could send. The kind that can actually roam the Grove's halls."

"None with such thick ties to the Lafertti Clan."

"I'm sure Leonas can find a few if he looks hard enough. He's disgustingly resourceful like that." Leinus grimaced, before leaning forward. The sleeve of his robe obscured the hole Dwyn had come from, and Tiv's vision along with it. "So," he began, dropping his voice an octave, "what exactly does Leonas want to know?"

"Everything."

"Of course. While I'm always glad to make his life more difficult, even I'm infuriated with the sluggish pace around here. My former college mates aren't exactly known for their patience, so I'm stunned that nothing more has happened."

"What do you mean?"

"Don't you get it, boy? I'm saying that I have nothing to report. The Institute is running, the forest is striving, and water is wet. Nothing's changed."

"Bullshit," Dwyn spat. "I've barely been here a week, and I can already see that the Lafertti Clan is putting the entire Grove on edge. Not just that either. They've been pressuring the Alps for months. *Months.* Elder Dace even suspects them of plotting the murder of not only the Grove's Potentate Union, but also some of the Elders on the Zenith Council."

"And you think that's new?" Leinus asked harshly. "You're young, indeed. Some ideas are a prison, and the Lafertti Clan is full of them. Their current masters are driven by the belief that freedom isn't given, it's won. While there is truth in their words, it's also not the type of notion likely to be followed by the majority. It reeks of revolution and blood."

"Yet they're following them now."

"Only listening." Leinus corrected. "The practitioners are getting impatient, but that's only to be expected. The Alps was wrong to announce their decision to abolish the Potentate Union so quickly. They should've waited until after the Summit, so that change could be immediately implemented. Now, they've stirred doubt and fear in the hearts of the practitioners here."

"Perhaps," Dwyn said, low and careful, "that was the point."

"Oh? It seems you might have more information to give me than I do you."

"Nothing that concerns a prisoner like yourself."

Leinus' eyes narrowed in disdain. "I could say the same to you, boy. We don't need any Vanguard Circle lackeys here. The representatives are smart. They'll leash their men until the Summit is over or until the Lafertti Clan makes a move. Whichever comes first."

"Why do I get the feeling that the latter is more likely?"

"Because it's no surprise that the Lafertti Clan wants more power. They've been pushing for this the hardest. But entitlement is a dangerous thing. It makes fools of men. Give it another week, and I'm sure you'll hear something about Master Zacarias wanting to take Arch Poten Cole's title right from under his nose. Now," Leinus sighed and leaned back, "if that's all, then I'd appreciate it if you left me be. I don't get paid to tolerate the Circle's pawns anymore."

"Wait!" Tiv interrupted. The pair turned at the sound of his voice, and he immediately crawled out of the tunnel so that they could get a better look. He knew Dwyn was warning him with his eyes to step back inside, but Tiv focused solely on the aged master before him. "I have a question."

"And you are?" Leinus raised an eyebrow.

"That's not important," Tiv dismissed. "I want to know why the Lafertti Clan hired men to capture practitioners from the Tower."

"What?" Dywn asked.

"I was carted away from the Tower's shores by a group of slavers," Tiv explained. "Before we got rid of them, they mentioned the Lafertti Clan. I was eventually taken by a different group, but I do remember them mentioning that they wanted practitioners."

Dwyn turned to Leinus with a heated glare. "Why would they do something like that?"

"I'm truly starting to question Leonas' sanity." Leinus sighed again. Infinitely more stressed than before. "Perhaps the job is getting to him. This is what happens when you send ignorant children that know nothing about the Grove's inner workings."

Dwyn growled. It was followed by an inarticulate string of his own frustration. "Then help me understand."

"The Potens did it," Leinus revealed, already tired of this conversation. "The Lafertti Clan is the Grove's oldest college. They've been around since it was first established, and will be for long after it has withered away in this ancient forest. They have a hand in every underground operation on this side of Ferus Terria, including the agreement with the Alps regarding the production of *Orivellea*."

"What do Orive crystals have to do with this?"

"Are you se—" Leinus cut himself off with a laugh, "—your uppers have kept you in the dark, I see. Understandable, considering. Visit the Anvil and you'll see that Orive crystals have *everything* to do with this. They're cages for a heinous being, furious from ages of captivity. Do you think imprisoning a god can be done without sacrifices?"

Just as the words left his mouth, a loud crash erupted from above them. It shook the ceiling, showering them in clouds of dust and ash. Stray pieces of chipped wood fell, just large enough to hurt Dwyn and Tiv's tiny forms. While all around them, prisoners looked up. They tried their hardest to poke their heads out of the small gaps between the bars of their cells, but the guards were quick to pounce on them. Some screamed and poked their weapons menacingly at their faces to get them to reel back, others quietly stated their commands in a manner so threatening that the prisoners obeyed without question.

Before they could recover from the sudden noise, there was another crash on the ceiling. Far louder than the last. It was followed by another, then another, until finally, a circular chunk of twenty-inch thick wood fell directly in the middle of the Slates' hallway, crushing one of the guards and cracking the wooden floors. A deluge of fire flew in right after it, effectively forcing everyone to retreat as deep as possible into their cells or, in the guards' cases, deeper into the Slates. The crushed man screamed in agony at the unyielding blaze, stopping just before it finally relented.

Both guard and prisoner alike gasped at the sight of the torched man. None quite able to muster the proper words. The shaft of light made it hard to see at first, but as soon as their eyes adjusted, they all did their best to look up at the hole above them, where a flood of enraged voices were currently bursting forth. The practitioners above were clearly fighting, and judging from the insults being thrown around, it wasn't over anything simple either. A number of them yelled about a missing man, while the rest tried to calm them down.

They failed spectacularly.

It wasn't long before their fury was misdirected. Blue glows filled the air, causing pulses of light to flash into the Slates below. The engraved enchantments along each cell glowed with every burst, prepared to explode and kill their captives should the surrounding magic become too intense. Tiv wasn't about to let himself die here. He slowly inched toward the hole in the wall, fully prepared to make a run for it as soon as the situation took a turn for the worse because judging by the intensity of their shouts, it wouldn't be improving anytime soon.

Only a scant few seemed to actually care about the damage they were causing in the first place. Tiv looked up to find two practitioners peering down the hole, disbelief on both of their faces. But then they yelped, moving away just as spears of ice rained down and a frozen pillar filled the gap from floor to ceiling. The voices were promptly muffled by the makeshift cover, though it didn't mask them completely. They couldn't make out what they were saying. The stark anger in their shouts, however, were as clear as day.

"What has them in a state now?" Dwyn commented, ignoring the chaos around them as half of the guards ran topside, while the rest tried to calm the excited prisoners. "I thought you said that the colleges were only listening. It sounds to me like their engaging in full-on brawls now. Whoever blew that hole is going to be spending a lot of time with you down here."

"The others know better than to humor the Lafertti Clan," Leinus said, examining the spire of ice like it could give him a reason for this madness. "And despite their prestige, the Lafertti Clan's practitioners know that they can't do anything without the proper support. Their smarter than that. I doubt that fight started between two colleges."

"Are you trying to tell me that there are—"

"Intruders? It's likely... You!" Leinus suddenly roared, turning to the tiny tunnel. He ignored the dozens of eyes that swiftly turned at the sound of his voice. The prisoners pressed themselves up against their cages once more, hollering at him in more languages than he could count, while the guards shot him their nastiest look to date. Their expressions were sour enough to curdle milk. "The little one that's always guarding that godforsaken rat hole," Leinus went on. "Has there been talk of any newcomers recently? A wave of new practitioners from another Institute, perhaps?"

Mox tentatively crawled out of his hole. He stood with his

head bowed and his tail curled in an arch before his legs. "Only the rescued slaves, sir. My partner is the one in charge of overseeing who leaves and enters the Mending Willow."

"Useless." Leinus sneered, before directing his gaze back to Dwyn. "I assume they were hired to support the Lafertti Clan. Instigate chaos, then involve the other colleges. Not a bad plan."

"That doesn't make any sense," Dwyn argued. "How can there be intruders in the Institute? Wouldn't they have noticed?"

"You've always lived in an open Institute—one with intense security thanks to the Vanguard Circle. Institutes like the Grove and the Tower are different. More isolated. Perhaps it's because of that you believe we would know everyone inside, but you're wrong. For one reason or another, it's the isolated ones that house the greatest number of practitioners. We get the highest number of transfers, both in and out. Couple that with relatively lax security and it's easy to see how they could sneak a few intruders in. The Grove is large enough that you can't possibly know everyone, but small enough that the faces in your own college become familiar. Perhaps the Lafertti Clan hired deserters with ancient grudges. I wouldn't put it past them. There are quite a bit roaming Ferus Terria, so I doubt they're in short supply. But they'd need to be older deserters. Experienced ones. Those who've had their names listed on the official handout for years and whose appearances have changed drastically." Leinus rubbed his forehead in thought. "Or maybe they're mercenaries. Maybe even slavers. I heard two of the Fetter's leaders were taken down recently. Perhaps the third is lashing out."

"If that's true, then that's... unfortunate for us."

Tiv nodded. "There's only one way to stop mercenaries: cut off the cash flow. But how do we even go about doing that?"

"That's assuming they're mercenaries," Dwyn said, "and that they're being paid with coin. There are some things worth far more than a fat sack of gold. For all we know, they could be a different organization entirely. Elder Dace is in charge of getting rid of quite a bit of them, and I can't think of any that have a great deal of love for the Institute."

"I would hurry if I were you," Leinus butted in. He squinted up at the pillar of ice. It shook once, twice, then a third time, as something—or *someone*—was repeatedly banged against the ceiling. "Numbers are a terrifying thing. When enough men in the same clothes think they're right, the world becomes a dangerous place. Those that have hidden their insecurities will rise up alongside those revolting and take part in whatever bloodbath will follow."

"We aren't done yet," Dwyn said vehemently.

"Oh, I think we are." Leinus glared. "Go on now. If you want answers, then this is the perfect opportunity for you and your friend here to slip into the Anvil. It's only when you find out the whole story that you can think of a plausible solution."

"You'd rather we waste our time searching the floors below than intervene and save lives up there?

"Spare me your fake moral high-ground speech. Corrections specializes in two things: information and torture. If Leonas sent you here, he wants to know exactly what our practitioners are doing. Not just the run-of-the-mill activities either. I guarantee you that everything Leonas wants to know about the Grove can be found in the Anvil. Guard rotations shift, but the main entrance is usually guarded by one of the higher ranking members of the Lafertti Clan. Show them this," he rummaged inside of his pockets, removing scraps of paper, lint, and... corks, until he found a garnet pin. Leinus blew on it, then wiped it on his shoulder. "These are given only to representatives of the Lafertti Clan. Flash this, and they'll let you pass."

"It would be easier if you just told us what we needed to know," Tiv said, holding his tiny claws out to take the jewel. He held it to his chest, careful not to scratch its polished surface.

"Some things are only believed when seen," Leinus said wisely, before shooing them away with a wave of his hand. "Run along now, and when you return, bring a gift. Preferably Potem Pramm's head." He drew a zigzag across his eyes. "I never did get to sew that mouth of hers shut. I'd like to finish the job."

Tiv recoiled at the revelation.

"You're vile." Dwyn sneered, before nudging Tiv back in the direction of the rat hole. "Let's go. I can't stand the smell of this place any longer."

Tiv opened his mouth to comment, only for an undignified squeak to escape instead, as an unexpected squall blew them harshly back into the hole with unrelenting force. Tiv flew two meters, before he collided with Mox, who cushioned his fall. Dwyn, however, wasn't so lucky. He went on for another meter, until he slapped into a curved wall that led away from Leinus' cell and back into the upper sections of the Grove. Dwyn bounced twice on the ground, pathetically moving his tiny legs in circular motions, as he tried his hardest not to lose control of his form.

"*Filan vahs!*" Dwyn rolled back and forth on his back. From the looks of it, he couldn't get up. "I didn't know he could use his magic. What in Silas' holy flames are those manacles for then? Decoration? Oh, for Snuff's sake, I think that *glari na vidaris* cracked one of my ribs!"

Tiv could understand some *Íarre*, but nothing that deep. That was no average slur, and judging by how venomously he spat the words, Tiv didn't even want to know how insulting it was. He rushed over, carefully setting aside the garnet pin, before helping him roll onto his feet. Dwyn wobbled, before leaning against the wall with an exhausted huff.

"Creator, he really did crack a rib," Dwyn said, trying to reach around his furry torso to feel his backside. "Breathing *hurts*. I need to get this healed."

"Are you sure you aren't just being dramatic? You're slouching. I think your back is the problem."

"You think he fractured my spine?" Dwyn panicked.

"No, calm down."

"How do you expect me to calm down when I'm basically a crippled rat?"

"You're not a—"

"You're not the one who's injured!"

"Relax." Tiv strolled closer.

"Shut up!"

"Breathe," Tiv ordered, before he slapped his lower back with enough force to send Dwyn flying onto his stomach.

"You little *filan vanaresen!*" he swore, though the squeak that followed made it sound considerably less threatening. "Thelarius help you because I'm going to make a stew out of your—" Dwyn fell silent when he realized that he was able to stand on his own. He stretched his tiny limbs in all directions, then jumped as high as he could in the cramped tunnel. "—I'm cured."

"I *told* you."

"So you did," Dwyn agreed, looking down at himself in awe. "Are you actually a Healer under all of that fur?"

"Are you actually part of the Vanguard Circle?"

"... That's fair." Dwyn wrinkled his nose. "Now, let's get out of here before that Ireldium fiend decides to conjure another gust of wind. Do you have the pin?"

Tiv promptly held it up.

Dwyn nodded in approval, before facing Mox, who did his best to hide his laugh behind his claws. "Watch him."

With that, they were off.

That wasn't so bad, Tiv thought, even as his gut churned in unease with each step they took back to the Grove's upper floors. Because deep in the pit of his stomach, he knew that this was only the beginning, and that whatever they found hidden in the Anvil wasn't something he'd soon forget.

16

"I got yelled at by your Potens before we left." Vidal sighed at the remembrance. "Please tighten your hold over them."

"It's you I should be tightening my hold over," Monet retorted. "Every time I turn my back, you've done something to upset them."

"Then stop turning away."

"This might surprise you, Vidal, but I do have other things to think about besides you and the problems you cause."

"But you do think of me."

Monet sighed, utterly done with him.

Vidal gave her his most charming grin, before tilting his head up to stare at the first flights of snow falling upon them. Light and easy at first. A soft blanket of cold that tinted their cheeks and noses, before it turned into a flurry of icy winds that were as biting as knives. It turned their skin gray, then blue. The snow buried them, unforgiving as it was. Shuddering, he raised his hood against the biting breeze, sparing his wife a glance to make sure she'd done the same before continuing on his way.

Biting gusts of wind tried to topple him on more than one occasion, and when that didn't work, the frosty temperature tried to take one of his limbs away. Fortunately, he was no stranger to this place; the magic that spread warmth all throughout his veins wasn't either. Heat pooled in his stomach. A mixture of blood and power and a soft, bubbling emotion he couldn't name. Every part of him remembered just what to do to keep him as warm as possible in this unforgiving landscape, despite the fact that he'd been living in the relatively warm climate of the south. Decades of experience couldn't be so easily erased, especially not by a body built and honed by the cold, a body that was specifically crafted to wage war in an icy backdrop that had no end.

He was always front and center here. When only dying trees and nothingness existed as far as the eye could see, there was no other choice but to stand proud amidst the drear, to scream at the rest of the world in a dramatic announcement of his presence—he was here, the lone streak of color. Vidal loved showing off his might. He thought of this place with every rise and fall of his chest, with each word that left his lips, and every passing thought unencumbered by his affection for Monet. Because this was his home... and he'd missed it terribly.

Vidal stopped to take it all in.

The Gelid Mountains were a magnificent sight. He recalled the days he'd wander the icy slopes with Leonas by his side, hands blazing, as they did nothing but walk. For weeks, they travelled these mountains, trying to find some form of liberty amidst the white and cold.

They found it in the frigid air they breathed, in the long and distant expanse that stretched farther than their juvenile minds could imagine. But most of all, they found it in each other's company. Because there was something indescribably satisfying about finding another person that thought like you, that had the same ideas and simply understood what you wanted out of life. They had their differences of course—Leonas would never willingly leave the Alps—but they were similar where it counted and, in the end, that's what truly mattered.

He still remembered whenever they returned from their impromptu treks. There were always a few snappish Elders ready to reprimand them by the front gates.

"You both have so much potential," they'd say in those high-pitched voices that grated on his ears. "You know the rules, yet you waste all of your talents breaking them."

Those were good times.

They were right though. Leonas quickly rose to prominence once he was old enough to be considered an adult. Vidal did the same until he met Monet. After that, he rose through the Veld's ranks instead, earning the respect of their Potens and establishing himself as an equal, despite his lack of title. And he'd done so in the most *un-practitioner* like fashion imaginable. Vidal smiled wistfully at the thought. He almost regretted leaving it all behind. Almost. There were some things that were worth more than his childhood home and a handful of memories. Things like freedom and new experiences; like helping Nebbin directly instead of sitting through meetings and ordering lackeys from across the country to do so in his stead; like having a family to dote on and call his own.

He'd met all kinds of people. Men as dangerous as any blade, children too grave for their age, and adults too naïve for this world, but only once did he stumble upon a woman with a fierce storm constantly waging war within her. A woman that's every move was followed by raging waves so powerful that her peers were left insecure. A woman that rendered him speechless whenever her eyes lit up in fury.

It was thrilling, and Vidal had always loved thrills. So, it was no surprise that he'd been gone from the start. Not once did he regret his decision to leave. But his resolution didn't keep him from wondering. Vidal often thought about all of the changes that must've occurred since he left the Alps. Oh, he received letters from old friends, but those were few and far between. Work and family life were demanding. So much so that it left little time for much else. Not that he was particularly hung up about it. Written accounts could never do present moments justice anyway. It didn't matter how well his colleagues wrote or how much they prided themselves in their ability to accurately pen a narrative, they'd always pale in comparison to the experience of actually being there to witness it. There was a certain rush to standing in the thick of things, to seeing and feeling it all with every fiber of his being.

But as they arrived at the sealed gates that led into the Institute, Vidal thought that maybe not so much had changed after all. As if mimicking every experience he'd ever had after a long time away, two Elders stood there with *very* grumpy looks on their faces. He even recognized them—Kenna and Rocous.

Vidal squinted to get a better look.

Kenna's frown dug more into her cheekbones than he remembered. The lines on her face had etched themselves deep, it seemed. Even Rocous was frowning. His lips were pressed down in a manner entirely unlike him.

Vidal halted when he realized that they were headed towards them. Oh, but he didn't want to deal with anyone yet.

"Smoke, blended perfume, and snow," Vidal said, breathing in deeply. He ignored the oncoming pair. "Have you ever smelt anything more intoxicating, Monet? Creator's holy scepter, I *missed* that scent. Missed that gray sky above even more. Two Elders are even here, fully ready to ruin our arrival."

"This place is as dreadful as I remember," Monet commented. Her lips drew upward into an unattractive sneer. "I can feel the arrogance sinking into me."

"I'm sure the cold will numb it."

"I don't plan on staying here long enough to allow it to do so. Silas curse this weather. How do you stand it?"

"I'm used to it. You will be, too, before the end of this."

"The cold isn't something to get used to. It's something to endure until it's finished."

"Shall I ward you against the chill then?" Vidal suggested. He twirled his fingers in her hair, marveling at the loose snow that glinted like stardust around her. "I make a splendid shield."

Just as the words left his lips, Rocous and Kenna stopped before them. As if to prove his words, Vidal stepped in front of Monet with his arms stretched out wide before him.

"It's been too long," Vidal said good-naturedly. "I see that Elder Moress isn't with you. A shame. I distinctly recall his evil smile whenever I returned half a minute later than usual."

"Moress?" Rocous asked, his eyebrows rising in disbelief. "Rincer Moress? You're joking. The man can barely ask for a glass of water without sounding apologetic."

"Now, that's news to me." Vidal smiled. "I'll make it a point to visit him then. Perhaps seeing me will help him regain some of his vanished luster."

"You're late," Kenna interjected, before they all fell into Vidal's pace. She scowled sourly at him, then swatted one of his outstretched arms away, so she could see Monet standing behind him. Kenna was quick to launch into a tirade. "The Council has sent multiple missives to the Red Veld regarding the Summit, all of which have either been returned or—"

"I'm here now," Monet declared. "I'm an Arch Poten, not another practitioner that the Council can call on whenever it suits them. I have my own responsibilities."

"I taught you better than that, Monet."

"You? I studied under you for two months when I was barely seven. You taught a child."

"One that clearly didn't learn the meaning of respect."

"I've yet to see you do anything worthy of my respect," Monet said obstinately. "I refuse to let anyone look down on me. I didn't come here to be lectured. I came here for the Summit. Be thankful I'm here at all. Because from what I've heard, I'm the first Arch Poten to arrive, am I not?"

Kenna pinned her with a glare so dark it could crack glass. But no one missed the small, upward tilt of her lips that gave away just how impressed she was by her unwillingness to yield. Monet was everything a Veld practitioner aspired to be—strong with her words and confident in her abilities. She had a secureness about her that made others falter.

"Open the gate!" Kenna abruptly yelled to a cluster of practitioners standing guard on top of the walls that surrounded the Institute. They scrambled off immediately, and after a moment, the groan of metal could be heard echoing throughout the mountain as the outer gate was lifted. The inner one swiftly followed. It was pulled open by half a dozen men each.

From his position, Vidal saw a group of anxious practitioners watching them like trapped rabbits. Their backs and shoulders grew rigid as the entrance was shut with a loud bang.

Vidal ignored them in favor of turning to Rocous. "Did you see Elder Kenna's stare when she saw me?" he began. "*Ghastly.*"

Rocous shot him a look. "Your wife isn't exactly the most charming creature on the planet."

"Nonsense. She's—"

"Spare me your gushing, Vidal. I suffer plenty of that from Leonas."

"Oh, he did learn from the best, didn't he?"

"He got that from you?"

"Of course he did," Vidal said smugly. "Not all words ripen with age, Rocous. Most simply rot into nothing after they've been left to stew for too long. That's why you need to be gaudy with your affections! Admit how much you love not being able to take your eyes off of someone!"

Rocous wondered how many people had shaken their heads at him for lines like that over the years. He didn't bother asking, however, not wanting to know if Vidal actually counted.

"Silas, purge you from this plane."

Vidal laughed at that, pausing just long enough for Monet to pass him. He made it a point to walk behind her. Vidal didn't like the atmosphere of the Alps at the moment. It felt tense. Stifling. He expected it to some extend; an Elder was murdered after all. But this was far eerier that what he had considered. Vidal blamed it on the lack of life on the streets. Where was everybody? He heard distant shouts, but they were muffled, as if screamed into closed space. Were they all crammed into a building? If memory served, the only buildings in that direction were the dorms. Had the apprentices banded together? But for what?

He looked cautiously around them as they walked, noting the small groups of practitioners that were littered here and there, sitting on frozen steps or nestled in obscure corners. They were older; better friends with murder and death. More than that, they looked experienced. Hunters, perhaps? Some dared to meet his gaze, but most kept their heads low and whispered amongst themselves. Definitely Hunters. If not, then they were Leonas' underlings. He did see the Dace family symbol stitched on a few of their shoulders, although they tried to hide it.

"This way." Rocous pulled him down a side street that led to the Vanguard Circle's main building.

Vidal dug his heels into the ground and pointed at Monet's retreating figure. "But my heart is that way."

Rocous rolled his eyes. "From what I've seen, she can handle a quick meeting with the Council on her own. This is the best time for us to slip inside of the Vanguard Circle's prison."

"Only Leonas has the key to the prison, and he's extremely territorial. He'll strap us to one of his interrogation tables if he so much as catches a whiff of us down there."

"He won't be interrogating anyone for a long time. Not if Roderek has anything say about it."

"What do you mean?" Vidal asked. He looked at Monet once more, worry etched on his features. As if sensing him, she craned her neck back to give him a look that told him to hurry up, but he merely waved her off with a tacit promise to follow.

"Leonas is locked in a cell down there," Rocous revealed. He quickened his pace when Vidal finally began following him down the street without his assistance. "They apparently have reason to suspect him for killing Dels Drakone."

Vidal stopped to gape. His jaw dropped from the sheer absurdity of his words. He remembered the letter Monet had received. While they did consider that the Elder might've been a member of the Vanguard Circle, maybe even a Drakone, but to actually hear it—and for them to suspect his partner of all people! Why would Leonas even bother risking his position? What motive could he possibly have? The Dace family was a trusted one in the Alps. He had nothing to gain and everything to lose.

Leonas had always been unfailingly loyal to the Institute,

despite his rather vocal disagreements regarding their more outdated customs. Customs that could only be considered legitimate because of their deep ties to the Institute's history. Vidal knew that a number of the Elders on the Council were sore about Leonas' blatant disregard for tradition, but that wasn't enough reason to murder an Elder. Let alone an esteemed member of the dwindling Drakone family. Leonas had other ways to get what he wanted from the Zenith Council, and contrary to what his work as the figurehead of the Corrections Division entailed, most didn't involve violence. If anything, diplomacy was one of his strong suits.

"Even now, you have sway amongst the members of the Council," Rocous said, snapping him back to attention. "The Verne family name has always rang strongly here. If anyone can get Leonas out of there, it's you."

"I'll see what I can do. But frankly, I'm shocked Leonas hasn't managed to talk himself out of this yet."

"Only the other two heads of the Circle have been allowed to visit him."

"And why is that?" Vidal asked. "The Elders are standing on shaky ground now, what with Elder Serach deserting and another one of their members dead. I'd expect clearing Leonas' name to be at the very top of their list of priorities. How can they do that when they aren't even allowed to speak to him?"

"The Council is too busy squabbling about other things to properly look into Leonas' case. Roderek is pushing for the election of a new Grand Elder, despite the number of absentees, so we can at least pretend that we're in control of the situation. When in reality, we're a far cry from it. He says it needs to be done in order for calm to return to the Alps. Once that happens, then we can safely reopen the gates. There are many in favor of his plan simply because they know that the atmosphere in the Grove is tense. Considering all that's happened, it would be strange if it wasn't. None of us want the Grove's practitioners to feel like we've abandoned them to the fury of their Potens right after announcing to the world that they'd soon be overthrown by the colleges."

"And the rest?"

"The rest want to wait for us to catch the murderer. If we open the gates prematurely and allow practitioners to leave and enter whenever they please, then we'll never catch the culprit. This wasn't just an ordinary practitioner. A *Drakone* died. Some of Maurice's more devout followers are demanding answers. It's only a matter of time before they resort to violence. If we don't have a better suspect than Leonas by then—"

"They'll go after him," Vidal finished. His expression twisted at the thought. "That's a fool's move. Leonas might kill them."

"That's what scares me," Rocous muttered. "They might as well etch a line on their necks now, so he knows where to swing."

"Oh, I wouldn't go that far."

"Don't lie to me. I've heard the stories. The one where he plunged a blade into a prisoner's mouth before she could say a word is famous among the practitioners in his division."

"Now, who's perpetuating such old tales? Back in my day, Remon would have your mouth sewn shut for such insolence."

"So, that brutality runs in the family then?"

"It's more accurate to say that it's a trait common to all Heads of Corrections. They take no pleasure in their actions."

"Try explaining that to the Elders," Rocous said, as he opened the Vanguard Circle's doors and led him down a familiar hallway, where they were greeted by two underlings. A Conjurer and an Amorph. Twins, though one was noticeably scrawnier than the other. "These are Leonas' men. They'll lead you to him. I'd rather not risk going into his sector."

"So, I'm the only one risking my life here?"

"I have to talk to Victor." Rocous shrugged. "He's advising Elder Meese regarding what to do about the practitioners that keep lighting his robes on fire."

"How fulfilling."

"Don't mock him. He's the only reason the older members of

the Council haven't mindlessly agreed with Roderek's plan in the first place. They aren't accustomed to saying no to a Drakone."

"Victor's *defending* Leonas?" Vidal asked, astonished.

They made for an odd pair. Victor wore silence like armor. Leonas, on the other hand, preferred exuberant spectacles. His partner had never been one to keep his fondness for someone secret, so if he actually liked Victor on some level, then Vidal would've known about it. He could only think of one reason for the Council's top adviser to willingly help his partner, and it wasn't because he was concerned about his innocence.

"You look like you want to say something," Rocous said.

"Does this have something to do with his daughter travelling with Leonas' son?"

"Where did you hear that? Don't tell me... did you meet them? If so, why didn't you bring them with you?"

Vidal's lips turned up into a perfect smile as soon as he realized his mistake. He shouldn't have said that.

"They're young," Vidal purposely dropped his voice an octave. "Who am I to take away their time alone?"

Rocous' eyes widened. "What do you mean their *time alone*? Just what are those two do—"

"Lead the way!" Vidal said to the two practitioners standing before them. They were patient little things. Quiet, too. Their expressions were polished masks of steel that didn't bend, even when his lethal hands settled on their shoulders. Leonas trained them well. "We don't have all day now."

"Wait, Vidal!" Rocous shouted. "Don't just end with that— *acrivas na galladen!* Do you hear me?"

"Language!" was all Vidal said, before disappearing with his escorts and leaving one extremely unhappy Elder behind.

***

Someone was coming.

Leonas heard the echo of footsteps approaching. Two pairs. They were brisk and followed a very specific rhythm that he taught all of his men to walk in whenever they entered the lower chambers of his division.

One, two... the scrape of a heel against concrete... *three, four, five, six...* another scrape.

To anyone else, it would sound as though they were dragging their feet, then simply picking them up again, which wasn't unusual for men that wore boots built precisely for rough terrain. But in reality, this was Leonas' extremely meticulous way of identifying them. One wrong move, and they could very well be nursing third degree burns the next morning. In fact, Leonas distinctly recalled one of his older apprentices shoving a greenhorn across the wall and pressing a knife to his throat for accidentally forgetting to scrape his heel after the sixteenth step. It was a memory he looked back on with a mixture of fondness and distress. The former because his teachings bore such splendid fruit, and the latter because they couldn't afford to lose another newbie. Practitioners apt enough to withstand even the first week of his rigorous training methods seemed to dwindle with each passing year.

But his declining department wasn't the problem now. There was only one reason for two of his men to be heading his way instead of laying low—someone was with them. Who that was, Leonas couldn't say for certain. But if his guest was important enough for his men to openly escort them rather than follow in smaller, less conspicuous forms, then he could only suspect an Elder. If so, then this Elder was remarkably light on his feet because no matter how much he strained his ears or in what angle he tilted his head, he couldn't hear anything. Leonas knew only a few Elders that took care to quiet their steps. He knew even less that naturally walked with such discreetness. Most wanted others to know that they were coming, fully expecting whoever they passed to either bow their heads in greeting or acknowledge their presence in some other way.

"Were you expecting anyone?" Javis asked, turning to face the sound. He squinted, like he believed that he'd be able to see through the walls if he stared hard enough. "I thought you weren't allowed any visitors."

"I'm not," Leonas answered. "Are you worried?"

"Why would I be?"

"I'm bad news apparently."

"For the moment."

Leonas eyed his colleague, trying to find any sign of nervousness. He hummed in satisfaction when he found none. Javis merely stared back at him with that deceptively calm face of his. He reminded him of Victor. Although he was less inclined to help the Council sort out their problems and more concerned about whatever experiment that was next on his long list of insane ideas. Javis was undoubtedly learned. A true erudite. And the only man worthy of the word... or so people claimed. Then again, those were the same people that described him as homely.

Shallow fools, the entire lot of them.

Leonas accepted plain, maybe even unimposing, but he wouldn't go so far as to label him unattractive in any way. Javis just never took care of his appearance enough for people to see past the disheveled beard and messy rags he liked to call coats. He always looked as if he hadn't showered in a week, despite the common knowledge that he actually did so twice a day. How Javis' personal hygiene routine became public knowledge wasn't something Leonas knew the precise details about, but he did know that it involved a large amount of alcohol. The information fueled the already existing curiosity regarding why his skin was always covered in unknown stains or why there were always tiny rips in his robes. It probably didn't help that one of the more putrid scents from the bacterial cultures Javis grew in his office clung to him like a second skin, no matter how much he bathed.

"Here they come," Leonas said.

His back straightened at the flicker of shadows across the wall. They wavered with the torchlight, their blurred dips falling into the tiny cracks in the stone. Their appearance was quickly followed by the protesting screech of metal as doors were opened and bolts were unlocked.

The ominous drip of water in the distance ceased, drowned entirely by the loudness of their movements. Endeavoring to distract himself from the anxiety of not knowing who was coming to see him, Leonas took to trying to hear that steady drip once again. There was something comforting about its unceasing stream; an assurance that time still flowed outside of his cell. But whatever philosophical train of thought his mind was about to get lost in came to a grinding halt once his eyes fell upon the familiar face that stepped through the doorway.

Vidal Verne stood there, his mouth pressed into a thin line that spoke only of malcontent. He inspected him in that overly pointed way of his that let the person know that he was doing so. And by his stone-faced expression, Leonas knew that he was unimpressed by what he saw.

Leonas was the opposite. He admired how the air shifted upon Vidal's entrance. It was as if he'd breathed it in, expelled it, and made it his. He'd always been like that; able to make the surroundings move aside to fit him in it. The sheer confidence in which Vidal held himself never made him seem out of place.

"What have you gotten yourself into now, Leonas?" were the first words that flew out of Vidal's mouth. "And how can I reap the rewards?"

"Vidal!" Leonas exclaimed. He pressed against the bars of his cell in a sudden rush of delight.

"Javis is with you, too, I see." Vidal smiled at said man. He barely registered Leonas' underlings leave the room to stand guard outside, allowing them some semblance of privacy. All of it was done without so much as a look from Leonas. His partner really was good at what he did if he could inspire that kind of obedience.

"It's good to see you again, Vidal," Javis acknowledged. "But I think we both know that you aren't allowed to be here."

"Correct as always."

"Where's your keeper?"

"My heart is currently speaking with the Zenith Council, getting reacquainted with their snooty ways and whatnot." Vidal waved the topic aside. "But that's not important. Besides, I can always feign ignorance if I get caught."

"Wilfully lying to authorities is a crime," Leonas chimed.

"Spare me your superficial preaching. The mere existence of your department is a breach of a thousand ethical regulations."

"All ethics are subject to perspective."

"Don't say things I can't argue with either." Vidal made a face. "Not having the last word leaves a bad taste in my mouth."

Leonas laughed at that. "You haven't changed, I see."

"Oh, but I have!" Vidal argued. "I've taken on a primary apprentice. Clever boy. Very talented. He has a scalding tongue though and an appalling temper. He also has this nasty habit of provoking those that shouldn't be tested."

"Sounds like a handful."

"Very much so. Though I'm not exactly looking to break his tendencies. He'd be bland otherwise. Kind of like soft oats."

"Are you really comparing your apprentice to food?"

"Yes, because I think of him as the spicy kind. He should be honored that I believe he has enough seasoning to be interesting. Not many do."

"You need to cleanse your palate then. You've always been partial to exotic spices. Those are hard to come by."

"It's why I like them."

"They'll ruin you one day," Leonas warned. "Still, this is a surprise. I never thought I'd see the day when you'd take on a primary apprentice. Who's the unlucky sap?"

Vidal simply smiled.

"Well?" Leonas prompted.

"Your son."

"... You're joking."

"I'm afraid not."

"Jack loathes the idea of having a master. What did you do to him Vidal? Don't give Cheryll a reason to spite you."

Vidal rolled his eyes. "While I'd love to give you all of the exciting, gory details about how we met and how he practically begged me to be his master, we, or rather *I*, don't have the time."

"Oh, that was a low blow."

"Rest assured, I fully meant it to be. So, what's this about you being framed?"

Leonas straightened at his suddenly serious tone. There was no more joking around now, and though he was curious about his son, there would be time to catch up later.

"They assume I murdered a Drakone," Leonas whispered. His eyes darted around in fear that others might be listening. "Dels Drakone, to be precise."

"And why, pray tell, would they *ever* assume that?"

"I sent Hunters outside right after the incident occurred. It just so happens that they took out a few practitioners as the gates were being shut."

"Now, that *does* look suspicious."

"With no other leads," Javis butted in, "and countless other problems springing up, it doesn't look good for him right now. It also doesn't help that he has a... prolonged history of harassing Dels in meetings and a reputation for snapping necks to get what he wants."

"That's part of my job!" Leonas defended.

"Why did you send them out?" Vidal questioned.

"Cheryll asked me to look into a few things in the Grove."

"Always the devoted husband."

"I don't want to hear that from you." Leonas scoffed. "It's not like it was purely for her benefit. I sent Dwyn, one of my best, to meet up with an old spy I stationed in the Grove a few years ago. I was hoping they could keep me informed and prevent things from getting out of hand, while the Alps waited for the other Arch Potens to arrive."

"Which college is this spy of yours in?"

"I wouldn't be much of a politician if I just told you now, would I?" Leonas smiled, before clearing his throat in a not so subtle manner to brush the subject aside. "Thankfully, it's not all bad." He gestured vaguely to his small cage. "I'm not chained, they feed me twice a day, and they even leave me to my own devices for the most part. That's the best anyone has ever been treated in these dungeons. I can vouch for that."

"I'm shocked that you haven't broken out yet."

"I'm sure the Council would *love* that. That'll make me look all sorts of guilty."

"... Are you?"

Leonas' eyes widened, before they hardened into a menacing glare. "Did you really just ask me that?"

"I had to make sure." Vidal shrugged. "It's strange for you to be this compliant, Leonas. I thought you might've been feeling guilty and decided to repent by staying locked up in here."

"Should I feel bad for every flogged fool in my dungeons?" Leonas spat. "Guilt is *poison*. That's an emotion I crushed long ago. Back when I first donned this bloody mantle."

"So you say," Vidal contended. The corner of his lips curled upward in a taunting manner that never failed to rile anyone. Even the calmest, most stoic of individuals weren't immune. But unlike most, Leonas possessed enormous amounts of self-control. A consequence of age, no doubt. A shame, really. Vidal missed riling him up.

"There's no need for me to do anything but wait," Leonas explained. "I get information well enough from here. If not from my men, then from the Tippings."

"The Tippings?" Vidal asked, looking between Javis and Leonas to confirm that he'd heard that correctly. When all they did was nod, he spared a glance around the room, as if speaking about them might suddenly make one appear. "Why would a guild of highly trained assassins care about Institute politics? I thought they claimed to be above all of that nonsense."

"They're concerned about what's currently happening in the Institutes. I think they're afraid that we might start chaining up Nebbin again."

"That's not surprising, considering—"

"The mistakes of our ancestors?" Leonas interrupted.

"History has a tendency of repeating itself." Vidal shrugged like none of this concerned him. "But you have the Tippings *and* Victor Sirx on your side? I'm impressed, Leonas. Very impressed. How did you manage that?"

"Possibly the same way you managed to get my son to become your primary apprentice," Leonas replied. "I heard he was with Victor's daughter."

"You heard right."

"Why didn't you bring them with you?"

"That's a discussion for another time."

"Is it about the stone?" Leonas asked. He watched Vidal's shoulders tense at the mention of it. "I'm going to assume that means, '*yes*.' Were they alright at least? Eating well? I'm afraid they might feel the full force of the First Zenith's wrath should they keep walking around with something they locked away."

"That being is the work of a jealous man, not an angry god."

"... What?" Leonas looked him in the eyes, trying to decipher the strange mix of emotions that he found whirling there. "What do you mean by that? What did you find?"

"Another time," he repeated, stronger this time.

Suddenly remembering that they weren't alone, Leonas glanced at Javis from the corner of his eye. He obviously knew exactly what they were talking about, and from the curious look on his face, he wanted to be present when Vidal explained. Leonas didn't blame him. The Heartstone's disappearance had caused the Council an absurd amount of distress over the past few weeks. It didn't help that Leonas lied about not knowing where it was in order to cover up for Cheryll sending it along with Jack. Why she did, he still didn't know. But he trusted her judgement, if nothing else.

"I thought you'd only just arrived," Leonas abruptly said, hastily changing the subject before any questions about the stone could be asked. "How did you learn about Victor?"

"A little bird told me." Vidal smiled, before turning to Javis. "Do you happen to know who Victor's already convinced to vote against rushing the vote for a new Grand Elder?"

"A good number of the older Elders," Javis said carefully. He was clearly having trouble leashing his own curiosity because his expression looked brighter and more interested than a child's. "Those with nothing to lose and those secure enough in their positions that currying the favor of a Drakone would do them little good. I believe he's trying to convince Elder Violet now."

"Violet?" Vidal muttered, then faced Leonas. "Is she the one that wore that shimmering silver band on her head that blinded the Peose at the winter gala elev—*no*, twelve years ago?"

"She might've been." Leonas paused at the sudden question. "I don't quite remember."

"Neither do I."

"Weren't you both there?" Javis asked, not even realizing that he'd fallen victim to Vidal's pace.

"We stepped out to compose ourselves when Elder Llorens, oh, excuse me, Spiri now, isn't she? When Elder Spiri walked in with a live bird on her head," Vidal enlightened. "The poor thing. I heard all of the ducks near the outer lakes run when they see her now. What was that about anyway?"

"I honestly don't know," Leonas said. "But Elder Nevaris made her leave."

"Oh, Nevaris had always been sour. That austere attitude is the reason why no one ever filled his requisitions on time."

"I prayed to Thelarius once to grant him a sense of humor."

"I prayed he'd choke on an egg."

"Didn't he though?"

"It was a strip of beef that got him."

"Ah, close enough."

"Indeed."

With that, they lapsed into silence.

They each took a moment to glance at one another. Vidal's gaze was especially intense. He was obviously holding back on account of their company. Leonas wanted to tell him that there was no need. Javis was a friend. But he knew that it would be for naught. Vidal wasn't one to share information easily, especially if it was so important that he didn't even dare to drop a few hints.

Vidal would return to tell him. That much, he was sure of.

Leonas' main concern was *when.*

Few stood a change against Vidal's persuasion, and he took every chance he could get to bend others to his will. Leonas knew that once Vidal stepped outside of that door, he'd be too busy re-immersing himself in the atmosphere of the Alps to return.

They were similar, so much so that he knew exactly what he'd do once he left these dungeons — first, he'd acquaint himself with all of the new faces and dig around for information while he was at it. After that, he'd seek the Elders and their primary apprentices out individually, before *accidentally* bumping into Roderek. Only then would he start dropping hints about what he knew, leading others on or obstructing them based on their usefulness to him.

Vidal had always been an outlier. Moving to the Red Veld clearly hadn't changed that. And for one reason or another, Vidal *always* knew more than he let on. But this wasn't the time to act independently, neither was it the time to hoard information. If he knew something, then it would be best if he told him as soon as Javis left. Unfortunately, Leonas knew that Vidal wouldn't do that either. One, because he was already bouncing on the balls of his feet, craving exploration; two, because Vidal would take immense pleasure in the fact that he'd be stuck here, wondering incessantly about his words and slowly driving himself insane, while he was out and about.

Leonas didn't even try to hide his grimace at the realization.

"I should be going then," Vidal said.

"So soon?"

"Your presence tires me." Vidal dusted off his already pristine sleeves in a way that indicated finality.

"When will you be back?"

"A day. Maybe two."

Leonas sprang forward just as Vidal gripped the iron handle. His hands slipped between the bars of his cage only to grasp air. "Wait!" he yelled, ignoring Javis' raised eyebrows. "I have a cat."

There was a long, judging pause.

"You're getting lonely, I see. Did you miss Cheryll so much that you replaced her with a cat?"

"Oh, you know me well. As expected."

"So, you have a cat," Vidal repeated with a sigh. "What am I supposed to do with that information? Take your cat home with me? You know my daughter's allergic to them."

"Don't you dare take Peaches!"

"Peaches?"

"That's Peaches Quilts McAnchovy to you!"

"I almost forgot about your *stellar* naming sense."

"I need you to drop by my office and feed him," Leonas said. "Do you remember that drawer where I keep all of my important letters? The ones from Jack and Cheryll."

"Jack sends you letters?"

"On occasion."

"Are you sure those weren't delusions?" Vidal asked plainly. "You have been here a while."

"I wish you'd stop making me question my sanity."

"Granted, and yes, I do remember that drawer. The one your father kept his hunting knife in. What about it?"

"Peaches has a small bowl there. You can buy milk from one of the stalls outside of the public archives."

Vidal hummed when he realized what he was getting at. There was another long pause, although less judgmental than before. But then he remembered where he needed to be, and his fingers tightened over the iron handle once more.

"Don't tell me what to do," Vidal said, before disappearing.

Leonas smiled. That wasn't a no.

17

"Let's see now…"

Vidal hummed, milk bottle in one hand and Leonas' spare office key in the other. On the floor behind him were two knocked out practitioners and a red-stained vial that anyone but him would likely get arrested for brewing.

He swung the bottle by its neck in small, circular motions, as he looked at the stale surroundings of Leonas' office. Curtains blocked most of the night sky, though a slim strip of stars found just enough gap to illuminate the outlines of the room.

Lighting a nearby oil lamp with his fingers, he thought that maybe he shouldn't have waited so long to drop by. But he had so many other things to do that rummaging through his best friend's belongings—for what was possibly the thousandth time in the last decade—just didn't sound like fun. He knew Leonas' office like the back of his hand. He even knew about the multiple stashes of vintage *G'orggio* he hid underneath the fake bottoms in his desk drawers. Though when confronted about it, Leonas would vehemently deny their existence, regardless if he was shown damning evidence of the contrary. Leonas stuck by his position like glue mixed with *Bournabee Extra Sticky Wax.* An unholy combination.

Besides, if they hadn't found whatever Leonas was hiding by now, then they never would. There was no reason to rush. The Elders were at a standstill, the other Arch Potens had yet to arrive, and that precious stone the Council liked to claim as their own was in safe hands.

So, Vidal had opted to greet a few friends first. They were scattered across opposite ends of the Alps, so he took it upon himself to bother entire classes of apprentices along the way. Then, he went to scare his former underlings enough to make them wary of every moving shadow until his departure. He'd even gone to the office of the head ambassador, Sanclen Sibyl, a devout follower of Ferus Terria's latest fashion trends, to get his opinion on his clothes. The haughty bastard had turned his nose up and sent him out... as expected.

His final stop before going to Leonas' office was an infuriated Monet, who'd been caught in a one-sided conversation for the better part of the afternoon with an overly enthusiastic apprentice that had the thickest northern accent he'd ever heard. The boy's mouth needed a warning sign—*Dear Foreigners: do not engage in conversation.* Monet had tried to speak, only for the boy to nervously talk over her at every turn. It would've been funny had Monet not already been incensed from her unnecessarily long meeting with the Zenith Council. The sight of his lovely wife stressed was never enjoyable. Luckily for her, *íarre* jumped from his lips, and he'd swept her away.

Vidal would've liked to stay with Monet, but she apparently had her own catching up to do with a few of the more tolerable Elders, leaving him with nothing but his boredom and the looming order from Leonas to feed his clearly imagined cat.

Just as he thought it, Vidal spotted a ball of pink yarn in the corner of the room. He stared at it for a moment, blinking twice in revelation, before looking around again for his partner's pet.

Nothing. He was alone.

Not here, he concluded, placing the milk bottle on Leonas' desk. *Dead cat then?*

It did smell strangely briny. He wrinkled his nose at the scent. Now that he noticed it, the smell seemed to double in strength. The windows were closed, and as far as he knew, the Alps wasn't near any bodies of water. So either Leonas recently began keeping a hidden stash of food that expired while he was locked in his own department, or his cat really did die in here. He prayed it was the former.

Vidal settled in Leonas' seat. He leaned back, examining his office as he did so. It was cozy... yet cold at the same time. Family portraits were mounted on the walls, although none could be considered immediate. Each painting was of a grumpy former Elder that came from the Dace clan. There was a velvet throw on the couches, but it was folded and placed meticulously on its arm. Two sets of playing cards sat on the table before it. They were piled into neat stacks inside of an elegant leather case. Beside them, sat a round carton of tobacco and a small mountain of wound scrolls.

Leonas wasn't this neat. Someone had definitely cleaned this place, likely after they finished tearing it apart for any and all of his partner's secrets. But even with the relative sterility, traces of his friend still remained. There was nothing over the top about Leonas' office. It was neither gaudy, nor sparse. But what he did have was expensive enough to make even the most spendthrift of nobles blush. From the solid gold frames around each portrait to the rare tomes rotting on the shelves. The Dace coffers were deep, and Leonas had a very subtle way of flaunting it.

Vidal spun around once, before reaching over to fiddle with the many statuettes by the edge of the desk. He picked up the heavy stone *Pinsore Beetle* first. A bloodsucking parasite. *Pinsores* had fangs that could pierce even the thickest of hides and razors on their legs that they used to bury deep inside of their hosts. Their spit had analgesic properties, so they could stay attached to their host for weeks, before the host eventually succumbed to the strings of venom that they released along with their feces.

Barring their lethality, they were cute creatures. Some practitioners kept entire colonies inside glass enclosures. There was even talk once about using them as Peose, but when the practitioner that had proposed the idea died from *Pinsore* poison, the idea was scrapped.

Leonas isn't one for cute things, Vidal knew. *So, where did this come from? Well, not that it matters. It's too fine.*

He exchanged it for the rudimentary one beside it. This was carved out of a finer slab, although the unrounded protrusions and skewed proportions didn't suggest skill. It looked like the work of a child.

A pillar? Vidal guessed by its size. *Not this one either.*

The next was a square with a moth embossed on top. *Too obvious.* When he reached the fourth, he paused. It had been years since he'd last seen it, but *this*, he did recognize—a robed woman.

There was just enough detail for him to make out her parts, but not enough that she had any clearly defined features. Her face was blank, and the only intricacies her clothes held were the occasional slopes toward the end that emphasized billowing. She stood on top of a thick pedestal. It had no embellishments. No engravings along the bottom or the side.

Only an enchantment.

Casting a furtive glance around the room, Vidal nicked his thumb on a nearby quill. He let the blood flow for a moment, before he pressed it to the statue's unshaped face. Slowly, features formed under his thumb. He felt the slanted eyes, the sharp nose, and the open mouth.

Is it screaming? Vidal mused, pressing his finger harder. He winced when the statuette's features dug into the small pinprick. Vidal was tempted to take a peek at her face, but knew from the engravings that suddenly framed the statue's pedestal that he'd lose his hand if he tried.

The woman glowed. She lit up the corners of the room in a momentary flash of brilliance… and Vidal almost strained his neck when a pair of curious eyes appeared in his periphery.

No one was there.

A *'pop'* came from underneath the desk, distracting him. He noticed that the statuette had ceased its shine, so he returned it to where it belonged. There was no blood on its head. Its face was unshaped. Even the cut on his hand was gone.

A healing enchantment, too? Vidal thought, impressed, before looking around again. He spent a full minute searching for an intruder—a crafty Amorph mostly—only to find that he was well and truly alone. *Every practitioner leaves traces of their magic,* he assured himself. *If someone was hiding here, then I would've noticed. Monet's right. I really do need to stop being so paranoid.*

Vidal knelt to inspect what had opened. To his wonder, it wasn't a drawer, but rather an entire stone slab. Leonas had evidently made some changes to his father's secret storage over the years. The tile mysteriously disappeared, and in its place was a gaping hole embedded right into the rest of the floor. Inside were four stacks of letters wrapped with twine, a leather-bound journal, Remon's hunting knife, an empty purple bowl, and a tin container with ashes inside.

He recognized that container.

"Hello, Master Remon," Vidal said with a mischievous grin. "It's been too long. Pardon the intrusion."

He rummaged around for a bit. Under the journal were more dispatches. Though these were shorter, mere sentences per page, and not nearly as well kept. They weren't from Cheryll or Jack, but several others—Euphemia, Vince, Reno, Gallahad. All names that Vidal couldn't put either a face or a memory to, which led him to believe that Leonas didn't care for them. If he did, then he would've mentioned them at least once in his letters. They were similar in that regard.

There was a stamped 'T' beside each of their entries. The responses, too, were short. They had no signatures at the end, but Vidal recognized the penmanship.

"Javis," Vidal said under his breath.

He read through the pages. Each entry was dated. The more important ones were even underlined for convenience. Those with names at the top detailed the current happenings within the Grove. Some even mentioned the general mood of the Institute, and included questions about certain high-ranking practitioners. Those written by Javis were primarily about the Zenith Council; inside information that the Tippings, who relied heavily on rumors and the public for information, had no access to.

Does Leonas want me to gather information for them or is this just his way of keeping me informed? Vidal debated. *Possibly both.*

He noticed that the latest string of missives had no response.

60.27.CA - Reno
Arch Poten Cole is planning on heading north soon. The Lafertti Clan are buzzing like flies.

62.27.CA - Vince
There was a cave-in inside one of your underground tunnels. They're guarded by a particularly ferocious Amorph, so I doubt they've been compromised. But it looks like it'll take some time to repair. I don't know what those scurrying between the walls do exactly, so I'm unsure if it'll affect their duties in any way, but I'll keep an eye on them.

66.27.CA - Vince
Mercenary camps have been spotted a distance away from the Mending Willow. Our agents have reason to believe that they've infiltrated the Institute as well.
We'll continue watching them.

73.27.CA - Gallahad
A band of freed slaves were brought to the Grove. I'm uncertain if there were practitioners from the Alps among them, but you should expect a message from the Grove's Potentate Union soon.
Nothing else to report.

74.27.CA - Euphemia
More practitioners arrived. One of them is an Arch Poten. My agents are gathering more information about the pair, but relay to us what you know. They're hesitant to approach.
Dwyn has made contact with Leinus.

Vidal could write an entire page in response to the scant

information they gave. He refrained, however, and simply wrote two lines about Monet's arrival and another about keeping their distance from the duo.

He held the quill to his lips, wondering in a brief moment of decency, if it would be alright if he ordered them to do his bidding. The doubt was promptly thrown out the window as he decided that he was going to do so whether they liked it or not.

Vidal added:

Search for owls in the mercenary camps.

If you find them, notify either of the two practitioners that recently arrived—tell them Vidal Verne sent you. I will warn you that they're horrendously difficult to get ahold of once you let them out of your sight, so don't bother if you feel as though your men may be stepping into a danger zone. They're an energetic pair that's always at the center of something awful. I advise you to keep your distance if you can.

I also need you to contact a red-headed Astonian and a pint-sized rogue on the other side of the Wymeran River. Both are Amorphs. They're travelling with the Hellion. Escort their party to the Grove.

Just as Vidal finished returning the pages, he saw those same eyes at the edge of his vision. He turned with a start and roved over the empty distance between himself and the imposing bookshelf pressed against the wall. Vidal stayed like that for an age, unblinking, unmoving. His every sense on the alert. Vidal's pulse jumped beneath his skin, while his magic hissed in his veins with every breath, waiting, *wanting* to be cast-off.

Then, he saw it.

Two horrific slits that appeared out of thin air to gaze at him in the darkness. Faster than he could register, his magic roared to life. A blinding flash of blue bloomed between his fingers, but just before he could let loose a torrent of spiked ice, the creature appeared in full before him. It was small and terrified. More than that, it had pointed ears, four paws, and a lithe body. Suddenly, all of his doubts were blown away—this was Leonas' cat.

His *very real* and *very alive* cat.

Vidal smothered the magic in his hands. The cat changed colors as soon as he did to blend in with the surroundings.

"I traumatized his cat." Vidal panicked. "Of all the stupid things to do, *of course* I do the stupidest one possible. Thelarius, guide me."

Vidal swiftly grabbed the dish from the hole, before closing it with another press of his uninjured finger to the statuette. He'd light himself on fire if someone stumbled into the room and found Leonas' cache because of his negligence.

He poured a generous helping of milk inside of the dish.

Then, he waited.

Peaches was distraught by his presence. But hopefully the allure of sustenance would win him over. Thankfully, it did. Because not a moment later, the milk was visibly lapped at.

Vidal watched as Peaches appeared in full before him. He eyed the cat's tabby fur and black spots. Peaches was plain, save for the few exaggerated features that showed him that this was no ordinary house pet. His claws were monstrous, and his tail was two times longer than his body. It curled in and out like unfurling petals. He had two sets of proud ears that stood at attention. They twitched every time Vidal so much as breathed.

This cat was definitely an experiment at one point or another.

"I thought there was a ban on genetic crossbreeding," Vidal whispered, glaring when Peaches lifted his head to hiss at him. "Vicious little thing, aren't you?" he deadpanned, not afraid in the slightest. "No wonder Leonas likes you."

Instead of attacking like he expected, Peaches stilled.

"What?" Vidal raised an eyebrow. "Do you like being called vicious or did you just recognize your owner's name? Vicious. Leonas," he repeated, watching the cat come closer. "Vicious. Leonas. Vicious. Leonas. Leonas. Leonas."

Peaches sat right before him now. Green eyes fixated on his red ones. Ever so slowly, Peaches extended his paw, before batting it towards him in a vague motion that seemed to gesture to his entire body.

Vidal didn't fancy himself an expert in animal behavior, but he could get the gist of what the cat wanted. He held out his hand, palm up and fingers splayed wide. The effect was immediate. Peaches strode over, sniffing in-between his fingers and moving all the way up to his wrist, before distancing himself again. Peaches seemed satisfied with what he found because when he returned to his bowl, he had no trouble showing Vidal his back. Even his ears stopped twitching with his every breath.

"You're more like a dog, aren't you?" Vidal commented, smiling. "I wonder if you have the genes of one."

He ran his hands all along Peaches' silken fur.

"So, if you're here and *alive,* then what's that smell? Has Javis been feeding you raw fish?"

"Who are you talking to?" someone said in answer, making Vidal jump for the second time that night. A spectacular feat, considering his usual vigilance. Vidal turned to the open door, staring at the intruder with wide, guilty eyes. Before him, Peaches shifted colors again. He darted out of his hands and padded somewhere he couldn't see in swift silence.

"Roderek!" Vidal exclaimed, gathering his wits. "What are you doing here?"

"I felt a trace of magic," he explained in that menacing way of his. "This area is off limits, Vidal." Roderek looked pointedly at the knocked out practitioners in the hall. "Or did the guards not tell you that?"

"They might have." Vidal held up the empty dish. "I was feeding Leonas' cat."

"… I don't see a cat."

"Neither do I, but that doesn't mean it isn't here."

Roderek raised an eyebrow, but easily let the matter go. He knew how conversations with Vidal went. He had no desire to start one about this.

"I almost forgot how unreasonable you were." Roderek said. He looked at the practitioners on the floor. "You didn't have to knock them unconscious, and with an illegal brew at that. That tonic had Levic Leaves, didn't it? There's a reason they aren't on the market, Vidal. Their aroma lingers. I can still smell traces of their foul stench."

"I would cover my nose if I were you. Those fumes will have you right down there with them if you dawdle for too long."

"I needed these men. They had other duties. Now, what am I supposed to do?"

"Do it yourself?" Vidal suggested, before finally rising to his full height. He placed the dish on the table, along with the half-empty milk bottle. "Men aren't born for their leaders, Roderek."

"But they'll die for them."

"They'll also die for their next meal. Which one do you think is more dangerous?"

"The answer will always be the one with less to lose."

Vidal sighed dramatically. "And *I* forgot how disgustingly amazing you were at word games."

Roderek paused just long enough for the silence between them to become uncomfortable. "I heard you met with Javis."

"Who told you that?"

"He did."

Vidal doubted it, but he ran with the lie all the same. "He was pontificating about rocks. Demented lizard. I'm shocked that no one's tried to bludgeon him with a metal rod yet."

"I could say the same about you. You have more enemies than friends here, Vidal. That's no secret. Although, unlike the other Elders, I'm not surprised that you decided to tag along with your wife. Leonas was imprisoned after all. It's only natural that you'd come running."

"I will always be here for Leonas."

"Fifteen years ago, you said something similar about staying in the Alps. How long is '*always*' to you, I wonder?"

"I don't like what you're implying," Vidal said, dropping his lighthearted tone.

"If there's nothing to lose by having it, then hold onto it,"

Roderek replied with an ambiguous tild of his head. He walked exactly two steps away to crush the red-stained vial under his boot. His face was an apathetic mask that gave away nothing, as blank as the faceless woman on Leonas' desk. "That was something an old Master of mine liked to say. Wise words, although a tad too vague. They don't take into consideration personal feelings like love or loyalty, or even nobler ones, like sacrifice. You, however, might benefit from them."

"Whatever I'll lose by maintaining my friendship with Leonas will be things I'll be happy to give."

"Strong words," he commended. "You're the first person that's ever told me the truth and lied to me in the same sentence. But I know you, Vidal. I know that there are some things that you absolutely won't sacrifice. You know that, too. So, if you don't want to risk losing them, then I suggest you keep your nose out of the Alps' affairs. Behave until the Summit ends, then return to the Veld. Go back to the practitioners there and to your little auction house. It's where you belong now."

His words felt like a blow to the chest, but Vidal kept up his stony façade. There was no room for hurt expressions or regretful wailing here. He made his choice. He left with Monet all those years ago, despite the shouts that begged him otherwise. The Alps lost a Master that day, and the Veld gained an old, unwelcome blueblood. Roderek was only stating the obvious.

Instead of answering with a snarky remark and an expletive like every fiber of his being wanted, Vidal asked the only question that truly mattered now—to the one person whose opinion on the subject had the ability to sway both the Council *and* the general public.

"Do you really believe he killed Dels?" Vidal asked.

"… I believe he's our only suspect."

That wasn't a '*yes*,' although it wasn't a '*no*' either. That was enough. For now.

"I forgot what a talented embrocologist you were," Roderek told him then, clearly wanting to avoid the subject. He tilted his head at the unconscious practitioners. "Wake them up, make sure they can walk straight, and then send them back to their rooms. I'll send more guards in an hour. *Don't* be here when they arrive. I won't be so forgiving a second time."

Roderek waited for him to nod, before turning to leave.

"For what it's worth," Vidal said, "I am sorry about your brother."

"So am I."

Vidal watched him go. His footsteps were silenced by the crisp night air. He took a deep, soothing breath. It had been a long time since he'd gotten into an *almost-argument* with someone like Roderek Drakone; even longer since he'd been silenced by a lack of anything to say rather than simple astonishment. His throat was dry. His pulse was still pounding in a mixture of regret, embarrassment, and petty anger. Even his mind felt overworked.

There were some things that could only happen in the Alps. A stretched mind was definitely one of them. Vidal could already feel the early aches of an intense migraine stemming from the center of his forehead. Absently, he made a mental note to get into a few more arguments with the Elders here. Preferably after he got Leonas out of that sad, little cage.

Because he really did miss this place. Even if it didn't miss him.

18

Jack sighed.

He wasn't one for sneaking around. He preferred to be out in the open, breaking through the front lines with his magic and being the main distraction—let those that were better at espionage hide within the shadows—but recently, he'd gotten quite a bit of practice at it. From wandering the crowded tunnels of the Pit to seeking information in the back alleys of Yorn; he might've even considered himself good, had he not known people like Pom and Khale that had steps as light as feathers. But even if he was skilled at it that didn't mean he liked it. He especially didn't like it when the people he was trying to hide from were his fellow practitioners.

It took a special kind of caution to avoid their gazes. Dodging the occasional roamer was easy enough, but following Philip's every move, while surveying the nooks and crannies they passed for Amorphs was a little trickier. About half an hour's worth of sneaking around trickier.

"If Dalis asks, tell him we got here in fifteen," Philip said, as they pressed themselves against the final turn that led to the Anvil. "There are two guards there. A Healer and an Amorph. The guard patrolling this hall should be rounding a turn on the left right now. That one's usually an Elementalist. But if you're lucky, it'll be a Conjurer. You take out that one. Drag him back here if you can and see if he has a key. I'll deal with these two."

With that, Philip rounded the corner.

"Oh, thank the Creator!" Philip exclaimed, holding his head.

"I've been looking for a Healer for the past two hours. They're all occupied by some fight on the upper floors and those on duty in the clinics have been inundated with new patients."

"Philip?" one of the practitioners said. A woman, if her squeaky voice was any indication. Jack heard her come closer. "What happened to you?"

"A few Gavinists got into a rather nasty argument. One of them threw the biggest damn gemstone I've ever seen. Luckily, he missed. Sort of."

"The gem didn't happen to be dark pink with small purple streaks, did it?"

"That's the one," Philip lied easily.

"You're joking! Creator, I heard that members of the Sanct Union were sent all the way to Redmount to collect those samples for them. Talk about ungrateful."

"Let me guess, it was those trainees on the third floor?" another said. A man this time. "Which college?"

"Libersta, I think," Philip said. "Although, they might've been from the Closions. I wasn't exactly paying attention."

"Bah! Those brats with their fleshy little meat hooks are *always* stirring up trouble. But it is pretty amazing they were even able to hit someone like you."

"I can't dodge everything," Philip defended.

Philip said something else, but Jack didn't stick around to listen. He made his way toward the corridor where Philip promised the guard would be. Jack found him easily, given that he was the only person there. It was an Elementalist. Bigger than most, but not as large as an Amorph. Still, he was at least two times bulkier than Jack. There was no way he'd be able to drag him back without Philip's help.

The guardsman crossed his arms, and Jack saw a ring of keys at his waist. Nine of them. Plain metal and polished. Three were bigger than the rest. He looked around the hall to find two orbs of light and a total of three doors, all opened wide. Jack could just make out a stack of wooden crates inside each room.

Storage areas, he concluded. *No other threats... hopefully.*

Jack pushed away from the wall with a casual, cattish grace. There was no hesitation in his movements. He'd done this too much and too often to feel any qualms now.

The lights of the Grove weren't like the usual torchlight he'd grown used to. They didn't flicker or wane in ways that could hide his moving shadow. The guard saw the long, dark stretch of shade. He turned with his hands glowing dangerously in front of him, releasing a precise thread of fire as he did so. Jack knew it was more out of instinct than anything. He could tell by how small and controlled it was. Standard protocol for when you were in a safe place and didn't know who might be sneaking up on you. The guard was well-trained.

Not well enough, however.

Jack tilted his head just enough for the fire to stretch into the air behind him, within an ace of his skin. Every nerve in his body hummed as he seized the man's outstretched wrist. Before he could step away, Jack wrenched him forward. His ice unleashed itself. It coated the man's entire left side. Swift and noisy. A cool wind of vapor drifted out in an arch around them, chilling the air.

Now was his cue to scream.

Jack needed to knock him out. But to his surprise, the scream died when red eyes met red. Did he think that just because he was an Elementalist, too, that he wouldn't hurt him? That was naïve. Jack watched, fascinated, as the man's eyes drifted down to where the Heartstone sat above his robes. The guard trembled.

Can he hear her? Jack wondered. Because he could. A soft, edgeless whisper that made him want to stick a candle in his ears and destroy his eardrums. They were words spoken in a foreign tongue. The stresses were so harsh that they made his ears itch. *Is this what Sylvie feels?*

Jack wrinkled his nose at the sudden scent of piss. He looked down to find that the guard had wet himself.

"Wonderful," Jack muttered, before coating his fist in ice and punching him square in the jaw. The guard collapsed. Jack would've grabbed him to silence his fall, but he wasn't about to risk dirtying his hands in *that* way. Instead, he snatched the keys from his belt, then circled around just in time to see Philip emerge from the corner.

Philip grimaced as soon as he stepped foot into the hallway. "What's that smell?" he asked. His gaze shifted from him to the guard, and then back again. "Don't tell me... did he seriously piss himself?"

"Don't remind me."

Philip walked over, only to squeeze his nose once he got too close. "Oh, that's not all either. *Lovely.* What did you do, Dace?"

"What does it look like I did? I iced him."

"That can't be all," Philip argued. "I had my doubts what with you only having one element, but you're good."

"You don't need to state the flaming obvious."

"Just accept the compliment."

"… I have the keys." Jack held them up. "But what do we do with him?"

"Stick him in one of these storage rooms. We can't just leave him here."

"Well, I'm not touching him."

Philip rolled his eyes. "Alright, silk stocking. I'll do this. You get that door open."

"What about the other two?"

"Already dragged them into a storage room across the hall," Philip said dismissively.

Jack stood there for a moment, wondering why there were so many storage rooms in this area. He snapped back to attention when Philip rolled his sleeves up to move the soiled man. He'd rather be trapped in a room with Vidal for a week than stick around for that. Jack hastily made his way back to the door. The coast was clear, but Jack kept an eye on the corners for any lingering Amorphs just in case.

The entrance to the Anvil was set at the end of a flight of stairs, comprised of no less than twenty-two steps. There were no orbs of light here, only a single candle that sat atop an ornate one-light candelabrum on the floor. It was lit, and had been for quite some time, judging by the wax all over the floor. The door itself was twice his height and made of solid black steel. If they were going for subtlety, then they failed miserably.

Jack couldn't see how thick the door was, but he knew that he'd struggle just to open it. There were circular engravings all across its middle. Jack traced them with his finger. He'd seen these before, back in the Drowned Tower. They were explosive enchantments that the Mentalists used to safeguard areas of importance. The marks could be attuned to a practitioner—usually the Arch Poten—so that they could turn anything within a thirty meter radius into ash. They were frequently etched onto the doors of underground annals or crudely scratched onto the walls of rooms once used for heinous sacrifices.

This was definitely the latter.

"What's the hold up?" Philip asked from behind him. He was rubbing his hands on a stained white cloth filled with holes. Jack suspected rats, only because he likely picked it up from whatever storage room he'd thrown the guard into, and places like those were always filled with vermin.

"These markings..." Jack trailed off. "They're a mess just waiting to happen."

"You've got a good eye," Philip commended. "These enchantments are so old that most just think they're for decorative purposes. The few that can place them never remember what they're for or what they do."

"Has this room always been used for Orive Crystals?"

"The Mentalists used to dump bodies down there. They must've been doing something with them or else they wouldn't even bother putting that mark up. I don't know who these enchantments are attuned to right now, if to anyone at all, but Arch Poten Cole's young, so I think it's safe to assume that one of his Potens has control over it."

Jack levelled him with a stare. "You're joking."

"Afraid not." Philip shrugged. "Horrifying thought, isn't it?"

"So, what's stopping them from blowing an entire section of the Institute as soon as they're ousted?"

"Respect for human life? Love for the Grove? Common decency?" Philip listed off, the frown on his face becoming more pronounced with each one. "Creator, I don't know. None of those sound right. We'll cross that bridge when we come to it. For now, just open the door."

"Are there guards on the other side?"

"Let's hope not."

Jack sighed.

This was turning out to be more trouble than it was worth. Though he knew that it would be from the start, it was another thing to be burdened with the Heartstone in an unfamiliar place, while Sylvie was off somewhere he couldn't reach. He knew that divvying up jobs was efficient and it wasn't as if Philip was an incompetent partner—on the contrary, Jack respected the fact that he knew how to both lead and follow, and although Jack wasn't comfortable with having him guard his back, he did acknowledge Philip's skill—but he would've preferred to be kept in their usual groups. Because with familiarity came ease. Jack knew how Sylvie thought, how she moved in the heat of the moment when men pointed their swords at her. Philip was new territory. They'd worked independently thus far, but assuming there were more people behind this door, then they'd have to get used to fighting alongside each other very quickly.

Jack just hoped they'd even be able to.

He distinctly remembered a trial partner he once had in the Drowned Tower, before he was officially paired with Tiv. The needy Amorph had gotten in his way so many times that by the end of the exercise, Jack had purposely begun shooting balls of fire in his direction. Jack didn't offer active support, neither did he expect or want it. He could only hope that Philip got the hint.

What am I even going to do down here? Jack thought. *Kill the workers? Freeze whatever tar is down there? I have to put a stop to it somehow, but I can't blow the place up or make it fall over itself. The Institute is sitting right on top of it.*

He fiddled with the keys, taking the bigger ones in hand first because surely a door this huge required a huge key to match. Luck found him when the first of the keys that he tried fit. It spun smoothly, the pins regularly oiled. Jack motioned for Philip to help him push open the door, and together, they slid it open just enough for them to squeeze their way inside.

Jack gagged as soon as he did.

The air was foul. Arid enough to make his lungs struggle to expand. But he fought the urge to breathe too deeply because, although his lungs craved more oxygen, the stench alone cautioned him against breathing at all. It felt like a desert. There was an ashy substance all around him that made tears well up in his eyes. He didn't think *sinister* had a smell or a taste, but this was definitely it. Jack was justifiably afraid for his health. He didn't want to risk damage to his insides by inhaling something so obviously filthy. Whatever taint that lingered in the room might actually kill him.

"Is this place poisoned?" Jack asked, coughing.

"Look up," Philip said.

Jack did—

—and he regretted ever doing so. This wasn't a finely shaped room like the rest of the ones in the Grove. This was a cavern. Dark and dry. The ceiling extended upward, half-wood, half-earth. There wasn't enough light for him to tell how high it stretched, but it couldn't have been far, since the Grove was right there. The walls looked grainy, even from where he stood. The rocky portions layered on top of wood, and then on top of each other. Uneven, but stable. Some of them even spiraled down, creating stone icicles with jagged tips. Jack hoped they stayed up there, but his track record for getting caught under falling ceilings kept him wary.

The walls curved smoothly to the floor... or what should've been the floor. Instead of stone or packed dirt, there was only a gaping hole that stretched farther than he could see. Jack leaned forward as far as he deemed safe, then gaped at what he saw.

"Are those bodies?" Jack swallowed, staring at the enormous piles of corpses. Was that why there was so much ash? Creator, help him. He had people's remains trapped inside of him now! But they weren't all bones and dust down there. Jack saw sinewy carcasses, too, and even fresh ones. "What is this?"

"Man's mess," Philip answered.

"Is this where you keep your supply for Orive crystals?" There was a moment of silence that confirmed Jack's suspicions.

"When those above wage war, it's always the ones below that die," Philip said, looking down at the hole and muttering a prayer under his breath. "This is where they go."

"*Lerno vinasera!*" Jack yelled. "This is flaming vile! I see fresh corpses down there, too."

"Prisoners with death sentences and Nebbin found dead on the streets, mostly. There are a lot of people that don't have anyone to bury their corpses for them. They're taken here," Philip explained, patient, despite Jack's fury. "Yes, I admit that some are robbed from their graves, but there's no use getting angry about it. What's done is done. Aren't you here to put a stop to this? Now, help me close the door, before someone slips in behind us."

Jack hesitated, not wanting to seal their only source of fresh air. When Philip gestured for him to hurry, however, he acquiesced. Philip was the only rational one between them at the moment, and they certainly didn't need someone slipping behind their backs and giving them trouble later on. Jack could acknowledge that much.

"This way," Philip said.

He led him down a flight of stairs. It connected into a back area, away from the massive pit of corpses. The smell lingered even here. The ceiling was lower; the ground made of compact stone. While there were still pointed spikes that could end him in a moment's notice, they were also smaller and less terrifying.

No fumes, Jack noticed. *If there's a lake here like in the Pit, then where and how are they redirecting the fumes?*

Before he could ask, Philip crouched behind an uneven stone pillar and pulled him down with him.

"What?" Jack asked.

"Arch Poten Cole is in the tunnel ahead of us."

"*What*?" Jack repeated, peeking around the pillar. He found a child with an owl trailing behind him. He was looking around the corner at the very end of the passageway. The hood of the cloak he'd been wearing had been thrown off, exposing platinum blonde hair and childish features.

He looks like Reed, Jack couldn't help but think. After casting his judgment, he asked, "What's he doing here?"

"How would I know? I thought he was with the Elder." Philip cursed. "This is the only entrance I know of that leads to this section of the Anvil. I could go out there, but I don't exactly want to tell him what I'm doing down here. We could try to find another way around if you're okay with getting lost for a bit. But I think it would be best if we wait until they clear *ou*—" he cut himself off when he realized that Jack wasn't even looking at him. "Are you listening to me?"

"Doesn't he look like he's trying to peek at what they're doing, too?" Jack said, inadvertently giving him his answer.

"You really weren't list*e*—*wait*, what?" Philip looked around the pillar as well. He found Lucian pressed against the wall. The boy peered over the edge for a few seconds, before shifting back to hide.

"He's definitely snooping." Jack smirked. "I can work with that. Follow me."

"What do you m*e*—*oh*, wait and listen, will you? Jack, wait!" Philip hissed, but his pleas went ignored, as Jack strolled over.

"What are you doing, kid?" Jack asked.

To his bewilderment, Lucian showed no signs of alarm. The boy merely turned with his head tilted to the side. His eyes were deader than any he'd ever seen. An amazing feat, considering the number of depraved people Jack had come across over his short life. Was this what it took to lead an Institute at such a tender age? If so, then Jack certainly didn't envy him.

Lucian's owl sprung onto his shoulder. It spread its wings wide, exposing blue veins that told him that this was no ordinary bird. Did the Vanguard Circle gift him with a Peose? Some things just weren't fair.

"Relax." Jack held his hands up. "We're all friends here."

Lucian shot him a suspicious glance. He hadn't had a friend since Master Elsevian, and he could still see his bloated purple corpse bobbing up and down the Wymeran River. That was the day he learned that not everyone knew to cut open the stomachs of the dead before throwing them in water.

"Friends?" Lucian repeated. His voice was deeper than Jack expected. "Us?"

I don't believe it either, Jack thought. But realizing that Lucian was growing warier, he said, "Why not? Thelarius knows I could use more of those, and it's not like I'm here to hurt you. I only want to sneak a look at what's going on over there." Jack followed Lucian's eyes as they drifted to a point over his shoulder. He knew exactly who he was looking at. "He's a friend, too. In fact, he's the one that led me to this part of the Anvil. You know him, right? He's a primary apprentice here."

"Philip," Lucian acknowledged.

"Arch Poten Cole," came Philip's automatic response.

"And you are?" Lucian asked.

"Jacques Dace."

"Son of Leonas and Cheryll Dace?"

"The one and only," Jack said. "I was curious about the Orive crystals. Are you the one that oversees their production?"

Lucian grimaced in a way that told him all that he needed to know. "My father was enamored by them," he revealed. "Elder Borris wanted to check on our current operations. He's in there now. I think he wants to put their production on hold until the colleges take over and those that don't know are brought up to speed. They may even choose to stop it permanently."

"The Council doesn't want us to make them anymore?" Philip asked.

"Or so Elder Borris claims," Lucian said. "Master Zacarias is in there arguing with him now."

"What about you?" Jack prompted, impressed by how well-spoken he was. Maturity at that age was rare, but perhaps it was to be expected of the so-called, second coming of Maurice. If more children were like this, instead of the little pests he knew them to be, then he'd be infinitely better with them. "What do you think about the crystals?"

"I want them gone," he said with finality. Philip stared at him, expecting him to explain the reason why he did, but Lucian merely pursed his lips and turned back around—done with the conversation.

Jack grinned.

Wicked eyes, this one, he suddenly heard. The most flawless whisper yet. *Blue like Maurice. A knife behind a smile.*

His grin tightened.

"Is something wrong?" Philip asked.

Jack didn't answer, not wanting him to know his troubles, but also refusing to lie. He waved vaguely instead.

Philip shot him a look. The concern was plain on his face, but also quickly forgotten in light of their current situation. Without speaking, Philip clasped his shoulder in assurance—a reminder that he was there if he needed him—before he went to stand beside Lucian, so he could peer over the wall; also allowing Jack a moment to gather his bearings in private.

It didn't take long.

She took to whispering nonsense in his ears again. Although he wouldn't lie to himself by saying that he preferred *her* speaking in the trade tongue—because he didn't. Not a chance. Foreign and ancient languages were easy to ignore. Whenever *she* whispered something he could actually understand, he ended up stopping in his tracks, forgetting everything else around him. That would get him killed one of these days. It was also another reason Sylvie needed to take the Heartstone back. It felt heavier than any necklace should.

Jack took three deep breaths, mentally preparing himself for whatever *she*'d be throwing his way, because surely *she*'d be speaking to him again. Soon. They were so close to another roomful of raw *Orivellea* that his stomach was already churning in anticipation. There was no way *she*'d leave him be. Jack had a sinking feeling that as soon as he saw it with his own eyes, *she*'d force him to get rid of it, once again unconcerned for his safety. So long as he bent to *her* will and finished the job, then they were on good terms.

Sylvie was Silas' descendant. A man that had somehow won *her* favor for himself and the rest of his line. Jack hadn't yet. Not by a long shot. He didn't delude himself into believing that he was anything more than a vessel; someone whose magic she controlled and whose body she could cause crippling pain to whenever *she* pleased. Why *she* didn't continuously do so was—

Jack pressed his hand to the back of his neck. He swore he felt Sylvie's pinching fingers, scolding him, dragging him away from his cynical train of thought. If he tried, he could even hear her voice: *'She's not going to hurt us, Jack. Not intentionally anyway.'*

"Pernelia, guide me," he muttered. "I'm going insane."

"Dace," Philip called, waving frantically for him to come see. "Elder Borris and Master Zacarias are arguing."

Walking toward the pair, Jack opted to stand behind Lucian, so he could press his hands on the smaller boy's shoulders to balance himself as he twisted his neck. Half of his view was obscured by Lucian's blonde head, but what he did see was enough to leave him breathless.

This was nothing like the crude working conditions in the Pit. There were orbs of aqua-colored light littered across the ground, enough to illuminate everything from floor to ceiling. Engravings ran all along the floor and around the room, no doubt fueled by magic. Even the people were healthier. Well-fed and clean. There were no fetters on their wrists or ankles, but they did have multiple Demar spells on their limbs.

Fitting replacements, he thought.

Corpses were piled onto wooden barrows, washed and disrobed, then dumped into the large black pool in the middle of it all. Conjurers and Elementalists served as mixers, swishing the water around with their powers. No signs of overwork to be found. They were likely replaced every few hours before their circuits gave out. Deep in the water's depths, he saw blocks of *Orivellea* already forming, floating to the top, before being pushed out of the water by the mixers. The blocks were carted off towards a section in the back that he couldn't see. To be cut into more wieldy sizes, he assumed. Not that their sizes mattered at this point. Jack had already gotten a glimpse at the darkness trapped within. The very same tendrils in his eyes, caught within those crystals.

No ancient beings hiding there. Only power.

Astounding, what a few key differences could make. What caught Jack the most, however, was the lack of fumes from this method. There was only clean air and a pleasant minty smell that completely masked the scent of death two corridors down. Was that because practitioners were actually dissolved here and not just Nebbin? Did that even make a difference?

How dissolved bodies could even be used to trap pieces of *her* wasn't something he ever truly wanted to know the secret to, although he had no qualms about hazarding a guess.

Since *she* could inhabit Nebbin—and to some extent, practitioners, without eventually killing them from an overdose of magic—then their substances mixed with the natural sealing properties of *Orivellea* created the perfect container for the pieces of *her* that unconsciously multiplied, despite being separated from the main body... or in other words, the very thing he carried around his neck.

This place truly was marvelous. Vile, but marvelous. When it came down to it, the Anvil was the only true legacy left behind by Maurice. Not the Grove, not the books he wrote, or the systems he built, but this. *This* is what Maurice wanted to leave behind. It was his life's work...

... And it made Jack's head feel like it was going to explode.

Because no matter how much he reassured himself, no matter what mental fortitudes he built, it still didn't prepare him for what he knew would happen. The last thing Jack saw before drawing back and crumbling to his knees was—who he assumed—Master Zacarias unleashing a violent spire of ice at Elder Borris. That couldn't be good. But neither was his current situation.

Jack cradled his head between his knees as blood gushed to his temples. The back of his eyeballs felt hot. The voices grew louder. Jack ran his hands through his hair like a madman, trying in vain to silence them. They wanted him to move.

Move, move, move.

How could he though? Jack could hardly stand with how much they made his head pound.

"What's wrong?" someone asked.

That was Philip's voice, he knew. A whip to snap his mind from his thoughts. He was close. Too close for comfort. Jack couldn't be touched when he was like this.

His eyes snapped open.

Hovering an inch above him, Philip's hand stilled.

"Don't touch me," Jack warned through gritted teeth. His voice was low and tight with fear. The surroundings seemed to slip through his fingers. Unreal. Unable to be trusted. His blood felt hot, surging through his veins like gushing river water through a too small sieve.

Jack bit his bottom lip to contain the shout that threatened to escape him. He crushed the heels of his hands against his eyes and waited for the feeling to pass.

He could have Philip use his magic, could have him turn it against the black tar wrapped around him, constricting his insides, and sucking what little color that was left in his skin— could have, as if it mattered. The words sat on his tongue like stones. Jack wasn't entirely sure why he was uncomfortable with revealing *her* secrets, but what he did know was that the weaknesses of the Heartstone weren't for others to realize.

Where's Sylvie? Jack wondered. Her touch was grounding. An easy, unselfish comfort. Philip's would be decidedly... not.

"Flames!" Jack half-hissed, half-yelled. He grabbed the side of his neck when what felt like a stack of books fell on top of it.

Before he could bite through the skin of his bottom lip, there was a blinding glow of light. Someone touched his shoulder, and then the pain cut off like a blow candle.

Jack collapsed at its absence. He opened his eyes to find an engrossed Lucian watching the tendrils recede. Behind him, Philip gawked at the darkness. But just as Jack opened his mouth to explain, a yell caught their attention.

"Did you see that glow? Someone's there!"

"Run!" another screamed, presumably Elder Borris. "Now, Lucian! Run!"

"Get him!"

There was no time for explanations now.

Jack did the first thing that came to mind; he picked Lucian up from under his arms and made a mad dash toward the nearest pillar that was wide enough to cover them. Lucian's owl flew up to the ceiling, hiding amidst the jagged deposits there without having to be directed. His Peose was smart, Jack would give it that. A short distance away, he saw Philip settle behind another pillar. It was thinner and shorter than the one they were hiding behind, but there was nothing to be done about that now.

The practitioners poured in.

Judging from the number of footsteps he heard race through the corridor they'd just left, there were at least forty of them. It was one thing to face a crowd of Nebbin, but a crowd of practitioners? Impossible. Some he could take. Forty at once, however, was a death sentence. That was a tiny army. There was no way he could handle all of those men, even with someone as powerful as Philip by his side.

Jack pressed his back against the raw stone. His hands settled on Lucian's shoulders. They were small and bony in his grasp. He squeezed them, tacitly trying to reassure him that everything would be alright. He always found a way out of the most awry situations. This time would be no different. And while he wasn't always whole by the end of it, he was alive. That's what mattered.

Truthfully, Jack comforted him more out of reflex rather than any actual concern for his feelings. Some part of him actually doubted that Lucian needed solace, but when he turned to face him, Jack saw the concern in his eyes. If he was the cause of an Arch Poten's death, especially one as young as this, he'd never forgive himself.

His lips twisted, as he thought about what they needed to do. They were in an open space and beset on all sides. It was only a matter of time until they found them hiding behind the columns. But Jack wasn't sure if the fact that they were in an open area was good or bad for them, since he didn't know what kind of practitioners they had or if they even cared about accidentally injuring each other in the process of trying to get to them. They likely had Healers that could clean up their wounds in case of friendly fire anyway.

A pebble rolled forward. It skidded to a stop a short distance away from Jack's foot. He didn't dare turn to find out who had kicked it... he didn't have to. From his periphery, emerged a booted foot and a full head of black hair. Jack held his breath when he saw the violent sparkle of serrated daggers.

Filan vahs, he thought. *Now what?*

***

Sylvie leaned against the rails on one of the upper rooms in the main section of the Grove. It was an open space meant for small gatherings. Low tables and half-pushed in chairs littered the area. There were no walls here, only one staircase that led up and another that led down. Both were framed by the same bannisters that circled the room. While there were certainly more comfortable and more private places to stay, this gave her a ringside view of the fighting below.

It started out innocent enough.

The Lafertti Clan was searching for their representative—Master Zacarias, or so she gathered from their constant shouting. They claimed he was missing; the rest called them dramatic. Sylvie didn't want to involve herself in their affairs. But when hands began glowing and it looked as if they'd start shooting more than just warning shots at each other, Dalis couldn't be convinced to leave. It didn't help that they had no clue where the Elder was. So, her brother was more than happy to stay right where they were to keep an eye on what was going on.

Where are the Potens? Sylvie wondered. *Or better yet, where are their Masters? Someone needs to put a stop to this. Are they really going to leave it to the senior practitioners?*

From the corner of her eye, Sylvie looked at Dalis. He had a very crabby look on his face. She knew that look. It was the one he gave her whenever she said or did something so unbelievably stupid that even he couldn't find amusement in it. She'd been on the receiving end of it only twice in her life—and both times, it had terrified her enough to avoid him for a week.

Dalis crossed his arms, as he examined the faces of every practitioner that entertained the Lafertti Clan's words. It wasn't long before those same practitioners began involving the other practitioners around them. The regular taunts were thrown around. Along with some more creative ones that Sylvie had never heard before—feckless biff, *nimici,* Maurice's beard—but seemed to be common amongst the practitioners here. There were a few that even hinted at secrets only the older colleges knew. Thankfully, nothing too drastic. They were all ignored by those that didn't get them.

Unfortunately, Dalis wasn't one of them.

"I don't recognize a lot of them," Dalis told her.

Not recognizing any faces herself, Sylvie took his word for it. She grouped them by their beliefs. On one side were the

Lafertti Clan and their supports—radicals that kept repeating a baseless theory about the Potens taking away Master Zacarias and dragging him down into the Anvil in an endeavor to stop the college takeover from happening. They demanded that the Potens be dragged from their rooms and held accountable for their crimes. Arguing across from them were the outliers in the Grove that still supported what the Potentate Union stood for. They didn't want the Potens gone, only replaced. Those were the ones that likely had something to lose from the Union's abolition. Then, interspersed in between, were those that were dragged into this fight. Most had opted to spout their own beliefs, somehow thinking this a good time to do so. It, predictably, caused even more chaos.

"They're from a different college," Sylvie finally answered when she realized that there would be no lull between their shouts for her to speak without raising her voice. "It's only right that you don't recognize them."

"I know the faces of my enemies," he argued. "Those aren't members of the Lafertti Clan, yet they're standing beside them."

"Another college then? I'm sure the Lafertti Clan has supporters from all parts of the Grove."

"Maybe." He squinted. "See that man on the side? The one standing with the crowd of Scripts?"

"The gray-haired one?"

"Him." Dalis leaned dangerously forward. "Why is he with my college? I don't recognize him. He's even talking to them. An old friend, maybe? No, I'd definitely remember a face like that. He looks old enough to be a Master. The Grove doesn't have any regular practitioners that age."

"I don't think he's the Elder we're looking for either," Sylvie said. "He's not wearing the official robes. Although, he could've changed."

"To blend in?" Dalis made a face. "Why would he do that? He's a member of the Zenith Council. Why even try looking like a regular practitioner? I'd understand if it was outside of the

Institute, but those brassy robes are instant respect here."

"He could be travelling with the Elder," Sylvie suggested, "or he could've entered without him."

"Now, there's a theory." Dalis nodded to himself. "Why are members of my college even here in the first place? Who brought them? I know they're antsy for change, but if they don't walk away now, then the younger ones might see, and you know how easily influenced they are."

"Then go down there and force them to leave," Sylvie said.

"I was going to, but now that an Arch Poten *ordered* me to do it, I'll be able to justify myself to them."

Sylvie grimaced. "You're a great person."

"I take offense to that."

"Well, as long as you're following my orders, then break up that fight while you're down there, and be quick about it, would you? You promised you'd help me find the Elder."

"I will," he said. But just as he was about to head down, one of the practitioners caught his attention.

"Applesauce!" the practitioner yelled, loud enough for everyone to hear. He was a Conjurer with a small nose and round spectacles—young. Too young to be caught in the middle of such an acerbic crowd.

"Was that supposed to be an expletive?" an Elementalist with a square jaw and hard eyes shouted back in disbelief. He looked like a dented suitcase. "Ashy fucking spirits, you're making my ears bleed! Go home to your mother, you depraved Snuff-humper."

The young practitioner was more explosive than his appearance suggested because fire spiraled out of his hands. A wave of heat washed over the crowd. The air above them blurred, as he directed his fingers at the man that had the audacity to shout back. But with youth came inexperience. He'd chosen the wrong opponent. An Elementalist with eyes as merciless as the one he was facing was too much for him to handle. He was the type that wouldn't go easy on anyone. Sylvie had seen many practitioners like him over the years; those with unrivalled reaction times. Once they realized an attack was coming, their instincts kicked in. Block, retaliate, repeat. Thinking came after the threat was dealt with.

Not one of the Grove's patrollers then, she knew. He didn't have the temperament for that. *A guard then? For one of the higher ranking practitioners no doubt. He might even be someone's primary apprentice.*

Sylvie saw the exact moment the Conjurer realized his mistake. The boy's eyes flew open, certainly not expecting to have both of his wrists seized by the Elementalist at the exact moment his magic burst forth. The man was fearless, utterly indifferent to the flames that licked at his clothes. He put all of his attention to redirecting the boy's hands to the ground, where they blew a hole into the floor. A scream echoed up to them. High-pitched and girlish. If it actually belonged to a woman though, no one could say. But someone had definitely gotten caught in the crossfire down there. Their pain was promptly drowned by the noise of the blazing tornado.

When the boy finally registered what had happened, he cut off the flow of his magic. But it was already too late. The Elementalist switched his grip so that he was holding him down with one hand. He raised his free arm up to the elbow, angling it in such a way that his fingertips were pointed directly at the boy's face. Chilly smoke emanated from his palm. His entire right arm shook from the amount of magic concentrated in it, but before he could spear him with his arm, the boy was yanked out of the way.

The Elementalist's hand was abruptly grabbed and pointed into the open hole left behind by the boy. He reflexively released his magic, creating a spire of ice that's peak threatened to stab a hole right through him. It would have, too, had the tip of the glacier not been systematically sliced off as it ascended.

It was only when the Elementalist stopped releasing his magic and the surroundings settled in a moment of peace that Sylvie saw the one responsible for putting a stop to their impromptu fight.

"Dalis," she gasped

He stood in the middle of it all, eyes wild and chest heaving. His naked dagger shone in the sparse light. Its edge was sprinkled with remnants of hoarfrost. Sylvie called out to him, louder this time, but it was masked by the sudden clamor of practitioners. Dalis ignored them. He took a moment to look up at the mass of ice before him, not at all impressed by how it glittered in the light. Instead, he snarled like a mad dog.

"What do you think you're doing?" Dalis demanded, slamming the Elementalist into the ice. Before the Conjurer could make a break for it, the members of the Scripts that were in the crowd sprang out and tackled him to the ground. "Answer me!"

"Back off, Sirx!" came an enraged shout from the crowd.

Dalis knew that voice. It belonged to a man that he really didn't want to see. Not now. Not ever.

"Tobias," he said venomously. Dalis didn't even turn to look at him. "I'll deal with you later. I've got business with this man here."

"That's a member of the Lafertti Clan, Sirx. Touch him and we'll split your neck faster than aged wood."

"Do you really want to defend someone that almost killed a fellow practitioner?"

"As far as I'm concerned, that was self-defense," Tobias argued. "If you want to talk about murder, then look at that fresh-faced shit from the Sanct Union that your college mates are pointing their blades at. The Red Scripts are on duty in the Slates, aren't they? If that wasn't a prisoner's scream we heard, then it was one of yours. That's his fault. Let go of him."

"So, he'll be pardoned because he didn't kill anyone?" Dalis challenged, holding his blade up to the Elementalist's neck. "He was about to, and he would have if I hadn't stepped in."

"You can't punish someone because they were *about* to do something! For Maurice's sake, you don't even have the authority to punish a member of your own college, let alone a member of another. Stop acting like you do!"

Their argument sparked the animosity of the practitioners around them, and before she knew it, the chaos returned, stronger and more violent than before. Sylvie saw a fist fight break out on the sidelines. The instigators were jeered on by their college mates. If there were any pacifists among them before, then they were gone now. All had fled at the first sign of magic being used to physically harm other people.

Sylvie pushed her way toward the middle where Dalis was. By the time she got there, she saw that he'd let go of the Elementalist and was now chest to chest with Tobias. A group of angry practitioners stood behind each of them, waiting for an excuse to lash out. With weapons or fists didn't matter. In the distance, she saw a group of younger practitioners running all around the Institute, calling everyone they could to the main section. If it was out of panic or excitement, she couldn't tell. But practitioners poured in by the dozens. Some asked questions, but most opted to jump right into the fray after seeing a friend of theirs get socked in the jaw or elbowed in the gut.

What's wrong with these people? she thought. Dalis had told her that most of the Grove's practitioners were divided; that they were looking for any excuse to snap, band with who they could, and then handle all of the Grove's "problems" themselves, but actually seeing it unfold before her eyes was downright insane.

At this point, Sylvie knew that the appearance of any Masters or Potens would just make things worse. She prayed that none would come, though by the way those adolescents ran around, shouting like heralds, she doubted it.

"Dalis!" Sylvie called, grabbing his elbow to pull him away from Tobias. "You were supposed to *stop* the fighting."

"I did!" he defended. "It's this *sih tovash* that instigated it."

"You're blaming me for this?" Tobias stubbornly lifted his chin. "If you hadn't pointed your knife at our college mate's throat, then this could've ended quietly."

"Quietly?" Dalis repeated, incredulous. "That man of yours

was spieling about the Potens dragging Master Zacarias to the Anvil against his will before any of this even started. Tell me how an accusation like that can end quietly? He's lucky none of the representatives heard that garbage!"

"Then *you* tell me where Master Zacarias is!" the Elementalist shouted from where he was being held back by other members of his college. "We've checked everywhere. The only other option is the Anvil, and he *hates* it down there."

"That doesn't mean the Potens dragged him there!"

"How do you know?" he cried. "Do you know where the Potens are? Because we can't find them either. They've all just magically disappeared! That can't be a coincidence."

"Oh, for the love of—this is why everyone avoids the Lafertti Clan." Dalis threw his hands in the air. "You're all impossible."

"Dalis!" Sylvie chastised, once again trying and failing to pull him away. "We—I don't have time for this!"

"And who's this?" Tobias asked, turning on her.

"Steady there, Tobias," Dalis said dangerously. "Don't drag my sister into this."

"Sister?" Tobias recited. He looked her up and down, before grimacing. "I heard about you. Aren't you the new Arch Poten of the Drowned Tower? They told me that you were here, but I didn't actually believe it until now. Why aren't you in the Alps?"

"Shouldn't you be trying to barter peace, instead of arguing with me?" Sylvie retorted.

"I don't want to hear that from someone obviously avoiding their duties. Why did you decide to stop by the Grove? To see your brother? If you'd gone north, instead of taking this useless detour, then the Summit might've been over with by now and our representatives would be in power!"

"You're pinning this on me? Did you forget about your own Arch Poten?"

"He's a child." Tobias scoffed. "His opinion hardly counts. The Zenith Council has been known to make exceptions to their rules. I'm sure they could overlook the absence of a twelve-year old boy."

Flames, she felt like she was talking to a barrel.

"Dalis was right," Sylvie said, all traces of anger tempered behind a controlled voice. It was the same tone her father employed whenever he was aggravated, and it had a knack for igniting fury. "You're impossible. I've never met anyone with such an assuming mind. Are you sure your representative didn't just run away?"

Tobias grabbed her by the collar. "What did—"

Dalis threw him off. "Back off, Tobias!"

"You again, Sirx?" Tobias shouted, jumping to his feet. His hands glowed with his wrath. All of the practitioners in the immediate vicinity tensed. Hilts were gripped and hands were raised in anticipation. "Come on then. I've had a bone to pick with you for *years*. If you really want to test your skills against me, then be my guest. It's time you remembered that no matter how hard you try Conjurers will *always* outrank filthy Healers."

Insulted shouts were heard from all around. Heads swiveled in their direction and entire throngs of people shoved their way to get closer to the suddenly surrounded members of Tobias' little crew.

"You're just awful with people, aren't you?" Dalis whistled at all of the angry Healers unsheathing their weapons. One of the younger practitioners had no specialty, and so brought out a grimoire the size of a pocketbook instead. That was new.

"Dalis." Sylvie tugged on his arm. She pointed to a group of practitioners spilling out of a hallway. They were all members of the Lafertti Clan. Sylvie squinted, trying to see where they were coming from. It looked to be from a floor below them. She heard footsteps coming from all around though, which led her to believe that the practitioners from the other colleges were still on their way.

Absently, she noted that two fuming Masters had arrived on the scene. They kept shouting, trying to get their practitioners into some semblance of order. While in the farther corners, a

Poten had made the mistake of showing himself. His arms were currently being held behind his back by a particularly burly Amorph, while another held a saw-toothed dagger to his throat.

That wasn't good.

Getting rid of the Potens now would only result in needless bloodshed. They needed the Hunters from the Vanguard Circle to keep the practitioners that still supported the Potentate Union in line for when the representatives took over. They also needed them for damage control once a larger portion of the Grove found out about how *Orivellea* were made. If they got rid of them now, while the Alps was still preparing for the Summit and unable to send aid, then working with the Hunters would be difficult afterwards. Most would resent them for leaving them to overthrow the Potens themselves. A resentment that would only double once they realized what was going on in the Anvil.

This is why I wanted to leave as soon as possible, Sylvie thought, internally panicking.

"We should go," she said, but Dalis brushed her aside, too concerned with Tobias. He motioned with his chin for her to leave. That was the only warning she got, before he charged. The practitioners behind him followed his lead. "For Silas' sake, Dalis!"

Sylvie surveyed her surroundings, careful to dodge any incoming practitioners that stepped in her way. People were still coming in. Once in a while, a Master flew through the halls, trying to calm everyone down. Their robes stood out amidst the rest of the practitioners. She couldn't find any representatives though, and the only Poten there was the one pleading for his life. Sylvie doubted the Elder was here.

What now? she thought. *I could find Jack. Maybe he's with the Elder. Or... no, it would probably be better if I found the representatives first. They'd be able to stop this madness. But I'm sure they must've heard the noise by now.*

She stilled in realization.

Was that boy right then? Are they being held somewhere?

Her gaze drifted to the one still being threatened by the Amorphs. They seemed harmless enough. If they actually wanted to hurt him, then they would have by now. Sylvie could hear his undignified squeals from a mile away. She doubted he knew where the representatives were.

It would have to be a private place. Closed off to the general public. Her hands flew to the space above her collar, hoping to get an answer. She paused when she grasped air. *The stone's with Jack… right. I hope he's doing better th—oh, Jack! The Anvil is under lock and key. If the representatives are down there, then he's going to have his hands full. I should go see him.*

But then again, so are the—

Sylvie made her way toward the two Amorphs, lighting a few sleeves on fire as she did so.

"Back up," she told them.

The effect was immediate. Both of them straightened. The one with the dagger brandished it threateningly in her direction.

"Who are you?" he asked.

"Someone that has business with him." She pointed at the sniveling Poten. Her hands were already glowing, prepared to do whatever it took to take him from them.

"Then get in line!"

"Didn't you hear her?" someone said from behind him. "She said she had business with him."

Before he could even turn to face the newcomer, he was kicked in the tender spot on the back of his knees. The man gasped. He caught himself with his hands. Without even giving him time to recover, the blade's hilt came crashing down on his neck, knocking him out cold. Two booted feet jumped on the man's back. She followed them up an unexpectedly short distance.

Sylvie's eyebrows rose at who stood before her.

"Myrrh?" she asked, doubtful. But the grin the Amorph gave her was filled with so much fire that whatever else she was going to say lodged itself in her throat. Sylvie's head snapped to the side when the larger man crumbled to the ground in a heap of relaxed limbs. His tongue lolled out, numb and out of his control. Her eyes widened even more when she was greeted by a familiar head of auburn curls. "Ethil?"

"You're gaping, Syl," Myrrh said.

Her mouth snapped shut. "Of course I'm gaping," Sylvie said, exasperated. She couldn't keep the smile from her face. "Cheryll said you were both headed to the Alps! How did you wind up here? No, better yet, *why* are you here?"

"Same as you." Myrrh shrugged. "Sightseeing."

"Oh, joy. You're lying to my face again. I have so many questions, but first..." Sylvie hauled the Poten up by his upper arms. He was taller than her, but also skinnier. Her hands heated. A tacit warning that she had no qualms about using her magic on him. "You're a Poten, right?"

The man shook his head.

"His name's Aldrid Grieves," Myrrh enlightened. "His robes are different because he works as their communications overseer. It's basically a glorified clerk's position. He's in charge of any missives the Potentate Union receives."

"What about their records?"

"That, too." Myrrh nodded. "Historical documents, old texts, practitioner reports, assembly transcriptions, you name it. He has no real power, but he does have access."

"That's good enough for me." Sylvie faced him. "I need you to take me to the archives' restricted section."

19

Jack didn't know what happened topside, but when a man shouted for backup and several of them suddenly started arguing about who would go and how many, he was only thankful. They fussed like kids, while he internally cheered in triumph. He didn't dare question his fortune, too afraid that it would abandon him midway.

Over the years, Jack had grown adept at counting men by the sound of their footfalls. It was a good skill to have for patrols, even better when wandering lands as threatening as the south. He didn't claim to be always right, but he could give a close estimate. It was child's play for him to listen to their dragging feet. At first, only a few followed the faceless godsend back through whatever entrance he'd come from. Five, ten, twenty, and then a few more stragglers after that.

Twenty-five at most. Fifteen at least.

More would come once they heard the screams, but he'd deal with them later. It would be easier to off them as they entered than as a group. All that mattered now was that the practitioner had cut their force by half.

A wild laugh bubbled at the back of Jack's throat. The whole of the group he couldn't take, twenty at once he couldn't take, but with half gone and Philip there to take more, he had — ten? *Ten?*

He'd wipe them from the face of Ferus Terria.

As quietly as possible, Jack switched positions with Lucian, so that he was the one with his back pressed to the stone. Lucian looked up in concern. Jack pressed a finger to his lips, before he shifted on the balls of his feet. His eyes met Philip's from across the cavern. Familiar orange orbs that glowed in the darkness.

Jack smirked when Philip nodded in understanding. Battle-ready practitioners always made the best partners.

He waited, silent, his right ear angled in the direction of the vanishing footfalls. He listened to the breaths of those remaining, listened to their whispered exchanges. Nothing more than idle talk lost in the distance. The cavern already felt emptier. It was in a physical sense, but he hadn't seen the exact number of people inside, hadn't observed them as they occupied the space. Walking amongst them was out of the question. So, then how could he ever truly feel for himself that the cavern was cramped? Perhaps the feeling of emptiness was just a trick of his mind. His body wanted to move. He wouldn't be able to if he believed it was still crowded with enemies. Not that it mattered now. Because in a few minutes, the cavern would be even emptier. He'd see to that.

The tendons in his forearms flexed as he spread and fisted his hands in turn. His mouth went dry in anticipation. Warmth spread behind his ribs. All a part of the intangible rush of a fight soon to come. Jack took a second to channel his fury — the coil of heat that bubbled in his stomach at what they were doing — into the magic that coursed through his veins. He'd need it.

For the first time since they entered, Jack chanced a peek. His vision was limited, made more so by the sparse light. He saw four that lingered in the back shadows. A pair to the right, talking quietly. A group of five across from them. Two that wandered on their own. The rest were lost to him.

He met Philip's eyes a final time, then Lucian's. Jack took the boy's hands and placed them over his mouth.

"Don't move," he ordered.

Lucian nodded.

Good, he thought. *No more waiting.*

There was no hesitation in his movements. No nerve-wracking instant for him to comprehend what he was about to do. No draw of breath before the wild world of blood and gore caught up to him again, with arms as tender and open as a parent welcoming home a child.

Jack simply *moved.*

He set his sights on the nearest wanderer first. A small, lean woman that Jack easily pulled behind the pillar as she passed. He knocked her out with a well-placed strike behind the neck before she even realized what had happened. With Lucian's help, they managed to lean her silently against the wall. But it wasn't long before another woman followed when she didn't see her emerge. This one was taller and broader than most, including Jack. Knocking her unconscious wouldn't be easy.

It took him the quarter of a second to make a decision.

There was a flash of light, and a narrow spear of ice flew from Jack's hand to the woman's throat, turning the warning she was about to shout into blood.

The rest, having seen the light of his magic, managed to raise their weapons. But it did the closest pair little good, as Philip charged and punched one of them in the mouth. The man reeled back, while Philip sidestepped the downward swing of his more delicate partner. She stumbled forward, and Philip elbowed her hard between the shoulder blades, forcing her the rest of the way down. He followed it up with a harsh stomp to the back of her head. Philip had just enough time to grab the dagger from her nerveless fingers, before the first man came at him again. He had one hand cupped over his broken nose and the other on the hilt of a long sword.

The man was coated in ice before he could even swing it.

Philip watched as the blade was casually plucked from his hand and used to pommel him into oblivion. Instead of keeping it, Jack tossed it to the side with a displeased frown on his face.

"You don't use weapons?" Philip asked. He spun the dagger with his thumb. "Because you should."

"I have my hands, don't I?"

Jack bared his teeth in a feral smile, while the rest of the practitioners finally gathered their bearings. *No Amorphs,* he noted, pleased by the fact. *But one Elementalist, seven... no, eight Healers, and a mess of Conjurers.*

Jack's hands smoldered in preparation.

This was going to be a massacre.

Four came at him at once, clearly seeing him as the bigger threat because of his eyes. They weren't wrong... not really. He'd need to use his magic sparingly, lest they find out his secret.

Two Conjurers blasted fire at him, forcing him to roll to the right, where an Elementalist waited. She ensnared his boots in a layer of ice that reached just above his ankles. Jack moved his legs, but they wouldn't budge. Before he could even attempt an escape, a shout from Philip rose from behind him. Jack swiveled without hesitation. A Healer stood there with his hands reaching towards his back.

So, they intended to capture him? They wouldn't for long.

Jack unleashed slender spires of ice from his hands. The man blinked twice at him, before he reached down to touch one of the many icicles staked in the spaces between his ribs. Jack tugged roughly on the Healer's arm. Once he got a good grip, he pulled with as much strength as he could muster and mercilessly slammed him into the sharp ice at his feet, freeing his boots. The Healer shrieked. But Jack didn't bother watching him suffer.

He turned on his heel, narrowly dodging a blazing sword thrown at him like a javelin by a furious Conjurer across the cavern. Jack bent to place his hands upon the ground. His ice sprayed forward, successfully trapping the thrower's legs. Fire bloomed from the man's hands, but Jack's magic travelled faster than most, courtesy of the stone around his neck. His ice spread up to his opponent's knees in an instant. The Conjurer only had a second to gawk, before Jack's magic entombed him. His flames were doused before they could even blow past his fingertips.

Without warning, that pesky Elementalist that first hurled ice in his direction appeared behind him. She had a frosty blade in one hand and magic budding in the other. She swung her sword in a downward arc that Jack nearly tripped trying to sidestep. It was followed by a punch to his shoulder.

That was no regular hit. Jack felt the gale she unleashed in his very bones. It made the surrounding muscles ripple, as he flew until he slammed into a wall. The rocky protrusions cut into his cheek, head, and back. Jack wheezed, trying to catch his breath. He got on all fours, absently noticing that there was a dead man beside him.

Philip's work?

He didn't have time to speculate. The practitioners gave him no time to rest. A Conjurer abruptly kicked him on the side with a stone-encrusted leg. Jack coughed out blood. Before he could gather his wits, the Conjurer stood above him with his hands outstretched, seeking death.

"Vaklas," Jack cursed. He blindly reached for something— *anything*—beside him and found the sharp edge of a naked sabre. Jack's fingers wrapped around it. Blood trickled down his palm, but desperation masked any pain he felt.

With frantic movements, he twisted it as best he could, before launching it forward to stab the Conjurer just below his throat. The man's voice vanished upward into a sharp scream. He gurgled twice, then fell.

Jack rolled away from him just in time to catch that Elementalist raising another hellish gale. No devastating hurricanes or tunnels of fire here. None of them let their magic spiral out of control... and he was glad for it. He'd be in a world of trouble if they did. But they knew the consequences of destroying the Institute's base.

He'd use that to his advantage.

Jack sprinted toward a slender pillar in the far corner of the cavern, away from Philip and Lucian. The Elementalist followed with a Healer behind her. A Conjurer stood back in the distance, providing long-range support.

"Pests," Jack said under his breath. He ignored the almost hysterical whispers in his ears. They grew louder whenever he unleashed his magic. Their foreign words were charms that boosted his power. "That's perfect. Stay on the sidelines," he warned *her* between breaths. "Try to take over and I guarantee you that neither of us will make it back topside."

Jack saw the Elementalist from his position behind the pillar first. She was a short distance away. Her arm outstretched in his direction, intending to blow him straight out of his hiding place. She was going to be a *pleasure* to kill.

He threw himself at the cave's wall opposite of him. His magic exploded as it left his hands. There was a hiss in the air, followed by a thousand cracks. Ice sheathed the wall. Spikes emerged from floor to ceiling. An exceptionally large one sprouted outwards to stab the Elementalist through the ear. It sliced half of it clean off, before piercing through her skull.

There were a number of terrified shrieks from all around. The Healer that had been following the Elementalist stopped in his tracks, horrified by the sight. A few more practitioners entered from the next room. Guards, perhaps. Laggards meant to protect the mixers. Nowhere near enough to overwhelm them. They gasped like the rest when they saw the wall of ice, and the Elementalist held up by the spike embedded in her head.

Jack took their moment of collective shock to look out at how many remained. *So few left,* he thought, *yet still too many.*

A frightened Conjurer unleashed a battle cry that bolstered his companions. Jack fell to his haunches to place his fingers upon the cool ground, promptly engulfing him in a block of ice.

Across the room, Philip curled his hand around an enemy's throat until the skin bruised. He sunk his borrowed dagger into the man's torso, leaving it there, before he threw him to the side. The man fell straight into another motionless practitioner that had been burned alive sometime during the fight.

There was no pause in Philip's movements. No instant to second guess himself. It was only him against everyone else. Philip bent to shift the ground beneath another practitioner's feet. Jack saw just how immense his control over his power was. The ground under his enemies shifted only in the areas he wanted them to. No excess trails like Jack's, even when he still possessed all of his powers. Every so often, Philip's magic would screech by in a froth of dust and sharp little rocks that darted like needles. Bits ricocheted off to the side to the pain of a few unlucky men.

Fighting with Philip was different than he expected. With Sylvie, it was like being at the back of a perpetual explosion. Fire turned the world into day. With Tiv, it was a competition. Who could finish the most, the fastest, and with the least amount of injuries? But with Philip, it was like having someone with black-bottled anger looming behind you in an alleyway. Silent and terrifying. He held an unfathomable power that he never fully showed. Every few seconds, Jack heard the sickening crunch of stones crash against bone. Thunderous roars echoed around them. Metal scraped whenever a man got too close. It was the sound of larger blades being parried by one not even half their size. Daggers were built for speed and efficiency. Jack heard Philip's whistle in the air whenever he swung.

Seeing him, Jack could see why so many favored it now.

Jack twisted when a woman with cropped hair abruptly charged at him with a spear. He dodged and wrapped both hands around the wooden end just as she began to jerk it back. Her palms slid loose on the shaft from the unexpected resistance. She attempted to turn, only for Jack to yank the weapon free. Momentum carried them both. Jack spun the bladed end around his back and then forward again, guiding it until he could grasp it with both hands.

The woman drew in a breath.

Jack drove the spear hard into the space below her collar, where the top of her jerkin sat unfastened. The force of the blow sent the spear's head wholly through her. Its sharp tip protruded from her scapula. He looked on as she wrapped her hand around the wooden shaft in disbelief, but he was soon distracted by another angry shout and a volatile tornado of fire headed his way. They were finally past the point of regulating their magic.

Too late now, he thought.

In the end, Jack lost count of those that fell.

There were so many corpses littered across the cavern that he'd almost stumbled more than once. His boots skidded on blood-slick stone. There were moments when even his magic faltered. Their destructive paths blocked by bodies that slowed his powers down, if only for a second. Jack wondered if they realized that he could only use one element or if they simply thought that he was toying with them. It was probably the latter.

With crooked fingers, Jack pressed his hand onto another chest. Until suddenly, there were no more. His hands rose only to drop again when he realized that it had gone completely silent.

Jack breathed—once, twice—before he slouched forward with a relieved exhale.

"Filan vahs," he cursed, wiping the sweat from his brow. Jack winced when he accidentally touched a gash on his forehead. When did he get that? "Flaming Conjurers and their intolerable stubbornness. If they had just run instead of charging with those quaking knees, then we could've been done fifteen minutes ago."

"You handled yourself just fine," Philip said. "When you tossed that sword in the beginning, I thought it was because you'd never been trained to use a weapon. But," he looked at the woman with the spear lodged in her chest, "seems I was wrong."

"You weren't," Jack revealed. "I was never interested in running around with steel edges strapped to my waist."

"Then how do you explain that?"

"I have a lot of experience turning them on people."

"Do you fight a lot of Healers?"

"Nebbin actually." Jack's mouth twisted at the remembrance of that long fight outside of the Pit. "Most of the Healers I've fought so far have been pacifists. They had their grimoires, their magic, and little else."

"The grimoires of the Healers in the Grove are smaller than most. They're only ever brought out for grievous injuries that require specific information regarding certain body systems."

Jack opened his mouth to speak, only to snap it shut when

Lucian emerged. He looked at the piles of dead on the floor with wide, anxious eyes.

"I almost forgot about him," Philip muttered, walking over.

While Philip went to see if the boy was all right, Jack fiddled with the Heartstone. He rolled it between his fingers. The regular wisps stirred within. One of the few constants in his life since the fall of the Tower. It soothed him. Eventually, the tension in his shoulders eased and his breathing evened out. He continued to stare at the calm ceaselessly spinning within. Barring that one mishap that almost got them all killed, *she*'d been on relatively good behavior. No tendrils tried to choke him. No slender shadows obscured his vision. There hadn't even been an order to get rid of someone — or something — throughout the whole fight. Sure, he'd heard whispers and lullabies, but nothing that hadn't already been on the edge of his hearing from the start. There was only constant support.

Sylvie was right. *She* did keep him safe. Jack really hated that.

He tucked the stone under his shirt, before turning back to the pair. Philip looked strangely spritely for a man that had just fought a dozen practitioners. Lucian had definitely healed him while he had his back turned. Thinking of the boy, Jack took a moment to inspect him. He searched for any signs of injury and was pleased to find that there were none. Although he should've expected that from the start. Even if he had been caught in the crossfire, Lucian was still a Healer. An exceptional one at that if the rumors across Ferus Terria were to be believed.

There was a sudden flap of wings above them.

Jack and Philip ducked their heads in caution, not wanting to get mangled by an Amorph. But they swiftly realized that there worries were for naught when Lucian's owl emerged. The bird circled above them once, letting out an ear-piercing caw that made them wince. Jack stared, as it landed on Lucian's shoulder. The useless thing. It could've at least clawed the faces off some of their enemies.

"Are you ready?" Jack asked them.

"Let him heal you first," Philip said.

Without missing a beat, Lucian walked over and grabbed his hand. Jack felt the healing wash of his magic. It was a potent thing. Absurdly efficient. Most Healers his age had to concentrate for a good minute, before their magic spilled into another's veins. Lucian's moved as fast as any Master's, and it sank all the way into his bones. It was a prodding stream that zoomed up the length of his arm, then fanned outward to the rest of his body.

All it took was a second.

By the time Jack blinked, Lucian had already pulled away. *She* hissed something venomous in his ears, but he hardly noticed in the face of his own shock. Lucian was something else.

Just as he thought it, Lucian stood on his tiptoes. His fingers curled over the Heartstone. Alarm bells sounded in his mind. Fear gripped his stomach when *she* shouted. Time seemed to lurch to a stop when tendrils shot out of the stone to wrap around the boy's hand. He knew what those shadows were about to do. Jack reacted instantly. An icy hand grabbed Lucian's wrist, squeezing hard until the tendrils receded.

Philip cried Jack's name, though it was lost to the frantic woman screaming inside of his head. He didn't seem to notice the darkness that had just tried to consume the boy.

"What are you doing?" Jack snarled, unable to keep his fury at bay. It didn't disappear even as Lucian's grip slackened.

"On your neck..." he trailed off warily. "You had the same tendrils as those in the Orive crystals. But they retreated into the stone."

Jack's eyes narrowed. He knew that Lucian saw the same tendrils in his eyes, but the boy seemed to know better than to comment.

"Let him go, Dace," Philip warned. He grabbed his forearm with a viselike grip, cautioning him from unleashing his magic on the boy. "He was just curious."

Jack doubted that. If he wanted to simply look, then he would've asked instead of trying to snatch it from his neck.

Despite his appearance, Lucian wasn't a child.

"It isn't mine," Jack said. He loosened his hold, then looked pointedly at Philip for him to do the same. "So, I'd appreciate it if you didn't touch it."

Lucian didn't answer, not that Jack expected him to. He eyed the glaring Peose on Lucian's shoulder, before tucking the stone under his shirt. Jack hated the impossible sense of security it gave him. Hated more, how protective he was over it. But he didn't come this far just to have it plucked from his neck... or to have it slay an Arch Poten because of his own carelessness. Sylvie would shout at him until his ears bled. His mother would stick him in a cage with her Peose for a week. And if that didn't kill him, then Vidal certainly would. The flaming bastard might even find a way to revive him just to do it a second time.

Jack wasn't here to murder any figureheads.

He was here to get rid of that black lake that they were *still* dumping bodies into. He couldn't allow any more people to die for the sake of Peose and Elementalists. More than that, *she* wouldn't let him. Pieces of *her* were trapped there, and *she* wanted them out. Jack could practically taste *her* displeasure. It settled like burning tea in his mouth. Sylvie really needed to take the Heartstone back. He'd go insane if she didn't.

"Let's get this over with," he muttered, more to himself than to the two practitioners currently staring at their feet.

They jumped at his words. But Jack didn't stick around for them to respond. He strode onwards, slipping past the dimly lit entrance to go straight into the center of the Anvil's production room. Only pure willpower fueled him now. He was going to destroy that lake, save Elder Borris, and then force him to call one of the brothers from Thelarius' temple to ferry them down the Wymeran River.

What Jack didn't expect was to find every mixer in the room unconscious or as well as. Farther away, Elder Borris dangled Master Zacarias by the back of his robes over the sweltering lake. Entire crystals had been destroyed. Their pieces were little more than heaps of twisted slag strewn across the floor.

Elder Borris tilted his head back. Jack couldn't quite control the impressed breath that left his lips when blue eyes met red.

"Who are you?"

***

The restricted section was as grand as Sylvie imagined, or rather, the walk to it was. Aldrid led them past winding staircases adorned with vines and lengthy hallways decorated with murals that dated back to the Tempest Age. Each intersection had no less than three relics. They sat upon long-legged tables with silver plaques that bore the relic's name and a concise paragraph about its history. Framed notes that read: *'Thank you for not touching,'* in elegant script hung above each. It was scarcely heeded, judging by the fingerprints Sylvie saw all over them as she passed.

The walk to the archives was long, but Sylvie took to passing the time by catching up with Myrrh and Ethil. They'd been busy since they left the Tower—Myrrh, especially. Her eyes shifted whenever something about the east was mentioned in passing or when Ethil asked Sylvie about what she knew. Myrrh was clearly uncomfortable speaking about it, perhaps unsure of her own boundaries. Sylvie didn't blame her. She'd been an undercover Hunter there for years, lying to everyone... even her.

Sylvie could still recall the hours they spent inside Archive 19. Myrrh had bothered her to no end then, asking rapid fire questions about the outside world and what it was like to be a primary apprentice. Myrrh had told her once that it was her dream to trek across the Eirinne Mountains.

Sylvie knew better now. She knew that her friend had experienced far more. Both as a Hunter and as Cheryll Dace's primary apprentice. While Sylvie was happy for her, all that time they wasted talking about things she'd already done made her feel like an idiot. It was Myrrh's job to lie, and she did it better than most. But that didn't stop Sylvie from wanting to kick herself for falling so easily for it.

They asked other questions, too—about the Veld and its Arch Poten, about the cities across the Yovakine Plains, and about recent happenings across Ferus Terria that she might've known more about. Sylvie chose not to answer most of their inquiries. She shrugged her shoulders, then followed it with a thoughtful hum that made it seem as if she couldn't find the right words. It was a habit she picked up from Jack. He did it whenever he didn't want to offer an explanation either because of personal reasons or to avoid saying a white lie.

To her chagrin, Ethil noticed this and wasn't afraid to call her out on it. Ethil had either gotten more observant during her time in the Alps or she always had been, and only now decided to show it. Sylvie believed it was the latter.

"By the way," Ethil began, "where's that stone you had around your neck? I've been curious about it ever since I first saw it in the Tower. Did you lose it?"

Sylvie schooled her expression into neutral. "It's with Jack," she said, struggling to keep her voice even instead of suspicious.

"And where is he?" Myrrh pressed.

"Wandering the Grove with Philip."

"Master Rhone's primary apprentice?"

"That's the one. He's Dalis' friend."

"He's your brother, right?" Ethil asked. "I saw him in the center of the commotion back there. You two don't look like siblings, well, except for the hair. He's more… block-ish."

"Dalis is all sharp angles," Sylvie agreed. "He gets that from our father."

"That explains it."

"We're here," Aldrid announced.

Sylvie could've jumped in relief at the timing. Dodging questions about the Veld was one thing, but skirting around questions about Jack and the Heartstone was infinitely harder. Sylvie was still in the dark about how much they knew regarding their present situation, if anything at all, so she figured it would be best if she just avoided the subject completely, lest she get caught in a lie and have to answer for it later on.

Myrrh's eyes raked over her. Her old friend certainly didn't go to great lengths to hide her suspicion. But if there was one thing Sylvie could handle, it was unnerving stares. She'd been on the receiving end of a fair few over the last few weeks. Enough to make her nearly immune. It took a truly piercing look to give her pause, let alone make her uncomfortable enough to spill her deepest secrets.

The jangle of keys caught her attention. Aldrid chose the largest; a solid hunk of gold metal that spanned the length of his forearm. He needed both hands to properly lift it.

Tailored pockets? she wondered distractedly. *I need those.*

Aldrid fit the key into its gargantuan lock. He didn't turn it right away. First, he took out four smaller keys of the exact same design, then placed those into tinier, separate locks. Just when she thought all of the keyholes had been filled, he fished out *another* ring of keys and began placing those into their respective places. At that point, Sylvie didn't bother watching him anymore.

She was more fascinated by the door. It was situated at the end of a short hall. Empty, save for the orbs of light littered across the ceiling and a gaudy purple sparrow painted on the wall. It was, quite frankly, appaling. Unapologetically so. It clashed with the embossed tree on the door that Aldrid was *still* inserting keys into.

The tree, in contrast, was a sight. From the detailed leaves to the chiseled trunk. Everything about it was of the finest quality. If the sculptors had been trying to mimic the grandiosity of the Grove, then they succeeded. Without a doubt.

The sparrow, however...

She couldn't even begin to fathom what that represented.

The click of a lock had her snapping to attention. Aldrid turned every key in a meticulous order. First one on the corner, another across, two beside it, a larger one straight down. It continued on like that for a full two minutes until eventually, only the immense center key was left. Aldrid huffed as he turned it. Even with both of his hands, the key only budged an inch. The tree on the door shifted with each centimeter it moved. While it was an appealing sight, it was also too slow for her liking.

Tired of his pace, Sylvie tapped him twice on the shoulder, then gestured for him to step aside. Aldrid followed obediently. He wrung his hands together, still jittery, despite the fact that they hadn't harmed him. His eyes kept shifting from the door to the hall, where Myrrh stood with her arms crossed like a sentinel.

He's scared... too scared, Sylvie realized. *But of what?*

"Be careful," Myrrh cautioned. Her eyes never left Aldrid. "I have a bad feeling about this."

Ethil took her words to heart. She smartly moved to the side, where she wouldn't be seen if the door suddenly slammed open.

Sylvie waited for them to nod their assent, before she looked back at the key. It really was large. Maybe even bigger up close. How Aldrid carried it around with him all day was the true puzzle. Sylvie wiped her hands on her robes, grabbed the end of the key with both hands, and then twisted with all of her might.

Click.

Sylvie almost slipped face first onto the cold floor when it turned smoother than a newly greased door.

"Spirits!" she hissed. "I'm going to—"

Aldrid's shriek drowned her threat. He huddled as close as possible to the ground, as if that might make him less noticeable. The door swung open of its own accord. Only to be stopped midway by Ethil, who pushed against it with one hand before it could crush her. The first thing Sylvie saw through the narrow strip wasn't a line of lofty bookshelves or a long table cluttered end-to-end with cornucopias and loose pages, but a glinting spear with an oiled tip. It looked mildly green under the light.

A warning from Myrrh echoed all around them just as Sylvie leaned back. She bent as far as she could go, scarcely avoiding the weapon. But the spearman followed her movements. He changed his angle to strike in a downward thrust, forcing Sylvie to slam into the ground. She held tightly onto the wooden shaft. Her hands trembled, as the tip of the spear hovered above her jugular.

There was a flash of light, and then a giant frog hopped on Sylvie's hands. It was midnight black with blue-spots on its head and back. Both Sylvie and the spearman faltered at the sight of it.

The frog opened its ginormous mouth. Its tongue lolled out, licking Sylvie's finger and making her shudder in the process. A glob of venomous spit darted out to cover the man's eyes. He screamed and dropped his spear in favor of trying to wipe away the poison currently burning his sockets. But he only made it worse, and it wasn't long before he was rolling on the ground.

Sylvie hardly noticed, too busy screaming right along with him. She shook the creature off and scrambled to her feet. The frog landed a foot in front of her. By the time she gathered her wits, it was gone and in its place was a smirking Myrrh.

"Really?" Sylvie stressed, wiping away the leftover mucus on her hands. "You couldn't have chosen a less revolting animal? Like a lizard or a snake? It just *had* to be a godforsaken frog?"

"It's my go-to form," Myrrh defended.

Her amused smile fooled no one.

"We have bigger problems," Ethil interrupted.

They looked up to find a dozen armored men that were a mix between practitioner and Nebbin. Those that had weapons, drew them, and subsequently pointed the steel edges of their blades at the fettered practitioners that knelt at their feet. Those that didn't, merely turned with smoldering hands and a threatening look in their eyes that cautioned them against any rash moves.

All of the practitioners before them were gagged and straining to speak against the cloth. Their manacles had magic-draining enchantments that sapped the strength from their bones. At least half had blindfolds wrapped around their eyes, while the rest had theirs pushed down to their necks.

Were they taunting them? Sylvie counted the practitioners off in her head. *Nine, ten... a little over a dozen.*

While she'd never seen any of them personally, she did recognize a few of their faces from books and recently published journals. These were the Potens and the college representatives. If a few were missing from the collection, then she couldn't tell.

Her eyes drifted to their surroundings. She couldn't use her fire here, not extensively anyway. The tomes were too precious. It didn't help that they'd ransacked the place. Entire shelves stood empty, their books carelessly tossed to the ground. Paper was scattered everywhere. The remnants of broken lamps and potted plants were littered between them like useless treasure under a mountain of dirt. Two steps away from her, Sylvie saw an ink puddle sacrilegiously staining an upturned crate filled with priceless scrolls. She could already imagine the hundreds of wailing scholars that would lament for years over it.

"Who are you?" Myrrh asked. The first to recover. "What do you think you're doing?"

"They're mercenaries," Sylvie said. She took one look at the blazing eye that adorned their shoulders and recognized them as members of the Hellion… but that wasn't all. Two had a ball and chain stitched onto their backs, another had a boar, then an ox, even a dragon's head. "… All working together?"

"That's what coin can get you," a man said. He sat on a desk with his legs crossed and a roguish smile on his lips. His long dark hair was tied into an unkempt ponytail at the base of his neck. In his hands, was a thin dagger with a triangular base. It had a turquoise hilt that contrasted sharply against his skin. "The name's Gil, sweet thing." He rotated the blade's tip to gesture around the room. "Temporary leader of this merry band."

"Temporary?"

"What's a mundie like me got to do with upper-crusts like these?" Gil shot back. "I'm the little man. Well, not so little anymore." He kicked one of the practitioner's behind the shoulder. The woman struggled, but eventually gave in when he stepped on her back. "We've got a job to do, and that involves restraining these folks here for a little while long—can someone please shut that whiner up?" Gil shouted. He pointed his blade at the spearman loudly whimpering over his seared eyes.

A sword was promptly shoved into his open mouth.

The spearman gurgled as the one responsible twisted his blade by the hilt. Blood sprayed in an arc, staining floor and wall alike, until the man finally stilled.

"Thank you," Gil went on, not even sparing the man a glance. "Now, where was I? Oh, threatening... right. Don't even think about making a move. These boy's will slice open one of your precious leaders if you do."

The three of them looked at each other, then back at Gil. Sylvie was the first to step forward with her hands in the air.

"Good girl." Gil smiled, then beckoned for the others to follow. Ethil and Myrrh dragged their feet, while another mercenary grabbed the shivering Aldrid from the floor and threw him into a pile of hardcovers in the corner of the room. As soon as they were all inside, two men slammed the door shut.

The mercenaries formed a circle around the three, but none of them yielded.

Sylvie looked around her. Myrrh was to her right, Ethil to her left. There was only one practitioner on Ethil's side. The rest congested around Myrrh. It seemed even deserters still preferred the company of their own kind. Before her, was Gil and four Nebbin that shared the same symbol on their leathers—a blazing eye. If they were his closest aides, then they were likely a part of his original group.

He's a member of the Hellion then? Sylvie thought. She'd heard about them from Vidal in passing. They weren't a big group. Much less significant than say, the Crystal Cartel or the Tippings. They skirmished with other Nebbin and had very few deserters in their service. Sylvie recognized the mark of the Ocean's Still on two of the practitioners near Myrrh. They were leagues above the Hellion. *So, why is he the one leading them? Unless... he's one of the Hellion's higher members. Who hired him though?*

Gil suddenly laughed. "I know that face. You look like you have questions."

"I haven't asked you anything," Sylvie said.

"So you haven't. But that doesn't mean you won't. I'm telling you now that it's better to save your breath." Gil gave her a slimy grin. "You'll need it."

"Why is it that every man I meet loves the sound of his own voice?" Myrrh spat. "*Na nia leraseva,* you insufferable cock."

Gil's eyes narrowed. Before any of them could move, he plunged his dagger deep into the shoulder of an aged man that hadn't seen the strike coming. Myrrh slammed her mouth shut. There was a collective widening of eyes, even by the other mercenaries in the room.

"We aren't supposed to touch the Potens!" one protested.

"Yet," Gil emphasized. "We're allowed to do as we please once we receive the go-ahead. I'm just having myself a taste."

"Lynol will have your neck, Gil," a woman warned. "His orders were clear."

"Orders? You mean those three lines he wrote on that soggy yellow parchment? You call that half-assed instruction an *order*? If he wanted to command us, then he should've gone to see us himself! Not send one of his oversized pigeons."

"If you aren't threatened by Lynol, then what about the Lafertti Clan?" she confronted, placing one hand on the hilt of her rapier. "They're scattered all around this Institute. They'll slice you open and heal you just to do it all over again!"

"The Lafertti Clan?" Ethil repeated.

Her voice was barely a whisper, but Gil heard it as if she'd screamed it into his ear. He faced his subordinate with a glower that told her to quiet down... or else. "You've said too much. Now, look!" He pointed at the three of them with his dagger. "They're curious."

"What does the Lafertti Clan have to do with this?" Sylvie asked.

"I'd like to tell you, sweet thing. But then I'd have to kill you, and that would be *such* a shame."

"You're going to kill me anyway," Sylvie said, certain. "You're just prolonging the predictable—and for what? To alleviate your boredom? Any other person would've given the order to kill us as soon as we stepped through the door."

"Do I look like any other person to you?"

"No. You're more like a caged dog." Sylvie put her hands about six inches apart. "The small, energetic kind. This isn't your usual kennel."

"Oh, don't be like that, Syl," Myrrh added, catching on to what she was doing. "He's lonely because his master isn't around to say *jump*."

Gil's lips twisted, not allowing them to get to him. "You say that now, but don't forget that it was me that captured your Institute's greatest leaders, and it's *me* that currently holds them hostage. Their lives are in my hands now."

"Captured them? *You*?" Sylvie repeated, changing her strategy. If insults didn't work, then... "No, I don't think so."

"And why is that?" Gil asked. "This place is a joke. Half of you would die as soon as you stepped into the Plains. It's no wonder you lot hole yourselves up in these elaborate fortresses."

"You couldn't have done this without an insider's help," Sylvie pressed, ignoring his jabs. These weren't regular practitioners. The representatives were the elite among the elite. They were likely taken off guard, but she didn't bother reasoning that out to him. "You couldn't have even made it through the forest without a practitioner to guide you... oh, I suppose that's where the Lafertti Clan comes in. But why would they ever work with the likes of you?"

"If you're asking that, then you're a blunt tool that knows nothing about what's happening inside her own home."

"The Lafertti Clan is currently the Grove's oldest and most distinguished college," Sylvie said, reiterating everything she'd learned growing up. If blatant taunts didn't work, fanaticism against what they believed in would surely do the trick. "Their sway here is second to none. To even think about hiring outsiders is prepos—"

"That college you hold in such high regard is just another

power-hungry faction like the rest of us," Gil said sourly. "They're short on men, whether they want to admit it or not. Lynol is somewhat of a living myth in the Plains. He controls half of Ferus Terria's underworld and has his fingers dipped in the rest. I don't know how they managed to get a hold of him, but he had the connections to bring us all together."

Gil paced back and forth, full-on ranting now. "Bleeding good it did me taking up his offer though. Sure, I'll be receiving a fat pouch on my way out, but any try-hard greentip can do this job. What's the point of gathering experienced mercs if they're just going to have us hole up in here? And just to set the record straight, we aren't here because we're afraid of you lot. The *only* reason we're in this abyss is because of these wrinkly cysts."

He stomped on the back of the one he'd previously stabbed.

"What about them?" Sylvie asked quickly, trying to needle more information from him before he lost himself to anger.

"Why don't you use your head sometime?" Gil sneered. "Only they're allowed entry here, aren't they? If those Snuff turds out there figure out that the representatives are in here with these old bags of Poten flesh, while all of that noise and animosity is stewing around outside, what do you think will happen?"

"They'll..." Sylvie trailed off, her mind racing with ideas. "They'll believe the Potens captured them to try to put an end to any talks of abolition."

"You got it. Now, if we kill them all, before they rush in..."

"The practitioners here will hold the Alps responsible for their deaths," Ethil was the one to say. Her eyes widened at the realization. "They'll believe they abandoned them because they closed their gates immediately after making the announcement. That could spark a civil war."

"And who would benefit from the looming threat of war?"

"The Elders that want a rushed vote for the Summit," Ethil said, at the same time Sylvie said, "Those that could use the Anvil as leverage."

They shared a glance.

Gil smiled at their wide-eyed expressions. "I heard the Clan has a hand in a lot of shady business down under. Whoever they have supporting them in that snowy castle up north must have promised them a bigger share... or a comfier seat."

Myrrh looked around. "Master Zacarias isn't here."

"See, this is what happens when you ask questions." Gil sighed. "Now, I have to kill you."

At his word, weapons were raised and stances were taken.

"The Lafertti Clan will throw you and everyone else here away as soon as this contract ends," Sylvie said in a sorry attempt to get him and his men to back down.

"I'm expecting them to."

"You'd risk your life and the lives of your band for a few sacksful of coin?"

"I'd risk more," Gil said with a thin, unfriendly smile. "If they have a problem with me, then they'll have to catch me first."

"I told you, Syl," Myrrh bared her teeth at the oncoming mercenaries, "He's an insufferable cock."

Sylvie's gaze drifted around her. She committed all she could to memory—a ticking Conjurer too close to Ethil, seven near Myrrh, an Amorph that stared at her from behind a shelf, and a spattering of Nebbin that gripped their swords in preparation.

Three, maybe four of the hostages would die before they could get to them. More, if Gil took it upon himself to cut them down while they were busy with his lackeys.

Realizing that they'd be caught helpless in the middle of a fight, the Potens and representatives struggled even more against their restraints. The fetters around their limbs may have zapped them of their strength, but it only tripled their will. Some thrashed from determination alone. Adrenaline eased, if not numbed, them from the pain of their chaffed skin. However, a few of the older ones—Potens with less to lose—had simply chosen to stop trying. Ironically, they were the first to be pommelled into the ground as soon as Gil gave the order to attack. The neck of a particularly aged male had even snapped when he was shoved.

That's one, Sylvie tallied.

They moved until they were standing back-to-back.

"Running away already?" Gil goaded. "At least make this last for me."

"I need to heal the one he stabbed," Ethil whispered. Her eyes roved over those captured, compiling any injuries she found into a mental checklist. "He'll die from blood loss at this rate."

"You'll need a way forward first," Sylvie said. "I'm going to clear a path ahead of you. Run when you see it. I'll deal with the Nebbin on your end."

"I'll distract the practitioners," Myrrh volunteered. Most were gathered in front of her anyway. "Feel free to send a few fireballs my way, Syl."

"We need to save the books, too."

"Tell that to them."

"If either of you find the keys to their manacles," Ethil said, getting them back on track, "then give them to me."

Their eyes met for the briefest of moments, before they sprang into action. Myrrh was the first to move. There was a flash of light and everyone around the room stilled, suddenly rattled by the appearance of a nine-foot snake with abysmal eyes. But that didn't last long. Myrrh opened her wide jaw with a demonic shriek. A glob of venomous spit darted out to cover a Conjurer head to toe in burning slime. The man screamed. His pain snapped them all out of their trance because the resolve in their eyes shone anew.

They all charged at once, hoping for advantage in numbers.

Ethil sidestepped a man with a crooked dagger and a vicious sneer. He was fast. Too fast. She found herself unable to get close because of his constant shifting. So, she shuffled backwards until her shoulder met Sylvie's back. Nebbin closed in around them. To the side, Myrrh distracted the practitioners as best she could. She slithered in front and around them, not letting them get close.

"Get ready," Sylvie said.

That was all the warning Ethil received, before a burst of fire exploded around them. It didn't last long. Merely a cautionary display of power to push those that had gotten too close back. But then it was followed by a quick siphoning of breath in the room. The air seemed to boil around them, making it hard to breathe. Ethil knew what this was. She'd seen it many times before on the coasts of the Zexin Sea. It was the ocean drawing back into itself before a surge, then—

A tsunami of lawless fire.

Brilliant and terrifying to everyone in the vicinity. Black smoke spread outward. A cloud of poisonous air released into the room. Ethil knew this was the only opening she would get. She ran blindly to where she remembered the Poten coughing out blood. Ethil felt the uncomfortable touch of flames lap at her skin, but they never lingered for more than a second. They were carefully controlled by Sylvie, who still, even in this highly combustible enclosure, managed to limit her power and spare some of the books around them. But the same couldn't be said for the other practitioners that immediately began spewing tunnels of ice and wind in an attempt to dispel the haze. Amorphs shifted into mighty birds and beat their wings, while the Nebbin swung their weapons around. The more composed of the lot simply waited with bated breath for their vision to clear.

Ethil stilled when a Healer stumbled in front of her, choking on smoke. His hair was crisped to his ears. He opened his eyes to find her, took two breaths, and several paces... before a tongue wrapped around his torso and pulled him back into the smog.

Myrrh, she thought, before running forward again. She had her own job to do.

Behind her, Sylvie was caught in the thick of things, barely able to see through her own doing. The Nebbin here weren't like the minions she fought outside of the Pit; they had experience fighting practitioners and weren't afraid to brave her magic. They found her heaving within the smoky blackness, despite their own limited sight, and then shouted to their comrades for help.

Before she knew it, a man with his glaive planted on the ground like a rooted oak stood before her. Sylvie didn't even get to focus on him because a rogue emerged from her side with his daggers poised in her direction. Its slanted edge nicked her cheek as she evaded. She grabbed his extended arm just below the elbow. Flames met exposed flesh, and the man roared in pain. Sylvie drew one of the spare daggers from across his chest and smashed its hilt across his unguarded temple until he dropped like a stone. She whirled around, attempting to bury the blade in the ribs of a man that had snuck up behind her, only for it to clang pathetically against his armor.

The man raised his sword high above her.

Sylvie braced herself for impact.

In an instant, a snake slithered all around him, snapping armor and back alike. Sylvie gaped at the sight of Myrrh, but her surprise didn't last long because the man with the glaive charged. An ox among men. Sylvie scrambled to her feet. She slipped past Myrrh to run directly towards him, fearless and desperate. Her magic surged in her veins like a cry. The man swung his glaive. Sylvie dodged...

... She tried to.

For all of her speed, the pointed edge where pole met steel still embedded itself in the spaces between her ribs. The glaive's swing was stopped only by the fire that burst forward to fry fingers and arms alike. It rushed, reaching his face this time. The heat melted his armor onto his skin. Blisters emerged. They grew and popped in succession. His expression twisted into a horrified gasp filled with realization, before he fell sideward.

The glaive slipped and dropped to the ground with a thunderous boom along with him. Cracks webbed out from the point of impact.

Sylvie gritted her teeth. Her eyes watered, as she covered the fresh wound with shaking fingers.

A stray blast of ice burst in her direction. Sylvie raised one hand to shield herself. The attack sheared away to either side of her like a forking river. Then, she countered, flinging forth her flames in a wide scything arc of raw power. Hidden somewhere in the haze, a woman cried in anguish.

Sylvie struggled to see through the occasional smears of light and the chaos of pitched violence. When a grunt sounded from behind her, she whirled around. It was hardly loud, but it sliced through the cries of death and the hiss of fire like a knife. Unease brewed inside of her. Myrrh was no longer there, having jumped once again into the fray while she had her back turned. But in her place was an unamused Gil. His hair had fallen loose from its ponytail and he had a slice across his right shoulder.

Did someone turn on him? she speculated.

"Half of those you were trying to save are dead," Gil told her. "Perhaps more, depending on how many my men offed while you released your cursed magic. Can you live with that?"

"It's better than you killing them all, isn't it?" Sylvie reasoned, not letting her mask slip. She made her choice to fight him, and she'd live with the consequences. "I ruined your plans."

"And you fulfilled them at the same time. The practitioners here will still feel animosity towards the Alps for not providing the support required from them."

"At least they'll have a few guiding voices left to keep them from an all-out war."

"For how long, I wonder?" Gil asked, as he lifted his blade. "I don't suppose you're just going to let me pass, are you?"

Sylvie's grip over her ribs tightened. There was already a lack of oxygen in the room — *this* just made the struggle for breath even worse. She couldn't move around like this. But there was no time to worry about what she could and couldn't do because Gil was already charging. She only had two choices now: give up and let him pass... or take her chances.

It wasn't much of a choice.

Sylvie raised her hands in dogged determination. She didn't back down, not even when his lips peeled back in a snarl. Gil twisted his dagger, aiming right for her neck. Its glinting edge reflected the fire that bubbled in her hands. It started out as an unruly curl that blew upwards into the open air above, but it transformed into a storm as it was unleashed.

No holding back now. No room for that here.

Her magic shifted course just as Gil brought his blade down to slice her neck open. He succeeded in cutting a line of agony too close to her jugular, though it wasn't as deadly as he'd hoped.

The room grew silent as a tunnel of fire consumed him.

Throughout her years, Sylvie had learned that humans burned just as well as the straw training dummies modelled after them. They went up in flashes of flame and smoke. Gil was no different. He screamed into the sky above him like a man that sought the Creator's salvation. The fire slid pain over his skin and insides. He rolled on the ground, inadvertently spreading the flames across the destroyed papers at his feet.

Gil gripped his head, his sides, anything he could reach. But Sylvie didn't stop. She unleashed all of the bright shreds of her magic until she reached the tapped out bottom of her soul, until she found herself bled dry with nothing left to give.

She'd exhausted her magic circuit. Again. Jack was going to be furious when he found out.

Sylvie heaved, then gripped her side in pain. This was no time to fall to her knees. There were still people around her that needed to be dealt with. She grabbed Gil's discarded dagger, knowing she'd need it while her magic replenished itself.

She left his body there. It was a long time before Gil stilled, nerveless and at peace. By then, all that was left of him was a warped black husk.

The floor still smoldered, ember-red at the edges.

20

It's strange, Jack thought, how much his perception—of Healers, Nebbin, and even Elders—had changed throughout the course of the last year. And it still did. Even now.

Elder Borris wasn't at all the weathered down codger that his title suggested. Even from where he stood, Jack could make out the muscle beneath Borris' impeccably fitted robes. They were lined with scarlet and gold. His trousers were a shade lighter. They peeked out from the space where the front of his robes opened for mobility. His dark hair hung in a loose braid down his neck, and he wore heavy silver jewelry on both ears.

"Answer me," Borris bellowed.

"Jack," he said mechanically. "Jacques Dace."

Borris' eyes widened, before he averted his gaze back to Master Zacarias who still hung too close to the water's surface.

"Of course." He growled. "Why am I not surprised? You're just like your father. Sticking your nose into the deepest, dirtiest affairs of the Institute. Did he send you?"

"I haven't spoken to my father since the Drowned Tower fell. I'm here because I want to be."

"And why, pray tell, would you ever *want* to be in a place like this? It isn't for children."

"Neither is it for ignorant elders that don't know who they're hurting by continuing to let this happen," Jack replied scathingly.

Borris faced him again. "You're an Elementalist. You of all people should be grateful for the *Orivellea.*"

"Why?" Jack challenged. "All it's done is make me another

pawn of the Institute. I didn't ask for these powers."

"You know much… too much. Why is that? Did your father tell you? Your mother? I doubt you learned on your own." Borris paused to look at the pair behind him. "Leonas mentioned that you and your Arch Poten companion were heading to the Alps for the Summit, yet I don't see her here."

"Her whereabouts are none of your concern." Jack scowled. "And just what do you think you're doing to him? Isn't that the representative of the Lafertti Clan?"

"And he calls me ignorant." Borris laughed. It was sharp and devoid of amusement. "Stand back, boy. I'm not your enemy. This *revonarahs karis* is plotting with someone from the north to kill Poten and representative alike, while the north is under isolation. He wants to spark the embers of war. You just caught me trying to… *coax* a few names out of him."

There was a bewildered shout from behind him—*Philip,* Jack placed. He ignored him. It was easy when the voice in his head pounded like a hammer.

Hurry, *she* chanted. A path of black tendrils even emerged, as if that might get him to move faster.

There was no time for surprises now. No time for questions either. Borris could tell him that birds couldn't fly for all he cared, and he'd still run with it. Jack wanted to get this over with, so he could return this godforsaken rock to Sylvie.

"If you're going to throw him in, then do it," Jack said, merciless. His voice brooked no barter. "I'm ridding the world of this place. *Now.*"

"What a coincidence," Borris said. "We have the same goal."

"You want to destroy the Institute's sole source of *Orivellea*?" Jack asked, skeptic. "I doubt the Council signed off on that."

"Why would they? But listen," Borris pointed at the ceiling. At first, there was only silence, but after a minute, Jack heard the distant echoes of fighting. "It's only a matter of time before a few errant practitioners make their way from the chaos up there to the one down here. I can't let them find out about this mess.

They'd resent the Alps even more. They might even grow to hate their Elementalist brothers. You carry dead men in your heads. Nebbin *and* practitioner.

Jack's lips twisted.

"How typical of an Elder to only care *wh*—" Jack cut himself off with a furious shake of his head. He fisted his fingers in his hair when *she* screamed. *She* heated his blood in that intolerable way that made him weak all over. "I *know* what I need to do! Stop shouting in my head with that ear-piercing voice! For Thelarius' sake, we need him! I can't just do it because you insist..."

Jack abruptly lifted his head.

"*Filan vahs*!" Borris cursed when his grip accidentally slackened and Master Zacarias went tumbling into the lake. The man wasn't even able to cry for help, as he sunk like an anchor into the thick water. He thrashed, flailing his arms and legs, but it only made him sink faster. Borris almost fell into the lake himself when he saw the black tendrils in Jack's eyes. "Creator, I didn't mean to do that, well, I *did*, but not so soon. Still, your eyes..." Borris trailed off, before blindly stumbling towards him, "is that what I think it is?"

"Syl might burn me for this," Jack said, "but she'll just have to deal. She isn't here, so she gets no damn say about what I do."

"Dace!" Philip ran up to him. He didn't like the revolted look on Borris' face. Philip clasped Jack's shoulder and tried with all of his might to get him to meet his gaze. "Dace! Hey, Dace! Can you hear me?"

Unfortunately for him, Jack only had eyes for the open space before them. He didn't even notice Master Zacarias' untimely demise or the half-curious, half-nauseated look Borris shot him. All he saw was that dreadful lake and the darkness that lurked within it.

"I needed you to call a brother from Thelarius' temple for me," Jack muttered. "But if you want to stick around here as this place crumbles, then—*fine*. I'll find another way. I can't stand this relentless shouting anymore. Feel free to die here with the rest."

Jack unleashed his magic. A wave of cold air blew out from his body. Thousands of frosty webs emerged from his feet, and then...

... Nothing.

The world grinded to a halt when Philip seized the Heartstone from Jack's neck and pulled. Jack's eyes widened. He reached out to take it back, only for Philip to use his height to his advantage by holding it high into the air.

"You *idiot*," Jack yelled, coming to his senses. "You can't—"

It was too late.

Tendrils emerged faster than he could see. Jack watched, sick with shock, as they wrapped all around his body. Philip didn't even realize that something was wrong until after he looked down to find that they'd wound their way across him. One moment, he was as healthy as any practitioner could be, and the next, his skin had gone completely grey. He gasped, but nothing entered his lungs. Philip's veins bulged from his temples and cheeks. He keeled over, unable to support his own weight. His strength was abruptly snatched from him by an unknown force.

His insides felt like they were being boiled. His body turned into a furnace, too hot to contain anything. Philip wanted to shout, to demand to know what was happening, but the words died in his throat. He could *feel* the tendrils slither through him. They were cool at first, a relief to the burning, then they swelled, expanding at a pace that made him think he'd pop into oblivion.

Jack tried to get the Heartstone away from his slack fingers, but a cover of wisps had glued itself over the appendages. He smashed his fists against them. Predictably, they were stronger than mere muscle and bone. He needed something else.

"Shit!" Jack shouted, as he tried and failed to get his hand to light. *She* was clearly upset with him. With Philip. With everyone and everything in this room. But that didn't mean *she* could just... "Shit, what, I can't—*why* can't I..." Jack faced Borris with wide, panicked eyes. "Use your magic on him!"

"What?" Borris asked, unable to comprehend the situation.

"Your magic!" he shouted, urgency driving every muscle in his body. His mind was at peace. His eyes, pure of everything. *Her* voice was gone—and that *terrified* him.

Borris ran over with his hands shining. He placed them on Philip's shoulders and watched in morbid fascination as the tendrils began to recede.

"No, not there!" Jack said.

He wrenched his hand away to replace it over Philip's arm. The darkness withdrew, and as soon as a piece of the stone became visible, Jack squeezed his fingers inside to grab it. He bit his tongue when he heard screaming in his head again. A blaze erupted in the pit of his stomach. It sprinted outward, before settling in a sizzle behind his eyes.

It hurt. It *always* hurt.

But this pain was good. It meant that *she* was safely within him and not attempting to kill anyone else. For a split second, Jack wondered if Sylvie could hear *her* from wherever she was now. He hoped not. He *really* hoped not.

Jack looked up to find Philip passed out and breathing heavily. Borris knelt above him, performing a cursory check with his magic. When the Elder turned those glowing hands onto him, however, he immediately shook his head.

"We have bigger things to worry about," Jack said.

He pointed up at the entrance, where he assumed the many men from before left through. They were back now... and in greater numbers. Jack couldn't see the end of their little troop, but he knew from the clamor of voices alone that they'd be too much for him to handle. Philip could barely stand. Jack didn't know how powerful Elder Borris really was, but he wasn't about to stake his life on an assumption of strength.

"We need to go!" one shouted into the cave, as he uncapped a tonic that Jack was too far away to see. It was likely something to numb the pain of his slung shoulder.

Jack's eyes widened when he realized that he wasn't a practitioner. His eyes were light brown and there was a common sword at his waist. *Nebbin?* he thought, looking at the rest of them. *No, not all of them.* There was a sprinkling of both amidst the crowd, but he knew that none of the practitioners among them were part of the Lafertti Clan. They didn't have the robes. *Deserters? Why are deserters here?*

"Did you hear me?" the man continued to shout. "We need to go! They found out about the archives!"

"Who's he talking to?" Jack wondered out loud.

As if in answer, the man screeched, "Lynol!"

Behind you!

Jack turned just in time to find Lucian standing behind him. The boy plunged a small curved blade, no bigger than a letter opener, into his back. It was shock, not pain, which made him gape. The pain came after. After he looked down to find the blade protruding from one of the spaces between his ribs, red and gory; after he saw the venomous blots of black tar on the steel edge.

Poison, Jack realized absentmindedly.

He gasped for breath, but it only made his chest ache.

Lucian stepped back. His eyes were harder than Jack's own. "Remove them," he ordered, before walking casually to the exit.

Borris made to follow him, but stopped when Lucian's owl almost clawed his eye out. It drew two deep lines of blood across his forehead. A warning to stay away. It was only when Borris realized that he'd have to fight the horde of men currently fighting to get inside that he turned to Jack. He didn't waste any time. Borris was too experienced for that. He pulled the knife from Jack's chest without warning. He gurgled in pain. Blood fell like a waterfall down Jack's clothes, and he coughed out more.

He'd ease that soon.

"*She* told me there was something wrong with him," Jack whispered in between pants. The surge of Borris' magic relieved him in ways he couldn't properly express. "I should've listened."

"You have the Heartstone," was the only thing Borris said — the only thing he could say. The revelation about Lucian had yet to fully register in his mind. He didn't *want* it to register. He had to focus on healing.

"For the moment. It belongs to Sylvie," Jack revealed. He pushed him away, despite the still open hole in his chest. "Get out of here."

"What?" Borris asked in confusion. "You can barely stand!"

"Take Philip and escape through the back entrance." Jack coughed out another glob of blood, then reached into his pocket to throw him the key to the door. "Now. They're coming."

"I can't—"

"You can and you will," Jack shouted with as much vehemence as he could muster. "I said that I would destroy this place, and I don't lie!"

Borris' throat went dry at the uncompromising tone of his voice. He turned back just in time to see the first wave of men charge. Behind them, practitioners lifted their hands. He couldn't get rid of them all. Especially not while protecting two practitioners... but he could at least save one.

It didn't take him long to come to a decision. He hoisted Philip over his shoulder and with an apologetic tilt of his head, made a beeline for the tunnel.

"Good riddance," Jack murmured.

He watched Borris go with a listless expression on his face. There was something about being left behind by someone that believed he was valiantly sacrificing himself for their sake that made him want to laugh like a madman. Jack wasn't that noble, nor did he ever pretend to be. He'd simply stated the truth—he didn't lie. If he said he'd destroy this place, then come hell or high water, he was going to do it.

He struggled to stand. The battle cries and mocking laughter of the men in front of him went ignored, as he focused all of his attention into making sure he didn't accidentally slip.

She'll keep you safe, he remembered Sylvie say.

Jack knew that already.

But who's keeping you safe? he thought, while looking up at the crowd rushing towards him like he wasn't a lone man. They seemed so trivial when it came down to it. In the face of all that he'd been through — rapidly falling ceilings, a forest full of Peose, throngs of manic Nebbin, *her* — they hardly mattered. *That's my job. Right, Syl? It's supposed to be me. It's why she let me keep this wretched ice in the first place. Because I'm the goddamn puppet.*

He needed to get back up there.

Jack squeezed the Heartstone. A ground and an anchor, while his actual one was beyond his reach. This single remnant of Sylvie that she'd forced upon him was the one moor he had left to hold onto in this blood-spattered world.

"Help me," he whispered, desperate. "*Please* help me."

What do you seek? *she* whispered in his ear. Old and familiar.

He breathed, ignoring the pain that bloomed in his chest as he did so. Jack didn't even need to think about it. He'd thought about this moment for weeks. Had dreamed about it for more.

"My power."

There was a second of stillness. Jack swore that the Nebbin stopped mid-step and that the swirl of elements headed his way ceased right in the middle of their onslaught. In that moment, when reality seemed to end, he thought *she* wouldn't grant his wish. Perhaps it was too much of him to ask *her* to return his powers, even if just for an instant. Her strength was a gift *she* bestowed only upon Thelarius. Jack wasn't him. He was a poor imitation at best.

But then that split second of doubt passed.

Jack felt a scream claw its way up his throat. The sound was lost by the time it pierced the air. His eardrums were clogged with the unknown… or so he hoped. They could've easily been shreds of broken tissue at this point. He wouldn't have noticed. It hurt. But so did everything else.

His ears were like the sails of an abandoned ship, useless and riddled with holes. No longer reacting to the howling winds. All Jack knew now were empty vibrations. A listless tap set to repeat, droning on with numbness and a distant echo of pain. It was akin to a song that he could just scarcely recall the words to. It had no tune, and the headache that came with trying to remember wasn't one so easily appeased. So, Jack stopped trying. Both his mind and his soul were consumed by the burning sting that travelled across his flesh.

Practitioner and Nebbin alike faltered at the sight of him. He didn't blame them. Jack would have, too, had he seen someone howling in pain for no apparent reason. But there was no going back for him now—no, he'd known that from the start.

I asked for this.

As soon as the thought was born, feelings too dense for him to pick apart rolled out. Hate, confidence, skepticism, faith. It was a mash of emotion that made him want to vomit. It cut through him, through flesh and bone and trained muscle, sharper and more deadly than any blade. The emotions knotted themselves until only one large mass of animosity was left. It boiled in his belly. Seethed, then grew until it pulsed in his veins like water frozen too quickly.

Jack shut his eyes in an effort to calm himself. To no avail. The pain in his chest disappeared. The wound cauterized itself until all that was left was tender, pink flesh. But now the heat in his stomach was making him delirious.

His skin was electric. His blood, an inferno.

He felt *her* yearning wash over him, followed by a surge of raw, malevolent power that flooded his insides and made his exhausted limbs quake in protest. His fatigue, however, was soon forgotten. It was replaced with an ache that begged for release. The strength that ran through his fingers was terrifying in its sheer might, dormancy shaken off as the unchecked beast inside of him roared through his blood.

Jack smiled dementedly. How many days had passed since he last felt as if he could command fire? Wind? The very stones he stood over? Far too long.

For the briefest of moments, he wondered how he could've ever lived without this. But reality came crashing down upon him when he heard *her* voice.

This won't last long.

It won't have to, Jack thought.

His mood turned an ugly shade of black, tethering on the brink of barely sane. He watched the closest of his opponents straighten their backs and set their jaws in an attempt to bolster their confidence. They were like a clowder of cornered kittens that hissed and thumped their claws to appear more menacing before a predator that they desperately feared. But Jack knew better than most the way an anxious animal crouched with its hackles raised, only to make itself small and quiet before the hunter. This was hardly any different.

Jack's lips twisted into a smile dark enough to inspire terror. Fire bloomed between his fingers like an unfurling sun.

He was going to burn them alive, and they were going to die screaming.

***

The entrance to the Anvil wasn't as grand as Tiv expected. It was nothing more than an oversized, over armored door that stood between him and where he wanted to go.

On their way down, at least a dozen guards had allowed them to pass without so much as a second look. All they had to do was flash that garnet pin. Once the guards realized that they were friends of the Lafertti Clan, nothing else mattered. Tiv had expected that same treatment at the door. But what he didn't expect was to find no guards at all. And with no keeper to grant them access, they were at a loss.

They'd found storage rooms in the area, but after peeking inside two of them, they decided against searching for a key. It would take days to sift through all of those boxes. The smarter move would be to wait until someone came to inspect the area.

"Can't you pick it?" Tiv asked.

"I could," Dwyn said, staring at the lock, then up at the rest of the door. "But see that pattern? Those are explosive runes. This door is definitely enchanted. It might go off if I try."

"Let me guess, the Mentalists?"

"How'd you know?"

"Their markings always have circular patterns," Tiv said. He'd traced the ones on his manacles enough times to recognize their handiwork.

"Now that I think about it, you're right. They always were obsessed with the moon."

"What does the moon have to do with this?"

"Elder Dace once told me that the first enchantments were instigated by the heavenly bodies. The moon was of particular interest to them because of how it made the tide rise and fall. Conjurers were desperate for a taste of that might, so they tried to mimic its appearance. They created veined inscriptions that raw magic could run between. Some even carved them into their bodies, so they could enhance their magic. Once they realized that that couldn't be done without permanently damaging their magic circuits, they moved onto everyday items instead. They wanted edges to be more than edges. They wanted stone walls to do more than just protect. They wanted everything to be at the mercy of magic's might."

"Do you remember all of the stories he tells?" Tiv asked, genuinely curious.

"More or less." Dwyn shrugged. "I wish my Peose was here. He's got these ice claws. Maybe he could use them to freeze the door just in case it explodes. Though I don't know if it'll be strong enough. These enchantments look heavy-duty to me."

"You have a Peose?"

"I was a proper Hunter, before I transferred to Elder Dace's division."

"Where is it?"

"I hid him in my sister's room. My Peose limits what I can transform into, and want to be able to turn into something small without having to worry about him."

Before Tiv could ask just what his Peose was, there was a loud crash from the other side of the door. The sound echoed ominously around them. They leaned in, trying to hear it again, but all they heard was a low, frantic jingle. Keys? The loose metal slid into something in the door. From their side, the lock turned left, then right. It happened a total of five times, all in rapid succession, before the metal slipped out. Definitely keys.

Dwyn placed a finger on his lips and gestured for him to back away. Once they were a few steps from the door, he whispered, "Someone's opening it."

"More like trying to," Tiv said.

"Let's slip in."

They shifted into tiny lizards as soon as the door clicked. With quick feet, they crawled their way up the side of the door, as the stranger struggled to push it open. Once it opened more than a crack, they slinked inside... and almost choked as soon as they did. The chamber beyond the door was foul. It was difficult to breathe, but they held their tongues. They continued to crawl until they were a safe distance from the old man struggling to push open the door. There was a passed out Healer by his feet—was he saving him?

Maybe, Tiv thought, looking out at the pit full of dead below. He would've shivered had he been able to. Instead, a needle-like tingle crawled up his spine. It was enough to have him backing as far away as possible from the mess in front of him.

A tail slapped against his backside.

Tiv turned to find Dwyn motion forward with his head.

"Do you hear that?" Dwyn asked like he wasn't the most fearsome predator in the area. Tiv struggled to keep up with him, not used to sprinting in a lizard's body. "Doesn't that sound like magic?"

Dwyn must've had supersonic hearing, too, because Tiv didn't hear anything.

"Those whooshes," he explained when Tiv didn't answer. "They sound like... fire? Wind? Maybe even both. It's definitely magic though. Are practitioners fighting down there?"

On cue, a dozen pained screams erupted from below.

They shouted random phrases—*fire, stay away, help, no, please don't*—that were made more terrifying by the utter fear in their voices. Their cries rang in their ears, lingering around them like a warning not to come. Neither of them heeded it. Not out of excess bravery or some form of morbid curiosity, but because retreat simply wasn't an option.

There was a distant rumble that made the walls around them shake. It showered them in pebbles and ash. Loose rocks that were just large enough to cause damage to their tiny forms. That was never a good sign. If whoever was causing that was allowed to continue, then it wouldn't be long before the stone spires hanging upside down above them began falling as well.

Tiv wasn't keen on death by impalement.

"This way," Dwyn said, following the screams.

Why am I here again? Tiv thought, hesitating.

But when Dwyn turned to see if he was following, he knew why, and he cursed his own impatience.

***

Madness.

That's what they walked into. Complete and utter madness. They didn't stumble upon a fight. Fights involved two or more parties struggling; involved some degree of equivalence between the combatants. There was nothing like that here. This was raw power overwhelming fools that thought they could beat it.

The area looked as if a dormant monster had been awakened, frantic and starved for battle. A red-stained field of corpses and gore. Nebbin and practitioner alike curled in on themselves. Some coughed blood, groaning from wounds too horrifying to look at. Others lay motionless, as good as gone—and frankly, better off. There was no hole to dump them in here. No bones or ashes either. These were fresh men that reeked of fear, courtesy of the Elementalist currently engulfed in a tornado of flame that scorched the ceiling and everyone within a three foot radius. Men wept, as they stumbled out of the blaze. Some were so disfigured that Tiv wondered how they were able to walk at all.

"He's at the center," someone yelled. Encouragement to his wavering companions. "Don't hesitate. He's only one man! Kill him!"

Ice was flung by practitioners in a futile attempt to draw the Elementalist from the storm. His fire consumed all traces of magic in an inexorable swarm of heat that made it difficult to breathe. Black smoke descended around them, before it was subsequently blown away by gusts of wind from the tornado's center. Tiv guessed that it was a tactic to lower their morale. If they saw the destruction around them, then it was only natural that they'd recoil in fear, and eventually, flee.

But that was a strategy employed by people that wanted to regulate their magic. The Elementalist hiding within showed no signs of relenting. He discharged magic like a child that had yet to learn the meaning of restraint. It was as if he was unafraid of his magic circuit suddenly giving out on him.

As if to confirm Tiv's suspicions, the wildfire spread. Raging trails struck out from the tornado's center and emblazoned everything in their path. The temperature increased as the seconds ticked on, until even Tiv found it difficult to breathe.

The magic that coursed through the Elementalist's veins was so intense that Tiv found himself taking a few steps back in fear of accidentally getting in his path. He'd never seen magic like this before. It travelled quicker than anything he'd ever known, fueled by something greater than desperation and fear. This wasn't a practitioner; this was a monster pretending to be.

Tiv yelped when Dwyn pulled him back just as a ten foot spear of ice rose from the ground. More emerged at random intervals. They killed any unfortunate souls that happened to get caught by them. Not that there were many left. Most of the spears only further mutilated those already dead.

This couldn't all be from one man. It just couldn't.

Magic roared around them. Tiv shielded his face with his arms when a stray stream of—*something* brushed all against his front. He shuddered when he realized that it was black and wispy. It brought his attention to the murky water behind the incessant spiral of magic. Its contents swirled high into the air, slowly evaporated by the sheer intensity of the Elementalist's flames. Black tendrils shot out as it was incinerated. Frantic coils that smashed into the walls and the ceiling. A living being that struggled against its demise.

Tiv recognized those tendrils. How could he forget? The last time he saw them, they were in the eyes of his partner. Small. *Contained.* Why were they here now?

Just as he thought it, his eyes widened in realization.

"No," Tiv said, stepping closer.

Dwyn shouted a question above the explosions and screams that his brain didn't care to register.

"That's—"

Without warning, all of the coils retreated back into the center. The world around them faltered at the stillness. Those remaining looked up in a mixture of apprehension and disbelief. The absence of terror was more intimidating than the terror itself.

They gaped, too shocked to retreat. Tiv knew what this was. It was the quiet flash between heaves of storm... and it was over in an instant. The air in the room pulsed. *Physically* pulsed. Dwyn hauled him back by the elbow, knowing that whatever was about to happen wasn't something they could afford to get caught in.

Thick tendrils shot out from the dark mass once more. A whirlwind of desperation that hit everything and nothing. They slammed through the bodies of men and women alike, striking craters into the ground and walls to raze the cavern. Screams bounced against the walls, as broken parts of the ceiling fell onto the unfortunates below.

It was like witnessing the death of a god.

The spiral of fire was steadily overpowered by a trail of ice that came from within. It encompassed the black mass, swiftly spinning until it reached the ceiling, where it shot out like a cobra's venom. The Elementalist's magic was a relentless blast of cold that battled against the burning liquid. Steam rose in all directions. Until eventually, there was a crack. It was followed by thousands more.

Ice blossomed from the darkness' center. Layers extended to cover the mass. The tendrils reacted almost hysterically. They curled to slap against the ice, only for the magic to consume them as well. With each hit, they were covered with frost. It wasn't long before they slowed to a stop, finally done in by the greater force.

They only had one moment to breathe, before a loud thud came from within the ice.

Bang.

Bang. Bang.

Bangbangbangba—

Once, twice, three more times. Tiv heard the frustrated grunts, despite the sheets of ice that separated him from the Elementalist inside. It was obvious to all what was happening.

He was coming out.

There was a blinding spark of white and blue, before it all came tumbling down—the spire, the frozen black mass, the wisps. They all dropped like they'd been thawed just moments before. It was an underground avalanche. No one was spared, save for those smart and able enough to shield themselves behind outcroppings of sturdy rock.

"Silas' sacred blaze!" a man shouted, too jovial for the situation. "That felt good."

The Elementalist walked out with his hands in his hair. He shook out the glittering remnants of hoarfrost that clung to it. His hands were still awash with a blue glow that made his skin look gray from the sheer intensity. There were cuts littered across his body, presumably done by the dead men at his feet. He even had a hole in his tunic that exposed a freshly cauterized wound. The thought of how he was even standing after such a fearsome display had both Dwyn and Tiv stepping back in caution.

They watched, as he looked all around him with those electric red orbs. Sharp and merciless. The Elementalist counted those still left, then smirked insanely at the sorry number. None of them were escaping this cavern alive—and they knew it.

But Tiv couldn't be bothered with their fright or with the Elementalist's demented grin because... he knew that face.

"Jack," Tiv called, before he could stop himself.

Red eyes snapped in his direction. Those destructive tendrils twisted chaotically within, even as the glow in his hands died.

"Tiv?" Jack said, disoriented. He eyed him up and down, then rubbed his eyes as if not quite believing he was there. "What happened to your hands?"

Tiv flinched. It was in that moment that he found out exactly *how* he missed his partner. It was akin to missing a yapping dog. Nice in the beginning, but after that, he remembered just how annoying he really was. Nevertheless, Tiv was happy.

"Jack!" Tiv shouted, sprinting forward. "You're awake! Why didn't you tell me? What are you doing here? No, where have you been all this time?"

"I should be asking *you* that." Jack grabbed his wrist to inspect the missing digits. His eyes were wide and furious. "What happened, Tiv?"

"I—"

"Jack?" Dwyn interrupted with wide eyes. "As in Jacques *Dace*? Elder Dace's son?"

"Who are you?" Jack turned to him. He was still blinking dramatically like he was trying to expel the darkness in his eyes even though they did nothing to hinder his vision.

Dwyn reached into his pockets to pull out a golden button with a moth emblazoned proudly on its surface.

"That's my father's sigil," Jack said, as sure as anything. It was a family heirloom that had been passed down for twelve generations. There were only three reasons he'd have that, and Jack quickly crossed out two of them. Because he doubted his father's death just as much as this Amorph's adoption into his family. There was a limit to absurdity. "Are you one of his men?"

Dwyn nodded. "What's going on here?"

Just as he asked it, there was a loud crack from above them. They craned their necks up toward the ceiling, where three dozen craters continued to break. The cracks spread to connect with the rest of the damage around them, forming an unsteady, stone web.

Jack's mouth went dry at the familiar sight.

"Please don't fall. Please don't fall. Ple*a—filahn vahs*!" He covered his head when a spray of sharp rocks rained down upon him. His hands lit up just as a section of the ceiling came crashing down. "We'll talk later. I need you two to take care of these leftovers, while I keep this place upright."

"Us?" Dwyn asked, looking at all of those left. "Who are these people, Dace?"

"They're after me. I'll fill you in on the rest later."

"You can't just ask me to back you up without—"

"I don't have time for this." Jack whirled around. His eyes never left the ceiling. "If you're not going to help me, then stay out of my way."

"I'll help," Tiv declared. He clasped his partner's shoulder in reassurance. Jack turned to him with his usual dark glare, except it was heavier this time. It was bogged down with weight that Tiv couldn't even begin to fathom. An exact mirror of his own.

They looked at each other for a moment, immeasurable trust and a thousand words exchanged with a mere glance, before they nodded and turned back-to-back against drastically different opponents. There was no need to swivel around. No need to check if the other would falter from what they were about to face. Such doubts had no place here. Tiv couldn't help but grin, even as he fisted what was left of his damaged hands.

He missed this. It was a reminder of freedom.

You're free, his mind insisted. *Free.*

The word itself came with the promise of a new world. He could do anything he wanted. Yet, the only thing he associated with it was the way everyone around him smiled at the thought.

21

By the time the battle ended, Sylvie had gone past the point of exertion. Breathing was slow and difficult. Bone-deep aches permeated from every limb. Even her thoughts were sluggish, as if pulled through deep water.

Dozens laid dead at her feet. The smell of rust in the air was so strong, she could taste it. Her hands were covered in ash and dried blood. Her clothes hardly fared better. They were stained with varying shades of scarlet and brown, their edges singed beyond reprieve. She tried to summon a small ember to set alight the remnants of the fight on her skin, but her magic struggled to cooperate with any of her commands. It was little more than a lambent candle now, doing its best to maintain itself in the pool of wax trying to extinguish it.

She knew the exact moment she'd exhausted her magic circuit. How could she not? It was enough to bring her to the brink of unconsciousness. But she also knew, without a sliver of doubt, that she'd do it over and over again if it meant that she came out alive. Now that the battle had been won, however, now that the adrenaline had faded and she could properly ruminate over her actions, she feared them. She feared what she was capable of in the heat of the moment. While her reactions always seemed wonderful at the time, the after made them look senseless. Needless violence in a world already brimming with it. No one deserved to be scorched until only a charred, black husk remained. She'd been injured, but not to the point of having to resort to such cruelty.

Sylvie wiped her hands on her tattered sleeves with a distant urgency. The grime wouldn't come off.

Why isn't it coming off?

Being able to react without a hint of thought was a superb quality in a practitioner. It was one of the many reasons why Columbus Cephas chose her as his primary apprentice. But recently, she'd been coupling that with her tendency to not look three steps ahead in a fight because of her expectance that someone would be there to watch her back; that wouldn't always be the case. She needed to manage her powers better or else she'd end up passed out on the floor in the middle of a battlefield.

Sylvie sighed. Thinking about her shortcomings made her dread her own familiarity with Jack. Because she just *knew* that he was going to have something to say about all of this, and it would definitely be about the Heartstone. She hoped that he was at least using it and not having arguments with *her* in his mind.

After the fight, they'd removed the gags and blindfolds of those still left. A grand total of seven. As it turned out, only one representative had died—Master Ivy of the Sanct Union—the rest had been Potens. Only two remained. The one Ethil tended to and another that could hardly be called alive at all. Frankly, Sylvie was shocked to learn that the mercenaries hadn't tortured her beforehand. Her eyelids were sealed shut and she had an impressive collection of scars littered across her body. Their appearance suggested age, but the red edges and puffy centers of a few indicated otherwise. Either she'd been hurt fairly recently or she was prone to infection. Perhaps both. Sylvie wondered if they left her alive because they believed killing her to be the greater mercy. Her appearance alone could haunt men for years.

Poten Pramm, they called her. *Amiria Pramm.*

Sylvie recognized the surname. Someone from her family had been a renowned embrocologist an age ago. Credited with the discovery of no less than sixteen new plant species and a genus of nettle that grew only in the Pulka Ruins. They'd also crafted a potent numbing salve and an amber-tinted alcohol that was made from the combined toxins of a snail and a fish.

Myrrh searched the bodies for the key to their manacles, while Ethil healed the wound on Sylvie's ribs. Some of the representatives spoke, explaining how they were captured. It was an ambush by Master Zacarias and Arch Poten Cole, as it turned out, much to the collective bafflement of everyone in the room. Others tried to help Myrrh by suggesting areas where the key might've been. Truthfully, Sylvie thought she burnt it into ash, along with the rest of Gil. But she didn't bother saying so. She had an inkling that the quieter ones among them knew anyway.

Eventually, their discussions faded into the background, as Sylvie looked up at the ceiling, lost in mindless contemplation. Had it always been so low? It looked strange to her, as if it was ever so slowly tilting. Sylvie's head cocked to the side to follow its movement.

It took her some time to realize that someone was calling her; that Ethil's hands had slipped from her ribs to her neck; that the strange mass in her mouth was actually her tongue. Numb and thick. Another part of her that simply refused to obey.

"Sirx," the voice called again.

Sylvie turned to it. A man. One she didn't recognize. He was tall, even when seated. His shoulders were larger than others his age. They were strong and thick with vigor. His beard was full... once. Half had been seared clean off sometime during their fight.

"You are Sylvie Sirx, aren't you?" he asked. "Dalis' sister? The east's new Arch Poten?"

"That's me," she said slowly. Her head spun whenever she spoke. That couldn't be good. "At your service."

The words came out more mocking than she wanted them to. Thankfully, the man didn't seem to mind.

"My name is Rhone," he introduced. "I'm the Red Scripts' representative. Dalis is under me. I'm glad to see that you're alright. Dalis went to the Yovakine Plains hoping to find you, only to return empty-handed. He came running into my office when you arrived. He was absolutely thrilled."

Sylvie stared in surprise at the revelation. She squinted, as if that would help her focus on the olive-toned blur that began to replace Rhone's features. Her fatigue was catching up to her. An endless tide that rose without end to swallow an ocean. What's worse was that it wasn't something Ethil could heal. Magic could only be replenished naturally with time and, preferably, bed rest.

Oh, how she wished she had the luxury.

Instead, what she got was a profound moment of clarity. Absolutely staggering in its intensity. It was the peaceful sedation at the pinnacle of exhaustion, where all she wanted to do was fall over herself, yet was denied even that. Sylvie thought of nothing and everything at once. An effort by her mind to keep her awake.

Rhone continued, undeterred by her indifference. "I heard your conversation with our... charred captor. Would you mind telling me what you know about the Anvil?"

There was only silence, before...

"I get it now," Sylvie rambled, more to herself than to Rhone. She stared hard at the ceiling as she spoke, watching it with a distant look in her eye. "Why Maurice betrayed Thelarius and stole *her* from him, despite the hardships they shared."

Every single head in the room turned to her.

"What are you going on about?" came an indignant, high-pitched shriek. "Maurice didn't betray anyo—"

There was a loud smack, followed by the sound of a body hitting the floor, then stillness once more. Rhone prompted her to speak again, but she'd already gotten lost in her thoughts.

Silas and Thelarius dreamt of a world where practitioners could be free. The Institutes they claimed and built reflected that vision—

Jack at the bottommost floor of any structure isn't safe.

—Maurice and Pernelia were bluebloods that might not have agreed with all of the Institute's laws, but abided by them nevertheless—

I need to find the Elder soon. Dalis, too, if he's done picking fights.

—They grew up fully believing that they would one day rule, that they were superior... until Thelarius came along and—

Myrrh's a Hunter. What's she doing here? Don't they hunt

deserters? Has she been dispatched to watch over the Grove or is she here for another reason?

—Their changes over the years shows in the Institutes they governed—

Tiv is here, they said. Did he come this far on his own? Was he searching for Jack? Will Jack go with him?

—The Drowned Tower has always been accessible by Nebbin, though they might not have always been welcome. The Grove, on the other hand, is filled with traps only a practitioner could get through—

It really is sloping. Slow. Steady. A falling book? How long until it slams to the ground?

—Maurice wanted to rule... he wanted...

"To create a world where only practitioners existed," Sylvie muttered out loud. An exhale, then, "What a worthless dream."

"What?" Rhone asked. "What was that? Explai—"

"She's clearly not thinking straight," Ethil intervened on her behalf. "Her magic circuit is fried. She needs rest."

Sylvie would love to. But reality was never so kind. There was the slightest of rumbles beneath her feet, then the distant boom of something loud and heavy falling. That was familiar to her. Uncomfortably familiar.

Sylvie looked up again. It definitely wasn't her imagination.

"The ceiling's tilting," she said, causing everyone to look up in panic. "... Isn't it?"

Just as the words left her lips, a scream erupted from outside. It was followed by a hundred more exactly like it. There was the sound of footsteps, broken only by the occasional curse, as entire troops of practitioners ran in the seemingly same direction.

"The Grove is sinking?" Ethil repeated, just barely making out their garbled voices. She looked back up again. "Wait, were you serious? The ceiling is actually—"

The ground beneath them suddenly dropped. The floor tilted in a sharp left angle that toppled all of them. They slid sideways. The surrounding furniture and corpses followed along for the ride. Books fell from their homes and attempted to crush them under their weight. Sylvie both cursed and thanked her luck. The former because she didn't want to die buried under a mountain of tomes and bodies; the latter because if she had the strength to burn these texts, then she would have, and she'd hate herself for it afterwards.

Sylvie grasped blindly around her. Eventually, her fingers found purchase on a wooden chest that was nailed to the ground. She tried to pull herself up, only to fumble when the world around her spun again. She settled for hanging onto it instead.

I could rest here, she thought. On cue, a tome no less than twelve-hundred pages slammed into her shoulder. *Never mind.*

Dragon Cults, she read, before flinging the tome aside. Sylvie looked around her, trying to make sense of her now skewed surroundings. There was a severed arm pressed against her leg. *Thelarius' wind! As if I'm not filthy enough.*

Another rumble came from below, except much louder this time. *Is that magic?* she wondered, pressing her ear to the floor. *Yes. Definitely. Someone's conjuring gravel down there.*

The Grove didn't stop completely. Not yet. It was too soon for that. But it did slow down enough for any furniture that was left standing to tilt instead of fall over. It was then that Sylvie noticed a bookshelf looming high above her. It cast a dangerous shadow just above where her fingers were. She had no doubt that a hit from that would snap them like twigs.

But just as soon as she saw it, the bookshelf was pushed away. A pair of large, callused hands grasped her by the arms, and she was pulled straight from the floor and onto her feet in one smooth motion.

"Are you alright?" a man she didn't recognize asked. He gripped her shoulders to keep her from stumbling back.

"I will be," Sylvie replied, then wrinkled her nose at the distinct scent of pine coming from his robes. When she looked down, she noticed that his wrists were free. *Did he find the—*

"I found the keys," Myrrh shouted from across the room, as if in answer. Behind her, the representatives shook out their limbs and tested their unbound magic. "They were under some man's crotch."

"Something we didn't need to know," Ethil chimed.

"I see you've already introduced yourself, Flax," a woman said. She had golden-brown hair that ended just above her ears and dark skin. A scar curved along the side of her cheek, ending just below her bottom lip.

"You're not the only one curious about what she said, Tabriel," Flax shot back.

"Indeed," another man walked up to them. A Healer this time with a feathered overcoat and an immobilizing stare. "But the Primordians get priority in these things."

"Varron," Flax acknowledged. "Need I remind you that the Primordians only get priority access to new publications and interviews by visiting members of the Scholar's Shift? Their youngest member is sixty-two years old. She's barely," he paused to turn to her, "how old are you?"

"Twenty-three."

"Not even half that," he went on. "She's free to speak to whomever she chooses."

"Not entirely," Tabriel piped up. "The forty-second clause clearly states that the Libersta's are in charge of any visiting Arch Potens—"

"We have bigger issues," Rhone intervened. He pointed at the floor. "The Grove is sinking! I'm sure she'll tell us everything we want to know in time, but we need to go out there and stop this madness before it gets any worse."

"No!" Sylvie shouted, causing them to turn to her. "I mean, *yes,* you should, but focus on righting the Grove from here. Have practitioners level the ground and plop up sections of the ceiling. I doubt this place will collapse because of a little dip. The An—"

"Is not spoken about in public," Tabriel cut in.

"Is none of your concern," Sylvie corrected with a scowl that dared them to question it. "It's a trench filled with corpses that should've been given a proper burial a long time ago, not cast into boiling lochs for the Institute's gains."

Tabriel's mouth opened and closed twice in shock by how much she knew. The other three were no better. They stared at her with wide, disbelieving eyes.

Varron was the first to gather his wits. "How do you know about that?"

"What does it matter how I know?" Sylvie's eyes hardened. "What matters is that I do, and I disapprove."

"So, what? You mean to put a stop to the *Orivellea's* production?" Tabriel challenged. "The Zenith Council won't take kindly to that."

"Neither will we," Rhone added. "It's a vile practice, to be sure, but it has brought the Grove prosperity throughout the years. The Alps relies on us to craft them, so we do. With *startling* efficiency. Ending or even limiting their production must first be discussed by all parties involved. You're young, but not young enough to not know that you can't just decide to end something because you disagree with it. Go through the proper channels. Present a statement to us and to the Zenith Council, and then we'll talk."

"That, there is the problem!" Sylvie exclaimed. "You talk as if you have a right to the remnants that multiply within that lake. Needing to sacrifice bodies—alive *and* dead—to create containers should've been your first clue that some powers simply aren't meant to be contained."

"Watch your mouth," Tabriel warned. "That's Maurice's legacy you're slating."

"It's a bloody and undeserved one!" Sylvie argued, breathing heavily. Her vision blurred at the edges, but all traces of exhaustion were stubbornly pushed aside. Vehemence took its place. "What do you think the practitioners out there will have to say about them? Because sooner or later, they *will* find out. Flames, for all we know, they might have already. It wouldn't be surprising, given this commotion. Peose carry those crystals. *Elementalist's* carry them. Those are dead men in their heads. Do you even know about their true nature, or has your greed kept you from thoroughly questioning the Council about why Elementalists need them in the first place?"

"That's enough," Myrrh interrupted, butting in before the argument could escalate. She didn't know the exact details about what they were talking about, but she'd find out. Soon. For now, they had bigger things to worry about. "We don't have time for petty squabbles. The representatives need to get the practitioners *and* the Grove in order. While you," Myrrh shoved a vial filled with orange liquid in Sylvie's unsuspecting hands, "need to drink that."

Sylvie rubbed her forehead with her fingers, trying to calm herself down. She didn't get much time because Ethil appeared behind her. The Healer placed her hands on her shoulders and rubbed them in a soothing gesture. They lit up, smothering her fatigue, before Ethil led her away. The representatives brooded behind them, but allowed her to leave without complaint. Despite their desire to question her about what she knew, they *did* realize that they have more important things to deal with and getting their practitioners in order took precedence over any arguments about the Anvil.

Little did they know that Jack was already down there. Even if they were to send a few of their higher ranking practitioners, the Anvil would be nothing more than scattered slag by the time they arrived... if they could at all. Judging by the Grove's slow descent, Jack and Philip were burying the workshop in a mountain of conjured rubble.

"Drink it," Ethil quietly urged. Her voice left no room for argument.

Sylvie popped the cork and brought the concoction up to her nose. Fruity. Sickeningly so. "*Hessroot* potion?"

"It'll give you a boost."

"The taste alone will make me want to vomit."

"You and I both know that it won't. It's good for you, and it'll last much longer than my magic will in your current state. I promise."

"A potion can trump magic?"

"It depends on how drained the practitioner's circuit is. Yours is weak right now. Flooding it with magic won't do it any good. You need a pick me up, not outside forces in your system." Ethil raised the hand Sylvie held the bottle in closer to her lips. "So, take it. *Please.*"

"You're the Healer," Sylvie said, then downed the brew — as easy as death, and two times more upsetting — it burned all the way down. She screwed her eyes shut at the sour aftertaste. The leftovers seemed to react to her spit by frothing in her mouth. Sylvie swirled her tongue at the alien sensation.

While *Hessroot* might not have been her first choice because of how absurdly long it took to kick in, it was likely the only potion Ethil had. Sylvie just hoped that one would be enough to last her through the next few hours. If not, then she'd need to raid one of the Grove's embrocologist centers... or get to her private stash. She'd been a fool not to take a few tonics from her pack. But she also hadn't expected to do anything but sit by Jack's bedside for the next three days. In retrospect, Sylvie should've known better than to assume a few days of reprieve.

"Thank you," Sylvie said.

"Anytime."

"Anything else?"

"Try to avoid using magic," Ethil advised. "If you decide to take any other potions later today, avoid anything with — "

"Wanewood," Sylvie finished. "Got it."

"Then that's it."

Sylvie looked up at the ceiling once more, shook her legs out to make sure that they wouldn't give out on her, then spun on her heel to open the door. A cacophony of voices flooded inside. The representatives stopped whispering amongst themselves at the sound. Even Myrrh halted her tedious task of passing the unconscious Poten into Varron's reluctant hands.

They spoke, asking where she was headed and what she

planned to do. But their breaths were wasted on her. Sylvie raced back to the main section of the Grove. It wasn't long before they followed, clearly having decided that dawdling in the archives wouldn't do any of them any good. She didn't bother waiting up for them. Sylvie only had three things on her mind now — finding the Elder, Dalis, and Jack.

***

The first one she found was Dalis.

Unsurprising, given that he was caught in the very heart of the chaos. Practitioners loosed their magic from all corners of the Grove. Bursts of every primal force could be seen erupting across the crowd. Some were so uncontrolled that they triggered nearby orbs of light into exploding. The magic veins hidden within each coiled, destroying floor and ceiling alike. Although the Grove never grew completely dim. The constant flashes of white-blue light ensured that.

Amorphs soared through the air or prowled the masses, taking on the forms of gnarly beasts and lethal insects. In one area, there was even an entire colony of ants that scurried on the legs of any unfortunate practitioners that happened to pass. They screamed, not in pain, but from the fear of it.

The younger practitioners, as well as those less talented in their skills had taken to hiding themselves. Some, however, were a little more courageous. They cheered their college mates from the sidelines. But the number seemed to dwindle as the fight progressed. Most jumped into the fray, either to save a friend or to make the most of this opportunity.

Sylvie could tell those that were a part of the latter. Their voices were loud. Their magic, gaudy. Pointless extravagance meant to draw attention, so that they could showcase their skills to the senior apprentices in their respective colleges. Then there were those—the older ones—that did this because they were actually angry. Because they were jilted at one time or another. Previous transgressions that piled onto one another to spark animosity over time. Those were the dangerous ones. They violently vented their frustrations on their longtime enemies, using this time to settle grudges, quite unaware that they were making a dozen more in the process. These were the practitioners in the very center of the fray.

Many were heavily injured, both intentionally and otherwise; many were healed on the spot. The most experienced Healers in the Grove were there. Traces of their magic remained in everyone they cured, creating a network of indecipherable streams throughout the room. The veins of those newly mended glowed like faded ghosts. These Healers were the easiest to find. They stood out without meaning to. Their magic lit, as brilliant as any star, then faded into nothing. All within the span of a second. There was no pause to wonder about the depth of a wound. No second to debate if they should waste their magic or throw the injured soul a potion. There was only the sight of blood and the instant reaction to it.

For that reason alone, Sylvie knew that a number of those being dragged away were practitioners that had exhausted their circuits.

If any of them noticed that the Grove had tilted, then they did a spectacular job of ignoring it. *Though*, Sylvie amended, *those that care more about that than this fight are probably already racing to the lower floors to investigate.* She just hoped they didn't catch Jack in any compromising situations.

Sylvie peered into the center, trying to catch sight of Dalis again. She saw a Conjurer whose shoulder was slashed by an errant blade that was viciously knocked out of a practitioner's hand. The woman's jaw slackened at the sight. She didn't scream, too shocked by the suddenness of it all. Fortunately, it was healed by a passing Healer that disappeared as quickly as he'd come. He offered no assurances or gentle nudges. There was no time for that here. Off to the side, an Amorph was buffeted by a storm of ice mid-transformation. The howl of pain that ripped through his throat sounded somewhere between a wolf and a dying seal. He wasn't so lucky.

"Sylvie!" Dalis shouted from the distance.

He held his hand up high, as he made his way towards her. Sylvie couldn't help but notice how frazzled he looked. His hair and clothes were in disarray. He was covered in sweat, blood, and an unknown magenta liquid that had an oddly potent aroma. She could smell its floral scent a good six meters out. There was a gash on his temple that trailed a thin line of blood all the way down to his neck. Despite this, he had the most satisfied grin on his face.

She could see why.

Beside him, was an older man in Elder's garb. His earrings reflected the flashes of light around them. Philip followed a few steps behind, just far enough that he could keep his eye on a particularly flamboyant Elementalist. The boy was no doubt a member of the Red Scripts. Sylvie wasn't sure if he was trying to impress the Elder or his senior practitioners—perhaps both. She didn't dwell on it, however, too busy inspecting Philip under the shifting light. He was noticeably pallid. His skin had a greenish tint to it that suggested illness. If Dalis and an Elder weren't enough to heal him, then he needed to be confined to a bed.

"I told you I'd find the Elder," Dalis said once she was in earshot. "Syl, meet Elder Borris."

"I wish it was under better circumstances," Sylvie said.

"As do I." Borris nodded solemnly. "Regardless, I'm always glad to meet a new Arch Poten, especially if it's before the rest of the Zenith Council. I assume you're here to force these practitioners back into line, but I'm afraid that will need to wait. I have to speak with you about the Grove's current political climate and a certain... incident that occurred. It's urgent."

"I'm glad you sought me out. I have a few things to speak about with you as well. But first..." Sylvie looked behind them and met Philip's gaze. "If you're up here, then where's Jack?"

Philip's gaze shifted to Borris, then back to her. "He's—"

"That's what I need to talk to you about," Borris interrupted.

Her heart spasmed. She didn't like the look they were giving her. Troubled. Shifty. *Remorseful.* Sylvie looked wildly around her, searching for Jack. Her nails almost broke skin when she didn't find him.

"How long have you been here?" she pushed. "Weren't you the one conjuring stones below?"

"I just regained consciousness," Philip defended.

"This isn't the place," Borris said.

Sylvie turned to him with a furious snarl. "The Grove tilted, is *still* tilting, and you're telling me that this isn't the place? Where is he?"

"Easy, Syl," Dalis said, putting an arm up to keep her from attacking someone. "I'm sure he's fine."

"You don't know that!" she shouted. "Jack can't—*he* isn't— *h*is magic isn't like other Elementalists. If he exerts himself too much, *she* might intervene. He'll turn into Rior!"

"Rior?" Borris questioned, but it went ignored as Dalis grabbed Sylvie by the shoulders and shook hard.

"Relax!" Dalis yelled, breaking through the panicked haze that he knew clouded her thoughts. "We're going to find him, okay? We'll go right now if you want."

"You're not going anywhere," Rhone said, emerging from a long hallway. His mouth was pressed into a thin line. He crossed his arms in displeasure at the sight before him. The rest of the representatives followed a second later with the exact same expression on their faces. "What's going on here?"

Dalis sobered immediately. All exuberance replaced by grave composure. "Master Rhone."

"Are you deaf now, Dalis?" His eyes moved menacingly to the practitioners around them that abruptly stilled at their arrival. The noise of those that had yet to see did nothing to mask the fury in his tone. "Explain yourselves."

Sylvie used that moment to boldly seize the Elder's wrist in a viselike grip. Borris turned to her with a start, though there was no question hiding behind his eyes.

"Where is he?" she asked.

"The Anvil," Borris said.

The words had barely left his lips, and Sylvie was already running across the chamber to head deeper into the Grove. She shoved dozens of practitioners out of her way. Those that retaliated were subsequently dealt with by a well-placed kick to their nether regions or by a merciless press of firy fingers on their jugulars. One had come at her with a knife, which she countered with a blow to the woman's elbow, before turning the force of her own strike against her. The woman's blade had embedded itself deep into her own eye. Those that saw it were quick to step away, taking the display as a precursor of pain to come should they get in her way.

Absently, she noted that Borris was following her. He was a lot more lenient, using his powers to turn those that stepped too close into piles of nerveless goo on the floor. His magic flowed out of him in quick bursts, faster, stronger, and more controlled than any Healer she'd ever seen. But perhaps that was to be expected.

Far behind her, Sylvie heard the enraged shouts of her friends and family across the room—Ethil, Dalis, Myrrh. They demanded to know where she was going. Dalis yelled at her to wait, clearly having every intention of coming with her, despite Rhone's disapproval. Sylvie ignored them all.

She kept running until the crowd of practitioners finally thinned and all she could hear were distant echoes and Borris' heavy steps as he trailed after her. He told her where to turn whenever she reached an intersection, rested his hand upon her shoulder when she had to stop to catch her breath, and led the way when she stumbled over her own two feet. Her muscles felt overused; spent beyond their capacity. Sylvie had run across longer distances in shorter times without food or proper sleep, so she knew that it couldn't have just been due to fatigue. The lack of magic in her veins was clearly taking its toll.

"This is it," Borris said.

Sylvie halted, taking care to quiet her steps as she descended the long staircase. The first thing she saw was a closed door and three practitioners attempting to pick the lock. Their robes had scorch marks along the edges, and they were covered in sweat. She was right then. Those that cared more about the Grove sinking than the internal conflicts between colleges had already come here to investigate.

She looked at the symbols etched onto the door. Full circles that tapered the farther they were from the center. Those were Mentalist markings. Explosives that could wipe out everything within a thirty meter radius.

"What are you doing?" Sylvie asked.

The three turned to her with their hands raised defensively.

"Do you want to die?" she went on, undeterred by their stances. "That door is equipped with explosive enchantments."

"And just who are you?" one of them asked. "What college are you from?"

"She knew what the marks were," another said, nudging his companion. "She's probably a Primordian."

"I should've known." The man grimaced. "You've got the sour face of a Primordian. Stay out of our way, you second-rate scholar. We're here to see why the Grove is sinking. We can't do that with this chunk of metal here."

"You open it without the proper key, and it'll wipe this entire section of the Grove from the face of Ferus Terria," Sylvie warned. "Back away from the door."

"Or what?" he challenged. "You'll make us?"

"If that's what it takes," Sylvie said. "But are you really willing to risk your lives for this? That's an Elder of the Diamond Alps standing behind me. Even if you do survive picking a fight with me, he can make you wish you hadn't."

The three turned to Elder Borris, who stood there with his head cocked. The shadows cast by the lone candle on the floor made him appear all the more frightening.

"Leave," Borris ordered. "All of you."

It didn't take long for them to come to a decision. They looked at each other, nodded once, then took off running. Sylvie would've smiled had it been under different circumstances. She walked up to the door and placed her hand on the cool steel.

"Why not use your title?" Borris asked from behind her.

"Would they have believed me?" Sylvie shot back. "I'm an Arch Poten, though I don't consider myself to be. My Institute is destroyed. Its practitioners, scattered. What exactly do I have to brag about?"

"The title holds weight, regardless."

"Not now," she disagreed, "but it will."

Borris paused at her answer. Realistic. Firm. But most of all, determined. She had a good head on her shoulders. Sylvie had all the makings of a splendid leader, whether she knew it or not. So long as she was given the proper guidance, she'd become one. A plan formed in his head, but he didn't bring it up. Now wasn't the time for future promises. He'd wait until after the Grove calmed down.

"I have the key," he informed. Borris showed her a ring full of them. He chose one of the larger ones with a scratch on its side. "Here."

Sylvie didn't waste any time. She inserted the key into the lock and pulled with all of her might. It was harder than she expected. The door barely budged, not even when she planted her heels on the ground and bent at an odd angle. Borris got the message. He grabbed the handle to help her. Together, they opened it just enough for them to slip inside.

She went first, only to lurch to a halt before entering.

"What's wrong?" Borris asked, peering over her shoulder.

A wall of rubble blocked their path.

22

It had been raining for days.

Khale looked up at the gray sky above him, then towards the outer line of trees that marked the beginning of the Mending Willow. The trees were so tall that even from meters away, their shadows still loomed above them. It was too dark for him to see through the foliage, and the evening fog did nothing to aid that. The area itself seemed to breathe like a dormant monster. But Khale had a feeling that standing beyond it was more ominous than standing within. It was the same feeling he got whenever he watched the Zexin Sea roar before a storm, as if something might suddenly emerge from the shadows and swallow him whole.

But that was paranoia talking. Exhaustion, too.

They'd been travelling at an extraordinary pace, moving well into twilight. He could smell magic in the air. It was so strong that he wondered if a new type of Conjurer had brought this boundless torrent to life. The rain spared nothing. Even his hard glass bracelets had adopted a misty cover across their surface. Behind him, members of the Hellion huddled together under sorry tents and thick blankets. There weren't enough for each of them, so they'd opted to spreading them out wide. One for every four. They spoke of their hometowns—the way light fell like a hammer through broad-bladed trees at noon; how the grass changed from scarlet to gold; the bone bare fields in the winter.

The livelier ones sharpened their blades. Some even sparred in an effort to generate warmth. Pom was one of them. He stood in a corner of the camp with Celina, where they swung their daggers at each other until their arms fell limp. A Healer quickly approached them. He dug his fingers into the sorest places on their backs until they slouched, boneless from relief.

Deserters weren't all bad. Khale knew that now.

He stared blindly at the silver-green leaves, watching them tremble under the downpour. Until eventually, his solitude was interrupted by an unhappy Drage. Khale was familiar with the hard look in his eyes. Something was bothering him, and Khale knew he wouldn't like it.

"Where're you from?" Khale asked, before he could speak.

Drage blinked twice at the question, before waving vaguely behind him. "Some backwater village farther south. It's not even on a map, so you can guess just how politically important it is. Peaceful place. Neatly trimmed paths and green fields. They had decent cheese. The locals were all proud of their sheep."

"Sheep?"

"Sheep," he confirmed. "If you're done asking stupid questions, can I tell you my problem now?"

"The rain's got you impatient, yea?" Khale grimaced at the sky. "Me, too."

"Then you'll love this." Drage pointed eastward. "I found some wandering men—Nebbin. They were talking about waiting for a signal to enter the Grove. Know anything about that?"

"Why would I?" Khale asked. "Overhear anythin' good?"

"Just that they already sent a group in. I'm guessing whatever's happening in the Grove has already started."

"A few Nebbin won't do much. Not unless they've got themselves some inside support, yea?"

"It's possible that they were hired by someone inside. They looked like mercenaries. Well-equipped ones at that. Definitely not the type to come this close to practitioner territory without a cartful of coin."

"Maybe they decided to venture to saner pastures. Too many slavers an' that 'round here for my taste."

"As if the Institute is any different."

"True." Khale shrugged. "See anyone familiar?"

Drage paused to think. "No. But I recognize the symbols on their crates. They're a mix of groups from the Plains."

"That include the Hellion?"

Drage nodded solemnly.

"Think Gil's amblin' 'round then?" Khale went on.

"He could never resist a well-paid job."

"It's pourin' an' we've been barrelin' through all hell for leather, yea? How much vim do you think we got?"

"Enough for a fight."

"D'you really think weedin' 'em out is a good idea?"

"Gil's elusive. This might be our only chance in a long time."

"Fine." Khale sighed. "Whatever you say, boss. But the men're exhausted. I think I'm on solid ground when I say that you ain't clearin' anyone with a troop like this. Have a small group move in first, yea? Surprisin' 'em is definitely best. An' everyone knows that the adrenaline from sneakin' 'round tends ta put a few springs in bushy steps. It's good for you!"

"Does that mean you're volunteering?"

Khale grinned eagerly. "Me an' Pom step in ta distract the lot. We'll all have a sweet, civil word. Maybe we can pretend ta be patrollin' Grove practitioners an' that. Then when they're well an' focused, you thin 'em out with a few arrows."

"We're doing what now?" Pom butted in. Celina followed a few steps behind him, rolling her neck around her shoulders like she knew what they were about to do.

"Just the 'morph I was lookin' for." Khale wrapped his arm around Pom's shoulders. "We need ta bait some men. Flash a little skin and bounce some vanes, yea?"

"*What?*"

"Honey-trappin'!" Khale shouted loud enough to make a few heads turn. "Stop sweatin' the little details an' follow me."

Pom's protests were muffled as Khale dragged him off.

"Do you even know where you're going?" Drage asked.

"East." Khale beamed, inordinately proud of himself. "You

gather the men an' leave the grunt work ta us, yea? Bein' delightful is what we do best!"

***

They moved east around the forest.

Pom knew how to track movement in the dirt, and Khale had the nose of a bloodhound. Between the two of them and a waylaid trader with a bruised face and a ransacked wagon, they followed the path to an outcropping of trees not twenty minutes from the Mending Willow. Although unfamiliar with this forest's terrain, they were acquainted with the general hazards of woodlands. They knew better than most the way a forest settled into deep stillness before opening itself to dawn. It was an easy thing for them to blend in with the trees in their regular forms.

Pom had better eyes for broken twigs and marks scratched into the bark, but here and there Khale would point to other signs: an overhanging branch cleanly sliced; the leftover core of a green fruit; moss crushed flat from many feet; the rough, repeating divots of a walking stick held by a heavy hand. All obvious, especially for skilled trackers like them. It helped that the ones they were after made no efforts to hide their movements. They found them quickly, despite the swift-falling dark.

"There," Khale said, slipping behind the bole of an old oak. There was a small pool hidden between the roots that he took care to side-step.

"How many?" Pom asked.

Khale's eyes flickered over the whole, counting them. He grimaced at the number. "You don't wanna know."

"Shit."

Thirty men, perhaps more, scattered like ants across the field. If they were waiting for a signal, then they didn't look it. The men had nestled like pregnant birds inside of their camps. Torchlight flared through the trees. Some were held steady by lower-ranked members, while the rest were fixed, standing upright with the help of heavy metal canisters.

Hounds circled the vicinity. Khale only saw two well enough for him to transform into—a curled-tail one with a black spot on his eye and another with beige-fur and a stumped tail. Hopefully both were well-liked, but not so much that he'd need to be wary about minute details like scars. He'd need to take careful note of their sizes, too. Khale clenched his fists. This was going to be more trouble than he thought.

As if sensing his frustration, Pom asked, "Why do you volunteer for things?"

"It keeps me outta trouble."

"This is out of trouble?"

Khale flashed him a smile full of pointed teeth.

"At least repent, fool."

"They've got dogs," Khale said instead.

"I hate dogs," Pom muttered. He checked his blades to make sure none of them caught moonlight. Skirmishes like this had become routine since they joined the Hellion, but no matter how many he found himself caught in, he could never get used to the low, insistent hum in his blood before the first draw of blood. "What are they doing?"

"The dogs?" Khale asked, though he didn't wait for an answer. "One's eatin'. Four're leashed an' sniffing the dirt."

"Let me guess, those four are all heading this way?"

"You know it. They've got some real staggerin' senses, yea?" Khale praised. "We need ta move quickly. You got my back?"

Pom lifted his face in the dark, and Khale saw the ferocity in his eyes. "Do you even have to ask?"

"Then let's go."

The silence that spread as they strode into the camp was amusing. Astonished faces were interspersed by reflexive alertness from battle-hardened men that hefted their unstrapped blades across their bodies. Most of them carried swords, but there were a few scattered archers with longbows. Khale could hardly contain his grin when he realized that some had unstrung them for waxing and now struggled to bend them back into shape.

Their leader stood a ways from the center of the camp with his arms crossed and his lips pursed in wariness. His ebony curls were tied in a loose ponytail that left just enough hair to cover his eyes and frame his swarthy skin. Torchlight glanced off of his armor. His shoulder's tensed like iron when they realized his position and stepped closer. Although he had yet to draw his saber, his hand dropped to its hilt as soon as he saw their eyes.

"Evenin'," Khale greeted, shading his eyes against a nearby torch. How they weren't doused by the rain was a question for the ages. "Strange place ta be campin', yea? Mind me askin' what business you cats have so close ta the Grove?"

"We're just passing through," the man said with a thick accent that neither of them could place. "And yourselves? This is an unfriendly place for practitioners."

"Patrollin'," Khale lied smoothly.

"Really," he drawled, tilting his head emphatically at their leathers. Robes were the mark of a practitioner. Only those considered special cases were allowed to wear anything else. "Are you sure you aren't out of your jurisdiction?"

"They are," a man stepped out from the shadows.

They all turned to find a Conjurer with slanted eyes and a clean jaw. His lips twisted in displeasure at the sight of them.

"Well, Snuff nuggins. I wasn't expectin' this," Khale said, changing his strategy. "Catchin' me in a lie—how embarassin'. Ta tell you the truth, we're here ta catch up with an old friend."

"Gil," Pom interjected. "He should have the Hellion's mark somewhere on him."

"Nobody like that here." The leader spread his arms wide. "So, I think its best you two leave."

"I can't allow that," the Conjurer interrupted. "The Scripts' are in charge of these parts, and I'm in charge of the duty roster. I've never seen you two before."

"We ain't very memorable," Khale said.

"Give yourselves more credit. I don't know you, so that only means one thing."

"An' what's that?"

"Don't you know?" the Conjurer held up a knife. "Deserters get dealt with."

"And what about passing mercenaries looking to invade the Grove?" Pom asked.

"Now, that's interesting." He turned to the group and barred his teeth in a feral smile. "Are you going to defend yourselves?"

"There's no need." The leader raised his hand. "Kill them."

Swords rang like a cry as they were drawn from sheaths. Khale only had time to meet the eyes of the Conjurer across from them in a silent plea to help them fight against the bigger threat, before two arrows came soaring through the air. One was aimed at his chest, while the other was uncomfortably close to his crotch. Before him, two men charged with their swords drawn.

Khale shifted into a large spider, charging forward before either of the bolts could hit. The men in front of him wavered at the sight of his long, hairy legs. He took advantage of their fear by sinking his fangs deep into their necks. Every single one of his eyes rounded in their sockets, before settling on a group of bowmen with unstrung weapons around a campfire. Flashes of white-blue light and panicked cries echoed behind him. Some were more distant than others. Khale didn't bother turning, knowing that his partner could handle whatever came at him. At one point, he even heard the deafening squawk of a vulture, followed by a man's gurgled scream—that was definitely Pom.

The Conjurer was a different story. It was like fighting beside a hurricane. Ice screeched by in a froth of pointed shards. It was like witnessing the release of glassy silver jewels that sparkled even when they were embedded in someone's face. Some were so big that they speared through muscle and armor alike. Khale came across one man with his hair plastered over one eye from too much blood. His calf had been impaled by a lance-shaped block of ice. Not lethal on its own, but enough to leave him shouting for help in horror.

"Khale!" Pom shouted. "On your right!"

He shifted into a bird just in time to dodge a fatal blow to his shoulder. The man lurched forward when his swing met air. Khale retaliated by using his claws to lift the mercenary's helmet, successfully tearing a chunk of his face along with it.

Pom was quick to approach. He slammed the butt of his dagger into the man's unguarded back. Not a good enough blow on its own, the swing too low and slipping on heavy leathers to do much damage, but it was enough for Pom to adjust his footing and follow with a sideward thrust. He embedded the cold steel in a small opening on the larger man's side. It slid between rib and sinew. Pom twisted it until the man stumbled, before pulling it out and stabbing him a second time, then a third. No extra twists now. Only a swift retrieval of his blade and a listless look as the man dropped to his knees and fell face-first into the dirt. More came at them. They nicked Khale with their daggers, splitting his leathers in half a dozen places. He groaned as his left side spiked agony from shoulder to wrist, courtesy of an arrow he scarcely remembered getting hit by. A woman invaded his personal space. The curved edge of her blade managed to slice Khale's collar, before she was roughly knocked to the ground by a defensive Pom, who cradled his stomach in one hand, while trying his best not to stagger back. Khale saw blood on his partner's fingers, undoubtedly his own. If his wound was as deep as it looked, then he wouldn't be able to last much longer.

Where's Drage? Khale thought, searching the surrounding trees and sidestepping a desperate swordsman all in the same instant. His eyes drifted to the Conjurer, who was engaged in a heated stare down with the leader of the group. A broken arrow dangled just below his left elbow and his hands glowed so brightly, it hurt. The men around him were blue in the face and encased head to toe in blocks of ice that were eight inches thick.

He didn't need help. His magic ran strongly in his veins, and he was nowhere near as physically exhausted as either of them. It was obvious to anyone that this Conjurer could wipe the floor with anyone foolhardy enough to approach, and it showed when the younger, greener mercenaries lingered on the sidelines, despite their initial bravado. But Khale was never one to stand on the edges in the middle of a fight...

... And he didn't like the way the leader's upper lip curled into an entertained sneer.

Khale only had one moment to take in the man dropping his saber in favor of sweeping the hair on his face back over his head. The Conjurer breathed in. Hardly loud. But enough to break through the cries of death and the clang of iron. Behind him, Pom burst out a cry of warning. But Khale realized too late that the orange glow in his eyes wasn't from the reflected torchlight.

The leader clenched his hand, and the world stopped.

A hurricane of bottomless fury erupted all around them. It pushed all of them back. Khale covered his face with his arms, trying and failing to hold his ground. He screwed his eyes shut. Khale heard the wind hissing in his ear. The air was sharp as it pushed him back, cutting his arms and chest at random intervals. The leader's magic clearly wasn't directed at him. He didn't have to be a genius to know his primary target.

Before Khale could even think about stepping in to help the Conjurer, a battle cry emerged from the trees. A cacophony of different voices followed. He opened his eyes just enough to see Drage leading members of the Hellion out into the clearing. The mercenaries that were left unscathed by the squall turned with a start. Khale turned his back on them, knowing they could handle the bulk of the group. His eyes scanned the area. How many were left before him? Four? Five? Pom was already taking out one. A stray blast of ice tore through another—it seemed the Conjurer was alright after all. Celina had even stepped in with her daggers drawn and her lips tilted upward in a violent smile.

When Khale jumped back into the fray, he set his sights on their leader. Gusts of wind blew all around him. While the Conjurer was able to shoot back trails of ice, they were always swept to the side as soon as his magic emerged.

Birds won't do, Khale plotted, his gaze roved over the distance between him and their leader. *I need somethin' heavier. Not too big though. I don't wanna be an easy target. Quick then. Lithe. A—*

A monstrous roar made everyone in the clearing still.

Heads swiveled in Khale's direction as the glow of his magic receded to reveal a massive feline with black striping and russet fur. Pintle Panters were native to the Eirinne Mountains. They hunted in packs, but one on its own was capable of taking down a bear. They attacked their prey in a stunning rush, dodging behind trees and doubling back to charge without warning. Practitioners were taught to avoid them. Khale, however, had opted to ignore that lesson. During a particularly lengthy patrol, he took it upon himself to blend in with an entire pack to integrate himself into their clan. Half of his ribs were broken by the end of it, but he was proud to say that he'd succeeded.

Taking advantage of their astonishment, Khale stalked forward at a hideous speed, aiming to sink his fangs into their leader's neck. Unfortunately for him, his prey had gathered his wits and did the only thing he could in such a dire situation— hold his arm up as a sacrifice.

Khale's teeth sank deep into bone, easily tearing through skin and muscle like a knife to hot butter. It wasn't long before his jaws were opening again. This time, they found their mark. His mouth clamped down hard on the leader's neck and the bottom half of his face, mutilating it beyond recognition.

Those around him were silent as he leapt back and shifted into his normal form. Blood coated his front. It was all over his mouth. Khale spat on the ground, futilely trying to get rid of the vile flavor.

"Works a killer, yea?" he said to no one in particular.

"Show off," Pom shouted from somewhere behind him.

It didn't take long for the remaining mercenaries to stumble back in terror at the sight of their disfigured leader. Drage whistled sharply, getting his men's attention. The enemies' morale was down, and they were fully willing to capitalize on their weakness.

The tide of battle quickly turned. But before Khale could even breathe a sigh of relief, a hand fell on his shoulder and squeezed—*hard*. He craned his neck back to find the Conjurer there. His orange eyes spoke nothing of amusement.

"Skilled or not," he drawled in a short, angry breath. "Don't think I'll let you off so easily, deserter."

"Impatient," Khale muttered. He tilted his head to the sky. "Don't tell me you don't like the rain either?"

***

The Conjurer's name was Lyss.

He was a member of the Red Scripts and had been escorting a wayward child back to Curran. He'd been watching the mercenaries for some time, and was about to return to the Grove to inform his college about their presence when they stepped into the clearing. It was fate, some of the more wishful thinking members of the Hellion said. Drage called it a coincidence, while Khale dubbed it a stroke of unbelievable luck—because finally, they found the reason they were here in the first place.

As they were healed by a deserter that Lyss eyed with disdain, they told Lyss the minute details of who they were, why they were with the Hellion, and what they were doing so close to the Grove. They found common ground in Tiv. Lyss knew him. He could even describe him. It wasn't long before Khale and Pom were forcing him to lead them to the Grove. Lyss, however, wasn't open to escorting so many Nebbin through the Mending Willow. Drage wasn't offended. On the contrary, he was more than happy to remain on the outskirts with his men, where he knew the deserters among them wouldn't be arrested.

"I've never seen you turn into that before," Drage said, leaning on a tree at the edge of the forest. "What was it?"

"A Pintle Panter." Khale smiled proudly. "My trump card. They're vicious things. Three-hundred an' fifty pounds a' pure muscle. They knock down trees for fun."

Drage matched his grin, before facing Pom. "What about

you? He can't be the only one with an ace up his sleeve."

"Mines a griffin," Pom boasted much to the disbelief of Lyss, who stood a distance away with his eyebrows raised at both of them. "It's leagues better than his sorry transformation."

"That little thing?" Khale scoffed. "It's yer height, Pom. I bet its yer weight, too."

"And its *leagues* better."

"So," Drage grinned mischievously, "Pom's stronger then?"

"Hey, you keep that kinda appallin' musin' ta yerself, yea?" Khale said. "We're friends an' that, but tasteless is tasteless."

"It's called honesty," Pom said.

Drage laughed and rested his arms over their shoulders. "How about a quick match once you two get out? We'll be here making bets on you."

"And we'll make sure no extra groups decide to stake out," Celina chimed from behind him.

"Sounds good," Khale said.

"Oh, and if you see Gil..." Drage trailed off, his voice low.

"We'll deal with him," Pom assured.

The sun had set in earnest by the time they finished saying their goodbyes. They walked behind Lyss. Silence followed them like a shadow. Lyss eyed them with a certain degree of wariness that, while expected, made it uncomfortable for them to speak openly. It didn't help that he wasn't talkative either. The only time Lyss opened his mouth was when he needed to clue them in on certain aspects of the Willow that could get them all killed... like the glowing orbs that doubled as explosives. Those were dangerous. They really should put up warning signs for those.

Nevertheless, their surroundings were beautiful. It was strangely broken in places, as if a fight had recently occurred. Were there wild animals here? Khale wouldn't doubt it if Lyss told them there were, but he questioned the animals' safety, considering the copious amount of orbs in the vicinity. He didn't think they were that reckless. If they were, then an explosion must've gone off every other day. No, a smarter explanation would be that the practitioners held their lessons here. He did see scorch marks on the ground. But that only brought up more questions. While this was the perfect playground for Amorphs, he wouldn't feel safe letting any Conjurers or Elementalists invoke fire here. That was just asking for trouble. Everything around them was incendiary.

Maybe they have some kinda preventive measure, Khale thought. He certainly didn't see any. *Or maybe their Masters watch ta keep 'em under control... ugh, no, that sounds like trouble. Are there even enough Masters for that?*

Khale didn't dwell on it. While it was an issue he'd like to know the answer to, for now, he focused solely on Tiv and what he'd say to him when he found him.

The walk was short. Almost boring compared to their earlier dilemma. But the dark branches stretched above their heads was entertaining enough to keep them from running off on their own. They were high and flecked with enough brilliant color to cut away the sunlight.

Somewhere along the way, Pom picked up a small pebble and began tossing it higher and higher into the air, until it eventually got caught in the leaves. Khale was less inclined to play with random objects. He laced his fingers behind his head and whistled instead, much to the collective annoyance of his companions. They didn't have to deal with him for long though. After another few paces, Lyss pointed to a colossal structure.

"We're here," he said, stopping in his tracks. "It's... loud."

"Really?" Pom cupped his ears and leaned dangerously forward. "Sounds like regular clamor to me."

"No, that's noisy even for a crowd." Lyss searched the area. "I don't see any of the guards."

Khale cocked his head to the side as he stared at the Institute. It was certainly grander than he expected and just as mystic as all of the books said, but...

"Lyss," Khale pointed at the Grove's base. "Is it supposed ta be tilted like that?"

23

Jack loved his magic.

He found evidence in that his thoughts were dominated by its loss. Although he never admitted it out loud, his magic was his treasure. More than his brilliance, certainly more than the so-called perks that came with being a practitioner. His heart was filled with adoration for it. Those four elements and his mastery of them defined him. While he didn't consider it more important than his freedom or his principles, it was certainly worth risking his life for. He'd walk along the edge of a cliff for weeks if it meant that he'd be an Elementalist again once he reached the other side.

He'd spent years honing his skills, so to have that power taken away—*again*—was devastating... or it should've been. He expected it to be. When he felt *her* power leave him, when the blazing heat in his stomach died and he could no longer conjure everything he trained so hard to use, strangely enough, all he felt was numb. Relieved. Maybe even a little disappointed.

Jack expected the feeling of grief to hit after. Once he filled the Anvil with conjured gravel; once Tiv helped him escape the overflowing hole, where pieces of unsteady ceiling still crumbled; once he was safe in a dimly lit hallway with a grotesque fresco of an old war mounted on the wall and breathing deeply in exhaustion from all he'd done.

But it didn't.

The adrenaline drained from his system like water poured over parched roots. He slumped against the wall, barely registering falling to the ground in a heap of aching limbs. His entire body was sore from the overuse of magic. The whispers in his head receded. His fingers wrapped around the Heartstone out of instinct, as if to reassure himself that it was still there. It pulsed in his grasp, responding to him.

She said something that his ears failed to register. But Jack didn't care enough to ask *her* to repeat it.

He wasn't disappointed when he lifted his free hand and tried to conjure something other than ice. No brief feeling of disillusionment or frustration passed through him. He didn't even grimace. Rather than being unduly annoyed by something he already knew would leave him or worrying over his own state or that of his partner sprawled out on the floor by his feet, he was more concerned about Sylvie.

And perhaps that was the most concerning thing of all.

That his wellbeing was secondary. That he thought of her even during times like this. A flare of possession welled up inside of his chest, and he forced himself to stand. It didn't matter that he slouched against the wall just to support himself. He needed to find her.

"The things I do..." he trailed off, purposely ignoring Tiv's concerned look.

Before he left the east, he didn't think it possible for his world to break and remake itself within the span of a few hours. He rejected the thought so completely that he felt mortified at the remembrance of it. Now, he knew better. And once again, as he was standing there with his mind running a mile a minute with worry. He was in another one of those strange points in time when his world spun in a new direction. His realization of what these feelings were came quicker this time. So much that his own denial could scarcely keep up. But perhaps that was to be expected. These buried emotions had coursed through him for some time now, so the weight in his chest wasn't new, although it certainly felt like it.

Jack absently looked up at the orbs of light that hung from

the ceiling. They were kept in place by vines. Every one of them still shined bright. A warm glow that spilled over wooden floorboards and old walls that remain unchanged, as if they hadn't just witnessed how the last few seconds shifted his life into another course.

For once, he wanted to see the sky. He wanted to see night dress it in varying shades of purple and blue, and breathe in the frigid air. Jack's lips twisted upward into a sudden smile, before he swiftly killed it.

Creator's teeth, he felt sappy.

"Hunter!" Jack barked at Dwyn, who'd taken to pressing his forehead against the cool wood in respite. "Give me your shirt."

Dwyn pushed away from the floor and was halfway toward him by the time the command registered. "… Give you my shirt?"

"Did I stutter? You *are* wearing an undershirt beneath those robes, aren't you?"

"Damn touchy," Dwyn muttered. "Is that a Dace thing?"

"Hand over my father's sigil while you're at it," Jack said, as he tore what was left of Dalis' shirt from his shoulders, before donning Dwyn's black one. This one was a much better fit. Snugger across the shoulders and small enough for the fabric to actually sit against his lean frame. Dwyn tossed him the golden sigil, and Jack promptly pocketed it for safekeeping. "Thanks."

"Oh, would you look at that? Genuine gratitude and no plastered smile to speak of. Not entirely like your father then."

"Should I tell him you said that?"

"Should I take back my shirt?"

Jack hummed in lieu of a response, before glancing at Tiv still spread across the floor like a starfish. He was spindlier than he remembered, his muscles atrophied. Jack never once recalled being able to see his partner's ribs, but there they were in full, disturbing view. He was definitely starved.

Tiv had new scars on his body. More than one spanned the length of his torso. They were pink, but not inflamed, meaning they'd healed naturally. No Healer worth their salt would leave a scar. Had he been held captive somewhere? Tortured? It was likely. The lack of fingers didn't suggest happy times.

Where and for what? Jack wanted to ask, but now wasn't the time. Instead, he waited until Tiv realized that he was staring. When their gazes met, Jack threw a thumb over his shoulder. "Are you coming?"

"Who's the one that can barely stand between us?" Tiv jumped to his feet in an impressive display of sprightliness. "You look like you're going to pass out."

"I could say the same to you."

"My depraved state is a separate issue entirely."

"That's not comforting at all."

"It wasn't meant to be."

"Good."

Tiv rolled his eyes. "You just destroyed what I heard was an important section of the Grove. What's the rush topside, Jack? They're going to maim you when they find out."

"I need to find someone."

"Sylvie?"

Jack blinked. "... How'd you know?"

"I saw her with you when you were first brought in. But we can talk about that later. We came down here for answers."

"Exactly," Dwyn butted in. "Care to explain what you were doing in the Anvil and who those people were?"

Jack's eyes drifted to Tiv. "As long as you explain what happened since we lost contact."

Tiv shrugged. "Done."

"Then I'll talk," Jack said, before looking out at the long hall ahead. He took a deep breath at the sight. His legs felt like they'd give out at any moment, but he'd rather grit his teeth and struggle on his own than ask for their help.

Tiv, however, already knew him well enough to wordlessly sling his arm across his shoulders. Jack stiffened. His mouth opened to say something acidic, but the protest died in his throat once saw his eyes. The look Tiv shot him wasn't filled with pity like he'd expected, neither was it threatening him into silence, it was just understanding. Complete and utter awareness of his difficulty to ask for help when he needed it. The old Tiv would've taken his arm and spouted an abrasive comment. The one beside him now was disconcerting for an entirely different reason.

What happened to him?

"You first," Tiv said, as if in answer to his thoughts. "Start with those tendrils in your eyes."

Jack's lips twisted in displeasure. Whenever someone brought up his eyes it felt like the harsh, overconfident prod of a rookie Healer poking a bruise still too fresh to touch.

"I wonder how many times I'll have to explain this?" Jack muttered. "But fair enough. Now, walk."

What Tiv and Dwyn found out during that short trek back to the main section of the Grove made their blood run cold.

***

Cheers.

That was the first thing Jack heard when they arrived at their destination. Voices bounced along the walls. The echoes of marching footsteps shook the already unstable ground. They hid behind a round pillar, watching from the sidelines as the practitioners crowded around a makeshift stadium made from an errant heap of fallen wood and conjured gravel. A representative that Jack didn't recognize stood atop it with his hands raised high. His voice boomed, silencing the crowds, but Jack didn't care to listen.

Jack swept the masses for Sylvie, but he found Dalis instead. It wasn't hard. The Healer stood in front of the stage where the representative spoke. His locked jaw didn't suggest joy. Neither did his crossed arms. His gaze was carved from pure steel, just daring any of them to step out of line. Philip leaned against him, breathless, as if he'd just run across the Yovakine Plains and back again. Frankly, Jack was just glad to see that he was alright.

But where's the Elder? Jack thought, searching. It was difficult with so many people, and before long, he gave up. There were more important things to worry about than a missing Elder anyway. He'd turn up eventually. If it just so happened that he turned up dead, then there was still an entire Council that could help them get to Thelarius' Temple.

It was only later, when more representatives he didn't recognize stepped up onto the already crowed stage and gave their speeches that he found out that they'd been held captive and that all but two of the Potens had been killed in an epic ploy to frame them, so the Lafertti Clan representative could be named head of the new Assembly. They all would've died had it not been for the valiant efforts of three practitioners who they proudly mentioned by name. Jack's eyes grew wider with each one that left their lips—and when Myrrh and Ethil both stepped up on stage, his jaw slackened in disbelief.

Although the fact that Sylvie was the only one missing just made him all the more concerned. Still, it was good to know that she was racking up favors while they were here.

The cries of outrage that followed and the sudden, mass turning on the members of the Lafertti Clan were expected. Jack stood back, watching the chaos unfurl around him. It wasn't much of a revelation to him, since Master Zacarias had attacked Elder Borris. But he wondered if they also knew that their tyke of an Arch Poten was a traitor as well. He'd gladly be the one to break the news. Jack was still sore about that nasty parting gift Lucian left in his chest. If there was one thing he didn't appreciate, it was more cauterization scars.

But why is Lucian even doing this? Jack wondered. *What does he have to gain?*

By the end of their speeches, it was clear to all of them that the representatives were going to take control. Somehow, Jack just knew that they'd weed out any traitors in the most gruesome manner imaginable... starting with the senior members of the Lafertti Clan. The Grove would no doubt be covered in blood before they left. Jack only hoped that what would soon transpire here didn't affect the Zenith Council's decision to wait for the remaining Arch Potens for the Summit, but considering that Lucian abandoned his title, then it just might.

If the election was rushed without them knowing who on the Council supported the radicals in the Lafertti Clan, then their leftovers might still have a chance to hold a seat on the new Assembly. Even worse, the new Grand Elder might just end up being their biggest supporter — and the cause of this bloodbath in the first place.

If the mastermind's plan was to stir enough trouble in the Grove that the Summit was rushed, then he succeeded tremendously. He'd even driven a divide between the two Institutes. Jack had no doubt in his mind that the practitioners here would remember their neglect for decades to come. Under isolation or not, the Diamond Alps not offering aid now wouldn't be met with understanding.

But, Jack amended, *at least this slims down the list of suspects. The only one that would benefit from a rushed election would be someone already in the lead. Someone the other Elders would undoubtedly vote for as the new Grand Elder.*

Jack could think of three, perhaps four names. One of them being his own father.

Then again, the head could also just be a puppet.

He groaned in despair. This was getting him nowhere, and the escalating noise was starting to give him a headache. He needed to find Sylvie and get out of here, preferably with the Elder in tow, so they could make their way to Thelarius' Temple. In the back of his mind, Jack hoped that she was visiting the Grove's archives. It was the perfect time. Everyone was distracted. He doubted she'd get another chance like this; he doubted *he*'d get another chance like this. Jack couldn't waste any more time scanning this crowd of hotheads.

But before he resorted to asking *her* for help, luck found him in the shape of Dalis noticing him from across the room. Dalis quickly shoved a path forward. If he noticed Philip struggling to keep up, then he didn't show it.

"Where's Sylvie?" was the first thing that left his lips.

"That's what I want to know," Jack said.

"You didn't see her?" Dalis pressed. "She went with Elder Borris to—"

"Tiv!" came a loud cry. "Jack!"

They all turned to find a head of fiery red hair.

Khale crashed into them, nearly toppling them both. Pom was next, although much more subdued than his counterpart, likely noticing that they were already struggling to stand.

Lyss followed after them. His gaze zeroed in immediately on Dalis and Philip, and when he spoke, it was with a grave face. Jack heard snippets of their conversation—a brief introduction of Khale and Pom, a status report regarding Conor, questions about the current situation, and... a mercenary camp?

Jack wanted to know more, but he was distracted by Khale tugging on his arm.

"It really is you! We've been lookin' all over the Plains for you slades, yea?" Khale shouted in their ears, nearly deafening them with his voice. His hands flew across their faces, their chests, even down to their hips, as if needing more affirmation that they were really there and not just figments of his imagination. "Huh? Is it just me or have you gained a tad too much weight, Jack? Or, no, maybe Tiv lost some?" His eyes drifted to Tiv's hands. "You lost some sausages, too?"

Tiv kicked him in the shin.

"Snuff muffins!" Khale cursed, caressing his leg. "Sorry, yea? Sorry. I'm just a spell too excited. I didn't mean it. I'm concerned. Honest! I do want ta know 'bout that."

"*We* want to know," Pom chimed.

"Yea, that. *We*," Khale corrected. "We were worried! But we knew that no explosion would be enough ta slow either of you loons down. No sudden capture either. But what're you doin' all the way out here?"

"That's what I want to know," Jack said. "What are you two doing in the Grove?"

"It's a long story. Breathless spiels ain't meant for reunions. Not ones with no booze an' no places to sit at least."

"Are the practitioners still scattered?" Jack pressed, ignoring his rambling response. "I thought my mother was rebuilding."

"She is," Pom said. "But we were looking for you two. Well, Tiv mostly."

"Touching."

"We figured you'd be together or at least know each other's whereabouts! And guess what? We were right."

"Real nice of us, yea?" Khale looked out at the mass of practitioners. "But seems like you two've yer own mess right now. This sight reminds me a' the Tower. Y'know, just before things spilled south. I still remember Tiv gatherin' all those madcaps an' firebrands an' makin' a mess a' the Institute. Don't tell me yer messin' with another?"

"We'll explain later," Tiv promised. "Right now, I need to get Jack to the clinics."

"I just said I was looking for Sylvie," Jack argued, pushing him away.

"You plan on finding her amidst all of this?" Tiv gripped his shoulder. Hard. "Besides, is finding her really more important than your condition right now? You can barely stand."

"But I *can* stand."

"Stubbornness won't keep you up for long."

"Then I'll hobble."

Tiv elbowed him in the ribs. The effect was immediate. Jack crumpled against the wooden pillar behind him. He would've fallen over, had it not been for Dalis, who held him up by the arm with one eyebrow raised in question at their sudden fight.

"Still think you can hobble?" Tiv challenged. "Your circuit is exhausted. *You're* exhausted. The magic in your system needs time to replenish. Not to mention that wound on your chest is still newly pressed. You're no good to anyone like this."

Jack breathed deeply. He gripped his face, willing the heated tendrils in his body to calm down. But it was difficult to keep his composure when the pain of Tiv's blow made it hard to breathe. In the end, Tiv's words went in one ear and right out the other.

"You think that love tap hurt me?" Jack drawled. He rolled his shoulders, undaunted by Tiv's quickly locking jaw.

"What did you just say?"

Jack swatted Dalis' hand away. Tiv was clearly upset over his lack of concern over himself, and he knew just how to provoke him. "Once I'm through with you even the monsters in the Zexin abyss won't know what you are, you six-fingered piece of shit."

"Man, that's some vintage Jack," Pom commented, whistling when Jack's arms coated themselves in a thin layer of smoking ice. "How long's it been since we've heard that mouth run off?"

"Too long, yea?" Khale said, watching them fight with rapt interest. Tiv's right hook had always been a little too mean, but it was something else to see him swinging at Jack with a barely closed fist and still twisting his nose a sickening angle.

Compared to Amorphs, Elementalists were almost always at a disadvantage in terms of size and raw strength. Jack was no exception.

"Left!" Khale shouted, throwing his own fist in the air as if to hit Jack himself. "Hit 'em on the le—*no*! You call that a punch, you milk-toothed bastard? You barely grazed him!"

"Jack, you wuss!" Pom jeered. "Stop dodging and take it like a man!"

"I'm going to look around," Dwyn said, loud enough for everyone to hear. He stepped forward without hesitation. He'd much rather take his chances in an angry crowd than witness this bizarre reunion. Dwyn looked at Philip. "Dace may seem lively, but Tiv's right. His circuit is exhausted. Could you take hi—them," he corrected when he saw Jack use Tiv's own momentum against him to knee him hard in the stomach, "to the clinics for me?"

"Gladly," Philip said, recognizing the trace of his magic. He was definitely one of the Hunters Poten Pramm called out in front of the Clave. But what was he doing here?

"Philip," Dalis urged.

"I know." Philip seized Dwyn's arm before he could disappear. His grip was as strong and unyielding as stone. "I'd refrain from revealing your position to anyone that doesn't already know it. As you can see, the practitioners are a mess right now. You might hear something... unpleasant."

Dwyn rolled his eyes. "Noted."

"Who do you report to?" Dalis questioned. "What are you doing here? Is the Vanguard Circle concerned about the Anv—"

"Just make sure that hothead doesn't keel over and die," Dwyn pointed emphatically at Jack. "Elder Dace might actually burn this Institute to the ground if he does."

There was a flash of light and Philip was left grasping air, as Dwyn shifted into a nondescript bird. He beat his wings once, before flying off and blending in with the rest of the transformed Amorphs scattered above them.

Dalis cursed him under his breath. He turned to the squabbling duo. Jack was sporting a broken nose, while Tiv had two full rows of bloody teeth. Their companions were off to the side. Dalis didn't know if they were verbally abusing them or rooting for them, but their voices were making his ears bleed.

Jack snarled when he caught his eye.

"Don't tell me you agree with him?" Jack asked.

"I don't," Dalis said honestly. "But weren't you the one that said you'd be fine down there? So, the question is: would you rather have Sylvie see you in bed, healed and properly bandaged, or sporting a bloody nose and standing half-mast?"

As if just realizing his injury, Jack touched it, then flinched all in the same instant. "*Filan vahs,*" Jack cursed. How could he be so careless? He scowled because he knew Dalis had a point, and when his eyes watered from the pain of changing his expression, his scowl only deepened.

"Don't give me that. This is your own fault. Don't you dare show my sister that dark look either. It's distressing."

"And we wouldn't want to mar that pretty face now, would we?"

"... You've got a problem with her?"

They glared at each other, but Jack was quick to concede, knowing that whatever he said in response wouldn't be a good answer anyway. "Fine, *kivesera,*" Jack spat, all venom. "I'll go. But I'm leaving right after."

"That's all it took?" Tiv asked in disbelief, while he nursed the fresh bruises on his ribs. "You're joking."

"Afraid not," Dalis was the one to answer. He put on his best wise tone. "You see, Dace here knows that people are mirrors. If you smile, a smile will be reflected, and all of that nonsense. He even learned that it's not worth letting something that can be avoided spoil the mood, since effects tend to, you know, ripple."

"Him?" Pom pointed. "If you're going to lie at least make it believable. This is Jack we're talking about. *'I-don't-care-about-you-I'll-do-what-I-please'* extraordinaire."

"Exactly," Khale agreed. "As if somethin' like that can be learned so easily. An' by this maroon, no less."

"I'm right here," Jack deadpanned. "And even I have no idea what you're going on about, Sirx."

"He admits it!" Pom said.

"Enough with the nonsense, Dalis," Philip intervened.

Jack couldn't be more grateful for his presence. He was a pillar of sanity amidst the hurricanes of madness that were these four.

"Heal what you can," Philip went on, "then bring them to the sixth floor. They always have free space."

"I'll help," Lyss volunteered, already slinging Jack's arm over his shoulder.

"You two," Philip turned to Pom and Khale, "are you familiar with the marks of the mercenary bands from the Plains?"

"Very," they said in unison.

"Then that settles things. I have to stay here in case Master Rhone needs me, so I'm going to need you two to explore the lower floors for any stragglers. I'll send some of the Scripts down with you, so you don't get lost. Think you're up to the task?"

They looked at each other, before nodding.

"Good." Philip regarded each and every one of them. "Any complaints?"

Their silence was heartwarming.

24

Sylvie's fingers bled.

She pounded on the compact stone, throwing smaller rocks behind her and clawing as deep as she could go. It was a slow process; one she knew wouldn't bear any fruit in the end. But that didn't stop her. The deeper she went, the harder it became. It was as if an entire granite slab had fallen from the ceiling to clog the entrance. As solid and sturdy as a grave.

Heaps of twisted slag littered the floor. But even she knew that this was getting her nowhere. Time was of the essence. She knew of only one way to do this swiftly.

Sylvie bunched her back and took a deep, calming breath.

Lazy tongues of fire curled up her forearms. Her body protested immediately. She recalled Ethil's words: '*Avoid using your magic.*' This was certainly avoidable. Dalis' reprimanding tone came next. The loud, booming one that frightened her as a child. He reserved it for special occasions. Sylvie could almost hear him yelling at her that this wasn't safe, that she needed to let her magic recuperate, or else she'd end up hurting herself.

Sylvie threw it all away with a violent shake of her head.

She thought of what mattered now instead. What was most important to her at this exact moment—*Jack.* A strong hand to keep her steady, while the rest of the world burned and bled and *smiled.* Her finger's tensed until all of the muscles in her arms were ignited with the blaze of fire. She dug her blunt nails into the rough granite and pushed, driving her hands in as far as they would go. It hurt. Needle-sharp steel against callused skin. Her magic melted the rock into lava that fell like thick droplets of rain around her. A few stray globs dripped onto her forearms, searing them to the bone.

Sylvie screamed at the sensation. She wouldn't be shocked if those in the main section heard her cries. Behind her, Borris said nothing. He didn't try to stop or reprimand her. He only squared his shoulders and placed his hands on her back. His magic surged into her very being, as intense as water gushing into a river. It wasn't quick enough for her not to feel her skin being melted from her bones, but her arms did heal over... and right now, that was all that mattered.

Heal. Burn. Heal. Burn.

The cycle continued.

If he wanted her to learn some lesson from all of this, then he'd have to wait until her stubbornness gave way first. Sweat trickled down her nose. Sylvie couldn't keep this up. She'd been drained already. The strength of her circuit would run dry soon — and what then? She'd pass out. Useless to all. But she couldn't bring herself to stop.

She swallowed, straightened her shoulders, and flexed her hands to slam once more into the unyielding stone. Dirt cascaded around her. Stray pieces of wood fell with it. They were remnants from the ceiling that mixed with the thick slab before her.

Every minute she spent there fueled her fury. It seemed to stretch her thinner and more hollow. It scraped at her careful walls like razor-sharp talons that wanted to drag her down into a pit of endless wrath. The constant rumbles she felt beneath her feet didn't help. They were so close that the slightest vibration was enough to leave her unsteady.

Then suddenly, the Grove stopped.

Sylvie's heart stilled along with it.

Her eyes widened. If whoever was down there finished conjuring dirt and Jack was left buried, then...

"Jack!" Sylvie shouted. She banged her fists against the rock, disregarding the way her vision bent along the edges. Her flames diminished without her consent, naturally slipping away. She breathed to draw it back out, but even that was a chore; a testament to how drained she was.

"Jack! Can you—"

"Sylvie?" someone said from behind her.

She whipped around so quickly that her neck strained from the motion. Sylvie caught the gaze of a man emerging from the shadows. He didn't wear the usual practitioner's garb, but rather, a fitted tunic and faded trousers. Even then, she knew he was an Amorph. Those eyes were unmistakable. He was broad at the shoulders and had a slanted nose. Sylvie squinted when his features came into focus. The first thing she noticed was his hair. The redness stood out like a royal duvet in a peasant's shack.

"Khale?" Sylvie blinked, then rubbed her eyes to make sure she wasn't seeing things. He was still there when she stopped. "You're... Khale, right?"

"The one an' only," he said, his Astonian accent was thicker than the atmosphere around them. Khale ran over to crush her in a bone-shattering embrace. He completely ignored the Elder that tilted his head at his sudden appearance. "I didn't think I'd find you here, Syl."

He was uncomfortably close. While they were acquainted with each other, she wouldn't go so far as to call him a friend. But Sylvie couldn't find it in herself to step away. He'd suffered the same fate when the Tower fell. Khale, however, had the type of laidback nature that eased the burdens of everyone around him. It lightened the heaviness in her chest, if only a little.

"What are you doing here?" she asked once he finally gave her a little room to breathe. "How did you even get here?"

"I should be askin' you that, yea?" He peeked at the melted hole behind her. "You aspirin' ta be some kinda Gavinist now? Meltin rocks an' that? Sorry ta burst yer noddle, but their cutoff age is sixteen. I asked."

Sylvie's eyes widened. She looked behind her, then back at him. "Khale!" she suddenly shouted.

"What?" he asked, bewildered when she gripped his arms with enough force to crumple steel.

"Help me! Please! You need to transform and dig into that."

"What?"

"Jack is... is..."

"That maroon?" Khale cocked his head to the side. "What about 'em?"

"He's in there!"

"In those rocks?" He pointed dubiously. "Like... cemented?"

"Crushed," she stressed, then shook her head. "No, *trapped*. He was down in this section when it came crashing down. He's definitely trapped, and I need you to help me get down there!"

"What're you talkin' 'bout, Syl? You gone full loon since I last saw you? Ain't no way that pyromaniac's down there."

"He was down there when the Grove started sinking."

"Wait. Don't tell me... that whole mess was cause a' him?" Khale asked, then laughed in delight. "Jack never hid his temper, yea? But this is an Institute we're talkin' 'bout. Don't tell me he sunk it, then escaped? That's bold, even for him."

"He's still down there," Sylvie said, exasperated. "Please, Khale, please help me get him out!"

"Like I said Syl, what're you goin' on about? I just saw that maroon topside. Besides, I wouldn't've lent a hand even if he was down there. Do you *see* those rocks? Jack's got a hard head, yea?

But even his skull ain't hard enough ta withstand *that*."

Her mouth went dry.

"What?" Khale's eyebrows scrunched together. "Don't tell me you don't believe me? I can take you ta see 'em if you want."

Sylvie's grip on his arms tightened even more. Because apparently that was possible. Khale wasn't fragile enough to not be able to withstand it, however. He simply met her gaze with one eyebrow raised in expectance.

"Well?" he asked.

Sylvie was pushing him back up the stairs before she even realized what she was doing.

***

The walk to the clinics was a short and undisturbed one.

They spoke in clipped sentences that often ended in uncomfortable silence. Khale disappeared halfway through, muttering something about Pom and stray mercenaries under his breath. He promised Sylvie that he'd return as soon as he could, and even wrapped her in a hug that she felt more comfortable receiving now that she wasn't in a state of utter panic.

"Careful not ta trip, yea?" Khale advised. "They're brimmin' with grievances. You fall over yerself an' I guarantee you'll break a bone. Not necessarily yers."

Sylvie quickly realized what he meant. Before they even reached their destination, they could already tell that the clinics would be packed. Men and women groaned in the hallways, waiting to be treated. Doors were left permanently open as people came and went, sporting everything from pulled muscles to broken bones. Outside one of the busier rooms sat a particularly disturbing patient with third-degree burns all across his arms and torso. The blistered flesh oozed a pungent liquid that had Sylvie wrinkling her nose in disgust. It was translucent, with just enough white and yellow flecks to put her off of solid food for the next week. On the floor beside him, lay a woman with her entire left side frozen solid. She shook uncontrollably, rubbing her hands as if that would ease the stinging cold. Her teeth chattered as she repeated the words, *'I'm sorry,'* over and over again.

Those inside were worse. Some were so terribly disfigured that she wondered just how much bad-blood existed between the colleges for them to go so far. It was one thing to bruise someone's face because they were perpetually rude, it was another thing entirely to twist their arms until they popped from their sockets and their bones stuck out like bleached branches from their flesh. That required hate. Long, festering hate.

Elder Borris was quick to spring into action. He aided those he could, although a number of them flinched away whenever he got too close. Not out of fear, but out of reflex; the bright light his hands emitted was simply too much for their fragile states. Borris even opened their herb stores to brew healing tonics of his own design. They had a spicy scent, but judging by the ingredients he mixed together, Sylvie doubted they'd taste anything short of atrocious.

Sylvie lingered here and there, assisting some of the busier Healers and helping the younger embrocologists concoct a few salves. She asked anyone that would stop to listen if they saw an Elementalist with deathly pale skin and an abrasive mouth. To her luck, a startling number of them had. Jack had apparently caused quite the uproar when he arrived with her brother.

They pointed her in various directions until she eventually ended up in a circular extension with multiple levels. Each floor had only one hallway with doors on both sides. There were no torches or orbs here. Instead, light flooded in from half-opened doors that she peeked through to find cozy, double bed rooms filled with sleeping practitioners. Every so often, she'd find a

Healer checking in on them, making sure they were comfortable, before disappearing just as quietly as they'd come. Others had friends and family fortunate enough to do it for them. They slept in stools and faded leather seats, hunched over their beds. It couldn't be comfortable.

Finding Jack was easy enough. The guard assigned to the floor called out to her once she reached the end of the short flight of steps that led to the fourth level. He had a chiseled jaw and short hair that was shaved at the edges.

"Dalis said you'd come," he said with a vague wave behind him. "Fifth door on the right."

Sylvie muttered her thanks, then made a beeline towards the door. Her steps slowed with each one she took, until eventually, she was left standing there, faltering before the thick panels of light wood. Her hand lingered on the handle in uncertainty, terrified of what she might find. But her doubts were swiftly expelled when she realized that if something awful had happened, then he wouldn't be here, resting with the rest of the barely supervised.

There was no reason to hesitate now.

She opened the door, expectant, only to find a blond man with round cheeks and a portly frame. There was a burlap sheet tangled around his legs. He shook suddenly with her entrance, shattering her hopes in an instant. He must've been having a nightmare because he twisted around like a dog coming in after the rain. There was another man curled up on a worn sea-green seat beside him. Scrawnier, this one. Younger, too, judging by the distinct lack of lines on his face. The color of his hair, however, was the same as the man in the bed.

Brothers? she speculated. They didn't look anything alike, but that could've just been her skewed view. The boy's mouth was ajar. Even from where she stood, she could hear his soft snores. They were broken every now and again by a sniffle that had him exhaling rapidly through his nose.

Sylvie's gaze swept the rest of the room in a last minute, methodical rush. There was a golden-brown dresser beside her with a writing desk shoved up against it. Three dozen books were piled haphazardly on the floor, unopened and caked with enough dust to suggest their owner's passing. She wrinkled her nose at the sight. Sylvie didn't care enough to read their titles. Instead, her eyes trailed to her feet, where a feathered overcoat sat in a rumpled heap, either having fallen from her quick entrance or left there by a negligent hand and a tired mind. But seeing as how she didn't hear anything drop to the ground when she entered, she decided that it was the latter.

Only the beds were well-kempt. This room clearly wasn't occupied often. Perhaps it had something to do with the floor number she was on. This was higher and in a place not so easily reached, so it was likely made for patients with no severe injuries. Jack's previous room had been cleaner and better furnished in comparison, but it also smelt more like doused alcohol swabs to offset it. Nevertheless, this was still a downgrade.

Sylvie found a rust-colored curtain in the middle of the room, half-closed with noticeable tears along the sides. Behind it was a mussed bed with another occupant. He had dark hair and red eyes that stared unwaveringly at her.

"How long are you going to stand there?" he asked, caustic, while shielding his eyes from the dim glow of the orb above his bedside. It wasn't exactly obtrusive, but she knew him well enough to know that he preferred sleeping in complete darkness. Unfortunately for him, there was no way to turn that nightlight off. "Close that curtain, would you? I'm tired of watching those two wheeze."

Despite his grumpiness, Sylvie could only sigh in relief.

Palpable wasn't a strong enough word for what she felt. The emotion sat stone-cold in her chest, stifling her breath and knocking bruises on her rib cage.

"Jack."

***

Sylvie smiled at him. It was different from the ones he'd seen before—more unsure. She tucked her hair unnecessarily behind her ear, before closing the curtain and falling into the empty seat beside him. Sylvie molded against the flat cushions, seemingly unaware of just how tired she was until she sat there. He wasn't surprised. A part of him even expected it of her at this point.

Still, Jack couldn't keep his smirk back at the sight of her. Unharmed and intact. For the most part anyway. He didn't like the state of her robes. It indicated injury. Jack gave her a thorough once over, only half-satisfied when he didn't find any. While he was glad that she had likely gotten herself healed before coming to find him, it also meant that her wounds were serious enough to warrant a trip to the infirmary.

"Your robes are a mess," he said at the same time she asked, "What happened to your chest?"

Jack looked down at his exposed torso, while she did the same with her robes. The scar on his chest was small compared to the ones he'd gotten from the Tower, but it was pinker and angrier, suggesting newness. Sylvie's eyes honed in on it like a starving man unearthing moldy bread.

"I got stabbed," Jack said nonchalantly.

There was a short, judging pause, before, "By who?"

"Does it really matter?" Jack didn't want to admit that he was caught off guard by a child. Genius or not. Arch Poten or not. He just didn't. Because then he'd also have to explain Philip taking the Heartstone from him, however brief.

"Of course it matters," Sylvie maintained.

"Later then. When you're less..."

"Less what?"

Cagy. Tired. Capable of responding irrationally, Jack thought, though he said none of those things. He didn't want to get into an argument. "Less sleep-deprived," Jack settled on, before changing the subject. "What happened to your robes?"

Sylvie frowned, then crumbled forward to lie against the bed. If it was the question or the answer that made her do so, he couldn't say for certain, but it was clear that he wasn't the only one with things he didn't want to discuss.

"I thought you were still down in the Anvil," Sylvie said. Her voice was muffled by the linens. The top of her head was pressed against his thigh. It took all of his willpower to not gently knock against her because of her blatant disregard for his question.

"What a coincidence," Jack said agitatedly. "I thought you were still in the main section with Dalis. But when I go upstairs, what do I find? You, gone. If that wasn't bad enough there were also a horde of practitioners fighting and representatives making grand speeches about the future. They were saying some pretty impressive things about you, Syl. How many are true? Did you really save them?"

"It was an accident. I just wanted to go to the archives, but once I arrived, I found them there. All tied up and weary. They were being held hostage by mercenaries."

"Don't tell me you feel bad about receiving the credit?"

"I don't care about that."

"Then what?"

"I..." Sylvie inhaled shakily. "I destroyed most of the books in there. Ages of history, of knowledge—*gone.*"

Jack rapped his knuckles hard against her head. "I destroyed the Anvil and possibly a few backrooms with priceless artifacts in them when I did. On *purpose.* So, don't feel too bad."

Her head snapped up, as if just remembering that the Grove had shifted barely two hours ago. "What happened down there?"

Instead of answering, Jack scooted forward until he was sitting in front of her. Sylvie scrunched her eyebrows at him in question. With quick fingers, he lifted the Heartstone over his neck and leaned forward to return it to its rightful owner.

She accepted it gratefully.

Jack pressed the stone against her for a moment with his thumb, as if trying to fuse them together and make her whole, before he let it fall naturally. He cocked his head, inspecting the way it settled against her chest. The effects of its removal were immediate. The nigh constant burn in his blood subsided and the voices quieted considerably. Even the ache behind his eyes diminished. Jack was sure that by the time he got some proper rest, it would be gone completely.

He breathed a sigh of relief. His neck felt lighter than ever. It made him wonder if that weight was an effect *she* had on everyone or if *she* did it to him on purpose. He wouldn't be surprised if *she* did. But if it was the former, then did Sylvie actually like the heaviness that came with wearing the stone?

Better to leave it a mystery, he supposed. Because he wouldn't know how to react if she did. One thing was for certain though: it definitely belonged with Sylvie.

She seemed to agree because the tendrils within stirred. There was a brief flash, brighter than usual, and then a contented hum. That lullaby echoed just on the edge of his hearing. He'd memorized every word by now and unconsciously sang along under his breath. Vibrations rattled the air, followed by a whisper of cold that made a shiver run down his spine.

"*She*'s thanking you," Sylvie said softly.

"It's concerning that you know that."

"It's concerning that you don't."

"Cut me some slack," Jack muttered. "I'm still getting used to the idea of *her* actually being an ally. Those tendrils *hurt*, Syl."

The worry in her eyes couldn't be imitated.

"What happened down there? Did *she* hurt you again?"

Jack shrugged. He didn't want to lie and say that she hadn't, but he also didn't want to dismiss the fact that she'd assisted him as well.

"*She* helped me, too," he said, then shuddered in realization once the words left his lips. He just admitted that Sylvie was right when she gave him the Heartstone. Jack expected her to question him first, then to give him that smug look she saved only for the sweetest of victories, before muttering a stinging, *'I told you.'* But she didn't. There was no triumphant grin or overly zealous jump in the air. Sylvie didn't even pull away to put some much needed space between them. Then again, perhaps it was foolish of him to assume she would.

Sylvie's eyes brightened, revealing happiness so stark that Jack wavered at the sight. It was a strange thing to behold. It was even stranger to realize that the reason for it was him. Because somehow, against all odds, he'd actually gotten along with that being in the stone. It might not have been long, but it was enough to barter a deal. He didn't even lose himself from the taste of all that power once again at his fingertips.

Sylvie really was right. The Heartstone kept him safe. But that she was pleased just by the thought of him being so made his chest feel like it was going to burst. Jack decided then that they could talk more about the details of their mini-expeditions later. Right now, he was caught by the look on her face. There was a brief lull in his movements, a momentary pause where he simply stared at her, etching her expression to memory. But then it passed, and before he knew it, he bent at the waist, closer, sinking over her, helplessly drawn like a line had yanked him forward. It was a simple thing then to return her half-smile, to match the intensity of her gaze, to acknowledge the bubbling heat unfurling like late petals in spring between them.

He was close. So, so close.

"Jack," she breathed.

And he stilled.

His chest heated in anticipation and joy and—

Faster than he ever could've imagined, his fingers wrapped behind her neck. His own impatience ruined whatever iota of self-control he liked to think he had. Sylvie was small and soft against his frame. A bit cooler than he imagined she'd be, bearing in mind her affinity, but a comfortable fit nevertheless. The entire situation reminded him of that warm feeling he had whenever one of his limbs slipped from out of the covers in the middle of the night. He was simply bringing it back in to warm it up.

Without preamble, he drew her towards him.

Closer.

Not enough.

Closer.

But before he could bring her all the way, and before the nigh instantaneous decisiveness he liked to boast about reared its head, Sylvie launched forward, clearly tired of his pace. She crushed herself to him, and he shuddered from the force. Jack shivered from the foreign touch of chapped lips against his own, but all coherent thought was lost as soon as she moved against him. Careful at first, despite her initial enthusiasm. The kiss was chaste, cautious, and so much gentler than he expected.

But then the moment passed, and when her shoulders eased and he mastered himself enough to return her soft press of lips, the rest of the world turned to dust. In that one instant of fervent desperation, passion and fire coiled together in his stomach. Jack matched everything she bared before him, then upped it tenfold.

She shrunk back in the face of his ardor. Startled, yet pleased. Ignorant to how simple it was for him to up the ante. He'd always been intense, lacking certain inhibitions that others scoffed at him for. It was only right that he'd put so much more into this. Besides, he'd wanted this too much to show restraint now.

Jack knew himself best after all.

Strangely enough, it was that same knowledge that kept him from losing himself entirely. His desire was something he realized early on in life. From the very first time he held an old transfigurations book to the numerous occasions he'd looked upon his father's seat and pretended to take his place. It had always been there, and his unmatched willingness to do anything for what he wanted was something he advertised proudly... until now. That wouldn't do him any good here. Because no matter how close Sylvie got, it wasn't enough. It would never be.

The pragmatic part of him leashed his own greed, before it grew into something unreasonable. Something like he'd seen in Vidal and even his own father. Jack didn't want to fall into whatever cursed cycle seemed to follow the men that he looked up to. He wanted to change his world, and this—whatever this was—would be a definite start.

But not two minutes in, and he was already failing miserably. Because he knew—*knew*—that if given the privilege, he could be blessed with a lifetime of gasping breaths, scant space, and heated exchanges, and it still wouldn't be enough.

He'd seen hate enough times to see how it changed a man. But he'd seen love do it, too. And when Sylvie's fingers twitched from where they rested over his chest, it was, indeed, love that spread through him.

Love, Jack thought. Those four letters were such a peculiar thing. He could hardly handle the enormity packed into the word. It was overwhelming, like a flood of sunshine after a long night. Yet it was small as well, as if the stars had all been fitted into one person to shower them in brilliance.

Jack hauled her up, then inched backwards until they both fell onto the bed in a mess of breathless pants and intertwined limbs. Sylvie sighed into his mouth. He pulled her closer in response. Jack swallowed every noise she made, memorized every drag of her fingers across his skin. He stored up the moments like a man turning for one last glimpse at the sea.

When she pulled away to breathe, he chased her, appalled by his own desire. He could bear it, he thought, if the world diminished to only this. Because Jack knew, without a shadow of a doubt, that he'd be perfectly content to live the rest of his life in the spaces between these soft, measured breaths.

It was at that exact moment that he felt it. A thin chain being forged between them. Shining, twisted links of metaphysical iron and gold that bound him to her in something deeper than either of them knew. Jack pulled away just long enough to take in her half-lidded gaze and red cheeks. His own face burned brilliantly at the sight. He felt the heat spread all the way to his ears, but he couldn't find it in himself to care.

The only thing that mattered now were his emotions, and how they swelled as proudly as an eagle unfurling its wings after an age of captivity, as profoundly as sunlight dribbling over a man that had been buried too long.

Bright...

She was so bright.

And he needed more.

25

The sling of the curtain jostled Jack out of his thin doze.

When his eyes blinked open, he found the world to be precisely as he'd left it. Well, almost. Sylvie's back was pressed against his side. The weight of her head numbed his arm. The two practitioners across from them were speaking in low voices. Their bleary-eyed looks and half-hearted greetings told him that they'd just gotten up, too.

Then there was...

"Did I wake you?" Khale asked, uncaring. "Sorry 'bout that. But you two've got a baker's dozen out there all gutted an' callin'."

Jack didn't respond.

Instead, he extracted his arm, careful not to wake Sylvie up, before blinking at Khale through the dim light of the oil lamp he held. The shadows seemed to have shortened with the hours, but when he recalled that no actual light penetrated the Mending Willow, he looked up to find that the orb above him had died out. He didn't think those had an off switch.

Sensing his confusion, Khale explained, "I heard all the orbs 'round here were supplied by the Arch Poten."

Jack's eyebrows raised, despite his dislike for the boy. Even he couldn't deny that was impressive.

"They're settin' up a team ta fix it," Khale went on. "Reps were discussin' some kinda rotation schedule. Like patrol duty! But more complicated. Somethin' ta do with their individual ability to control their magic stream. It sounded borin' an' I didn't wanna stick 'round for borin', so I left ta call you two instead."

"What else is going on?" Jack asked, stretching. "Anything I *need* to know?"

"Nah. Just cleanin' an' partyin' mostly."

"What?"

"You deaf now, too, Dace?"

"Shut it. I'm just having a hard time believing they're..." Jack trailed off, unable to even say it. "Please tell me you're joking."

"Araid not." Khale grinned. "Don't get me wrong. They're not all a bunch a' slugs, yea? I mean, their seniors were all workin' on gettin' things in order. Y'know, creatin' some synergy while they could an' contactin' all the right folks up north. But then the lights went out. Practitioners started complainin' 'bout the dark. So, everyone broke out these ancient oil lamps. Problem is, they aren't used ta this kinda dark. Not like us Tower kids. Before we knew it, they started breakin' out all kinda things! Pots, pans, cleanin' supplies. Claimin' that they were gonna start cleanin' up the Grove from the bottom up. Literally. A real energetic bunch, yea?"

"The kind I hate dealing with."

"This is yer mess though, so yer gonna have ta. But you should be safe. I don't think anyone really knows yer the one that made this place sink, save for the uppers. An' all the grunts are too busy switchin' between cleanin' up the mess topside an' drinkin' their injuries numb ta pay you any mind."

"It's not the grunts I'm worried about," Jack said. "But it's nice to see that you haven't changed. Still thinking about the moves of the little people."

"I got more handsome," Khale declared. "Don't tell me you haven't noticed?"

Jack scoffed.

"I did!" Khale shouted, loud enough to startle Sylvie into wakefulness.

"Damned pest," Jack muttered. "Do you have to be so loud?"

"Maybe if you stopped lookin' at me like I said somethin' fetched, then maybe—"

"Khale?" Sylvie interrupted. They found her already rising in concern. Jack placed a hand on her shoulder to keep her from getting up. "Is everything alright? What are you doing here?"

"Obviously I've come for a tryst," Khale quipped, then rounded back on Jack. "Now that you brought it up though that makes me wonder... what are *you* doin' here, Dace?"

Jack raised an eyebrow. "This is my room."

"But I thought you wanted ta leave as soon as possible. You kicked up a fuss an' everythin', yea? Yet here you are, sleepin' of all things."

"Keep implying things, Khale, and I swear Tiv won't be the only one missing a few fingers."

"Easy." Khale raised his hands in surrender. "No need for threats. We're all rational, civilized people here. Right, Syl?"

"Don't bring her into this."

"Jeez." Khale clicked his tongue. "Barely five minutes in an' this maroon already looks like he wants ta rattle my bones an' freeze me all sorts a' different colors. Hey, Syl. Help a guy out here, why don'tcha?"

Sylvie looked between them, before mumbling an uncertain, "Did you do something, Khale?"

"Straight suspect, huh? I'm innocent. He's the prickly one."

"I'm still here, you *adrinas rivaren*," Jack cursed.

"See what I mean? Easy with the curses, Dace. The magic, too. I can feel it flarin' from here," Khale said, before ambling up to Sylvie. He bent at the waist, making sure to get right in her face. "So, Arch Poten, huh? Snazzy title. Bet you've got all kinds a' new perks."

"None at the moment," Sylvie said, leaning back.

"In the future then."

"... Probably."

"Perks are always nice, yea?" He gave her a winning grin.

Sylvie's eyes thinned at the sight of it. "What do you want?"

"Well, I'd rather live with pigs than ask you this, but—"

"Then don't ask."

"—how 'bout makin' me an apprentice?"

Sylvie sighed, regretting even acknowledging his presence in the first place. "We're the same age, Khale. What exactly do you hope to learn from me?"

"Embrocology? Better hygiene? How ta torch an egg without oil," he listed off.

"Scram, before I do something I'll regret."

"I see this maroon's black personality's rubbed off on you. Don't be so touchy, Syl. I'm serious, yea? Really! I'll even swear on Thelarius' holy wolf pelt or somethin' just as sacred, so consider me, will you?"

"*Khale*. I already told you to—"

"Scarper, yea, I heard you the first time." Khale saluted. "I'll be seein' you then, princess."

Beside her, Jack choked… or more like gagged. "Thelarius, return your sight," he prayed. "I need to clean my ears."

"That sounds like a good idea ta me. Distance an' all that keeps friends, *friends*, yea?"

"What's that supposed to mean, you damn mutt?"

"Means I know what yer doin', Dace. Cozyin' up ta our new Arch Poten, wantin' ta snag yerself somethin' good once the Tower's rebuilt. I've got my eye on you."

"Just go already," Jack said, exasperated.

"I will. Soon as you two haul yer heavy's outta bed. Like I said, there are some loudmouths callin' for you out there. Both of you. They wanna talk, gossip, maybe even have a few glugs."

"And what?" Sylvie asked.

"Drinks," he clarified.

"No, I got that, but," she faced Jack, "why are they breaking out the booze? Just how long were we asleep?"

"You're asking me?" Jack shot back.

"Long enough, yea?" Khale interjected, before pulling them up with such force that they stumbled. He was so tall and gangly that sometimes it was easy to forget that he was an Amorph. One trained in the Drowned Tower at that. But once they took that into consideration, they realized that his strength was simply a matter of course.

They struggled against him, but Khale dragged them all the way to the door and to the corridor's dim and yawning throat without breaking a sweat.

"I don't have all day," was all he said, before pushing them right into a group of practitioners loitering there.

The broken string of curses that left their lips were expected.

***

The rest of the evening passed in a blur for both of them.

They were greeted by people they barely recognized, berated by those they did, and then pulled away to be introduced to even more. They learned quickly that the practitioners really were bothered by the lack of light. It was the first thing they mentioned upon seeing them, and also the sole subject they complained about. But to them, it felt nostalgic. Comforting. Reassuring even. They reveled in the way the candlelight cast dim orange streaks on the polished floors. It illuminated just enough for them to see shadowy figures and the smooth metal handles of distant doors. They even took to the old practice of tapping the walls to announce their presence whenever they were looking for someone in a crowded hall. It never failed to make every single person in the room turn to them, if only for a second.

It was an old habit, and one that clearly hadn't died yet.

They discussed what they knew with their friends from the east, and even the added extras they travelled with, making sure to keep out a few of the bigger details that were only for them to know. In return, everyone explained where they'd been all this time and what they were doing. It was a long talk, filled with passed mugs and damnably infectious enthusiasm. Not all of them could speak so lightheartedly about their experiences, however. Some had chosen to clamp their mouths shut and let their eyes do the talking. Cera was the first on that list.

The highlight of the evening was when Jack stopped Ethil

from handing Sylvie a goblet full of wine.

"We don't let her drink anymore," was his explanation. "She drank once with Vidal and ended up setting a sofa on fire."

To his surprise, neither Pom, nor Khale batted an eye at the revelation. Instead, they spat out their drinks and shouted Vidal's name like an ancient curse.

"You know him, too?" Jack asked. "Silas, spare you both."

"Isn't he your Master?" Pom questioned.

The astonished queries after that were predictable and wholly unwelcome. What followed was a full-on discussion about Masters and titles. Unfortunately, they were forced to leave in the middle of an argument between Myrrh and Dwyn when they spotted Master Flax in the distance.

In that instant of wariness, they tacitly agreed on avoiding all of the representatives and leftover Potens for as long as they possibly could. Dodging talks that could very well end with them being thrown into the Slates and kept there until their superiors decided if the Heartstone was a threat or not was definitely in their best interest. And if there came a time when they couldn't, only then would they play the '*Sylvie-saved-you-card*' to sneak out of any trouble.

It was only when they stumbled upon Elder Borris that things finally slowed down again.

They found him in a deserted hall, leaning against a pillar twice his width with a bottle of malt in one hand and a crumpled missive in the other. Borris covered his face with his sleeve as they passed, but promptly dropped it when he realized who they were. He was obviously hiding. Neither of them blamed him. They knew from experience what practitioners with acerbic tongues and too many questions could do, and answering them never helped. Because they always twisted your words into something beyond frustrating.

"Elder Borris," Sylvie greeted. "How long have you been here?"

"Ten minutes," he said, taking another swig from his bottle.

"I didn't think anyone would find me so quickly."

"We weren't exactly searching for you," Jack said. "But we did want to ask you for a favor."

"Does it have something to do with the stone?" Borris pointed at Sylvie's collar, where the Heartstone sat beneath her robes. "The Council has been searching for that."

Jack and Sylvie shared a look.

"Don't look so anxious. I'm not going to take it away," Borris assured. "I was simply curious. I heard it was lost in the Zexin abyss, along with the rest of the Drowned Tower. Now, the question is, did Serach hand it to you or did you two take it from him?"

"*She* chose us," Sylvie answered.

"*She*?" Borris looked at her like she'd just sprouted a second head, before he recalled the incident in the Anvil. He glanced at Jack warily. "You mean... those shadows that inhabit the stone? I didn't realize it had a will of its own."

"Few do," Jack said. "But if you know about the stone and the *Orivellea*, then that must mean that you know the secret behind Elementalists, too?"

Borris threw a cursory glance all around them, making sure that no one was listening. "My title as Elder isn't just for show. I know all about the Institute's affairs. Even the unpleasant ones. But how do you two know about that? Don't tell me you had a child while we had our backs turned?"

"As if that would happen." Jack sneered. "But now that you mention it, what's going to happen to the Alps now that their sole source of *Orivellea* is gone?"

"Quite a bit of argument and resource wasting, I suppose. They'll search every corner of Ferus Terria for that stone. They can't form another lake without first getting their hands on a piece from the main source, and any crystal without those sealed powers are useless. Hide it well enough and you two might just be the cause of Elementalists dying out completely."

"Fine with me," Sylvie declared. "It's a bloody practice."

"But one passed down to us from Maurice, himself. Would you break ages of tradition for the sake of a few rotting corpses?"

"The fact that you choose to continue letting people die for tradition is exactly what's wrong with the Institute. Power isn't given, it's earned."

"How can you, a Conjurer, say that? You were born with a magic circuit. Just like all of those in your family before you."

"Then I'll say it," Jack said. "I love my magic, but knowing that so many died for it, years before I was even born, isn't a burden I ever wanted to have. And what about all of those mediocre Elementalists that sit on their haunches and do nothing with their powers? Were their sacrifices worth it? Even the Grove's Arch Poten hates them. Though he is a special case, so I'm not sure how true that is."

"It's true." Borris gave them a wistful grin. "He hates them."

"Good to know he wasn't lying to me the entire time," Jack said, disgruntled.

"I've watched Lucian since he was a boy, and I can tell you for a fact that, more than anything, Lucian hates violence. His father showed him the Anvil when he was barely six years of age. He'd drag him down kicking and screaming. It didn't come as a surprise when he led me there without question after I told him that I'd destroy it."

"I don't understand," Sylvie said. "Then why would he aid the Lafertti Clan with capturing the Potens and representatives? Why stab Jack? Why become a head of the Fetters? Why even get in our way? It makes no sense."

"He could've been promised by the one supporting the Lafertti Clan in the Alps that they'd get rid of the Orive crystals permanently if he cooperated," Jack offered. "But even that's a bit fetched. There are better ways to go about doing things, especially with his position."

"He's still a child, Jack," Sylvie said. "Don't forget that."

"If he can kill a grown man without batting an eye, then he's not a child. He's a *threat*. Nothing less."

"I see you two already have a few theories," Borris said approvingly. "While I don't have any concrete evidence about who might be behind this, I can tell you one thing—Roderek is the one currently pushing for a rushed election. He's also the one that suggested the Alps isolate themselves after announcing the Potentate Union's abolition. Now that Lucian has… gone, Roderek's urging might finally bear fruit. We need to keep quiet that Lucian has betrayed the Institute. Stall for time until all of the important figureheads are present, then tell them about Lucian's desertion. We can't have a vote until you get to the Alps."

"What if Lucian makes it there before us?" Sylvie asked. "What if he convinces them that we aren't on our way and that it would be better to hold the Summit immediately?"

"He won't. I'll send a letter to Javis regarding Lucian's… transgressions. You just focus on Roderek."

"And if he decides to use force? What if he gets rid of all those that oppose him and takes the seat for himself?"

"Then that proves his guilt, doesn't it?"

"Do you doubt that Drakone so much?" Jack asked. "Isn't he the head of the Vanguard Circle's Hunter Division?"

"He is, and the title was well-earned. But underneath that impeccable veneer, Roderek is a purist. Always has been. Over the years, many have come to accept that side of him. He's a great practitioner that hails from an even greater family, so it's not like they could do anything else. But believing in the superiority of your own kind is a dangerous ideology to have. More so if you're in a position of power."

"Just like Maurice," Jack said under his breath.

"Many Elders would bow to him because of his name alone, but they fail to realize just how grave his ideas are. They believe he won't act on it, and they're fools for even thinking so."

"Assuming it is him," Sylvie said, turning to Jack, "then he's going against Maurice, isn't he? If Maurice created the Orive to create a world full of practitioners, then…"

"Roderek wants to restore it to the former order," Jack finished. "I know that there are more than one type of purist, but why can't we find one with, I don't know, a method that isn't so stupidly extreme?"

"You shouldn't be talking about extreme methods, Jack."

"What's that supposed to mean?"

"Maurice," Borris interrupted, before Sylvie could respond. "You two know something about Maurice?"

Jack caught Sylvie's eye, before motioning to her neck. Sylvie got the message. She revealed the stone that housed their most prized possession, and said, "We have Silas Drayr's journal."

"You... *what*?"

"And his sprog, too," Jack added, wrapping an arm around Sylvie's shoulders.

Borris choked on his own spit. He placed the bottle down in fear of dropping it at the revelation. "His descendant? How did you find that ou—" Borris cut himself off with a cough. Twice to clear his throat, and three more for good measure. "No, that doesn't matter. I need to see his journal first."

Jack held his arm out in front of Sylvie, effectively stopping the Elder in his tracks. "We'll let you see it, but in exchange, we'd like you to call one of the priests from Thelarius' temple for us."

"I do remember you mentioning that in the Anvil. Does that have anything to do with what you found in Silas' journal?"

"Call one and find out."

"It'll take a few days," Borris said, eyeing the stone around Sylvie's neck. "Perhaps longer, since I can't accompany you."

"Is that a problem?" Sylvie asked.

"It might be." Borris frowned. "Protocol dictates that the Elders watch those they allow inside, but I can't leave here. Not now. I need to remain as an envoy for the Zenith Council. I'll be overseeing the formation of the Assembly, and making sure that they treat the remaining members of the Lafertti Clan properly. There can be no more blood spilled here. Not until the Council gets wind of what's happening and announces their decision regarding the Clan. I also need to oversee the extraction of the door's connection from Poten Pramm. I'll transfer it to one of the new members of the Assembly."

"If you're staying here, then what are you going to do about the Summit?" Jack asked. "Will you just cast your vote aside?"

There was a moment of silence.

Borris' gaze flew to meet Sylvie's. She raised an eyebrow in question, but otherwise met his stare head on, undaunted by the way he openly judged her. He didn't find any burning sparks in her eyes. Not like Jack's. No, Borris found something else. He was met with pure steel. Firm and unyielding. Obstinate to a fault. But if given enough heat, he knew she could bend.

A surge of approval washed over him.

"I'll give you my vote," Borris declared, surprising them both. "On the condition that you carry it not as the Arch Poten of the Drowned Tower, but as my primary apprentice."

"Your primary apprentice?" Sylvie repeated, caught off-guard by the sudden offer. They'd barely spent a day in each other's company. "Why?"

"Why not? I've seen enough to know that you'd flourish under my tutelage."

"But surely there are others in the Alps… those with better skills and from better families."

"Syl," Jack said, exasperated. "You're a descendant of Silas Drayr. Your blood can't get any bluer."

"We have no proof," she retorted.

"We have a talking stone!"

"That's the most suspicious thing in the world!"

"Suspicious? It's like a living prophecy. You can say—"

"Family names are important," Borris intervened, sensing that they'd had this discussion many times over and that if he allowed them to get into it, they wouldn't be stopping any time soon. "But in the wake of those legacies, sometimes people forget that it's the capability of the individual that truly matters. Damon made the Sirx name great, your father made it even greater. You have the potential to extend that legacy. I can help you make it soar to far grander heights."

"But you're a Healer," Sylvie contested. "There are plenty of Conjurers that could teach me more about my own magic. My previous Master was also a Healer. He relied heavily on books and second-hand information. How will becoming your primary apprentice be any different?"

"I don't presume to know what the future holds," Borris said. "But in the north, there are many families able to contend with your own. You'll find dozens of Conjurers jumping at the chance to teach you when you arrive, though few of them will be truly happy to see you succeed. I can't even begin to count the number of Masters up there that only take apprentices in the hopes to further their own names should they thrive in the future. Luckily for you, I'm not one of them. I'm the last of my house, and I've already attained one of the highest seats possible... a seat you could take upon my passing."

"You want me to become an Elder?"

"When the time comes, I'm offering you a chance to step down and leave the Tower to more experienced men. Unless you want to be trapped there for the rest of your years?"

"I..."

"So, you're saying doors will open for her if she agrees," Jack cut in. "Well, we already knew that. That's why we're having this conversation."

"Watch your tongue, boy, lest you hurt those you care for with your careless handling of it," Borris warned, before turning back to Sylvie. "What I'm saying is that you shouldn't turn down opportunities. This is the first time I've extended an offer of apprenticeship to a non-Healer and the first I've even considered taking a primary apprentice. I can assure you that it will be the last."

"But I'm not looking for a Master," Sylvie said.

"And before today, I wasn't looking for a student," he replied. "You don't have to give me an answer now. Take your time. This isn't the kind of decision you should jump into with your eyes clenched shut."

Just as he said it, a teenage boy called him from across the hall. He was shorter than average and heavy around the waist. Before he was even halfway down the hall, he doubled over and held on to a nearby table for dear life, clearly having overexerted his lungs. Just how long had he been running? The boy looked ready to keel over.

"Work calls." Borris stared at the huffing practitioner with disinterest. "We'll speak again."

"Contact the temple," Jack reminded.

"Of course. But as I said, it might take some time."

"Could you also find someone to escort us to the Alps once we return?" Sylvie asked.

"Return?" Borris questioned, before firmly shaking his head. "There's no need. There's a way to the Gelid Mountains from the temple. It's a wide passage concealed in a great rift. It was once used by the Mentalists and is far from any easily-traveled mountain passes. Statues of their gods linger there, crumbling in time with their once grand altars. But don't let it deter you. Despite how cursed it may appear, I assure you that it isn't."

"Wait," Jack said, fetching his wrinkled map and pointing at the southwest corner where Thelarius' island came near the mountain range. "Do you mean here?"

Borris spared all of his notes a glance, before nodding. "That's the one. Large beasts linger there due to the number of wild Snuff in the area. It's a perfect hunting ground for them. Unfortunately — or fortunately in this case — that keeps most from approaching. The local legends about travelers jumping or being flung from those heights don't help either. But if it's you two, then I'm sure you'll be alright."

"How do we know we're on the right path?" Sylvie asked.

"You'll find jagged spikes lining the way forward like teeth. Follow them up, and you'll see the walls of the Diamond Alps when the sun is at its highest. It's a long trek, but not impossible.

You'll waste more time returning to the Grove."

"Thank you," Sylvie said.

Borris nodded in acknowledgement, before taking one of their hands in each of his own. His voice dropped to a whisper as he said, "Always keep in mind that secrets are a dangerous thing. The truths that hide between those that keep them are like ivy rooted deep and strong under rocks. They'll burst all at once into the light. Be careful when they do. Listen and absorb truth and hurt alike. I guarantee you it'll spill between the fingers of every practitioner nestled in that mountain. Be calm. Be open. And remember that words are as much a lance as they are a salve. You need to be careful with them. The things you say there will determine your future."

Borris' eyes settled on Sylvie once more.

"I trust you'll consider all of your options during your travels."

There was a twinge of finality in his voice that Sylvie could only nod at. And before they knew it, he was already walking away. They looked at each other once he was well and truly out of their periphery. They'd be going soon. But it wasn't only another Institute they'd be leaving behind this time; it was all of their closest friends. Yet, for reasons she didn't want to get into, Sylvie wasn't as disheartened as she thought she'd be.

Let the rest of the world wait. She just wanted to travel with Jack once more. The Institute's reigning powers could squabble to their heart's content, so long as they left her out of it. Sylvie's first priority was returning *her* to where *she* belonged. It was why she decided to take so many detours in the first place.

As if reading her thoughts, Jack said, "We're close."

The grin that split her lips then could only be described as joyful.

26

Rhone leaned against his seat, as he ruminated over the last seven days. A lot had happened. Too much. The two that knew all of the tiny, intricate secrets at the very heart of the matter would be leaving soon. Although they didn't say a word about departing, he wasn't naïve enough to think that they'd actually bother with an announcement. As soon as he took his eyes off of them, Rhone was *certain* that Jack and Sylvie would slip away. They'd do it when all of the representatives were too distracted by the innumerable practitioners they had to supervise. It wouldn't be long now. The Grove was getting busier with every hour, even more so now that the orbs were functioning again. Once they left, it would be too late for him to ask questions.

He could place a guard on them to stall their departure, but Sylvie had the authority to send them away. Dalis was out of the question. He would never agree to do so. Spies might work. Although he doubted their effectiveness, and if found, they might end up straining his relationship with them. If Philip's haunted recollection about the Heartstone was to be believed, then it would be easy for them to loosen any man's tongue.

Rhone doubted they'd ever return to the Grove, considering how sickened they were by their operation in the Anvil. Reaching out to them once they were gone was also out of the question. Their positions and his own tedious schedule would make it next to impossible. They'd have to initiate contact first. But Rhone couldn't see them doing that... not unless he made himself particularly memorable. If he did that, then they might speak to him of their own free will in the future. That kind of trust would surely benefit him in the long-run.

While he had managed to get ahold of them more than the other representatives due to his tactic of casual conversation—as opposed to vehemently questioning them about everything they knew—it still wasn't enough to break their barriers. Rhone wanted to hear more than opinion pieces about the Institute's system and the Demar Spell. Sure, he received the occasional report from Philip, but he was a second-hand source. They were faulty by nature. On top of never having all of the information he wanted, Philip could've misheard or misinterpreted what they were saying. His apprentice was biased as well. Philip liked them, and therefore, didn't pry as deeply as Rhone wanted.

Rhone spent years watching young practitioners grow. Some flourished. Most, however, didn't. The majority were left to either content themselves with a life of mediocrity or to keep on striving until they realized that life could be cruel without reason, and sometimes hard work got men nowhere. But neither of them fit into that category. They could be so much more if nudged in the right direction. He could be the one to do so. He'd even get the answers he wanted in the process.

Two birds with one stone.

The only trouble was finding a stone large enough to throw when he was standing upon a coast filled with pebbles.

I need to use something that would hold their attention, Rhone thought. *Something only I have.*

Rhone thought of their families.

He'd had the fortune of meeting Leonas Dace and Victor Sirx on a number of occasions. With Leonas, it was a game of expression, so subtle and so delicate that he'd felt an immense sense of pride having mastered it so well. But despite their similar looks and unfortunately similar tempers, his son was a different creature entirely.

Not two minutes into their first conversation, Rhone knew that Jack preferred blunt honesty over careful wordplay. He spoke with an openness that didn't just border on the shores of insolence, but waded knee deep in its waters, then trailed it all over brand new floorboards. Vehemently.

What's worse was that Jack expected the same unnerving honesty from those he worked with. He never said so, but the command was clear, regardless. It was in his eyes. Those fiery red orbs demanded, if not respect, then fear. More often than not, it was the latter. The air he exuded was as intimidating as the name he bore. It didn't help that Jack was a bloodhound when it came to sniffing out lies. Neither did his scalding tongue.

By the end of their first discussion, Jack had called him out on every pleasantry and *'waste of breath'* — as he so amply called it — word of small talk that left his mouth. It wasn't an experience Rhone looked back on fondly, and for the first two days, their run-ins were about as welcoming as a poisoned needle directed at his eye. Thankfully, it was the kind of dread that faded with exposure. Jack wasn't entirely unlikable. Once Rhone became accustomed to his overall brashness, avoiding the infamous Dace mood swings was as easy as breathing.

Rhone learned quickly that there were two telltale signs of Jack's anger: a threatening stone-faced look, as if he was physically trying to control his own snarl; followed by a horde of people running in the opposite direction. Only a small handful could calm Jack down once he started, and even then, it wasn't without a fight. But Rhone found a safer way. Jack's fury was self-limiting. Give him a few hours, and his foul mood always simmered down into controlled annoyance.

Jack liked being left alone.

So long as Rhone steered clear of the usual pitfalls that sparked his... passion, Jack was an easy man to get along with. If nothing else, their conversations were never dull. Jack's mind was sharp, his mouth, clever, and his talent, undeniable. He was eager to learn all he could about the world. The only real flaw he had as a student was that he bored easily, then disappeared once he did. Jack's ability to immerse himself in his work didn't help with that. There were times when he'd be neck deep in ancient scripts written by some backwater figure that even he didn't know the name of, then reading the obscure ramblings of an entirely different scholar by the next hour.

Now that Rhone thought about it that wasn't too different from Leonas; the Elder was interested in all sorts of things, always jumping head first into different focuses as soon as he was done with the last. It was the same with people. The more interesting someone was in Leonas' eyes, the better. Jack was more grounded. A trait he got from his mother. Along with his tongue, which gave him nothing but grief whenever he was revved and looking for a fight.

He was also easier to get ahold of. If he wasn't with Sylvie, then she knew exactly where to find him. Cheryll had never bothered calling Leonas for his sake. He was only glad that Sylvie wasn't the same. She was an unharrowed lake in a world constantly ripped apart by greed. She knew peace, and taught others what exactly the word meant without imposing her views upon them.

While Sylvie didn't have the steadfast disposition of her father, it was close enough. Far closer than he'd ever seen. Perhaps that was to be expected. Her blood ran strong in her veins. While she wasn't as eager to learn as Jack, her mind was no less full. Her upbringing under Columbus Cephas showed even if she didn't flaunt it.

Rhone questioned their friendship in the beginning, not quite understanding it. They were oil and water when it came to handling their interests. Particularly Jack's willingness to endure nights absorbed in his passions and Sylvie's bizarre detachment to the things she, herself, deemed fascinating. But that was where he saw the stem of their relationship. With Jack's prompting, Sylvie looked beneath the layers, no longer content with what she'd initially seen. Drive, evidently, was contagious. That, or Jack bothered her enough to spring her into action.

They were similar at their base, however. In core traits they shared once the pricklier ones had been shed. They seemed to have learned early on that they were able to bounce thoughts off of each other in a way that benefitted them, and did so frequently. From errant ideas to well-placed remarks. They spoke with the ease of partners forced for decades into each other's company.

It was evident that if given the proper lessons, Jack would make a splendid, if not hard to please, teacher. Unlike those well-spoken masters or power-hungry elders, however, he was made for the Vanguard Circle. Jack's disposition was meant to serve the underbelly of the Institute, and to be its leader; to have men following his orders, acting apart from the rigid structure of the Zenith Council.

His nature demanded it. His blood assured it. His own talent sealed it.

Sylvie was the politician.

She was bred for it. Sylvie knew when to step forward to defend and when to draw back in their turn. Knowing when to concede battles was necessary in order to win the war. But, more importantly, she had the temperament for it. She listened to others, took their opinions into account, before making her decision. All she needed was the learning touch of time and a guiding hand, lest she end up an adviser like her father.

Practitioners were only worth the expectations they exceeded. By that logic, neither of them could be considered disappointments. Far from it, in fact. They were ice and fire; the world broke against them. The Alps would surely benefit from their presence.

Rhone would be a fool not to take them under his wing... and Rhone was no fool. Already, he saw the scheming eyes of the other representatives, searching for ways to best use them to their advantage, to hone them into their own personal puppets. Although he was among them, better him than another, more vicious man.

He was a Master. The entirety of Ferus Terria recognized his skill as a practitioner. Dalis trusted him. Tiv respected him. That was all the backing he needed. The only thing to watch out for would be their parents. Maybe Rocous. Masters, if they had any. He doubted it. They couldn't have been scouted that fast. Even if they were, Rhone knew that any practitioner worth their salt would be shoulder deep in the Alps' affairs now.

Surely, they wouldn't disallow them... acquaintances.

But what do you give two practitioners that don't need anything from you? A personal gift? Would they even appreciate it if it wasn't practical? Victor might. Leonas, definitely. But them?

There was no use dwelling over it.

Rhone jumped from his seat, startling the girl arranging documents on the requisitions table beside the door. She wore thick spectacles that reflected the light at just the right angle. They masked the color of her eyes. Rhone paid her little mind, only looking at her long enough to make sure that she was steady on her feet and in no danger of scattering the piles of documents on his desk. Before she could even open her mouth to ask him where he was headed, Rhone was already rushing down the hall.

He checked the public archives first. When he didn't find either of them there, he visited all of the halls they were seen frequenting over the last week. Rhone even went so far as to check the blocked entrance to the Anvil. He checked their private quarters in the Red Scripts' section last. It was empty, save for an empty vial on a nightstand beside one of the beds. Their room was always strangely sterile whenever he dropped by to visit, so he doubted they left.

But...

Rhone searched for Philip.

He found him leaning on a wall and eating from a wooden bowl, unconcerned with life's worries. Expectedly, Dalis was nearby, though he was far more animated. Dalis stood before a long table, roving over a one-page letter that seemed to make him angrier with each passing second. A crowd of practitioners were clustered behind him, either trying to get a second-peek at the page or making a ruckus because of it.

Not one of them were from the Grove, Rhone realized. The Hunters from the north were there. Ethil, too. There were two others that he only recognized because of the reports Philip gave him. They spoke rapid-fire about ill-mannered Elementalists and having to meet someone outside the Willow.

Tiv and Cera were off to the side, speaking in hushed tones. They nodded their heads at him as he passed, but quickly returned to their previous conversation. Rhone didn't care enough to bother them. He walked up to Dalis instead. The Healer dropped the letter immediately. His face was scrunched up in displeasure. Rhone could practically hear him cursing in his mind.

The Hunter that nicked it from Dalis' hands groaned in dismay once he read it in its entirety. "Elder Dace is going to kill me for not getting him to write a personal letter or, flames, even a *note* would've done!"

The boy seemed to be exaggerating, but Rhone believed every word. His expression was a mix between horrified and outraged. Rhone had no doubt that if the others hadn't taken the letter from him, he would've handed it to the lively crab on his shoulder and just let it tear the thing apart. No evidence of spare time was always better.

"What happened?" Rhone asked.

"See for yourself," Dalis said. He took the paper from Ethil's unsuspecting hands and shoved it close enough to blind him.

Rhone smoothed the edges of the page.

Partner,

I'm writing this to avoid a maddening spiel of common decency from Sylvie. Even though I already told her that this letter would only piss you off, and I certainly don't need you of all people angry at me. I have enough on my plate as it is. But no... it's always no.

That woman is heartless, I tell you. Those gutted glances are going to be the death of me. Creator, I can practically feel the veins on my temple pulsing. I'm afraid they might actually pop soon. Or, *then again, it could be the herbs. Sylvie's brewing something foul right now, and my eyes are suspiciously itchy. I don't know how much more of this I can take. Tonics are good, but with a stench like that, I'd rather take my chances. Also, I just noticed that there aren't any windows in these rooms. For the love of... **why** aren't there windows? Whoever designed this place clearly never shared a room with an embrocologist before.*

But back to the matter at hand, we've got some business to take care of before we head to the Alps for the Summit. We'll return to the Grove in due time. Maybe. Likely after our business in the north is concluded.

Feel free to direct any missives to my Master, Vidal Verne. He'll open them. I have no doubts about that. So, keep any sensitive information to yourself. He has enough ammunition against me as it is. Don't you dare add to it. Don't direct anything to my father either. Elder Borris told me his letters are being vetted. He didn't give me the precise details, but if my father's involved, then I doubt it's anything pleasant.

It was good to see you. Try not to die while I'm gone. Sylvie left a week's worth of 'enhancement draughts' for you in our room. She said they'll help you regain muscle mass and keep you looking like, well, an Amorph (take that however you want.) Sylvie left instructions there, too. While the contents of each vial might look like mucous, they smelt like oranges, so they're safe. Probably.

Until next time.

Jack

P.S. Tell Elder Borris that Sylvie said she'd accept his offer of apprenticeship.

A red wax seal with the Dace insignia was stamped beside his name. The postscript looked sloppy compared to the rest of the letter. The sentence sloped downward to avoid the seal, as if he'd scrawled it in just before their departure. A last minute decision then. But the knowledge that it was didn't stop Rhone from almost tearing the page in two.

Vidal and Borris were quick. He'd give them that. While he didn't expect anything less from such renowned practitioners, his expression still warped in disappointment at the news.

It seemed he was too late. Well, no matter.

Rhone's gaze shifted to those around him. Skilled Amorphs, a stellar Healer, and an Elementalist from an affluent family. The room was brimming with talent. He wouldn't make the same mistake.

***

Lucian rubbed his eyes.

He glanced at the scroll in his hands and reread it for what must have been the fifth time in the last ten minutes, before finally giving in. He'd have to send it sooner or later. His father had taught him many things—both good and bad—but the best was to hold his head high and do what needed to be done. Never save a task for tomorrow when it can be accomplished today. Lucian lived his life by that rule.

He was always productive, moving from one job to the next until night fell and he woke again. It wasn't because he enjoyed being occupied. He just hated having things weighing on his mind. Stress could kill. He'd seen it happen. To Nebbin, to practitioners, to the ordinary unfortunates that couldn't cope with life's hardships. It wasn't a pretty sight. Death rarely was.

Lucian firmly believed that if he postponed this report for another day, then the lack of sleep might actually kill him. Because every time he read it, all he wanted to do was alter it in some way.

He tucked the dispatch on the leather strap around his owl's talon, then watched it spread its great wings with an ear-piercing cry. Sure, there were a few sentences he could reword and maybe even some notes he could scrawl into the already packed margins, but it wasn't anything truly important.

Lucian was tired of ruminating.

His owl flew off into the blue-grey sky, as quick as a bolt that glided with the wind. Lucian rolled his shoulder, already missing his Peose's weight. No matter how much he trained it to be gentle, its talons still dug into him whenever it landed — or more often, perched. On particularly stressful occasions, his owl even drew blood. He would've had an impressive display of scars had he not been a Healer.

Lucian distinctly remembered the first few years of its life after an Orive crystal was embedded inside of its chest. He'd spent a ludicrous amount of time simply staring at those razor-sharp claws and wondering what else his owl might be doing if it wasn't stuck with him. He liked to imagine that it would be the bird king of some distant forest in the Pulka Ruins or a fearsome predator that circled the Eirinne Mountains, but the more pragmatic side of him knew that it would probably be dead.

His owl was the runt of the parliament. Lucian still remembered the day he received it. The tiny thing was barely the size of his fist and had only one foot and half of its tailfeathers. Even its hoots were pathetic. Meek and feeble. Nothing like he was used to. He hadn't thought twice about healing it. Lucian simply placed his small hands upon its tiny body, and then smiled when its foot suddenly remade itself.

Then, before even his lightning quick mind could register, he was labelled the second coming of Maurice.

Lucian sneered and buried the memories as deep as he could. He looked out at the snowscape to distract himself. What surrounded him was a land of white as far as the eye could see. More rained down upon him, falling over his head and collecting between the strands. Cold overwhelmed his senses. He watched, fascinated, as his breaths visibly escaped him in a tiny cloud of smoke that dissolved into nothing.

It's cold, Lucain thought blankly.

He spared a glance at the group of mercenaries that trudged along behind him. They fared better than he did, undoubtedly used to travelling long distances under spotty weather.

At least I don't have to worry about them. They aren't the best, but they're good enough. More than I could hope for with the other Fetters leaders gone. I should've used those networks while I had the chance.

Lucian sighed.

Not that any of that matters now. I need to get to the Alps. I'm sure they're against announcing my desertion in fear of a rushed election. No one wants to risk one amidst this chaos, lest the one that instigated it be crowned head without their knowledge. Kings already voted in are harder to deal with than candidates searching for support.

He looked out at the long trail ahead of him.

The last time he'd walked this path was when he was seven years old and his father wanted to show him off to the Zenith Council. Elder Borris had arrived to escort him. He brought a royal purple scarf that was so long, it wrapped around him no less than eight times. Lucian recalled a passing herd of Snuff, too. They hid in a forest full of fir trees, where he played hide-and-seek with Borris until he suffered from frostbite on his toes. Borris had healed him afterwards. Lucian still recalled the surge of warmth from his hands as it spread all throughout his body. He was so much bigger back then. Tall, tender, and impossibly kind. Lucian couldn't have imagined that Borris knew about the Orive crystals.

Jewels made from flesh and blood, he thought, his mind drifting to all of the horrors he'd seen in the Anvil over the years.

When the corpses of those already gone weren't available, they'd take the next best thing: prisoners, slaves, Nebbin. Even the occasional deserter that had rebelled one too many times. Lucian used his position as Arch Poten to limit the number of Nebbin and prisoners they got their hands on, and as he grew older, he started an underground network to limit the amount of slaves and deserters as well. But he could only do so much on both fronts. In the end, his efforts only made his fellow leaders in the Fetters suspicious of the crystal's power.

Lucian could say with certainty that they were allies he'd never miss. His memories of them were all bad. Which was quite a feat, considering his standards for what constituted a bad memory. If his recollections weren't so vivid, he might've thought them false. Maybe they were hallucinations from a toxin he'd mistakenly ingested or stories from another life that were planted inside of his mind. But that was a child's hope. One that he didn't want—didn't *need*. Because, if nothing else, their deaths were a weight off of his already bogged shoulders.

Ever since he was young, Lucian recalled even the slightest of instances—a passing face, a useless sentence in a book, an endless list of numbers—it was as if his brain had deemed everything to be of equal importance. So, it was easy for him to conjure up images of death and gore in his head. Especially since it was all that surrounded him. The things he'd realized because of his memory were surprising.

For one, a good number of those he'd met believed that only a scant few didn't deserve to die in a hole underneath the Institute. Them being amongst those few of course. Perhaps it was tradition that spoiled them. If their forefathers did it, then they should continue their legacy. Or maybe they were all purists inside and that was the only way they could really express it. He didn't know how anyone could think like that. How they could be filled with such unquenchable hatred. When he, a mere child, would wake in the middle of the night screaming loud enough to injure his vocal cords because his entire bed was covered in imaginary blood.

Lucian could still hear the screams of those that were dragged down into the Anvil by their haunches; could still see their anguished faces as they were enveloped in a toxic pool of heat. The thick waves of black water ate away at them until not even ash remained. Then, after all that hurt, after all that agony and sacrifice, a tainted crystal would emerge.

Power, they praised. Like it was something to be coveted.

They were worse than the Mentalists. At least they never hid who they were. They showcased their beastly natures with puffed chests and delighted smiles, making reputations out of the number of tortured souls they left in their wake. Beasts that prideful about their misdeeds made caution a simple thing.

Them, on the other hand...

He had to put a stop to it.

One, final appearance, Lucian thought, bolstering his spirit. *Once I get there and give them my twist of what happened, I should be able to convince them to speed up the election even without the Tower's Arch Poten present. She's new anyway. Her opinion can be disregarded in the face of so many overlapping crises.*

Lucian closed his eyes and breathed to steady himself.

I'll cast my vote, and it'll finally be over. He's already agreed to rid this world of Orivellea upon his election. I can't rest until the secrets to their creation are buried in history.

27

Vidal almost forgot how charming the Alps was. Almost.

He didn't want to grow too attached, lest he moor himself to somewhere he'd already been told he had no home. But this close to the center square, he couldn't help it. There were more greenhorns than seniors here. Most didn't recognize him, but they did stop to bow. If it was because of his flashy attire or because of the self-important way he held himself, he didn't know, but he smiled all the same. It was nice to be respected for no other reason than because he deserved it. Vidal was a bonafide Master with all of the documents in the Alps' annals to prove it. But he also inspired fear in so many that after a while, it became the only reason they dropped their heads when he passed.

It was early morning, and already, men and women rushed by on either side of him. A fair few were laden with crates and overfull carts that they pulled behind them. Vidal made a game out of it by guessing what was inside each, and then approaching them under the ruse of a Master sent to inspect their goods. Their staggered faces were the most thrilling part.

He looked on at the half-assembled market stalls that lined either side of the street. Their brightly-colored canvases draped over their rickety roofs were for appearance more so than shade. This high in the mountains, the sun was always covered behind a grey sky. Baskets of fruit and worse, fish, spilled out around the feet of their hawkers.

Vidal stopped for a moment at a stand filled end to end with glass chalices. They were bathed in the synthetic light of a nearby oil lamp. The woman responsible for them jutted out a saucy hip at his appearance. She batted her eyes at him, and it was then Vidal noticed the thin line of gold paint along the outer corners. If it was out of genuine interest or a simple desire to make a sale, he wasn't certain, but he ignored her in favor of staring at her wares. They'd make a fabulous addition to his collection in Yorn.

"Price?" he asked.

She said something that his ears failed to register. The words grated on his ears like screeching iron when she reached over the scant space to place a hand on his forearm, unintentionally bunching up the plum silk in a manner he couldn't ignore.

"Hands off," Vidal commanded. He scrunched his eyebrows at the unwelcome touch. "My robes are considerably more expensive than yours."

The woman reeled back as if she'd been burned. Vidal regarded her with crippling patience, blinking twice for good measure, before continuing on his way. There were pests everywhere, but he supposed he deserved that for bothering so many others so early in the morning. Karma's blade was swift.

The jangling of shop bells faded as he proceed farther into the city, and by the time he turned through two more avenues, the everyday workers had mostly vanished, leaving behind only the higher ranking practitioners and large groups of stone-faced Hunters. The old-fashioned ones wore heavy robes with fur trimmings. Their faces were powdered white; their lips blown with dark blue dye. Even the shop fronts became more elegant. The swinging placards were etched and filigreed. Their well-dressed proprietors nodded politely as he passed.

A number of Elders lingered here, giving speeches and arguing about things he didn't bother listening to. Roderek was among them, towering above the rest in fine form. Sunlight caught in his eyes like wildfire, causing more than one person to stop dead in their tracks as soon as he opened his mouth to speak. When Vidal caught his eye, Roderek stepped forward into a beam of sunlight that made his entire being flare gold. He nodded briskly in acknowledgement, before retuning to his previous conversation. That brief action, however, was enough to make more than a few heads swivel in Vidal's direction.

Vidal could see why so many supported him. It wasn't only because of his family name or his title as Elder and Vanguard Circle Head, but because he was one of the most amazing speakers he'd ever seen. Greater than Leonas, who had a proclivity for unnecessary dramatics; perhaps even greater than himself. Roderek was passionate, but not fanatic. Wary, but unafraid. His confidence never waded into arrogance. All were lethal combinations. Sometimes all it took was a good speech to sway those still unmoved, and those around him were swayed, indeed.

That wasn't good.

Vidal turned on his heel. He needed to go to Leonas' office and check if any new messages had been left for him. He stepped inside a lab full of embrocologists on the way to nick a few dried herbs from storage. But before he could leave, there was a smart rapping at the door. A younger man with a curly beard walked in with his hands folded behind him. Every practitioner in the room immediately stood up and bowed. Without having to be told, they lined up into three orderly lanes that left him standing out like a sore thumb.

The man looked at him with a raised eyebrow that Vidal only smiled at. He recognized him as a fledgling Master that most described as too committed to the Institute's rules. He had light hair and red eyes that sparkled like jewels under the light.

"What are you doing?" he demanded.

"What does it look like?" Vidal quipped. "I'm taking a few plants. I've been experimenting with a new poison recently, and I'm afraid that it's too corrosive for my liking. I need to tame it with the proper ingredients."

"Only specially appointed Masters are allowed to test poisons. Even then, nothing so lethal that it needs to be tamed. You need a permit from one of the Vanguard Circle Heads for that."

"Rest assured, I have one."

"You arrived with Arch Poten Verne, didn't you? Masters from the Veld aren't given such privileges."

"How fortunate then that I earned my title in the Alps."

He gave him a look chockfull of skepticism, and Vidal savored every second of it. "You shouldn't lie," he said. "But I wouldn't expect anything less from someone from the Veld."

"What do you have against Veld practitioners?" Vidal asked. His jovial tone dropped so fast that everyone around him took a cautious step back. "We help people and we kill them. Not much different from anyone else, if you ask me."

"I didn't."

"Clearly. Go and leave me to my devices. You wouldn't want to lose an eye in front of your own students now, would you?"

Vidal sighed when the man crossed his arms. All it took was a brisk nod of his head, and then his students were leaving. They looked behind them as they crossed the threshold, hoping to see a glimpse of the oncoming fight. Unfortunately for them, Vidal was a patient man. He didn't move. Not even when the door slammed shut, as piercing as a hammer to a blade, and they were enveloped in silence.

Vidal cocked his head to the side. The light from the nearby window illuminated his features into something cold and beastly. The man jerked when the temperature in the room dropped just enough to be uncomfortable.

"What now?" Vidal raised an eyebrow. "Don't tell me you actually want to exchange blows? Here? Are you trying to get into trouble with the Council or is this just your foolish way of getting them to notice you?"

"Threatening a fellow Master is a crime," was all he said.

Vidal wasn't impressed.

"And they call Veld practitioners hot-blooded?" he muttered under his breath. Vidal walked over, casually disregarding the twists of fire that shot out as soon as he did. The flames came too close for comfort. They grazed his cheek, just near enough for him to feel the blazing heat; they even singed a few stray hairs, before receding. It reminded him of the small snakes that hid in the grassy plains of the south, striking out with their jaws wide open, only to retreat a second later. Nothing more than a warning to stay away.

Vidal wasn't so merciful.

Magic was a tool, same as a bow or sword. If his emerged, then he might as well use his powers to the best of his ability. No use sparing something that could be incinerated from the start. But it seemed he finally found the exception to that rule. Allies could be such a hassle. More so if they were easily... excitable.

Vidal put his hands on the man's shoulders.

"Relax," he said, squeezing. There was a flash of light, then a thin layer of hoarfrost slowly enveloped him. Vidal felt him shiver under his hold. "This will hurt less if you do."

He jerked back, but Vidal was already reaching up with ice-tipped fingers, prepared to remove his eye in the most basic sense of the word. He got close. Close enough that a thrum of excitement tore through his body at the prospect of actually being able to do it. So, when the Master regained his wits and seized his wrist in an unyielding hold, he was both upset and delighted. More so the former, despite the trouble he'd undoubtedly get in if he actually did gouge his eye out.

His grip was a gritty thing. Tiny pebbles fell in the scant space between them. Sharp and dusty. They chaffed his skin. Before long, three long rivulets of blood travelled down his forearm, soaking his robes a dirty brown. The sight only made his grin widen.

Not all bark after all.

Though he obviously wasn't the brightest of the bunch. To openly challenge him and assume he wouldn't make good on his promises was proof of that. Vidal could ignore many things, but blatant disrespect of the Veld wasn't one of them. The man's reflexes were sharp though. He'd give him that. Almost as sharp as the frosty look in his eye. It was a good glare. Strong. Unwavering. He must've had a lot of time to perfect it. Unsurprising, considering where they were. The power of a glance could make someone submit mid-conversation here, and with an attitude as haughty as his, he was no doubt born and raised in the Alps.

Vidal's methods had built him a reputation when he worked with Leonas under Remon Dace in the Vanguard Circle's prison. One that clearly hadn't held through the years. Perhaps it was time to rekindle the rumors.

Just as he thought it, the door opened and Rocous walked in. He had a bundle of letters in one hand and a long piece of twine in the other. Rocous blinked twice at their position. It wasn't outright hostile, but it wasn't exactly friendly either. His eyebrow chased his hairline when he felt traces of magic in the room.

"Careful, Mand," Rocous said, silently praying that he'd misread the situation. "Vidal has a tendency to go for the eyes."

"Oh, he knows!" Vidal laughed. He freed his arm and stepped away in one smooth motion. "There's something about that split second of horror on their faces when they realize what's about to happen that just makes the mess worth it. It's so... *unsuspecting.*"

"Leonas said the same thing." Rocous gestured to his mouth. "Except for the tongue."

"Truly the perfect partner."

Rocous shook his head. "A missive came in from Gillot Verathin's daughter. She was apparently saved by a group of wayward practitioners that fled the Grove to search for their missing family members from the Tower."

"The Grove?" Vidal repeated, confused for a moment, before the thoughts clicked. His eyes lit up in sudden understanding. "Did they find her in a slavers den past the Narrow Marsh?"

"I don't know the precise details, but if you've already heard something about this, then it's likely. A few other letters came in, too. They're addressed to you."

"Me? From who?"

"That's what I want to know."

Rocous showed him the cream envelopes with his name elegantly scrawled on each. It was all done by the same hand. Did one person suddenly decide to send him a string of messages or were they all sent at once, and his name was written by one person for efficiency?

There was only one way to find out.

Vidal swiped them from his hands. He read through each one with slowly widening eyes. They were complaints mostly. A lot of well-worded threats meant for Jack; brief regards and stories sent to Sylvie. There was a particularly angry one from her brother that made the corners of his mouth turn up. He even found one from the man Leonas sent to the Grove. That was interesting. Not only because of its contents, but because he'd have more information to hold over Leonas' head.

Despite his name scrawled on the letters, only one was actually meant for him, which led him to believe that Jack had them forward their missives here while he was off making another mess some place else. The letter was placed in a thicker envelope with buttery parchment. Barely two sentences in, and Vidal already knew that it was a report regarding what had happened in the Grove. He checked the pages—fourteen in total. Long, but informative. There was even an official-looking wax seal stamped at the very end. The Red Scripts' representative's name was signed in huge letters. More signatures trailed after almost sheepishly.

"These are good," Vidal said. "No, more than good. They're brilliant. Fantastic. Flaming *excellent*. If I use this report as evidence and claim that rogue members of the Lafertti Clan plotted to overthrow the Grove and plunge the Alps into chaos, then I'll be able to free Leonas."

"The Lafertti Clan? What do you mean the *Lafertti Clan*? That's a serious accusation, Vidal."

"Serious enough to free a suspected murderer?"

"It sounds insane."

"Don't talk to me about insane. Leonas locked up in his own bleeding dungeons is insa—"

"Wait," Rocous interrupted. "This isn't the place."

Vidal's gaze drifted to Mand. He found him silently standing there with one hand over his eye, noticeably shaken. His shoulders heaved with each breath. It was as if he hadn't even registered them speaking. Vidal gave him credit for being able to grasp his wrist in the face of fear. Few could swallow their doubts and put on a brave face when the moment counted. He'd remember him for that. It might be useful in the future.

"I think you broke him," Rocous remarked. "What did you do, Vidal?"

"Does it matter? We have better things to worry about."

"Of course it matters."

"Then get a Healer," Vidal said, walking towards the door. "I'll be with Leonas."

***

That rat was back.

The black one with the boils on its back and head. It even brought a friend. Just as hideous and twice as vicious. It scurried along the corners of his cell, sniffing the ground and hissing in a cattish way whenever it found a scent it didn't like. Leonas took a step back the first time he'd heard it. Tiny, yet monstrous. As if it had been possessed by a starving predator. Even its teeth were disturbing. They were long and rectangular. Each looked as if they'd been coated in dirty yellow paint.

Gnarly things, he thought. They were better suited for a beaver, given their size. The sight alone was jarring enough to make Leonas avert his gaze. Not an easy feat, considering his profession. Leonas had a sneaking suspicion that it carried the plague, but he let it stay. *Because—*

He turned when he heard the soft echo of footsteps from outside of his door. Leonas could tell that their owner tried to quiet them. It was obvious by how the sound weakened after every second or so, only to begin again, except faster. As if they were still deciding between making noise and staying silent. But their worries were for naught. This was his domain. Very few could successfully sneak up on him here.

Those that could, were either dead or far too busy to come down—at this time anyway. It was still morning. He knew this by the contents of his meal: two pieces of cold sausage and a slice of stale bread. It was the same thing day after day, but he didn't complain. It could've been worse. Far worse. They could've starved him the same way he did his prisoners. With random periods of no food until they begged the guards for a sliver of crust as they ate their meals in front of them... or they could've given him oats.

The horror. Leonas shuddered.

He'd rather fry one of the diseased rats.

Leonas angled his ear so that it was facing the door. He tried to hear—a cough, a sigh—anything that could tell him who it was. All of his usual visitors came in the dead of night. After the good boys and girls of the Alps were asleep, and the real leaders came out to properly run things. So, who had the free time to visit him now? More importantly, who was brave enough to venture this deep into his dungeons without an escort? It couldn't have been Vidal. He'd never be so loud. Not one of his men either. They knew that Leonas didn't approve of morning visits.

Maybe Rocous, no, he hates it here. Dark, he says. Well, of course it is. Victor then? Leonas sighed at the thought. *His face isn't much better than these flaming walls. Perhaps it's Cheryll. Oh, I hope so. But she's still in the east. No, this has to be an Elder. But who? Javis?*

His question was promptly answered when the door swung open to reveal an old friend, and someone that made his eyebrows chase his hairline in disbelief.

"Roderek." Leonas stood. "Now, that's a face I didn't expect. Was the weather spotty?"

"I see you haven't lost your spark," Roderek replied. No stiff lines of awkward tension to splint together broken conversations here. They were both too outspoken for that. Roderek looked behind him. "Leave us."

There was a flash of light and a fly that had been following him morphed into a man with coarse, sun-dyed hair and a strict jaw. Leonas recognized him as one of Roderek's personal guards. He'd seen him often in meetings and had even had the pleasure of working with him at one point when he was tasked to hunt down a deserter with sensitive information about the Zenith Council's previous Grand Elder.

The guard piled his hands behind his head, before walking out the door. Tough *and* obedient. Leonas was more than a little jealous. He went through men quicker than any other division, so he was always searching for fresh prospects. The men in Roderek's personal guard would be perfect additions to his crew. The sort that would live to a long ripe age, despite his demands.

Leonas schooled his features once the door slammed shut. No need for him to see his curious smirk. That was just asking for trouble. More ammunition was the one thing Roderek could do without.

There was a moment of silence between them, where all they did was stare at each other. Leonas looked at him appraisingly. He was often told that it made others uncomfortable, but Roderek's cool glare didn't falter. Rather, its relentlessness was what made it so intense. Leonas would even go so far as to call it unforgiving had he not been accustomed to seeing the wild, unbroken eyes of the select few in his cells that could withstand his methods. Those were gazes that only cared about one thing: vengeance. Roderek's could hardly compare.

This isn't about Dels then, he concluded.

"You trained under my father," Roderek said.

Leonas tilted his head at the subject. Roderek wasn't like any of the other Elders. He wasn't even similar to the eccentric sort like Vidal; a riot in and of himself that used a courteous, yet threatening voice that no one could refuse. Vidal's determined cheer was daunting, but Roderek was far worse. He spoke in demands. Questions that they ended like sentences. It terrified almost everyone he spoke to. Although Leonas was sure Rodereks' family name and rank helped quite a bit with that.

That was another thing. Roderek wasn't like the other Drakones either. He'd earned his position; he'd even earned his respect—not an easy feat. Leonas acknowledged his skills as a practitioner, despite how their ideologies clashed.

"Answer me," Roderek prompted.

You didn't ask a question, Leonas thought bitterly, but bit his tongue. "I did… for a time. Roldeak helped Vidal and I transition from practitioners to Hunters. My father officially took us under his wing in Corrections soon after our first few missions."

"He liked you."

"I recall him threatening to spear my head outside of the gates on a blunt stick if I ever disobeyed him."

"I recall Dels threatening you in a similar manner."

Leonas' lips twisted at the comment. "Why are you here?"

"So quick to change your tune. Why do you think I'm here?"

Oh, Leonas could hazard a guess. But he wasn't used to being the one hounded for information, and so blatantly at that. The tables had turned. Leonas didn't appreciate it one bit. So, he kept his mouth shut and lifted his chin to glare at him. If Roderek wanted answers, then he could at least provide a few of his own.

"All of this can end, Leonas," Roderek said. "You can be free, keep your position, and put all of this behind you."

"You talk as if my life isn't moving forward. Although I've been spending a good deal of it in a cell, don't trick yourself into believing that I'm trapped."

"Then think of your name. I'm sure your descendants would appreciate it being cleared."

"You care too much about bloodlines. You always have."

"You don't care enough. Perhaps that's the Nebbin in you."

Leonas' glare hardened. "Don't you have an election to fret over? Currying favor surely isn't an easy task. Oh, but I'm sure all the pity thrown your way does help. Funny, how family losses can be so beneficial to some. Though I'm sure that your main contender also being suspected of murder helps, too, doesn't it?"

"You're rambling, Leonas. Am I making you nervous?"

"Aggravated, more like. Has anyone ever told you that your presence is mentally taxing?"

"Vidal. Once."

"Good man."

"And yet another practitioner whose family doesn't deserve its prestige."

Leonas rubbed his temples. "If you've come to speak about untainted blood, then you've come to the wrong place. I don't share your ideals. I'm an Elementalist. How could I?"

"I thought you, of all people, would respect those with true power. Those that gave you what you have today."

"You speak as if Elementalists were born crippled, and it was you that saved them. What do you want? Praise for a personal dream your ancestor forced upon the rest of Ferus Terria? You won't find that here. I didn't ask for a crystal."

"But you received one, and it's made you who you are."

"I can't exactly remove it. Tell me, does it pain you to know that I'm one of the best practitioners alive today? It does, doesn't it? Few can compare. That's a fact. That Elementalists rise so high is another. But I earned my position, regardless of whatever else you might believe. I earned it the same way you did."

"You shouldn't have had the opportunity to do so."

"And the truth comes out," Leonas said, his voice was as rough as stones grinding against each other. "Careful, Roderek. Someone might believe that you want to get rid of Elementalists. Oh, now that's a thought. Tell me, is that why you got rid of Dels? It must pain you to know that someone from your family was born without a circuit. Is your blood as pure as you believe?"

They gazed at each other for an age, before Roderek turned to look at the rats. His eyes lingered too long for Leonas' liking. He was definitely checking to see if they were Amorphs.

"You know where the stone is," Roderek said, finally cutting to the chase. "I know you do."

"I don't," Leonas denied. "Why would I?"

Roderek reached into his robes and pulled out a cream-colored strip of parchment. "Arch Poten Cole claims otherwise."

"… And what does he claim exactly?"

"That your son is in possession of it and has committed a few rather atrocious acts in his Institute. Shall I send my men after him?"

Leonas glowered.

"Step back," Roderek went on, "support me, and together, we'll claim it was one of the Tippings that killed Dels. Perhaps even vagrant rebels from the Lafertti Clan. I'm not so blind that I can't see the sway you hold over the Elders, Leonas. Convince them to support me, and I'll allow you to keep your position. I'll even let your son take it upon your passing."

"How generous of you."

"I want to change the current order," Roderek said, turning a blind eye to his mocking tone. "Not destroy it completely. Help me do so."

"You focus too much on your personal dreams, Roderek. You always have. If I were an ignorant man, I would tell you something cliché—something that Masters who knew little about life outside the Institute have told me. Over and over again. You know, word vomit like dreams are worth pursuing no matter how childish they may seem."

"So that when death comes, we can greet him with a smile," Roderek finished. "I've suffered through Master Karim's spiel before."

"I'm not like him, so I'll tell you this: if attaining your dream requires trampling on lives, then it's better left unrealized."

"All dreams require a little sacrifice."

"That's easy to say when it's not your life being thrown into the gutter. You keep going on about how you want to change things to better suit this notion of an ideal world in your head that you disregard the vibrancy of the one around you. The one out there, filled with practitioners and Nebbin that you'll have to deal with when the time comes. You're just like him."

"Who?"

"My son," Leonas said, both amused and affronted by his declaration. "Jacques has no other desire than to change his world for what he believes is better. Let me tell you what I've been telling him for the past decade—it's impossible to change. Not his way and not yours either. The two of you would kill and claw your way to the top to see your dreams realized. But segregation and hierarchy is what the Institute knows. Crowning another king would change nothing. Least of all if that king is you. Not everyone agrees with what you consider ideal."

"Unlike your son, I don't want freedom."

"You want freedom from Nebbin. But if you cast out every ounce of Nebbin blood from these walls, then you'll be left with empty streets."

"I'll content myself with knowing that I purged the Institute of fakes like you."

"If you tell the world the truth about Elementalists, you'll spark a revolution. The likes of which this land hasn't seen since Thelarius freed the slaves. Is that really what you want? Is it worth undoing ages of development?"

Roderek didn't speak, but silence was also an answer.

"Consider my words, Leonas." Roderek turned his back on him, effectively ending the conversation. "I advise against taking too long. Unless you want your first sight after leaving this place to be your son's limbs strewn across the Circle's entrance."

Leonas snarled, more beast than human. Once the door slammed shut, he turned, not wanting to waste another second.

"Did you hear that, Javis?" Leonas asked.

On cue, the bigger of the two ugly rats scurried up to him. Leonas was sufficiently appeased when it really was Javis' voice that emerged. "How did you know it was me?"

"I didn't."

Javis shook his boiled head, and Leonas was tempted to kick him out of reflex alone.

"I'll gather my men and try to find Jacques," Javis said. "I'm sure Vidal will be here soon, so stay put and listen to what he has to say. We can't afford to have you running off just yet."

"I know."

"Truly? Because you ignore my words all the time, Leonas."

"Only when they're worth ignoring."

"Then promise me you'll stay. I'll even contact Cheryll for you," Javis added because he didn't trust the way Leonas' lips thinned in a rare display of his aversion.

"Just find my son, Javis."

It wasn't the black look in his eyes or the straightness of his frame that made Javis rush off, it was the unspoken violence in his voice should he fail to.

28

The Jade Sea was calm.

Calmer than Sylvie expected with a river as volatile as the Wymeran rushing into it. They were currently on a small boat with an elderly man dressed head to toe in cream tones. He stood tall on the stern floor with one hand on the dark wheel and the other fisted at his hip. Beside him was another man, even older than the first. He twisted dried leaves into little bundles for what she assumed was an offering. They were both Amorphs, and had rusty voices that croaked whenever they spoke.

The brothers from the temple had picked them up some time ago. Sylvie couldn't say for certain how many hours had passed, but it was enough for Jack to have fallen asleep against the rails. It would've been faster had they just transformed and flew them across the sea, but vows against the use of magic for anything other than protection were taken by all that entered the priesthood. It was a strange tradition, considering Thelarius' expertise, but not one she didn't understand.

Thelarius used his magic to defend those in need. But who exactly did they hope to defend when they were locked away on some remote island? She wouldn't be shocked if their skills had dulled over the years.

The wind picked up in a sudden rush of billowing sails. The white cloth snapped forward, straining to break free from the mast. Weightless sprays of water flew across the deck to shower her robes. Salt was on every twist of wind, thick enough to cup in her hands. Before her, steel-grey clouds broke and a shaft of light tumbled down, staining the leading sea as green as glass.

The helmsman turned to her then. He nodded once, before jutting his chin out to sea in a silent indication of their proximity. Sylvie wasted no time. She approached Jack. He tossed his head in a fit of panic. She was familiar enough with his sleeping habits to know not to get too close.

So, she called his name instead.

Jack stirred at the sound of it. Slow and confused at first, before his entire body tensed with realization and something else Sylvie couldn't name. It rattled his bones, winded up his spine, and twined at the base of his neck. He straightened like a jolt of electricity had spread across his shoulders. Before she realized, his eyes had flown open. Full, wide, and furious.

He snarled something acidic, his words as sharp as breaking glass. But it was his expression that alarmed her the most. Wrath. So plain on his face that it drove through her heart like a blunt nail. Sylvie frowned at the sight. She stepped forward, despite his darkened gaze. That didn't belong there. Not here. Not with her.

"Are you alright?"

His eyes met hers, and she saw the displeasure behind them. "Don't make me lie to you, Syl."

"Then don't. Was it something about the First Zenith again?"

"You have this way of asking questions that begs more questions." His gaze dropped to the glowing stone around her collar. "If you're curious, ask *her*. I'm sure *she*'ll be glad to tell you. Why'd you wake me?"

He looked her dead in the eyes. Jack was unsurprised to find them steady. Levelled. Perhaps even calculating depending on the situation. She was always unruffled. Until he'd grip her hand and realize her mask was one of the most perfect he'd ever seen.

"We're close," Sylvie responded, tolerant. For now.

Just as she said it, she saw a flash in her peripheral. A gold sun, shining and proud, calling home its worshippers. It stared down at them like an unblinking eye.

They'd read enough about Thelarius' temple by now to

recognize the looming edifice on sight. It was raised on a sudden prominence that jutted out from the flatland. A long avenue of grey paving stones swept before its doors, curling around artfully-placed rosebushes. Each plant was well-cared for and trimmed to perfection.

Marble spires rose up before them, imposing and stark against the endless sea behind. Distant carved walls that climbed in levels along with the echoes of hymn and prayer. Rock giants stood motionless before the temple gates. A brutal addition, given their purpose, but no less beautiful.

Jack's eyes lit up at the sight of them.

Another minute of sailing and then the rest of the island resolved into detail. Lush vegetation. Cultivated fields. The brothers here were entirely self-sufficient. There were no other buildings in the area, save for a lone silo at the very edge. Ships, much like the one they sailed on, were lined in neat rows and moored to the docks. The ropes that tied them were old and worn, but sturdy enough to fulfill their purpose.

They quickly found that the temple was even grander up close. The front alone was three times the size of Curran's shoreline. A dozen thick pillars of shining marble rose from the front steps to brace the white-slated roof. There were no walls here. Nothing to guard against prying eyes; the temple was built to be seen, a proud sanctuary for the one whose spirit dwelled inside of it.

The helmsman let out a cry, while his companion dropped rusted iron to the sea below. The water frothed at the weight of the anchor. Ripples extended outward, then settled into nothing once the spume disappeared. Brothers emerged from the temple like bees. They heaved planks in place and wrapped ropes thrown from the rails onto pylons with practiced ease. Above them, a flock of birds wheeled great dark circles that dispersed once the ship knocked against the wharf. A great, hollow boom, despite its size. It rocked dangerously once, then settled at last.

Excited tendrils burst forth, guiding them forward.

Sylvie's heart hammered loudly in its cage.

She held out a hand to Jack, who grasped it without thought. The familiar, honest calluses were a welcome comfort that quelled her stirring gut. She met the eyes of over a dozen priests, all openly staring at them in curiosity. If they were wondering who the Elder was between them, then they were going to be sorely disappointed.

Jack stood beside her, muttering something unpleasant under his breath.

"Where do you think *she*'s leading us?" Sylvie asked.

He tilted his head to glance sideways at her. "Let's find out."

***

The seniors in the temple took one glance at the missive Elder Borris wrote for them, then a longer glance at their faces, before ushering them inside with snappish voices that only meant one thing: they weren't welcome here.

Jack scoffed. He didn't come all this way to let the opinions of a few codgers stop him. He'd go in whether they liked it or not. Thankfully, they didn't put up much of a fight. They kept their opinions contained to barely audible utterances and hateful glances. All very easy to ignore, considering how their gazes ventured away in alarm whenever he made eye contact.

They exchanged their boots for a pair of ill-fitting indoor shoes and were provided basins of water to clean their hands and faces before entering the main hall. It was cool, spacious, and, to his delight, dim. Jack might've called it pleasant, had it not been for the heavy stench of incense that lingered in the air. The smell settled over him like a second skin. His nose itched with every inhale.

Jack examined the broad marble stones under his feet. They were polished and smooth just like the rest of the temple. There were no errant blankets of dust or smudges on the floors. Only priceless rugs with baskets of fruit on top. Beside them, were golden dishes that had soft white wax pooled at the bottom.

Depictions of cloaked, kneeling figures were etched along the walls. Words were written below them in a language long dead.

"This way," one man said. His voice brooked no barter. "The seniors have granted you permission to browse the lower archives. I'll come fetch you in four hours. A guard will be posted at the door for the duration of your stay. Should you need anything, then he'll call for one of our brothers to assist you. Wandering the temple without permission is strictly forbidden. Am I clear?"

"Crystal," Sylvie said for both of them.

Satisfied with her response, he led them to a library with thick emerald drapes half-drawn over the narrow windows that stretched two stories high.

They ambled through the long aisles of bookshelves, ignoring the wide-eyed stares and hushed whispers that echoed up the high stone walls. Their escort showed them into the grand recess at the very heart of the archives, before withdrawing. Jack inspected the area around him. He stood behind a high-backed chair that faced an enormous desk littered with papers. Behind him, Sylvie leaned casually against one of the overburdened bookshelves.

When one of the younger scholars stared unabashedly at him, Jack raised his eyebrow in a delicate threat. The boy straightened like the lash of a whip. It wasn't long before the only thing left of him was a glimpse of his far-off figure pulling on the collar of his shirt.

"Are you already scaring people, Jack?"

"If you want someone gawking at you while we walk out of here, then feel free to call him back."

"Point taken," she said, walking off. "Over here."

Jack looked up to find those dark tendrils leading them to a path outside. He could practically feel *her* excitement. It stirred the air and made it hard to breathe. They followed the trail to a double set door. Jack caught Sylvie by the elbow before she could open it. There were practitioners all around them. Given, they were either hiding behind shelves or seated a distance away, but Jack could *feel* their wandering eyes digging holes into the back of his head.

"*She*'s slipping," Jack said. He didn't think that was possible. "People are staring at us, Syl."

Sylvie stopped to look around. From the corner of her eye, she saw a practitioner duck behind a table. He stammered out an excuse to air about being late, before running off. He took extra care to cover his face with his sleeves.

"Subtle," Jack said dryly. "Why are there so many kids?"

"They did say it was the lower archives."

"We've been reduced to learning with novices."

"Would you rather be with a horde of snobbish elders?"

"I'd rather have my own archive," he said with a nostalgic look in his eye. "Those were the days."

She shook her head at him. "So, how do you propose we get out of here?"

"You distract them by burning a shelf, while I ice the guard. Then, we run hell for leather to wherever *she* wants."

"Quietly, Jack. I meant how do we get out of here quietly."

"I gave my suggestion. It's your turn."

Sylvie eyed their surroundings. They were circled by innumerable rows of shelves lined with artifacts and tomes, dark-wood tables, and matching chairs with tall backs. In a corner, there was one scholar hunched over himself. He had silver spectacles and a full head of sand-brown hair. Piles of leather tomes surrounded him. From what she could tell, he was reading four different books at once. He wasn't young, but he wasn't old either. They had passed a few smaller than him, which told her that he wasn't a child genius, but rather a passionate worker. He was definitely the sort to get absorbed into his own world.

Perfect, Sylvie thought.

Directly beside him was a beautifully stained window. She noticed two guards patrolling the hall, coming and going every few seconds. With that kind of turnabout time, it was likely that they only oversaw that one hallway. That would be a problem. But nothing a little teamwork couldn't solve.

"There." Sylvie pointed.

Jack grunted, swiftly catching onto what she was thinking. He wasn't against her idea, but he wasn't excited about it either.

"And what do you plan to do about that poor scholar?" he asked. "More importantly, what about the people around us?"

"Ask to go to the bathroom."

"You're joking." He scoffed, then ran his hands through his hair when he realized she wasn't. "Of course you aren't. *Filan vahs.* Your plan has too many holes, Syl."

"It's better than being chased from the start. Besides, simple plans work best."

"I'm astounded they work at all."

"It helps that you're great at executing them."

"Okay, that was a stellar save. I'll give you that." Jack rolled his eyes. "But if you want to slate them, then this is one hell of a way to go about doing it. I'm not too keen on going to prison, so if you think we're surrounded by cretins just say so. I'm one-hundred-and-ten percent certain that they'd rather have their egos bruised, than their bodies."

"Of course I don't."

"This plan says otherwise." He stuck his thumb in some vague direction over his shoulder. "You do realize that there's a bathroom here, right? And how exactly am I supposed to leave once you sneak out?"

"Make a fuss," Sylvie said, already walking toward the window. "You're good at that."

Jack scowled, but didn't deny it. Before he could think better of it, he made his way to the door and rapped on it a solid three times. He took care to open it only a smidgeon. Just enough for the guards beyond to get a glimpse of his face. Jack waited until they neared to open it fully.

Leaning against the doorframe, he said, "I didn't know the temple had guards. People guards. Not those golems. Oh, what

I'd give to face off against one of those."

The amount of suspicion packed into their gazes made him feel all sorts of guilty.

"I'm just curious," Jack went on, holding his hands high in peace. "Or what? Can't talk without some senior's permission?"

"Watch your mouth," one of them said. He angled his head in a way that let him look at Jack from under his nose. "We didn't take the Oath of Opposition like the rest of our brothers."

"Why not?" Jack asked, loud enough to garner the attention of everyone in the immediate vicinity. "Don't tell me you didn't make the cut to become full-fledged scholars?"

"Of course we did. We wouldn't be allowed in the temple otherwise."

Jack hummed in deliberation. He took that moment to glance inconspicuously at Sylvie, and he wasn't at all disappointed by what he found. She had already slipped out. Sylvie ran ahead, presumably to hide until he got himself out as well. As if it would be that easy. Unlike him, she didn't have to deal with anyone. The boy she'd slipped past hadn't once looked up from his books.

"Sorry," Jack said, returning his gaze to the pair. "I'm just having a hard time believing that. I know looks can be deceiving, but you two don't look like the studious type. You remind me of a few friends of mine. Amorphs of course. Bold. Reckless. Always looking for a fight."

"We aren't meatheads!" the guard shouted, red in the face.

Jack raised his eyebrows at that. "Now, when did I say that?"

"Your implied it, you li—"

"Name-calling. Always with the name-calling. It's hardly civil," Jack said, feeling very much like a hypocrite as he did so. "No hard feelings though. I'll let it slide."

They rolled their eyes.

"Should we be thankful?" the guard asked patronizingly.

"Absolutely," Jack replied, perfectly mimicking his tone.

Then, he flashed them his father's sigil. It had a red imprint from the wax he used to mark his letter to Tiv, but the moth was still visible. They looked at it, then at him, before stiffening in realization. Jack smirked at their rigid postures. Showing it was always a gamble. He never knew who would recognize his family's crest or who would even care. But judging from the looks on their faces, Jack guessed that they'd met his father personally... and he'd scared them enough to wet themselves.

"I want to see one of the upper archives," Jack went on. He wasn't lying. "I've got a few documents I want to copy. A lot was lost when the Drowned Tower collapsed. I assume the higher floors have the originals?"

"The seniors only permitted you to browse the lower archives," the guard denied, all forced politeness.

"Then lead me to one of your seniors. What I'm looking for isn't here."

They exchanged an uncertain glance.

"I'm not against going myself," Jack continued. "But if they find me unescorted, who do you think they'll blame?"

That did the trick.

The more prideful of the two sneered in open disdain, before gesturing with his head to his companion, who stepped up to escort him. Jack grinned in triumph, as they began walking down the hall in the direction Sylvie disappeared off to. He saw those tendrils still lingering above him. They beckoned him forward. To his luck, they followed the path perfectly until the other guard was long out of sight.

When they reached a T-shaped intersection, Jack knew Sylvie was there waiting. Not because he saw her shadow or had some innate sense for where she was, but because those voices that were always on the edge of his hearing grew loud enough to startle him.

"Left," his escort ordered.

Jack looked up to find the tendrils going in the opposite direction. Nevertheless, he turned left. He seized the guard by the elbow when he followed, then pulled with all of his might. The guard drew back out of instinct, at the same time Jack let go. The fall on his back was inevitable, and Jack could only gasp when the top of his head collided with someone's feet.

Sylvie stood there with an iron helmet that she slammed against the side of the guard's head. Its pointed tip hit his nose, causing it to twist in a sickening angle. Jack twitched at the sound.

"Where did you get that?" Jack asked, lifting an eyebrow.

She pointed behind her, where two guards were piled on top of each other. Both of his eyebrows rose this time. Okay, so he was a little impressed. Not that he'd ever tell her that.

"You couldn't avoid them?" he taunted. "I'm shocked."

"They didn't believe me when I said I was lost," she said, gently dropping the helmet. "And I didn't see you trying to lose him peacefully either."

"Oh, like I had the time." Jack shook his head. "Nevermind that. We need to hurry. Once those trainees in the archive realize you're gone, they'll notify the seniors. I told you your plan was flawed."

"A twenty minute head start is better than nothing."

He couldn't disagree with that. But that didn't mean he liked it. "We're never going to be allowed in here again."

Her lips twitched in amusement, and he watched, fascinated, as she struggled to suppress it. But before he could make a smart remark, she was already walking down the hall... that didn't stop him from muttering it under his breath, however.

They sprinted down the halls, taking care to avoid the occasional worshipper. Three times, they had to find another route because the hall was littered with singing brothers. And each time, they nearly ran into the same exact practitioner. He seemed to be wandering aimlessly, too busy memorizing a long book of tacky chants to pay them any mind. Jack didn't envy him. They realized quickly that the guards were only stationed around rooms of significant importance such as annals and ostentatious altars. Those were easy to spot. They had stained glass windows that they could see from meters away, and in front of their doors were golden statues of Pernelia's falcons.

It wasn't long before they reached the end of the trail. They lurched to a halt when they saw that it stopped at the top of a flight of stairs.

"What the…" Sylvie looked around. "Are we here?"

Jack stepped back to take it all in. Everything about the room was tall. The coffered ceiling stretched higher than most, and the smallest statue was no less than eighteen feet in length. There was no furniture, save for a dark-polished table in the center of the room that ran a dozen places too long and foreign chairs with high, curved backs and striped-ivory fabric. Silver candelabras were set all across the table; their candles cold and unlit. Jack doubted the room needed them. Not when the ceiling was filled with pulsing blue inscriptions that faded in and out of view.

"Enchantments," he said, eyeing them. They were unlike anything he'd ever seen before. "Are they stopping *her*? Is that possible?"

Sylvie took out the Hearstone just as Jack bent to inspect it under the waning light. The tendrils were still there. They were wound in a tight coil at the very center of the stone, as if they were trying to protect themselves from something.

"Hey!" Jack's thumb glided over the stone. "Anyone there?"

There was no response.

"Silent treatment again?" he grimaced. "What about my eyes?"

"Same as alw—" Sylvie stopped, abrupt enough to make him panic.

"What?" Jack asked. To his chagrin, Sylvie grabbed him by the chin and directed his face this way and that. He grabbed her wrist, stopping her, before she could twist his head any more. "Flames! What do you think y—"

"They're shifting," she interrupted. Her grip slackened under the weight of his own.

"Shifting?" Jack asked. "What do you mean shifting?"

"I see them now," she said. The light above them brightened. "And now they're… retreating?"

"Can't you be a little more descriptive?" Jack asked dryly.

"It's hard to explain. It's like," she looked down at the stone. Sylvie lifted it with her free hand. "... Like this."

His eyes widened. "I knew there was something wrong with these enchantments. Look at them. Those signs are ancient. Do you recognize any of the words?"

"I can barely see them from here."

"Well, they aren't like anything I've ever seen."

"Where is everyone?" Sylvie asked. She leaned forward and peered at the table. "The table's... dusty. The rest of the temple was spotless. This area must be restricted."

"And for good reason," Jack said. "Let's go back down for now. It's not safe here."

"Wait." Sylvie pointed to the corner of the room. "Look."

Jack squinted through the dark to find a stone door half-hidden behind the statue of a deer. It was set-double with more inscriptions along its surface. It seemed almost... alive; breathing like a dormant monster. He was about to argue against going inside when he heard voices echo up to them from below. They ranged from outraged to stunned, and Jack just knew that they were the cause.

"Looks like we don't have a choice." Jack frowned when he heard half a dozen doors shouts ring out in the open. "Come on."

They ran towards the door, and together, they pulled it open. It was heavy, far heavier than either of them had expected. And damn all the shadows of the harbor, if moving it wasn't a thankless task. Jack flinched when it dragged against the pristine marble, but there was nothing to be done about that. They focused on opening it just enough for them to slip inside.

It creaked and gasped, too loud in the hush of their surroundings. When that was done, they helped each other close it. Sylvie pressed her back to the stone and used her legs to push, while Jack did the same, except with his shoulder. He made sure to hold onto the handle, so he could stop it just before it slammed shut and alerted everyone in the building.

"That's good enough, Syl," Jack said.

Sylvie backed off, while Jack pushed it the rest of the way. They breathed a sigh of relief once it finally closed.

They grinned at each other, before turning to look at their surroundings. This room was markedly smaller than the last. It was nothing more than a square with a wall on one side and a long line of tall windows on the other. The view, however, was breathtaking. The sea went on for miles. A boundless body that made them feel large and small all at once. Jack saw Sylvie's eyes widen at how the evening sun dressed the sky in a lovely red and orange gown. He didn't blame her. The sight was striking enough to inspire a thousand songs.

But that wasn't what really caught him. No, what he saw in the center of the room was far more overwhelming.

"Another one," Jack said.

They looked upon the large *Orivellea* together. Blue and throbbing. There was no black liquid here. Not in a place like this. But they couldn't be wrong. They'd seen the Orive crystal in all of its different states, and this was definitely one of them. It was larger than even the one in the Pit. Brighter, too, despite the dark wisps that swirled within.

Without warning, the darkness withdrew. It moved backwards in the blink of an eye, as if to make way for something even greater. The haze slowly cleared. A trail of blinding white was left in its wake. They shielded their eyes against the glare for all of an instant, before feeling compelled to lower their arms. It wasn't long before the light paled into something manageable.

And then... footsteps.

A figure beyond.

Intimidating, even in the luster.

Jack gawked for one unending moment, red meeting red, before he averted his gaze to the ceiling. He muttered every great name he knew—the first Zenith, the Creator, a few heroic figures of the past, Vidal, even his own father—praying for someone to come rinse his eyes out with the strongest, most potent cleansing tonic they could find because surely he was hallucinating.

He'd obviously suffered from some sort of neurological damage sometime during his journey here. Maybe he'd been hit one too many times over the head; maybe he'd exhausted his magic circuit so much that he was actually in a coma; maybe he was still with Sylvie in the Red Veld, trapped in bed and caught in a nightmare. For an instant, he wished Serach would step out, flash that fake smile and tell him all about his grand scheme to take over the Tower. Anything for some blessed sanity.

After a minute passed and the sterile ceiling was still there, he looked around, purposely avoiding the... *thing* in front of him.

Jack stared at the rich marble tiles and intricately carved tales along the walls, wondering if the stories they told were just as boring as the ones he was forced to learn growing up. Before he could examine them more closely, Sylvie grabbed his forearm. Tight and shaking. Jack looked down to find Sylvie's pale hand gripping him hard enough to bruise. Her fingers twisted into his sleeves, as if she were trying to clean them for an evening meal. The desperation was clear in her eyes, and when she met his gaze, he knew. Knew that, at this moment, he was a sturdy dock amidst rolling waves. The only real thing left for her to hang onto.

Oh, but he was already half-drowned himself, and the disbelief didn't burn any less clear in his gaze.

Jack's mouth pressed into a thin line as his entire body stilled. His muscles contracted with unease like the first aches before illness. The frantic tremble of his lips was the only sign of his inner panic.

"New priests?" A man's voice. Low and casual with power. "Younger than usual."

Two pairs of eyes flickered to the giant standing undeniably beyond the crystal. With broad shoulders and an easy two heads excess of height, he strode as close as he could towards the edge. There was no gladness on his face, only uneven composure. It was far more threatening than the dark sneers and open threats they were accustomed to.

The way he watched them was decidedly creepy. His eyes moved, but his head remained still.

Although they'd never met him before, they'd seen his face enough times in their dreams to have memorized every premature wrinkle, to have found him in a crowd of thousands, to have—

"Don't listen to the hokum these incense smelling vicars tell you," he went on, clearly unamused by their presence. "I can't absolve your sins."

Darkness burst forth, and the thrilled shout that followed made them falter in surprise.

Thelarius!

29

Their first instinct was to go still.

They watched, unable to tear their eyes away from the sight of Thelarius Merve, himself, focusing on the sound of *her* voice. The darkness that sprang forward recoiled as quickly as it had jumped. Jack grabbed Sylvie by the arm when she was knocked back by the force of something unknown slamming back inside of the stone around her neck.

"Are you okay?" Jack asked. Sylvie nodded, but he didn't trust the way her chest heaved as she did so. His grip tightened. "Don't lie to me, Syl."

"Is this really the time for this?"

Jack faltered. It wasn't, but this was familiar. Easy. The sight behind them was decidedly *not*. Creator forbid it ever be.

"Is that what I think it is?" Thelarius asked. They swiveled around at the rusty sound of his voice. "You even turned. Does that mean you can hear me? See me? Does that make you special or has everyone ignored me all of this time? Don't tell me they heard me bawling?"

"You," Sylvie swallowed the lump in her throat, "you've had visitors before?"

"Many nights ago, when Maurice actively disallowed people from entering this room, I had none. But once he disappeared from this world, there were a few brave enough to disobey his rules. I suppose curiosity does that to a person. They always left shortly after though. It's... cold here."

Now that he pointed it out, they realized that it really was. It felt like all of the cold air from the levels below rose to freeze the floor to keep the air as chilly as possible.

Jack and Sylvie shared a glance. Together, they stepped forward into a strip of orange light. Thelarius squinted at them. He took in their appearances with a thoughtful absorption, from the dirt on their shoes to the grease in their hair.

Eventually, his gaze settled on Sylvie.

Thelarius shook his head like he was trying to clear the haze around his memories. They *saw* the moment when he was able to place her features because he bent forward at the waist, leaning so close that his hands pressed against the crystal.

"What's your name, girl?"

"Sylvie," she paused, then tacked on a hesitant, "Sirx."

He seemed to deflate at her words. But when Jack chimed in '*Drayr*' at the end, Thelarius regained his enthusiasm. Before he could even comment, however, his eyes flickered to Jack. His mouth opened and closed in horror.

"Your eyes," Thelarius began. Jack flinched at his sudden attention. "They're red. Red! Don't tell me Maurice succeeded? Has it really been so long? And what about yo—Sylvie, was it? What's your relation to Silas? Granddaughter, great grandda—"

"Try descendant," Jack intervened with a look of icy scorn. "The Oak Age was over three hundred years ago. We're in the Crown Age now."

"Crown..." Thelarius trailed off. "No, that can't be. So long? But what about..." His head shot up. He looked at the stone around Sylvie's neck. "What happened? Is *she* alright?"

Sylvie's hand settled on the Heartstone. "I can't hear *her.*"

Thelarius looked wildly at the various inscriptions along the walls. They couldn't fathom how he could possibly see beyond all of those tendrils shrouding him, but they also didn't question it. Thelarius Merve stood before them now, surely, impeccable eyesight wasn't a stretch.

"This room is enchanted," Thelarius said. "Maurice created it to keep *her* from escaping the crystal. It slams *her* back inside as soon as *she* tries. As for me, I bounce along the walls whenever these pieces of *her* do try to leave. I've been trapped here because of it."

"I don't understand," Jack cut in. "Why would he even bother? Why not just kill you and be done with it?"

"Maurice kept me anchored here, knowing that *she*'d never truly disappear if I didn't." He raised his arm as if to grasp the stone. "Thank you for bringing *her* back to me. All I've ever wanted was to fulfil my promise to *her*."

"*She*'s not with you yet." Jack met Sylvie's gaze. "We need to disrupt these enchantments."

"Cut through the important bits with shards of ice," she suggested. "I'll ask him to translate Silas' journal."

Jack grinned in approval.

Before they could even take a step, however, there was a loud bang on the door. It was followed by two angry voices screaming at the top of their lungs for them to come out. Jack turned on one heel with an inarticulate sound of frustration

"There's always something," he muttered darkly.

"Shall I?" Sylvie offered, but Jack nudged her back in Thelarius' direction. He gestured with his hand to get Silas' journal out.

"I'll take care of it," he said, sparing a moment to watch her mutter the opening incantation for the Heartstone. There were two bright lights. One as she reached her entire hand into the now engorged nugget to grab Silas' journal and another as he placed his hands upon the large door.

Ice sprayed out from his fingertips, scattering across the door's surface with a thousand tiny cracks. He purposely let it slip between the slits underneath and between the two doors, before making it spike upwards. Jack smirked when one of the men beyond was silenced mid-shout. His blood dripped in from the bottom, while his companion yelled in a strangled mix of horror and hysteria at the sudden death of his partner. From what Jack could make out of his frightened ramblings, his feet were stuck. Jack called upon his magic once more, letting it spike upwards blindly until the remaining man gurgled.

"May Pernelia's wings guide you to where the First Zenith dwell," Sylvie said instinctively, though her words held no passion.

"The first Zenith?" Thelarius perked up. "Oh, if Silas could hear that."

"Don't we have to renew that?" Jack asked.

"One thing at a time," Sylvie said. "Hurry up. I'm sure more of them are on their way."

Jack shrugged, as a short spike of ice emerged from his hands. He dragged it across the walls in long, restless streaks. It felt akin to profaning an altar. Jack didn't know why it felt that way, but he blamed it on how costly the marble looked. When he came upon a particularly thick line, he savagely thrust the ice right into it and left it there.

All three of them turned when a part of the crystal around Thelarius cracked.

"A little more, Jack," Sylvie hollered.

She ran a hand down the crystal, as if to clear it of invisible dust. It felt like the fine grit of a shark's skin, and she rubbed her fingers together at the unexpected sensation. Sylvie pressed the journal to its surface, praying in the back of her mind that its coolness didn't smudge the words.

"Could you translate this for us?" she asked. "Or scrawl an alphabet somewhere?"

Thelarius gaped, bewildered by the familiar penmanship. "Where did you get this?"

"The Pit. It was being used by someone to create *Orivellea*."

"I had an inkling those crystals would become a problem when Maurice first pitched the idea, unfortunately he was able to get Pernelia on his side. Together, they convinced me that it would be worth it. I brought it up to Silas once, but he never cared for Gavinism. Are you the same?"

"I'm an embrocologist," Sylvie said, smiling when Thelarius' eyes lit up.

"Like Silas!"

"Not entirely. I hated Silas' poetry. He published dozens of epic poems during his time in the Alps. They're regarded as classics now. Every practitioner has to read at least ten of them."

"Forgive my lack of sympathy, but I'm proud of him. No one deserves it more. Silas wrote a bit of everything, compiling pages like a sailor unearthing gold. If you'd like to know more about this code, then you need only look at the *Tevëre* alphabet. The basic version taught to children. We crossed the letters with *Ognum* glyphs and *Íarre* symbols to mean different things, but so long as you know the fundamentals of *Tevëre,* then you should be able to get a gist of what Silas wrote."

"*Tevëre*?" Sylvie stared at him, lost.

Thelarius mimicked her expression. "Is that gone now, too?"

"I've never heard of it."

"Well, then," Thelarius deadpanned, just as bewildered. "If it helps, I believe the public archives within the Diamond Alps had a linguistics section. I assume that's still standing?"

"I hope so."

His eyebrows scrunched together in dismay. "Pernelia spent much of her time perusing the books there. It would pain me to learn of its destruction."

"What happened to her?" Sylvie asked, the question rolling off her tongue as easy as a song.

Thelarius stopped unexpectedly at her words. His voice caught in his throat, and he lowered his eyes. Strange, for a man so tall; for a man with tales larger than life. When they'd first stepped into the room, his silent anger made it hard to breathe. Intimidation that stretched far beyond the breadth of his shoulders. Now, like this, he looked remorseful. Guilty. Like a man begging to no longer be alone.

"Maurice chained her inside of his temple when I ran off to destroy the crystals he kept here," Thelarius revealed. He refused to meet her gaze. From the corner of her eye, Sylvie saw Jack angle his head to listen in on their conversation. "As you can see, I failed. Maurice had always loved her. Locked away in that sacred place, I wonder just how much she suffered from his hand. It's not something I like to think about. Maurice used to regale me with stories about her well-being, but that ceased once he realized that this cage he built didn't just slow time down... it stopped it completely. Last I saw him, he was a weak, limp-wristed man with yellow teeth. He was furious at me for avoiding the clutches of death. But... I think that in all of his jealousy, he forgot that death can also be a blessing."

"If I disrupt these enchantments," Jack piped up, hoping to escape the grief that drowned his words, "what'll happen to you?"

"I assume this body of mine will return to dust," Thelarius said, disturbingly peaceful. His eyes softened at the look on their faces. "Worry not. I've had a good life. Certainly better than most I've come across. Growing up in chains, I never once thought I'd have my own home, let alone a temple. Funny, how things turn out. It's strange to be worshipped when, like so many others, all I did was murder for a living."

"You had a larger purpose," Sylvie insisted. "A cause."

"You flatter me. I simply did it better than most." Thelarius sighed in resignation. He looked up at the swirling darkness gathered around him, and then at the open sea. Thelarius reveled in the sight of the grey waves, in the stars about to show. He knew that this would be the last time, and so he didn't hate it as much as he did yesterday. "I am *tired* of waiting here—caught in empty space. I'd like to fulfill my promise to *her*."

"Was all of this," Sylvie trailed off, struggling to find the words. "Was it worth it? Gaining *her* power, being trapped here... would the alternative have been easier?"

"Easier? Certainly. Ages alone would take its toll on anyone. I'm just grateful that I've had those... voices here. They've kept me sane. We've spoken a lot throughout the years. Sometimes I think they understand me. I won't lie and tell you that my life hasn't been difficult, but I feel that the alternative would've been less enjoyable. Less memorable, too. Days blot together when you're trapped in routine. Repetition is everything for a slave."

"No, not easier as a slave!" Sylvie immediately corrected once she caught on to what he was saying. Her cheeks heated in embarrassment. "I meant," she coughed, "as a practitioner with Silas in the Drowned Tower. To not be caught in the politics of the rest of the world. If Pernelia and Maurice never noticed you, you could've kept your abilities hidden. Was your suffering for the rest of the world—like this, in here—worth it?"

Thelarius didn't answer. Not really. Instead, the corners of his lips twitched upwards into a half-smile.

"Silas asked me the same thing once," he recalled fondly, "when he was tired of signing documents, tired of fighting, and of being criticized for decisions that need not have been so closely examined. He even corrected himself when I believed that he was referring to my time before all of this. As if the thought of me once being chained had never even crossed his mind. Those slip-ups... they remind me of him. *You* remind me of him. His genes are stronger than I thought or perhaps I'm simply seeing what I want to see."

"What you want to see?" Sylvie repeated.

"His spirit." Thelarius pointed at her. "It's chosen to reside in you. Silas has always been stubborn."

Before she could respond, there was another bang on the door. It was followed by a dozen footsteps and a blast of fire.

"They're melting my ice," Jack said.

Sylvie inclined her head. She angled it in such a way that she could just scarcely hear those on the other side. But their conversations cut to nothing after a stern reprimand by a man with a particularly guttural voice.

Her eyes met Jack's for the briefest of instances. He was already moving to the far right. Jack dragged his spire of ice with enough violence to risk its breaking.

"Syl," Jack called. He made a sharp, derisive noise in the

back of his throat. Solemn, but not quite urgent enough to be considered a warning. A plea to move then. "Get ready."

Sylvie placed the journal by Thelarius' feet, along with the Heartstone that contained *her*, before facing the door without an ounce of hesitation.

"How seriously do you think they take their oaths?" Jack asked. "Because it sounds to me like they plan on striking first."

"*You* struck first, Jack."

The door slammed open just as the words left her lips.

Two guards muscled their way forward. They carried hefty tower shields with enchantments all across their metal surface, symbols meant to redirect certain elements. Behind them, the once empty room was now full to bursting, the clamor of their outrage spilled into the air like a rush of water over a broken dam. Sylvie recognized a few of the faces. Did they really send some of the younger scholars from the lower annals? They were livid, but anger didn't make up for experience or skill. She wondered just how well they'd be able to fare… or perhaps they were only here to confirm their identities. Yes, that seemed more likely.

Sylvie trained her eyes on a particularly scrawny Conjurer with thick spectacles and a quivering lip. He wrung his hands in front of him when he realized that she was staring. He'd make a good hostage.

There was a brief moment of pause, where everyone just stared at them, as if shocked that they hadn't attempted to blast them with magic when they entered. Frankly, Sylvie was as well. She expected Jack to unleash a barrage of hoarfrost, not stand there with his lips twisted into an annoyed grimace and his hands doing—*nothing.* But it wasn't long before the group gathered their wits and charged. No questions. No threats. No useless attempts at getting them to surrender. They simply raised weapons and hands alike to cow them into submission.

Practitioners rushed in. Despite the frenzy, Jack and Sylvie held their ground, too used to this already. Besides, there was nothing to fear here. Thelarius was at their backs, albeit locked away and invisible to his own worshippers, but he was still there.

There was something about knowing for certain that a living god was watching over them that made them stand straighter.

Sylvie met Jack's gaze, and with a meaningful point at the walls, grinned when he nodded his head.

***

Personally, Jack was pleased that they'd come.

They were infinitely more efficient at destroying the walls than he could ever hope to be. Magic erupted around them. Controlled chaos that damaged, but never truly broke. It seemed even they were wary of the unspoken consequences that came with tearing apart a temple as precious as this. Sharp pebbles scraped against the enchantments, followed by storms of ice that left marks deep enough to cut off the flow of magic that stemmed from a place none of them knew. Fire was generally avoided, evident by those few that used weapons instead of magic. Jack pegged it on some misguided belief that a higher temperature would negatively affect the crystal.

From the corner of his eye, he watched as Sylvie dodged the tip of a practitioner's sword. It shrieked across the floor, dragging a vicious line into the pristine stone. She twisted sideward, almost stumbling, before dropping a heated hand on the swordsman's shoulder. It was so hot that Jack heard the sizzle of flesh a good four meters away.

He didn't have time to keep an eye on her, too busy with his own mob of furious brothers. So, he yelled a brief— *"Have it under control?"*—instead. Jack cracked a smile when she snarled out an answer.

Crabby, Jack thought. He wasn't worried. The crystal around Thelarius was breaking more and more. Soon, he'd be free… and they'd be, too.

Jack huffed, as he placed his hands upon the nearest wall. He froze half of it in a flash of blinding white. Jack made certain to time it just as Sylvie released a long line of fire that rose from floor to ceiling. Practitioners all around them gaped at the partition of dense heat, barely able to run back as it leapt towards them. It forced more than half a dozen straight into Jack's ice. His magic latched onto them, spreading over their torsos like an arctic web, before they could move away from Sylvie's flames.

Their screams rang in the open air. The sudden display of power made the group around them falter because, for an instant, their attacks ceased. But when a young boy, barely sixteen, charged with his chest puffed and his mouth opened in an ear-piercing cry, they moved to back him.

The boy didn't last long. Their bolstered fury, however, was another matter entirely. Threats rang in the open air. Jack zeroed in on a man that screamed something vulgar about his mother. While he didn't go after him—far as he was—he did feel a twisted sense of satisfaction when the man was accidentally bludgeoned on the side of the head by his own clumsy comrade.

Crack!

Jack swiveled to his left, where a deep fissure had finally formed on the crystal's surface. Flaws spider-webbed out from the center. White and gleaning. Inside, Thelarius regarded the newfound imperfection with a face carved from stone. Jack would've handed over his pack—money, belongings, and all—to know what Thelarius was thinking at that moment. After being held captive by that sorry sparkler for so long, it couldn't be anything pleasant.

He turned just in time to see Sylvie grab a discarded blade from the ground. She fueled the enchanted weapon with magic, before striding up to the crystal. Her march was purposeful; her gaze unwavering. Jack knew what she was going to do. So, he lingered behind and stood at her back, prepared to block anyone that sought to stop her.

Sylvie exchanged a quiet word with Thelarius that he wasn't close enough to hear, before she closed her eyes and squared her shoulders. He knew her well enough by now to know what she was doing. Sylvie was counting—*one, two, three*—waiting for her pulse to slow to something less than racing.

She raised the blade.

The tendrils beyond the surface swirled in excitement. Sylvie took one last breath, and then brought the iron edge over her head down with every shred of strength she had. The blade broke off, flying in wide spirals over their heads to clang against the ceiling with a shrill, hollow shriek. The hilt followed, forgotten, as Sylvie dropped it to the ground.

Jack looked on. It was so simple that it astonished him how easy it was. Her blow was enough to make the crystal crack and for fresh air to grace its insides since the Oak Age.

One blow.

It cost them nothing but a moment, and finally, *finally*—

Wind whistled from the slit on the crystal's surface. The practitioners around them gasped in apprehension. They took a collective step back when dark tendrils rose high and menacing above them. Mist darker than coal formed, encompassing everything they knew. A physical manifestation of power twisted by the unknown. It tainted the air like a swarm of locusts.

"You've saved me," a voice cut through the haze. "Allow me to return the favor."

Jack and Sylvie looked up to find Thelarius standing there, glowing silver-white and divine. His arms were spread wide. The darkness bounced around him, as if made for him—and him, alone. There was a purr in the air. Voices chanted his name. Beyond that, deeper, was a willowy figure in the strands. A woman that Jack hadn't seen since the Drowned Tower's fall. She was beautiful beyond compare. Her features emerged, smoky and restless. She appeared behind Thelarius to swathe him in an embrace that far surpassed the banal descriptions of intimacy.

There were shocked cries all around the room.

Jack drew his eyes away for a second to find that the rest of the practitioners had dropped to their knees in sudden veneration, praying as if they'd prepared for this day their entire lives. Perhaps they had. Those wisps that had caused him such pain time and time again wrapped lovingly around him and Sylvie in gratitude. A satiated beast returned home. He couldn't make out the whispers in his ears. They were too fast and too numerous to count. A muddled mix of apologies, thanks, and sentences in different tongues. For once, his head didn't throb.

"You owe us nothing," Sylvie said. She splayed her fingers as far as they could go, letting *her* bleed between the gaps. "We wouldn't be here if it wasn't for *her*—for you. Rest assured that we're going to go to the Diamond Alps and turn it into what you and Silas meant it to be. A place for harmony, where the Demar Spell is used for protection and not restriction. Where men aren't sacrificed for power. Don't check on us once you leave. Not yet. Because you'd be sickened if you saw what the Institute has become."

There was a beat of silence.

"You're young." Thelarius placed his hands on Sylvie's shoulders. "Yet you say you want to fulfill our dreams. An admirable aspiration, but those are the dreams of men long pronounced dead. They're the ideals of youths from ages past. Would you really be willing to risk your lives for them?"

"We already have," Jack cut in. He ambled forward until he stood beside Sylvie. "I decided a long time ago that I'd change my world, and using the Demar Spell for its intended purpose is a start."

"If its glory you seek, then don't bother," Thelarius assumed. His face turned graver by the second. "For it's found only amidst valleys of blood and gore, atop piles of hardship made slick from the rotting bodies of men and women exactly like you. I've met hundreds of practitioners that placed excessive weight on labels like Elder, Master... *Mentalist*."

There was enough black-bottled hate in that word to make anyone falter. Thelarius carried on.

"I bore witness to lives being formed and guided by those words. Do you want to be caught in that? You'd be little better than those practitioners that spent their youths sharpening their claws, only to find that they'd been useless all along. Because no amount of gold is worth the night terrors that comes from fighting for a cause that isn't yours. No title is worth the disgust or the red that never seems to fade from your hands." Thelarius' face hardened. "Go home or seek one out. The path you're on can't be called a life."

"Did the tendrils clog your ears?" Jack sneered, sudden enough to give Thelarius pause. Sylvie grabbed his wrist to distract him so that he wouldn't run his mouth.

"This is still the path I've chosen. The one *we've* chosen," Sylvie answered properly. "We're perfectly content to be right in the middle of everything."

"Then you are fools," Thelarius stated. "Small, reckless fools. But... I don't hate that. You two remind me of myself when I was young. So, I'll hope for your well-being instead. Keep in mind, however, that it's only the living that know victory."

Thelarius eyed them both. He hardly thought his opinion mattered, even more so now that he was preparing to leave this plane, but their eyes were so bright, and they looked at him as if he could give them the secrets to existence itself. He couldn't disappoint them. Thelarius watched them glance at each other, one disapproving, the other defiant. Beyond that, he saw focused gazes that lingered and fists that clenched in protectiveness.

They were on equal footing then.

Good, he thought.

Silas taught him many things. One of them was that, sometimes, it was better to be beside someone and not behind them. They cared for each other; it was evident in their eyes. That was all he needed to see to know that they'd be okay.

"I've made my companions wait," Thelarius announced. "It's about time I go to them. Thank you. Thank you isn't enough. Leave now. This temple won't be here for long."

They looked up at that.

"What are you going to do?" Sylvie asked at the same time Jack said, "It's going to crumble, isn't it?"

"I've wanted to burn this temple down since it was erected. Today, that dream will be realized." Thelarius smiled wistfully. "Allow me to bestow upon the two of you this final gift. It was the first, and today, it will become the last. It is the true piece. Any others are mere mimics. Even the one you've had in your keeping was merely a second-rate vessel. This will keep *her* powers rooted to both of you until your eventual passing. Watch over *her* in my place."

"What is *she*?" Jack asked, unable to help himself.

"A being that was lost in the darkness. One that awoke to find an endless expanse of loneliness. Since you have those eyes, I'm sure you were taught that magic is a gift limited to those with the ability to harness its power. That is only a partial truth. Magic exists in the air we breathe and the ground we tread upon. Channels upon channels of untapped potential can be expelled in a single breath. But there exist a select few able to concentrate it and turn it into something more—those once led by the Creator, those that passed circuits on to us, the temporal keepers of this realm, so that they might endure infinity in slumber."

"You mean," Sylvie paused, stunned, "the old gods?"

Thelarius didn't answer. He only grabbed the thick chain around his neck and showed them the dangling black mass coiled within the amulet at the end. The same mist was there, but far more condensed than the Heartstone where *she*'d been stored. He placed it in Sylvie's open palm, along with Silas' journal and the broken remnants of the stone they'd kept for so long in their keeping. It was nothing more than useless shards now.

"Stand tall and lead the coming era," Thelarius said, soft and strong all at once. He piled their hands on top of one another, so the belongings were crammed between them. "Together."

They looked at each other. A faint lullaby grew louder in the room, and then—

Brilliance.

30

Jack couldn't see.

Someone grabbed his arm—Sylvie, he realized, shaking his head desperately in a futile attempt to clear it—slung it over her shoulder and dragged him in an unknown direction. Her face was a muddled mess of smeared blood and dirt. She had an angry bruise blossoming under one eye. When did she get that? Her voice sounded distant and frantic, despite their proximity. Before he knew it, the floor pitched dangerously beneath his feet.

How far, he meant to ask only for it to come out slurred.

"Come on," she said severely. Her fingers blazed hot on the back of his skull, igniting a throbbing agony that made him huff.

"Syl," he managed to wheeze.

She pinched the back of his neck, intense and piercing from the remnants of her magic, and for a moment, the world solidified again, sharpening into the bright, red-burnt horizons above the infinite sea. The acrid scent of smoke and salt hung around him. Bones shattered like glass somewhere nearby, flesh burned, and a man screamed.

Wait, Syl! No! Jack wanted to say through the dim fog. His vision came in sporadic bursts, but he was certain that wherever she was, wherever she was leading him, it was *wrong.*

Dangerous! His mind shouted the warning in his ears like he didn't know that already. *Three steps. Half a dozen more. But we're already five steps too far. She's headed towards the...*

Suddenly, the window's edge.

He wanted to back away, but the room behind them was

currently being taken over by hellfire as Thelarius' figure glowed bright and god-like. They were so close that Jack could *feel* the air ripple from the heat he emitted. Beads of sweat trailed down his back uncomfortably, making him feel stickier than he already was. He needed to get away. *They* needed to get away. But not here. Through the stairs, through that large door he remembered icing, anywhere but the godforsaken window.

There was no way they'd survive the fall, and even if they did, the ground would surely kill them. They were too far from the island's border to even hope to tumble into the water. Even then, there'd be no guarantee that they'd survive a dive from this height. Jack doubted he'd be able to resurface. His mind was still foggy, his senses as dull as the blunt edges of an herbivore's teeth. Jack only remembered pieces of what happened. Fragments that blurred together and echoed too loudly for him to piece together.

Shattered plates, he likened, struggling to stitch his thoughts into something coherent. Jack recalled Thelarius piling their hands on top of one another. Sylvie's small and warm and *right* in his own. Jack had looked at her for the briefest of moments, before white dominated his vision.

Thelarius burned before them. A god willfully falling to his demise. Heat siphoned all of the air from the room, then spread outwards to boil marble and man alike. *Her* tendrils framed them both, protecting them from the onslaught of ceaseless power. It was enough to make him choke on his own breath. He couldn't breathe. He didn't want to breathe. Thelarius' magic was simply too much to face, let alone take in. Jack bowed his head in unconscious surrender, trying to make Thelarius stop. Sylvie pulled him towards her, shouting reassurances like a prayer. The amulet in their shared hands glowed, red-hot and sweltering, and then—

Pain.

It was always pain.

The familiar pounding behind his eyes was never welcome, but it was especially uncomfortable then. He staggered from the ache that emerged from his gut, spiraling out of control and extending until every part of him felt branded. A singe that settled deep in his marrow. Jack gasped for breath, feeling electric pinpricks spear all across his chest. They centered on his heart. An intense zap of something spindly and thick shocked him, before clutching his insides with a tightness that bordered on deadly. It wrapped around every part of him. His throat, his lungs, even the muscles that made up his limbs. For one insane instant, he could feel every individual fiber throb, before his body hissed in reaction. Sylvie held him tighter, despite the steam that escaped his pores, as if he'd just summoned a ball of flame.

His senses flared, then eased. Jack's body hurt, but more distantly now. Pain easing for no apparent reason was never a good sign. Jack couldn't afford to fall unconscious now.

A gift, she whispered in his ears.

Jack bit his tongue to keep from cursing *her* back to Thelarius' side. There was another whisper from a different voice. Sylvie's. Far lower and more distant than he ever wanted it to be. It was hard to pick apart sounds when chaos swelled around them like blots of ink. But Jack knew what a tightened grip meant—worry, fear, desperation—Sylvie pulled his arm farther across her shoulders, straightening him out in the worst way possible.

His side ached with the sudden jerk, and although he knew it was unintentional, that didn't stop him from biting out a booming expletive. He would've given a more coherent complaint if given the chance. But not a second later and they were *flung* from the room into the waiting sea by a coil of heavier air. Like a shipwreck, they dropped from security and straight into something malevolent and bottomless. Jack screwed his eyes shut, unsure if a scream managed to escape his throat, but it felt raw and he could feel the bile rising, so it likely had.

They fell.

Wind howled in his ears. The impact of the water made Jack lose his train of thought. Everything was replaced by—*cold*. The Jade Sea was freezing and bitter. Its waters, strangely thick. He struggled to hold the small breath he had, keeping his mouth and his eyes shut amidst the undercurrent.

If he thought that standing before Thelarius was bad, then this was a different league entirely. His arms spread out in wide arcs, trying to find something to hold onto. Every second stretched into eternity as he fumbled in the vast emptiness, willing himself to not sink more than he already had. He didn't want to die. Not like this.

He jerked when something solid and forceful grabbed a fistful of cloth and skin alike. Harsh digits dug into the spaces between his ribs. Jack reached out, holding on with as much strength as he could muster. He found purchase in the shape of a forearm. Thin and slick. Hard to grasp. Harder to see. His eyes opened, only to shut again when all he saw was black and the bubbling blur of an inferno.

Flames under water.

He was going insane.

Jack reeled back out of instinct when the hand attempted to pull him upward. But he stopped resisting as soon as he realized where up meant: the surface. It wasn't long before his head broke it. He gasped for air, then choked from the sheer amount of it. Jack was barely able to see through the rivulets of stinging salt water that fell down his eyelids. A voice rang in his ears. Urgent, yet soothing. It told him what to do.

Breathe, Jack. Stay with me.

Relax your legs, spread your arms.

No, you… like this… there we go.

Just like that. You're doing great.

Breathe.

He waded his arms through the waves, but even that was a chore. There was nothing solid in sea foam for him to embrace. So, he reached out and grasped Sylvie with enough force to shatter a boulder. She gasped, caught between wanting him to let go and wanting to draw him closer, so he wouldn't slip and drown. Jack opened his mouth to speak. He needed to warn her about the pain he felt and his bending vision—to no avail. If he managed to get a word out, then he didn't recall it. Jack tried to retain his senses, tried to move his legs and keep his eyes open for longer than a second, but, entirely against his will, the world turned spotty once again.

Jack fought against it. He did. Jack didn't want to leave her out here like this. He didn't want to be a burden. They needed to work together to get out of this mess just like they'd been doing for the last few months.

… But the caw of birds echoing above them was so soothing. A stark contrast to the noisy flames that consumed everything in their path. Sound seemed to bend as the seconds ticked on. Moments winded into something long and endless. There were no more pale streaks of light out now. Only the blackening sky and clouds of midnight smoke. The stars were gone.

Sylvie screamed his name.

It was a relief when his vision finally faded.

***

Partner,

You better be prepared for a good scrape once I see you again. While I didn't expect you to trumpet your departure around the Grove, a goodbye would've been nice. Instead, I had to find out that you left from that stupid letter with the rest of those seconds.

You're always busy with your own piffle, so it's not like that's anything new. But I have to admit, it's… strange not being the one by your side to help you through it. Next time, I'd appreciate a heads-up (or an offer to tag along. I might not accept, but it's the damned thought that counts.) I dropped pots of paint over Masters' heads for you for years to help you sneak away. The least you could do is give me a shout-out, before you go gallivanting into Creator-knows-where.

Pernelia, I want to hit you.

But speaking of maybe not accepting things I normally would have, Myrrh called me 'wilted' today—as if that intolerable midget has any right to speak to me about not standing quite as tall as I used to. But funnily enough, I... don't disagree with her. I'm just not as enthusiastic about tempting the Creator anymore, and I'm not afraid to admit that. I'm already down a few fingers, good sleep, and a lot of muscle. It's lost its appeal, I suppose.

Still, watch yourself out there, Jack. (Please.)

I'm not so rich with my friends that I can risk losing a few. The world's a dangerous place, and whether you know it or not, you can be a perfect fool sometimes. Sylvie will agree with me, I'm sure.

In other news, I'll be heading to the Diamond Alps with Cera and a few others. Dalis and Philip, I think. Maybe Lyss. The Grove is preparing a group of their finest to go up there and hammer out a few agreements that I don't really know all that much about, but they're willing to let me come along. I've never seen the Alps, so I think it'll be good for me. If you're interested, I'm sure Dalis can tell you more.

I hope this reaches you before we arrive.
Until then,
Tiv

***

"Jack!" Sylvie shouted.

A bolt of fear shot down her spine when he didn't respond. She tried again, a third time, and then a fourth, but he was limp and sinking. She couldn't hold him up any longer. His hair was matted to his face, deathly pale, as always. She couldn't tell if he was getting better or worse, but his skin was cold and that was never a good sign. Her eyes drifted above her to where Thelarius' temple raged. Stray pieces of wood and furniture exploded from within to fall into the waters beside them. One had come dangerously close to hitting them. If she hadn't ducked their heads underwater in time, then it would have.

She needed to get away.

Sylvie looked frantically around her. Surely there must've been a strip of land somewhere. Something low and small that she'd be able to haul Jack onto, so they could wait until he was well enough to ice a path for them. Her head bobbed up and down the water's surface. She took deep breaths and spread her arms as wide as possible with Jack currently leaning his full weight on her. He was heavier than he looked. Every second made them sink a little deeper. Sylvie wouldn't be able to accommodate both of them for long.

She wasn't going to die here. *She wasn't.*

"Neither are you," she swore.

Then, like an answer to her plea, she saw it. A ravaged strip of land that led into a cavern with a rocky mouth. It looked like the beginning of a secret passage, but she couldn't be certain. It was too dark to tell much of anything right now. She could just barely make out the water as it swirled around it. Tiny whirlpools that circled the gravelly contours. She'd seen the same thing at the Wymeran River. Water always orbited what it couldn't break. It was enough for Sylvie to deduce that the land there was sturdy enough for her to haul Jack onto and rocky enough for her to hold. Absolutely perfect.

It was far, but it was there. Oh, sweet Pernelia, it was there. Alone, the swim might take her a quarter of an hour.

With Jack, however...

Sylvie searched the murky waters for something usable. Anything that could float. She found it in the form of a wide strip of half-burnt timber that nodded dangerously with each passing wave. She thanked the Creator in her mind only because that sorry piece was infinitely more precious than nothing. Sylvie grabbed it as soon as it drifted within arm's reach. It was a soggy thing, but thick enough for her to shift a good portion of Jack's weight onto. She could only pray that he wouldn't fall; that the tattered strip wouldn't split apart halfway and kill them both.

Carefully, she kicked her legs. Sylvie placed all of her focus on making sure Jack didn't slide straight into the Jade Sea's depths. There was no room for mindless worries now. The errant pellets of furniture that blew out into the sky hardly bothered her.

Some landed close enough to rock them back a few feet. The water bubbled as the charred objects broke the surface, hissing like a cat doused in the rain. But cats didn't let out steam, and the hot moisture from the furniture blinded her almost as much as the evening breeze—cold, biting, and filled with salt. It was an added displeasure. One she very much wanted to just blow away. Not for the first time, she envied the power of Elementalists and other Conjurers.

Four times, Sylvie had to stop, exhausted both physically and mentally. The fear of drowning weighed on her mind. Thankfully, the tide was on her side. Every time it rose, it pushed her farther away from the wreckage and closer to where she wanted to go.

It's the little things, she thought, distractedly placing a hand on Jack's cheek to check his temperature. It was dropping. No surprise there. She needed to hurry.

Picking up the pace, Sylvie focused on getting them to safety. It was a long time before she got to the rocky outcropping, but when she did, she swam to the least jagged protrusion she could find and abandoned the splitting timber. Sylvie hauled Jack up by his armpits. As soon as half of his body left the water, she felt the full weight of his unconscious form. It threatened to sink them both. Planting her feet into underwater ledges along the side of the ground, she used her legs to propel him the rest of the way. His shoulder and hip roughly collided with the rocks. Sylvie panicked when his head hit the ground with a loud thud, but relaxed soon after when she saw his chest move up and down.

Steady. His breathing was steady, and he was...

Safe. She heaved a sigh of relief. Barring a few scratches and a bump on his head, he was okay. That was all she could ask for. *Okay, my turn.* Sylvie snuck her fingers between small gaps in the rocks. *One, two...*

Her fingers slipped a few times, numb as they were, but she was able to crawl her way up. Then, in a mess of tired limbs and wheezing breaths, she collapsed on her back beside him. She grasped the empty space around her neck out of instinct. The lack of pulsing there made her eyes open wide in alarm for one, mindless second, before she settled back in realization.

Sylvie craned her neck, so she could see the burning temple. She stared, entranced by such a great pillar of fire. It was collapsing in on itself now. The stone golems that Jack had spoken so ardently about must've been playful fairytales because there they were, dead and motionless, despite the marble columns falling over them like saplings in a storm. The fire spread to the fields across the rest of the island, laying waste to the lush gardens and painstakingly sewed crops.

Thelarius' flames were as powerful as would be expected from the leader of the First Zenith. They'd soon turn everything on that island into ash, if they hadn't already. It wouldn't be long, however, before they were forced to stop from a lack of kindling. Then again, this was Thelarius. For all she knew, his flames would continue on until the entire island melted straight into the ocean. It certainly wasn't beyond the realm of possibility.

As she laid there, trying to muster the energy to sit up, Sylvie realized that she could no longer hear the brothers shouting for help or the fire eating up all of the oxygen in the atmosphere. She only heard the water; the birds flying in great circles above her; and Jack's unsteady breathing. Even closer, a whisper in the wind. Content. Grateful.

Sylvie swore something caressed her cheeks. She screwed her eyes tight, utterly spellbound.

I've found what I sought.

Her eyes snapped open.

Have you?

Sylvie rubbed her ears. They were tingling. Almost itchy. She was hearing things—or so she hoped. The Heartstone wasn't with them anymore, but Thelarius *had* given them something else in its place.

That amulet… Her thoughts came in sluggish bursts that were interspersed with long moments of nothingness. It was getting harder to focus. *Where is it?*

Sylvie twisted until she was facing Jack. She inspected him. His right temple oozed blood. He had a few more minor scrapes from the fight in Thelarius' temple. Nothing life threatening. But he was shivering now.

Fantastic, she thought bitterly. *Now what?*

"Shit," Sylvie cursed, as she inspected her belongings. Silas' journal was ruined. She'd carelessly stuffed it into an inner pocket inside of her robes, along with the broken shards of the Heartstone. The entire thing was cut in various places *and* folded at a strange angle. Even worse, it was soggy. The words, illegible. It was a sorry sight. She could practically hear the hearts of every scholar across Ferus Terria breaking. "I doubt this is reparable. Maybe if I dried it?"

She put it back inside of her pocket for now.

Sylvie eyed the cavern she'd seen in the distance. It was dark and seemed to be lined with… ice? She couldn't tell if it led into a deeper path. Sylvie didn't want to bring Jack there. She also didn't want to push herself more than she already had by using magic to warm them up. But Sylvie knew that in a few hours the open land they were on now would be worse. In her current state, her flames would be little better than a flickering candle in the face of the midnight breeze. Sylvie prayed that no other stranded creature had taken residence inside, and if one had, then she hoped it wasn't vicious. She didn't think she could handle it.

But first...

She scooted up to Jack and gently took his arm. His hand was shut in a limp fist. The chain of Thelarius' necklace was knotted all around his forearm.

When did he do that? Not that it mattered. She pried his fingers open all the same, prepared to claim their memento and tuck it somewhere safe until they were both ready to evaluate just what exactly they had in their possession.

Sylvie paused when all she saw was an empty chain.

Did he drop it?

Upon closer inspection, she saw a mark on his hand. Sun-shaped and ashy. As if Silas' emblem had been scorched right in the center of his palm. She traced the edges. They were too pointy. The rays of light were thin and curved. There were no extra lines to depict fire.

Not Silas, she decided. *Too plain. It looks more like the Institute's. The Zenith Council's then? No, that wouldn't make any sense.*

Sylvie drew nearer, so she could use both of her hands to properly splay his own. Hers were, unsurprisingly, smaller in comparison. Cleaner, too, she would've thought. But once she flipped her left hand up, she was proven wrong. Terribly wrong.

Her eyes widened when she saw the very same mark.

What happened next was done purely out of reflex. Sylvie called upon her magic, hoping to singe the dirt off of her into nothing. Her veins lit up, followed by her skin. There was a spark. Red and orange flashed. And then...

Nothing.

"What—"

The sentence ended in a startled shout as her hand erupted with fire beyond her control. She tried in vain to calm it. Between moving away from Jack to keep him safe and her utter panic, she looked down to find that his hand was glowing, too. More important, however, was the way it flared in response.

Sylvie almost fell back into the water when his hand ignited.

***

Ashy spirits, Sylvie!

Horrors on you, your title, your Institute, and your future. I'm going to spew curses on any lands you might own, crops you might sew, even your descendants' fortunes—all of it! Do you know how many bones I rattled trying to find you this morning? I was ready to storm the Zenith Council's headquarters!

What if I suddenly decide to run off of some high cliff for some personal vendetta and give absolutely no notice to anyone about my whereabouts? I know you'd be cursing me to the Zexin abyss and back, maybe even marching out of the door to haul me back to beat some sense into me. I don't care that this situation is different, and I know you're not marching off to your death, but... [A string of blotted profanities and illegible words follow.]

Do you have any idea how long I spent searching for you, yet you couldn't even leave me my own flaming note? Weren't you supposed to be the decent one out of the two of us? Pray our great ancestor keeps you under his wing because if you come back with so much as a scratch I'm going to make you run laps—laps— around the Grove until you've learned your lesson. If you thought father's drills were hard, then you haven't seen anything yet.

And father! Oh, please tell me you sent him a letter. Please.

Thelarius' stars... I don't want to go to the Alps anymore. I'm going to ask Master Rhone if I can sit this one out. I doubt he'll let me, but it's worth a shot. I blame you for this!

Stay safe. For both our sakes.

Dalis

***

Jack's head *hurt*.

And that voice wasn't helping.

"Wake up, you bleeding heartache!" the voice yelled, close enough to deafen him. It was agonizingly familiar. Jack tried his best to put a face to it. "Wake up!"

He groaned. Jack couldn't muster the will to move. Every muscle in his body felt as if it had been pushed past its limits. His clothes were drenched in... something. It couldn't be sweat. There was far too much. Whatever he was laying on was too hard. Even the room was too cool. Too. Too. Too. He couldn't properly express how much he hated it.

Jack's face contorted into a grimace. He searched blindly for a blanket, but finding one was harder than he expected. He could barely extend his arm without a spike of pain shooting up the limb and making the rest of his body ache in protest.

"Jack!" That cursed voice again. The one he so adored. "Why

must you choose now of all times to sleep like the godforsaken dead? You need to get up. *Now!*"

Creator, free him.

Couldn't he have one moment of peace?

Then, as if the world wanted to spite him for simply existing, he felt a blow to his stomach. Just below the ribs, where he was most tender. His eyes snapped open. Half a dozen curses flew from his lips, while more danced along the tip of his tongue. Before any more could escape, a familiar set of hands cradled his face and he was forced to look at their owner. Two pairs of eyes met in a clash of red and orange that put the setting sun to shame.

Sylvie stared at him. The lines on her face were more severe than he was used to. Her grip made his headache so much worse, and the place where her right hand framed his cheek stung. Was he bleeding somewhere? Now that he thought about it, he did taste the iron tang of gore in his mouth. He'd definitely suffered a few injuries. Jack hoped she packed a few pain relieving tonics or, at the very least, the ingredients to brew one. He didn't want to limp *and* battle a migraine all the way to the Alps.

From his periphery, he saw the tall black husk of Thelarius' temple. Thick clouds of smoke rose from somewhere he couldn't see, fueling the toxic haze above them. That meant a part of the island was still burning, so he couldn't have been sleeping for long. Jack opened his mouth to ask her what in the world she was doing jostling him, but she beat him to the punch.

In the poorest attempt at evenness possible, she said, "Your hand is on fire."

Jack blinked. Deliberate. Owlish. He pursed his lips in a noiseless request for her to repeat herself because surely he'd misheard. *Surely.*

"Your hand," she echoed, slowly losing her cool with each word, "is on fire."

His eyes travelled down, uncomprehending, until he saw the great torch that encompassed his right hand from fingertip to wrist. As soon as he registered the fire, his arm lit up to his elbow.

"What the—" Jack shouted. He extended his arm as far as it could go and moved his torso back, as if he could actually get away from his own rebellious arm. He swore Silas was trying to kill him. Jack didn't know why, but he had no other explanation for this.

His stirring emotions seemed to act as a kindle because not a moment later, the flames travelled up to his collar. Jack gasped. He shook his arm like a madman. Everything he was taught about dropping and rolling was promptly shoved off of the nearest cliff because all he could think about now was how bright the flames were and how unbearably hot they made him.

"What are you doing?" Sylvie shrieked, scooting away.

"My hand's on fire, Syl!" Jack yelled. He was so stunned that he didn't even notice just how oddly high-pitched his voice sounded. "*Why* is my hand on *f—no how* is my hand on fire?"

"Put it out!"

"What do you mean put it out? How do I—"

"It's magic, you spoon!"

His eyes widened in realization. Jack harshly shook his head. Of course it was. What else could it be? If he had just focused for a moment, he would've felt the power leaking from his veins like an open faucet. Jack closed his eyes and concentrated on controlling it. Slow, just like he was taught growing up.

Wind it down, he recalled in his father's encouraging tone. *Steady, Jacques. I know it's frustrating, but you can't be impatient now. You don't want to smother the flames too quickly. Your mother will string me up by my ears if you pinch another nerve.*

Slowly. Take your time… good.

Remember, this isn't like blowing out a candle. You want to control it like we do with the hearth. Douse it as close to your skin as possible… that's it. Now, imagine fresh dressings. Wrapped careful, but firm all around you. None of that green ointment though. That's foul. Oh, there we go. You're getting it. Find a long strip of mental tape to hold those bindings in place. You want just the right amount of tightness.

… Perfect.

When Jack opened his eyes again, the flames were gone. He was tempted to undo his handiwork just to see if his hand would ignite again, but he stopped himself, not wanting to be the reason for Sylvie going into hysterics. He flexed his fingers instead. His palm tingled. Everything from wrist to shoulder felt heated in a way that he was no longer used to.

Jack raised his eyebrows in shock when he saw the dark mark that blemished his otherwise ghostly skin. It stood out like a patch of wildflowers among a field of weeds. He inspected it with the curiosity of a child that had just found a new toy.

"What is this?" Jack asked.

"I don't know." Sylvie held up her left palm for him to see. "But I have it, too."

Jack squinted at her mark, before looking back down at his own. They were definitely identical. He didn't trust any symbol that looked like the Zenith Council's, more so if they mysteriously appeared on his person after an encounter with a god he thought long-dead. That was just common sense. But... he had conjured fire, hadn't he? He'd been sleeping, but those flames definitely came from him. They were now being actively suppressed by him, too. He didn't want to hope. Jack didn't fancy himself that daring.

Still...

Jack called upon the magic sleeping beneath his skin.

Something less dangerous, he decided. *Less frightening.*

Dirt poured from his hand.

Jack's jaw slackened in disbelief as piles and piles came spurting out. He didn't care about how it mixed with the water in his clothes, muddying them; didn't care that he'd conjured enough to bury his legs. The only thing that mattered now was that a different element, the element he *chose*, leapt from his hands. He looked at his left and tried to conjure wind. His shoulders sagged when only ice appeared, but he wasn't disappointed for long because his powers were here—*with him.*

They were back where they belonged.

"Jack," Sylvie called, but he didn't seem to hear.

He was transfixed by his hand. Jack watched it come to life with the elements that he loved. Then, easier and more open than she'd ever seen, Jack smiled, absolutely delighted by the return of his magic.

"Syl," he said, almost choking on the word. "*Look.*"

"I see it." Sylvie smiled, as she reclaimed the lost distance.

They turned, shocked, when her left hand abruptly glowed. Then, as if mimicking his own, dirt gushed forth.

***

Jacques Dace,

*Do you **want** me to burn at the pyre?*

I want to claim that I never saw you, but you took that damned family emblem with you. Now, I have to go back to the Alps and stand before Leonas-flaming-Dace, arguably the most terrifying man in all of Ferus Terria, and give him my full report of everything that happened in the Grove.

*What exactly do you expect me to tell him? That you ran off into the wicked unknown, while I had my back turned? He's going to berate me for my negligence. **Me.***

You better watch yourself out there, Dace.

Dwyn

[Dozens of crude drawings of stick figures being decapitated and a shaded crab's claw bludgeoning a head litter the bottom of the page.]

Sylvie Sirx,

I'm not sour about it... not really. But a goodbye hug would've been nice. I know you're busy, but really, I think I deserve a proper farewell, considering everything we've been through over the years. Just know that I expect one the next time we run into each other, which I assume will be in the Alps. I'm heading back there to report to Elder Dace, though I'm not sure if I should return to the east first to assist my Master. Regardless, I'll see you when I see you.

Ethil said she'd prepare a bucket of Roco sauce just for you next time you two cross paths. She knows how to make her own extra-sweetened version of it that I'm sure you'll love. (Frankly, I don't know how you two can stomach it.) So, look forward to it. Ethil's inordinately proud of her concoction and she's even made a dozen jars for the children here.

I also wanted to say that I'm sorry for lying and keeping all of those things about myself secret for so long. It was part of the job description, but now that you know, I'll do my best to avoid it—lying, that is. I don't think I can avoid secret keeping.

I'd like to remain friends if you're okay with that. Ethil tells me I could use more of those. I'm not sure I believe her, but... I mourned Reed's loss, too. I don't want to forget the time we spent together.

Be careful, Syl.

Myrrh Amaurisse

✻✻✻

"How do I stop this?" Sylvie shouted, panicking for the hundredth time that day.

"How are you even doing that?" Jack yelled right back. "You're not an Elementalist!"

"Stop stating the flaming obvious, and help me!"

His lips twisted in a moment of petty anger, but he was quick to walk her through the steps just like his father had once done for him. The words were clumsy as they left his lips. Incorrect here and there, and with none of the same humorous delivery. He'd never had to teach someone how to control their magic before. Even he didn't consciously think about it at this point. Halfway through, he watched her mumble her own technique that must've been taught to her by Master Cephas. Funny, how a lesson learned a lifetime ago could still be useful now.

She had an easier time stopping the magic that leaked from her system, though he didn't expect anything less. She was more experienced at dealing with errant seeps than he could ever hope to be. It was only a matter of adjusting how much she wanted to suppress, and she'd always been good at regulating her powers. Sylvie's flames came in measured bursts. She had an effortless control that even he envied. It would be absurd to think that she wouldn't show the same talent when it came to stopping any of the other elements.

"Try using ice," Sylvie said.

Jack complied.

This time, they weren't dumbfounded when a thin layer of white frost crept up to her wrist. Instinct made Sylvie conjure fire to melt it. Jack raised an eyebrow when steam emerged from his own hand and a red-hot blaze ignited up to his elbow. His fire had always been wild, but this was different. This was far more overpowering. Irrepressible. Was this a Conjurer's power?

"Maybe it has something to do with proximity?" Jack speculated. "You were fine when you were near the ledge."

Sylvie's eyes narrowed. "Do you want me to fall?"

"You know what I mean."

She did, but that didn't mean she wanted to be anywhere near the water's edge. Nevertheless, Sylvie swallowed her complaints and backed up until her feet touched the land's slippery corner. It was a generous ten steps away. More than enough space... or so she hoped. Jack eyed her, checking to see if she was ready, before he flicked his thumb outwards. Sylvie flinched, as a tiny twister of wind appeared in his hand. Gray and cutting. She almost collapsed in relief when her own hand remained completely still.

"What's wrong?" Jack asked, extinguishing his magic in one smooth motion.

"What do you think?"

"You're part Elementalist, Syl." He grinned, exuberant. "Be proud. The esteemed Breaker of Chains gave us these powers."

"Didn't these powers come from *her*? That container might've been his, but I doubt that black mass was. Thelarius said it would keep *her* rooted to us. It must've been a sealing spell."

"Don't ruin this for me."

"You still have those tendrils in your eyes," she said. Her words were more damaging than a blow to the chest.

"I *just* said not to ruin this." Jack scrubbed his hand over his eyes, as if that might get rid of them. He purposefully met her gaze, so she could see the burning animosity in his own. But just as he was about to say something cutting in return, he stilled... and then smirked.

"What?" she asked. "Why are you looking at me like that?"

He pointed right at her nose. Her pupils zeroed in on the digit. Without any adornment, he said, "So do you."

She blinked for a second, letting the words sink in, before she backed away with enough urgency to make him throw his head back in laughter. Sylvie searched for something she could see her reflection against. But all she found were hazardous waves that moved too frequently to see much of anything.

"Don't believe me?" Jack asked, more smug than offended.

"No, I do, it's just..."

"I mean," he amended because the frown that tugged on her lips then made him twitch, "it doesn't look bad. We match."

"I don't know if that's a good thing."

"It's flaming excellent! Now, I don't have to suffer all of those eye questions alone. They get very old, very quickly. You'll see."

"Oh, wait," Sylvie said, solemn enough to startle him. "Didn't Thelarius say that the amulet would keep *her* fixed to us? *Us,* Jack. Judging by our eyes, that wasn't a lie. I assume *her* core disappeared with Thelarius, but if she isn't gone completely, then does that mean we've become substitute anchors in his place? Because If we haven't, then—"

"Every Elementalist across Ferus Terria lost their powers," Jack finished, catching on.

"We don't know that for certain," she said desperately.

"Yes, but even if they didn't, *her* being tied to us is problematic. *Lavyana kahs.* What was that isolated oaf thinking? What'll happen once we die? Chaos, that's what! Does he expect us to take care of this whole Elementalist-Nebbin dilemma before then? *Vaklas in an den*! Why must gods be so *demanding*? As if I have nothing better to do than fix their messes."

Jack ignored the fact that they were the ones that told Thelarius that they had every intention of going to the Alps and doing whatever was necessary to change the Institute into something better; something more like his and Silas' dream.

"We don't even know if we've become replacements yet," Sylvie said. Always the voice of reason. Her tone wasn't pacifying in any way. Only factual, and even a little irate, but Jack found comfort in it all the same.

"I hope we did," Jack said honestly. Because the alternative was a thousand times worse. "But there's two of us. How do you think that works? If one of us dies, do half of the Elementalists become ordinary people or do we die together?"

"I'm more concerned about someone finding out."

Jack's expression hardened. "You think someone will trap us like Maurice did to Thelarius?"

"It's not impossible."

He didn't answer. Because she was right. It wasn't. But he'd be damned if he let the threat of confinement stand in his way. They'd have to be careful about what they divulged from here on out, which wasn't anything new, but this called for a different kind of secret-keeping. This was no longer about returning a wayward soul to another, and it certainly wasn't a situation that could be easily related to a sibling or an old friend. Personal relationships meant nothing in the face of something that had the power to affect the entirety of Ferus Terria.

If they didn't announce what they knew at the right time and in the proper setting, then they'd make a lot of enemies. More than they could handle. It would be best to figure out what was happening in the Alps and amass supporters, before making any bold declarations.

Patience, it seemed, was the key to everything.

He wished he had more of it.

Jack surveyed their surroundings. His gaze settled on a cavern a short distance away. He sighed, exhausted from the mere act of breathing. Now that the initial shock of his restored powers had died, the insane throbbing on his entire right side became a lot more noticeable. Suddenly, it was very important that he lay down.

Sylvie needed to brew the most potent pain-reliever possible because he swore he could feel his blood gushing through his veins. Thick and fast. At this point, only a borderline lethal potion would do. Anything for some blessed relief.

"Let's rest there for now," Jack said after a lengthy silence. He even pointed at the cavern for emphasis. "My head hurts."

Whatever protest Sylvie had died in her throat once those three words left his mouth. Jack couldn't quite contain his shock when she stared daggers into a nearby rock with a small red stain along one of its sharper edges. Well, that explained a lot. Now he knew why he felt like someone had slammed him against a wall.

"Don't tell me *you're* the reason for my splitting headache," Jack accused, before tacking on a distressed, "please."

"I'm not."

"*Filan vahs*," he swore. "It hurts more knowing you're lying."

"I saved you from drowning," she abruptly defended, confirming his suspicions. He couldn't fault her for that.

Jack settled for running his hands through his hair instead. Sylvie smiled at him. It was fond and much too warm for his liking. Jack doubted he got his annoyance across, but it was hard to when all he could think about was how much he appreciated the fact that he was still there with her to express it.

"How am I supposed to argue against that?" Jack muttered under his breath, before he tugged her forward. "Let's go."

***

Jack an' Syl,

I didn't doubt for one second that you two'd be up on yer feet an' gone before any of us even knew what happened. I was jugglin' when I heard the news. Pom threw some things at me an' that ended up happenin'. Don't know how exactly. You can blame my stunnin' reflexes, I s'pose. Wish you two coulda seen the show, but I'm sure elopin' must take a lot outta people.

(Dalis is glarin' at me while I'm writin' this. Well, hard-eyes and death's wishes ta you, too, strangely buff Healer... I mean, how is that even fair? Healers shouldn't 'ave bodies like that.)

Anyway, if you two really did set out ta wed behind our collective backs, consider adoptin' me, yea? Pom, too. We're a set, so you'll have ta take us both. Don't worry though, we've got a lot ta offer! I'm pretty decent at house chores if I do say so myself. An' Pom's wicked with a pot an' some ripe veggies.

Word of advice about marriage destinations though: do not, under any circumstances, get married up north. I read in a book once that you've gotta wear these masks with rubies embedded in 'em. Real ones, mind you, an' you even have ta pay for 'em! I'm sure you could get yer hands on a few paste ones, but I doubt any true northerner would be caught dead in those. Others'll probably notice, too, then you'll have a judgmental horde of people ta deal with. It'll be a huge pain. I don't recommend it. Just get yerselves a priest, a witness, an' a fancy three-tiered cake. I'll even bless it.

Oh, but I do like that whole mask idea. Y'know, without the fancy jewels an' all that. It can hide a lotta bitter expressions. (That maroon's got a lotta those, so watch out, Syl.)

An' I forgot ta mention this but me an' Pom made some friends that want ta meet you two. Nebbin, in case either a' you were wonderin'. All good people—okay, mostly good. Maybe.

You'll like 'em. They'll like you. It'll be perfect. I promise.

I've got a fair few more things ta say, but Pom just brought in a whole chicken. An' holy sin, it's alive. I've got no clue where he got it from or what he's plannin' ta do with it, but I have ta go.

We'll catch up with you blazes in the Alps, yea?

Khale (and Pom)

***

The hollow, as it turned out, was a tunnel.

A very short one with one mouth opened to the Jade Sea, and the other, to the icy slope of the Gelid Mountains. It was a peculiar place. A bridge between realities; a buffer that kept two edges of the world from colliding. The air was heavy, but refreshing. It almost felt as if magic ran deep underground here, working as an anchor to keep the path untouched.

Icicles gleamed along the outer edges closest to where the weather took a sudden turn for the frosty. The landscape beyond was a scattered mess of trees and small bushes hardy enough to stand the weather. Jack knew from memory that they'd disappear the farther up they went. But for now, there they stood, undisturbed under a miserable dusting of snow as white as dye.

There were no wild predators here. Not yet. No souls but their own. It was odd—this solitary wild, where the evening chill continuously chased the hour. Bundles of gathered leaves and branches were neatly stacked in the middle of the path. Either a remnant from the tunnel's previous occupants or an emergency supply for travelling Hunters. Perhaps both. The bundles were soggy; the leaves curled at the edges. But neither of them needed parched tinder to start a fire anyway.

By the time they had one going—small, so as not to alert any stray wanderers to their presence—night had arrived in earnest. True dark fell over them like a cloak to freeze their bones clean through. They stripped to their smalls and laid the rest of their clothes across the floor. It wasn't the best way to dry them, but there were no lines for them to use as hangers here. Even Silas' journal was thrown open amidst the rest of their belongings. It was far more dilapidated than it had been. Vidal would either laugh or butcher them once he found out. Jack had a sinking feeling that it would be a terrifying mix of both.

They knew that they couldn't stay for long. The Institute was nothing, if not efficient. At that very moment, scouts were likely being given orders to investigate the cause of that great fire. By morning, the area would be swarming with practitioners.

But for now, just for a little while, they could rest.

Jack watched the leaves hiss in their tiny hearth. It was a riot of gold and scarlet that swirled up and around, spreading echoes of warmth that weren't enough for his chattering teeth. They made eerie shadows dance along the walls. Jack tore his gaze away from them in fear of seeing something he didn't want to.

He settled for examining Sylvie instead. She sat beside him, packing away damp herbs and foul-scented balms. The potion she'd brewed for him once they settled had been bitter, but effective. His head felt better. The scrapes and bruises that littered his body still ached, but fainter now. He felt, for lack of a better word, healthier. Though it was a shame she didn't have anything for the overpowering taste because—at the moment—it bothered him even more than his injuries. The vile flavor lingered in his throat like an overcooked rabbit.

Jack pulled at the semi-dry cloak cocooned around her shoulders once she sealed all of her belongings into a stone.

That one's normal, he reminded himself. *There's nothing that can hurt us inside.*

Sylvie turned when he thoughtlessly fisted his hand into the cloth, and that was when he noticed just how slight her cloak was. It was too thin for the weather; thin enough that he was sure that he could tear right through it if he tried.

She couldn't be warm. There was no way.

Jack took her hands in his. Just as he thought, they were cold. Freezing, even. He didn't rub them, not wanting them to swell. Jack brought them to his lips and breathed, hot and heavy, over her curled fingers. She didn't move away. Instead, Sylvie looked up at him through lowered lashes, then sighed in content.

A narrow wind picked up, whispering winter. It slipped through the tunnel to make it moan like a drowsy beast. Jack turned his head so that its chilled edges wouldn't catch the tips of his ears, only to shudder when the wind slid into the empty spaces between them to grope at their bodies. They'd both be covered in ice if he allowed this to continue.

So, he didn't. It was as simple as that.

Jack didn't exactly know how to be gentle. He wasn't sure he wanted to be. But when he drew her closer; when Sylvie buried her cold nose into his neck and wrapped her arms around his waist; when she closed her eyes, leaning into him until there was hardly any space left for breath between them—

He tried to be.

"You're warm," was all she said.

"I would hope so."

Just as he said it, another wind picked up. He shuddered as the ice-touched air pinched his nose and cheeks. It blew particularly cool at his back, just above his shoulders, where there was nothing to guard him. Sylvie slid one hand from his waist to wrap around the back of his neck. Her palm spread cozy heat that untangled the knots there, before she slid it down even farther. She stopped between his shoulder blades.

"Not warm enough," Sylvie added after a moment.

He felt, rather than saw her smile. Jack laughed. It was low, but strong enough to stir her hair. "Rest," he murmured, while tapping an absent tune on her skin.

It wasn't long before she slipped into a light doze.

Because there were no threats in sight and because the sound of the sea beyond was so utterly soothing to his tired mind, he permitted himself to follow. Jack's pulse slowed, safe and silent inside of a wild tunnel between two worlds that had, against all odds, managed to grow warm.

✷✷✷

Sylvie,

I've just announced your acceptance of my offer to the Elders in the Zenith Council via an official missive that I'm sure they'll only grudgingly accept. They've been urging me to take an apprentice for years, but I doubt they expected it to be the newest Arch Poten.

You'll get a lot of nasty looks for your choice, but don't let them affect you. Most will be from envious practitioners anyway. All harmless, I assure you. It's the Elders that you need to watch out for. They'll test your loyalty as an apprentice from the start. Just like they've done with every fledgeling. It can be quite tiring, but I'm sure you'll be able to navigate your way through the Alps' politics just fine. Learning is only a matter of time and exposure.

Regardless, I do urge you to exercise caution once you arrive. The north is full of cutthroats that would rather see you fall to your death than step a single wrung above them. While this might seem extreme, it's the truth. I've lived there long enough to know how even the mountains breathe.

Trust few, believe none, and keep a watchful eye on those you deem worthy to be called your friends. You never know what might happen. I will see you again soon.

May Silas light your way.

Elder Borris

✳✳✳

They basked in the salty spray of the sea.

Neither of them stayed for long, only wanting to get one final look at the waters that Thelarius' Temple once stood so proudly over. For a split second, Sylvie wondered if he'd grown to hate the view. But the thought vanished when a stunning white bird flew across the green-blue waters. It dipped down, close to the foam, then cawed loud enough for the sound to ring in her ears.

It was striking. Nature always was. Sylvie had to consciously force herself to turn away from the sight. They still had a long journey ahead of them after all. The trek through the Gelid Mountains wasn't known for being easy. A day trudging through snow would be demanding, especially for eastern practitioners that had very little experience in such unforgiving weather.

She went first, crossing the tunnel they'd slept so peacefully in for those scant few hours when the moon dominated and all that was good in the world fell into darkness. She stared up at the tall slope they needed to climb, at the boundless expanse of silver-white that stretched beyond her vision. It was so much different than anything else she'd ever encountered. This was pure. Untouched by man. She could only imagine what the Diamond Alps looked like.

Sylvie turned when she heard Jack follow. He drew near, exultant and proud, while the sea surged behind him. As he strode coolly to his place beside her, Sylvie linked her hands together and lifted them high above her face. There was a gladness in her eyes caught by the yet young morning light. Warmth blossomed from deep inside of her when she saw bursts of sun slip over the mountainside, tumbling down in long strips over the snow. Not enough to melt it, but… soon.

Maybe, she amended. Sylvie didn't know how cold it got in the Gelid Mountains to be sure. But she did know that even if she was surrounded by ice, today would be beautiful. There wasn't a cloud in sight.

Jack tugged her arms down, so he could seize her hands in his own. The corner of his lips twitched up into a lopsided grin when she looked up at him, smiling, like he was a ray of sunshine after a ceaseless night.

Behind her, the day dawned gray and pale. Even the waves were tempered in the face of the coming morning. Excitement bubbled in his chest at the sight. It was the childish, rose-tinted exhilaration that came from the knowledge that he'd be returning to a home he'd been gone from for far too long. Jack imagined seeing the top of the Alps above the clouds. He imagined those pointed buildings carved into the mountainside breaking through the long expanse of ashen vapor. It was enough to make him tremble in elation because finally, *finally* he'd be back where he belonged; back in the center of the world and all of its messes.

He was so close.

They were so close.

"Are you ready?" Jack asked.

Sylvie gave him a look that was too much for him to bear. It was too full of—*everything.* Joy, excitement, wonder, fatigue, and an uncontainable delight that staggered him. So much honesty in that one look. More than words could convey.

She squeezed his hands to steady them, before taking two steps ahead. His ground and his anchor.

"Are you?" Sylvie shot back.

Jack only stared at her in response. He'd been waiting years for this moment. Her answer was far more important than his own. But she didn't speak again, so he focused on her expression instead. Jack examined every inch of her face. It was alight with the promise of the future. He could practically *feel* her excitement. She brimmed with the sort of euphoria that only came from the realization that she had the wild open sky laid out before her feet.

After a moment, Sylvie stretched out her hand. Strong and unwavering. She bit her lip, waiting for him. Sylvie didn't have to wait long though because Jack didn't hesitate to grab ahold of her. He fully seized her hand in his own with a firm, reassuring squeeze. An anchor himself, perhaps.

Sylvie smiled when he did. Jack intertwined their fingers in response, mooring himself to her of his own volition.

Together, they stepped away from the shaded tunnel and to the Gelid Mountain's steel-shining skyline; to the hopeful prospects that clenched fiercely around their hearts. She didn't release his hand, and he made no move to pull away.

So much of their time gone to other worries, and more left to drain on future hardships, but any reservations they had could wait. This transition would never come again.

All that mattered now, the only thing they wanted to matter, was this single sunlit instant.